KEEPERS OF ARDEN

The Brothers

Volume 2

By L.K. Evans

DEDICATED

To my mom. Thank you for always being supportive. Without your faith in me, I never would have published and would probably be back at a job that didn't make me happy. Thank you for always being a positive voice when things get rough.

To my sister. I've said it before and I'll say it again, if ever the Zombie Apocalypse were to happen, you're the person I'm running to. Not only because we're sisters, but because you're one of the strongest women I know, and no zombie would ever come close to touching a person in your family. And as always, you'd take care of me.

THANK YOU

A huge thanks to my editor, Lynda Dietz (http://ilovetoreadyourbooks.blogspot.com). It was a long one, and I appreciate all your hard work and time.

Thank you to my cover artist, Michael Evans. I wasn't the easiest to work with, so thank you for putting up with me and giving me an amazing cover.

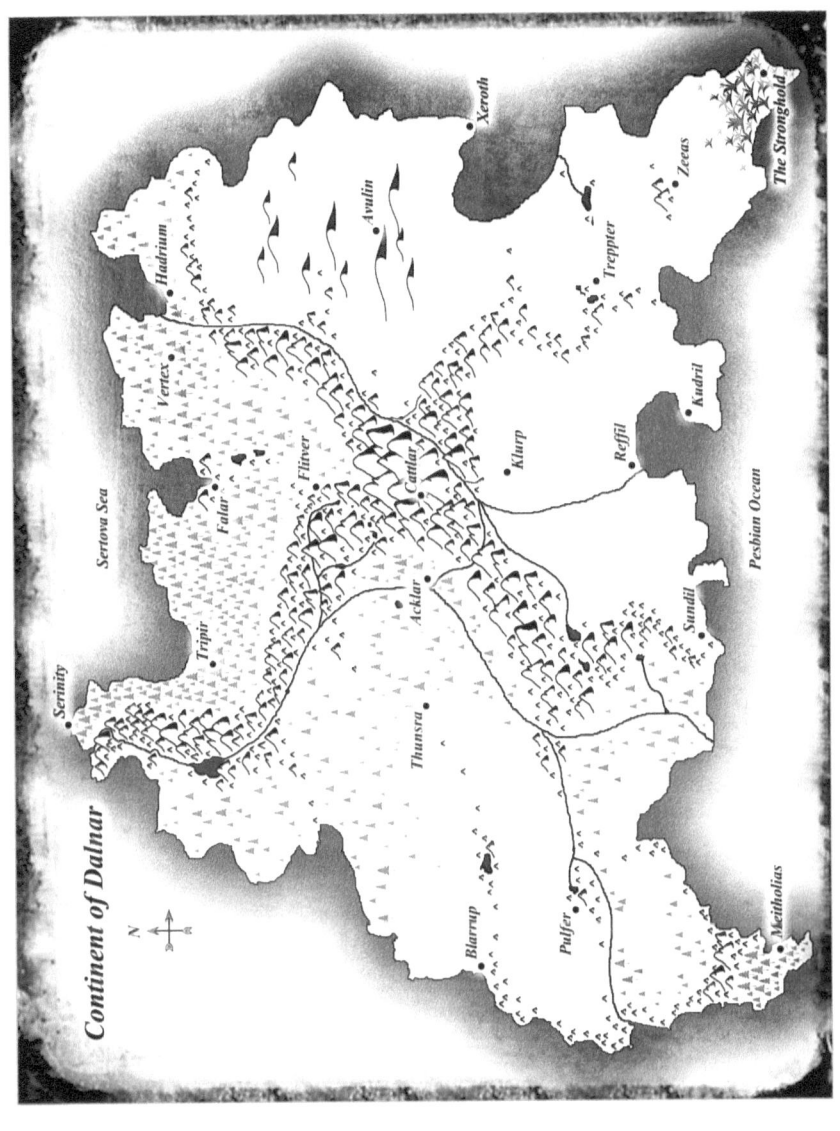

Continent of Dalnar

1

SPRING 1018 A.R

Unupture shrank into the shadows of the mossy stone pillars that climbed upward to support the towering roof in God's throne room. The swamp's humidity beaded sweat until waterfalls trickled down his smooth scalp. However, what unfolded in front of him made the muggy air and his damp robes the least of his worries.

At the base of the dais raising God's throne, Dethal was crumpled in a broken heap. His stark white femur protruded through his skin, contrasted by crimson blood trickling down it, and his twisted arm hung like a dead snake. His fire-red hair and beard were slick with sweat. The mage's groans and gasps added a dull background noise to God's rant.

Unupture clawed his gaze from Dethal and turned to Sansis groveling at God's feet, seeming not to notice his dislocated shoulder. Then again, Sansis could subdue pain with mere thought.

Unupture cursed the day he met his master, and groped for the courage not to flee. For years he had played the game flawlessly, for all the good it did him now. Sansis's foolishness and Dethal's stupidity would be Unupture's undoing. He would serve God for eternity, both in life and in death.

"We were so close," Sansis said. He seized the bottom of God's blood-red robes in his bony fingers. Weak layers of skin covered tendons, and the three white hairs on Sansis's balding head were stuck to his scalp. Decaying skin hung off in flakes, and his skull-like face made Unupture shudder. "I felt Salvarias sway toward your cause. I swear it on my life! It was Dethal's fault the boy escaped. I wasn't there to prevent it!"

God backhanded Sansis, sending him toppling to the ground. "Imbeciles! All of you! Do you realize what you've done to the boy?" God slammed his foot into Sansis's side. Something cracked. "You've unlocked whatever his mysterious power is, you've strengthened his magic, you've shown him where Zeeas is, and—" Grabbing Sansis's robes, God lifted him as if he were a small child and flung him across the room. Sansis collided with a pillar and crumpled into a ball, gasping. "And you've let him escape and delay our plans! Serenity was our most difficult battle in Dalnar! Lord Bellerum lives! And now there have been reports that he's building an army! An *army*! Do you know how he knew to do so? Do you!"

Sansis rolled to his knees, prostrating himself. Whatever grievous wounds he'd suffered were healed. "We do not know it was the boy!"

God marched down the three steps that raised his throne and closed the distance to Sansis. Without so much as a word, he planted his foot square in Sansis's face. Blood spurted from Sansis's crinkled nose. The bone should have impaled his skull, but Sansis's one power of healing prevented an easy death. His nose unfolded, and his watering eyes were the only evidence of what had been done to him.

"It was him!" God roared. "Who else would have told Bellerum to fortify? We'll never have another chance at Serenity! Not until I build additional forces! Do you have any idea what you've done?" He glanced around the room. "Unupture! Show yourself!"

Squaring his shoulders, Unupture left the shadows. "Yes, Master."

"Advise me! What can be done to rectify this catastrophe?" God strode back to the dais.

Unupture swallowed twice before he choked down the knot of fear in his throat. God was not a planner. He relied on those around him, and failure or ineffective advice meant certain death. Unupture licked his lips and glanced at Dethal's face, still twisted in pain, before he spoke. "We have options, Master. My suggestion is to use them all. Allow me to call forth my children from their slumber and unleash them upon Dalnar. The damage my creatures inflict will gain enough attention from the cities that they'll not be able to adequately train and coordinate amongst themselves. The time for secrecy is at an end."

God plopped down on his throne and sank his face in his slender hands. "We were saving them to reinforce our numbers. If we use them, how can we overpower the cities?"

Unupture bit back his sarcastic comment. God's army was three times the size it needed to be. Half of Dalnar could've been overpowered years ago if God hadn't been so cautious. Now, the most fortified cities knew danger lurked at their doorstep. "Our army is large enough, Master. With the cities protecting their denizens, they won't have enough forces to maintain order, much less join Lord Bellerum in any kind of mass army. That'll buy us time to coordinate our next attack, which must come swiftly. We must keep them disorganized."

God leaned back and stroked his smooth cheek. Sputtering torches mounted along the pillars flickered warm light across his face, complementing each chiseled feature, calling attention to his flawless beauty, and reflecting in his black eyes. There was something alluring about him—something that drew Unupture to him, despite the plethora of reasons to flee from his presence. "And the boy?"

Unupture shrugged, rubbing his hands over one another, frowning at his orange skin glistening with the thin layer of goo that had kept him alive. No matter how often he bathed, the goo never came off. Another gift of his former master. Veedran was a cruel god. Shaking off his self-pity, he said, "He's difficult to find. As you said, Dethal's teachings have made Salvarias a worthy adversary. We don't know his gift, but we can assume he has been given some sort of ability to see future events. We must be prepared for him to try to thwart our plans. However, with my children out in force, his path will be wrought with danger. There is a chance he might die."

"I want that boy."

"You want victory, Master. The boy would be a quick way of obtaining it, but as you've seen, turning him will be harder than we'd originally thought. His death would be tragic, although not wholly unhealthy to our cause. If we by chance capture him, all the better. I'll tell my creatures to watch for him, but as you know, some are more bloodthirsty than others. They may not heed my request."

"And the Protector?"

Unupture smoothed his plum-colored robes, grimacing against the patches of sweat. He really did hate the swamp. "Rumors of his expertise in swordplay are spreading across Dalnar. In spite of that, his true powers are not fully developed. I sensed it in the slave caverns. Granted, he possesses some, but as you said, his father never transferred them, so the boy is weak. From what I've learned in Falar, he doesn't lack confidence in his skill with a sword. We can use our knowledge—and his ignorance—to our advantage ... make him no more than a pebble in our shoe. To do so and with our lack in military siege techniques, I suggest you call upon the servants you mentioned: the ones you said could not be defeated. The ones who can plan our campaign. Then, we can not only shake the Protector's confidence, but we will finally have the minds needed to plot our path." Unupture spread his hands helplessly, nodding toward Sansis and Dethal. "I fear your current servants have no military genius. These new servants will be our hope."

God steepled his fingers. "So soon? I had only wanted to raise them if we were desperate. To awaken them will take much of my powers. It will leave me weaker than I am."

Unupture ran his hand along a knotted vine snaking around a column. Vegetation had overrun the Stronghold, providing unsavory blood-sucking insects with as many homes inside the walls as outside. "To wait could be our undoing. Lord Bellerum lives. Wilhelm Laybryth lives. Salvarias is free. The old Guardian and Protector are still at large. The odds are stacked against us, Master."

God sagged further into his throne, gazing off at seemingly nothing. When finally he spoke, his voice was tight. "So be it. I will call upon my military minds. Waking the Four will be my last feat of power."

The room spun around Unupture, and he grabbed hold of the vine to steady himself. "The Four? The servants of Veedran?"

God nodded. "The same."

"How ..." Unupture swallowed hard. "How, Master? How can you command them?"

"It won't be easy," God said. "As I said, it will drain my power."

Unupture shared a shocked glance with Dethal before smoothing his robes and gaining his composure. "I know much of the Four. I met them when I served Veedran. Should Salvarias or Wilhelm Laybryth try to thwart our plans, the Four will show our new Protector just how vulnerable he is. No mortal blade has ever killed any of the Four."

"And vice versa," God said. "No one can kill a Protector."

"We do not need to kill him," Unupture said. "We need to shake his confidence. He will not be so bold if he meets one who matches his skill. If Salvarias attempts to utilize the powers Dethal has coaxed to the surface against the Four, he'll discover they are immune to magic."

"It'll take much preparation on my part to awaken them." God rested his head back, staring at the ceiling for several moments before he spoke. "Your soul will remain your own, Unupture. You have pleased me once again. More so than my most favored servant."

Unupture nearly fainted with relief. He bowed. "Always will it be willingly offered, Master," he lied.

"For your next task, you must find a way to gain access to the boy. I want what resides inside his mind. His fears. His dreams."

Unupture tilted his head. "As you wish, Master. I will meet with the God of Magic."

God turned to Sansis. "What word do you have on the old Guardian and Protector?"

Sansis's hands shook as he wiped them along his robes. "Last report was that they left Windlous, Master. We have not learned where they were headed."

"If they come here, you'll be in danger," Unupture said to God. "The Protector's powers are double those of his son. One touch will harm you greatly."

"Perhaps," God murmured. "But his Guardian is weak. He will not be able to fight the Hunters for long. Soon, I'll have back what was stolen from me. Then I won't need the Soul. I won't need the Four. I will need no one. By my mere thought, Arden will be no more."

At seeing God's eyes light with maddened hunger tipping toward insanity, pity swelled in Unupture. What could make one so lost that his soul was filled with only anger and hate?

2

SPRING 1018 A.R

Salvarias hunched on a bench in the Bellerum gardens that overlooked the lazy sea. The towering estate loomed behind him, covered in sweet-smelling jasmine. Though spring, he tightened the new, thick black cloak his brother had bought him around his shoulders, warding off the breeze gliding in with the rising sun. He had given up the dream of being warm since he was a boy. Always a chill infused his blood, layering frost on his bones. Even during summer, when the beating sun coaxed sweat to his brow, he shivered. His sole respite was the warmth his magic supplied.

The ocean drumming the cliff supporting the city of Serenity soothed Salvarias with the now-familiar melody of the sea. The gardens were a forest of manicured hedges, a rainbow of flowers, and a bouquet of redwoods, aspens, oaks, and evergreens. Though trimmed and planned, the gardens were as relaxing as the wilderness, free and untamed as it was. Birds chirped, singing along with the trees' song Salvarias had listened to since childhood, although sadly, he could never understand their words, just as he did not understand the ocean's song.

As he shifted his gaze from the gardens to the ocean, he found comfort that their victory over a week ago had spared the Bellerum home from ruin. To Salvarias's surprise, Lord Bellerum had taken it upon himself to ramp up his army, though surely he did so to protect his own daughters, not to save the world of Arden. Regardless, it suited Salvarias's wishes, no matter the reason.

For the last few days, Humar had occupied his time by helping Lord Bellerum clean up the destruction left by the blackfurs' attack; Durak assisted in the smithy repairing armor and weapons; Okulu appraised various ales; and Wilhelm and Varila strolled the city together. Salvarias kept to himself and avoided Lunara as if she were a contagious, incurable disease. He had yet to see her since the night they had shared together in the gardens, though he had achieved such success by hiding in his room or sneaking out in the early hours of morning like a thief evading capture. He did not care how he obtained distance between them, simply that he did. In their shared dreams, he had been close to her when he had thought she was a figment of his imagination, but knowing she was real had changed their relationship. He could not be close to her and was accepting of this truth. Her safety was all that mattered to him, and the only way to obtain such was for her to be as far from him as possible.

Sighing, he rubbed his burning eyes. Sleep was as elusive to him as warmth. Ignorantly, he had hoped Serinity's victory would end his nightmares; however, it did no such thing. Instead, new cities smoldered and new horrors were inflicted upon the people of Arden. Unlike his nightmare of Serinity, the new ones were nothing more than a foreshadowing of Arden's future. There was no direction, simply a message of what to expect. As if those did not plague him enough, there were the dreams of his burning mother latching hold of him, spewing her hatred through melting lips. Tobin joined the nightly fun with his words of abandonment that speckled Salvarias's face with his father's blood. Salvarias hated sleep as much as ... he shook his head. Nothing compared.

Adok plopped his head in Salvarias's lap, discussing how soothing the ocean was when it thundered against the bluff. Salvarias ran his fingers through the wolf's sleek black fur, offering his agreement, and marveling as usual over the wolf's enormous size. Though merely a year old, Adok had grown into the largest wolf Salvarias had ever seen. When standing, Salvarias could pet Adok without the slightest bend in his stature, which attested to the wolf's height since Salvarias stood nearly six and a half feet tall. Adok's powerful, muscular build had allowed him to run long distances without tiring, all the while keeping up with the horses when they had fled Kudril. As Salvarias mulled over the wolf's abnormalities, a sudden boredom set in, and he no longer felt the need to ponder on it. Adok nuzzled his hand.

Instead, his mind drifted to his visions. As surely as the sun would rise, he merely needed to bide time until his next vision. He never questioned if their meaning would lead to anything other than relief from the growing darkness. The visions had to. In his mind's eye, he linked the fate of Arden to the fate of his soul. Perhaps if he delivered Arden into the light, his soul would follow and the evil within him would flee. He could not believe otherwise, lest the last thread of hope he clung to fray and snap. However, his patience had been wearing thin over the past week of waiting.

Though the visions or how he obtained them remained a troubling conundrum, he could not suppress the strong sense the visions were not his true purpose. There was a tug on his mind, a constant draw toward … something else. Whenever he focused on the nagging feeling, all he wanted to do was get up and roam the world, searching —but searching for what eluded him as a rabbit eludes the fox, darting from shadow to shadow, quicker than he could catch. The knowledge teetered just outside his grasp, and he swore he heard whispered instructions snatched away in the wind before he could discern their meaning. Therefore, he purposely ignored the thoughts and whispers. The visions were certain, clear, and helpful. The other thing did nothing except set his nerves on edge.

As if hearing his desperate wish for a vision, a flash of white light blinded him. When it dissolved, he found himself floating above stocky trees thrashed by a howling wind. Before him stretched a rocky plain with a muddied aqua lake nestled in its center. All around it, campfires sparkled like stars. Nearly a hundred thousand men in black armor and creatures Salvarias had only read about roamed between tents and circled fires. Terrified screams rose above the wind. Three hovel-sized tents had been erected toward the tree line opposite him. That was where the screams came from. He shuddered, recalling similar shrieks that had haunted the walls inside Zeeas.

Even though Salvarias was not a traveled man, the army's location was as clear to him as the sun on a cloudless day. As he surveyed the army's numbers, his heart recoiled further from hope. Serinity had only been the beginning, and the darkness would not wait long before attacking another helpless city. Therefore, it was Salvarias's responsibility to travel to the lake, confirm his vision and, by some miracle, destroy the army.

White light flashed again. Streaks of azure sky and hues of green charged him. Dizziness dimmed his vision, and he latched hold of whatever was in front of him. By the time his surroundings solidified, he was breathing heavily and Adok's fur was squeezed between his fingers. He apologized to the wolf and gasped in a few deep breaths, cursing his weak lungs.

A woman's voice spoke behind him. "Gentleman Salvarias?"

Glancing over his shoulder, he saw Madam Bellara standing behind him. She was one of five servants who attended to his room, though he had begged her several times to permit him to make his own bed. Being pampered made him uncomfortable.

"Are you all right?" she asked, reaching out.

Salvarias rose and dodged her hand. "Yes, madam. And please, call me Salvarias." He shifted to the side, allowing the breeze to rid the thick clove scent that clung to her. Sunlight sparkled like diamonds on her silvery-white hair, and her complexion was as bleak as snow. Not a single wrinkle flawed her face, and Salvarias had yet to guess her age. If based solely on her appearance, he would figure her no older than Okulu—late twenties, early thirties perhaps—whereas the hardness in her eyes betrayed a woman who had seen thousands of years.

She curtsied and smiled. "You left your room early. Have you eaten?"

"No, madam. I will eat with my brother."

"As you wish." She presented him a folded piece of cloth. "This is from the servants in the Bellerum estate. It's our thank you for saving our home."

Salvarias stared at her in disbelief. He had never received such a kind gesture from a person he hardly knew. He bowed deeply. "There is no need to thank me, madam. There were many who aided Serinity. I could not accept a gift. While I appreciate—"

"I'd be insulted should you turn it away. We know you helped Lady Lunara. It's just a small token of appreciation."

Humbled, he accepted. "Thank you, madam." He unfolded the cloth. Suspended by a strip of black silk hung a silver pendant of a tree that looked remarkably close to the tree in Salvarias's dream of the walking dead. "It is beautiful, madam. Please, express my thanks to the others."

"You'll wear it, won't you?"

Salvarias tied it around his neck. "Of course, madam."

She curtsied and left him alone in the garden.

Taking in a deep breath, Salvarias gazed around at the trimmed hedges, soaring trees, lush grasses, and multitude of flowers. His thoughts went to the Bellerum library and to the wonderful feasts he had dined on every morning and evening. He recalled so many laughter-filled conversations between Lady Talura, Lord Bellerum, and their daughters. Alas, peace was wrenched from his grasp. Even worse was the peace his brother would be denied. All due to Salvarias.

Yes, my pet, the presence in his mind hissed. *So much pain do you cause your beloved brother. I remain surprised you can live with yourself.*

I know what I do to him, Salvarias retorted. *I do not need to be reminded.*

If you truly understood his pain, you would leave your brother and spare him your evil. I fear time is closing in around you, my pet. Soon, you will kill him.

"Leave me!"

The presence receded. Battling the ache in his chest, Salvarias headed toward the dining hall to ruin the lives of his companions.

~

WILHELM WOLFED down his fourth helping of salty ham, boiled eggs, herb-roasted potatoes, and half a loaf of bread. The expansive dining table overflowed with his favorite morning foods, making him wish his plate was larger. Why people didn't eat off platters he'd never know. They were much roomier and permitted the food to be spread out in tidy piles. Plates made him pile up his food in heaps so he had to eat in the order it was uncovered.

Hearing a snort, he looked up at Varila sitting opposite him, watching with a raised eyebrow. His eyes roamed her leather armor that accentuated every curve of her seductive body. It took all his willpower to remain in his seat and keep his hands from finding the soft skin visible between her boots and armored skirt.

He winked. "I'm stocking up. Who knows when I'll eat next?"

She rolled her eyes, tucking a strand of wavy, golden hair behind her ear. "Lunch is but a few hours away. I think you may live to see it."

"You can never be too certain. As my father said, 'Food provides nourishment for the body and the mind.' So really, I'm nourishing my mind."

"Bah. I think not. If that were true, you'd be the smartest man alive."

"How do you know I'm not?" Wilhelm changed his tone to one of distinction. "One cannot give away all one's secrets to the first pretty girl one sees."

Varila let out that throaty laugh he loved.

Humar, Durak, and Okulu entered the room and joined them at the table. Humar wore his armor, as he did everywhere he went. Wilhelm could count on one hand the number of days he'd seen the knight without it. Today, Humar had apparently relaxed because his helmet was not tucked under his arm, nor did he wear his gauntlets. His mousy brown hair stood up from the number of times he'd probably run his hand through it, and his azure eyes sparkled a smile. Okulu, though covered head to toe in armor while traveling, had taken advantage of the safety of Serinity and wore deep brown trews and a midnight blue tunic. It offset his olive-tinted skin and brought out his grass-green eyes. Durak sported the leather armor he'd fashioned himself, nearly a replica of Wilhelm's, save for the bear that emblazoned Wilhelm's breastplate. Durak's gray face was etched with deep frown lines, despite the fact the short man was smiling beneath his waist-length beard.

"Morning"s were exchanged before the three men helped themselves to the feast laid out before them.

"Where's your father and mother?" Humar asked Varila. "They always eat breakfast with you."

"Mother is with Lunara in the library, and father is still in the process of interviewing candidates for the commander position."

"I'm surprised he's not interviewing you," Humar said.

"I'm not interested," Varila said. "I help train recruits, but as far as commanding an army goes, I'm not the least bit qualified, nor would I want to be."

Salvarias glided into the dining room and sat next to Wilhelm. As always, Salvarias's burgundy mage robes were twice the size needed and draped down his slouched shoulders, dragging an inch or so along the ground. The hood was pulled up, completely shadowing his face except for the set line of his lips and strong jaw.

After a quick exchange of greetings and once Salvarias had gathered a plate of food, he turned to Humar. "If Dalnar were threatened, how long would it take to amass an army and how many could be recruited in that amount of time?"

Humar reclined in his chair, running his hand through his hair, sticking it up even higher. "Hastily and ill-prepared, Dalnar could gather maybe … I'd say maybe twenty thousand strong in a month's time. Dalnar's army is too divided among the cities and travel times alone are a challenge. The knighthood is so inconsistent across the lands that none have the same training. Even if they flock together, their fighting techniques would be their downfall. Given a year or so, I figure they could get … maybe fifty thousand and conduct trainings to unify the men. You'll have to remember that Dalnar isn't threatened by war like Loutsil. Their armies are nothing more than guards and a few knights. Why do you ask? What's this about?"

Salvarias's shoulders slumped, and he pushed his plate of food aside. "Cities have hundreds of thousands. Why—"

"Farmers, merchants, drunks." Humar shook his head. "You could gather them and toss them at an enemy and they'll be cut down. Might take a few with them, but it'd be a massacre."

Salvarias sighed. "The time for me to leave has come. I ask you all again to stay in Serinity."

Humar leaned back in his chair and studied Salvarias a moment before shaking his head. "I'm coming. I think Dethal is still after you. And I think you're heading right for the center of this darkness. I want my chance to help. I want to fight."

Durak grinned at Wilhelm. "Aye, me too. Can't have this ogre lumbering around Dalnar. He'll make a mess of things."

Okulu took a swig from his flask and nodded. "I'm in."

"You need to eat, Salv," Wilhelm said over a mouthful of bread.

"When do we leave?" Humar asked.

"Tomorrow," Salvarias said.

"Where are we going?" Lunara asked, strolling into the room, her black hair dancing around her waist. The peach dress she wore was gathered under her bosom, falling loosely around her slender frame. She smiled sweetly at the group before sitting across from Salvarias.

Salvarias spoke barely above a whisper. "*We* are not going anywhere, my lady. You must remain with your father and help with the affairs of Serinity."

"My father can run the city perfectly well without me. I am going."

"No, you are not. You will remain here."

Lunara stood. "What has happened that I am no longer permitted in your presence?"

"We cannot all be focused on your protection, my lady." Salvarias rose from his seat, gaze locked on her, fingertips white as he pressed them to the table. "You refuse to fight, refuse to carry a weapon or armor. You put everyone in danger."

"Did I not break the orb? Did I not prove useful?" Lunara retorted.

"Once, you helped." Salvarias's voice was unusually loud and strained. "You did nothing to defend the city, nothing when Dethal showed. I or someone else protected you."

Lunara glared at the group. "Do you all feel the same?"

Wilhelm glanced at the others. Everyone mirrored his shocked expression as they stared at the ill-tempered duo. "No"s were murmured throughout.

She turned to Salvarias. "It appears only you have this opinion of me. I will go. If you sneak out, I'll follow you. I know men who can track."

"You risk our lives for your selfishness," Salvarias hissed, and stormed from the room.

Lunara's determined gaze melted, and she sank to her chair, tears filling her eyes. Varila wrapped an arm around her sister's shoulders. Stunned, Wilhelm left the room in search of his brother. He found Salvarias pacing in front of his bed, eyes unfocused, forefinger and thumb rubbing together.

"What was that about, Salv?"

"You have ears, Brother. We cannot protect her where we go. She must remain behind. Persuade Varila to talk to her."

"Whoa ... Varila would take my head off. Her first loyalty is to Lunara. This isn't like you, Salv. What's going on?"

Salvarias sat on his bed and rested his head in his hands. "I need to rest. Please, let me sleep."

"Sure, Salv. You know you can talk to me if you want."

After Wilhelm closed the door, he turned to see Varila standing behind him, face red. "Something's wrong," he said. "Salv's not like this. You've been around him, you know him."

"I know I don't like the way he looks at my sister. I don't like the way he looks at *any* of us. He hides his agendas and is self-serving!"

He flinched from the sting of her words. Regret flashed across Varila's eyes, but her lack of apology said the regret was for Wilhelm's wound, not her hateful words about his brother. Jaw tight with anger, he said, "No one understands him. No one sees what I see. None of us knows what he's been through, what he's going through. We're the ones who are self-serving!"

He marched to his room and slammed the door harder than he intended. Flinging himself into a chair, he glared at the smoldering fire. Though hardly any time passed, he couldn't fight the urge to check on Salvarias. His brother had never lost his temper. When Wilhelm opened his door, Humar was waiting.

The knight cleared his throat. "Odd, wouldn't you say?"

Wilhelm grunted in agreement.

"Let's go talk to him," Humar said.

"It might be better if I go alone."

Humar shook his head. "I want to see if I can get some additional information about where we're going." His mouth set in a determined line. "I will get him to trust me."

Wilhelm didn't argue. Maybe, just maybe, Humar possessed that ability. Wilhelm went next door and knocked before entering with Humar. Salvarias sat on his bed, crammed into a corner, knees drawn to his chest, head buried in his arms.

Salvarias did not look up when he spoke. "What is it, Humar? I am tired and need rest."

"I wanted to get any details you might have about our journey so we can buy appropriate supplies."

Wilhelm sat next to his brother. When Salvarias raised his head, his features were typically emotionless, his lips neither frowning nor smiling, and Wilhelm knew beneath the shadows of Salvarias's hood, his eyes were a dull lake, void of a ripple of emotion.

"We head southeast, past the barbarian lands," Salvarias said. "I ask—I beg you—again to leave us. The road ahead is dangerous."

"I'm going," Humar said. "It'll be nice to be the hunter, instead of the hunted."

"No, I fear we are still the prey. Our tiny flame of hope merely blinds us in the darkness." Salvarias paused, then said, "There is no honor nor glory in accompanying me. Only death."

"Tell me," Humar said. "You know me well. I won't stop searching for an answer as to what it is you're trying to accomplish. For once, trust someone, boy. With enough people, our tiny flame can become a bonfire, and predators are usually scared of fire."

Time passed with the anticipation thick enough to cut with a sword. When finally Salvarias spoke, his voice was lined with a dull reality, a cruel foretelling of their future. "I see cities burning; mutilated bodies cover the streets, and impaled children line what once were beautiful roads. Blood runs in the rivers and taints the oceans. I *feel* the evil of the world and see it growing in power. I dream it each night. Each night I hear screams of the dying. Each night I see women murdered by dark shadows, children hunted and butchered, men carved apart. I see people I knew in Falar burning in flames, their faces twisted with pain." Salvarias turned his black eyes to Wilhelm and then to Humar. His voice dripped with apology. "I had a vision ... an image before our mother was murdered. I saw Tobin lying dead on the ground. Yet I said nothing. I did not warn him. If I had just said something ..." Salvarias's words choked off.

"It's not your fault, Salv. It's those men who killed them, not you."

Humar ran a hand through his hair and leaned back heavily. He seemed to age years in a breath. Salvarias tensed under Wilhelm's arm.

Eventually, Humar whispered, "You were just a boy. So young to understand something like that. Even if you'd said something, no doubt the men still would have found you. The outcome was inevitable." Humar inhaled a breath and smiled. It didn't brighten up his eyes as usual. "It wasn't your fault, boy."

Salvarias shook his head, clenching his fist. "I could have prevented it, and I hate myself for my cowardice. I will live with the knowledge for the rest of my days. But I learned." Defiance set in his expression, his head rose higher, but still low to keep his eyes shadowed as always. "I do not ignore my visions any longer. I warned Lady Lunara of the men who entered her room. I warned her of the hidlu. I dreamt of Serinity in flames, disfigured bodies filling the landscape. I saw Lunara burning in an alley; I smelled her flesh, tasted the smoke. It was so real. At first, I did not understand what could do such a thing, then I had a vision ... an image of the creatures. The blackfur grabbed me and I experienced its power and, at that moment, I discovered how to fight them. We defeated them and saved the city." Salvarias lowered his head and shuddered. "I had a vision of an army mounted south of the barbarian desert. I do not know their purpose. All I know is I must go there and see it for myself. Perhaps even find a way to destroy it."

Humar cleared his throat. "Why have you not told me before? Why not tell me the truth, boy? I'd like to think I've earned your trust."

Though Wilhelm doubted Humar noticed, Salvarias seemed to draw inward upon himself, curling tighter, tensing, emitting waves of fear and uncertainty that had always assailed Wilhelm whenever Salvarias talked of his gifts. Those tangible emotions were why Wilhelm refused to allow others to question his brother's "oddities."

Salvarias's voice was soft, emotionless to others aside from Wilhelm, who easily heard his brother's fear. "I am not normal. I am embarrassed, afraid ... ashamed."

Wilhelm pulled the pea-sized wooden puzzle box from his shirt pocket. The instant his brother touched it, it expanded to the size of a grapefruit. All six sides were lined with smaller blocks that were somehow connected at the center, but expanded out to contort into odd shapes as Salvarias manipulated it. Wilhelm could never fathom how the box was constructed.

"There's no such thing as normal, Salv," Wilhelm said. "I think you were right when you said we were meant for something. You're meant to help Arden, to find out what these new creatures are doing here. I think these visions are going to help us. It's a blessing, not something to be embarrassed about."

"I agree," Humar interjected.

"These visions are not all I feel," Salvarias said. The pieces of the puzzle box whirled faster. "There is something else I must do, but it eludes me, always at the edge of my mind. The feeling intensified at Zeeas."

Humar's eyes lit with understanding. "This is what Dethal wanted from you. To learn about these visions?"

"Yes."

"You had them before you were taken?"

Salvarias's tense shoulders relaxed. "Some, but they became stronger, clearer during my time in Zeeas. Spells—pushing my magic —opened my mind somehow, allowed me to see them. The more I learned, the clearer the visions."

"How did they know you had them?"

Salvarias shrugged. "I have not figured that out yet. They do not know it is visions. They call it a 'gift.' I am not sure they even understand what is wrong with me."

"Thank you, boy," Humar said.

Salvarias paused in his manipulation of the puzzle box and met Humar's gaze. "It is I who owe you thanks. Your help has been invaluable ... frie—" Salvarias cleared his throat. "Friend."

Wilhelm grinned ear to ear at Humar.

A slow smile spread across Humar's face and melted into a toothy grin. He rose and inhaled a deep breath. "Well, there's much to be done. You boys get some rest. We'll leave in the morning. And don't worry, boy. I won't tell anyone about the visions. It'll be our secret. However, I want you to confide in me. Trust me to only tell the others what needs to be told."

"Thank you," Salvarias said.

Wilhelm conveyed his gratitude in his smile. "Thanks." After Humar left, Wilhelm wrapped an arm around his brother's shoulders. "I'm proud of you, Salv."

Salvarias's eyes sparkled a smile, the churning of his irises pulsing with every hue of gray imaginable. No white could be seen, only endless black. "Thank you, Brother."

His brother turned his attention back to the puzzle box. As usual, the pieces spun into shapes only Salvarias understood. Wilhelm squinted at the device, trying to see how his brother manipulated the box with such ease and, for the first time, realized Salvarias's fingers were larger than the smaller pieces, yet they moved at the slightest contact. As Wilhelm watched, pieces shifted that were not touched. His brother's mind as well as hands controlled the device, which continued to intrigue Wilhelm. He chose not to say anything. The puzzle box offered a strange relief to Salvarias, and he would not question it.

Salvarias eventually stopped and held up a finished product.

"What is it?" Wilhelm asked.

"My brother."

3

SPRING 1018 A.R

T alura rested a hand over her mouth to hide her smile as she watched her husband pace in their bedroom while their daughters stood with their heads lowered. Upon seeing the look in Varila and Lunara's eyes, she knew arguing was plainly pointless. Edium, however, seemed undeterred by their daughters' resolve.

"I won't allow it!" Edium roared. "Out of the question! Absurd! Ridiculous! What are you girls thinking? Varila, I expected more from you! How could you agree?"

Lunara raised her head, tossing her wealth of black hair from her face. "I will go with him, Father. By the gods, I'm old enough to be married! To have children of my own! I—"

Edium scoffed. "You're barely considered an adult, Lunara. No matter how much you think you've grown in the last year, you're still an innocent girl. A-a child!"

"I am not, Father!" She turned a pleading gaze to Varila.

Talura's oldest sighed. "I won't let anything happen to her, Father. I've kept her safe for the past year. I can—"

"That was before acid-dripping creatures were wandering our world in regenerating armies!"

Talura rose from her chair. "That'll be enough, all of you. Edium, would you be a dear and make me some tea?"

"Now?" Edium gaped at her. "You want tea at a time like this?"

Talura strolled in front of her husband and gave him a lingering kiss, feeling his whiskers tickle her lips. "Yes, my dear. I think tea would do us some good."

The deep crease in Edium's brow eased, and the anger clouding his hazel eyes faded. "Can't a servant get it?"

Talura kissed him again. "But you make the best tea, dear."

Her husband sighed and nodded. "This discussion isn't over, girls. We'll continue it when I return." Edium stormed out, muttering under his breath.

Talura turned to Varila. "Why don't you find out for me where the brothers are? I need to have a word with one of them."

Varila squeezed Lunara's hand and left. Talura motioned to the balcony, and her daughter followed her outside. "Wonderful day."

"I must do this, Mother."

"You and I have never been separated until last year. I could never get you to go with your father nor did you venture often from the estate. Now, you have no fears of traveling out into the world."

"I believe in Salvarias. I think Arden is in trouble. And I think he'll be the one to save it."

"Is that the only reason, dear?"

Lunara smoothed her dress and faced Talura. "I love him."

"I see. And how does he feel about you?"

"We've not talked about our ... feelings. Our relationship is ... complicated."

"You've never lied to me nor have you guarded your feelings. This is a new side to you."

"There are things happening to me that I don't understand. Nevertheless, *I* want to figure them out. It's time for me to be on my own."

Talura fought tears of joy. She'd feared Lunara would never dare experience life, all its hardships and joys. Though the timing was poor, Talura had a strong suspicion Salvarias would care for Lunara as strongly as Edium or Varila. "So be it. I'll convince your father. But you must promise to listen to Varila. The world is dangerous."

"I will. And Mother, please don't say anything to anyone."

Talura raised an eyebrow. "You've not told your sister?"

"Varila hasn't taken to Salvarias. She'd disapprove and, if she uncovered my feelings, she wouldn't allow me to go. I fear Father would react the same."

Talura pulled Lunara into a tight embrace. "I won't tell a soul. I like having our secrets."

SALVARIAS ABSENTLY STARED out his window, only vaguely aware of the bustling city sprawled out below. Worry knotted his gut and chewed on his conscience. He knew the group should remain behind. Tagging along would put them all in terrible danger. The more they knew, the more hazardous their road. He could sneak away, but a very tiny part—one he hated—wanted them to come. He needed help. He needed Humar's tactical mind.

A knock sounded on his door.

"Salvarias?" Lady Talura called.

He glanced at the window, entertaining the wild notion of scaling down the wall and fleeing deep into the forest. His absurd fear merely drove his tired thoughts further into depression, bringing back the tightness in his neck. Yes, his mother had beaten him, but nothing compared to the torture Sansis had done. Yet mothers sparked absolute terror in Salvarias and had done so his entire life. Eighteen years and he had not come close to overcoming it. He disgusted himself.

Cursing under his breath, he walked to the door and partially opened it. "Yes, my lady?"

"I was wondering if you were free for a walk," Lady Talura asked. Her rich brown hair was once again done in a braid decorated with white jasmine flowers. Her ice-blue eyes were a replica of Lunara's, and her smile simply lit the room with warmth. He found her petrifying.

With no excuse, Salvarias reluctantly nodded and stepped from the room, Adok at his heels, glaring at Talura. She beamed a smile at both of them before leading them down the stairs, through the entry room, and outside to the Bellerum stables.

Probing through the different horses' minds, he sought Mithal. The stallion latched on to his thoughts, immediately issuing a plea for help. Shifting by Lady Talura, Salvarias strode by the horse stalls until he came upon a grassy corral. Mithal was there with a stablehand who was holding a saddle. Mithal wanted nothing to do with it. He reared and kicked the air, nickering a warning to the stablehand.

Salvarias unlatched the gate and moved between the two, trying to calm the stallion while requesting the man leave the corral. After Lady Talura gave the order, the man marched out, mumbling that the stallion would never be rideable.

"You see none others can approach the stallion but you," Lady Talura said, entering the corral.

Mithal pranced back. Salvarias offered assurances that she meant no harm.

"How do you calm him so quickly?" she asked.

Salvarias stoked Mithal's neck, finding the horse's favorite spot. "I love animals, my lady. I am sure Mithal picks up on my affection." He did not lie. Mithal had sensed his care toward animals. Of course, Salvarias's ability to communicate with them sped up the horse's acceptance, but he would not disclose that to Lady Talura. His oddities were his own, secret and shameful.

"Mithal?" she asked.

"It is a name I selected."

"I like it. Your brother's choice of name for the horse he purchased surprised me. Lilly, I believe?"

"Yes, madam. Though it is I who is to blame for her name."

Adok trotted into the stable and picked up a friendly conversation with the horse, who oddly enough, engaged readily with a vicious predator of the forest. Salvarias found it mildly amusing.

"I see," Talura said, raising an eyebrow at Adok when the wolf sat in front of the horse. "I have a love of horses. The stallion was a gift from Edium. I've had him for several months; however, I've never been able to get close to him."

"He is calm," Salvarias said, communicating with the horse as well. "You should try again."

Mithal, with much cajoling, took a step toward her, no longer interested in Adok. The wolf growled and moved off to the side.

Talura held out her hand and approached with measured slowness. Though the horse was skittish, Salvarias provided continual assurances. Once they were past an awkward greeting and she had scratched Mithal's favorite spot on his neck, the horse warmed to her quickly. In no time, she was riding bareback, laughing. Salvarias sat on the corral railing next to Adok and watched the two with puzzled contentment.

Eventually, she dismounted. "He's wonderful," she exclaimed.

"Indeed."

"I want you to have him."

Though he wanted the horse more than he could express, he knew the price the stallion would fetch. Lady Talura's generosity far exceeded what he deserved. "You can ride him now, my lady. I cannot accept such a gift." He heaved himself down, leaning heavily on his staff to take weight off his weak leg.

"No, he's yours." She turned a steady gaze to Salvarias. "I would be insulted should you refuse."

He stumbled over a polite way to decline, but none presented themselves. He asked the stallion what he wanted, sure to outline the many dangers and uncertainties of being in Salvarias's company. Adok offered promises to watch for Mithal's safety, and the horse eagerly agreed to leave Serinity. Salvarias bowed to Lady Talura. "You are too kind, my lady."

"Shall we head back?"

Salvarias nodded and followed her out of the corral. Once he latched the gate closed, Lady Talura reached for him. Suddenly his mother stood before him, board perched over her shoulder, eyes wild with hate. Salvarias staggered backward.

"Salvarias!" Lady Talura snapped.

Her harsh tone drove away the apparition of his mother.

"What you see is not there, dear," she said soothingly.

Although it had happened quickly, his sheer fear had stolen his breath and raced his heart to such speeds he was surprised he did not keel over. He rested against the corral, gulping in huge breaths.

"Take your time," Lady Talura said, smoothing the front of her forest-green dress.

After gaining control, he stood straight. "I ... I am sorry."

She smiled. "Whatever for, dear? You apologize far too much. Come."

He followed her to the estate.

At the steps leading inside, Talura broke the silence. "My daughters will be in your company once again, I hear."

"Yes, my lady. I would be forever in your debt if you asked them to remain behind."

"Most men would leap at the opportunity to be in Lunara's presence. Yet you refuse her company."

"I fear for her safety. Our road is dangerous. Lunara does not fight. She does not—"

"I'm well aware of the conversation you had with my daughter."

Salvarias cheeks burned with shame. "I did not mean to hurt her, my lady. However, what I said was not a lie."

They passed through the entrance and started up the steps toward Salvarias's room.

Lady Talura sighed. "So many think weapons and armor are needed to defeat evil, but they are sorely mistaken. My daughter has gifts, Salvarias. Many gifts. Her mere presence will help you be victorious, and not because of some power or sword, but because her heart is filled with hope. When you are trapped in your darkest hour, she will be your beacon. She's strong enough to survive the horrors of the world. Varila will look after her ... as will you."

"Of course, my lady." Salvarias's heart overtook his tongue. "Her life will be guarded above my own."

"Then I have nothing to fear. She's safer with you than here in the walls of this estate. Of that, I have no doubts." She stopped in front of his bedroom door. "You are an honorable man, Salvarias. I hope our paths cross many times over."

She curtsied and left him standing rigid in the hall.

4

SPRING 1018 A.R

The morning breeze lifted Wilhelm's hair from his brow and cooled his forehead as he and his friends passed through Serinity's gate. The spring sun hid behind a veil of pale gray clouds, and the sweet perfume of flowers tickled his nose. He couldn't help his smile as he gazed at the farms his brother had cast a spell upon and saved from fires. Though the meadow was blackened, the fields of crops had managed to survive the attack without a single grain burned.

After the farmlands, the tree perched on the cliffside marking their parents' resting place appeared in the distance. The dark wood was silhouetted against the faded blue sky with its thick branches shading a growth of clover.

"Brother," Salvarias whispered.

Wilhelm tilted his head in understanding and moved his chestnut mare next to the Loutsil knight. "Salv and I will catch up." Wilhelm nodded toward the tree.

"Sure," Humar said, his gaze lingering on his brother's gravesite. "We'll keep a slow pace."

"Thanks."

Lilly lazily plodded along down the hill, and her bobbling gait stretched Wilhelm's back. He tugged her toward the tree line, but Salvarias waved him forward, dismounting Mithal. "They will not venture far, Brother."

Wilhelm swung his leg over the saddle and thudded to the ground. Lilly tossed her mane, nickering loudly, which prompted a chuckle from Salvarias.

"What did she say?" Wilhelm asked, giving the mare a firm pat.

"She said the ride will be long." Salvarias stroked Mithal's neck before releasing the stallion. "She wishes you would eat less."

Wilhelm grunted. "I will now that we're traveling. Talura was free with her helpings at dinner."

"I noticed." Salvarias smiled wryly. "I am surprised she found your threshold."

Wilhelm chuckled, rubbing his stomach. "After the fourth helping, I finally felt full. I don't ever remember feeling that before."

The black wolf padded soundlessly next to Salvarias, casting mischievous glances at him as they carried on a silent conversation. Wilhelm draped his arm around Salvarias's shoulders, lifting him slightly to offer any comfort. As usual, the act resulted in a deep breath from his brother and a relaxation of his tense shoulders.

"It was nice of Talura to give you the stallion," Wilhelm said.

"Indeed. The horse is worth much."

"She likes you."

Salvarias's response was a re-stiffening of his shoulders. For eighteen years, his brother had preferred solitude and shied from affection. Salvarias's social detachment never bothered Wilhelm, and, in honesty, he enjoyed the times alone with his brother. When it was just the two of them, Salvarias blossomed and shared his smile often along with his light, infectious laugh. His shoulders lost their slump, and his eyes lit with love and curiosity. All the wondrous gifts Salvarias possessed were brought to view. When alone together, Salvarias was a different person.

Wilhelm settled on the clover dotted by dull white flowers with his brother. Although the gentle breeze and rhythmic ocean soothed Wilhelm, the memory of their parents' death caused a ripple of the ill fortune that stalked the brothers to sneak down his spine, and his lost childhood brought a bitter lump to his throat. His resentment grew the longer he stared at his parents' names carved into the bark. The white letters seemed to glare at him in the morning sun as a confirmation of his failure to keep his brother safe. As if to stake down his gloomy thoughts, Salvarias's hand shot up to his missing ear. The carved names gleamed, and Wilhelm's mood darkened.

Salvarias's eyes were distant as his breathing switched to short gasps. Even as he curled into a ball of depression, Wilhelm was already moving an arm around his brother's shoulders.

He didn't wait long before suggesting they leave. Salvarias nodded in agreement, and Wilhelm kept hold as he rose, moving his arm around to a headlock. He flicked down his brother's mage hood and ruffled his thick hair. Once the familiar strong punch connected with Wilhelm's ribs, he chuckled. "Ouch. You're getting stronger."

Indeed, if healthy, his brother possessed alarming strength, built by nothing but his mere will. Though Zeeas had wasted Salvarias into a bag of bones, had taken his ear, and had ruined his left leg, the scrumptious food at the Bellerum estate had brought him to the healthiest weight Wilhelm had seen, adding those sculpted muscles Salvarias could obtain with no physical exercise. None noticed how strapping his brother had become due to the purposeful slouch Salvarias incorporated in his stance, as well as the overly large mage robes of deep burgundy he wore. Though curious, Wilhelm rarely questioned his brother's actions. He was sure Salvarias's shy, reserved nature was merely finding ways to detract from unwanted attention.

As Salvarias mounted Mithal, an ear-to-ear smile spread and, with it, the world seemed to come alive. "See if you can keep up, my dear brother."

Grinning, Wilhelm tossed his leg over Lilly's saddle. Salvarias's stallion reared, kicking the air, and landed hard, thundering ahead at a full run. Wilhelm's calves dug into Lilly when the mare bolted forward without permission, nearly tossing him from the saddle. Salvarias's laughter filled the morning breeze, and Wilhelm joined in the feeling of freedom paired with the excitement coursing through him. The myriad of colored flowers blurred to a rainbow from wind-stung tears while the cool breeze ripped through his hair. The short race ended at the thick tree line. Of course, Salvarias had won.

"She's getting used to my weight," Wilhelm explained, reining in next to his brother.

"I am sure that is why," Salvarias said dryly. He glanced at the mare and smiled.

"What did she say?"

"She said you ride too high."

By the time they rejoined the group, Salvarias's set expression had returned, his gaze once again cold and detached. Wilhelm felt Varila's eyes watching him but chose to ignore her stare. Her hurtful words about Salvarias lived crisply in his mind. His emotions played an annoying game of tug-of-war; one side the love he might hold for her, and the other his protective nature over Salvarias. Right now, his protective side was winning.

Salvarias withdrew his black leather-bound spell book from his pack and glanced at Wilhelm. "Why are you upset with Lady Varila?"

He grinned. "How do you know I am?"

"Brother," Salvarias said with a slight scold, flipping through several pages.

Wilhelm sighed, never understanding how Salvarias always picked out lies. "It doesn't matter."

"Lilly wants to visit Kinfer."

"Kinfer?"

"Varila's horse."

"No, she doesn't." Lilly started to trot toward Kinfer, but he held her back. "Knock it off, Salv."

"Brother, you know she cares for those who travel with us. What-ever she said was uttered out of concern. You must be more under-standing."

Wilhelm grunted, slumping in his saddle and accepting defeat dealt with his brother's next words.

"Please, Brother."

Wilhelm sighed and permitted Lilly to lead him next to Varila.

She turned her sea-blue gaze to him and winked. He wanted to rip out his stomach when it flipped with nerves. Her golden hair reflected the sun, braided loosely to allow a few strands to frame her face, tempting him to brush them aside. Her sun-kissed skin beamed with warmth, and his gaze moved to her strong thigh visible between her armored skirt and boot. His hand twitched with the memory of her smooth skin gliding under his callused hand.

"Okulu thinks he can hit that tree," Varila said, her tone a throaty, seductive hum. "The one with the moss growing from its branches."

Wilhelm squinted far ahead to a slender sapling no larger than his wrist, then back to the grinning, blurry-eyed half-Winsire who took a swig from his ever-present flask.

Okulu winked. "Bet an ale at the next tavern."

Wilhelm looked again at the tree clustered among pines and grinned. "You're on."

"Me too," Varila said.

Durak leaned back in his saddle, smoothing his waist-length black beard. "Aye, I'll take that bet, ye drunk fool."

"Salvarias?" Okulu asked.

Salvarias glanced at the tree and then the mercenary. "I think not."

Okulu laughed while drawing a dagger with fluid grace. A quick flick of his wrist sent the gleaming blade for the sapling, and ended with a deep thud in the slim trunk. The merc trotted nonchalantly ahead to retrieve the weapon.

"Bastard!" Varila called.

Okulu smiled ruefully over his shoulder. "My dear golden-haired warrior, don't be upset. I'm sure you'll never underestimate my abilities again."

"Go suck an ogre!"

Wilhelm shook his head at his own stupidity. "I don't know why I fell for it."

Varila muttered an oath. "Because he's drunk all the time. He shouldn't be able to hit those targets."

The tension between her and Wilhelm vanished. He glanced at his brother, engrossed in the pages of his spell book, and smiled.

~

VARILA ANGLED BACK in her saddle, stretching her sore muscles in the early hours of evening. Her hind end had grown soft during the near-month they'd stayed in Serinity. Now she paid the price for being lazy while at home and not riding daily as usual.

To top off her aching back, she was bored. Lunara talked with Durak, Humar with Wilhelm, and Okulu—at Humar's orders—rode ahead and scouted for dangers, leaving her no one to converse with. She didn't even have passing travelers to nod to or silently make fun of. Humar had kept her group from main roads, forcing them to weave through the forest.

She turned a cold stare to the mage, seeing his lips moving in the never-ending whisper of numbers. He sat astride her mother's black stallion, reading his spell book, unaware of his surroundings. She despised few things, but he was quickly heading toward the top of her list. Arrogant bastard. He kept his agendas hidden from the group, and he never engaged in conversation. Someone else had to try to lure him to talk and, even then, he replied in short responses, as if he were too good to associate with them.

Okulu trotted up to the group. "I've found a place for camp. Little stream nearby, clearing with few rocks, and concealed by a circle of dense trees."

Humar nodded. "I think we've gone far enough today."

Varila could've kissed him. They rode a short while longer before they came to the campsite. Her group, except for Salvarias, had traveled together for over half a year and setting up camp had become a quick routine. The only change was the fire. Wilhelm, instead of gathering tinder and lighting it himself, motioned to Salvarias.

The mage whispered a spell, and his voice raised gooseflesh on her arms. He sounded as if he stood behind her, his words caressing her like the touch of a lover. She shuddered off the feeling. After flicking his hand, a fist-sized ball of fire appeared. It moved to the wood and in no time, flames erupted.

Soon, they were settled near the fire, each with a plate of food. She admitted she might be slightly jealous of Salvarias. He consumed Wilhelm's attention. She'd gotten used to sitting by the fire in Wilhelm's lap, wrapped in his warm arms. Now his arm was always draped over Salvarias's scrawny shoulders. After she'd known the mage a few days, she'd been quick to side with Durak. Salvarias didn't deserve Wilhelm for a brother.

Once they finished eating, Salvarias gathered the plates and, with Wilhelm in tow, went to the nearby stream to clean them. Seeing Lunara's gaze follow the mage, Salvarias managed to leap to the number one spot on Varila's list of repulsive things.

When the brothers returned, Wilhelm remained standing while Salvarias sat near the fire, Adok resting habitually at his side. The wolf cast her a snarl, which she returned with a glare of her own.

Wilhelm cleared his throat and turned to Humar. "I've been thinking, and I want to try ..." He glanced at his brother and Salvarias motioned him to continue. "I want to try fighting with two swords."

Humar shook his head. "I don't have an extra broadsword. We'll have to wait until we return to Serinity."

"I ... I was going to try my broadsword and great sword."

Varila sat straight and Humar asked the same question that was in her mind. "Can you lift both?"

Wilhelm scuffed his boot against a rock.

"Yes," Salvarias whispered. "He can."

She'd never seen Wilhelm uncertain before. He was normally a towering muscle of confidence, and with every right to be so. With a height of over seven and a half feet, he possessed a body made of solid stone, and his square features were chiseled to capture the heart of any woman. His bright amber eyes dripped with warmth and honesty, and even men offered him quick friendship and trust. Yet here he stood, head downcast, a blush tinting his cheeks.

Humar slowly nodded and rose. "You're sure you can handle both?"

Wilhelm glanced at Salvarias. The mage's face was shadowed, but his hidden actions induced a grin from Wilhelm. The familiar confidence lit his eyes, and he drew his great sword, holding it in one hand while drawing his broadsword from its scabbard strapped to his back. His muscles bulged as he twirled them both, cutting through the air with powerful whooshing spins.

Varila ached with an urge to pounce on him and take what her body needed. Lunara giggled, and she nudged her to be quiet.

Humar grinned. "You'll be the first since Ctol Lilkous to wield two swords."

"It's been a dream of mine," Wilhelm said.

"You've never mentioned."

Wilhelm shrugged. "I didn't think I'd ever have the skill. Salv's been pestering me since I beat you in Serinity."

Humar drew his long sword. "We'll begin slow. Very slow."

Indeed, Humar moved as if stuck in a mud bog. It was obvious in Wilhelm's first parry that he didn't need so much handholding. He countered, moving quicker than Humar was apparently prepared for since Wilhelm's sword ended up grating against Humar's breastplate, sending a screech through the woods that made Varila's teeth stand on edge and startled off a night bird.

The knight grinned. "All right, Wilhelm. You set the pace."

Wilhelm winked and lunged. Varila had watched the two spar for six months, and if she hadn't, she wouldn't have picked up on how slow Wilhelm moved compared to his standard, one-sword training routine. Nevertheless, his agility was incredible, his feet seeming lighter than his tall, heavy frame should permit.

He didn't win a blow again. Regardless, by how quickly he learned, she had no doubt it was simply a matter of time before he mastered the technique.

Once the two finished, Wilhelm unbuckled his sword belts, set them by his bedroll, and returned to Salvarias's side.

"Thanks, Humar. I appreciate it," Wilhelm said.

"You're an easy student," Humar said. "Just remember, I get the credit when they write stories about your skill."

Wilhelm let out a rumbling laugh. "I don't think they'll be writing stories about me." Whatever Salvarias murmured caused Wilhelm to grin, and he mussed Salvarias's hair under his hood.

Varila leaned back on her elbows and watched the firelight brighten Wilhelm's eyes. Smiling, she imagined bards laboring over songs and stories written about a man who had the strength of ten men and a heart larger than all those in Arden combined.

Maybe, just maybe, she'd let the soon-to-be legend touch her again.

5

SPRING 1018 A.R

Humar ran his hand across his brow to rid it of sweat in the late hours of afternoon. Not knowing what might lie ahead made the thought of packing away his armor out of the question. He creaked neck to foot, living in his discomfort without complaint. The helmet was too much, though. He needed to feel the breeze on his face.

Glancing around the group, he took stock of the mood. His natural tendencies toward leadership had landed him the role without so much of a question in his abilities or a request for him to undertake the responsibility. His friends had mutually assumed it, and he preferred to be in control. With all that he'd witnessed since the brothers escaped slavery, he had no doubts the darkness mantling over Arden was readying itself for something big. And every choice he made propelled him one step closer to stopping it.

Upon cresting a hill, he saw inky black smoke weaving above the trees off in the distance. A scream sounded from far away and birds shot up into the brilliant blue sky. The wail did not trail off, but instead, turned to the bombarding screeches of someone suffering beyond imagining. Humar didn't need to see it to know a mage burned in the forest. Okulu came barreling into view.

"It's in our path, Humar," the half-Winsire said as he reined in sharply.

Humar rubbed his beard. Tobin's death was never far from his mind. He wanted to investigate the scene and, hopefully, the men were still there so he could question them ... or deliver justice. "Salvarias and Wilhelm, take the girls and go around. Durak and Okulu, you're with me."

"I would prefer to go with you as well, Humar," Salvarias said. "Perhaps Durak could accompany my brother."

Out of the corner of his eye, he saw Wilhelm tense. Though Salvarias seemed content to allow Humar's leadership, he had no doubt if he were ever to deny Salvarias's "suggestions", the boy would either assume the role himself or leave the group. Times such as these, Humar needed to tread lightly, giving Salvarias what he sought while controlling Wilhelm's reactive temper when it came to his brother. "I think that's a fine idea, Salvarias. If any are alive, you'd be best suited to offer treatment."

"I'm coming as well," Wilhelm said.

Salvarias shook his head. "Dangerous men could be wandering these woods, Brother. The sisters need protection."

Seeing Varila's eyes light with anger, Humar said, "I swear on my life that no harm will come to Salvarias. *Lunara* must be kept safe, Wilhelm."

"Please, Brother."

Wilhelm slouched and nodded. "Sure, Salv."

With that, Humar led his party one way while Wilhelm veered south with the others.

Setting a dangerous pace, Humar allowed his armor to accept the whippings of low branches. Although his horse tripped often over hidden moss-covered rocks or fallen branches, neither he nor Salvarias permitted their horses to slow. Okulu, however, had less control over his mount. He soon trailed farther until he went out of sight.

When the stench of roasted flesh wafted through the air, Salvarias picked up his pace. Humar nudged his mare with little success. The horse refused to go faster.

The charred body finally came into view. Fire still licked up the corpse, crackling and sending a spray of red embers to drift along the breeze. No other bodies lay strewn about and no men were in sight. At the nearby base of a tree, the leaves and soil were matted with blood.

Salvarias swung off his horse and took a few faltering steps until he stood directly in front of the dead person. Humar reached the area and dismounted, looping his horse's reins around a tree branch.

"We need to put out the fire," Humar said. He went for his water-skin and blanket.

"*Ich comad fyian eassa,*" Salvarias whispered. Reaching out a hand, he touched the flames, which immediately receded in upon themselves until nothing but a boiled person remained.

Humar startled. The spell wasn't in the list Mafarias had shared years ago. Only fourteen spells were known, and one that ended fire was not among them. Humar opened his mouth to question the boy, but stopped when he noticed Salvarias shaking, and his numbers were spoken instead of whispered.

"You all right?" Humar asked.

The boy turned on his heel and strode off until disappearing behind a house-sized redwood. Rain suddenly poured down, hissing and steaming off the corpse. Humar looked up at the sickly green clouds that had formed in a breath. The temperature dropped, making the icy rain better suited for winter instead of spring. The wetness made the sight even more ghastly. What looked like boils covered enough of the mage's face that Humar couldn't tell if it was male or female. The skin was sagging off, revealing the curve of a cheek bone.

Okulu cursed from behind. "Sick bastards. No sign of them?" The merc slid off his horse, mopping rain from his face.

"No, none. See if you can determine how many there were."

Okulu studied the pressed parts of soil, crushed ferns, broken branches, the blood splattered on the trees and ground, and finally ended at the pool of blood mingling with the muddy puddles of rain. "Seven, maybe eight. Hard to tell. The mage never stood a chance." Okulu pointed east. "The tracks lead that way. Looks like they moved faster than we did. Their horses must be accustomed to flight through wooded areas."

"Any chance of catching them?"

Okulu shook his head. "Not in these conditions. We're too far behind and the tracks will soon be washed away. Looks like they're headed our direction though, so we'll have to keep an eye out for them. Maybe set up a double watch at night." Okulu glanced around. "Where's Salvarias?"

"Over there. I need to talk to him and then I'll help you cut down the body." Humar gathered the boy's cloak and walked a ways to the tree. "Salvarias?" He continued around the trunk until he came upon Salvarias curled up against the trunk, gasping. "Salvarias? What happened? Are you—?"

"I beg—" He gasped. "Leave—" He clutched his chest. "Leave me a mo-moment."

Humar's growing suspicions seemed more factual. Why he voiced it, he wasn't sure. "You saw what happened to Tobin, didn't you, boy? You saw the truth."

"I beg—" Salvarias rocked violently. "I beg you."

Humar draped the cloak over Salvarias's shoulders. Adok, whom Humar hadn't noticed, parted from the shadows with teeth bared, taking a threatening step toward Humar. Hands up in surrender, he left the mage and headed back to Okulu.

"Is it just me," Humar growled, "or has that wolf grown irritable of late?"

"Odd beast," Okulu said. "I've noticed it as well. Except with Wilhelm and Lunara, he seems rather unfriendly. I've kept my distance."

Together, they dislodged the body from the stake and lowered it to ground. Using an axe that had been tied to his saddle, Okulu chopped off tree branches and respectfully covered the dead. Digging a grave would take more time than either man was willing to sacrifice, especially at the late hour and lengthening shadows.

A loud crack amid the trees shoved a rush of blood through Humar. He whipped out his sword and crouched, listening, searching. Okulu's sword slowly hissed from its sheath.

Rain thrummed through the leaves and deeper patters sounded against wood. A low roll of thunder echoed across the sky, followed by a soft pulse of lightning that sprang a raven from a nearby tree. Its flapping wings and piercing caw spiked the hairs at the base of Humar's neck.

"That wasn't the cause," Okulu hissed.

Humar didn't question the merc. The noise had to have come from something bigger.

Okulu sucked in a breath, and his eyes focused high up a tree. Slowly, he reached for his throwing knife.

"Steady your hand, half-breed," a man said. His voice had a musical quality to it, a higher pitch than most Erthlas.

"Who goes there?" Humar called.

"I would ask the same of you," the man said. "And since I have an arrow leveled at your throat, I believe I am at the advantage."

Humar eased his gaze up to the bushel of thick leaves Okulu stared at. "My name is Humar. This is Okulu. We saw the smoke and came to offer our help."

"There were eight," the man said. "They overpowered the cursed and tortured him brutally before burning him alive."

"And I suppose you sat up there in your perch, smiling," Okulu snapped.

"I mourn any loss of life. Though mages are unholy, none should suffer nor be slaughtered. Marooning them on an island where they can't hurt others is my preference. Regardless, even if I'd wanted to help the wizard, I couldn't have saved him. I arrived too late. I see you are a sympathizer of the cursed people, half-breed. It goes against the side of your superior breeding."

Okulu cast a disarming grin toward the voice. "You must not understand Erthlas. We're not as stupid as Winsires."

"Blasphemy!" the man hissed. "How dare you speak of your people so."

"We mean no disrespect," Humar said. "My friend is a passionate man."

Okulu snorted. Humar winked. Okulu believed in nothing and was loyal to even less.

"Enough," Salvarias whispered.

Humar jumped and looked behind to see the boy standing out in the open, arms in the sleeves of his robes.

"Show yourself," Salvarias said.

"I think not. I don't know the intentions of your group. I'm outnumbered and—"

Salvarias whispered, flicked his hand, and an icicle materialized. Within a blink, the boy's shard shot through the air and stopped shy of the bunch of leaves.

"I ask again," Salvarias said, "show yourself. I do not wish to send you to your death, but given the choice between these two men and yourself, I will spare them."

Only the droning patter of rain intruded on the silence.

Okulu's hand strayed toward his throwing daggers. Humar relaxed his stance, loosening himself in preparation of an attack, and blinked rain from his eyes.

A roar of thunder unfurled across the sky and a flash of lightning made shadows leap from their hiding place. When the rumble subsided, the humming patter of rain was the sole voice in the forest. Humar would normally have enjoyed the soothing sound if an arrow wasn't leveled at his heart.

"My patience has seen its end," Salvarias said calmly.

"Wait," the voice said.

The bushel of leaves parted and a young man scaled down the tree with such speed he stood in front of Humar within two breaths. Startled, he stumbled back a step.

The man was a Winsire, as Humar had expected, young, around Wilhelm's age. The Winsire's green tunic and trews were plain, but their quality betrayed the man's wealth. A well-crafted and deadly looking bow hung over his shoulder, and belted at his waist was a sword clearly of Cavrul making. The ice shard hovered at his throat.

Salvarias bowed. "I am Salvarias Laybryth."

"Prince Neithelas Frisliasi of Meitholias, home to the Winsires of Dalnar." He raised his head proudly.

"That's a mouthful," Okulu drawled.

"I am honored," Salvarias said.

"Humar," he said, extending his hand. The prince did not accept. "This is Okulu," he said, resting a hand on the merc's shoulder. "I think you can end the spell, Salvarias."

"*Rulose.*" The shard vanished.

"What brings the prince of Winsires so far from home?" Humar asked.

"My brother, first heir to the throne, set out shy of two seasons ago to investigate the unholiness sweeping over Arden. We Winsires have superior senses and for some time have known of a darkness threatening our lands. Initially, we discussed our fears with the trees, but they were too frightened to search the cause for us. That's when my brother left. We've not heard from in him in months. I have, with help from my beloved friends—"Neithelas caressed the nearest tree—"been following his trail for weeks. I'm determined to see him safely home."

"Why did your father not send warriors?" Humar asked. "Why only one man?"

"Sending more to their doom is not our way. My father has begun building defenses in our homeland. Soon, we'll call our brothers and sisters from the land and hide ourselves until the evil has run its course. I, however, am close to my brother. I couldn't leave him to suffer at the hands of darkness. I left unbeknownst to my parents." Neithelas glanced from Okulu to Salvarias before turning fully to Humar. "Though I find your choice of company unappealing, I'm in need of assistance. As a knight, you must honor your oath to help those who require it. I need protection and an escort through these dangerous woods. Of course, I have plenty of funds to pay you for your efforts. I head toward Hadrium for now, though my course may change at any moment."

"You listen here, you little half-wit, pompous bastard!" Okulu roared. "I'll—"

"Might I have a word with you both," Salvarias interjected.

Humar nodded. "Give us a moment, Neithelas."

Neithelas's upper lip curled. "Since you so rudely refer to me by first name, I assume you don't recognize my title? Do Erthlas exclusively bow to the vile pigs Loutsil breeds?"

"While I agree that Loutsil kings are unjust, I don't bow to any man," Humar said shortly. Grabbing Okulu's arm, Humar ushered them out of earshot of the prince. "What is it, Salvarias?"

Salvarias's head hung lower than normal, hands shaking. Whatever emotional torment he was experiencing was barely within his control. Humar would've offered help, but Adok's snarl made him keep his distance.

Salvarias rested a hand on the wolf's head. "While I agree that Prince Neithelas is ... difficult, ensuring his safety would be in our best interest. If what I have told you proves true, we will need the help of the Winsires."

Humar looked past Salvarias at Neithelas. Indeed, if such an army from Salvarias's vision existed, Dalnar would not stand a chance unless united. "I see your point. We can't follow him everywhere, but as long as he stays along the same direction as ours, I see no reason we can't keep an eye on him."

"Are you out of your mind?" Okulu snapped. "He's a snotty brat we'll have to handhold the entire way. I bet he's never left his mother's teat until now!"

"I'm sure his path will veer from ours soon," Humar said. "In the meantime, making friends with him is our mission."

"Count me out," Okulu said. "I'll leave right now before I kiss his ass."

"At least keep the insults down for me," Humar said.

Okulu grunted.

Mopping rain from his face, Humar traipsed to Neithelas. "We don't need any money; however, we'll escort you as far as we can. Eventually, I'm sure our paths will part. Until then, you're one of us. We won't pamper you, and we expect you to pull your weight in setting up camp, hunting, and so on."

"I will not hunt animals, but I will help collect fruits and vegetables. Is that acceptable?"

"Yes," Humar said. "We have two other non-meat-eaters in our group, so you'll fit in just fine. You got a horse?"

Neithelas nodded. "I do."

"All right," Humar said, squaring his shoulders. "Let's go meet the others."

LUNARA DREW her cloak under her chin and pulled her hood lower to shield her hair from the rain. The pine she had sought for shelter spread out to deflect most of the freezing rain, but a steady drizzle still snuck through.

Wilhelm, oblivious to the downpour, paced, casting scowls at the clouds, then in the direction Humar should be, and then back to the clouds. Clearly, he didn't like separating from Salvarias, and she wholly agreed. The mage needed guarding.

Durak grumbled a curse and wrung out his beard. Droplets fell from his eyebrows, streaming down his face like tributaries to connect at the base of his chin. "Just like the storms we used to get in Falar once a week. Damn unnatural!"

Wilhelm grunted and then paused in his pacing. "What did you say?"

"The storms," Durak said. "Remember 'em? Once a week it'd rain colder than frost, whether it be summer or fall. Me told Idolar it was a curse cast upon Falar. Somethin' unholy, me told him."

Wilhelm shook his head and picked up his pacing. The sound of horses snorting and hooves plodding along snapped the group alert. Varila yanked her sword from its sheath and stood in front of Lunara. Poking her head around her sister, Lunara studied the woods.

Adok bounded into sight followed by the rest of their group. Another person rode next to Humar. The newcomer was concealed in a thick green cloak she swore was made of leaves, but couldn't fathom how such a feat would be accomplished. All dismounted.

Humar motioned to the figure. "This is Prince Neithelas Frisliasi of the Winsires. He's going to be in our group for a while." Humar motioned to Wilhelm. "This is Wilhelm, Salvarias's brother."

"How opposite," Neithelas murmured. "A warrior, strong and proud."

Wilhelm's gaze had yet to leave Salvarias. He seemed unaware of the Winsire.

"This is Durak," Humar said.

"Ah, a Cavrul. A diverse group, Sir Humar."

Okulu snorted.

"Just call me Humar, Neithelas." The knight motioned to Lunara. "This is Varila, and her sister, Lunara."

Neithelas glided to Varila with entirely too much grace. He pressed the back of her hand to his lips. "Such a fine specimen of a woman. And one who fights. Women in Meitholias are experts with a bow and even a few are practiced with a sword. Accept my admiration for an Erthla woman who shows such strength."

Varila spread her arms open. "Admire away, Winsire."

Neithelas smiled politely. Lunara, still half hidden behind Varila, stepped around to politely greet him. When he turned to her, his eyes widened and he froze.

She curtsied. "Lunara. It's a pleasure to meet you."

Neithelas sank to one knee. "Pardon my rudeness. Your beauty has stolen my breath, my lady."

Okulu made a vomiting noise with which Lunara quite agreed. Still, she'd been raised properly. She tilted her head at the compliment.

He took her hand in his and kissed it, his lips lingering past her point of comfort, and she withdrew her hand. Thankfully, Wilhelm broke the awkward moment.

"What happened?"

Humar glanced at Salvarias, whose counting had switched from a barely audible whisper to one clearly heard. "We found a mage. Burned at the stake. The men who did it were long gone."

"That's it? That's all that happened?" Wilhelm pressed.

Humar nodded. "Why do you ask?"

Wilhelm shielded his eyes as he studied the clouds. "Nothing. Never mind," he muttered. "Salv and I are going for a walk."

Without waiting for a reply, Wilhelm draped an arm around Salvarias's shoulders and steered him into the woods and out of sight.

Unable to fight her curiosity since she knew few Winsires, Lunara used her powers to probe Neithelas's soul. It was pure, honest, and free of bitterness. There was peacefulness that drew her to him, a kindred spirit of sorts. He loved and valued life as much as she.

"A prince?" Varila said, wrapping her arm with Neithelas's and pulling him to his feet. "How utterly wonderful. Are you married?"

"No, my lady. I haven't been betrothed as of yet." He pushed back his hood and smiled at Lunara. He was more beautiful than handsome, but, then again, so were all the Winsires she'd seen. His large eyes were inviting, an innocent naivety mixed with a commanding air. Straight blond hair, almost white, flowed around his shoulders like a blanket of silk. His chiseled features were not as square or broad as other men, but still struck a masculine quality. Olive-tinted skin complemented his hair, accentuating his violet eyes framed by lush eyelashes.

"Such a handsome man and no wife?" Varila said. "Let's have a nice chat, shall we, Prince Neithelas?"

Varila shot Lunara a secret wink, and she rolled her eyes. Nothing stirred within her—no feelings moved, no desire swelled—but the instant she thought of Salvarias, everything stirred.

6

SPRING 1018 A.R

Three uneventful days passed before the dense forest parted way to a meadow wreathed by soaring pines. Tripir nestled in its center, spotted at the edges with farmhouses and fields of uniform crops.

Wilhelm followed Humar along the main road and into the village, keeping close to his brother, who had artfully concealed his robes. At least in small towns there were no guards to question mages.

Tripir huddled in depression, as Wilhelm mused most unwalled cities did during these dark times. As they plodded along the dirt road, he took notice that few women roamed the streets and even fewer men. Old folk and young children made up most of the village's denizens. Suspicious gazes tailed Wilhelm's group, and men hefted sickles with menace in their eyes while standing guard over the few women.

The honey-colored log tavern Okulu chose sported a decent-sized common room, home to a roaring fireplace, which, Wilhelm thought, made the room stuffy. His brother and Lunara appeared relieved to see it, and both settled in chairs next to the leaping flames.

After the other six companions took a nearby table, Humar

turned to Varila and asked, "How do we want to divide the rooms? They only have two with four beds each."

"We'll stay with the brothers." Varila gazed at Lunara while her finger circled the rim of her newly arrived ale pint. Her movement roused reminders of when her soft fingertips had traced the scars on his back.

"Very inappropriate for unwed women to share quarters with men," Neithelas said. "Perhaps the women should have their own room?"

Wilhelm had decided early on that he didn't care much for the prince. The man scowled too often in the direction of Salvarias.

Humar shook his head. "I won't leave them by themselves. Despite Varila's talent, times aren't safe."

"True," Neithelas said. "I offer my bow and arrow to you, my lady, should you want me to stay with you."

"Four to a room will be fine," Varila said. "Thanks though."

Okulu downed his ale and chased it with a swig from his flask. "Another six or seven days and we'll hit Vertex."

"We need to avoid Falar," Durak grumbled. "Place be swarming with those damned black-armored soldiers."

"We'll stop well outside the city limits and send Okulu and Varila in for supplies," Humar said. "They'll be less recognized. Just be sure to avoid your father's contacts, Varila. We don't want any knowing our route."

The worn-down owner, an older woman with curly gray hair, served beef stew and bread to Wilhelm's table, except for Neithelas who accepted a bowl of vegetable broth. She took the other two bowls of broth and additional bread to the younger siblings along with a glass of wine for Lunara.

"Here, you mage scum." The woman spat in the broth before thrusting it at Salvarias.

Wilhelm bolted up from the table, curling his fingers into a tight fist, but before he took a step his brother's hand raised as the sign not to interfere.

Salvarias accepted the bowl. "Thank you, madam."

Wilhelm glared at the woman when she turned around, and she hastened her steps to the kitchen. His brother tossed the broth in the fire and set the bowl aside, keeping the bread, and continued reading. Wilhelm cursed under his breath at Salvarias's patience, the same as their mother's. Ashra had gracefully avoided spit when she walked down the streets and ignored the taunts and cruel words, all the while offering help to any who permitted her, even if it'd been the same ignorant fools who'd spat on her.

Wilhelm blinked to remove the haze of anger clouding his vision and squatted beside his brother. "Let me get you another bowl. She won't spit in it this time."

"No, Brother. It is fine. I am not that hungry."

Wilhelm clenched his fist, glaring at his surroundings for something to release his anger upon. He felt a gentle squeeze of his arm by Salvarias.

"I promise, Brother. I am fine."

After ruffling Salvarias's hair and accepting a solid punch to the ribs, Wilhelm returned to his table, staring at his steaming bowl of stew while additional villagers shuffled into the tavern, cramming it full of warm bodies and spoiling the air with the stench of sweat. Three men chose a table close, clothes dusty and hands crusted with dried mud. Wilhelm pondered if the drawn lines on their sad faces were a recent addition. Whatever darkness brewed in Arden seemed to age people. He glanced at his brother's dark-rimmed eyes and the exhausted slump of his shoulders. Indeed, the evil added a weight to all.

"Did you hear about the black-armored soldiers in town?" one of the men asked another. "They're looking for a group of people. A man, large as can be imagined, a young mage, two women, one knight, and a Cavrul. Said any with information will receive a handsome reward."

"Bah! No city guards or knights wear such cursed armor. Evil, I tell you, pure evil is what those men work for."

The man snorted. "Maybe, but my wife and I need money. We had poor crops last season. And my son was taken. I can't plow as much land. I doubt we'll get enough food to make it through next winter."

"If these men are looking for them, further reason to help them. Mark my words: black-armored soldiers are not ones to get involved with."

The owner arrived with the men's food and the conversation switched to crops and the latest in plowing methods. With a shake of his head, Humar motioned to Salvarias, indicating a two-person table in the corner, and jerked his head to Okulu as well.

Salvarias rose and stood in front of the fireplace, his back to the group so Wilhelm was unable to see his brother's actions. A few breaths passed before he glided to the corner table with Okulu.

"Over by the fire, you two," Humar whispered to Varila and Wilhelm. "Send Lunara to me. Neithelas, go with Durak to the bar."

Wilhelm made his way to a stool near the fire and whispered to Lunara, "Go to Humar." He adjusted his sword for easy access.

She nodded and joined the knight. Durak had already moved to the bar with Neithelas. As Varila rose from the table, two men entered. They wore the same armor as those who had helped Dethal kidnap Salvarias, who had pursued them after Salvarias's rescue, and who had searched for him in Serinity. No skin or cloth could be seen beneath the plates of metal. The only opening was a slit in their helmets, yet even what lurked beyond the mask was nothing but darkness. Wilhelm had no idea how any could survive in a suit of metal, nor how they managed to move so fluidly.

Grabbing her drink, Varila staggered to Wilhelm and straddled him, taking a swig of ale. Wilhelm glanced at his brother sitting next to Okulu, head lying on the table, and the merc's ale pint in his limp hand, feigning sleep. The soldiers surveyed the room, and after a nod toward Okulu, they shoved aside any in their path to the corner table.

The black-armored man gestured to Salvarias. "Friend of yours?" The man's voice echoed as if he were on the other side of a massive cave.

"Yep," Okulu slurred.

"What's wrong with him?" the man asked.

"What's it look like? He's drunk off his ass! We're celebratin' his father's death. Got a sizable inher ... inherit ..." Okulu hiccupped.

"Inheritance?"

Okulu raised his flask. "That's the word!"

The soldier grunted. "What color are your friend's eyes?"

Wilhelm's heart squeezed a rush of blood. His hands went clammy and his life beat pounded in his ears.

Okulu sounded offended when he said, "Um ... I think green or hazel. I don't stare too long into his eyes."

The soldier lifted Salvarias's left hand. Wilhelm reached for his sword at the same time as Varila, who shook her head while applying pressure to his hand.

He struggled with his instinct to fight. There was no hiding the mark on Salvarias's palm, a mark only known by Wilhelm and whatever evil hunted his brother. Though Salvarias had always been artful in hiding the black, hollow ring circling a silhouetted black flame, it was impossible in this situation. One look and the soldiers would know they'd found their prey. His fingers glided over his own mark of a bear on his right palm.

The soldier dropped Salvarias's hand and wiped his armored glove on his breastplate. Something about the soldier's action raised a warning cry in Wilhelm, but the exact reason eluded him. Was it because the soldier wore a gauntlet and still worried about contamination? Or perhaps it was how jerky his motions were?

"What's that?" the soldier asked.

Okulu smirked. "Some infection he's had for a month now. I'd be careful. I think it's contagious. A woman he was with a week ago had the same sores on her—"

"I don't need to know anything else." The two soldiers turned their attention to the rest of the tavern and started toward Wilhelm.

Suddenly, Varila kissed him, turning her head to block the soldiers' view of him. His hands moved on their own to her thighs as her arms wrapped around his neck, her fingers tangled in his hair, her body pressed against his. He lived in a world of strawberry-oiled leather and sweet ale-tinged lips.

When her mouth left his, she looked over her shoulder. Wilhelm cursed at seeing the soldiers lingering near the bar. He'd hoped they'd venture on, not permitting further time to survey the patrons. They must've been inebriated not to piece together the companions, and luck wouldn't remain in their corner long.

"Easy," Varila whispered. "It'll be fine. You're too tense for a man sitting with a woman of my charm and beauty on your lap. You should act defeated, desperate."

He turned his gaze to her and grinned. "I'm not familiar with the feeling."

"What if I told you I'd never sleep with you?"

Wilhelm shrugged. "I wouldn't believe you."

She grinned. "I find your confidence repulsive."

"I find your lips irresistible." Wilhelm purposely slid his hands farther up her thighs.

In a blink, the cold blade of a dagger pressed against his throat and a seductive challenge glittered in her sea-blue eyes. "My lips are not all you would find irresistible should I allow you to pursue me further. Now lower your hands."

Cheeks burning from both arousal and her comment, he returned his hands closer to her knees. "I look forward to the possibility of learning what other parts can hold me as captive as your taste."

For the first time since he'd met her, Varila blushed. She grinned, lowering her dagger, and pressed her lips to his. Her touch lurched his heart to new speeds, and he was sure the entire room heard the thundering drum. Nails scratched down the back of his neck, making him battle a primal need only she had ever erupted. The heat between her thighs penetrated his trews, reminding him just how long it'd been since he'd felt the warmth of a woman. An unbidden groan of craving rumbled deep in his throat.

When she withdrew her lips, the tavern's sounds and smells battled through his layers of yearning. He glanced over her shoulder to see the soldiers leaving the tavern. Humar escorted Lunara upstairs, and Durak and Neithelas followed a moment later.

Varila's lips brushed against his. "I only did that to hide you."

"I owe you my thanks." Wilhelm watched his brother leave with Okulu.

"I'll be sure to collect your debt."

He turned his attention to her. "No time like the present."

"If you think I'll settle for a kiss, you're mistaken."

She suggestively bucked her hips, erupting his lust like a volcano. Crushing her close, he rose from the chair, mind racing for possible locations to sneak away. Her legs unfolded from his waist and, with aching restraint, he lowered her to the ground.

His blood felt on fire and his knees wobbled. The tavern spun for a moment before his heart found its rhythm. As his world cleared from its hazy dream, he realized she held him steady, and her eyes gleamed with triumph. She grinned wickedly before heading up the stairs. He inhaled a deep breath and admired the view while he followed her to their room.

When they entered, Okulu broke into a hearty laugh. "Well, you two had the best idea."

Humar shook his head. "You're lucky that didn't attract attention."

Varila snorted. "I knew what I was doing, Humar."

Wilhelm winked at the knight, sat next to his brother, and reached for Salvarias's hand. His brother pulled away and closed his fist.

"What did you do?" Wilhelm asked.

Okulu handed Salvarias a wad of dressings. "Looks like he burnt it on the fireplace."

Wilhelm reached for his brother again, but Salvarias shifted out of reach. "Are you all right?"

"It is fine, Brother."

Okulu shook his head. "It's pretty bad, Wilhelm." To Salvarias, he said, "I don't know what possessed you to burn your hand but, then again, they were looking for something, weren't they?"

Salvarias remained silent.

The merc shrugged. "Suit yourself. Do you have witch hazel? If not, I can get some or else that burn will get infected."

"I have some. Thank you, Okulu."

"Get some sleep." Humar motioned Okulu, Neithelas, and Durak out. "I want to leave early in the morning."

Neithelas kissed Lunara's hand before following Durak from the room. Wilhelm watched his brother dress his burnt hand, trying to catch a peek to see the extent of the damage, but Salvarias hid it from view. Finally giving up, Wilhelm flicked back Salvarias's hood and ruffled his brother's hair. After feeling the familiar strong punch to the ribs, Wilhelm leaned against the wall on his cot. Salvarias's rhythmic whispered numbers soon lulled Wilhelm to sleep, bringing dreams of strawberries and soft lips.

SALVARIAS GAZED over the rolling hills littered with the walking dead. He missed Lunara's conversations, her sweet smile, and soft touch. Regardless, he would not complain. This dream was his sole respite from the nightmares of burning cities or those where he relived his parents' murders.

He glanced up at the sole tree and its branches sprawling over the hill he stood. No blood glistened at its base, and it was all that seemed alive. Even the dull, wheat-colored grasses bowed in the steady stream of blood, and the breeze carried with it the stench of rotting flesh. In spite of that, by the tree, none of it reached him. Try as he might, he could not stay. He walked forward, even though he begged his feet to remain.

He parted through the dead, meandering up and down hills while gently avoiding outstretched arms. He kept his gaze downcast to avoid the blank eyes of the dead, and he focused on his footsteps sloshing through the blood in order to block their moans of pain.

"Young man."

Salvarias froze. No one ever talked to him here. No one kept him company save for the dead. A sense of danger prickled the back of his neck.

"Turn around, Salvarias. Allow me to look upon the man you've become."

Salvarias fled. He plunged through the dead, slipping on the bloody ground, scrambling to keep his balance.

"You cannot outrun me, young man. Save yourself the trouble."

Salvarias glanced over his shoulder. A man robed in deep plum floated toward him. His orange skin clashed against the pink sky, and he looked ... gooey.

"Come now," the man said. "You'll only weaken yourself. Let us get this over with."

Salvarias stumbled and toppled to the ground. He clambered to his feet to feel a cold hand grab his arm. The gaping hole in the dead man's chest did not seem to hinder his ability to restrain Salvarias with an iron grip.

The man robed in purple stopped in front of him. "Do you remember me?"

Terror froze Salvarias's limbs.

"We've met before. In the slave caverns, though I doubt you'd remember." He grimaced at the bloody ground and glanced around. "Is there no place clean we can sit?"

The instant Salvarias's mind went to the tree, it appeared within a few feet.

"Much better," the man said. He walked toward it but stopped shy of the untainted grasses. His brow furrowed, and he seemed unable to take a step forward. "How very interesting," he murmured. "If I must, we'll do it here."

The robed man settled on the bloody ground and motioned to the dead man. A forceful hand shoved Salvarias to sit.

"My name is Unupture."

Salvarias could not loosen his jaw to speak.

"I've tried to find you for a few nights. Seems you don't allow yourself to succumb to deep sleep often. How do you obtain such a feat?"

Salvarias's mouth went dry.

Unupture smiled kindly. "So be it. You don't have to tell me. Now, on to what must be done. You react poorly—extremely poorly, I might add—to my power. When last we met, you nearly died from it.

I assume your mind was too weak to handle what I did. However, you're stronger now. Regardless, I advise you to relax and permit me what I seek. If you do so, your pain will be minimal." Unupture pushed up his sleeve. "We'll start slow."

Unupture's index fingernail grew, lengthening to twice that of his finger. Utter terror clamped Salvarias's throat, pressing down on his lungs, forcing him to struggle for each tiny gasp. There was little cause for doubt that the unbearable pain he had experienced his last day in the slave caverns had come from this man. The lingering effects had lasted weeks.

Unupture frowned. "I cannot begin to understand the fear you must be experiencing. I'll make these visits as quick as possible. We'll slowly build your tolerance. I don't wish to inflict agony upon you, but I must."

Unupture moved his hand behind Salvarias's neck.

"Please," Salvarias whispered. "Please do not—"

White-hot pain seared down his spine. He convulsed, blinded by agony. What felt like maggots squirmed within his brain, compressing his mind, straining his skin to contain the bulge of his expanding skull. Desperate to relieve the pressure, he screamed.

"Please, don't fight me," Unupture said in Salvarias's ear. "You must relax your mind."

Salvarias latched on to whatever was near, squeezing with his entire might. The pain escalated as the number of maggots increased and began a frenzied exploration of Salvarias's memories, his fears and joys. Utter terror assailed him as he battled against the force, using every ounce of his mental abilities to block the man's power from finding what it sought.

"Breathe, young man."

Trying to gasp for air, Salvarias flailed about, thrashing wildly in an attempt to break free. He became aware of the man's fingernail rammed into the base of his neck. Any movement sent bolts of pain down his spine.

The nail burrowed in further, and the power surged with new desperation. Salvarias's muscles constricted, and he went rigid. He choked out a shout of pain, his stomach flipped, and he arced off the ground, gulping for air like a fish out of water.

"Breathe!" Unupture demanded.

Something warm flowed from his nose, spilling between his lips. Blood.

"Dammit!" Unupture cursed.

Salvarias lurched when the nail slid out of his neck.

"Next time we'll go slower. Forgive me," Unupture whispered.

Then Salvarias flew through air. The impact on dry land sent a sharp whoosh of air into his lungs, and his eyes flew open. One glance around and he saw a washbasin. Scrambling from wherever he was, he tripped over objects, rushing toward the table. He barely made it in time before becoming ill.

"What's wrong? What happened?" Wilhelm said.

Salvarias looked up to see his brother hovering beside him, lines of concern etched across Wilhelm's square features. Salvarias retched again.

"You need to take a steady breath, Salv."

He realized how harsh he breathed. Locking his gaze on Wilhelm, he watched his brother's measured breathing. Soon, they breathed in unison and the pain dwindled. He sank to the floor.

"Good," Wilhelm said. "What happened?"

Closing his eyes, Salvarias rested his head against a cool table leg. Sweat beaded his forehead and trickled down his neck. "Nothing, Brother. Just a dream."

"People don't react that way to dreams, Salv." Wilhelm's voice carried a paranoid edge.

Salvarias touched his fingers to his upper lip and they came away slick with blood. Accepting a cloth from Wilhelm, Salvarias clamped it over his nose, leaning his head back to stop the bleeding. He glanced around the room and finally recalled where he was. He tilted his head to Lunara who was pacing behind Wilhelm, and then to Varila who sat on her bed. "My apologies."

Varila lay back down, and Lunara offered a sweet smile before crawling into bed.

"I won't push you for answers," Wilhelm whispered, handing over the puzzle box and helping Salvarias stand. "But I'm here if you want to talk about it."

"Thank you, Brother." He doubted he would ever disclose his pain to anyone. What good would come of it? Wilhelm would only worry more.

After drinking a glass of water, Salvarias limped over to his bed crammed into the corner of the room. He sat up against the wall, smiling when his brother did the same and wrapped an arm around Salvarias's shoulders. Once Wilhelm's snore started, Salvarias gingerly felt the back of his neck. He winced when his fingers glided over the puncture.

A RAY of light falling across Salvarias's face woke him from light sleep. A low rumbling snore echoed in his ear, and a heavy arm draped around his shoulders, holding tightly even though Wilhelm slept. They had fallen asleep sitting up against the wall as they so often did, and Salvarias mused it was the only time he slept comfortably. Though his nightmares remained, an instant peace greeted him when he woke; the familiarity of Wilhelm's drumming heart and steady breathing, and now the smell of oiled leather that clung to him after he had received his armor from Durak. There was no urgent need to know where Salvarias was or who was with him. He was safe.

Wilhelm's arm tightened as he inhaled a deep breath. "Morning, Salv."

"Morning, Brother." Salvarias sat up, rubbing sleep from his eyes.

The sisters were standing at the window, heads together, and whispering softly to each other.

Beyond the door, Humar spoke as he knocked. "Wilhelm, Varila?"

"Come in," Wilhelm called.

Humar opened the door and peered in. "Let us eat so we can get out of here. I'd prefer you stay in the room, Salvarias."

Wilhelm nodded. "I agree. I'll bring you up some food."

"Thank you, Brother."

Everyone filed out, and Salvarias pressed himself into the corner of the room as Adok jumped on the bed and sat beside him. He performed his quick spell and ran a hand along his smooth cheek. Despite himself, he grinned. Shaving was tedious and, more importantly, required him to use a mirror, something he avoided so he was not forced to see his evil eyes. Developing a spell to keep a clean-shaven face was completely selfish with no benefit to the masses, but Salvarias was, after all, a selfish person. Such things were expected.

He began to unwrap the dressings covering his left hand that he had burned last night. The act had been impulsive, and he had cursed himself afterward. His left hand was his spell hand, and if it healed poorly, he would lose his dexterity to draw complicated runes.

He paused when halfway done, noticing the familiar tug on his mind—that calling he had heard his whole life—seemed more forceful this morning, more urgent. Frowning, he glanced around the room, battling his legs to keep seated instead of wandering Dalnar, searching ... he needed to search.

Shaking himself, he stripped away the last of the dressing and gasped at his perfect hand. Not a single blister marred his palm nor was the skin red or inflamed.

He had a sudden urge to chop off his hand. It was not normal. No matter what potion he applied, it should never have healed as it had done. Grabbing his dagger in a moment of sheer panic, he punched the blade tip into the mark's outer ring. He hesitated. He could lose his ability to draw runes if he did what his paranoia urged him to do.

Do it! the voice shrieked.

He sliced his hand. The pain was no greater than if he had pricked his hand on a needle, and it hardly bled.

He had a wild notion the mark was some sort of being living on his palm, and untamed fear tightened his chest and stole his breath. Rushing to the washbasin, he pressed the tip of the dagger into his palm, ran it around the black circle, and then dug under his mark, cutting away the center of his palm. He looked frantically around before hiding his chunk of skin in a cloth. He wrapped his hand in dressings, cleaned up the blood, and stashed the bloody washbasin under his bed along with the wad of cloth that hid his palm. He crawled into the bed, wedging himself in a corner.

Adok whined, mind firmly planted inside Salvarias's, repeating comforts that saw no results.

The door flung open, and Wilhelm entered with a heaping plate of food. "I got—what's wrong, Salv? You're pale as snow."

"Nothing, Brother." He cursed his trembling voice and took a deep breath. "I am fine."

Wilhelm frowned and looked around the room. Salvarias's gaze darted over the furnishings, floor, and washing table, and he inhaled a soothing breath when he saw no evidence of what he had done.

Finally, Wilhelm set the food on the bed, though by his roving gaze he was still trying to find the reason for Salvarias's peaked complexion.

Unfortunately, Salvarias's shaking hands would only worry his brother further, so he said, "I am not hungry. I will wrap it up and take it with me."

"You need to eat, Salv."

"I will. Once we leave. I promise." His hand did not even hurt, did not throb or spasm when he flexed his fingers.

Wilhelm shook his head. "I'll let them know we're ready."

"Thank you."

Once Wilhelm left, Salvarias gathered up the food and packed for everyone, desperately trying to distract his mind.

THE DAY of riding was torture for Salvarias. He battled the urge to unwrap his hand and see what horrors awaited him. When they stopped for the night, it took every ounce of willpower to wait until everyone slept before he snuck from camp, avoiding Durak on watch. Adok followed, whining and licking his hand, but the wolf's constant assurances everything would be all right did little to ease Salvarias's fears.

He marched far enough to ensure he could light his sparrow without any seeing him. Glancing around, he yanked free the dressings. "*Lumous.*" His sparrow of pure white light shimmered to life, illuminating his left palm.

His legs gave out and dropped him to his knees. He stared in disbelief at his hand. It was as if his discarded chunk of flesh had managed its way back to his palm and stitched itself together before healing completely, not leaving a single scratch or scar.

"What am I?" Salvarias breathed.

THREE DAYS HAD PASSED since Salvarias and his companions left Tripir. The ride to Falar's forest had been uneventful and—for Salvarias, who had withdrawn completely inward—peaceful. He had blocked out the companions, especially Lunara, and kept his spell book firmly in front of his face to avoid conversations and Lunara trying to catch his gaze.

His fear over what lurked within had sent him tumbling into an unshakable depression. With his fight draining, the evil that normally nibbled on his soul began tearing off minuscule pieces. If he had not monitored it so closely, he would have barely felt the increased feeding.

Now, another blow knocked him back, and a swell of utter grief clogged his throat as he stared at the meadow in the Falar forest. It was nearly the same as it had been eight years ago, perhaps slightly warmer, and he did not remember the sunny daisies being quite so dull. He moved to the spot where he had laid out a blanket with his mother. Memories of Tobin's tearful eyes when he had given Salvarias a book rushed him with such force he swayed. Times such as these he hated his ability to remember every detail of his life as if he were reliving it.

"This is as good a place as any for a camp," Humar said. "It'd be nice to rest in the open. Drink in some sun."

A strong hand rested on Salvarias's shoulder, holding him steady, and Wilhelm's voice rumbled, "I'd rather not, Humar. Let's move into the woods."

There was a long pause before Humar said carefully, as if knowing Salvarias's torment, "I suppose you're right. We'd be out for easy pickings. We need some rest, though. We'll camp tonight, and Okulu and Varila will go into town tomorrow."

"Salv and I will catch up," Wilhelm said.

Salvarias had not been able to rip his gaze from the spot. He swore he could still see the grasses bent from where the blanket had rested.

Once the companions were out of sight, Wilhelm said softly, "It's not all bad memories, Salv. We picnicked here often. Do you remember them?"

"Each one," Salvarias whispered.

"Come on," Wilhelm said, draping an arm around Salvarias's shoulders. "Let's go for a walk."

Salvarias had a foolish notion that if he left the sight, he was abandoning Tobin, condemning his father to be butchered again. Yet, Tobin's withdrawal had gouged a wound so deep, the mere thought of his father caused physical pain. Then again, could he blame him? Had Salvarias not withdrawn into empty darkness when he saw inside himself, what true horrors his soul was capable of performing?

Wilhelm tugged on him. "Come on."

Knees weak and thoughts consumed by painful memories, Salvarias followed his brother. Wilhelm's arm slid around his shoulders and seemed to give strength to lift his heavy legs.

He counted flowers and trees in his peripheral vision, trying to block memories. Unfortunately, his counting was becoming less effective. Since Zeeas, he was able to count up to five things at once. When emotionally strained, he ticked off a sixth object with his forefinger and thumb. Still, his mind raced with random thoughts he did not understand, hear, or initiate.

Even as he thought these thoughts, he also visualized Lunara's sweet smiles, contemplated the fate of his companions, remembered the lovely library at the Bellerum estate, listened to his brother's heavy left foot plop down harder than his right, and Salvarias carried on a conversation with a field mouse, sparrow, and squirrel while staying close to Adok's thoughts. It was all at once. He should go mad. It was a strain—one he neither wanted nor could he stop. Focusing on it made him want to scream, to rip out his hair, to crush his brain in order to cease its ranting.

"Here," Wilhelm said, startling Salvarias.

Glancing around, it took a moment to recall their location; the place Wilhelm and Salvarias had meandered to on so many occasions when looking for solitude on family picnics. This was the place they wrestled together; the place Wilhelm gifted Salvarias freedom from his pain. An instant smile sliced across his face when he looked up at his brother.

"You remember this spot?" Wilhelm asked, surveying the soaring redwoods wreathing the meadow.

Salvarias balled his hand into a tight fist and rammed it into Wilhelm's side.

"Ouch! You're going to pay for that, Salv."

Salvarias turned to dart away but found himself pinned to the ground. It happened so fast and gently, he had no idea how Wilhelm had caught him so quickly nor how his brother had managed to get him to the ground without causing the slightest discomfort.

He grinned up at Wilhelm. "You are too gentle, Brother."

Laughing, his brother mussed his hair. "You know you can use magic to beat me."

He squirmed under Wilhelm's inescapable hold. "I doubt it would work."

"Give up?"

"Hardly."

Salvarias was stronger than he had been when he was little, and had not wrestled with his brother since. Leveraging his entire weight, Salvarias rolled on to his stomach and used the strength in his arms and leg to shove his brother up and gain traction. No doubt existed that Wilhelm *let* him win. Knowing it would be short-lived, he bolted. He found it difficult to run when he was laughing so hard. Wilhelm, exaggerating his scramble to his feet, took up pursuit.

Salvarias's trips and near falls were no ploy. The uneven ground would have been a challenge even if he had the proper use of both his legs. Glancing at his brother fleeting along as though running on a smooth road swelled absolute pride in Salvarias.

"Surrender!" Wilhelm roared.

Salvarias had no breath to respond his defiance as he turned his gaze forward. Arms wrapped around his chest, and then he was falling, twisting in the air to land safely on his brother instead of the lumpy ground. Before even processing Wilhelm's flip, Salvarias was pinned yet again, his hair ruffled under Wilhelm's boulder-sized hand.

When laughter stole Salvarias's air, Wilhelm released his hold, a crooked grin cutting across his face.

"You've gotten stronger," Wilhelm said.

Salvarias sucked in a few deep breaths. "And you faster, Brother."

"Practice." Wilhelm plucked Salvarias up to sit.

Salvarias chuckled, helping brush twigs and grass out of his hair and off his robes.

"What's so funny?" Wilhelm asked.

Salvarias's chuckle rose to a laugh and he shook his head. "It sounds foolish, brother, but you handle me as if I weighed no more than a doll to a child."

Wilhelm shrugged, wrapped an arm around Salvarias's shoulders, and passed him the puzzle box. "Don't be ridiculous." Wilhelm gazed around the meadow and inhaled a deep breath. "See, Salv. Not all bad."

"No, not all bad." Resting against Wilhelm, Salvarias allowed the tension over the past days to fade as he whirled the box into the shape of a deer. Alone with Wilhelm, fears and uncertainties vanished, self-doubt and hate evaporated. No longer required to monitor his oddities, he gave voice to his conversations with various animals and slipped into a relaxed mindset.

Time lazily rolled by until Adok barged into Salvarias's thoughts by announcing intentions to backtrack for a rabbit he had sensed earlier.

Salvarias grinned at the wolf. "I warned it, friend."

A streak of black was all Salvarias saw before he found himself flat on his back with a slick, wet tongue licking his face. Wilhelm chuckled as he pulled the beast off Salvarias. Adok growled affectionately and bounded off into the woods.

Wilhelm stood, lifting Salvarias with him, immediately snaking an arm around Salvarias's neck, and headed toward the trees. "What did you do?"

"I warned a rabbit he might return." Salvarias jabbed his brother's ribs with an elbow.

"Ouch." Wilhelm chuckled, taking the box from Salvarias's hands. It shrank to the size of a marble, and his brother stuffed it under his armor.

Once they entered the dense woods, a shiver ran up Salvarias's spine. His happiness faded, and his gaze darted around the looming shadows while he fought the foreboding feeling twisting his gut.

When they came upon a clearing, he realized he had sensed evil; he had recognized his own stench. A group of thieves was restraining his companions.

A man with yellow hair and a scar on his chin grinned wickedly. "Well, look here, boys! A mage and his pets. I think it might be time for another lesson."

7

The scarred man spoke in the same merciless tone as he had eight years ago when he had slaughtered Salvarias's parents. Bandits restrained his companions, save Lunara. She was clutched in the arms of the yellow-haired man. Blood ran down her temple, and her wide eyes switched from overbearing fear to desperate hope.

Something very dark rippled the waters of Salvarias's placid lake of indifference. What lurked in the deepest depths was a terrifying emotion, one that fed off his pain and sorrow, one that had grown into a vile beast. When it burst through the surface of his lake, Salvarias had no choice but to obey its command.

His vision sharpened, Lunara's sobs sounded as though she wept them in his ear, and he shook—not from fear, but from the power of the beast within.

He chanted and drew his rune as the yellow-haired man yelled for someone to stop him. There was a rustle behind him, but Wilhelm had recovered from his stunned immobility and engaged the other attackers. Salvarias even heard his brother mumble, "I remember you."

Icicles appeared in Salvarias's rune, twelve in total, and he sent them flying to the murderers' necks, all except the yellow-haired man. The men grabbed their throats, their fingers slipping on the shards as they tried to stop their deaths. Salvarias reduced the speed of the icicles, allowing them to sink slowly into their victims. Screams gurgled and crimson blood spewed between the murderers' fingers.

The yellow-haired man was preoccupied with watching his men die, and Lunara struggled free. Salvarias advanced as the scarred man whipped out a sword Salvarias recognized as Tobin's. The murderer lunged, driving the blade straight for Salvarias's heart. Raising his arm, he used it to shove the sword off course. Cool steel sliced across his forearm and sank into his shoulder, but he did not flinch, did not stop his advance when the blade penetrated farther.

He felt no pain, only hate and rage.

The beast had taken over, standing protectively in front of Salvarias's naked sorrow and pain. That primal creature he so ardently shielded himself from flared to life, ridding him of the control he normally possessed. Like a drowning man needed air, Salvarias's rage, which until now had been hidden, demanded death.

He grabbed the man's throat, leaned close, and whispered scarcely loud enough for the yellow-haired man to hear, "Do you remember the *lesson* you taught my family? Do you remember slowly stabbing my father to death? Do you remember my mother's cries as you raped her? Do you remember her screams when you burned her at the stake?" The man's gaze darted toward the sound of Wilhelm's sword, then back to Salvarias. Recognition lit his cold eyes. "I, too, remember. With every step, I walk beside my father's mutilated body. With every breath, I hear my mother scream. Allow me to bestow upon you an equally harrowing education."

Salvarias's creature burst into life, rearing its ugliness in the form of black flames, more shadow than fire, yet it set aflame nothing but a deeper fury. It caressed his skin, flickering over every inch of him.

The fire surged with expectant delight, awaiting his command, and he ordered it to the man's wrist, breaking his grip on the sword. A raspy cry ripped from the man's throat as the skin on his hand sizzled and sputtered, and the satisfying aroma of burnt flesh wafted up to

Salvarias. Devoid of feeling, he yanked the sword from his shoulder and tossed it aside.

Suddenly, scenes of utter horror assailed Salvarias, stealing away the forest and replacing it with spectacles of death. As if he were the scarred man, he reenacted each of the man's brutalities, feeling what the murderer felt both physically and mentally, while simultaneously experiencing the terror and physical pain of each man, woman, and child the murderer had butchered. Each horror became as real as the air Salvarias breathed.

He raised a dagger and rammed it into a man's stomach. Warm blood gushed over his hand and a swelling sense of power over life and death bathed him in ecstasy.

At the same time, *he gasped when sharp bolts of pain shot through him as the blade penetrated his skin, yanking up to spill his insides. Fear and terror clogged his throat.*

Seamlessly switching, *he mounted a woman, using his weight to hold her down, and intense sexual pleasure coursed through him and satisfaction bloomed at his dominance over her as he violated her, not caring about the warm blood leaking from her side.*

Simultaneously, *his manhood burned and throbbed, and helplessness tore at his heart as he grew cold and the assailant's hungry eyes blurred into darkness.*

Next, *he drove a sword through a man's back, relishing in his sense of godhood. Life was at his beck and call, held in his hands, prey to his whim.*

Crying out, he looked down to see the sword sticking through his chest, and the heartache of leaving those he loved caused greater pain than the blade draining his life.

Murder upon murder he committed. Terror coalesced on his mind, and he trembled with physical pain. Though seventy or more agonizing scenes played out, only breaths had passed.

Then *he stood over Tobin, sneering in contempt for a man who befriended such sick creatures. In a blink, he parted open Tobin's throat, listening with rapture at his gurgled last breath and watching with satisfaction as his eyes—bathed in horror a breath before—dulled to lifeless orbs of hazel.*

Utter terror stabbed his heart at the thought of harm coming to his two sons and it gave him strength to battle the claws of Death coming to claim him. Then he heard her scream. His beautiful wife, the woman who had loved him, who had gifted him two sons, who had given him purpose, was consumed in flames. Loss ripped a cry from him and tore open his chest to expose his raw sorrow. He turned to his sons. Wilhelm was still unconscious, but Salvarias's eyes were wide. "No" choked in his throat as he fought to free himself, to shield the fragile boy from further pain. But then the child smiled, chilling and full of wickedness. It stole what little warmth he had left and disgust rose as bile in his throat. How could he have ever loved something so cruel as to grin while his mother burned alive? Imploring the gods for forgiveness, he recalled his love from the child ... from the monstrosity he had once cared for with every fiber of his being. Then pain seared across his throat and his world darkened.

Salvarias's heart nearly shattered, but the blackfire was too determined to let his pain hinder its course so it plunged onward.

He stood in front of the naked woman, reveling in the terror shining in her eyes.

"No!" Salvarias choked, begging not to relive what the man did to his mother.

It was futile.

Shoving her to the ground, he exacted his power over her, pinning and forcing himself upon her. Her screams intensified his pleasure, driving him to ravage her mercilessly until her fight had faded into submission. He stared at her tears mingling with the heavy rains and drank in her sobs as he emptied inside her. He had broken her. Then he held a bucket of burning liquid. He tossed it on her tortured body and watched her wither into nothing with nearly as much pleasure as when he'd taken her.

Salvarias's mind almost caved. Nevertheless, his beast had not finished and towed him into his mother's suffering.

Sickened by himself, he tried to hide in a dark corner of his mind, but he could not escape the man's wild gaze and his taking of everything he had held sacred. His fight drained until he merely lay sobbing. Then heat encased him. He screamed, looking down to see vicious flames eating his flesh. So much pain for what seemed an eternity. Then nothing. His thoughts drifted to the abomination he had spawned. He should have killed it. Now it would be loosened upon Arden. He had failed at everything. Despair claimed his life before the flame.

Salvarias's absolute sorrow and pain tore a cry from his throat. He nearly released the murderer, but his beast, the blackfires of fury, wrapped around those tender emotions and hid them away. His cry switched to a shout as rage erupted like a volcano suppressed for far too long.

Salvarias ordered his blackfire over the man's body. The murderer writhed and clawed at Salvarias's arm as the fire flickered and spat with savage hunger. With power he did not understand nor question, he poured the pain and horror of each victim into the man's soul, forcing the murderer to relive the harrowing last moments of his victims, just as Salvarias had done. The scarred man's eyes bulged, and screams rasped from his burnt throat.

The man's suffering ignited an intense wave of satisfaction within Salvarias. He savored the murderer's torment, the aroma of burning flesh and hair, the taste of vengeance on his tongue. A smile spread across his face when the light of life faded from the scarred man's eyes, and ecstasy—pure elation—heaved and gushed from Salvarias's soul.

He blinked and stood in a realm of horror that should have driven him mad with one glance. However, the scene held no fear for Salvarias and only stoked his rage to higher levels.

A fog blanketed the plane he stood, pulsating with hues of gray-black, swirling and shifting with an eerie light. There was no ground, no mountains, no rolling hills. It was as if he floated in the clouds of a stalking thunderstorm, the air stiff, lacking any scent of wilderness. But Salvarias clearly smelled the terror.

Before him, soaring higher than his sight carried, loomed a glassy black door, more like an impenetrable film than stone. The same odd light that gave the fog life cast sinister shadows on the faces twisting against the film, hands clawing at it for release. No fear crippled Salvarias when he saw the faces *move*, morphing from one terror-filled expression to another. His gaze slid left to right, smirking at the thousands upon thousands of doomed souls that made up a wall stretching farther and taller than his vision reached. Screams seeped through the film and wept down the wall.

The yellow-haired man knelt next to him, trembling, his gaze fixated on the faces, snot and spittle running down his chin.

The swirling black fog came alive, caressing Salvarias, searching his mind.

Instinctively, Salvarias reached out and touched a flat, smooth section of the door, one that resembled a hungry flame. The fog whirled with anticipation. The doors moaned open, cold air rushed from beyond, and instantly he shivered, his breath clouding.

A voice rose up, seeming to come from the fog itself, and its tone brimmed with hunger when it said, "His damnation is yours to sentence. Tell me, and I will carry out your punishment."

Jaw tight with anger, Salvarias turned to the murderer. "I want you to know what you did to her, know how she felt, and relive it. I want you to feel everything he felt—everything! I want you to know what you took from my brother, from me! I want you to know my pain, what I relive every night, and what I hear with every breath I take!"

Salvarias shoved the murderer through the door. Darkness enveloped the man, and the doors groaned shut, sending a resounding thud of finality echoing in the space. The murderer's scream pierced above the others, and Salvarias's smile broadened, listening with rapture to the cries of terror.

The fog encased him in warmth, driving away the chill, and seemed to approve of his action. His satisfaction rose to new heights, the screams soothing in his ears, the smell of retribution calming his mind, and the evil fog tasting sweet. He breathed in the feeling of power, of vengeance.

A laugh escaped when the murderer's face, brutally contorted in horror, pressed into the door, centered and eye level so Salvarias could clearly see the man's torment.

The fog's voice shook with anger. "Now you see what I see. Now you *feel* what I feel. Now you know that I am merciful." Its next words roared out. "Go and sentence them to eternal damnation, son of shadow and fire, son of anger, commander of the Blackfires of Vengeance! Offer quarter to none! All must die! All *deserve* to die!"

Salvarias blinked and the forest reappeared. The still-burning corpse was supported in his hand, the man's skin dripping in wilted chunks to the unharmed grasses, and Salvarias's laugh faded from his throat. He dropped the charred body, smirking at the cloud of flesh that puffed in the air.

The blackfire imploded, diving deep beneath the waters of Salvarias's lake, tunneling into depths that went beyond his understanding and reach. With its absence, his sorrow and pain were exposed, raw and too horrible to process, and his wilting smile shamed him.

What have you done, my little murderer? the presence hissed.

Salvarias stumbled backward, and his gaze fell to the looks of shock from his companions. His stomach churned, realizing they had seen his evil, discovered what he was capable of performing. Vengeance, yes. Torture, pure savagery, no. Lunara was the only one not watching, her face buried in her hands, and Wilhelm was doubled over on his knees. His brother had been ill.

He has seen your evil, my murderer. He knows now and weeps for the loss of his brother, the voice said.

Salvarias felt sick. He desperately needed to leave. His mind spun at his actions as the images of the scarred man's victims started settling into his soul. Their physical pain still thrashed his body, his mind still relived each tormented moment, and it bordered on more pain than he could bear. Fleeing consumed his thoughts. Then he heard Mithal. He grabbed the horse's mane and mounted. Without needing direction, the stallion bolted. Salvarias heard his brother's cry and urged the horse to take new speeds. He rode low in the saddle, but branches still cut his face. He could not see them through his streaming tears and the sudden torrent of rain.

Wilhelm stumbled to his feet. "Salv!" His brother disappeared among the thick pines.

A ripple of dizziness made him stagger back a step. Through pulsating vision, he stared at the charred corpse of the man who had changed Wilhelm's life, who had murdered his lovely mother and wonderful father, who had stripped away his happiness, who had stolen his childhood.

The stench of burnt flesh seemed to reach into his mind and exhume details of the fateful night eight years ago. Vaguely he remembered a scorched ground, an unnatural stench in the air, the smell of smoke in his brother's hair.

A sob left him. Idolar had lied. Wilhelm's parents had not died quickly. And a horrible suspicion began to worm its way into his mind: his baby brother had witnessed it all.

The thought shoved him to his knees. Thunder ripped through the forest, vibrating the muddied ground. He raised his gaze to the malicious green clouds pummeling the sky with bright pulses of lightning. Stinging sheets of rain flogged him, seeming to seek punishment for all his brother had endured.

"You must let me help him," Lunara said.

He looked over to see her trying to wrench free of Varila's hold.

"Trust me," Lunara begged. "I understand what he went through. I was connected with him the entire time."

His mind was shutting down. He couldn't deal with this. Not after so many years of locking his pain away in a blind smile of denial and indifference. Now, he was being forced to relive that night, to remember the empty year of his life that had followed. The five years spent in the dark tunnels and caves, being beaten and whipped ... So much darkness. So much pain.

"Please!" Lunara cried, twisting in her sister's arms. "You must allow me, sister. You must!" A flash of lightning lit up Lunara's ice-blue eyes, coaxing forward a memory that hovered just outside his grasp, leaving the sensation of trying to recall the name of a brief acquaintance.

His gaze drifted to the charred corpse, smoke hissing off its black-ened body. Salvarias's cry had carried so much pain. So much anger.

Something shook his shoulder. He couldn't tear his gaze from the body nor could he rid his mind of the image of Salvarias encom-passed in shadowy black fire.

A sting across his cheek focused his eyes. Lunara cupped his face and lifted his head. "He needs me," she said. "He needs *me*. Not you. Not Humar. Me. Don't follow until the morning. Mithal can cover long distances, and I'll need time with him."

Wilhelm grabbed her arm before she left. Whispering so only she could hear, he said, "There might be death around him. You have to convince him it's not his fault."

Though her brow furrowed, she nodded. "Give me time. I promise I'll help him. I promise." Without waiting for a reply, she mounted her mare and went out of sight before Varila's call of caution faded.

A strong hand squeezed his shoulder, and Humar said, "Let's get away from this."

Wilhelm barely kept aware of his surroundings as he followed a silhouetted figure. He tripped over rocks and logs, bushes and ferns. Someone caught him each time he nearly fell.

The person stopped, and Wilhelm trudged from the group, knocking aside arms and shoving people away when they tried to follow. Eventually he was alone.

All the memories of his parents before the murder—of Tobin's kind face, of his mother's soft hum while she prepared dinner—charged his mind. Then came memories of the fateful night and the hollow year afterward, the year spent living on cold streets only to be followed by cold caves and whips from the slavers. All that changed in his life was because of one man with a scar across his chin. One man. One.

Sorrow plunged its barbed hands inside him and purged him of strength. His knees buckled, and he collapsed to the soaked ground. Hot tears burned down his cheeks as he cried into the soil, unable to control his racking sobs, balling clumps of mud in his fists.

Soft hands slid around his face and lifted his head on to something warm. Through tear-blurred vision, he saw Varila's sea-blue eyes. A wet blanket covered him and fingers glided through his hair.

"You're not alone," Varila whispered.

Her words tore down the last of his walls protecting him from horrible memories and pain. He wept like a broken child.

8

SPRING 1018 A.R

Mithal stopped at a creek after nearly an hour of hard riding. Salvarias more fell from the horse than dismounted and became ill before scrambling into the deep part of the water, not even bothering to remove his robes. He felt tainted, unclean. He scrubbed himself in the freezing stream, desperately trying to remove the man's throat skin from his hand and the evil that clung to his flesh.

Rain poured down in biting sheets. Thunder boomed and lightning lashed out across the sky. Shadows pounced toward him, and the trees loomed threateningly overhead.

He hugged himself as the images of people flashed across his vision, their pain and horror rippling through his mind and ravaging his body. The murderer's face grew hazy and, in one blink, Salvarias no longer saw the scarred man inflicting the atrocities. It was Salvarias himself. He raised his shaking hands to see them covered in blood.

Yes, the presence hissed. *My poor, precious little murderer. You killed them. You killed them all.*

Salvarias became violently ill. He frantically stripped out of his clothes and gaped at his stained body. Not even the creek's flow rid him of the warm blood that soiled his skin. Uncontrolled sobs assaulted him as he grabbed nearby branches and leaves and used them to scrub himself with renewed vigor.

His thoughts flashed to his mother. Even though she had beat him, he felt sorry for her, guilty for making her deal with such an evil child. He loved her. Her anger and hatred toward him were his fault; what she withstood trying to drive the evil from Salvarias had been inflicted by him. Knowing the suffering she endured in her final moments tore through his heart. Tobin's pain, his sheer hatred for Salvarias was the last feeling the man had had before death. No happy memories, no peaceful thoughts crossed either parent. Both had been focused on their hatred and blame toward Salvarias.

His attempts to clean himself were futile. He could not rid the blood, and his sheer agony soon blinded him. Groping his way to solid ground, shivering from the icy rains, naked and alone, he curled into a ball, wishing he could disintegrate into darkness.

It was then he saw himself huddled on the bluff of sanity. It over-looked an ocean of ravenous red fog stretching as far as the eye could see. It roiled with thought, and there was no doubt it sought his soul. He looked up at the solid vibrant tree he clung to, but his grip was slipping as the cliffside eroded from the blood of those he had killed.

Despair, terror, and loneliness devoured the last of his fight and hope. His hidden bundle of fears and suppressed memories unrav-eled. His vision faded in and out: one blink a stream, one blink his mother's knife, one blink red smoke, and the next murdered faces. He wanted peace with such a hopeless hunger he fumbled for his dagger.

It is the only way to end the evil, my murderer.

"What was the black door?" Salvarias cringed from the cold ground beneath him and thunderclaps echoing among the trees.

Oblivion, my little killer of the innocent. Taken over by a dark force. A place you will end up, reliving your evil deeds along with those of the people you condemn there, the ones you whispered to which caused them to be in that cursed realm.

You are evil, my murderer. It is in your soul, in your heart. Only one truly belonging to darkness could touch the doors of Oblivion, could command the blackfires of death. Look again at the victims. Look again at what you have done. Look again at the blood on your hands.

Blood dripped down his arms, and the screams of the dying filled his ears. His mother's knife glittered in the sunlight, and he watched in horror strapped to a chair as she drew near. He grabbed the back of his head, curling up tighter when he felt the scar.

He could no longer bear the images and painful memories, could no longer infect the world with his evil. Gathering his courage, he clenched the cold metal hilt of his dagger and rammed the blade toward his heart.

"No!"

He heard Lunara's voice as she stopped the knife from penetrating his chest bone. She wrenched the dagger from his fingers. Lost in darkness, he felt her arms surround him, and he clung to her. He ached with a need to dissolve, to fade from life, nothing more than a speck of soil blown away in the wind. Burying his face in her neck, he sobbed in hopelessness. Her hair encircled him, shielding him from the world, providing comfort for the part of his soul longing for love and acceptance, and he hid in the raven mass, tucked in its secrecy.

His evil shrank from her light, and his own soul bathed in her compassion, acceptance, understanding, and care. He packaged the painful memories of his childhood into a tightly wrapped bundle and stowed it away once again, buried deeper, never to be remembered.

Lunara shivered by the stream, stroking Salvarias's wet hair, rocking his shaking body. Her tears mingled with his and her heart ached with his.

"You're all right," she whispered, pulling the blanket closer as her gaze darted from the dead animals to the ground littered with dead insects. Both horses had spooked and ran before the dying forest reached them.

"You must believe me," Lunara whispered in his ear, tearing her gaze from the gruesome sight. "You have done nothing wrong. I do not hate you. I do not fear you. You have nothing to be ashamed of."

"I am sorry," he sobbed, his fists balling her dress. "I did not mean to kill them."

"I know. It's not you. It's not your fault. You've done nothing wrong."

"Please help me," Salvarias wept. "I do not want to be evil. Make it stop. Please make it stop!"

Lunara lifted his chin so he could see the care and concern brimming in her gaze. "You're not evil. You're one of the kindest men I know. I ... I care for you, and I do not care for evil men, Salvarias. Wilhelm loves you. He doesn't hate you, he doesn't fear you."

"I am evil. You saw! He saw! They all saw it!" The intensity of his pain reached inside her and embedded a physical ache. "I cannot endure it anymore! I cannot!"

Keeping her voice calm, she said, "What I saw was a tormented man. I *felt* a man experience pain no one person should ever experience. You've done nothing wrong." By the gods, he barely choked in air through his sobs. She smoothed a lock of soaked hair from his face. "Salvarias, you must believe me. You're my friend. I care for you. Even after what I saw, I care for you. And I do not care for evil men."

He stared into her eyes long enough for her to think he didn't believe her, but finally he buried his face in the crook of her neck and curled up tighter. At that moment, the forest ceased dying and the rain abated to a light drizzle.

All she desired was a way to offer him greater comfort, to possess magical words that would ease his pain. A confession of her love almost left her lips, but now wasn't the time. Her admission would simply cause him further pain, of that she was certain. With nothing left to give, she kissed his forehead. The rain ceased altogether and bright rays of sunlight cut through sparse clouds. She welcomed its warmth.

Eventually, exhaustion must have towed Salvarias to deep dreams. Lunara shifted until she sat against a fallen tree, using her legs to help support his weight, and fervently ignored the death circling her. She wrapped her arm around his head, holding him to her chest, smoothing his hair from his forehead. "What cruelties have been done to you?" she whispered.

Hours passed before the sun dipped over the trees, sculpting dark shadows in the forest and bringing with it the chill of night. Salvarias stirred in her arms, and his warm breath caressed her neck. She pulled the soaked blanket tighter around his nakedness in a pointless attempt to stop his shivering.

After a deep breath, he sat up, drew his knees to his chest, and the blanket around his body. "*Lumous.*"

The sparrow glowed close, chasing off shadows and adding a horrifying illumination to the death surrounding them. He surveyed the forest with widening eyes.

"It's not your fault," Lunara said, shifting to face him. "It—"

He lowered his head, cringing from her and rocking. He must've thought she judged him, thought him to be destructive and evil. She cupped his face in her hands and raised his head to look into her eyes, which she filled with her love and understanding. His relief was palpable.

"Thank you," he whispered, quickly wiping his tears. He fumbled with his wet robes wadded by the creek and retrieved a cloth. Lowering her hood, he held back her hair and dabbed the dried blood from her temple. "Are you all right?" he asked.

She almost laughed. After what he'd experienced, he was worried about her well-being. She smiled and nodded.

Once he finished, she picked up his robes and kept hold of his hand, helping him rise. He followed her from the death scene with a look of one who'd been numbed by their pain.

Mithal was waiting by the first signs of life. She got a dry blanket, fresh robes, and a needle and thread from the pack, set the items aside, and began clearing a spot for a fire while Salvarias found dry firewood. After they situated the logs, Salvarias chanted and set them on fire.

He stared at the hissing flames, eyes distant, arms folded around himself. She moved in front of him and lowered the blanket so she could see the two wounds on his chest. After examining them, she looked into his haunted eyes. "I need to sew one."

She did her best in the campfire's light, seeing him wince every so often. When done, she glided her fingers over various scores, wondering what caused such odd marks. Ashamed at her ill timing but unable to stop, she admired his physique. He was not sickly thin as she remembered, but covered in thick, defined muscles with shoulders broader than she'd thought. Though his scars from Zeeas made her heart ache, his body ignited a new heat within her. She saw his strength, not his mutilation.

He shivered under her touch, and his eyes focused on her. Cheeks burning, she picked up a dry blanket, removed the wet one, wrapped the fresh one around him, and gave him a gentle tug to the ground.

"What happened?" she asked.

He bowed his head, gathering the blanket closer, and shuddered. She shifted closer, facing him and drawing her knees to her chest. She lowered her head to look into his eyes.

Fresh tears were welling. "I saw ..." His voice choked.

"You don't have to—"

"I saw the people he killed ... I know what he did to each." Salvarias's face paled, and he rocked himself. "I felt ... I *feel* their pain, their torment. I know what my parents thought in their last moments. Even now when I close my eyes, I see the dead; I see their blood on *my* hands. *I* killed them."

His rocking became aggressive while he stared at his hands. Lunara scooted closer and was surprised when he gathered her into his embrace. He buried his face in her hair, holding her as if she possessed some ability to banish his suffering. They sat for many moments, Lunara afraid to move, afraid if she stirred he would recall his warmth, erect his emotional wall. Eventually, he released her and rested his face in his arms propped up on his knees.

"We should get some sleep," she murmured.

He raised his head and nodded. Lunara curled up on the wet grass, teeth chattering without a blanket. She felt his eyes on her.

"It is a c-c-cold night," she remarked.

Salvarias settled behind her and drew her to him. Covering them with his blanket, he wrapped one arm around her waist while the other slipped under her head like a firm pillow. He folded his arm around her shoulders until she was encased in his embrace, and he inhaled deeply. She listened to his breathing steady and soften as he drifted to sleep. Gliding her fingers along his scarred arm, she closed her eyes and permitted her tears freedom.

LUNARA TREKKED THROUGH THE FLAT, desolate desert she did every night in her dreams. The arid land was barren except for specks of parched grasses wiggling between dried, cracked mud. She knelt at the edge of the pit, looking far down into the darkness at the shadowed figure huddled at the bottom. Always, the person—or possibly creature—sounded distant when it spoke, and the soft voice made it impossible to identify if the figure was male or female.

As with all the other nights, the conversation started the same. "Hello, Lunara."

"Hello," Lunara said.

"You must help him."

Lunara perked up, her attention fully focused on the figure. Normally, the voice asked for help, begging Lunara to find it. It had mentioned the mage only once before. "I don't know how to help him. He won't lower his guard around me."

"You must continue to try. Do not give up. You must break through." There were a few sobs before the voice hoarsely whispered, "What has he done to him?"

"Please, tell me what to do!"

"There is so much pain around me. I ... I am alone. So weak. So very weak."

"How can I help you? Tell me!"

The voice whispered softly, "I wish I knew, child. All I know is the Soul must be saved. Without him, we are doomed."

Before she could voice further questions, the scene vanished, and she woke in Salvarias's warm arms.

~

SALVARIAS STIRRED LAZILY from the deepest depths of sleep. His arms were wrapped around Lunara, her back against his chest, his face buried in her hair. She was awake, her breathing quicker than when she slept. He was ashamed of himself instantly. Especially after what had happened with the scarred man, he knew the risk of allowing her close. Nevertheless, he did not remove her from his embrace. The peacefulness of his mind was unfamiliar. However, holding Lunara was like returning to the embrace of a long-lost lover. She was ... right. He never wanted to leave this moment, to endure the stares of his comrades, see the judgment in their eyes. He did not want to go back to his sorrow.

Lunara's fingertips caressing his arm calmed his thoughts. "Good morning," she whispered.

He inhaled deeply, feeling more rested than he had in his entire life. For the first time, no nightmares had haunted his sleep. He had strolled through forests, gardens, or simply tranquil darkness.

Pulling her closer, molding her to him, he nestled his face in her hair, breathing in her intoxicating scent. His tiny soul rested in her light—safe and cared for, drinking her warmth. His evil ceased its vicious feeding, and he fought tears of relief.

She rolled over to face him. "We need to head back."

He absorbed her smile and the kindness provided in her eyes. When she ran her fingers through his hair, her hand glided over his eaten skin where his ear used to be, but she did not recoil or avert her eyes. She repeated the movement, not shifting from the grotesque area. She seemed unfazed by his mutilation, and his need for her acceptance, to grow the care offered in her eyes, nearly moved his lips to hers.

"How are you feeling?" she asked.

"Rested," he murmured. He closed his eyes, allowing her touch to hypnotize him, her fragrance to rip away his pain.

He was not sure how much time passed before she spoke again. "The images … are they still there?"

Salvarias pulled himself from his reverie, removed her from his embrace, and sat up. He shut his eyes tightly when his mind picked up new speeds. The normal images he had experienced since birth were there, but the people the yellow-haired man had killed were crisper than the others, slower to pass by, and their horror layered over Salvarias's mind while his body ached with their pain. He had no doubt he would endure this every waking breath.

Starved from its lack of feeding, his evil crept from its hole and its fanged teeth sank into his soul. He glanced up to see the world veiled by a thin haze of red. Blood. Everything was tinted the color of blood.

"Yes," he exhaled, resting his face in his hands. His mind was a great deal more painful, and his chaotic thoughts had doubled from what they were before he had killed the scarred man. Once again, the image of the cliff of sanity appeared. It was slippery with the blood of the people he had killed, and he tightened his grip on the root he had clung to since birth, cringing from the abyss of red smoke below.

Shivering, he pulled the blanket closer. He was petrified.

Her light touch reached him, calming his mind, erasing the images, and ebbing his pain. He took a shuddering breath and raised his head. The red haze still tainted his vision, and he swallowed his tears at the loss of vibrancy life once had.

Shifting to kneel in front of him, Lunara lowered the blanket to examine his two gashes. His cheeks burned with embarrassment. The wounds from Zeeas had healed poorly, and the sheer number of scars caused people to gawk at him with unwelcomed pity. Yet, Lunara's eyes were not filled with pity. They shimmered with desire. Her direct gaze made him want to shy away, but he was held captive by her eyes, by her rose-red lips parting, by her fingertips tracing a scar across his chest. Silky strands of hair fell along her cheek, making his fingers itch to brush them from her face. She leaned forward and every muscle tensed. Her hand flattened against his chest, sliding up to his shoulder as she inched closer, gifting him the feel of her warmth, the moisture of her breath nearing his lips.

As her hand caressed his shoulder, he could not help but notice something on her palm felt different; not smooth like the rest of her flesh. He desperately tried to ignore it, but his curiosity demanded satisfaction. Silently cursing himself, he caught her wrist. Gently, he turned over her hand to reveal a mark on her palm, round and white as a full moon.

"I've had it since I was born," she said, voice shaking. "My mother has one as well." After she took in a deep breath, their moment passed and she smiled, removing her hand, and pulled a fresh set of robes over his head. "I must admit, I did a good job mending you in the dark."

After he finished dressing, he held her wrist and traced the mark with his fingertip. A flicker of recognition crossed his mind, of some event he should recall, of some person he should know. It disappeared in an instant, and he was unable to retrieve it.

Her sharp intake made him raise his head to look into her eyes. They were wide, and her breathing was quick. "What is it?" he asked.

She opened her mouth to reply, but stopped short when a horse nickered. He looked past her to see a silhouetted man riding toward them. Salvarias instantly recognized his brother's frame.

This is your chance, murderer. Flee! Run from your brother before he withdraws his love! Run!

Scrambling to his feet, he staggered back as Lunara grabbed his arm. He was incapable of seeing his brother's judgment. He would abandon his brother, save him the grief of knowing the evil in Salvarias's soul. He pulled against Lunara.

"It's all right," she said. "Please—"

Her touch did not overcome his fear. Angry clouds formed within a breath and the sky spat rain.

"No." Salvarias pleaded with himself to stop, but a thundering roar denied his request.

Lilly bucked, throwing Wilhelm from the saddle, and her petrified thoughts pierced straight to Salvarias. Wilhelm never paused to calm or catch the mare as she whirled around and bolted. He marched straight for Salvarias.

Wrenching his arm, he cried, "Let me go!"

"He loves you!" Lunara said. "I swear he doesn't hate you."

His brother drew closer, and fear paralyzed Salvarias. This would be the moment when he was left alone in the world. This would be the moment when Wilhelm finally saw the demon he called "brother."

Wilhelm closed the distance quickly and, with reluctance and dread, Salvarias met his brother's gaze.

"It's all right, Salv," Wilhelm whispered. "I promise, we're all right."

"I-I do not understand," Salvarias said. "You have seen it. Finally, you have seen my evil. You know—"

"I don't see evil, Salv," Wilhelm said. "I see a man capable of killing someone who murdered innocent people. I see a man who avenged our parents."

"No, Brother." Salvarias's gaze slid to a rabbit floundering across the muddied ground, its agonizing screech slicing through his thoughts. The grasses lost their color. Leaves curled. Insects crawled from out of the soil, flailing about. "You saw the satisfaction I received from death. I am not normal ... there is ... something inside me."

"I love you, Salv. You're not evil."

Salvarias shook his head and stumbled back a step. "Leave before I hurt you!"

"You won't. I know you better than you know yourself. Look at me." Salvarias tore his gaze from the rabbit and looked into Wilhelm's eyes. "I'll protect you. You won't hurt anyone because I'll never let it get you. You believe me? I won't let it get you."

Deep in Salvarias's own soul, the tiny part belonging solely to him, he knew Wilhelm was right. His brother would not let the evil take him. Wilhelm was the root Salvarias clung to, the vibrant tree that protected him.

The guilt Salvarias harbored for his parents' death would never ebb, and the knowledge and understanding of their true feelings doubled it. Nevertheless, even with his shame and abhorrence at himself, he selfishly allowed Wilhelm's arms to encase him as they had done when he was a child, tucking him away in a place where no one judge him, where all that existed was love and safety.

"Forgive me, Brother. I beg you," Salvarias wept.

Wilhelm's arms tightened. "There's nothing to forgive, Salv."

Imbecile! the voice yelled. *This was your chance to save him!*

I am not ready to leave him! Salvarias pleaded with the voice.

Then you condemn him to death!

Salvarias buried his face his hands and allowed his tears and absolute sorrow to thrash him senseless.

He wished Lunara had never stopped him.

9

SPRING 1018 A.R

U pon riding into their camp, it was clear that Salvarias's preparation for the hurtful stares of his companions was grossly inadequate. Durak glowered at him, more disgusted and untrusting than before, if possible. Humar and Varila avoided eye contact with new lines of fear and distrust etched in their features. The turn of Humar caused a knife to twist in Salvarias's gut. Right when he had learned to trust the man, to call Humar a friend, the knight would no longer look at Salvarias. Yet he had known this day would come.

Yes, did I not tell you? the voice hissed. *I told you when they saw, they would turn from you. Just as your mother turned. Just as Tobin turned.*

Salvarias dismounted and stayed on the side of the horse blocking him from view while he unstrapped the saddle. He withdrew his aspen branch before Wilhelm lifted the saddle from Mithal and took it over with the others.

Salvarias took several deep breaths to calm his nerves, tucking away his hurt. The presence was right. He did not need their friendship. He had lived without such comforts for eighteen years. Wilhelm was enough. Another deep breath, and he turned to find Neithelas standing stiffly, violet eyes gleaming with hatred. Salvarias had figured the prince would be an issue. The Winsire race did not condone killing, and merely engaged in battle to save their families' lives or their own. Even then, their killings were swift and merciful.

Neithelas seemed to be waiting for an explanation, perhaps an apology. Salvarias was in no mood to offer either. By the prince's reddening face and clenched fists, Salvarias's silence had succeeded in sparking Neithelas's anger, which dredged up a secret hope: maybe Neithelas would kill him—carry out the act Salvarias should have had the courage to do after his first breath of life.

Instead of ramming an arrow in his heart, Neithelas punched Salvarias squarely in the jaw, sending him reeling until his staff caught his balance.

Wilhelm was there in an instant and leveled the prince with one blow. His brother balled Neithelas's cloak in his fist, hauled the prince to his feet, and punched him again, cutting open his bottom lip. Salvarias and his companions snagged hold of Wilhelm's arms and shoulders in an attempt to restrain him. Varila went so far as to jump on his back. He shrugged everyone off with ease and spun around with his fist raised and eyes wild.

Salvarias stepped into his brother's line of sight. "Brother."

Though Wilhelm trembled, his eyes calmed. He grabbed Neithelas and lifted him eye level. "You so much as look at my brother again and I'll dig out that arrogant heart of yours and feed it to the vultures!" Wilhelm tossed Neithelas aside and glared at the rest of the group. "Anyone got anything to say?"

Salvarias doubted any god, creature, or even the most heroic warrior would have been dense enough to speak. Everyone shook their heads, eyes wide.

"Good. Leave my brother alone." Wilhelm stormed over to the fire pit, hands shaking and shoulders rising and falling with deep breaths. Salvarias shot Lunara a quick glance that she understood, and she went to his brother's side. Durak returned to a stump, whittling at a stick and scowling at Salvarias. Humar and Varila meandered toward the fire, seeming to take a keen interest in their boots.

Salvarias gathered his spell book, chose a tree apart from the group but within sight of Wilhelm, nestled against its trunk, and gazed at Lunara conversing with his brother. She was an affectionate woman, resting a hand on Wilhelm's arm as she spoke, sitting close, oblivious to her beauty, to her allure. Innocent to the power she possessed in her smile, what she could evoke with a caress.

I am disappointed in you, my little murderer. Not only did you pass the opportunity to leave your brother, but you allowed the innocent girl closer to your heart. Your resolve is crumbling, pet. I sensed your desires, your barbaric response to her. Would you taint something so pure? Each time you touch her, her innocence flees further. Are you so selfish that you would sacrifice her purity to satiate your lust?

I did no such thing, Salvarias retorted.

Bah! Spare me your lies! I sensed what was in your heart. I sensed your desire to taste purity. She cannot be spoiled by you. You must spare her, above all others, from the evil seeping from your fingers. Surely you see now. You must maintain distance from her. Friendship cannot exist between you. You must *distance yourself, my murderer.*

Salvarias lowered his gaze. The presence was right. Lunara, above all else, must remain pure, untainted, and clean of evil. She was his beacon of purpose: that beauty existed in such dark times was worth his suffering.

He would not be the one to rid the world of her light.

"Ale?" Okulu asked.

Salvarias glanced up at the grinning merc and shook his head, purposefully lifting his spell book closer to his face.

Okulu shrugged and sat in front of him. "Love the whole black fire thing. Never seen that spell before."

The words tightened a ball of fear in Salvarias's chest. It was not a spell. Or at least he did not remember casting it. It might have been ... or not. His mind swam through the event, but he was unable to remember how he conjured it. All he remembered was anger.

"I've never seen a spell with twelve shards before either."

Again, he could not recall generating twelve shards. The most he had accomplished before was five. And it was draining. Though

Salvarias felt tired, it was more mental than due to magic. He ignited his magic.

Your anger blocked out all that interferes, my brilliant wizard, the magic said. *You have more power than I imagined!*

The black fire?

That I do not understand. But I will continue to search your mind, see what I can find.

Salvarias rested his head on his arms, drawing his knees to his chest. Now he felt tired. He was happy his magic was pleased, but he possessed yet another oddity, a power different from other mages, spells unknown to even his magic.

"So I assume you didn't realize you did that?" Okulu said.

"No, I did not."

"Brilliant!"

He wearily raised his head to look at the merc. "Pardon?"

Okulu winked. "I've always wanted to know a mad person."

Salvarias arched an eyebrow. "I am happy to oblige you. I assure you there is plenty in my mind you would find disturbing should I ever permit you to see."

"I look forward to the possibility." Okulu took a quick swig from his flask. "People are so ordinary. It's why I'm rather fond of magic. Shame I'm not a wizard."

"I think Arden is a safer place because you are not," Salvarias said dryly.

Okulu chuckled. "Perhaps. I would turn Neithelas into a rat and force him to live in Falar. It has the worst garbage."

"And you know from experience?"

"I've passed out in a few alleys."

Salvarias relaxed against the tree. "You do not like our new friend?"

"I don't consider him a friend, friend. I think he's a little stuck on his self-appointed throne. But Winsires usually are. They think their large eyes let them see into a person's soul."

"You do realize you are part Winsire."

Okulu's eyes widened, and he pressed a hand over his heart.

"Blasphemy!"

Salvarias shook his head, hiding his smile.

The merc cast his roguish grin. "Part. My mother didn't approve of the Winsire culture. It's why she ventured out of Meitholias. She wanted to experience the world, live. She never taught me how to listen to trees or anything about our culture."

"Do you wish she had?"

"Maybe a little." Okulu's tone lost its light air. "It would help in times such as these."

"You are skilled at tracking and using nature. More times than not, you have turned back for no other reason than whispered words. I think you listen to the trees without knowing you do so. Your mother probably knew, and that is why she did not teach you."

Okulu's eyes sharpened, gleaming with clear intelligence. Salvarias no longer had any doubt; the man was never drunk. Salvarias also suspicioned Okulu had been measuring his worth since their first meeting. The half-Winsire did not pass the popular one-glance judgment of most, and more than once Salvarias had caught the merc watching him closely. And, oddly, Salvarias felt more relaxed around Okulu than any other person he had met.

Friendships will hurt you, my murderer. Keep them at a distance. You have no friends. You need no friends.

Okulu's normal blurry eyes returned. "So now you're telling me I'm mad too?"

"I would not want you thinking you are normal."

Okulu chuckled. "I really don't have to talk to trees now. We've got birds fluttering around us all the damn time." There was an unvoiced accusation sparkling in his eyes. "I was going to kill that sparrow the other day. It seemed focused on you and never shut up."

Salvarias shrugged. "He had a lot to say."

Okulu laughed, shaking his head as he rose. "You're an interesting one. A very, very interesting man." After throwing on a broad smile, Okulu strolled back to the campfire, taking long pulls from his flask.

Salvarias settled comfortably against his tree, flipped his spell book to the most recent words his magic had discovered, and lost his mind to study.

~

LUNARA WOKE to a low rumble of distant thunder. The sun imbued itself in rolling clouds that darkened the northern sky. The spring storm would come in from the ocean and, for the first time, she desperately missed her home. So many times she had sat wrapped in her mother's arms and a blanket while she watched baleful-looking clouds churn up the sea as they billowed their way to Serinity.

She tossed aside her blanket and looked around her camp. Varila and Okulu must have already left for Falar. Humar, Neithelas, Durak, and Wilhelm sat around the fire in light conversation. Salvarias was nowhere in sight. With what had happened yesterday, she was surprised Wilhelm had left his brother alone. Then again, she hadn't told him that Salvarias had tried to kill himself.

After folding her bedroll and blankets, she joined the men by the fire. Wilhelm's eyes were dull and shifted often toward the woods as he sat with the sword he had retrieved from his parent's murderer. Apparently, it had been a gift from his father before the poor man had met his end.

"Morning," she said, extending her hands toward the flickering flames. "I see we're in for a storm today."

Humar nodded. "I'll take the relief. It's been warm since we left, and a day or two of rain just might cool down my armor."

"They never last," Neithelas said. "Spring storms are as flighty as a butterfly. I'm sure in a day we'll be sweating as before."

"Aye," Durak grumbled, never pausing in his carving of a chunk of wood.

"Where's Salvarias?" Lunara asked.

"He went to the stream to wash up," Wilhelm responded. He motioned off to the right. "It's just a ways over there if you want to join him."

"I think I will," Lunara said.

"I'll escort you, my lady," Neithelas said.

"No, no need," she said quickly. "I'll be fine."

Her savior came into view. Adok grinned and trotted up to her, snuggling his head under her hand. "Good boy. Adok will keep me safe."

Without giving Neithelas the chance to argue, she strode forward. Once the camp went out of sight, she slouched with relief. Neithelas's attention wore on her patience. She didn't want his affections, yet he seemed oblivious to her hints.

When she arrived at the thin stream babbling down the mountainside, she found Salvarias leaning against a tree and counting louder than normal while staring blankly at the water as it fought its way around rocks.

"Hello," she said.

Salvarias looked up and bowed. "Hello, my lady."

Her heart sank. So formal already; as if they'd shared nothing the day prior. Forcing a smile, she walked to his side.

"Chilly morning," she said.

"Indeed."

"How did you sleep?"

"Fine."

"Really?" She arched her eyebrow. "I heard you muttering the entire night. I doubt you slept at all."

"And what would it matter if I told you I had not, my lady?"

Lunara opened her mouth to respond, but found she had no answer to his question. Perplexed by his sudden change, she knelt by the stream, scooped water in her hands, and splashed it on her face, gasping as its frigidness shocked her fully awake.

She looked over her shoulder and said, "What does matter is that you would lie to me."

Salvarias's cheeks tinted pink, but he remained silent.

Lunara shook out her hands, dabbed her face dry with a fold of her dress, and moved to stand in front of him. He shied away, turning his head from her. She was sure something stabbed her heart. Gently entering his mind, she offered comfort through their connection.

"Please," he whispered. "I have asked you before not to sense my emotions. While I thank you for your help yesterday, for your understanding and care, our relationship has not changed."

She shifted until he had no choice but to meet her gaze. "What is our relationship, Salvarias?" One more tiny step and her body brushed against his. The lines of pain on his face relaxed, and he closed his eyes as he inhaled deeply. "What is our relationship?" She rested her hand on his chest. "Tell me."

He opened his eyes, and his emotions melted into emptiness. Taking her hand in his, he stared at it for several moments before he whispered, "Acquaintances, my lady. We are acquaintances." He dropped her hand and turned to leave.

"And our dreams?" she asked.

Salvarias stopped, back toward her. He turned his head slightly and said, "A mistake. I am not that man. And we are not friends." He paused only a breath before he left her alone.

The first raindrops snuck their way past leaves and branches to join the tears cascading down her cheeks.

10

Lunara shifted her hair over one shoulder in hopes the light breeze might cool her neck. She had considered herself an accomplished rider until the recent lengthy travels she'd undertaken. The past four days had caused her thighs to ache and tenderized the inside of her calves and knees. She'd been ecstatic when Wilhelm had, without asking, lifted her on to his saddle. He seemed to know when she was uncomfortable and, as he did with Salvarias, was quick to do anything needed to ease her suffering. Indeed, riding sidesaddle had helped relax her muscles and offered the tender skin on the interior of her thighs much-needed relief, but Wilhelm might as well have been the sun. His body emitted enough heat to simmer water. She couldn't decide which was worse: sweating or enduring aching muscles.

She decided heat was preferred, especially since riding with Wilhelm kept Neithelas at a distance.

"Sorry," Wilhelm said. "I'm a little warm."

Lunara smiled up at him. "We're halfway through spring. Our cool days are nearing an end."

Wilhelm chuckled. "Even in winter I'm warm. I don't get cold often."

"You're a damn skillet over an open flame," Varila said.

"I didn't hear you complaining when we were on our way to Treppter last winter," Wilhelm said. "Matter of fact, I don't think there wasn't a night that you spent out of my lap."

"Please," Varila drawled, rolling her eyes. "You couldn't keep your hands—much less your eyes—off me."

Wilhelm's lopsided grin spread. "Your eyes wander to all sorts of places."

He flexed his arm, winking at Varila. Lunara giggled when her sister blushed.

"We're here," Humar announced. "Look sharp."

Though not nearly as large as a major city, Vertex spread out a good mile or so. Lining the packed-down dirt road were old men, women, and young children. A few middle-aged women mingled among them and even fewer able-bodied men. As her group passed, whatever activity the citizens had been engaged in came to halt. All eyes were on Lunara and her friends.

"Unfriendly," Wilhelm muttered.

"Do ye blame them, lad?" Durak said. "This darkness is merciless. Just look at 'em. There be hardly any women."

They followed the main road to the opposite side of town where a tavern squatted along with the other two-story homes and shops. With no ruling lord present, the buildings were not tended to as regularly as larger cities, and it showed by broken windows, poorly patched holes, and an overall unstable appearance. Lunara wasn't sure it was safe.

A commotion a few buildings down gained the group's attention as they dismounted and handed their horses off to the stablehands. Men, the old and young alike, were rushing toward the edge of town, hollering for the women folk to help them. Lunara stood on her toes to see a group of ten or so children approaching the edge of town. They wore tattered cloaks stained with blood, and tears streaked their dirty cheeks. Lunara and her friends rushed to help.

The first villager reached the children and knelt in front of the oldest-looking boy. "Where are you from? What's happened to you?"

Lunara and her friends fanned out behind the few men that had gotten there first.

A little girl, no older than eight, reached out her thin arms smudged with dirt. "Help us!" Tears spilled from her doe-brown eyes, and her chin trembled with sobs.

Lunara started forward, but when the child looked at her, a chill ran up her spine, and she took a step back. Varila rubbed her arms. Though Lunara couldn't explain it, the children repulsed her. Despite her revulsion at her own disgust, her feet would not move to help.

The villager seemed unbothered by the child and swooped it up in his arms. "There, there, child. You're safe now."

The little girl threw her arms around the man's neck. Varila latched hold of Lunara's arm and both stumbled back. She didn't want to be anywhere near the children.

The rest of the children were already cradled in the arms of villagers while the men soothed them with whispered words. Her friends were intent on the children as well, except for Salvarias. Lunara didn't need to look at him to feel his stare.

"What is it?" Salvarias asked.

"I ... I don't know," Lunara said. "Something ... It just doesn't feel right." They were simply children: small, helpless, scared. Nevertheless, her lip curled when she looked at them.

Varila shook herself. "Those children give me the creeps. There's something—"

"Brother!" Salvarias called. "Stop!"

Wilhelm, who had been reaching for a child, turned to Salvarias.

"Those are not children," Salvarias said.

"What are you talking about, Salv?" Wilhelm said. "They're kids."

"No, Brother. You cannot touch them."

The little girl scowled at Salvarias. "I know you, mage." She shifted back to cup the villager's face in her tiny, dirt-crusted hands. In the sweetest voice, she said, "I want you to kill everyone, except for him."

As if she were an owl, her head turned until nothing but an empty hole existed where her face had been. No eyes, no features, no

... soul. Lunara clamped a hand over her mouth to keep from screaming.

A giggle echoed from the emptiness before it shrieked, "Kill!"

The villager unraveled the girl from his arms and turned around. Lunara gasped at his blank gaze. There was no thought in his hazel eyes. He stared as though blind.

"Herrel!" a woman cried, rushing toward the man.

Using his staff, Salvarias shoved the woman off balance and clear of the man's attempted beheading with his sickle. Not seeming to care who he killed, the villager whirled it to his left and sank the sickle into another villager's stomach. Lunara froze, gaping at the man's lifeblood spilling from his torn-open gut. His eyes, once holding the brilliance of life, dulled. A ring like shattering glass echoed in Lunara's ear, and as the gleam of life flickered out, she swore she actually felt the ache of the world as it lost one of its children. A sob escaped, and she clutched her heart.

Roars of anger from the villagers crescendoed behind Lunara as they rushed forward, packing them together like a bushel of wheat. Any man who had held a child whirled to face the town with the same mindless gaze.

"Brother!" Salvarias called.

Salvarias grabbed Lunara's arm and guided her behind Wilhelm, who plunged through the growing crowd. Try as she might, she could not block the moist sounds of weapons sinking through flesh or the crunch of breaking bones. She leaned to the side and became ill. The blood ... So much ... She retched again. Salvarias mercilessly kept her walking.

Roars of anger switched to howls of pain. Looking over her shoulder, only women steered clear of the scene, escaping into homes or scurrying for cover. Among the crowd, giggling children darted in and out of the mob, converting additional men toward their cause.

Salvarias stopped in a shadowed alley a few buildings clear of the fight. Varila wrapped her arms around Lunara's shoulders, whispering in her ear that everything would be all right.

"Where are the others?" Salvarias asked, keeping his gaze on the main street.

"I lost them in the crowd," Wilhelm muttered.

"We must find them." Salvarias turned to Varila. "If a child approaches you, stab it in the—"

"I'm not going to kill a child!" Varila retorted. "Not all of us are heartless bastards!"

Salvarias grabbed Wilhelm's arm. "No, Brother." He looked at Lunara. "Have you read of the Battle of Thonlin?"

Lunara merely stared at him. All she heard were screams, hacking bone. Varila shook her. "Lunara."

"B-briefly," she stammered. Her shock gave way to fear. "The deceitful Children of Thonlin."

"Now you understand," Salvarias said.

"They're not children," Lunara told Varila. "They're demons created by Veedran. They wiped out an entire army, pitted friend against friend with one touch. They empty the mind to their cause. We must kill them."

Salvarias nodded. "Women were added to the armies because only they can sense something about the child is amiss. Once a child is destroyed, whomever they touched is cured and their mind returned. The villagers do not need to be slaughtered. We must find the children and kill them. Only by stabbing the emptiness where the left eye should reside can the people be saved. Any other way, the curse will remain."

"Let's find the others," Wilhelm muttered.

"Lunara and I will stay here," Varila said.

Salvarias and his brother strode toward the mayhem and soon became lost in the brawling crowd. Lunara paced the width of the alley, gnawing at her fingernail, trying to block the sounds of death that churned her stomach.

"Dammit!" Varila cursed, drawing her sword.

Lunara peered around her sister to see Humar marching toward them.

"By the gods," Lunara breathed.

Humar's once bright azure eyes were dull of thought. His sword rasped from its sheath.

"He's better than me," Varila said.

Lunara reached out her mind to Salvarias. His attempt to block her from his thoughts was nearly flawless, but after they'd been attacked in the woods, he let her in a sliver so she could speak to him if needed.

Help us! It's Humar. Varila cannot best him with a sword.

Though he did not respond, she sensed his acknowledgement.

"Stay behind me," Varila said, shoving Lunara back. "Don't interfere. If he beats me, run and find Wilhelm. You understand?"

"Yes," Lunara said.

Humar raised his sword when within range and brought it down with enough force that it drove Varila to one knee. With a cry and a screech of metal on metal, her sister rolled to the side and clear of the knight. The curse had not stripped Humar of his agility and speed. Sword whipping through air, he put Varila on the defense, causing her to stagger back with each tight swing.

Hurry! Lunara screamed in her mind.

After a cursory sweep of the alley, she found a fist-sized rock. Varila just needed a distraction to gain her ground. Lunara threw the rock at Humar. It clanged against his breastplate. The knight's mindless gaze switched to her, and he marched toward her. She stumbled backward.

"Humar! It's me, Lunara!"

Varila smacked her blade against Humar's shoulder. It did nothing to slow his stride. He raised his sword. Lunara butted up against a wall. She had no room for escape.

"Don't make me do this!" Varila cried.

Varila's sword rose up behind Humar, aimed for the knight's sword arm.

"No!" Lunara screamed.

Humar drew his arm back for the thrust. Varila swung. Everything seemed to move in slow motion.

Wilhelm suddenly tackled Humar, twisting midair to shield the knight as he raised his broadsword to block Varila's strike.

Her sister's momentum was too great to stop, and Wilhelm's block was not aligned as he plummeted toward the ground, arms enveloping Humar. Without proper footing, he had no chance. Varila's sword knocked aside Wilhelm's in a shower of sparks.

"*Ich comad otec!*" Salvarias shouted.

A filmy distortion draped over Wilhelm right as Varila's sword connected with his neck. Her sister's cry cut short when she tripped backward, as if her sword had hit stone. Lunara looked up to see Salvarias standing near, ashen-faced with an expression of sheer terror. His mouth moved again and the film vanished.

Wilhelm pinned Humar to the ground, using his weight to hold the knight still. Varila's sword fell from her hands, and she sank to one knee. Rushing to her sister's side, Lunara whispered, "He's fine."

Blood trickled down the side of Wilhelm's neck. Thankfully, Varila's strike had barely grazed his skin.

Salvarias quickly checked Wilhelm before disappearing into the crowd.

"Stay here," Varila said. "I'm going to help."

With a shaking hand, Varila snatched up her sword and followed Salvarias.

Wilhelm grinned. "That was a little close."

"I think your brother's heart skipped," Lunara said, trying to steady her voice.

"Salv would never let anything happen to me."

Humar stopped struggling, choked in a breath, and wheezed, "I can't breathe!'

Wilhelm eased up his weight. "You in control of yourself?"

Humar nodded. "What happened? I … I was fighting a villager."

Wilhelm hauled the knight up and clapped Humar on the shoulder. "You let one of those creatures touch you."

The knight motioned to Wilhelm's neck. "My doing?"

"No, that was Varila. You're lucky Salv and I showed up when we did. Varila almost lopped off your arm."

Humar swayed and staggered until Wilhelm caught him. "I'm dizzy."

Wilhelm eased him to ground.

"Leave me and go help the others," Humar mumbled. Color drained rapidly from his face.

"I'm not leaving you or Lunara by yourselves. You're in no condition to defend her."

Humar exhaled sharply. "My head ..."

Salvarias and the others struggled through the crowd and sprinted for the alley. Varila was unsteady on her feet as Okulu supported her. Dark blood clumped her hair to the side of her head.

Salvarias gave Humar a cursory glance, reached into the pouch tied at his waist, and handed Humar what looked like tree bark. "Chew, do not swallow it. Once the flavor has left, spit it out."

Varila cast Lunara the "I'm fine" smile before sinking to the ground next to Humar.

"Suggestions, old friend?" Okulu asked. "We're out numbered now. No chance."

Humar shook his head, grimacing as he did.

"I can't find the creatures," Okulu said. "I think they've left. I guess there's no reason for them to stick around. They've touched over half the people. It's simply a matter of time before the mindless ones kill off the others. We can't have these deranged villagers leave for other towns." He took a rather long swig from his flask.

"Agreed," Durak said. He motioned to Salvarias. "Burn it down, boy."

She stared past everyone to see men hacking at other men as if they'd just entered the new profession of a butcher. She gagged at the trail of limbs and carcasses the mob left in their wake. Blood congealed the dirt road to a gory path of death, and white bones stood stark against the crimson road. "Kill everyone?" she breathed.

A light hand rested on her shoulder. "Do not look, my lady," Salvarias whispered, his hand sliding down her shoulder before his touch left.

She clawed her gaze from the sight and focused on Salvarias's shadowed face.

"Aye. These people will just move to another town and kill there, lass. We have a chance to stop it."

Wilhelm's jaw rippled. "You want my brother to burn down a town? Kill hundreds of people?"

"He's the only one who can, lad. And the only one heartless to do so, as we've seen."

Wilhelm bolted to his feet, looming over Durak. Salvarias quickly grabbed his brother and moved in front. "He is correct, Brother."

Wilhelm's jaw set, and he looked down at Durak. "What you're asking of him is ... is murder!"

Durak pointed to the people fighting. "Ye want to see that on the streets of Serinity? Or Falar? I've read about the wars too, lad. Me know those creatures will follow their horde 'til they amass it into an army. Thousands will die!"

When Salvarias spoke, his voice was soft as ever. No one else besides Lunara could sense the absolute dread his emotional wall could not conceal. "You must listen to him, Brother. This cannot spread."

"You don't have to do this, Salv," Wilhelm said. "There's got to be another way."

Salvarias opened his mouth as if to assure Wilhelm, but his brow furrowed and his gaze shifted to the forest. "Perhaps there is. Do you trust me, brother?"

"You know I do, Salv."

"You must stay here with the others. Allow me to do what I must alone."

"I don't like the sound of that," Wilhelm growled.

"They will not harm me. You heard the girl."

Wilhelm's fists clenched. "I ... I can't let you go by yourself."

"You must, Brother. Durak is correct. Unless I find another way, I will have no choice but to slaughter these people. You must let me do this."

Wilhelm stared at Salvarias for several moments before he said, "Promise me you'll be fine."

"I cannot."

Wilhelm turned a pleading gaze to Humar, but the knight shook his head. "You have to let him go."

"Curb your selfishness," Neithelas murmured to Wilhelm.

"Shut up," Wilhelm grated to Neithelas. He stared at the crowd before shaking his head. "Fine."

Salvarias strode toward the stables. Once out of sight, Wilhelm punched the nearest wall, leaving a smear of blood on the wood.

"Let's get inside the tavern," Okulu said. "After they've killed the rest of the villagers, they'll leave. If we stay out of sight, we might have a chance to live through this."

Wilhelm and Okulu helped Humar up. Varila was unsteady on her feet, and Neithelas and Durak were quick to wedge themselves under her arms.

Using Varila's injury and Okulu and Wilhelm's distraction to her advantage, Lunara slipped away from her friends and made her way to the stables. Though not well traveled, she was well read and had studied tracking methods extensively. She could pick up an easy trail and Salvarias had done nothing to hide his tracks. The sweep of his robes and cloak led her to Mithal's stall. The stallion was gone. Saddling her mare quickly, she set off after the mage.

His trail ventured through alleys and into the forest. Pine needles softened her horse's hooves as they wound their way between the sparse trees. She didn't go far before she heard Salvarias's voice.

"It is me you seek. Here I am."

She slid off her mare, keeping her movements light and soundless. After looping her horse's reins around a tree branch, she crept from pine to pine until she saw the mage. He stood calmly, staring ahead of him.

"You flatter yourself," a child's voice said from the shadows.

"Yet each of you avoided me in the village. In fact, one of you even killed a villager who would have landed a fatal blow against me.

Enlighten me, Children of Thonlin, how should I interpret those actions?"

Six children came from the shadows to stand in front of Salvarias. Two were boys, the other four little girls. They looked so innocent to Lunara, but the sinking feeling in her gut told her these were nothing shy of abominations. She picked up a thick stick the length of her forearm.

"We did not kill many of you," Salvarias murmured.

"That's because we're smarter than you," one little girl sneered. "Show us your hands, wizard."

Salvarias flicked his hand behind his back before raising them in surrender. Behind him, four shards of ice appeared, and he held his dagger, ready to hurl it toward the creatures. They seemed not to notice it.

"If you are not seeking me, why have you emerged from hiding?" Salvarias asked.

"We've been called by our father."

"Father? Veedran is no longer in Arden."

"Veedran's not our father. You pathetic Erthlas think you knew everything back then. Our father made most of the creatures you fought during the Long Wars. He's the one who sent us into hiding after Veedran left. But now he has unleashed us."

Salvarias stiffened. "Unupture?"

The children giggled. "You've met him?"

"In a matter of speaking. Why now? Why send you into Dalnar now?"

One little girl stepped forward. "I like this wizard. I want to keep him for myself. Imagine if we controlled one. We could make him do all sorts of tricks for us."

"*Lumous*," Salvarias whispered. His sparrow of light fluttered in the air.

The children laughed with delight as the sparrow floated around them, seeming nothing more than innocents enjoying a game of chase.

"Why now?" Salvarias asked.

"Because we need more time," a girl said, leaping at the bird. "We need to distract—"

"Shush!" the oldest boy snapped. "He's tricking us. Tie him up. We're taking him to Father."

"Allow me to see your true faces first," Salvarias said. "I have been curious what they look like close up."

"You're not scared?"

"Little frightens me, child. I have experienced horrors beyond your imagination."

"Everyone who sees us is frightened."

Salvarias shrugged and presented his hands, wrists together. "So be it. Such a shame to not behold what would surely be a terrifying sight."

The creatures glanced at each other and smiled wickedly. "With six of us, he's liable to go mad!"

A little girl giggled. "All the more reason. With his mind gone, his magic will be ours."

The children shared an eager glance before their heads turned, pivoting on their neck bones as if they were wooden dolls. Lunara averted her eyes, relying on hearing alone.

"*Rulose!*" Salvarias said.

She glanced at Salvarias as his shards shot from behind his back to land in the black depths of four creatures' faces while his dagger soared through the air. Lunara darted from her hiding place.

"Salvarias!"

He whirled as she tossed him the stick she'd been holding. Snatching it from the air, he rammed it into the eye socket of a child sprinting for him. The creature wailed, teetering backward, clawing at the stick. It crumbled to the ground next to the others, writhing on the forest floor, flailing about, screeching in an inhuman voice. Then all was silent. The small bodies seemed to fizzle from existence until the only evidence of the Children of Thonlin was a heap of clothes.

Salvarias walked over to her. "What do you think you are doing?" There was no anger in his voice, and his emotions were well concealed; however, she had no doubts he was upset with her.

"I-I wanted to help."

"You could have been killed, my lady."

"What would you have done with the last creature if I hadn't been here?" Lunara planted her feet firm, staring up at him in defiance. She'd done the right thing, she was sure of it.

"I had a protection spell."

Lunara scoffed. "I didn't see it."

"There are many types of protection spells, my lady. Though more draining, there is one that is invisible. It would be wise if you heed my words next time. I do not need your help."

He strode by her to Mithal.

Lunara bit her lip to keep her tears from breaking free. She felt foolish, like a stupid little girl who had just bragged about saving the world, only to learn it'd been someone else.

11

SPRING 1018 A.R

Lunara picked at her breakfast as her friends sat around a common room table discussing their route. The sun had just started to fade the blackness of night into the dull gray of morning, exiling the stars that had sparkled at her when Humar first awakened her. Apparently, the knight wanted to get an early start.

The tavern was mainly deserted save for the cook and owner. The town outside had spent the night collecting body parts and burying their loved ones. Her group, save herself and Salvarias, had helped. Her friends had returned late in the night, dusty and covered in blood. The memory still haunted her.

She snuck a piece of ham from a platter and passed it under the table to Adok, who had taken on a new habit of resting his head in her lap so he could easily snatch up whatever she stole from the table to feed him. Salvarias never seemed to notice, or if he did, he refrained from saying anything.

"Me say we go to Hadrium," Durak said, using his small dagger to whittle away at a stick. Wood shavings accumulated on the table in a tidy pile. "We need supplies, and these small towns don't offer variety or the essentials."

Wilhelm shook his head. "It's too dangerous. I'm sure there are black-armored soldiers looking for us in Hadrium. We'll hunt, camp outside cities."

"Wilhelm's got a point," Varila said.

Humar ran his hand through his hair. "But we can get lost in the crowds in a city. Once we make it to a tavern, Salvarias can stay in the rooms."

"What do you think, Salvarias?" Lunara asked.

Without looking up from his spell book, Salvarias said, "I think it would be best if everyone returned home. My brother and I can travel alone."

"Me tired of your ungrateful attitude, boy!" Durak roared.

"Hush!" Humar said. He kept his voice a whisper, though no other patrons occupied the common room. "He never asked us to come."

Salvarias looked up from his book, locking gazes with the Cavrul. "Indeed I have not, Durak. I would prefer to be alone on this journey. The choice to leave is yours, and I highly encourage you to do so."

"Me not goin' anywhere, ye selfish—" Durak started, but Wilhelm's anger cut off the man's rant.

"Leave him alone," Wilhelm said.

"Both of you stop it," Humar chided. "We're in this together, but Salvarias is right. Anyone can leave at any time." Humar turned to Wilhelm. "I know you're worried, but I'm sure Hadrium is our best course of action. There are no major towns between here and our destination. It's the last place to stock up on supplies."

Wilhelm's shoulders slumped, and he nodded.

Lunara finally gave up her attempt at eating and shoved her plate to Wilhelm. The sounds from yesterday, the blood she'd seen on the streets, and the weeping villagers were too fresh in her memory.

She allowed her sleepy gaze to rest upon Salvarias. She had seriously reflected on his words and actions when he had told her they were merely "acquaintances." Initially, she had wallowed in depression. But after the hurt passed, her hope and optimism worked through her problem. He'd lied to her, but worse, he had lied to himself. Her challenge was to understand why.

His gaze slid from his book to her, and his counting stopped. She hadn't realized she'd entered his mind. Withdrawing from it, she smiled at him. One day, she would break through his wall. Love and patience were all she needed, and she had plenty.

12

Varila steered her horse next to Humar, glancing back at her friends ... and Salvarias. Everyone looked worn. The horses' heavy hooves planted loudly with each step and their heads hung low. The day had been full of Humar pushing them with little rest.

"Humar," Varila said. "We need rest. Everyone's exhausted. Look at them."

Humar nodded. "I know, but I want to make it to Hadrium tonight."

"Why? Has our little savage given you some kind of deadline?"

"No." Humar glanced at Salvarias riding at the rear of the group with Wilhelm. "Nevertheless, I don't want to be stuck out in the woods. Those children in Vertex aren't the only creatures lurking in the night. I want the safety of a large town."

"What about the village by the river? We can camp there, and it's merely another mile or so. At least there's a few more people. I just don't think riding into Hadrium is a good idea."

Humar shook his head. "I know you're worried about Lunara, but she's doing fine. I want to be in Hadrium tonight."

"Then you're buying new horses after you've driven these into the ground, you stubborn ass!"

Varila reeled her stallion around and rejoined Lunara, who was engaged in a conversation with Neithelas. As Varila listened, it was obvious Lunara wasn't interested in the prince. Neithelas, however, was infatuated with Lunara. He complimented her at every opportunity, and since joining their group, he'd waited on her when camped. Not only did he tend to her comforts, but he seemed protective of her, riding close and keeping the mage at bay. Varila approved highly of him and made it her personal mission to sway her sister to accept his courtship, if ever Neithelas were presented the opportunity to ask Edium for permission.

Okulu trotted up to the group and slid off his horse. "The village is just ahead. We should walk the rest of the way. It'll give the horses a break."

Varila dismounted, stretched her cramped legs, and took the reins from her sister and Neithelas in order to give him the chance to walk close to Lunara. The prince was quick to take the hint.

After a short hike, wood shacks appeared ahead; their silhouetted shapes contrasted against the rosy pink sky. There must've barely been twenty or so homes. Some appeared to be nothing more than one room while others were twice as large. All were shoddy in construction and probably never repaired. It shouldn't be surprising. Few crossed the river. Most who visited Hadrium took a ship from Falar or a river barge from Acklar or Reffil. It reminded her of the old stories of how the world was before Nevlar struck it apart. Hadrium and Falar had once been prosperous cities, trading with one another, and even shared a ruling lord. After the Retribution, the divide of the river and the added mountain range had removed Hadrium from healthy trade. She'd visited the city several times with her father. It'd turned into a dive, worse than Falar, and wholly unsafe. She wasn't looking forward to visiting.

Glancing up, Varila was surprised no tendrils of smoke from chimneys or fires warmed the chill night. Uneasiness washed over her when she realized she heard no commotion, no birds, no crickets, no—

Suddenly Lunara gasped.

In the fading light, Varila made out a glistening carcass lying on the outskirts of the village.

Lunara whirled around, turning her back toward it, and her eyes darted every which way, her breathing rapid, and face as pale as the crescent moon hanging in the sky.

Neithelas folded Lunara in his arms. "The trees say evil is among them. They're frightened."

Okulu cursed and drew his sword. Still unable to see what lurked ahead, Varila followed suit and yanked her sword from its sheath.

"How enlightening," Okulu hissed at Neithelas. "I don't suppose they could tell us what exactly is out there?"

"They don't see as we see, half-breed," Neithelas said. "If you cared for your heritage, you'd know such truths."

"Enough," Humar said. "Everyone alert. Lunara and Salvarias, stay in the center of the group. Durak, take the horses and bring up the rear. Okulu, front and center. Varila and Wilhelm, stay with him. Neithelas, keep that bow ready."

"I think it wise for Prince Neithelas to be guarded, Sir Humar," Salvarias said.

Humar glanced between the two men before nodding. "Go into the center, Neithelas. Okulu, if something comes at us, be sure to duck out of the way of Neithelas's arrows."

"Brilliant suggestion, old friend," Okulu said. "I would've leapt in front of him the instant he raised his bow."

Wilhelm grinned. "Good thing Humar's full of friendly advice."

"We'd be dead if he wasn't," Okulu said. "I'm surprised I lived all these years without his guidance. However did I survive?"

"Ye numb-brained idiots!" Durak growled. "Now's not the time to be spoutin' jokes. Keep yer eyes and minds alert."

Okulu took a swig from his flask. "I don't know if I can take much more of these life lessons."

After they'd formed a circle, Humar and Salvarias flanking the group, they moved forward. Adok padded soundlessly alongside Salvarias, glancing at the mage and then the trees, then back to the mage.

"What's with the wolf?" Varila asked.

"Prince Neithelas is correct," Salvarias said. "We are not alone."

Varila looked over her shoulder at Lunara. Violent tremors shook her, and she gripped Neithelas's arm, keeping her gaze downcast. Whatever she'd seen spooked her enough to take comfort from the Winsire.

Varila rolled her shoulders and flexed her fingers around her sword hilt. A few more steps and she cocked her head to a strange buzzing. "What's that?" she whispered.

"Flies," Salvarias said.

"How—" Varila cut herself off. She could see a dark cloud of them swarming around the glistening lump. Then came the sour odor of excreted bodily fluids. The air was laden with the stench of death and decay, almost tangible the farther she walked.

The ground around the lump was soaked with blood, amplified by the red hues the setting sun stained in the sky. White bones were a stark contrast against what looked like heaping piles of ribbons in every hue of pink and red imaginable. Though Varila tried to tell herself it might be an animal, she knew otherwise. And the additional scatterings of shredded flesh and broken bones were a clear testament that the entire village had been ... eaten, torn into by something unholy.

"Neithelas," Humar whispered. "Are there any alive? Can the trees tell us?"

"There was a massacre here," the prince responded. "I doubt any survived it. They say evil hides within their branches during the day and slaughters when darkness comes. They said two moons have passed. Any that might have survived surely fled during daylight hours."

"We need to get across this damn river," Durak said.

Okulu clucked his tongue. "I advise against it. If there's something waiting for us, we'll be exposed. No place for cover."

"The sun's almost settin'," Durak snapped. "What do ye propose we do, drunkard?"

"Board ourselves up," Okulu said. "Find a defendable home and make a stand. It's as safe as crossing the river and we'd have a better chance of making it through the night. We can leave at first light."

Humar nodded. "Durak and Varila, go find a place for the horses. Wilhelm and Okulu, see if you can find a place for us to stay tonight. I want few windows, a space small enough to defend, but large enough to fight if it comes to it. Neithelas, Salvarias, and I will stay with Lunara."

"I prefer to settle the horses, Humar," Salvarias said.

"Go with Varila, then," Humar said. "Durak, stay with us."

Varila smoothed Lunara's hair. "We'll be all right. Don't look around, and stay close to Humar. Do exactly what he says."

Lunara nodded, head still downcast, a shaking arm pressing the sleeve of her dress to her nose.

With difficulty, Varila left her sister and followed the mage. The horses pranced behind him, snorting and casting nervous glances at the trees. They walked a little ways, choosing a path around mounds of intestines and bones, until they came across an enclosed barn with the door propped half open.

Varila moved in front of Salvarias and peered inside. Thick darkness cloaked the rafters and rear barn.

"*Lumous,*" Salvarias whispered.

A sparrow of pure white light appeared and flew inside, checking rafters, crevices, and dark corners. The barn was perfect for pinning the horses for the night: two already-boarded windows, plenty of hay, and a trough full of water.

Once Varila was sure it was safe, she motioned the mage inside. "I'll wait out here," she said.

"There is no need, my lady. Please join my brother. I will be along shortly."

Varila snorted. "You know Wilhelm would kill me if I left you alone."

Salvarias tilted his head. "Thank you, my lady."

"Just hurry it up, would you?" She glanced up at the trees as they whistled in a subtle breeze snaking down with the river, and she rubbed her arms to ward off an unnatural chill. "This place gives me the creeps."

"Of course, my lady."

Salvarias disappeared inside. Varila surveyed her surroundings, trying her best to ignore the flies buzzing around a corpse off to the side of the barn. Whatever could do such a thing made her skin crawl.

Durak strode up, his frown wrinkles deepened. "We be holed up in a home over there." He pointed to a shack with two small windows and two larger ones. As if reading her mind, he said, "Wilhelm and Okulu are boarding up the windows, lass. It'll be secure."

"How's my sister?"

Durak's face softened. "She's scared, no doubt about it, but she's being brave. That Winsire is keeping her company. Doin' a damn fine job distracting her from this—" the Cavrul looked around and shook his head—"death."

Varila jerked her head toward the home. "Go and help them out. We'll be along shortly."

"Aye, lass. Keep a watchful eye on the sun. It'll be disappearin' on ye any moment."

Varila absently watch the Cavrul march out of sight before turning her attention back to the village.

A jarring clang of metal on metal sounded in a home past a field of dried up crops. It was if someone had knocked over pots in the kitchen. She checked on Salvarias. The mage was talking softly to the horses, still removing saddles.

Adjusting her grip on her sword, she crept toward the home, one silent step at a time. She studied the trees and sky, the deserted streets and deep shadows, the bloated corpses and crimson colored soil. The air was eerily quiet, an unnatural hush among human dwellings. She became aware of a steady pounding from behind her, past the barn. It must've been her friends boarding windows.

She reached the home where she suspected the clash originated. Crouched low to the ground, Varila made her way to the front door. With a clammy hand, she gripped the lever and gave it a tentative test.

It wasn't locked. She edged open the door, peering through the widening crack. Someone—or something—moaned.

A raspy voice croaked from inside. "Hel ... help ... me ..."

Varila shoved open the door. The last light of evening fell across a man bloodied head to foot, sprawled out on the floor, weakly reaching for her.

"By the gods," Varila breathed.

A candle flickered next to him, making shadows dance on the wall and glisten off the blood soaking the wood-planked floor. The man's cheeks were missing, a chunk of his nose had been torn off, and three fingers were eaten clean to the bone. That wasn't what made her gag and turn away. The skin on his arms and legs had been ripped off to reveal strips of tendons and bone. His chest had chunks of flesh gouged out, and there was a hole in his side still oozing blood. He lay in a pile of his own excrement and bile.

"Help ..." Blood bubbled his lips.

"I ... I can't," Varila said. "You're past healing."

"End ... end ..." The man shuddered violently, and his face twisted in pain. His head rolled to the side, and his eyes widened. "No. No!" He pointed a shaking hand at the window.

Varila strode over and peered out. She hadn't realized the sun had set. Standing between her and the barn was Salvarias, face upturned. Varila bent down and craned her neck to get a better look at the looming trees. Littered among the branches, blocking the sky from view, were thousands of yellow eyes.

"What in Veedran's wickedness is that?" Varila cursed.

A deafening beat of wings drummed overhead as the eyes took flight. Varila dropped her sword and clamped her hands over her ears. Salvarias did the same outside. Vague outlines of what appeared to be bats dirtied the sky before the candle flickered out and an oppressive darkness enveloped her.

Spinning around, she no longer had her bearings. Everything was pitch black. Setting her jaw in expectation, she forced her hands from her ears. By the gods, it was so loud she couldn't hear her own thoughts. Scrabbling forward, she made her way toward what she hoped was the exit.

Something grabbed her ankle. She toppled to the ground, yelping when a blunt object rammed into her ribs. Whatever had clasped hold of her groped up her leg. She clawed forward. Then she realized it was hands, wet and bony fingers digging into her thigh.

A gust of wind crashed into her, pinning her to the ground. Something slimy brushed her face, her exposed arms, and her bare thighs. The liquid heated her skin like an itchy rash.

The man screeched with such horror it evoked a paralyzing fear in Varila. He released his grip.

White-hot pain flared up on her thighs. Something sharp sliced her forehead. She covered her head with her arms, curling up tight. She could feel things ... slimy wet things, beating against her.

Every inch of her exposed skin burned as if she were touching a kettle. Tears brimmed in her eyes. The creatures tangled in her braid, flapping loudly against her ears. Unable to contain her scream any longer, she released it and, as it left her lips, she felt teeth tearing into her flesh, tugging off chunks of skin and muscle. They were eating her alive.

Desperate to escape, she scrambled forward on her hands and knees. Splinters from the wood floor slipped under the skin on her palms, and debris littered across the floor jabbed her knees. The dark room gave no clues as to an escape route. Nevertheless, she refused to lie helplessly on the floor and allow the creatures to feast.

She kept her chin tucked to her chest, hiding most of her face. Cold sweat trickled down her brow, mingling with warm blood running into her eyes. She realized how lightheaded and disoriented she felt, how dull her wits were, and how sounds faded in and out. She was going to faint. The creatures must be draining more blood than she thought. Her mind grew heavier, pulling her toward sleep, and her fight ebbed with each lurching movement.

Then the mage's soft whisper sounded near her ear, a language unknown, but altogether soothing.

Icy wind brushed over her, driving a shiver down her spine,

clouding her rasping breaths. The beating wings stilled, and what felt like a pile of frozen river rocks dumped down on her, striking and bruising, wrenching grunts and yelps from her.

Then, only the drumming of wings from outside echoed in the home.

The weight of the rocks was torn away. She looked up through her arms to see Salvarias drop to his knees beside her. Blood clumped his hair, ran down the side of his face, and pooled in his eye. Parts of his robes were shredded, showing the white raised scars covering his body.

She swallowed the lump in her throat, fighting to remain conscious. "I'm dizzy." Her voice vibrated in her head.

"Eat this," Salvarias said.

She opened her mouth and accepted a crisp, pale green leaf. Two chews later and a sudden burst of energy infused itself into her muscles, and her mind snapped alert. She shoved herself up to sit. The floor was littered with what looked like bats. Their bodies glistened with frost, and their large yellow eyes were fixated on nothing. They were frozen solid. The man who had occupied the home no longer had his throat, and his belly had been emptied.

She reached out for the mage. "Help me up."

Salvarias stood and offered his staff instead of a hand. She grabbed hold, and he pulled her to her feet.

"We do not have much time," Salvarias said. "They will break through the window."

Indeed, the creatures flung their bodies against the glass, leaving smears of a gray liquid. One glass panel had already cracked.

"What are they?" she asked.

"Wretics. Not seen since the days of Veedran."

"I don't know how we're going to get out of here." Thankfully, the leaf had ended her pain. She didn't want to be awake when the effects wore off.

"We must think of something," Salvarias said. "My brother will come for you."

"You mean you."

Salvarias's shadowed gaze steadied on her. "Are you so blind to his feelings for you, my lady? And why do you deny yours for him?"

Shock at his directness parted way to anger. "Don't tell me what I feel, mage. And don't pretend that if given a choice, he'd save me over you."

Salvarias's brow furrowed. "He—"

"Are *you* so blind that you can't see he'll never allow himself the smallest moment of happiness until you have yours? He'd kill us where we stood if it meant making you happy." Curling her lip in disgust, she said, "You better think of something fast before Humar and Okulu run out of strength to keep him safe in that home. Eventually, he's going to overpower them and come looking for your pathetic ass."

Salvarias's knuckles turned white, but his tone remained as even as always. "I do not know a spell that can kill all those creatures, my lady."

"Lunara told me about the protection spell you used when Dethal showed. Can't you cast that over us?"

"To maintain that while walking is near impossible, my lady. I must adjust the spell for our slightest movements. Furthermore, the difficulty of holding the spell increases based on the number of objects trying to penetrate it. I doubt I would make it."

"Can't you make it a ... a bubble around us? That'd help the walking."

Salvarias tilted his head, as if curious about what she said. His lips moved a moment before he shook his head. "I cannot, my lady. Perhaps after hours of study, but not on a whim."

"Then your brother is going to get eaten alive. Live with that!"

Varila hobbled over to a table and leaned against it, bereft of the courage to look at her legs. She'd be disfigured now. So much for her armor. No man would be distracted in a fight by scarred up thighs.

"You must keep pace with me," Salvarias said, startling her from her thoughts. "Walk in step with me, and do not make any sudden movements."

Varila nodded and held out her hand. "You'll have to help me."

Salvarias passed her his staff. "Use this and Adok."

"It'd be easier if—"

"No," Salvarias said flatly. "Adok will help you."

Muttering a few curses at him, audible ones, she limped to Adok and accepted the mage's staff. He stood on the other side of the wolf, inhaled a long breath, chanted, and flicked his hand. A white film draped over them as if someone had tossed a see-through linen on them. Varila breathed in the crisp air, void of decay, and the perfect temperature, not too cold, not too hot. The deafening drumming of wings sounded miles away.

"How wonderful," she murmured.

"Three ... two ..." Salvarias met her gaze, and she nodded. "One."

They both took a step forward. Cool air brushed her ear but then the warmer air of the shield covered her. By the time they reached the door, they'd found their rhythm and hobbled together in perfect unison.

Salvarias mopped blood from his face before flinging the door open. Wretics assailed them, but none penetrated the shield. They both left the home and continued onward, blinded to what lay ahead, taking such slow steps she feared they'd never make it. The yellow eyes of the creatures were all she could see. There was no sky, no ground, no trees, no homes. Just eyes; hungry, mad eyes. A chill snaked up her spine.

"How can you see?" Varila asked.

"I ..." Salvarias's jaw clenched. "Remember the steps I took from the barn. I know ..." He sucked in a breath and shook violently before gaining control. "I must concentrate."

Miles seemed to pass as they walked in silence. Oddly, she missed the mage's constant counting that she'd grown so accustomed to hearing. Without his lulling voice, she felt alone in a world void of music.

As they walked on, she had no choice but to lean her weight on Adok and the staff. The dwindling potency of whatever Salvarias had given her made her legs leaden and wobbly. The burning heat she'd felt when first attacked slowly simmered up to a boil. She was sweating again; cold sweats. Her fingertips were nearly frozen. Glancing over, Salvarias wasn't in any better shape. Though her wounds were physical, she could see the mental strain of his magic. His mouth was set in a thin line, and he shook like a frightened rabbit. His breathing came in sharp, twitching inhales, making her lungs ache in sympathy. A single drop of blood fell from his nose.

And on they went.

Eternity. She swore it'd been hours. The darkness outside the shield was blacker than the deepest hole, thicker than pitch. The wretics had doubled their efforts, ramming into the shield, diving overhead at full speed.

Salvarias stumbled and fell to his knees, groaning deeply. A steady trickle of blood ran from his nose, dribbled from his ears, and bubbled on his lips. Adok wedged himself under Salvarias's arm.

"Get up," Varila ordered. "You selfish son of a whore, get up!" She kicked his leg. "Wilhelm will come for you if you don't get to him first." She glanced back to see wretics feasting on his ankles. "Watch the shield!" Using his staff, she whacked one in the skull, sending it rolling head over feet. "Hurry up!"

Salvarias shoved himself up and limped forward. His eyes had lost focus. Blood parted his lips, wetting his raspy breathing. Muscles under his robes tightened and spasmed. He shook violently.

Three more steps and the end was here. He couldn't go on. The fight and strength seemed to drain out of him and he collapsed.

"Salv!" Wilhelm's voice sounded leagues away.

"Get out of here!" she yelled.

"Salv!"

Salvarias's eyes focused, and he coughed up blood. Digging his hands into the ground, he pulled himself forward. Varila tried to stand on her own to help, but her legs refused her weight.

The film left him. Only Varila and Adok were covered. Wretics massed upon him.

"Salv!"

"Over here!" Varila yelled.

Adok pulled free from her and leapt on top of the mage. He

snagged hold of a wretic and clamped his jaw. Bones broke and black liquid gushed from the creature's pierced throat. Adok snatched up another wretic before a yelp escaped the beast.

"Help!" Varila called, clutching hold of the staff to remain upright. The white film shivered, flickered in and out, and then solidified.

A ruddy glow came into view, silhouetting a hulking man and gleaming off the steel armor of another. Okulu and Wilhelm. Wilhelm sprinted forward, swinging his torch wildly in front of him. The creatures gave the fire wide birth. Okulu, also wielding a torch, bolted next to her.

"What are you two idiots doing?" Varila demanded.

Okulu winked at her. "Why, saving you, lovely golden-haired warrior. Your sister remembered a book she'd read about wretics being opposed to burning."

Wilhelm passed the torch to Okulu and wrapped his brother in a blanket to protect him, ignoring the creatures that feasted on his arms.

"Release it, Salv. We're safe," Wilhelm said. "You've got to release it."

Salvarias was a ball of tense muscle in Wilhelm's arms as the white film expanded to all of them.

Varila turned to Okulu. "How far are we?"

"I'd say fifty paces," he responded.

"Salv, you—"

"Go!" Salvarias rasped.

Cursing, Wilhelm covered Salvarias's face with the blanket and nodded to Okulu. The merc, donned in full metal, darted forward, leaving the safety of the shield. He waved the torches at any wretic who drew near. Varila latched hold of the wolf and let him more carry than support her.

Finally, a door came into view. Okulu pounded on it with his foot, keeping the wretics at bay with fire. When the door opened, Wilhelm barreled through first, Varila right on his heels, and then Okulu dashed inside. A mere two wretics made it in, and Humar and Durak chopped them down quickly.

Lunara rushed to Varila's side, tears standing in her eyes.

"I'm fine," Varila said, forcing a confident smile. "It looks worse than it feels."

"We're inside," Wilhelm said. "Release it!"

The white film vanished. Wilhelm lowered Salvarias and peeled back the blanket. Blood covered the mage's face and still trickled from his nose and ears. He was out cold.

"By the gods," Okulu breathed, staring at Varila's legs.

She looked down to see blood and raw muscle. The room spun then blinked out. Excruciating pain was the last thing she remembered.

13

S alvarias stood under the vibrant tree, staring out over the low rolling hills littered with corpses. As he strolled down the hill and mingled with the throng of dead, he begged his mind to awaken. He had avoided this dream since Tripir by not succumbing to deep sleep. Now, he clung to the hope that the encounter with Unupture had been his last—a fluke. However, he only walked a short way before a voice spoke.

"Hello, Salvarias."

He closed his eyes. Running was futile.

"You've avoided me yet again."

Salvarias squared his shoulders and turned to face the man.

Unupture was situated on the bloody ground. "I assume since you haven't fled you've accepted your fate."

"I have."

"Then join me, and let us be done with this."

Salvarias settled on the ground next to Unupture, ignoring the blood soaking into his robes. "Allow me to make my own assumption."

"By all means," Unupture said.

"You are in cohorts with Dethal."

"More like Dethal is in cohorts with me. The mage is not as high in the ranks of my master's servants as I am, though I'm below Sansis."

The mere mention of Sansis caused Salvarias to tense.

Unupture's thin lips tightened to a frown. "I don't need to see your body to know of the horrors he inflicted upon you. Tell me, has he gone mad yet?"

Salvarias lifted aside his hair to reveal his missing ear and acid-eaten skin. "He would have done more if Dethal had not been there to remind him that I needed my tongue and eyes to perform spells. Yes, Sansis has gone mad."

Unupture grimaced. "My respect for you has increased. You're an apt adversary. To endure such torture ..." He shuddered.

"And you are abnormally kind compared to others I have met who serve your master."

Unupture smiled halfheartedly. "My nature, what I was made to do, tends to attract unpleasant people. Evil surrounds me. Some say what I do is evil. I create. I take one creature and breed them with another. I make new life, and I consider each my child. Is that so evil?" He sighed, holding up his hands and studying them as if they were the source of his power.

Salvarias's stomach knotted with understanding. "It is why you take women?"

The man nodded.

"I think you are a coward to say such things," Salvarias said.

Unupture's eyes saddened. "I see."

"I will not permit you in my mind. What you attempt is futile."

"Eventually, you'll adapt to my powers, young man. There will come a time when you can no longer fight me. Your suffering this night will be in vain. I can't change your mind. I say this to prepare you for your failure. Allow me in willingly, and you can avoid the pain I must inflict."

"I will not."

"And yet again, I respect you more."

"Why are my memories so important to your master?"

"I don't think it wise I disclose that information. Fortunately for us—"Unupture smiled ruefully—"and wholly unfortunate for you, we've found your lack of knowledge has played to our benefit. Revealing our intentions would not be prudent for us."

"Then let us hurry this visit along. I am eager to wake."

Unupture winced and looked out across the field of the dead. When he spoke, his voice was subdued, a hint of confession in his tone. "It's not what I wanted. Once Veedran left, I sent my children into slumber. I told them to leave Arden alone. Of course, there were some who disobeyed me, but most listened. I retreated to Windlous. For the first time in my life, I had peace. I didn't have to look upon a woman's face as I cut her open. It was in Windlous that I found contentment with what Veedran had done to me ... had embedded in me. I satiated my needs and desires with small creatures, mixing various insects and small rodents together. I hadn't harmed a person for near a thousand years. But when my master showed on my doorstep, I knew my time of peace had ended. You must understand, I do not wish to be his play toy. But my master knew what lurked inside me. He called upon my powers, what Veedran planted inside me, the need the dark god branded on my soul. A requirement. I can no more quit creating than I can deny myself water. And I knew upon first laying eyes on my master that if I denied him, my life was forfeit." Unupture set his jaw, guilt and a challenge set in his eyes. "And if I am being honest, I love what I do. I love to create." His eyes saddened once more. "However, I do not like to cause pain to others. But I must."

Salvarias looked over the rolling hills. "A man once told me, 'If a heart wants to be good, it can. We control our actions. Our actions do not control us.'"

"You believe it?"

"It is what I have lived by since first he uttered those words to me."

"A wise man. Who was he?"

"The only man I have ever called Father." Salvarias swallowed the lump in his throat. "Please, let us be done with this."

"As you wish. I'll use very little power." Unupture moved his hand behind Salvarias. "I beg you again, please let me into your thoughts."

"And I beg you, cease this effort. I will not stop fighting you."

As strong as Salvarias appeared, inside terror clamped around his throat, churned his stomach, and raced his heart. When Unupture's nail grew to double the length of his finger, Salvarias resisted the urge to flee. Gathering his courage, he moved his hair aside. "I am ready."

Pain jolted through Salvarias, freezing his blood, rippling along his skin as if someone stabbed him with a thousand daggers. The swarm of maggots massed in his skull, squirming in his brain. As he suspected, he was in no condition to endure Unupture's powers. Salvarias's surroundings vanished, and he lived in a dark cocoon of agony. Air abandoned him, control over his extremities fled, and he flailed about in the throes of torture. When Unupture pressed against Salvarias's thoughts, searching and seeking, he screamed. The energy to guard himself burgeoned such pain in his mind, he was sure it would kill him. Yet he refused to allow entry to his secrets. He would die shielding them not only from Unupture, but also from himself. No one could gain access to that dark corner.

"Lower your wall, young man. Accept my powers. You must stop fighting me!"

Salvarias latched on to Unupture's arm, squeezing as a river of ice flowed instead of his blood. Gasping, he gained enough air to scream again, trying to give the pain an outlet.

Unupture's tense voice rang out, but the man's words were indecipherable amidst Salvarias's screams.

Then a deep rumble sounded above everything. "Salv! Wake up!"

Salvarias lurched when the nail slid out of his neck.

"Call for the tree!" Unupture shouted.

"Brother ..." Salvarias coughed. "Brother."

The darkness fizzled into a dull yellow light and bright amber eyes appeared.

"Thank the gods," Wilhelm exhaled. "Breathe, Salv."

Salvarias gulped in air through his cough, choking on the blood running down his throat. His fingers were numb from clenching

Wilhelm's arms. Releasing his brother, he accepted a cloth and pressed it to his nose.

Once he got his breathing under control, he said, "I apologize."

Humar and Okulu were by the door, armored head to foot. The wretics' beating wings still drummed outside, vibrating the floor and walls. Durak stood guard by one of the windows, axe at the ready. Lunara was wrapped in Neithelas's arms and tears streaked her face. Salvarias turned to Varila lying next to him. Her arms were raw with chunks of flesh missing, and her thighs had no skin left between her boots and just above her armored skirt. Color had drained from her face and she looked near death.

Okulu motioned to Salvarias. Using his staff, Salvarias shoved himself up and joined the merc.

"The wolf had a deep bite," Okulu said. "But I cleaned it, and he seems fine. I'm surprised he let me near him."

Salvarias was already talking with Adok who passed along assurances that he was fine.

Okulu motioned to Varila. "I cleaned hers as well, but I don't know what else to do. If I wrap them, the dressings will stick to her, and we'll cause the same damage when we take them off. I have a couple herb mixtures I could try, but I've never seen wounds like this before."

Salvarias watched his brother smooth her hair, eyes somber. "I might have a potion we can use: a balm that covers her legs and provides a barrier between her skin and the dressings. We can do the same for her arms and my brother's."

"What do you need?" Okulu asked.

"Water. Warm, not hot."

Salvarias settled near the fire, accepting his herb pouch from Okulu, and busily went to work. He often glanced at his brother, reliving Varila's harsh words and swallowing the lump that formed when he realized she spoke the truth.

Yes, my murderer of the innocent. He gives up much for your pathetic existence.

So he does.

And yet you'll not leave him. You won't save him from your murderous ways.

I need him.

How selfish you are, my pet. Do you not remember whispering atrocities on the wind? Tempting honest people toward evil? Would he love you if he knew what you did? Would he stay with you if he knew it was you who raped his mother? Who burned her at the stake? Who sliced apart his father? Would he still care for you?

Salvarias regarded his brother before returning his attention to the mixture, adding warm water to loosen the texture. *Yes, he would. And I hate myself for it.*

As you should, my murderer. At some point, you'll be given the opportunity to leave him. Prepare yourself to do so. It's the only way to give him the life he deserves.

Salvarias's stomach knotted. The voice was right, but he feared he did not possess the strength to leave Wilhelm.

14

Humar leaned against the doorframe, staring at the sliver of sunlight that had snuck through a slat in the boarded window. The sealed home reeked of armor, sweat, and blood, making him anxious to leave its confines.

Salvarias roused from sleep and left the corner of the one-room home to peer outside, whispering numbers.

Humar joined him. "They seemed interested in you last night."

"A mistake, I assure you. Wretics are bloodthirsty creatures. I doubt they paused long enough to identify who I was." Salvarias's shadowed gaze leveled on Humar. "We are a mere thirteen days from Serinity. It is not too late to turn back, Sir Humar."

"I wish you'd stop asking. It's getting old," Humar said, not hiding his irritation.

Salvarias leaned closer and his dark eyes and barely audible whisper seemed to burn through Humar's soul. "And I wish you would come to terms with what you witnessed in the woods with your brother's murderer. I am not a man to follow. You have seen my true self, Sir Humar. Surely you know the safety of the group is in peril."

"Until you take me to the army, you're stuck with me, boy. Regardless of what I saw, Arden is more important than my dislike toward you." Salvarias's eyes flickered with the briefest passing of hurt. Humar didn't care. "Can Varila ride?"

Salvarias's voice was smooth, no hint toward his feelings. "I think it best she rides with my brother. Sidesaddle will not irritate her wounds."

He nodded. "We'll leave soon. Get everyone packed. Okulu, you're with me."

Humar went to the front door and cracked it open. The thumping of wings had ended what he guessed was an hour ago. All had been disturbingly silent since.

Outside, the streets were poised like a squirrel surveying for danger. The forest floor was mottled with blinding sunlight, sparkling the bloodied corpses to look like piles of rubies, and the air itself seemed tense.

Humar slipped outside with Okulu. They traversed two streets and passed three homes until they reached the barn. Okulu lifted aside the block of wood barring the doors closed and flung them open. The horses were huddled in a pack, nervous but unharmed. The worrying ache in Humar's gut unraveled, and he relaxed his rigid shoulders.

"Thank the gods," he said.

"Indeed." Okulu started saddling the horses and Humar helped. "Quite the night last night. How are you holding up, friend?"

Humar massaged his jaw where Wilhelm had landed a nicely dealt blow. "I think he merely used a quarter of his strength. I could feel his restraint."

"You're lucky he still had the mindset to control himself. Why in Nevlar's vengeance you decided to keep him from helping Salvarias, I'll never know."

"It was too dangerous."

"It was too dangerous for Salvarias and Varila to be stuck out there by themselves."

Humar chose not to respond. Okulu, however, continued along with his point.

"You're usually watchful of everyone in your company, but when it comes to Salvarias, everyone besides Lunara and Wilhelm seem to have no problem leaving the mage to fend for himself."

Humar ground his teeth, forcing himself not to fall into Okulu's trap.

Okulu's voice lost its light air. "How long have we known each other?"

"Too long." Humar sighed and moved around his mare to regard Okulu. "You saw it, too. And your expression was just as shocked and disgusted as the rest of us."

"It took me a little off guard, I'll admit. However, unlike you, I can stifle down my judgments. Salvarias didn't mean it."

"Which part?" Humar drawled. "Killing twelve men by slowly driving an ice shard through their throat, or leisurely burning a man alive while laughing. And let's not forget the boy was covered in unnatural fire that didn't even harm a blade of grass. It's not right, Okulu."

"The fact the murderer killed Tobin means nothing to you? Didn't you want him dead?"

"I did. And I'm happy justice has been served. But it should've been quick. You can't condemn an action, then go off and perform it yourself. What Salvarias did was hypocritical."

Okulu shrugged. "Fair enough. But if you'd looked into his eyes afterward, you would've seen he was horrified."

"I don't think for the reason you think he was. The boy isn't right, Okulu. Never has been."

"Neither is Wilhelm. But I don't see you judging him."

Humar glanced at the grinning merc. "Wilhelm's a good man. There's not a mean bone in his body."

Okulu tightened down the last saddle and clapped Humar on the shoulder. "Tell that to your jaw."

The merc left the barn. Humar patted his mare before trailing behind Okulu. There was a shame that gnawed at Humar, but it didn't feast enough for him to change his mind. Salvarias's soul was dark.

The companions were waiting outside for them and went to the business of loading the packs on to the horses.

"I dropped my sword in that house," Varila said.

Humar took notice that some color had returned to her face, and her trembling seemed reasonable with the extent of her wounds. He motioned Durak to go retrieve her weapon.

Varila turned to Salvarias. "Can't you"—she flicked her hand in the air—"make our stuff magically return to us?"

Salvarias stroked Adok's head as the wolf leaned against his leg. "That would be an enchantment, my lady."

"So. Enchant them."

Salvarias frowned. "I fear that power might be out of my reach."

Varila snorted. "You never know until you try."

Okulu winked at Salvarias. "When you figure it out, I'd love for my daggers to erupt in fire when they hit a target. Or maybe they could return to my sheath. Then I wouldn't have to pluck them from the dead. Always such a messy task."

After they finished loading the packs on the horses, Humar led his group to the bridge that would take them over the river.

"Ye be mad!" Durak said. "That bridge not be sturdy enough for horses."

Humar partially agreed. Several wood planks were eaten with rot and the ropes were frayed. Still, it was the only way across unless they turned around to Falar and took a ship to Hadrium.

"It'll hold us," Humar said. "Okulu, go first."

Muttering under his breath, Okulu guided his horse up the steps. To Humar's surprise, the horse seemed to have no qualms about crossing. It navigated well, avoiding less than favorable planks and walking light. Out of the corner of his eye, Humar caught Wilhelm's wink to Salvarias.

Durak was next, followed by Neithelas. Once the two were across safely, Humar motioned to Lunara. She cast a small, brave smile and climbed the steps. She took several deep breaths before boldly walking forward. Her courage continued to impress him.

Humar sent the rest across and lifted Varila to his horse before setting off himself. Once he climbed the steps, he realized the wood was indeed deteriorated past safety. Varila's soft curses did little to help his confidence. Planting each foot tentatively, he led his mare forward. Wood creaked and groaned, and the rushing river below seemed like a watery grave that yawned open in expectation of a potential victim. To his surprise, he made it across alive and fought the urge to kiss solid ground.

The day's ride was slow, even though Varila had taken to riding with Wilhelm. Okulu had set a relaxing pace, which seemed to lift the spirits of Humar's group. Durak's curses and tall tales of Cavrul adventures sent deer fleeing through the forest, and Wilhelm's rumbling laugh often startled birds from the trees. Lunara's smile eventually snuck out, and even Neithelas chuckled a few times. Varila dozed most of the ride, but each time she stirred awake, she seemed more alert and, by the time the crumbling walls of Hadrium came into view, wasn't even wincing or groaning when she shifted positions.

Hadrium had not changed in the two years since Humar's last visit. It wallowed in filth, disease, and crime—worse than Falar. The once imposing wall of ashy-gray rock had deteriorated, leaving boulder-sized chunks scattered at the base of what remained. The gate hung askew on rusty hinges, grinding metal against metal to set Humar's teeth on edge. Two guards stood watch, swaying on their feet, burping loudly and speaking in a slurred yell.

"Disgusting," Wilhelm muttered.

"Aye, lad." Durak shook his head. "This was once a great city before the Retribution. Now, no one wants to visit."

"The Knight Council won't allow any to be stationed here," Humar said.

"Why?" Wilhelm asked.

"Because it's past saving," Varila said. "I've traveled here a couple times with my father, and every time we've come, the city has worsened. He told me that after Nevlar smashed our world, Hadrium fell to riots and looters. The knights couldn't spare enough troops at the time. Those they did were crucified and tortured. The idiotic townspeople blamed the nobles and knights for Nevlar's Retribution. Now, gangs of thieves run the city."

"Why not send the knights now?" Wilhelm said.

"Why should they?" she said. "Hadrium offers nothing unique, no real reason to trade. What they can provide are crops the same as Serinity and Falar. Traders don't need to fear for their lives in Serinity and Falar. Why risk it? After how the citizens treated the knights, the Council saw no reason to send additional men to be butchered. Hadrium is lost."

Wilhelm shook his head. "The knights could put a stop to this."

Humar smiled at Wilhelm. "I happen to agree with you there. However, the Council is full of old men who have grown complacent with the state of things. They've come to think that the roaches that skitter across their floor is the only evil that still resides in Arden."

"Fools. Don't the new members see a chance for change?" Wilhelm said.

Humar shrugged. "Hadrium has been this way for hundreds of years. And the Council positions are inherited. Their sons take their place, and the same ignorance has been bred into them. No, not until the rightful heir is found will the Council ever change."

"Rightful heir?" Wilhelm asked.

Humar shifted in his saddle. "There were two commanders who fought side by side with King Ctol Lilkous during the Long Wars. Wilhelm and Travard Firth. They disappeared at the final battle that ended the goddess's life and drove Nevlar and Veedran into the forest. Before all that and under the watchful eye of Zerana, Wilhelm and Travard were the ones who created the Knight Council, trained them, set the rules, and strategized the battles. They were supposedly an impressive pair. It's written in the knighthood laws that the son of Wilhelm Firth would rule over the order."

"Tobin mentioned that I was named after a commander," Wilhelm said.

Humar nodded. "He asked Ashra once why she'd chosen that name. It's not common, and most view it as sacred. You're the first Wilhelm I've ever met."

"What did she say?" Wilhelm asked.

"She had her magic at the time of your birth. She knew she would be shunned by others anyway, so she picked the strongest name she could think of; one recognizable so her son would be known to the world."

Wilhelm chuckled. "She always told me I would do great things."

Humar regarded him for a moment before nodding. "I believe she was right."

Wilhelm's cheeks tinted pink, and he shifted in his saddle. "We'd best get going."

Durak chuckled. "Shy as a newborn fawn."

Wilhelm's deepening blush only sent Durak into fitful laughter. Humar nudged his horse's flanks and steered them toward the two teetering guards. Neither of them held a list of mages in their hands. They seemed too drunk to care or notice that a sliver of burgundy robes peeked from under Salvarias's black cloak.

"What's yer purpose here?" one guard slurred.

"Why's ther' so many of ... of ..." The other guard burped loudly. "Of you?"

Okulu swung off his horse and wrapped his arm around the nearest guard's shoulder. "We're looking for an inn to drink the night away before pillaging a nearby farm." He held up his flask, casting the two guards an empty-minded grin. "Toast me luck in finding endowed wenches and riches beyond my imagining!"

The men produced flasks from under their breastplates and raised them high. "To wenches and gold!"

Okulu took a long swig. "What's the best tavern for strong ale and full-busted women?"

"That'd be the Horse Trough," one guard said.

"To the Horse Trough!" Okulu raised his flask again, and the three men took a healthy swig. He tossed each man a copper. "Use it to pay the whores I'll send your way."

The guards grinned broadly and pocketed the money. Okulu swung on to his horse and led the group through the gate.

Music leaked out of taverns, drunken men and women mounted

each other in dark corners, children ran amok, and stray animals lapped up spoiled water and ate moldy food. Heaps of diseased citizens—coughing and groaning as they fought to survive—lined the alleys. The stench of feces, vomit, and rotting food thickened the air. Humar raised a gauntlet to his nose, preferring the sour smell of armor to the city.

The Horse Trough was a log tavern steeped in termites and wood rot. Though no breeze disturbed the stale air, the tavern groaned and croaked in objection to its existence.

"Nope," Varila said. "I'm not staying there. Forget it. We'll camp outside."

"We're staying here," Humar said. "Those wretics could venture this way and I'd rather have a city they can feast on instead of just us."

Either subconsciously or not, Varila ran a hand over her dressings and nodded.

They dismounted, and Wilhelm and Salvarias led the horses toward the stables. Okulu wrapped Varila's arm around his shoulders and helped her along while Neithelas took Lunara's hand, keeping the wide-eyed girl close. The couple on the side of the entrance writhing and groaning in the throes of lust stained Lunara's cheeks to the color of the deepest red rose. Humar shook his head as he made his way inside. More of her innocence had just been lost.

Inside, music filled the air, patrons danced and hooted in drunken delight, and barmaids—indeed very endowed—seemed content to let men do what they wanted for a couple coin. Humar was pleased to see the place packed, hoping it would provide cover for his group to slip into their rooms unnoticed.

He found the tavern owner behind the bar sampling his own ale. He was a devilishly handsome man with a smile that suggested he knew it. By his mischievous and shifty eyes, Humar wouldn't be trusting the man as far as he could throw Wilhelm.

"Two rooms," Humar said, slamming down coin to get the owner's attention.

The man snatched the coin and offered a wide grin. "Two rooms for the good sir! A few additional coin and I'll have some wenches sent up."

"If I'd wanted whores, I would've ordered them," Humar snapped. "Keep to your own business."

The owner laughed and tossed two keys at Humar. "I thought you were one of those stuck up knights from Loutsil. Seems you've got a mouth."

Humar grinned. "Armor's not mine. Ran into a highbred Loutsil snob roaming the woods and I killed him. Stole his armor." Humar leaned back so the owner could get a better look. "Fits as if it were made for me!"

The owner's smile dropped. "You must be good with a sword to beat a knight from Loutsil."

"Damn good," Humar said, keeping his smile friendly. "Keep that in mind when you send your men upstairs to rob us."

The owner chuckled nervously. "I wouldn't dream of doin' such a thing."

"Good." Humar tossed the owner a silver. "I'm not in the mood for a fight. There's another one of those for you in the morning if my friends and I are left alone."

"Consider it done," the owner said, rolling the silver between his knuckles.

Humar gave the sisters a key and sent them up with Neithelas and Durak while he waited for the brothers with Okulu.

Okulu flipped a coin to a barmaid. "Two ale." He leaned against the bar, surveying the loud crowd with his bloodshot, grass-green eyes. "Rowdy bunch."

Humar grunted. "I think we'll keep everyone in the rooms tonight. We'll bring up the food."

"Want to tell me where we're going next?"

Humar scratched his chin, feeling how thick his beard had grown. "South, past the barbarian desert. I've been debating taking a ship to Xeroth and going from there. Either that or stick to the mountains on the west side of the desert."

"Ship might be safer. Less dangers on the open waters, that is, if there are any Watythm sailors here."

"Watythms won't sail with a mage even if there are any here." Humar took a sip of his newly arrived ale, potent enough that it induced a shudder as he swallowed it. "I've never understood it." He coughed down the lingering effects. "Watythms adore mages, worship them, but they don't let them on their ships."

"There are a few who do. Every time, their ships are attacked. They think Veedran's old creatures follow the scent of magic."

"And what do you think?"

Okulu shrugged and downed his ale. He slammed the mug on the bar and wiped his chin. "I think it's just another round of bad luck for mages." He nudged a man next to him. "Any Watythm sailors ported here?"

The man scowled at Okulu. "No. Haven't seen one fer days."

"River barges?"

"Bah!" The man spat to the side. "No one is stupid enough to travel by river anymore."

Okulu motioned the barmaid for a mug of ale. "Thanks. This one's on me." He turned to Humar. "I guess that decides it. We follow the mountains."

"What about an Erthla boat?"

Okulu clapped him on the back. "Death wish, eh?"

"On the contrary."

"Erthla's aren't sailors. You know as well as I that most ships don't make it from port. Watythms is the only way to sail. And an Erthla boat wouldn't be permitted to dock in Xeroth. They only take their own."

Humar grimaced down another sip of ale. "I guess it's the mountains."

"Fool," the man spat. "Mountains 'er just as danger'us as 'em Erthla sailors. Mountain folk 'er flockin' to Treppter or here."

"What's been seen in the mountains?" Humar asked.

"Unholiness! Foul creatures frem the depths of Oblivion!"

"He's right," a harsh voice said next to Humar. "You'll die in the mountains."

Humar turned to see two Cavruls sitting beside him. They looked nearly as grumpy as Durak, and each smoked a pipe of some weed that smelled like sulfur.

"Pardon?" Humar asked.

A Cavrul with sleek black hair and a braided beard said, "The lands between the cursed desert and the mountains are piled high with unholy creatures. They flood around the desert as if it was the plague, but ravage the mountains like a winter storm. No road is safe."

"Aye." The other Cavrul's hair was as curly as Durak's and his beard was in four braids. "We Cavruls don't leave the mountains anymore."

"You're a contradiction to the statement," Okulu said.

The sleek haired Cavrul shrugged. "We're on our way home from Falar. We're eager to be in the safety of stone."

"Humar," he said, extending his hand.

"Hunz," the Cavrul said, shaking Humar's hand vigorously.

"And I'm Frink," the curly haired Cavrul said.

Humar tilted his head. "Pleasure. And thank you for the warning."

The two Cavruls whispered to each other, then turned to Humar. "How many are in your party?"

Humar shifted in his seat. "Eight."

"Eight? All healthy? Fit for travel?"

"Yes."

Hunz squinted. "All men?"

"No, we have two women with us." Humar rested his hand on the hilt of his sword.

The Cavruls glanced at each other before Hunz said, "We'd be willing to lead you through the mountains for a small fee."

"Cattlar is a little out of our way," Okulu said.

Hunz waved him aside. "We're not from Cattlar. We're from Catlin, a cave town about three days journey from Cattlar."

"Never heard of it," Humar said.

"Aye, few have. It's a new town, less than five winters old," Frink said.

"I thought Cattlar was the only Cavrul city," Okulu said.

Hunz shrugged. "We're outgrowing it."

Okulu looked at Humar. "That'd put us almost even with Avulin."

"Aye. Straight east for four days would take you to the barbarians' city," Frink said.

Humar leaned over to whisper to Okulu. "What are your thoughts?"

"Any distance inside the mountains will be less distance outside of them. If what they say is true, it'll be safer inside. Plus, once we leave, we'll be at the edge of the barbarian desert. Less chance of being eaten by the cannibals."

"The last time we ventured through caves, we were attacked by a thousand hidlu," Humar reminded him.

"Rare and a product of whoever is after Salvarias. Between the Children of Thonlin and the wretics, I'd rather take my chances in the mountains."

Humar nodded and turned to the Cavruls. "What's the fee?"

"One gold piece."

Okulu whistled. "You call that small?"

"For what you're getting, yes I do," Hunz said.

"A fair price for life," Humar said. "You should know, we have a mage in our company. A young one, barely a man."

The two exchanged a quick glance and nodded. "Acceptable."

Humar pulled off his gauntlet and spit in his hand. "You have a deal, Hunz."

Hunz spit in his hand and clasped Humar's. "We leave tomorrow at sunrise. Meet us outside the gate."

"Thank you," Humar said.

The two Cavruls sauntered out of the tavern.

"Durak's going to kill me," Humar said.

"Why?" Okulu asked.

"He hasn't been home for over a hundred and twenty years. You even mention other Cavruls and he starts chasing you around with that axe of his."

"Well then, my friend, the pleasure of breaking the news is all yours. I find myself terribly occupied at the moment."

Humar cast the merc a disgusted look. "I'll tell him in the morning, coward."

"You say coward, I say intelligent."

The loud ruckus of the tavern quieted to a hushed whisper of awed words. Humar looked to the entrance where Wilhelm had entered with Salvarias. It was because of the low ceiling, Humar mused. Other taverns were grander and complemented Wilhelm's frame better; didn't draw as much attention. The Horse Trough, however, was sinking in upon itself. Wilhelm had to cock his head to the side to avoid hitting it on the ceiling, and his frame was wider than the door. As usual, Salvarias stood half behind his brother, hood low.

"It be a monster!" the man next to Okulu breathed.

Okulu chuckled. "Hardly."

"Could it be Wilhelm Laybryth?" the man hissed.

Humar's gut knotted. "Who?"

"The boy frem Falar. Largest man alive. Unbeatable with a sword. Them says he can best twenty men by himself."

"Bah," Okulu said. "I've met Wilhelm Laybryth. I got in a brawl with him in Falar. I lost a few teeth, broke a few bones. Barely made it from the city alive. That's not him. Wilhelm Laybryth is twice his size."

The man narrowed his eyes. "It be rumored he has a brother spawned by demons. A mage. Could be that hooded boy next to him."

"I'm telling you," Okulu said. "That's not him. That man's with us. Name's Brack. The mage is Reedlin."

The man glanced at him and shrugged. "Shame. I'd love to meet such a legend."

Conversations started again as Wilhelm squeezed between tables, politely removing women's hands as they took hold of his arms to gain his attention.

Humar motioned to the stairs and joined the brothers as they climbed their way to the second floor. At the top, Wilhelm was barely able to stand straight. Once inside the room with the others, Okulu's breath exploded out.

"We need to be careful," Okulu said to Humar.

He nodded, looking around the room at the moldy hay piled up for a bed. He'd definitely be sleeping in his bedroll.

"What's this about?" Varila asked.

"Seems Wilhelm here is earning a reputation in Dalnar," Okulu said. "A man thought he recognized him, but we told him Wilhelm was someone else."

"Reputation?" Wilhelm asked, dropping his pack in the corner along with his brother's.

"You didn't expect to be that large, good with a sword and ladies, and not earn a reputation, did you?" Okulu asked.

Wilhelm grinned. "Is that jealousy I hear?"

Okulu snorted.

"No one's noticed before," Lunara said.

"No other tavern has been quite so confined," Humar said. "He couldn't stand straight. Calls greater attention to someone when they have to lean to the side to walk. Plus, the others were small towns. This is the first major city since Serinity."

Lunara giggled. "He is tall."

Humar ran his hand through his hair, and when he spoke, he focused on Varila, trying to convey his concerns for Lunara in his tone and gaze. "We're in for a dangerous road, more so than we've experienced. We've heard rumors that our path is littered with creatures."

A hush blanketed the room.

Varila glared at Salvarias. "Where are we going, mage? Why don't you tell the rest of us? We might—"

"Don't ask questions," Wilhelm said. "Go wait outside, Salv."

Salvarias had the sleeve of his robe pressed to his nose, and his breath wheezed in and out. The mage seemed eager to leave.

Wilhelm started shoveling hay out a small window. "I've told you before not to ask him questions. He'll tell us what he needs to tell us."

Varila's teeth ground together. "If he'd tell us, we could help. Instead, he keeps us in the dark. We're risking our lives, and he can't even trust us."

"We're heading south," Humar said. "Past the barbarian lands by about five days of travel."

Varila grunted. "Thanks. Someone who finally has a rational thought. Now, do you want to tell us what we're doing?"

Humar shook his head. "I've told you enough. There are no Watythm sailors in Hadrium. We've no other option but to risk the mountains. I'm warning everyone of the dangers."

"We need to avoid the barbarian desert at all cost," Varila said. "I mean at *all* costs. My father and I don't have the best reputation in the sands. But going into woods littered with creatures doesn't sound like a good plan. Maybe we should give up this fool's quest and go home. We already defeated whatever was stalking our lands."

Humar's eyebrows shot up. "You think we eliminated the threat? You can't be that naive." Her blushing cheeks told him she indeed thought the threat had ended. "We stopped an attack, Varila. We didn't find the culprit behind it."

"I'm sure it was Dethal," she said.

"Perhaps. But whoever it is, we need to find and stop them. That's our goal. That's why we travel."

Durak nodded. "Dull-witted as knights are, he's got a point, lass."

"Thanks," Humar said dryly. "We'll bring up food in a bit. It'll be an early morning tomorrow so get some sleep." He followed Neithelas, Okulu, and Durak from the room. Outside, Salvarias was leaning against the wall, doubled over, wheezing in gulps of air. "You all right, boy?"

Salvarias nodded. "Thank you, Sir Humar."

Humar left for his room, breathing heavier than needed.

~

VARILA JOLTED awake from a nightmare of bloodthirsty wretics feasting on her and Lunara. A shudder ran down her spine. She'd hoped she would sleep for the day in Wilhelm's arms once more, avoiding the pain of her eaten legs with the luxury of dreams. Then she realized there was no pain; no throbbing, no burning, no jabs ... nothing except a little tenderness when she pressed her thighs together.

She flung back her blanket and sat up. The faintest glow from Salvarias's sparrow shadowed Lunara sleeping soundly next to her. Wilhelm snored softly, and Adok was using Wilhelm's calf as a pillow. Salvarias had crammed himself in a corner with his spell book propped up on his knees pressed to his chest.

He glanced up and tilted his head in greeting.

"My ..." She bit her lip. What if she was losing feeling in her legs? What if they'd have to take them? She'd die. No one could survive—

"My lady," Salvarias whispered.

He'd risen soundlessly and now stood on the other side of Lunara.

"My legs don't hurt," she snapped. "What in Oblivion did you put on them? A slow-working poison?" Her anger toward him was unfounded, but she was in no mood to be rational. She rarely was.

Salvarias moved around to her other side and knelt down. "Perhaps we should look at the wounds. I assure you, it was no poison. I had intended the mixture to dull the pain."

"Intended? What does 'intended' mean? You didn't know the effects when you put that crap on me?"

"My lady, berating me will not change the fact that we need to examine the wounds. Please remove your dressings."

Varila yanked on the dressings. "Why do you always have to be so damn calm about everything? Don't you get angry? Pissed off?"

"Often, my lady."

She glanced up at his serious expression. "Go suck an ogre. I don't need sarcasm."

"I was being quite truthful."

Bastard. She wrenched off the rest of the cloth. Her thighs were still raw and red, but only the deepest gouges seeped the tiniest bit of blood, like through cheesecloth. Even so, she still should've felt pain by how ugly the wounds were, but she felt nothing. In complete gratitude, she breathed, "What was in that potion?"

"Simple pain relievers and herbs to help skin regrow," Salvarias murmured. His sparrow floated above her thighs. "You are healing at a remarkable rate, my lady. Faster than I thought possible."

When she reached to pull aside his hair, he flinched. "Oh, stop that! I'm not going to hurt you. I want to see if your bite is healing the same."

Humar's voice rose from the other side of the door as he knocked. "Varila? Wilhelm?"

Varila glanced out the window at the twinkling stars. "Have you gone mad, knight?"

He edged open the door. "I know it's early but we need to get going."

"I think we could use the rest," Varila retorted.

Humar shook his head and smiled at Wilhelm and Lunara stirring awake. "Sorry, but we need to get going. We'll eat as we ride. Okulu and Neithelas are gathering the horses. Meet us in the stables after you've washed up. No towns for ten days."

Varila groaned. She hated not bathing regularly.

After Humar left, Wilhelm pulled a blanket over his head and rumbled out a curse.

Salvarias offered his staff to help her rise. "You should bathe without the dressings. It might be painful, but it is imperative the wounds remain clean. Upon your return, I will have fresh dressings and a new mixture ready."

She nodded, gathered a clean dress for her sister, undergarments for both, their bathing liquids, and snatched her sister's hand and led the way out the room, down the dimly lit hallway, and outside toward the bathhouse.

"Damn knight," she muttered. "No baths for ten days!"

Lunara scrunched up her face in a dramatic frown. "I know. Hopefully we'll find streams."

"We'd better. I'm not going ten days without some sort of cleansing."

The tavern owner, yawning and sour faced, was waiting for them at the bathhouse. "That half-breed said there'd be two women looking for baths."

"That's us," Varila said.

"I've got one room, per his instructions, with two tubs. Water isn't that hot, but then again, it's the middle of the damn night!" The tavern owner spat to the side and stomped off.

"I think I agree with him," Varila said, glancing up at the sky.

"No, morning is close. Humar is planning something."

Varila drew her sword and eased open the door. Two lanterns lit the room enough she could see two tubs filled with water, two drying cloths, soap, and two dark corners. She strode in, grabbed a lantern, and marched to the corners. They were alone.

"All right," Varila said, setting aside the lantern. She grinned girlishly at Lunara. "I love baths!"

Lunara giggled, shed her dress and undergarments, and tested the water with her toe. She gasped and yanked her foot back. "It's freezing!"

Varila cursed. "It'll be miserable. Let's get this over with."

She poured a few drops of oil into her bath water to scent it with strawberries and then climbed in. The cold water stung her skin, but her thighs where the mage's potion had been applied didn't hurt at all. It wasn't necessarily numb either. She wasn't sure what in Oblivion was going on, but she was thankful.

She bathed quickly and, through chattering teeth, spoke of the traits she admired in Neithelas. She didn't miss her sister's rolling eyes, sighs, or snorts of disagreement, but none of it stopped her from carrying on. She'd do everything in her power to steer Lunara's lingering gazes from the mage.

After they bathed, they returned to their room. Wilhelm was waiting with the mage's herb bowl and a deliciously crooked smile.

"Mind?" he asked, holding up the bowl.

Varila hesitated only a breath, wondering if he'd see her disfiguration and grimace in disgust. Forcing a smile, she said, "Behave or I'll slice your throat open."

Wilhelm chuckled and patted the ground in front of him. "I'll do my best."

She plopped down in front of him and was very accommodating in her position to give him the most access to her wounds and make him confront the fact she no longer had thighs his eyes would linger on as they'd done since she met him.

Instead of a sneer of loathing, his quickened breathing and trembling hands were a confirmation that he'd not changed his mind. It felt good to be lusted after, and her grin spread in response to his wink.

As Salvarias and Lunara packed, Wilhelm applied the mixture, never inching his hands higher than her wounds crept. She admitted she was slightly disappointed in his chivalrous respect.

They were close as he worked, and she inhaled the rich aroma of leather and steel. She loved the way he smelled. Once he finished applying the mixture, he tightly wrapped her thighs with a frown of what looked like regret. Varila rested her hand over her mouth to hide her smile.

"All done," Wilhelm announced.

Salvarias glanced over and nodded. "Thank you, Brother."

Wilhelm shouldered on the brothers' packs, and Salvarias plucked up Lunara and hers, and led the way.

Outside, the night was not particularly chilly, but the cold bath and cool morning air made Varila shiver. Lunara's teeth knocked together until Wilhelm draped on his cloak and wrapped it around them both. Varila gave him a thankful smile. She'd rather be the one in his arms, but Lunara came first. Salvarias clutched his cloak closer, but the thick fabric didn't hide his trembling. She noticed his still damp hair.

"I'm guessing you took a bath in the same freezing water as us?" she said.

Salvarias nodded. "I d-d-do not blame th-th-the owner. It is early."

Varila grunted her agreement. The deep sky had lightened to a dingy gray and stars had faded from the eastern skyline. Only the occasional snore or dreamy murmur from homeless residents disturbed the hush that always seemed to accompany morning.

When they reached the stables, Humar motioned everyone to gather around. "We need to have a quick meeting." Once all circled him, he continued. "As I'm sure you've noticed, our trip so far has offered several concerns. The Children of Thonil and the wretics are testament enough to the perilous nature of our travels."

Durak rolled his eyes. "Get on with it, ye long-winded knight."

Humar smiled faintly. "As I told you last night, Okulu and I have learned the road we're taking is crammed full of the unsavory. It's a suicide path, and I refuse to take it and lead us to our deaths."

"How sage of you," Varila said.

Humar grinned. "I have my moments. Now, I've already made plans ... much, much safer plans."

"Oh do tell," Varila said dryly. "The only place safe is up in the sky or inside a rock."

Okulu chuckled. "Funny you should mention, because—"

Humar elbowed Okulu. "Last night in the tavern, we were discussing our route and challenges when two men offered up a solution. They've agreed to lead us through the mountain. Inside, there's a path of tunnels and caverns that'll take us half the journey in complete safety. The rest of it we'll follow mountain trails until we're past the desert. Then we'll go to the open plains."

"Inside a mountain?" Varila groaned. "I hate caves."

"I agree," Wilhelm said.

She looked over at him to see Lunara folded in his arms, as if he needed her comfort, not to keep her warm.

Humar ran a hand through his hair. "Salvarias? What are your thoughts?"

The mage rested a hand on Wilhelm's shoulder, and his hooded gaze fixed on his brother. Wilhelm slouched, and nodded.

Salvarias spoke to Humar, "I agree with your decision."

Humar smiled. "Good. We're meeting our guides outside."

"I'm surprised ye found anyone who knows those tunnels," Durak said, turning to mount. "I've never heard of another besides Cavruls ..." His voice trailed off and the reins fell from his hands. When he whirled around, his gray face was reddened, and his scowl caused her to cringe. "Ye best be careful what you say next."

Humar's look and tone was apologetic. "They've offered to take us to Catlin."

Durak's axe whipped free, and he barreled toward the knight. Humar danced to the side, hand resting on the hilt of his sword while he held up the other in an attempt to calm Durak. "Be rational, Durak. We don't—" He dodged right of Durak's charge. Wilhelm snatched up the Cavrul and wrapped his arms around Durak's chest. The oaths that spilt from him caused Lunara to gasp and Neithelas's eyes to widen.

"Listen to what he has to say," Wilhelm said.

"I'll do no such thing, ye overgrown ogre! Put me down!"

"Nope." Wilhelm winked at Humar. "I'll let Okulu chop off your beard if you don't calm down."

Durak stopped struggling. "Ye wouldn't, lad. Ye not be that heartless."

Wilhelm chuckled. "You willing to bet your beard on that?"

Okulu, with dramatic slowness, drew a dagger while smiling a chilling smile.

"All right! All right!" Durak sputtered. "Tell the drunk not to come near me."

Humar's eyes brimmed with apology. "I'm sorry, Durak. This is the only way to keep us safe. You've trusted me for years ... *years*. Trust me now."

"Put me down," Durak said. "Me need to think."

After a nod from Humar, Wilhelm lowered the Cavrul. Durak stomped off to the side of the group, Humar following. Varila inched closer so she could eavesdrop.

"I know you haven't been home in over a hundred years," Humar whispered. "Even though you've never told me what happened, anyone can see your pain when you talk of your homeland. Believe me, I don't want to hurt you. If it helps, we're not going to Cattlar. It's a new city called Catlin." Humar ran a hand through his hair, making it stick straight up. "I've been up all night trying to think of another way. If you know of one, tell me. For this, the lives of seven other people rest in your hands. The lives of Varila, Okulu." Durak's shoulders slumped. "Wilhelm." Durak's head lowered. "Lunara."

"You've made yer point," Durak snapped. He took a deep breath and shook his head. "It won't matter though. They won't take a mage."

"We've already told them. They still agreed."

Durak snorted. "Surely ye be mad. No Cavrul likes mages. None of us!"

"You lived with the boy, Durak. I—"

"If ye think I did so without hate, ye be wrong."

Humar looked away, and his gaze found Varila. "Then you understand, my old friend. These two Cavruls have agreed. That doesn't mean they do it free of prejudices."

Durak scuffed his boots on the cobblestones. "I've got a bad feelin'. It not be right. I agreed to let the boy in my home because I've strayed from my peoples' beliefs. If they be returnin' to a Cavrul city, then they haven't. Something else is going on, Humar."

"The decision is yours, Durak."

Durak thought a long moment before shaking his head. "We'll go through the caves. You know why Wilhelm doesn't want to?"

Humar glanced at the brothers. "I had a suspicion. I didn't think he'd mind so much. Especially since we spent time in the mountains when we were looking for Salvarias."

Durak grunted. "The boy wasn't of his right mind. Me doubt he knew where he was or who was with him. This will be hard on him. And Salvarias."

"Yes, it will." Humar smiled at Varila. "But I think someone can help distract Wilhelm."

Durak followed Humar's gaze. "Aye, indeed she can."

She rolled her eyes.

When the men joined the rest of the group, Durak said, "We be goin' through the caves."

Lunara looked at Neithelas. "And where will your travels take you?"

"I'll continue in your company," Neithelas said. "The trees have followed my brother to the sands. Our paths still align."

Humar nodded. "Happy to have your company."

"You are an apt leader," Neithelas said before turning his gaze to Lunara. "Furthermore, I find myself with another reason to travel with you."

Lunara's cheeks turned a rosy pink, and she looked away. Varila grinned. "How wonderful. I was hoping you'd stay awhile."

Neithelas tilted his head. "I find you and your sister's company pleasant. I'm in no hurry to part from such perfection."

Okulu made a gagging noise, prompting Wilhelm's rumbling chuckle.

They mounted, Varila bravely taking to her own horse since the gods only knew what they'd encounter, and made their way out of the city. By the time they passed the creaking gate, the sky was pale yellow, stark with the promise of a hot day. Varila didn't mind the prospect. After the cold bath and still wet hair, she needed the sun's unfiltered warmth.

At the edge of the trees, two Cavruls sat astride donkeys. Unlike Durak, these Cavruls were a lighter gray and their beards were braided. However, their scowls and frown lines were a mirror of Durak's.

Humar made quick introductions, calling attention to the wolf that had remained in the shadows until announced.

Hellos were exchanged until Hunz came to Durak. "Durak Boughlar?"

"That's none of yer damn business," Durak snapped.

Both Cavruls flung themselves off their donkeys and knelt. "It is our honor to escort you, Lord Boughlar."

"Lord?" Humar said, mouth agape. "Lord!"

"It be nothing," Durak grumbled. He waved an irritated hand at the Cavruls. "Get up, ye fools. I'm not a lord anymore. And we don't need to talk about it. Just ... let's just be goin'."

Both Cavruls cast Salvarias a quick glance. "Would you like us to rid the creature from your side?"

Humar quickly snatched Wilhelm's reins and cast him a stern look.

"No, ye idiots," Durak snapped. "If me wanted him dead I'd have killed him meself."

Humar said, "Is this going to be a problem?"

Hunz and Frink shook their heads and mounted their donkeys, eyeing the mage with clear contempt. Varila smiled. She was going to get along splendidly with their new guides.

15

E ver since Varila had planted the seed of thought, Salvarias had become obsessed with the idea of enchanting. It had consumed his mind during the prior day's travels as he tried to discuss the possibility with his magic. Oddly, his magic had dismissed it. Today, as his group embarked on the steady climb up the mountain, Salvarias decided to broach the topic again. And this time, he would not accept no as an answer.

Set in his resolve, he ignited his magic. Instant warmth flowed through his blood, driving away his chill. Confidence bloomed with such speed, he swore one flick of his hand would level mountains, call forth the sea, and vanquish the sun. He smiled to himself. *Hello, my friend.*

His magic wrapped around him like a heated blanket of care. *My wizard. Are we to study today? I feel it's been years since we perused the words of your mind.*

I am afraid not. Once again, we are riding. A quill and ink are unmanageable on horseback.

How maddening. I'd hoped to come up with a new spell or two. If we're not studying, how may I serve you?

I would like to discuss the possibility of enchanting again. I find—

As I told you before, enchantment is out of the question.

There was a hint of anger in the magic's voice ... or was it hurt?

Salvarias clearly conveyed his resolve by opening himself to the magic. *As you can see, my friend, I will not be dissuaded. I want to know why it is unattainable for us.*

No mage can enchant, the magic said shortly. *Let us move on from this tiresome discussion.*

Your statement is not true. My dagger is proof that mages can enchant. It—

No mage enchanted it! The magic's voice was strained, and the usual fondness lining its words was replaced with fear.

Keeping his voice even as if comforting a small child, Salvarias said, *We have grown closer together since first we talked seven years ago.*

Yes, my wizard, we have.

I understand we have many obstacles to cross before we blindly trust one another, but as I have done for you, I ask you to do the same. Trust me now with this confession, my friend. Tell me what causes you fear.

A long moment passed before the magic spoke again. *I'm not strong enough to enchant. Magic itself is not strong enough. As I said, no mage can. What is within your dagger resembles magic on the surface, but there's something different—something that reaches beyond magic. It's something that is similar to what is inside you.*

Salvarias tensed. *Explain.*

Remember when we first spoke, I told you that I sensed two powers within you?

Yes.

They are stronger than me. Those powers are what can enchant. I ... I'm worthless in comparison.

Questions flooded Salvarias. *How did I obtain these other powers? What are they? Where did they come from?*

I have few answers. One power you have unleashed on your own.

When? I do not—

Blackfire. That's the power needed to enchant.

Then I understand. Enchantment is outside our reach. Salvarias shuddered. *I will never use it again. I could not endure the pain.*

The magic sighed. *It's hidden in such a dark corner of your soul that I doubt you could ever find it on your own. I, however, can tap into it. I can control a very miniscule portion of it. It allows me to because it knows it's you who commands me.*

What are you not telling me?

I ... I'm afraid.

Salvarias's patience was wearing thin, and he snapped the words out in his mind. *Of what?*

Of you ... no longer needing or wanting me.

Salvarias's jaw dropped and a sudden urge to laugh rose up. He coughed it back and shut his mouth. *I will never stop needing you. You have cared for me, protected me, taught me, and are one I consider a friend. No matter what powers I possess, our relationship is more valuable than all of it. Without you, I have no confidence, no ...* He struggled for a word, but there was none. His magic made him who he was, stopped him from learning swordplay with his brother, gifted him a sense of worth. His magic, much like Wilhelm, adored his oddities. Without his magic, he would be ... "Hollow."

Relief flooded him with such intensity he swayed in his saddle. *I'm most appreciative, my wizard. I thought once you learned you didn't need me, you'd banish me, break our connection.*

I would not know how, nor would I seek the knowledge. You and I are locked together for all the days I live. Even after my physical body turns to dust, I doubt my soul will release you. As for the blackfire, I refuse to command it. The blackfire is something I never want to experience again.

As childish as I feel, I am honored by your words," his magic said. "And my jealousy toward this other power can easily be turned to a partnership. Don't dismiss it, my wizard. With it, we can accomplish great things. With it, we might have a chance at defeating whatever horror stalks the lands. I can tap into the surface of the power without igniting the blackfire. It can lend a miniscule portion to me.*

What about this other power? You say there are two?

Yes. The other power merely resides within you. I can access it if I choose, or not. However, the two powers will not ... shall we say, work together. I can only use one or the other.

Salvarias shook his head and pulled his cloak closer. *I am fright-ened of them both. We do not understand them. We do not know where they come from. We know nothing.*

True, but you knew nothing of me, my cautious wizard. Remember how tentative our relationship was in the beginning. Greatness can only be achieved once fears are evolved into knowledge. I have faced mine. Now you must evolve yours.

Salvarias closed his eyes. Every person his parents' murderer killed materialized. The faces of seventy-three innocent men, women, and children stared at him, all weeping, all savagely butchered. Deep red blood splattered his face, ran down his hands. Remembering them brought their pain, tearing apart his body with all they had endured. Then his parents surfaced.

I ... I cannot. Salvarias shut his eyes tighter, begging his mind to stuff the images into his peripheral vision, pleading the stabs to cease.

Memories, my wizard, his magic whispered. *Just memories.*

The faces dissolved, and he saw simply blessed darkness. His mind calmed, and his pain disappeared. A light hand was resting on his arm.

He looked over to see Lunara riding next to him, a frown tugging the corner of her enticing red lips. All he desired was to lift her into his saddle, hold her close, bury his face in her hair, and become lost in the comfort of her touch. Instead, he pulled away, grimacing against the rush of his thoughts and the normal images of slaugh-tered people. He swallowed the lump in his throat. "I am fine."

"Of course. I thought you might be dozing. I didn't want you to fall."

Salvarias glanced around. Wilhelm was the only one watching him, twisted around in his saddle, brow furrowed. Salvarias turned to Lunara. "Thank you. I am fine." His tone was a dismissal, and she smiled sweetly before nudging her horse forward.

It won't be the same, the magic said. *You'll not experience what you just experienced. Like a fortress shooting into the stars, this power has many levels, degrees of use. I assure you, if within my power, I will save you from such grief.*

Salvarias inhaled a deep breath and shook off the remnants of dead. They once again played in the corners of his mind, always there, but ignorable. Steeling himself, he said, *So be it. What must I do?*

We'll learn together as we try to perform it, my wizard. All I know is that it's not like me, but since you're accustomed to dealing with my power in such a manner, I'll instruct you in the same.

I do not understand.

There are no spells needed, no release, no commanding. It's more your will and thoughts that can achieve our objective. However, to ease the strain, we'll come up with a spell, we'll release it, we'll command it. I'll make it as similar to a spell as I can. Otherwise, the strain might be too much. This power is raw, and I doubt it understands the limits of the human mind.

None of what you say is building my confidence, Salvarias said dryly.

His magic chuckled. *Indeed. I'll see to that as well. If I may be so bold, when can we study once again?*

When we rest for the night. Perhaps we can come up with a spell to write without ink.

An excellent idea.

Salvarias rubbed Mithal's neck when the horse danced nervously at the proximity of a mountain lion Salvarias conversed with. He comforted the rest of the horses before refocusing on his magic. *And a bubble. We must make a bubble.*

Pardon?

A brilliant idea from my soon-to-be sister-in-law. A protection spell that does not cling to its target, but one that bubbles out. Imagine how much easier it will be to guide.

Indeed. A wise woman.

She was also the one to suggest enchantments. If I continue to irritate her, I am sure she will provide all manner of ideas for new spells.

How truly wonderful. I wish you success.

Salvarias smiled at his magic's sarcastic tone. *My mere existence provides fuel to her hate.*

Perhaps you should ride next to her and strike up a conversation?

Salvarias grinned. *I think not. I would rather enjoy a peaceful day of riding.*

Then I bid you farewell until tonight, my brilliant wizard.

Salvarias allowed his magic to rest, shivering as its presence faded into sleep. Pulling his cloak tighter about him, he took in his surroundings. The forest was not nearly as layered as Serinity or Falar. Patches of dirt were as common as the sprinkle of stones and the emerging of tree roots. Ferns dotted the dusty soil like the early stars of evening. He missed the lush forests of home.

It was midday when Adok growled, hackles raised, gaze darting around. The group reined in, surveying the woods. Adok told him there were creatures hiding in the woods right as twenty-five octrils darted out from behind trees and rocks.

"Dismount!" one spat. "Keep your hands where I can see them, all of you!"

Salvarias and his companions raised their hands.

"I said dismount!" it snarled.

The octrils formed a half circle in front of them. They could run, but ... Salvarias shared a glance with Wilhelm. His brother winked.

"Think it through, boy," an octril warned. "You can't defeat this many."

"Clearly," Salvarias said, "you underestimate my companions."

Salvarias whispered his spell and flicked his hand. Five icicles appeared in his rune. "*Rulose.*" They shot through the air and landed in the chests of five octrils on Wilhelm's left side. It gave his brother the advantage of not caring about his flank.

"I've got this," Wilhelm said to the others as he whipped his sword from its sheath. He hissed Lilly into a charge. The mare trampled one beast while Wilhelm cleaved through another octril's head. Bits of gore sprayed out.

Salvarias drew his second rune and sent five fire shards to the octrils rushing his brother on the right.

Apparently seeing Wilhelm as their target, the octrils coalesced around him. With him mounted, it was a massacre. Wilhelm's great sword lopped off arms and heads, splattering the dry pine needles with blue-green blood, and his crooked grin was sliced across his face. Seeming to think it was not a challenge, he dismounted with seven octrils left, slapping Lilly on the rear to prompt her from the foray.

Salvarias glanced at his gawking companions. Pride swelled up in him. His brother was a force to be reckoned with, and watching him slice through his opponents was simply something one would not believe unless they had witnessed his skill first hand. The scene had stunned their companions into a captive audience.

Salvarias held a shard ready to assist if need be, a simple spell, easily maintained, easily repeated. Wilhelm locked into a fierce fight with five, keeping them at bay with thrusts and flying fists. The other two octrils darted in and out of the closed-in brawl, jabbing swords in between Wilhelm's offensive lunges, causing his brother to narrowly avoid slices.

Throughout Salvarias's life, he had watched his brother spar not only because of how proud it made him to be related to such a man, but for situations such as these. He wanted to fight alongside his brother, to share the camaraderie. But swords were not his passion. Now he saw how unstoppable the two of them could be. He mused they could take on fifty men and walk away with minor scrapes.

Focusing on the fight, he anticipated his brother's next move. Waiting until Wilhelm's large frame would be clear, Salvarias sent a fire shard sailing through the air. It avoided Wilhelm by less than a finger's width and landed with a satisfying thud in the forehead of an octril.

Wilhelm's rumbling laugh infected Salvarias. He released his small icicle, timing it perfectly with Wilhelm's next lunge. Again, it missed him by a breath to penetrate the neck of an octril. Two remained. Ducking a beheading swing, Wilhelm rose up, arching his massive sword. Entrails poured like wine from the octril. Wilhelm's sword was already on the downswing to block the second octril's attempted thrust. His fist connected with the octril's jaw, snapping it sideways and sending the creature sprawling to the ground.

"Piece of crap," Wilhelm muttered. "When are you going to learn that you're not taking him from me again?" With that, he sunk his sword in the octril's throat. He yanked it free and raised a grin to Salvarias. "Nicely done, little brother."

"You as well," Salvarias said, a smile twitching on his lips.

Wilhelm turned to the companions. "Thanks. I needed a good fight." Not seeming to notice their dropped jaws, he wiped his sword clean on the grasses.

Humar cleared his throat. "You two fight well together, as if you've done it all your lives. I don't recall it, though."

Wilhelm shrugged. "We haven't." He chuckled. "Always knew it'd be like that. Invigorating, wouldn't you say, little brother?"

Salvarias patted Mithal's neck. "Very." He enjoyed these moments when his brother's pride rang in his voice. It was the only time Wilhelm called Salvarias "little brother."

"Where were your trees on that one?" Okulu asked Neithelas.

"Allow me to give you an education in your heritage, half-breed," Neithelas said. Okulu rolled his eyes. "Trees don't communicate the same as creatures. They don't have a brain, therefore, their presence is different from other living beings. They sense emotion; matters of the soul. Early on, Veedran defiled life, defiled souls. The trees sensed his abominations; warped souls, creatures bred by unholy means. The Dark God, however, grew savvy. If you'll recall your histories— you do know how to read, don't you?"

"Go screw a sapling," Okulu growled.

Neithelas smiled faintly and continued. "As history tells us, octrils were soon the species that made Veedran's numbers. They are more creature than human, more slave than bloodthirsty. They were bred to *want* to serve Veedran."

"I wonder what changed," Lunara said, eyes staring intently at the reins in her hands.

Salvarias glanced around at the bloody mess. He inched his horse to her side, blocking her view of the carnage, and motioned to his brother. Wilhelm nodded and nudged Lilly to Lunara's other side.

Neithelas frowned. "What do you mean?"

Lunara smiled at both of them and said, "Why do they now serve whatever evil is plaguing Arden? If they were made—created—for Veedran, how did this other thing get them to obey him?"

Neithelas shrugged. "Everything evolves, my lady. Without the Dark God, they've surely roamed Arden until finding another master." Neithelas sniffed. "I wouldn't doubt it if the darkness plaguing our lands is Crutar."

Durak shook his head. "If that damned god commanded the octrils, he would've wiped us out ages ago."

"The last of the Long Wars killed nearly all the octrils," Neithelas said. "I doubt Crutar was left with enough forces. I believe he's been breeding them in that wretched tip of Dalnar."

"My father told me stories of the lords of the cities sending armies to overtake Crutar," Lunara said. "He said they failed miserably."

"The southeastern point of Dalnar be protected by over a hundred miles of swamp," Durak said. "No clean water, no game, and no means for fires. There's hardly any dry land. There be no place to camp. Armies can't survive in such conditions. And Veedran's sea monsters flocked there after the Long Wars. An attack at sea isn't even possible."

"It's why I believe wholeheartedly that Crutar is the one carrying out Veedran's sick obsession," Neithelas said, nodding his approval at Durak. "It's no secret that Crutar worshipped Veedran."

Lunara shuddered. "How could one care for something so evil?"

Neithelas raised an eyebrow, glancing at Salvarias. "I have wondered the same."

Salvarias doubted any others noticed the prince's delicately placed insult.

Neithelas turned back to Okulu. "In case you didn't know, half-breed, trees give a part of themselves to Winsires, even half-breeds such as yourself. Their energy and vibrancy are imbued in our souls. Without their presence, we grow weak, almost as if starved." Neithelas turned to Humar. "Within these caves, Okulu and I will feel hollow, half of our energy taken away."

Okulu curled his lip and looked away, shifting in his saddle.

"Once we are free of the caves," Neithelas continued, "they will focus on feeding us." He frowned slightly at Okulu. "Though you are stubborn, the trees sense your empty soul. They offer you extra attention, but you've refused to learn the ways of your people. You don't know how to accept their gift. You must feel half alive."

"Go to Oblivion," Okulu growled.

"Do the trees sense everyone's souls?" Lunara asked, clearly trying to turn the conversation.

"Only the soul of a Winsire is open to their viewing," Neithelas said. "With other races, they sense intense emotions. It's how I can track my brother, yet why I couldn't foresee this attack."

"Might I suggest we continue?" Salvarias said, watching Okulu wring his horse's reins in his hands.

After Okulu had stolen a few daggers from the dead and Humar had checked for other useful supplies, they set off, all gathered around Wilhelm as they praised his skill.

16

T he afternoon waned, and the buzz and excitement of the group faded with the passing time. The sun burned through the trees, making it feel like the second month of summer instead of the last month of spring.

In the remaining few hours of daylight, a young sparrow caught Salvarias's attention. It flitted from limb to limb, singing as loud as its little lungs could muster. When he connected with it, the sparrow's young mind was awash with songs. So eager was it to share that it dove from its perch and circled Salvarias, singing and switching from tune to tune. He begged the sparrow to return to the trees, but the bird saw his group as no threat. It was not even scared of Adok.

The companions twisted in their saddles to stare at him. Of course, it was Varila who spoke.

"What's with the damn bird?"

"Looks like it's a young one," Wilhelm said. He cast Salvarias a pained look.

"So it is." Salvarias returned the same look to Wilhelm.

"Funny," Okulu said casually. "I've noticed a number of sparrows that seem very vocal around us."

"Birds enjoy spring," Wilhelm growled. "Forget about it."

The sparrow's dizzying flight had yet to cease.

"Perhaps it ran into a tree and knocked its brain loose," Okulu said, stroking his mustache. "Or maybe fell from the nest when he was little. I knew a mother who dropped her baby once. Dreadful mistake. The child never was right after it."

"It's damn annoying," Varila said.

"I think it's delightful," Lunara said. "It sings lovely songs."

"If only you heard the trees," Neithelas said. "Their song is the sweetest even among the birds." He turned to Lunara. "Perhaps one day, my lady, you could visit my homeland. I would love to show you the wonders of the trees."

Lunara's smile was anything but genuine. "Perhaps."

You should drive her toward the prince, the presence said. *If her interests are steered from you, you might be able to save her from a horrible fate.*

Indeed, the prince could provide her a solid, caring life. Safety from darkness, from pain. Neithelas would no doubt protect her as much as Salvarias wished to do. He shoved aside a surge of jealousy. Lunara's safety and happiness were all that mattered. Better for her to obtain it without him, without his evil devouring her light.

"I have heard Meitholias is a beauty to behold," Salvarias said. "You should be honored by his offer, my lady. If what I have read is true, no Erthla has been allowed in the city for well over a hundred years. To refuse would be insulting." He ignored the knife twisting in his chest.

Neithelas tilted his head. "You are correct."

Lunara turned in her saddle to face Salvarias. Steel lined her voice when she said, "Thank you for your opinion, Salvarias. I, however, won't be traveling to Meitholias. I wouldn't want to break Winsire tradition."

"The prince has requested—" Salvarias gritted his teeth when the sparrow landed on his shoulder, tweeting away.

Okulu burst out laughing. "I like that sparrow. He has good taste in company. Shame your trees can't sit on your shoulder, Neithelas. I'd like to see you compete with that!"

"Let's get going," Wilhelm said, motioning to Hunz. "We don't want to be out here at night." The companions continued on, but Wilhelm held back until he was beside Salvarias. "Can't you make him go away?"

"I have tried, Brother. He is very excited."

Wilhelm's grin spread. "You're the most amazing man I've met, Salv."

"So you say. However, I cannot stop a bird from circling a band of humans and a bloodthirsty wolf."

Adok growled.

Salvarias glanced down at him. "If you would be more intimidating, my dear friend, perhaps the sparrow would wander off. It appears you are no threat."

Adok bared his teeth.

Wilhelm chuckled and leaned over to ruffle Adok's fur. "He's a softy. The wolf doesn't have a mean bone in his body."

Adok nipped at his hand, and then turned to the sparrow and gave a sharp bark that startled the bird enough to cause it to leave.

Frink's voice rose up. "Up there." He pointed to a steep hill that ended at a sheer slab of granite half a mile long and nearly as tall.

"I don't see anything," Humar said.

"Aye. Not visible from here. But the entrance into the caves is up there."

"Shhh!" Okulu said.

Everyone tensed and cocked their heads.

"There! Did you hear it?" Okulu hissed.

"What is it?" Neithelas whispered.

"There it is again!" Okulu leaned back in his saddle and spoke loudly, causing everyone to jump. "It's the mountain laughing its ass off at Frink. I think it agrees with me. The Cavrul's gone mad. There's no entrance to a cave up there. Trust me, I've got damn good eyesight."

Durak spewed oaths. "Ye drunk bastard!"

Hunz swung off his saddle. "We walk from here."

Salvarias stiffened. He had never thought to ask if the horses would be permitted into the caverns. They were his friends, as much a part of the group as Okulu, Durak, Varila ... all of them. They could not leave them in the wilderness.

The horses pranced, whinnying their agreement. Before he voiced an argument, Wilhelm spoke in a low, chilling tone, jaw set. "We're not leaving the horses."

All turned a surprised look.

Humar recovered first and dismounted. "We'll get new ones in Catlin."

"We're not leaving the horses," Wilhelm repeated.

Humar shook his head and started untying his pack. "Sorry. We don't have a choice."

"Then Salv and I are leaving," Wilhelm growled.

Humar raised his gaze to Wilhelm. "You're being unreasonable."

"Can the horses fit through the tunnels?" Salvarias asked. "Is there ever a point in which they could not make it?"

Hunz rubbed the back of his neck. "No, they can fit. But there's no hay. And most horses go mad in the caves after a few days. It's not in their nature. It's better to release them."

"There are grasses that grow within caves that the horses can eat. And I assure you, they will not go mad."

"I didn't pay for Lilly to leave her behind," Wilhelm said, patting the mare. "She's coming with me. All the horses are. Salv and I will be responsible for them."

Humar's eyes narrowed, and his gaze darted between Wilhelm and Salvarias. "All right. If you're sure it's the right choice."

Wilhelm nodded. "It is."

"Thank you, brother," Salvarias whispered.

Wilhelm shrugged. "I've grown fond of this cow." Lilly glared at him, and Wilhelm chuckled. "Is it just me, or can they understand us?"

Salvarias leaned closer. "They can. I have taught them our language. It is basic, but effective. Adok as well."

Wilhelm winked at the wolf. "I think he's understood us since we first met him."

Salvarias turned his gaze to the wolf, staring at him absently.

There were several odd traits about Adok. First there was ... Salvarias frowned as he lost his trail of thought, suddenly very bored with wherever his mind had wandered.

Lunara steered her mare next to Salvarias, and mischief twinkled in her eyes and danced on her smile. "I think I'd like to race you to the top."

Salvarias glanced at the steep hill. He was about to shake his head when she spoke again.

"We'll make a wager. What would you like if I lose?"

Salvarias thought a moment and came up with a bet shy of brilliant. "You must never enter my thoughts again."

A frown tugged on the corners of her mouth. She stroked her mare's neck while gazing at the hill. He could not believe she was considering it. He decided to seal his case. "And you must accept Neithelas's request to court you, when he does submit it to your father."

Lunara's eyes flared with anger, but she doused it quickly and replaced it with the same sweet smile that made his stomach flutter with nerves. "Agreed. Now, if I win, you'll take me for a walk ... alone, we'll read a book together, alone ... and you'll ... brush my hair ... alone."

Salvarias's mouth dropped open. She grinned and dug her heels into her mare's flanks. The horse shot up the mountain. Before Salvarias even processed what had happened, Mithal lurched forward.

Wilhelm and Varila's cry faded into the pounding hooves of the horses, the rush of Salvarias's blood flooding his ears, and Lunara's giggle. Mithal's long strides caught up to Lunara.

She turned a grinning face to him; eyes alight with happiness and a life-defying thrill. Even as he clung to his horse, he felt as if each perilous step led him further from his problems, his pain, his responsibilities. They fell away from him like a rockslide, freeing his shoulders of their burden. Nothing existed except the exhilaration of the climb, Mithal's muscles pumping beneath him, the horses' frothing pants, and Lunara's beaming smile. In that moment, he was free.

The horses were neck and neck when a flat ledge at the cliff base came into view. It stretched out about twenty paces and followed the length of the sheer face. It would barely be enough room to stop. He did not care. He was lost in the excitement, in the competition of the moment.

He urged Mithal on, taunting the stallion. White foam lined both horses' muzzle and sweat ran down their chests. Still, both bolted on. They were close. A mere five paces. Lunara squealed in delight as her horse leapt on to the landing a step before Mithal. The loss did not bother Salvarias. He was lightheaded and reeling with excitement. He slid off Mithal and leaned against the cliff, gulping in air. Lunara sagged by his side, breathing as hard.

"Wonderful," she said. "For a moment I thought you might beat me."

All of Salvarias's burdens assailed him with such ferocity it drove him to sit. He had agreed to a walk. Nothing more. A walk and to read a book. And to brush her hair. To be close to her. To smell her.

Ah, my little murderer, the voice hissed. *Do you think you did so accidently? You carelessly fell into her plot. Must I remind you of your evil? Of her innocence? Would you taint something so pure because of a wager? A bet that could harm her?*

Leave me! Salvarias dropped his head in his hands. How could he have been so dense? How could she have won? Lunara was a talented rider and her mare fully capable of besting Mithal, but had he done all he could? Did he give Mithal full rein?

You cannot do these things, my murderer. The voice was kind, comforting. *You cannot fall into her plots. You cannot befriend any of them. Either you'll kill them with your evil, or they will abandon you at the first test. She is no different. One day harm will come to her because of you. One day, she will see your evil and leave you. Humar has already withdrawn his friendship. He has already abandoned you. Your heart cannot bear such pain again. I know it's hard, but you must deny any of them friendship. You are free of them all. You must remain so. It is the only way to save them.*

Neither Lunara nor Salvarias spoke until the companions joined him.

Varila's anger was expected. "What in Oblivion did you two think you were doing? You could've lamed one of the horses! You could've fallen! The horse—"

Boulder-sized hands wrapped around Salvarias's arms and lifted him. Guilt would not allow him to meet Wilhelm's gaze. "They're fine," Wilhelm said. Though his brother tried to hide it, Salvarias heard the worry in Wilhelm's voice.

"I am sorry, Brother."

"Don't apologize, Salv. Everything's all right. Everyone's fine." Clearly, Wilhelm was consoling himself.

"Where is this mysterious entrance?" Okulu asked.

"This way," Frink said, heading down the ledge.

Humar whistled. "Quite the concealment. Is this natural or was it designed by the Cavruls?"

Salvarias glanced at the smooth cliff and it took a moment to see a slight line in the rock. Curious, he slipped by Humar for a better look. The cave entrance was more of a tunnel that ran along the inside of the cliff face. From straight on, one could not tell the tunnel wall apart from the cliff.

"Remarkable," Salvarias murmured, peering into the darkness.

Durak grunted. "Rumors be that Nevlar created these entrances throughout the mountains. None can see 'em, and only Cavruls know where they be."

"Let's get going," Hunz said. "We've got a long way to go before we stop. And no need to be tense. Nothing lives in these caves."

Once inside the tunnel, Salvarias lit his sparrow. The musty odor of stale water and moss crammed the air, and the walls were damp with condensation. The cool tunnel immediately made him shiver, and he tightened his cloak. Air, ever elusive, would become a ghost in the caves.

The tunnel turned sharply and dumped them into a smooth domed cavern. The walls had been polished to a glossy surface that reflected like a mirror. Meticulous etchings of Veedran's creatures decorated the walls, and among them were Cavruls fighting with fierce-looking swords, axes, and spears.

"Your work is beautiful," Neithelas said.

"Took years," Frink said.

Salvarias sent his sparrow high in the cave, lighting the carvings as it drifted from scene to scene.

"How long can ye keep that spell up?" Hunz asked.

"Days if need be," Salvarias said.

"Then do it so ye Erthlas don't get yourselves hurt."

"Of course," Salvarias said.

The coal black ground of the tunnel Frink took was dotted with puddles formed by dripping stalactites. It was wide enough that they could walk together in pairs, and Salvarias was relieved when Wilhelm stayed beside him. The tunnel brought up memories of his days in slavery: how sick he had been, how each stinging bite of the whip had felt, and how bright his brother's blood seemed when it dripped from his back.

Wilhelm wrapped an arm around Salvarias's neck. "How are you feeling?"

"Fine, Brother."

"You told me in order for you not to have nightmares that you don't allow yourself deep sleep. You've only had a few bad nights since we left Serinity."

"Our travels are dangerous, Brother. I cannot attract attention. When it is safe, I will sleep."

"I think you're doing it to avoid nightmares."

Salvarias craned his neck to look up at his brother. So many times Wilhelm's insights into Salvarias's feelings caught him off guard. "There is one that is disturbing. You are correct; I do not wish this dream so I try to keep myself in light sleep. I can scarcely make it a few days at a time, though."

"It's the dream that gives you a bloody nose?"

"Yes."

Wilhelm sighed and shook his head. "I wish I could help."

"You help in more ways than you know."

Wilhelm looked up and then behind him. He shuddered.

"What is it?" Salvarias asked, surveying the cavern.

Wilhelm inhaled a deep breath and pulled him closer. "Nothing."

"Brother."

"It reminds of the years we spent in the caves. All the whippings and beatings."

Salvarias rested a hand on his brother's shoulder. He knew what lay beneath armor and cloth. Scars on top of scars covered Wilhelm's back. For the first time, Salvarias saw his carefree brother for what he truly was: a stoic warrior, enduring suffering without complaint, trudging through hardships to rise above them. The grins and laughs were not false, but hidden behind them was deep pain.

"Truly, you are a courageous man, and I the luckiest," Salvarias said.

Wilhelm ruffled his hair.

The next hours of walking were tiring. The tunnels themselves sprouted stalagmites like a forest, causing the companions and horses to weave and squeeze between them. The stalactites dripped down the walls like tendrils of charred honey, wet and glistening. Some tunnels were a steep climb while others a precarious descent where the horses slipped and whinnied their irritation. Most tunnels were wide and open, but a few were claustrophobic, making it feel as if the walls were closing in around Salvarias. Several times, he battled the urge to scream and flee back the way they had come.

Caverns were welcomed and all that kept Salvarias sane. Hylim plants cascaded down the walls and speckled the ceilings like stars with their soft rose glow. Caverns were every mile or so and only in those open, hylim-illuminated spaces did the companions talk. A few caverns showed just how small his group was in comparison. One in particular seemed endless; stretching far enough that Salvarias's sparrow could not find the other end without plunging them into darkness. It made him feel vulnerable, and he found himself walking next to his brother the entire time, tripping over him in an effort to keep close. Wilhelm's bright eyes dulled the farther they trekked, and he shuddered often, absently flexing his back and resting a hand on his sword hilt, the slightest noise causing him to jump and half draw his sword. The Cavruls kept up conversation and seemed more chipper with each passing step. As annoyed as Salvarias was, he found he rather enjoyed this merry side to sour-faced Durak.

The changing temperature added to Salvarias's discomfort. Most tunnels were freezing, but on occasion, they happened across one so hot it drove the cold from him in a breath. The fluctuation gave Humar a stuffy nose that Salvarias reminded himself would need to be treated before the knight succumbed to a cold.

Try as he might, Salvarias could not ignore the fact that air wanted nothing to do with him, nor how sore his chest was from laboring for each tiny breath. He wheezed and full out gasped several times. Miserable was a significant understatement.

After what he determined was three hours, they stopped for the night in a cavern lit by hylim, which he had not had the opportunity to study yet. He took advantage and emptied a jar of willow bark and carefully dug up a plant, soil and all, and put it in the jar. Frink and Hunz also removed jars and made one for each companion.

As they set up camp, Wilhelm's grumbling stomach echoed loudly, making their group snicker beneath their hands.

Once Salvarias set the wood aflame, he unsaddled the horses and removed packs, giving each horse an apple and accepting Mithal's nudges of affection. The earthy aroma of mushrooms filled the damp air, mixed with boiled potatoes and rosemary—what would be their meal for the next few days in the caves. Salvarias smiled to himself as he withdrew a strip of dried ham from his brother's pack. When he turned to head back to the group, Wilhelm popped from behind Lilly carrying two bowls of steaming stew.

"Oh, thanks." Wilhelm traded a bowl for the ham. "I don't know how much of these vegetables I can take," he muttered.

"I assure you, brother, there are those who survive just fine without meat."

Wilhelm shook his head. "It's unnatural, Salv. Eating meat is ... it's part of living a long life. It's like you're eating accompaniments to the main course. Half a meal, half the nourishment."

Salvarias settled a nearby rock. "Of all my oddities, you find the fact I do not eat meat 'unnatural'?" He felt a tug on his hood and leaned forward, pulling it from Mithal's lips.

Wilhelm grinned. "I do. Everything else is a gift. Not eating meat is a choice. Big difference. Besides, that's what they're raised for: cows, chickens, pigs, and there's an abundance of deer."

"Trust me when I say that they would prefer a different occupation." He smiled when he felt the horse nibbling on his hood again.

Wilhelm plopped down next to Salvarias. "Maybe. But they taste too good to give up."

Salvarias chuckled. "Eat quickly or Humar will fall asleep before your instruction." He wrenched his hood from Mithal's mouth.

Wilhelm winced. "I'm a little out of practice. It's been a couple days since I sparred with him. I'm sure it's set me back."

"Highly unlikely. I have never seen you forget instructions when it comes to fighting." Salvarias rested his head on his brother's shoulder. "Your skill has grown with each lesson. Soon, no one will survive your blades."

"Ah, so now I'm supposed to be unconquerable. That's a lot of pressure, Salv."

"My dear brother, there is nothing you cannot accomplish."

"Humar's starting to teach me some new techniques. He said my sword skills are nearly perfect, but he said there are things I can do with my mind. He said eventually I'll be able to fight without relying on my eyes."

Salvarias frowned. "I have not read about any fighting conducted that way."

Wilhelm shrugged. "He said not many know about it. It's supposedly only taught to those who were from privileged families, and even then, only a handful of knights could master it." Wilhelm batted Mithal away, snatching his hand back before the horse bit him.

Salvarias grinned up at the stallion. "Fun is over, my friend. And Lilly stole your apple."

Wilhelm chuckled. "She needs it. I think she's getting thin."

Lilly, wholly insulted, kicked Wilhelm's shin. His brother yelped, dropped his bowl, and clutched his leg. "Why'd she do that?"

Salvarias reprimanded the horse gently. "You insulted her, Brother. Horses see thinness as a weakness."

Wilhelm rubbed his leg, hopped up, and patted Lilly's flank. "Sorry, old cow. Didn't mean it."

Lilly nickered and shoved Wilhelm to sit. Apparently, only the horse could knock Wilhelm off balance. Usually his brother was as solidly planted as a mature redwood.

"She accepts your apology," Salvarias said, passing the rest of his stew to Wilhelm. "I have had my fill, Brother."

Wilhelm downed it in a few gulps.

"Do you find it odd?" Salvarias asked, absently sending his sparrow fluttering around in front of him.

"What?"

"Hunz and Frink's help. The octril attack outside the caves. Something is beginning to feel terribly wrong."

Wilhelm frowned. "I don't understand."

"The timing of Frink and Hunz's offer. Their presence in Hadrium. It seems … too convenient. Then there are the octrils. I find it odd a group would be meandering the mountainside randomly searching for us. Furthermore, I have thought of the event often, and Hunz and Frink never discussed it. They seemed unsurprised by the attack."

"There're all kinds of creatures roaming the mountain, Salv."

"Yes, but not once did they bring it up. They did not mention it as odd, or make a comment about the frequency of attacks recently." Salvarias shook himself. "Perhaps I am merely tired."

Wilhelm scratched his chin. "Maybe. I'll keep an eye on them." He chuckled. "If you think about it, coincidence seems rather fond of us. After all, Humar returned home after a ten-year hiatus just a few weeks after Tobin had been killed. Uncle Mafarias seemed to show up when we needed him most. Okulu came into our company and helped me find you after Dethal took you. Oh, and the sisters came to Falar the same night you were taken. And don't forget Vuddruk, that mage who helped after we got you out of Zeeas."

Salvarias frowned, a tingle of importance tickling his brain. "Indeed," he murmured. Too coincidental to be coincidence.

After getting Mithal another apple, Salvarias followed his brother to the group.

"Where were these glowing plants last time we were stuck in caves?" Varila asked.

Durak shrugged. "Those were uncharted tunnels. Cavruls help spread hylim through the major thoroughfares."

"So how extensive are these tunnels?" Okulu asked.

"They run through all of Dalnar," Hunz responded. "The Retribution shifted mountain plates, making pockets and tunnels everywhere. In the mountains though, there be the true jewel. They run in a web only Cavruls can escape. It's in our blood to listen to the mountains."

"I think it's disconcerting," Neithelas said. "I don't like to think that one person can go from Falar to Meitholias underground without detection."

"Bah." Durak waved his hand. "Ye misunderstand. Not all be connected. Only in the mountains. Everywhere else is just pockets of tunnels and caverns."

"I see." Neithelas draped his cloak around Lunara's shoulders, followed by his arm. "You had me worried."

Lunara smiled and shrugged from under his hold. For some reason, that made Salvarias feel better, though why he did not understand. He simply cared for her as an acquaintance. The way firelight danced off her hair in a rainbow of dark colors meant nothing. Nor how her red lips were soft and full, beckoning him—

Weak, my little murderer.

Salvarias lowered his head.

"I hate not knowing the time," Varila said, rubbing her arms. "I can't tell if I should be tired or not."

"The sun has been set for over an hour, my lady," Salvarias said, opening his spell book. "We are but another hour from sleep."

She snorted. "There's no way you can tell time here."

Salvarias set out his quill and ink and ignited his magic.

"Salvarias," Okulu said.

He looked up. "Yes, Okulu."

"How do you know the time?"

"He doesn't," Varila snapped.

Ignoring Varila, Salvarias said, "In the past, I have counted from sunset to sunrise. Depending on the season, it ranges."

"What do you mean, counted?" Okulu asked, winking at Wilhelm.

Salvarias glanced at his grinning brother. Wilhelm shrugged.

"I do not understand your question, Okulu. I have counted; one, two, three, four, and so on from sunrise to sunset. In doing so, I can track time."

"So you're counting right now? Even as you're talking to us?" Okulu asked.

"Yes."

"You can count a bunch of things at a time, can't you?" Okulu said.

A blush crept up his cheeks when he realized he had confessed one of his oddities. He did not respond.

"A brilliant mind to accomplish such a feat," Neithelas said. "I was curious why I heard different—"

Wilhelm kicked Neithelas's foot. "I warned you."

Salvarias frowned, studying his companions who looked away uncomfortably, as if they had a secret. He turned to his brother and raised an eyebrow.

"It's nothing, Salv. Get to studying." Wilhelm rose and motioned to Humar. "Up for a little practice?"

The knight nodded. "Yes, I am."

Salvarias lowered his gaze to his book, trying to figure out what had just occurred. It was apparently something everyone knew but himself. As curious as he was, his magic soon consumed his thoughts.

Coming up with the spell to write without ink was much easier than he would have thought. It only took half an hour to devise one.

Barely containing his excitement, Salvarias set aside his quill and leafed to the back of his spell book where he documented the new plants he had discovered. Of course he remembered all he ever studied without the need to document his findings, but he had discovered early on that it gave him a sense of normalcy.

He whispered, *"Ich comad trasibe,"* and thought the word hylim, and it appeared on the page, letter by letter, as if he had written it by hand.

Brilliant! his magic exclaimed. *Perfect!*

But I feel the drain of maintaining the spell, Salvarias said.

With time it'll become nonexistent, just as your light spell. We'll eventually be able to keep it active for days! Weeks! Months!

Salvarias tried to tame his own excitement. *I will practice it several times a day. Are you tired, or would you like to continue studying?*

Please, allow us to continue. I've been thinking of enchantments and what we should do tonight. It should be something simple, something we're already familiar with. And we need an object to test it on.

Is there potential for the object to be harmed?

No, no. Nothing will happen to the object. You, on the other hand, I don't know. That's why I want to start simple. Neither of us knows what to expect.

Salvarias ran his hand over his staff, feeling every indent and knot that he had memorized. The staff was his most prized possession, more so than his spell book.

Light. And we will use my staff. When commanded, it will supply as much or as little light as I need.

Brilliant, his magic said. *A safe object, and the light spell is as common as breathing to you.*

Salvarias shook his head. *A poor choice of analogy, my friend.*

"Salv."

Salvarias startled and looked over to see his brother settling into his bedroll.

"Could you douse the light?" Wilhelm asked. "And you need to get some sleep."

"Sorry."

After ending the light spell, Salvarias crawled into his bedroll, hugging his spell book close, and waited.

It did not take long before a chorus of rumbling snores intruded on the quiet cavern. Soundlessly, Salvarias picked up his jar of hylim and tiptoed to the tunnel they had taken, Adok padding along behind him, lecturing Salvarias to be cautious.

He sat in a dry spot, trying to curb his excitement, and ignited his magic. *I am ready, friend.*

Let us begin. I've spent much time with the power today and have devised what I think should work. The strain on your mind is what remains a mystery, but this is the safest way without allowing the blackfire to surface. First, I want you to focus on the energy. Become aware of it. Be one with it. Let it flow through you. Blackfire and I will protect you, fear not. Once I sense your level of relaxation, I'll prompt you to cast the light spell.

I will do the longer version.

The short one will suffice.

Salvarias shook his head. *I want them separate. If I want the staff, but not the sparrow, I must have a different command.*

Ah. Very wise, my wizard. So be it. The longer spell. After you've spoken it, I want you to command the staff to accept the energy. Command me, and I will command the blackfire.

I am not sure I understand.

Think of the staff as a living being. It must link to the energy. It must be open to receive it. You are imbuing it with the power to do so. Enchanting is connecting an object to the surrounding energy. With your command, the object will pull from the expended life force of whatever surrounds it.

Salvarias battled with the concept. *I think I understand.*

Once you solidify the link, once you feel the staff accept your instruction, release the spell. That will lock the link into place.

I understand.

I am beyond myself with excitement. Shall we begin?

Salvarias nodded and settled comfortably against the wall. He reached out his mind to the expended energy, surprised by how much existed in the dark caves and tunnels. At first, it was nothing new. He had been connecting with energy since he could remember.

He had even developed the ability to trace it to its source: to each worm, each sprout of plant life, each bat, each spider. Every tiny creature he could find by the signature of energy.

Seeming satisfied, his magic surged forward with the power of the blackfire. It erupted like a volcano in his veins, simmering his blood, churning with mind-bending command, raw need, anger—such loathsome rage—and an overpowering demand for Salvarias's attention.

Gasping, Salvarias doubled over. His muscles flexed and pulled against the strain of controlling the power, as if he had gorged himself on too much food and his skin needed to split to accommodate his mass. Pressure burgeoned in his brain like an instant hurricane. Sweat burst over him, rolling down his back, neck, forehead, everywhere.

He exhaled sharply, clutching his head. "Help me!" he cried.

You must not fight it! his magic warned. *You must accept it!*

No! Salvarias wanted nothing to do with it.

He became aware of the weight of air. It was burdened with expelled life force. The energy was a power unlike anything he had ever experienced, and he cowered in awe of it, humbled and meek. He understood in that pivotal moment that energy was not just what once was and is, but what was to be. It was everything. Everything. The beginning and the end. Life and death. Creation and destruction.

He felt insignificant in its presence. An ant to a mountain. He curled up, drawing inward, cringing from the power, too frightened to scream. So small. Nothing but a speck of dust. Weak. Helpless.

Then the energy took notice of him, and he immediately sensed its anger. The knowledge he had gained was sacred, secret, and something not meant for mortals. Like a predator starved for weeks, the energy devoured chunks of his life force, ripping him apart from the inside out. Cold set into his bones, his mind was sluggish to think, and each breath was more trouble than it was worth.

He was so very tired. He stopped breathing. His heart faltered. The energy was nearly done consuming him. And he did not care. He wanted to sleep.

"No, you may not," a deep voice whispered, seeming to come from all around him, yet muffled as if behind a wall. The presence behind the voice was so massive and powerful that Salvarias's entire being recoiled from it. Yet even as it drove a dreadful fear into him, it felt oddly familiar, like a long-lost friend from childhood. "Life obeys *you*. It is yours to do with as you please, son of shadow and fire." The voice switched to address the energy. "He is part of His family. Treat him as such."

The oppressiveness of the energy morphed to be a reverential servant to Salvarias's will, but its unbending loyalty and love crushed him to the floor. It jolted through him, mending what it had done to his body, stitching his unraveling mind, forcing air into his lungs, shocking his heart to beat. The pain ... by the gods, the pain. He screamed.

The spell! his magic called. *Hurry!*

"*Ecia Lumenious!*" Salvarias shouted the spell to give his pain an outlet.

A hazy wave of power exploded from him, splattering the contents of puddles on to the walls, drying the ground. The stalactites shuddered and pebbles rained down on him. The pressure that had nearly exploded apart his body sucked out of him, leaving his skin sore and tender to the touch.

Think of the staff! Command us! his magic said.

The wave of power had turned, rushing back toward him with the force of death.

The staff! his magic snapped.

Salvarias directed as much of his thoughts to the aspen branch as he could.

Release it! his magic shrieked.

"*Rulose!*" Salvarias cried.

The wave switched at the last moment to slam into the staff. The force flung Salvarias against the wall. He gagged on blood gushing from his mouth and cried out from the tenderness of his body. As he crumbled to the floor, darkness came, but it was a peaceful darkness, very quiet and terribly heavy. And Salvarias allowed his mind to be devoured by it.

~

WILHELM JOLTED AWAKE. His hand moved for Salvarias before his head even turned. He groped a pile of blankets. Fear clamped his throat closed. He sat bolt upright. Salvarias was nowhere in sight. Then his brother screamed.

Scrambling free of the blankets, he snatched up his father's broadsword and darted toward the tunnel they'd taken the day before. When he rounded the corner, a rolling wave of hazy air greeted him. Its force lifted him off the ground and hurled him into a stalagmite, pinning him, pressing the air from his lungs, bending his bones close to snapping.

As quickly as it came, it sucked backward, disappearing into the tunnel. Wilhelm fell like a pile of bricks, rolling on his side and gulping in air.

He heard cries of alarm from the group, but he didn't wait for them nor did he wait for his breath to return. He tripped his way to the tunnel.

His brother lay motionless, illuminated by a soft pink glow. Adok stood by his side, licking his hand and whining.

"Salv!" Wilhelm sank to his knees beside his brother. Fear almost prevented him from turning Salvarias over. Steeling himself, Wilhelm gently lifted Salvarias into his arms. Blood trickled out his brother's nose and ears, while pools spilt from between his lips. His breathing was wet and shallow.

"What happened?" Okulu said, dropping next to Wilhelm.

"I don't know. I ... I think he was testing a spell." Wilhelm turned his brother over to drain the blood from his mouth.

"Quite the spell," Okulu whispered.

When the blood stopped, Okulu pressed a cloth to Salvarias's nose and tilted his head back. Wilhelm almost cried with relief when his brother's brow furrowed. He took the cloth from Okulu. "Don't touch him."

Lunara sank to the ground beside him, pale and trembling.

"Can you connect with him?" Wilhelm asked.

"He blocks me even when he sleeps," Lunara said. "I reached out to him right as I woke. He was in pain, but now he's sleeping soundly, peacefully. I can't tell much else."

"No nightmares?" Wilhelm asked.

Lunara shook her head. "Oddly, no."

Wilhelm grunted. He'd never known Salvarias to sleep peacefully.

"Let's head back and get some rest," Humar said from behind.

Wilhelm lifted his brother and followed the group to camp. Instead of his bedroll, he chose to sit against the wall. After settling Salvarias beside him, Wilhelm covered his brother in blankets and wrapped an arm around Salvarias's shoulders, holding him tightly.

Sleep did not bless Wilhelm. He replayed his time in slavery and the dead mages he'd seen, blood running from their mouth, ears, and nose. This was the second time Salvarias had been in the same condition. *If* his brother woke, he could be mad. They'd seen it happen in the slave caverns: mages screaming and flailing about, sputtering words in a foreign language, yanking their hair out, clawing their own eyes out.

Of course, Wilhelm could easily command Salvarias to stop, just as he commanded his brother to leave Bartle in the slave caverns. It would simply take that slight influx in his voice—that ordered command that his brother would obey without thought. Matter of fact, Wilhelm had no doubt he could command Salvarias to slit Adok's throat, and his brother would do it without question, without pause. He clearly remembered Salvarias's subservient eyes, that blind obedience to Wilhelm's tone. It'd haunted him every day since he'd forced his brother.

Closing his eyes, he tightened his arm around his brother's shoulders and reminded himself of his promise. Never would he coerce his brother do to anything. Salvarias's choices would always be his own.

Regardless, it did nothing to alleviate the boulder sitting on Wilhelm's chest.

SALVARIAS'S MIND clambered up from deep darkness. There was a low murmur of conversation. Then Adok barged into his thoughts, furious over the risk Salvarias had taken. He heard the wolf's claws clicking on the stone floor as Adok paced. It took Salvarias a moment to remember what had happened. As it returned, he became aware of every muscle aching as if someone had pounded on him with a hammer, and his brain thumped against his skull.

He groaned, wanting nothing more than to return to deep sleep.

"Salv," Wilhelm said, voice thick with worry. "Salv, wake up."

Forcing his heavy eyelids up, Salvarias looked at his brother. Relief flooded across Wilhelm's square features.

"Thank the gods," he breathed.

Adok's rant faded off into the distance, and darkness once again wrapped around Salvarias. This time, it was not peaceful.

When he woke again, his mind was clear, though his body still throbbed, and his brain was clawing to escape his skull.

Humar hovered in front of them.

"Finally," the knight muttered. "What happened?"

"Forgive me," Salvarias said, sitting upright on his own. Everything tipped and turned. "I am fine to continue."

Wilhelm rose and offered his hand. Salvarias grabbed hold and sprang up with Wilhelm's strong pull, reeling as the world heaved around him. A strong hand gripping his arm held him in place.

"Why don't you go ahead?" Wilhelm said to Humar. "We'll be right behind you."

Latching on to Wilhelm's solid presence steadied Salvarias's surroundings. The companions, who had been loitering around the cave, set off with the horses.

"Were you enchanting? Is that what happened?" Wilhelm asked.

Salvarias nodded. "I am sorry, Brother. I did not know it would take so much energy."

Wilhelm inhaled a deep breath and turned his face toward the rosy-pink ceiling. Guilt clogged Salvarias's throat, and he stared at the dark floor.

"Forgive me, Brother."

Wilhelm wrapped an arm around Salvarias's neck and steered him in the direction of their companions. "Don't apologize, Salv. So did it work?"

Salvarias stifled his doubt and whispered, "*Ecia Lumenious.*"

His entire staff lit with a soft white light. He stumbled to halt, as did Wilhelm.

"That's brilliant, Salv!" Wilhelm exclaimed. "Absolutely brilliant!"

Salvarias was swept up in a tight embrace. He could not take his dumbfounded stare from the staff.

"I cannot believe I did it," Salvarias whispered. He had never fully trusted it would work. But here was proof. Salvarias, a self-taught mage, could enchant. Excitement overcame him, and he flung his arms around his brother, laughing in half shock, half delight.

Wilhelm's voice boomed out, echoing through the caves like a fast approaching thunderstorm. "My little brother is the most powerful mage alive!"

17

SPRING 1018 A.R

The day passed with fast travel due to the late start Salvarias had caused, supper was quick, and the companions had taken to their bedrolls early. Salvarias, however, could not sleep. He had spent the day talking with his magic and learning what errors he had committed. Though he had survived, his magic adamantly stated they should not try again unless he willingly accepted the power, merged with it. He would not, nor was he content with his one enchantment. He would try again.

When the familiar snores of his companions started, he unraveled himself from his blankets and quietly headed toward the tunnel. A light rustle from behind made him glance back. Durak was sitting up, staring after Salvarias. He turned and took the tunnel out of the cavern. Durak never cared when he left camp. He mused the old Cavrul secretly wanted him to die.

He found a dry spot to sit and propped himself against the coal-black stone. Adok plopped by his side, still lecturing Salvarias about the dangers of enchanting.

He ignited his magic.

I advise against this, my wizard. It's too dangerous.

I was not prepared. I will do better tonight.

What if I refuse?

Salvarias grinned. *My friend, you want to master this as much as I. Let us stop with the veiled threats and begin.*

You know me well. Can we use the woman? When you are touching her, your mind is calm. You can focus on me. Your power ... it doubles when with her.

No. I would not be comfortable doing so. I will do better this time.

So be it. Now, what are we attempting?

A protection spell.

Protection spells are not the easiest. It'll be more difficult than last night.

Salvarias grinned. *But think of the possibilities if we succeed.*

There was a pause before the magic could no longer hide its excitement. It mingled with Salvarias's joy like a giddy schoolboy stealing a first kiss. *As my wizard commands. Whenever you're ready.*

Salvarias closed his eyes and focused on the energy. In his ignorance, he thought this time would be different because he knew what to expect. But his knowledge merely intensified the effects. The humbling power of the energy made him curl up, once again feeling small, miniscule. No matter his feelings, the energy was as reverent. It did not rip apart his being. It did not try to devour him. Instead, it hung heavy in the air, awaiting Salvarias's command. Intentional or not, the weight of it pressed him to the wall and lay upon him like an anvil. He gasped with little reward for his effort.

As the magic surged up, bringing with it the blackfire, Salvarias's blood simmered with unnatural heat. Before he even thought of his command, the blackfire took charge. Frantically he tried to control it as did his magic, but it dissolved his will with hardly any effort. Its desire—clearly understood by Salvarias—was to test the boundaries of his tolerance for its presence, of his physical endurance to its power.

Blackfire's swelling force rendered him listless, crushing against his skull with the strength Wilhelm could muster at the forge. Salvarias screamed a silent wail in his mind. Muscles constricted, sending his feet thrashing, bowing his spine, and locking his fingers in tight claws. Blood drained from his skull and spurted from his mouth, spraying across the walls. Skin along his biceps split open from the burgeoning might of the power, brimming tears in his eyes. He was breaking apart. His mind and body were not made for such power. Just when he thought he reached the end, his magic surged up and attacked the blackfire.

You must give it an outlet, his magic commanded. *I'm too weak to pull it back when it's this strong! Command it!*

Salvarias gurgled out his spell. The power shot from him in the same hazy wave, drying puddles, throwing Adok against the wall. When it bolted free of him, he fell to the floor like a wet cloth, unable to move, unable to think.

The wave of power receded, surging toward Salvarias like a tsunami. He lacked the energy to direct it to the staff. Paralyzed by pain, beaten of his strength, he could only watch his death approaching.

Instead of striking him, the wave hit his staff. Limp from fatigue, Salvarias sailed backward, rapping his head smartly against the wall. He was not sure if it was the effects of enchanting that yanked him into deep darkness, or if it was due to the blood running down the back of his head.

The last thing he felt was his magic lashing out in anger at the blackfire.

SALVARIAS WOKE to a familiar steady drum and his head rising and falling with the measured breaths whooshing in and out of Wilhelm's lungs. Warm blankets covered him, and a heavy arm was wrapped around his shoulders. The thick aroma of oiled leather and polished steel sent a calm ripple down Salvarias's spine. He was with his brother, and nothing else mattered.

"Salv," Wilhelm said. "Are you all right?"

He nodded and forced his eyes open. They were apart from the group, leaning against the cavern wall within reach of the soft pink glow of hylim.

"Let me guess," Wilhelm said. "Enchanting?"

Salvarias closed his eyes and snuggled down in the blankets, sagging in complete safety, and he let the tension drain from his shoulders. "Yes," he whispered.

"Next time, you need to get me. You shouldn't wander off on your own."

His brother's voice rumbling in his chest tempted Salvarias with sleep as it had done when they were younger and Wilhelm would read to him. "You need rest, Brother. There are no dangers in these caves."

"Next time, wake me."

Salvarias kept quiet.

"You hungry?"

"Not really," he said. He desperately wanted sleep.

"Everyone is ready to leave. Do you need more time?"

Salvarias sighed and pushed away the approaching darkness. "No. I can leave now."

Wilhelm gave an affectionate squeeze and called out to the group, "We're ready. Why don't you all get a head start? We'll be right behind."

Rustles sounded, horses nickered, and soft conversations started. Salvarias waited until the echoes of shuffling footsteps faded and silence blanketed the cave before opening his eyes, squinting against the dull light of the hylim. His headache escalated, churning his stomach, bludgeoning his brain, stabbing his eyes. He groaned.

In a tight voice, Wilhelm said, "That was a lot of blood. More than last time."

Salvarias shifted and regretted movement. Every muscle felt beaten and sliced apart. His head actually moved with each thump of his brain. He ignited his magic.

What happened? he asked.

The power, my wizard, the magic said in a voice tense with anger. *It thought to test your endurance to its force. It came at you stronger than when you used it in the woods. I was unprepared and I failed you. Please, accept my apology.*

Failed? I do not understand.

I discovered it when the power was testing how much your human body could endure. I can offer you a ... protection of sorts. It showed me, but too late to ease your pain. I've discussed at length with the power and made it clear to never do such a thing again.

You can make the pain stop?

To a degree. I'm still trying to understand, my wizard. Rest assured, the power won't attempt again what it did last night. I won't allow it.

Thank you, my friend.

Your life is thanks enough. I feared I had lost you. Until you're ready to merge with it, my wizard, until you accept it, I fear we must use the smallest amount needed to enchant. I can't control it alone. If it ever chooses so, it could break us apart. Only you can control it, and even then, you could only do so if it's a part of you.

The force is evil, my friend. You know what it did when I killed the scarred man. I cannot merge with something so repulsive.

I agree, my wizard. Therefore, we'll proceed with caution. I'll only call forth the minimal amount that, together, we can control. It might reduce the potency of our enchantments, but it's worth your life. Rest now. We'll talk tonight.

The magic receded.

"Ready?" Wilhelm asked.

Salvarias nodded. "Thank you, Brother."

Wilhelm rose, lifting Salvarias, and shifted an arm around his neck and ruffled his hair. "So, what did you do last night?"

"It is a protection spell, of sorts." He fought to control his stomach with each wallop to his brain.

"Let's give it a test."

Before Salvarias could object, Wilhelm snatched the aspen branch and raised it overhead. Salvarias heart stopped, which did nothing to help his aching skull. Using what he assumed was all of Wilhelm's strength, his brother whacked the branch on the ground.

When the staff vibrated and remained whole, Salvarias sucked in a breath and grabbed the branch from his brother, hugging it close. "I think you stopped my heart."

Wilhelm grinned. "I don't think it's within your ability to fail. Let's give it another test." He wrapped a hand around the hilt of Tobin's broadsword.

"No!" Salvarias clutched his staff protectively. "Let us work up to such a test."

Wilhelm withdrew the sword, grinning wildly. "Hurry up and perform what you want, because I'm about ready to do a test of my own."

Salvarias yanked his dagger free from its sheath. Begging the spell to hold, he ran the blade over the wood. No matter how hard he pressed, the blade glided just over the surface of the branch. Next, he nicked at the wood, but nothing penetrated the shield. Steeling himself, he was about to ram his knife into it when Wilhelm snatched it up.

His brother tossed it in the air and, as it fell, swung his sword, muscles bulging, stance giving him the most momentum, and struck the branch. It flew across the cavern, ricocheting off the stalagmites to clatter to the ground.

Salvarias swallowed down his fear and raced for his staff. He gingerly lifted it and checked it over. The staff was perfect.

Wilhelm ruffled his hair from behind. "See, nothing to worry about."

"Your faith is moving, dear brother," Salvarias said. "But for my heart's sake, please do not use my most prized possession to demonstrate your confidence in me."

Wilhelm clapped him on the shoulder. "You're the most powerful mage alive, Salv. Like I said, you don't know how to fail."

Salvarias accepted his brother's headlock and followed him from the cavern toward their companions. Elbowing Wilhelm in the ribs, his brother's laugh and feigned pain plastered a smile on Salvarias's face.

18

Varila was overjoyed when Hunz announced they would stop early. It wasn't the break from trudging through damp darkness that sparked her broad smile. It was the promise of a natural underground spring that provided a pool suitable for bathing.

After they'd unpacked and set up camp, Salvarias approached her. "I think it is time to look at your wounds, my lady."

Varila plopped down and unwound her dressings. When the last fell off, she gasped at her smooth skin. It was pale, as if she'd never seen sun, but flawlessly free of scars.

"Remarkable," Salvarias murmured, leaning close to examine her skin.

"Remarkable?" she scoffed. "It's a damn miracle."

Okulu gaped at her legs.

Stifling a grin, she said, "Eyes to yourself, merc."

Okulu squatted beside her and ran his hands up her thighs. "Brilliant! What was in that potion, Salvarias?"

His gesture was innocent enough, but Varila didn't like to be touched without permission, and she did have a reputation to uphold. She slapped Okulu across the cheek; hard enough he got the point, but not cruelly.

Okulu cast his devilish handsome wink. "I couldn't resist."

"Next time, my sword won't be able to resist slicing off your head."

Salvarias cleared his throat. "The potion was grinnd, hfial, and willow bark oil."

Okulu laughed as he withdrew his flask from underneath his armor. "You've got a talent with herbs, Salvarias. I think I'll leave the mending to you from now on." He took a long swig.

Salvarias tilted his head at the compliment. "My lady, I see no further need to cover your legs."

"Best news I've had in a while," Wilhelm said.

"I'm sure it is," Varila said. "Come on, Lunara, let's get a bath."

After gathering fresh undergarments and two jars of hylim, she followed her sister and Hunz from the cavern, spirits higher than they'd been in a long time. They took a tunnel a good fifty feet before it twisted to the left and sloped down, making the floor slippery and dangerous. Varila gripped the wall, edging down after Hunz. Once it flattened out, it took a right turn and dumped into a wide high tunnel blanketed with hylim. The natural spring was more like a babbling creek, deep in some parts, perhaps as deep as she was tall, while the rest was shallow enough she saw the ebony rocks beneath. In the middle, a pool had formed, looking absolutely inviting.

"It'll be cool," Hunz said. "But sometimes the rocks heat from below."

Varila caught a faint whiff of sulfur. It'd be heated enough to allow them to take their time.

The instant Hunz left, Lunara stripped out of her clothes and dipped a toe in the water. She giggled and slid in the pool, smiling as she submerged herself completely.

Varila checked the tunnel and stood guard while Lunara bathed, using the time to unraveled her braid.

After a short time, Lunara, with a heavy sigh, left the pool, dried off, and dressed. "At least we didn't have to wait too long. How many more days are we in here?"

Varila shrugged as she tugged off her boots. "I'd say five or so days."

"I don't think I could've waited that long." Lunara wrung out her hair.

"Go ahead back up," Varila said when she heard her sister's stomach gurgle. "Get some food."

Lunara smiled sheepishly and rubbed her stomach. "I'm starting to sound like Wilhelm."

"I don't think that's possible. He's a damn bottomless pit."

"You'll be all right by yourself?"

"Fine. I won't be long." Varila stripped out her armor and undergarments.

Lunara gathered up their dirty clothes and left. Excitement hardly contained, Varila slipped into the warm waters. She cleaned grime from under her nails and washed her hair twice to rid her curls of dust. Sighing in contentment, she floated to a corner free from the current and closed her eyes.

"Varila?" Wilhelm's voice startled her awake. "Varila? Are you there?"

"I'm here," she said, climbing out of the pool. "I just dozed off." She wrapped a drying cloth around her. "You can come in."

Wilhelm rounded the corner wearing an unbelted tunic and trews. In his hand, he clutched the broadsword he'd taken from his parents' murderer.

"Lunara was getting worried," he said, setting his sword by the stream. His gaze darted over her, and he looked away quickly. Smiling, she realized it was probably the most skin he'd seen in near a year.

Wilhelm yanked off his shirt, reminding her how long it'd been since *she'd* seen that much skin. The pink glow from the hylim shadowed the indents of his muscles, rippling as he kicked off his boots. The body she had assumed hid behind soft fabrics paled to what truly existed. Stone-solid and gorgeous.

He started to unlace his trews and stopped halfway done. He looked up at her and grinned. "Mind?"

Reluctantly she faced the wall. Casually, she shifted around her armor, using it as an excuse to steal a peek. He'd already turned around and was stepping into the pool. Her smile fell as she stared at the scars stacked upon his back. So many times she'd forgotten what a hard life he'd led. He was a man quick to smile, affectionate, and with a hearty laugh. Few would ever guess that he'd lost his parents during the last years of his childhood, that he'd spent a year sleeping in the cold, dirty streets of Falar, and that he'd been a slave for five years, whipped and abused. Shaking herself, she dressed with reluctance, battling the urge to crawl into the water and take from him what she desired.

She heard a splash and looked over her shoulder to see him emerging from the pool. He tugged on clean trews, not seeming to care he was still wet.

Droplets of water followed a trail she ached to trace. Her feet moved on their own. Before she knew it, she stood in front of him, hand extended, eyes fixated on his chest rising and falling with each massive breath. Her fingers twitched.

His callused fingers glided across her jaw, caressing her cheek, brushing over her lips. He angled forward, locking his gaze with her until his breath caressed her lips. He waited for her to meet his advance.

She didn't love him. She used men, just as they used her. So why shouldn't she kiss him? She could take him now. Use him. Then toss him aside. She—

His lips brushed hers, lightly, tenderly. Every muscle tensed, and a tingle shot through her. His next kiss was deeper, tinted with a growing passion that weakened her knees. Relaxing her hand on his chest, she felt his quickened breathing, his heart beating faster. His smooth skin was warm, almost hot, and she glided her hands over his chest, drinking in every indent, bulge, and scar.

The way he kissed her, the way his hand slid around the back of her neck, the way he trembled, brought her emotions she'd never felt before. She didn't want to be used. She didn't want to be an exploiter. She wanted him to love her as she loved him.

Her own thought ripped her lips from his. She stumbled until she butted up against the wall. She couldn't love him. She'd heard the stories when she'd been stuck in Falar waiting for Mafarias; she had learned quite a bit about his appetite for women. She didn't care he slept around, but she didn't want to end up being just another girl on his list. She realized that's why she hadn't slept with him. She wanted more from him than mere sex. But why hadn't he slept with her? Why—

Scratchy fingers hooking around her chin stopped her ramblings. "This isn't meaningless to me," he whispered. "I don't want to see you with another man. I don't want another woman. I don't know where this is heading, but I want to find out."

He exuded confidence, quiet control. She was a strong woman, could handle anything thrown at her, but here with him she could be ... her. She could be ruthless in a fight. She could lash out with her sharp tongue. She could wear a dress as easily as her armor. She could cry when she heard a beautiful song. She could be tough enough to take down a man bent on hurting her and gentle enough to cradle a newborn. Most importantly, she could be frightened. And through it all, he'd see *her*. She wouldn't have to hide her fears and tears. He wouldn't see them as a weakness, he'd see them as her strength. Someone else besides Lunara saw *her*. And it was a man. A man who tore down the wall she'd built, all the bricks she'd piled up to keep herself safe. And she loved him for it.

Reservations fell from her shoulders, melting her against him, allowing her to succumb to her desires and heart without her usual fear. He had freed her.

His arms circled her waist, lifting her easily off the ground in his embrace as he kissed her with renewed fervor. She wrapped her legs around him and tangled her fists in his hair. The tremors that had rippled through him vanished and along with them his passive demeanor.

His hands gripped her thighs as he shoved her against the wall. His lips ventured to her neck, exploring her exposed skin. Tilting her head, she gifted him free reign. The left side of her breastplate loosened, exhuming a mewl of desire she'd never heard from herself before. By the gods, she needed him, and her extreme want caused her to rake her nails down his back. An animal-like groan rumbled in his throat, instinctual, primal, and it reached out to her own unguarded, untamed desire. He shoved her harder as his hand slid up her side. Rough fingers caressed her breast, and she whimpered in a painful need fully upon her. His massage deepened, and his body ground against her. The throbbing between her legs brought tears to her eyes, building a hunger only he could satisfy. Pleas were leaving her lips, begging him to release the arousal that neared painful. Then his hand slid up her thigh. Higher. Higher. Higher.

"Wilhelm? Varila?" Okulu called from the tunnel.

Wilhelm's moan dripped with agony. For a moment, she feared she might kill Okulu.

"Humar's a little worried," Okulu said, voice filled with amusement.

Wilhelm gently lowered her and walked to the edge of the pool. Buckling her armor, she watched his back rise and fall in deep breaths.

He snatched up his clean tunic, pulled it on, slung his sword belt around his waist, and tightened it as he turned to face her. His gaze slid over her as his hands had done moments before. He walked to her, put an arm on either side, and leaned forward.

A grin sliced across his face as his lips pressed against hers. "Based on that, I think I was right."

Varila spoke between each soft kiss. "About what?"

Wilhelm's lips glided down her neck and his words played on her skin. "In the tavern you said you'd never sleep with me. I said I didn't believe you. Looks like I was right."

Varila grinned, angling back to accept more of the pressure of his mouth. "You'll never know. I might have, I might not have."

"Ahem," Okulu said. Varila turned to see him standing in the tunnel entrance, smiling. "I see you two found the baths ... satisfying."

Wilhelm stood straight. "I would have if you hadn't interrupted. This, I won't let you forget, my friend, nor will I forgive you."

She didn't think she'd ever forgive the merc either.

LUNARA KEPT her hand over her mouth after dinner to hide her smile. Whatever had happened in the bathing tunnel between her sister and Wilhelm had plastered a permanent grin on Okulu that seemed to have the sole purpose of goading Varila into curses. Wilhelm merely sat with a content smile on his face.

Salvarias rose from his bedroll and retrieved a fresh set of robes. When Wilhelm started to rise, Salvarias rested a hand on his brother's shoulder. "Please stay. I need time alone."

Wilhelm frowned, but nodded. "Just be careful."

"Of course, Brother." Salvarias headed toward the tunnel.

Lunara hopped up, calling to her sister as she sprinted forward, "I'll show him where the stream is." She gave neither Varila nor Neithelas time to argue.

Salvarias paused once she entered the tunnel. "I can find my way, my lady. I do not—"

"I know," she said, running her fingers through Adok's soft fur. "I need to move around a bit."

Of course, she lied. She wanted nothing more than to rest her weary, sore feet and aching back. Regardless, any time she could sneak away with Salvarias alone, she did so.

He opened his mouth, and before he uttered a word, she slipped by him and led the way.

"The stream is warm," she said. "Smells a bit off, but I don't think it gets in the skin. At least, I haven't noticed it."

"*Lumous,*" Salvarias whispered.

White light glowed from behind. Looking over her shoulder, the sparrow floated above Salvarias, gliding as if on a breeze from the ocean. The bird always offered her a comfort, and his spell seemed to embrace her as if his word was tangible.

"Are you ill?" she asked, seeing his peaked skin in the light of the sparrow. Now that she mentioned it, she remembered how low his hood had been throughout the day's hike. She stopped to peer farther into the shadows of his hood. "You look pale."

"I am fine, my lady." He inched by her. "I am tired, nothing more."

Frowning, she followed him. "Have you not been sleeping?"

"In a way, I have."

"What has—"

Salvarias sighed audibly. "You are full of questions."

"It was you who said to never apologize for curiosity."

Salvarias glanced over his shoulder. "So I did."

The steep tunnel was even slicker than before with her friends clearing the dust that had provided traction earlier. Now the rocks were smooth as glass.

Lunara clung to the wall as she took tentative steps, extremely jealous of Salvarias's staff that kept him upright.

Adok, who'd been walking behind her, planted his head in the small of her back and gave her a push. The force sent her slipping down, scrabbling for any hold along the wall. A yelp of surprise escaped her. Her feet tangled with one another, and somehow she ended up in the opposite direction, tumbling backward. She caught site of Adok's grin before she snapped her eyes closed in expectation of hitting the hard ground. Instead of stone, strong hands caught arms, and Salvarias drew her close. They skidded to the bottom where Salvarias grunted when his back smacked the wall and she collided against his chest. She sank into his arms, trying to get her wobbly legs to stand on their own.

He inhaled a deep breath close to her hair before he said, "Are you all right, my lady?"

Fighting her smile, she found her own two feet and stood. "I am. Adok tripped me."

Salvarias's hands lingered on her arms before he pulled away. She caught the stern look he cast to the wolf, who simply grinned again.

"Why would you do such a thing?" Lunara asked, cupping Adok's head in her hands and kissing his muzzle.

"The wolf has a ... playful side," Salvarias said, continuing down the tunnel.

"Playful? Is that what you call it?"

When they rounded the corner, the babbling stream greeted them.

Salvarias glanced around before turning to her. "Thank you for showing me the way, my lady."

She smiled. "Why are you so tired?"

She felt his hooded gaze study her. "I have ... I have been enchanting. It takes much out of me to do so."

"I see. What have you done?"

"Ecia Lumenious," he whispered.

His staff lit up in the same pure white light as his sparrow. It rid the shadows under his hood and she gasped. His face was pale and shiny, and rings around his eyes were deep black. He turned his head to the side, casting his face in shadows once more.

Squinting in the light, she caught sight of his hood crusted with dried blood. "You're bleeding."

Salvarias touched the back of his head and winced. "I had forgotten."

She held out her hand as she knelt by the stream. "Give me your cloth and I'll clean it."

"Thank you, however, I can take care of it, my lady."

"It's not a request," she said, shooting him a determined gaze.

Sighing, he handed her a cloth and sat on the ground next to her. As she dunked it in the stream, he lowered his hood and rested his head on his arms supported by his knees.

"You should probably consider not enchanting tonight," she said, allowing a stern note in her voice.

He shrugged.

Shifting behind him, she parted his crusted hair and found a nice-sized welt with a nasty gash on top. As gently as she could, she dabbed the cut clean. Her fingers grazed over another raised line, and she shifted his hair aside.

"You have a scar," she murmured, tracing it from the middle of the back of his head to the middle of the top. "A rather large one."

He fumbled to find it, and she guided his fingers. The cut was even, planned, not accidental. He followed it and then yanked his hand away.

"What's it from?" she asked. "Zeeas?"

"I do not know." He shrank away from her and took the cloth, keeping his gaze downcast. "Thank you, my lady. Adok will accompany you back."

Adok growled at Salvarias before nudging his head under her hand and supporting her as she rose and left for the exit.

Before she entered the tunnel, Salvarias asked, "I am curious, my lady. Have you been able to read my soul yet?"

"I haven't tried since our first meeting."

"I would be grateful if you tried once more."

She reached out her mind to his, but as it was before, she sensed nothing. Even with their connection, his true heart and soul were hidden.

"I sense nothing," she said.

Salvarias shook his head, clenching his hands into tight fists. "I do not understand. With our connection, you should be able to see my true self."

"Why are you so curious? Do you not know your own soul?" The instant the last word left her lips, she regretted them.

Salvarias snapped tenser than a lute string. "Thank you once again, my lady."

"I'm sorry. I ... I ..."

"Thank you." His tone was a dismissal.

"I didn't—"

"I beg you, leave me."

Battling with her need to comfort him and the need to give him the distance he required, she smiled her sweetest smile. "I'm sorry."

He tilted his head, his eyes dismissing her. She walked back to her friends, leaving the man she loved alone.

19

S alvarias gazed at the roiling waters in front of him. He wondered if he just fell forward if they would consume him in their eternal darkness. He forced his gaze up and surveyed the tunnel. Trying to shake off his depression, he shoved himself up and followed the stream against the current, hoping exploration could tame his rampant mind.

Enchanting had finally caught up to him. The strain he had endured both times made his muscles so sore they hurt to be touched. His mind, always barely within his control, had freed itself. The number of things he thought about were so many he no longer could identify what they were. Some part of himself withdrew totally inward, to a secret and quiet spot, but there was a drumming that pushed against the walls of his new home, a pressure that made him physically ill.

The tug on his mind was near desperate now. It was becoming an old friend, just as the images of death, but it took his concentration not to roam the world. He wasn't sure, especially with his exhaustion, how much longer he could restrain himself.

The tunnel opened up to reveal an indent in the stream where another pool had formed. Hylim reflected pink tendrils along the stream like tentacles of an octopus. The smell of sulfur was suffocating. Nevertheless, he needed something to ease his aching muscles. Stripping from his clothes, he lowered himself into the pool. The too-hot water reddened his skin within breaths, but he did not care. He stayed until sweat beaded his forehead.

After washing, drying, and changing into a fresh set of burgundy robes, he noticed another tunnel, short and narrow. Curious, he peered inside. It opened to another cave no larger than a bedroom. Moss blanketed the floor and grasses sprouted. The horses would have loved it. A pond was filled with inky water; motionless, peaceful.

He ignited his magic.

My wizard, his magic greeted. *I have hopes the strain today will be less.*

I as well.

You're exhausted. I can sense your mind is weak. Are you sure you want to continue?

I am.

The magic warmed him, excitement mingling with his own. *I have the highest regard for your dedication. Indeed, you challenge me.*

Salvarias settled by the pond, resting his back against the cool rock. *I would not want you to become bored and leave.*

His magic chuckled. *With you, my ever-curious wizard, that would be an impossibility. Boredom isn't something you'll ever experience in your lifetime.*

A shame, my friend. Sometimes I would like nothing more than to sit and think of nothing.

After experiencing it once, you'd never do it again. Your mind wasn't made to be complacent. You hunger for knowledge as much as I.

Salvarias closed his eyes and inhaled a deep breath. *Let us begin.*

Are you certain you'll do this without a spell?

Salvarias nodded. "I understand it better. There is no need."

You spoke aloud.

Sorry.

Don't apologize. It's not I who cares if our conversations are heard.

I need no more fearful looks from my companions than I receive already.

Indeed.

"Let us begin."

You spoke aloud. Your mind is tired. I'm doubting this again.

I will do it.

As you wish, my wizard.

The energy responded quickly, casting its sense of reverence and obedience, weighing on him with its power, causing Salvarias to groan at the tenderness of his body. He tensed in expectation of the blackfire, gritting his teeth at the memory of it burning through him. However, when it rose it did not tear him apart. Instead, it merely boiled his blood, a much-preferred side effect. The pain was still intense, straining his muscles, stretching his skin, pressing against his brain, but compared to what he had endured the last two times, this was nothing.

Focusing on the staff, he commanded the blackfire with his thoughts. The staff would provide heat or cold, depending on what Salvarias longed for. It was a selfish enchantment with no purpose than a hope to expel the chill in his bones. Nonetheless, he thrust his wish at the blackfire. It surged with understanding, shooting from him in a wave, sloshing the pond water on him, leveling the grasses, draining blood from his skull to drip out his ears, nose, and lips. Salvarias collapsed into the darkness he loved before the wave even receded.

SALVARIAS JOLTED awake when a slick tongue ran up his hand. A chill had settled over him, and he felt faint, lightheaded. He shoved himself to sit and spat out the last of the blood in his mouth.

Blinking to try to clear his mind, he saw the fabric resting against his legs shift. It was subtle, but he was certain his robes moved. Icy fingers of fear trailed down his spine. With a violently shaking hand, he raised his robes. Feasting on him were slick black leeches. He then realized they were on his neck, back, arms, everywhere.

Terror robbed him of rational thought. Everything went black. Tears burned his eyes, and he wiped them away. Suddenly he could see again. He was staring at a stone ceiling while lying on his bed. Lightning pulsed outside his bedroom window, licking across muted green clouds. Ropes cut into his wrists and ankles as he writhed against his bindings. He looked down at his thin, naked body: so small, so helpless.

"Drive it from you!" his mother screeched. She stood near, holding a bucket.

"I am trying," Salvarias whispered, fear gripping his throat, tightening his chest. "I promise, Mother." He yanked against the ropes, stretching his fingers toward her. "Please, I am scared."

"I don't care," Ashra said, tears streaking her cheeks. "I've asked you, I've begged you!" Her jaw clenched, and she stood straight. "I know now. I know it lies in your blood. Your evil is coursing through the very thing that gives you life."

Salvarias craned his neck so he could see in the corner of his room. Shadows concealed a figure, and a single stream of light fell across slate-blue mage robes pooling on the floor.

"Help me," Salvarias begged. "Please, help me."

"He will not," Ashra said. "I give you one last chance, monstrosity. Force the evil to leave you!"

"I cannot! Please, Mother. I have tried."

She dumped the bucket's contents on him, and slimy leeches cascaded over him. It merely took a breath for the first one to bite.

"Brother!" Salvarias screamed, wrenching his hands against the ropes. "Brother!"

"He will not help you." Ashra settled on Wilhelm's bed and opened a book. "Now hush. I want to read."

Salvarias bit his tongue, shutting his eyes tight, sobbing with each sucking bite, begging his mind not to remember the sight of them slithering over his skin. He was not sure how much time passed that he lay there before the rustle of his mother's robes made him open his eyes. His vision blurred in and out of focus. He felt drained of life.

"There. That'll be enough for today. If you weren't so sickly, we could do this longer." She untied his hands. "Be careful—"

He scrambled up, swaying at a sudden lightheadedness. "Help me!" he cried. "Get them off!"

He swatted the leeches, smashing them on his skin, clawing others off, raking his fingernails over his skin hard enough to draw blood. He heard himself choking on sobs, crying for his brother. His mother just stood there, arms folded, watching him with tears raining from her eyes.

VARILA SNUGGLED CLOSER TO WILHELM, listening to his rumbling snore, smiling at his heavy arm hung around her shoulders. Finally ready to accept the call of sleep, she closed her eyes.

Wilhelm jerked awake. "Salv," he breathed.

He rose so fast she fell from his lap. Grabbing his sword, he dashed down the tunnel. Varila snatched up her sword and ran after him. His pace was slowed because he bounced between the walls as his frame nearly took up the entire tunnel. It gave her a chance to keep up.

He slid down the steep slope, keeping his balance easily. She managed her way down, though not nearly as gracefully. When they burst into the tunnel with the spring, it was empty.

"Where is he?" Varila said.

Wilhelm breathed raggedly, his head whipping left and right. He darted upstream.

Salvarias's screams tore down the tunnel, overpowering the babbling of the water. Wilhelm spewed oaths as he slipped over smooth rocks, scraping his knuckles each time he scrambled on. At one point he stopped, cocking his head and listening. Salvarias's cries ricocheted off the stone walls. Her heart pounded loud enough that she couldn't get a bearing on his location.

Wilhelm closed his eyes and inhaled a deep breath. When they popped open, he ran forward. Salvarias was begging for Wilhelm, sobbing in a tone of terror that raised Varila's flesh to bumps. Wilhelm stopped at another pool.

"There!" Varila called, pointing at a tunnel.

She darted behind Wilhelm into a cave where Salvarias was backed up against a wall, frantically hitting his arms and legs. What froze her were the mage's eyes. He wasn't where they were.

"Salv." Wilhelm fell to his knees beside his brother. "I'm here, Salv. You have to calm down."

"Help me, Brother! Get them off! Get them off!"

Wet stains glistened on the mage's robes. She went to his other side and yanked up his robes to see leeches flattened like a blanket on his legs.

Wilhelm grabbed Salvarias's shoulders and shook him to gain his attention. When Salvarias looked at Wilhelm, she wasn't sure what he saw. He seemed to recognize his brother, but the look in his eyes ... she shuddered.

Salvarias latched hold of Wilhelm. "Help me! Help me!"

"I'm here. I can help you, but you have to calm down." Wilhelm grimaced. "Salv, you have to calm down."

The mage's knuckles were white as he clung to Wilhelm's shoulders. "I cannot get them off! Help me!"

Varila had seen a man gripped by such debilitating fear once before. He'd been past reason, and her father had swiftly ended the man's misery with a firm blow to the head. When the man came to, he was rational and alert. Wilhelm, however, didn't possess the strength to do what was needed.

"Do you trust me?" she asked, raising her voice to be heard over Salvarias's frantic sobs.

Wilhelm met her gaze, rocking his brother in his arms.

"Do you?" she snapped.

Wilhelm nodded.

"Leave him with me. Go back to the stream and wait."

Wilhelm shut his eyes tight as he whispered to Salvarias, "I love you, Salv." He pried his brother's fingers loose.

"No!" Salvarias screeched, clawing for Wilhelm. "Do not leave me! Help me!"

"Go!" Varila ordered.

Wilhelm darted to his feet, dodging Salvarias's outstretched hands. Clenching his fists, he spun around and stormed out of the cave, roaring like a wounded animal.

Salvarias's eyes filled with hurt. He wrapped his arms around himself and rocked violently.

Futilely, but still worth a try, Varila said, "Salvarias, can you hear me?"

When she reached out her hand, he scrambled to the opposite wall, his distant gaze darting back and forth. Balling her fingers into a tight fist, she followed. She'd wanted to hit the mage for a long time, but this felt wrong.

Furling up on the ground, Salvarias softly wept, "Please, I am trying. I promise." He jerked, hugging himself tighter, squeezing his eyes shut.

Varila leaned her weight back.

"Please, Mother. I am trying!"

She froze. Impossible. Wilhelm had told her that Ashra was a loving, wonderful mother. Impossible.

"Brother," Salvarias sobbed. "Help me."

She dropped to her knees by his side and rested a hand on his shoulder. "Salvarias, your mother isn't here."

His brow furrowed, and his trembling doubled.

"You need to snap out of it. You're in a cave. Wilhelm's close by. Just open your eyes and—"

Salvarias's trembling switched to short convulsions.

"Salvarias!"

His eyelids fluttered, and his body hitched. A drop of blood fell from his nose. He wasn't breathing. Varila bolted up to fetch Wilhelm, but Salvarias's gasping breath stopped her shy of leaving the tunnel. She turned to see him roll on his side, gulping air and shuddering. When he opened his eyes, they were alert. His gaze swept the cave then focused on her.

"Where am I?" he said.

"A ..." Varila motioned around her. "A cave. You went for a bath. You must've come here."

Salvarias's peaked face was beaded with sweat. "I am sorry, my lady. I do not remember ..." His voice trailed off and a glint of fear surfaced in his eyes as he ran his hand over his arm.

"Don't look," she said soothingly.

His trembling was renewed, and he met her gaze. "My brother ... was he here?"

"Yes. You were panicked. I sent him away so I could knock some sense into you."

"Tell me everything I said."

Varila shrugged. "You said, 'I am trying,' and kept screaming for Wilhelm to help you."

"That is it?" Salvarias pressed.

Varila nodded.

Salvarias's eyes narrowed. "And when my brother left?"

"Pretty much the same," Varila said. Regardless of her hatred for him, she knew all too well the pains of abuse. Her pity fed her lie to sound sincere enough.

Salvarias's jaw tightened. "Whatever else I might have said does not need to be repeated to my brother."

Varila shrugged. "Didn't hear anything else."

Salvarias swallowed hard. "Where is he?"

"He's outside. Can you walk?"

Salvarias used his staff to haul himself up and followed her out. When they came to the stream, Wilhelm bounded over and scooped Salvarias up in a hug.

"What happened?" Wilhelm asked.

Instead of answering, Salvarias buried his face in Wilhelm's shoulder.

Wilhelm glanced at Adok. "Take her back." His eyes were filled with gratitude as he smiled halfheartedly at her. "I need time alone with Salv."

Varila nodded and headed down the stream with the wolf snarling at her.

"Let's clean you up," Wilhelm said.

A broken sob escaped Salvarias and seemed to trail her for eternity. When she rejoined the group, Humar was pacing by his bedroll, and Lunara was waiting by the entrance.

"Everything's fine," Varila said. "Unless you want a nasty glare from Wilhelm, I suggest everyone go to your beds and leave them alone when they get here."

Time passed. Hours, breaths, she wasn't sure. It felt like years before Wilhelm appeared, carrying Salvarias. Instead of taking the mage to his bedroll, Wilhelm propped himself against the cavern wall and settled Salvarias by his side. The mage stirred briefly to tighten his grip on the puzzle box and curl up before drifting off again.

Varila retrieved a few blankets and took them over to him. "How is he?" she whispered.

"Fine," Wilhelm said. "I finally got him to sleep."

She raised the blanket to cover Salvarias, but Wilhelm motioned her to stop. Keeping an eye on his brother's face, Wilhelm slowly hiked up the mage's sleeve and looked closely at his arm.

"What is it?" she asked.

Wilhelm lowered his brother's sleeve and added all the blankets to Salvarias. "Just trying to piece together a puzzle from our childhood."

"What do you mean?" Varila asked.

Wilhelm shook his head.

"You can tell me," she persisted.

Wilhelm sighed and rested his head against wall. "Those bite marks look like the same ones he used to get when he was little. I thought it was something that bullies did to him. I'm not so sure now. I swear the marks look identical, but leeches don't live in alleys."

Trying to sound casual, she said, "What did your mother think they were?"

"I never asked her. Salv wasn't close to her."

"You said she was an amazing mother."

Wilhelm frowned. "She was ... to me. Salv ... he's not an affectionate person. He never allowed her to touch him. He probably wouldn't have let her look at them."

"You said bullies beat him?"

"Once a week, when my father took me to the guardhouse, Mother took Salv to the market. He'd sneak off, and each time, bullies got a hold of him."

"Your mother didn't stop him?"

Wilhelm grunted. "*I* can't stop him. He sneaks from camp nearly every night. If he wants to go somewhere, he's going."

"You've got a point there. I guess we'll find out when he wakes."

Wilhelm snorted. "He won't talk about it. He never did. Now won't be any different."

She smiled at him. "Need anything?"

"No, but thanks."

She went to her bedroll, mulling over how Wilhelm could be so oblivious. He'd never let anyone harm Salvarias, and she had no doubt he'd have killed his own mother if it meant Salvarias's safety. And what did it matter, anyway? Salvarias was an ass, a selfish bastard who consumed all of Wilhelm's attention. The mage was grown now, free from her. Matter of fact, he disgusted her even more. He was a coward for not telling anyone, to keep the true nature of his mother hidden. What if she'd turned her beatings on Wilhelm?

She shifted in her bedroll until she faced the brothers. Wilhelm snored, but Salvarias's eyes glittered beneath his hood, reflecting the light of the hylim at his side. He was focused on her. She wondered if he'd kill her to keep his secret. Yes ... yes, he would.

20

S alvarias walked in the rear of the group; head lowered, exhausted, tripping when Mithal nudged him in affection. The memory of his childhood had emerged from his neatly wrapped bundle and refused to go back. Now, those dreadful hours he had spent in his room strapped to his bed with leeches feasting on him replayed over and over.

On top of that was a growing suspicion he had said more in front of Varila than he would want anyone to hear. If Wilhelm ever found out ... Salvarias shuddered off the thought. His brother's anger would be unmanageable, but his brother's guilt would be the death of Salvarias. He had lied to Wilhelm so they could stay together, and he would suffer a thousand more beatings at the hands of his mother if need be.

To add to his fears and depression, Unupture's patience had found its reward. Over the past several nights, Salvarias's mind had adapted to the man's power. No longer did he vomit or get bloody noses. Despite all the torment, Unupture surpassed kind. He was caring, giving Salvarias time to prepare, and talked freely about himself, though careful never to reveal information about his master. To Salvarias's alarm, he found he enjoyed his talks with Unupture.

The man was intelligent, if not misguided, and had a vast knowledge of history. Each night, their conversations had carried on longer.

A low growl ahead snapped him from his thoughts. They were in a cool cavern where water dripped down the walls to branch across the ground like roots of a tree. The stench of wet dog mingled with the musty odor of dirt and stagnant water.

"Wolf!" Varila shouted.

Swords hissed from their sheaths. Salvarias darted forward while connecting with the wolf. It was a female, lost, afraid, hungry, and desperate. Worse, she was protecting two cubs. His companions formed a half-circle, cornering her.

"No!" Salvarias ordered.

Only Wilhelm halted. The others advanced toward the dark corner where she was trapped. Frantically he assured the wolf everything would be fine, begging her not to attack his companions. He would handle it. Even as his thoughts left, Durak tossed a chunk of hylim in the corner. The pink light cast a rosy shade to the wolf's rich brown coat, streaked with gray and cream. Her white teeth gleamed as she snarled and growled. Behind her, two cubs stumbled over one another to shrink into the corner. Ribs stood up beneath their coats and the mother was in far worse condition.

"Surround her!" Humar ordered. "Be prepared for her to attack!"

"Enough!" Wilhelm roared the words with such commanding presence that the group halted and turned to him. "Step back!"

Everyone obeyed.

"Salv, handle it."

Salvarias slipped between Okulu and Hunz and knelt a few feet from the wolf. Adok joined his side, offering her assurances.

"We mean you no harm," Salvarias said. "We are merely passing through. You are lost?"

The wolf confirmed his suspicions. She'd yet to lower her guard.

"I will give you food, and my friend"—he motioned to Adok —"can provide direction out of the tunnels."

The wolf's snarl softened, though her gaze darted from him to his companions.

"Salv," Wilhelm whispered.

Salvarias turned to see his brother holding dried ham. Nodding his approval, Wilhelm tossed him the meat. He glanced at his companions staring at him with wide eyes, and realized in all his exhaustion that he had given voice to the words he had conveyed in his mind to the wolf. Shame and fear burned his cheeks. They would question him and learn of his oddity. He already saw Humar's clenched jaw and accusing stare. Wilhelm would not be able to intimidate the knight into silence.

"Everyone, put your swords away," Wilhelm said.

Steel raked against leather behind Salvarias. The wolf's posture relaxed as he laid out food. The cubs could no longer wait and dashed between her legs to accept the meat. Adok scooped up a chunk of ham and placed it at the mother's feet. Keeping her eyes on the group, she ate.

Wilhelm slowly walked to Salvarias and handed over the rest of the ham. "It's all we have."

"It should do," Salvarias murmured. He looked up at his brother. "Thank you."

Wilhelm winked. "I'm going to get the others further along the tunnel."

Adok, understanding that Wilhelm had sacrificed his stockpile of meat for the she-wolf, licked Wilhelm's hand.

Wilhelm patted Adok's head. "Don't mention it."

After ruffling Salvarias's hair, his brother rounded up the others and left. The she-wolf relaxed and trotted up to Salvarias, accepting ear rubs and any meat he offered her. Adok gave directions out of the cave while Salvarias tore off a chunk of his robe and made a makeshift pouch. He tied it around her, loose enough so she could reach it, and told her that once she pulled a strip of cloth, the knot would untie and spill the contents. It would provide enough food to get them to the exit.

After many thanks, a few belly rubs, and several licks from the pups, the family went on their way.

Salvarias watched them until they went out of sight. He shoved himself to his feet and followed the path toward his companions. "Why did you not sense her earlier?" he asked Adok.

The wolf growled in annoyance at himself, saying he had not been concentrating on smells.

Salvarias stopped walking and met the wolf's gaze. "It is instinctual, my friend. You are not the only wolf I have conversed with. Smell is as common as breathing to a wolf, or dog. You should not need to 'concentrate' to smell." Frowning, Salvarias thought back on their travels. "It is why you did not give us warning of the octrils sooner. But it is completely out of character for a wolf to—"

He suddenly lost track of his thought. Adok grinned at him and licked his hand.

"Very soon, my dear friend, you and I are going to have a serious conversation. I have many questions, and next time, I will write them down so I am not distracted."

Adok rolled his eyes.

Wilhelm's booming yell thundered in the tunnel and urged Salvarias into a sprint.

"Don't ask him!" Wilhelm roared. "I told you to leave him be, Humar!"

"He just had a conversation with a wolf!" Varila yelled. "What do you expect? We want to know how in all of Oblivion your brother talked to a wolf!"

"I'm done!" Humar said. "You will tell me what I want to know, boy!"

"Boy? Boy!" Wilhelm's voice quivered with anger. "I'm no boy, Humar! I swear to all the gods in all the worlds that if you even bring it up to him, we'll leave and you'll never see us again!"

"Why, when it comes to your brother, are you a different person?" Varila said. "Where does the kind man go? All I see is a bully protecting a ... a demon disguised as a man!"

Those words hit Salvarias with force, causing his feet to stumble over one another, making him cling to the wall for support. A sharp pang of utter hurt lanced his heart.

Why, my littler murderer, are you surprised by her comment? the presence said. *As I recall, your mother called you demon on several occasions. The truth is not always easy to hear.*

Salvarias darted into the cavern before Wilhelm could say something to Varila he would surely regret. Lunara's hands were fisted at her sides, face flushed. Okulu was reclining against the wall, a frown on his lips. Neithelas, Frink, and Hunz stood off to the side, looking uncomfortable at the confrontation. Durak, Humar, and Varila had taken an aggressive stance in front of Wilhelm. His brother trembled visibly, face red, jaw clenched. Salvarias rested his hand over his heart. It hurt.

"Thank you, Brother." The pain they had caused Wilhelm simmered a dreadful anger in Salvarias, but worse, the pain he had forced upon his brother clouded Salvarias's soul with shame. Together, they stripped him of his patience and understanding. He tossed back his hood. If they wanted a demon, a demon he could provide. "I can speak to animals and have done so since I was a child." He strode forward, not hiding his eyes, merely his pain. "It is why I knew the horses could make this journey. It is why a wolf accompanies us. It is why no bears have attacked our camps at night. It is why no snakes crawl into your bedrolls while you sleep. It is why no insects have infected you with disease." He did not hide his eyes from the light of the hylim and, instead, raised his head, allowing the full horror of his demonic eyes to be seen. "I will not answer questions, I will not listen to your whispered conversations and hateful words." He locked gazes with Varila. "Call me a demon if you wish, my lady, but never insult my brother again." He motioned to the horses. "There is no need to lead them any longer. They will follow us on their own accord." He turned to Frink. "Let us continue. There is nothing more to discuss, and we have wasted enough time."

Durak spat to the side and stormed off behind Frink and Hunz. Humar and Varila muttered curses as they left the tunnel. Neithelas took Lunara's arm and led her past Okulu. The merc grinned and cast Salvarias a wink before leaving with the others.

Salvarias raised his hood and stepped next to his brother. "Thank you for trying."

"You didn't have to do that, Salv." Wilhelm's fists were clenched so tight, blood oozed under his fingernails.

"I know." Bottling his hurt, hiding his shame at yet another of his oddities discovered, Salvarias met his brother's gaze and grinned. "But beating our companions to Oblivion is not what I had in mind when we set out on this little journey, Brother."

Wilhelm's shoulders relaxed, but no grin.

Salvarias locked arms with his brother and guided him forward. "Although I think it would have been a sight to witness you battle Varila. I doubt we have seen her full potential."

Wilhelm's voice tightened. "I don't care to ever witness it."

"My dear brother, if there was someone in our company who possessed traits no other human did, would you be so willing to allow that person to eat at my side? If someone in our company erupted in black flames, set a man on fire, and laughed about it, would you permit him to share a room with us?" That last statement coiled Salvarias's stomach.

"Yes."

"You are most stubborn, Brother. You know as well as I that you would not. You care for me. You would never allow another near me you did not trust. Varila has the same care for Lunara." He shifted to catch his brother's gaze. "Surely, if there is one man in all of Arden who can understand her outburst, it would be you."

"I'd never say such things, though."

Salvarias grinned. "Is it not her mouth that you find so appealing?"

A slight smile twitched on Wilhelm's lips. "She's a very outspoken woman."

"A trait you admire. You would not care for her if she was any less."

"I ... I just wish you two would get along."

Salvarias rammed his fist into Wilhelm's side.

"Ouch!"

Salvarias's heart lifted at his brother's rumbling chuckle. "It is not

I who is interested in her. I am sure our relationship will work itself out eventually."

Wilhelm locked his arm around Salvarias's neck. "You're the most understanding man I've ever met, Salv. You don't deserve the way people treat you."

"I give them plenty of reasons, Brother. You are blinded."

Unupture felt the familiar tingle from the amulet hanging around his neck. Eager for intelligent conversation, he strode through the corridors of the stronghold, startling black-armored soldiers from his path. He reached his room out of breath, not waiting to calm himself before jumping in bed.

He clutched hold of the tree pendant, slipped his mind free from his body, and floated among the thoughts streaming through the air like seeds from a dandelion. Salvarias's waves of thought were different from others, stronger, multiple where others simply had one.

The ghastly pink hue revealed which thought was the dream he so easily accessed with help from the pendant the God of Magic had enchanted. The surging power blossomed up, snagged hold of his consciousness, and used the connection to Salvarias's amulet to drag Unupture's mind into the rivulet of Salvarias's dream.

One blink later and Unupture stood amid the dead, blood soaking the hem of his robes. Only thinking of the mage, he whispered, "Hello, Salvarias."

Salvarias appeared from behind a plump woman void of a head. He bowed. "Unupture."

"How have your travels been?"

Salvarias grimaced as he sat on the bloody ground. "Uneventful."

"How wonderful for you." Unupture sat beside the young man, resting his arms around his knees and staring at the legs shambling by. He tried to ignore the blood seeping into his robes. "I am pleased to hear no harm has come to you."

"Thank you. How is your master?"

Unupture sighed. "Angry, as always. He rants through halls, devouring anyone dense enough not to flee from his path."

"It pleases me to hear so."

"I'm sure it does." Unupture studied the mage a moment before looking ahead. "Something has happened."

Salvarias shrugged.

"Are you well?"

"In a manner of speaking, no. My ailment is mental, however, not physical."

"I'm as relieved as I am worried."

Salvarias tilted his head. "Once again your concern goes against my assumption of your character."

"Thank you for noticing. I hope to show you I'm not what I serve."

"Then why not leave?"

Unupture heaved a deep sigh. "If only. My master would hunt me until the end of my days. My punishment for abandoning him would surpass even what Sansis could concoct."

"If you help me, I could defeat him."

"That you might. However, I'm not willing to bet my soul on a maybe. He's experienced with his power, whereas you are not. He's not afraid to unleash its pure glory. Even if you chose to do as he does, you're not cruel. And I'm afraid cruel people rarely lose. Such is the way of life."

Salvarias lowered his head to stare at his hands.

Unupture bent forward to catch his gaze. The man's eyes swirled with shifting shades of gray, churning like an eddying current in a raging river. What struck Unupture each time was how Salvarias's bone structure mirrored God's: beautiful, flawless to the point of being unnatural. "You believe nothing in yourself."

Salvarias shrugged. "Perhaps, perhaps not." He squared his shoulders. "I am eager to move past this event tonight. Shall we continue?"

Unupture raised his face to stare up at the pink sky. "Such an unpleasant hue. Still, I'm happy it's not orange. I fear Sansis has turned me from that horrid color." He rubbed his orange hands over one another. "Even mirrors sicken me."

"I pity you. I would not want to be reminded of him every time I looked in a mirror."

Unupture cast a wane smile. "You're a very polite man."

"Rudeness is abundant. Judgment is the way of our world. I find it a shame and have no desire to add to its power."

Unupture sighed, realizing he didn't have the heart to hurt the mage. Not tonight anyway. "I won't use my powers. I'll let you enjoy this dream as you once did. Let us merely talk."

Salvarias's shoulders slouched and all pretense of courage drained from his face. "You have my thanks."

Unupture smiled at the vulnerability shining in the mage's eyes. Slowly, the young man was trusting him. Though they were on opposite sides, he had a strong desire to maintain that trust.

They talked for some time of the creatures Unupture had created. He shared his dreams with the young man, what he'd wanted for each of his monstrosities, and Salvarias graced him occasionally with an opinion or different perspective. They could've talked for hours or breaths. Time was immeasurable in the never-changing sky.

When finally Unupture ceased speaking, Salvarias whispered, "I have become accustomed to your powers." It was a statement, not a question.

Unupture rested a hand on the man's shoulder. "You have. When next I enter your mind, my power won't debilitate you."

"I ..." Salvarias raised his gaze to Unupture's. Pain filled the black irises. "I am tired."

"You've remembered something."

Salvarias nodded. "What hides in my mind frightens me. I beg you, tell your master you were unsuccessful. Tell him you tried and could not pry apart my mind."

Unupture squeezed Salvarias's shoulder. "My master can pick out lies. He would know. But I can reveal a secret. Your body will be accustomed to my powers. You'll function while I search your mind. *You* will function."

Understanding lit Salvarias's eyes. "I can still fight you. I can block you."

Unupture smiled. "Yes, you can, but doing so will cause you greater pain than you endured before. Up until now, think of it as being given the same poison over and over until you made yourself impervious to it. My powers can no longer kill you. Now, just as a duel with swords, ours will be a duel of the minds. Steel yourself from distraction." Unupture rose to his feet and helped the mage to his. "Take care, Salvarias Laybryth. I can grant you a few nights of peace to prepare yourself." He looked around the dead. "I will leave you alone as long as I can."

Salvarias nodded. "Thank you, Unupture. Again, I am taken aback by your kindness."

Unupture smiled at the vibrant tree. "I wish you and your brother safe travels."

Salvarias's gaze steadied on the soaring branches. "And may our souls always remain our own." He started forward and stopped shy of the dry ground. "Though I appreciate your offer of solitude, it would please me if we still met."

Unupture's mouth dropped open. He snapped it closed and nodded. "I will visit you every night, if you so desire."

Though his face remained shadowed, Unupture felt Salvarias's probing gaze. When the mage spoke, his voice was void of the caution it usually contained. It was filled with warmth. "I do desire such visits."

"Why?" Unupture breathed. "Why would you willingly offer your company to a man sworn to find your darkest secrets and exploit them to your enemy?"

"There is more to you than what your master uses. You are capable of great things. I hope to know the man who would protect the lives of the innocent over his own when finally presented with the opportunity."

"I fear death. I fear the loss of my soul. I would never sacrifice myself. Your hope is misplaced."

"Death awaits us all. When my time comes, I will stand before the doors of Oblivion and be asked: Did you try? And I will, without hesitation, say yes. I will accept my fate because I have done everything within my power to be a good man, to fight what lives within me."

Unupture shook his head. "I don't believe trying will save me from that cursed realm."

"It will not save me either," Salvarias said. "Make no mistake, Oblivion awaits me. Some acts I have committed will ensure my entrance. I, however, will walk through the doors willingly for I know I tried. There was nothing further I could have done."

"You are brave."

Salvarias laughed, light, airy. The dead seemed to perk up at his mirth, smile themselves, and the dull pink hue of the sky brightened. The plane of death almost seemed ... beautiful.

"Brave is not a word I would use to describe myself," Salvarias said. "Fear drives me. Fear for my soul is what makes me fight your master. What you call bravery is a desperate attempt for redemption, selfish in every sense of the word." Salvarias bowed. "Until tomorrow night."

Unupture bowed, smiling at the young man despite himself. "Until tomorrow, Salvarias. I wish you safety."

Salvarias tilted his head and stepped on to the dry soil. The pink sky was replaced with a moss-covered ceiling.

"I hope I'm not disturbing you."

Unupture sprang up and looked over to see Sansis lounging in a chair by the fire. "Of course not. I was merely connecting with our young mage."

A hungry gleam lit Sansis's milky eyes. "How is he? Is he in good health?"

Unupture left his bed and sat in a chair opposite Sansis. "He is."

"I miss him, you know." Sansis's eyes distanced as he stared at the flickering flames that lit his exposed tendons and muscles in an eerie red. Where translucent skin covered bone, the flames imbued it with its orange hue, clashing against his pumpkin-colored robes.

"He mentioned he suffered much at your hand," Unupture said.

"Mmm ... so he did. I've never met another that can heal so quickly. His tolerance for pain is ... is nothing short of astounding."

"To what do I owe the pleasure of this visit?"

"I am leaving and wanted to bid you my farewells."

"God failed to mention."

"He doesn't tell you all," Sansis said. "Although I've noticed that he seems to trust you more than me these days. I, however, do not. There's a reason for my trip, but I won't tell you what it is. I prefer you to fret over it."

Sansis caught Unupture off guard when not with their God. Sansis's demeanor was confident, assured, and sneaky. Around God, he appeared to be a groveling fool incapable of defending himself. Some ploy, surely.

Unupture turned his gaze to the fire and shrugged. "It's of no matter to me. I have my purpose—which, because of you and Dethal, has been expanding to areas I don't desire. I assure you, you've nothing to fear from me. You've always been his closest disciple. I simply serve where I can."

Sansis rose from the chair and rested a hand on Unupture's shoulder. Sansis's powers crawled inside Unupture, caressing his insides as if they were cradled in Sansis's raw hands. Pain flared along his shoulder, stabbing from Sansis's hand down Unupture's arm, blinding thought and ripping a cry from his lips. The man might as well have raped him for how violated he felt.

"Shush now, my friend," Sansis said. "I sense a strained muscle. I'm merely healing you." His rancid breath brushed Unupture's cheek. "Your heart is not in our cause, Unupture. I can see through your skin as you can see through mine. Be thankful I've kept my suspicion from God. But know that I'm watching you. I advise you to stay in your dungeons with the whores you've infected. The boy is mine."

Sansis glided from the room. Unupture doubled over, falling from his chair and clutching his shoulder. The violation was beneath his skin, *inside* him, still licking over his insides with residual pain. Curling up on the floor, hugging himself, he wept.

21

L unara decided she hated walking. The tunnels were too low to ride through, the caverns too short-lived, and the stone floor was wearing a hole in the bottom of her right boot. She was cold, tired, sore, and wanted her own bed to sleep off the stiffness and rest-less nights since entering the tunnels, or rather since leaving home.

At least tomorrow they would leave the mountain. Perhaps Humar would let them stay in a nice warm bed in the new city of Catlin where she could bathe every hour until she finally felt clean. She sighed, running a hand along her arm and feeling the thin layer of moist dirt. It'd only been a few days since her last bath, but the walking and the dripping stalactites ensured cleanliness didn't last long. Their water supply was running low, so no rinses were allowed. The brothers seemed equally irritated. She was surprised by their hygiene compared to other men, and guessed their mother must've wanted a daughter for how well both maintained appearances. Salvarias's face was always smooth, as if he shaved every morning, but she never saw him with a shaving knife. Wilhelm, borrowing her sister's hand mirror, shaved every few days, keeping it to thick stubble versus a full beard. Neither brother smelled, in contrast to the other men, except Neithelas. The prince was as attentive to his appearance.

Even so, the time in the caves had affected him. His face was drawn with lines she'd never noticed, he slouched, his feet shuffled, and he was the last one to rise each morning and first to succumb to sleep. Okulu wasn't much better.

Speaking of Neithelas, she'd forgotten he was talking to her.

"Do you agree, my lady?" he said.

"I'm sorry," she said. "I didn't catch your last question."

"Do you agree that each soul is paired?"

She resisted the urge to glance at Salvarias. "I do."

"As do I. I believe when you first meet a person you know whether they're your soul's mate."

"I disagree with you there. I think love grows over time. One cannot possibly know if they love someone when they first meet. They can be physically attracted, but not love. Furthermore, I don't think souls always find each other. Some souls love another, even one not meant for them. I believe it's rare for a soul to find its true mate."

Neithelas frowned. "Winsires believe that souls seek each other. No amount of land can keep them from finding their mate."

"Or you drug them," Okulu said, voice rougher than usual, as if he'd not drank water in days. "That is, if they don't want to submit to the whole soul mate thing." He took a long pull from his flask.

Neithelas stiffened. "You don't know what you speak of, half-breed."

"I know that's why my mother left," Okulu said. "A man was pursuing her, and she wasn't interested. She knew about the thryn plant, so she left before he could use it on her."

Neithelas snorted. "How did a woman learn of it?"

"The women know more than you think. It's wrong to do what you do."

Lunara fell back a step to walk with Okulu. "What's thryn?"

Okulu leaned over to whisper near Lunara's ear, "Salvarias always seems lost in that book of his, but I've been testing a little theory. He hears everything. Watch." Okulu called over his shoulder, "Salvarias? Care to explain?"

The mage, who'd remained distant since the encounter with the wolf yesterday—nose planted in his spell book—looked up. "Thryn is a tree native to lands of the Winsires. It produces a fruit whose juices act as a ... love potion, for lack of a better term. It clouds the mind and makes it—from what I have read—impossible for a person to resist advances. Winsire males have been using it for some time to ... persuade women to accept courtship."

Okulu winked at her. "Thanks, Salvarias."

"Your facts are misguided, mage," Neithelas said. "Women are creatures of whim. The fruit merely curbs their nature to allow rational thinking."

"Oh, my," Okulu said. "You realize you said that aloud?"

Lunara glared at the prince. "Whim? Women are creatures of whim? We must be drugged in order to think rationally?"

Neithelas's brow crinkled. "Yes, my lady. You flight around with no care of the—"

"I'm going to stop you right there," Varila said. "Your Winsire women may 'flight' around, but Erthlas don't. We know what we want. And Erthla women take what we want."

Neithelas shook his head. "I've seen otherwise from you, Lady Varila."

Varila's eyes flashed with anger. "Would you care to explain or stop while you're ahead?"

"Oh, please do explain," Okulu said, grinning broadly.

Lunara felt a pang of guilt. Neithelas's gaze was filled with confusion. He'd been raised with a certain way of thinking. It wasn't his fault. The poor man continued, though.

"I've seen your glances at Gentleman Wilhelm. You seem interested, but you change your demeanor toward him daily, if not hourly."

Varila snorted. "I know what I want, Winsire."

"Then why not take it? Clearly he feels the same."

Lunara held her breath. The two hadn't talked since Varila made the comment about Salvarias being a demon.

"You obviously don't know anything about how I feel," Wilhelm grumbled.

Lunara knew her sister well. Wilhelm might as well have hit Varila.

Salvarias rested a hand on his brother's arm and spoke without looking up from his book. "What you see as irrational behavior, Prince Neithelas, is the paradigm of rational. All races are flawed. The head and heart battle each other with every emotion. Of that, men are no different than women. How many marriages using the thryn fruit are faithful?"

Deep red blossomed on Neithelas's cheeks. "That's beside the point."

"Is it?" Salvarias said, voice cold. "The man drugs the woman his cock wants at that moment then moves on once the thrill of the hunt has passed. Even those men who might remain faithful have wives who seek another bed. Forcing a woman with thryn is no different than rape."

Lunara started at Salvarias's direct words. She'd never heard him so blunt before, and now that she studied him closer, she saw his tense shoulders and jaw rippling as he ground his teeth. The caves were apparently affecting everyone except the Cavruls.

"Women play with men's hearts," Neithelas said, turning to face Salvarias. "They're cruel with leading us on, even as they turn their heads when we offer our attention. Your brother is prey to Varila's deceitfulness."

Salvarias's spell book snapped closed, and his voice was sharp when he said, "My brother is prey to *nothing*, and Lady Varila is far from deceitful. What you see is the natural dance of courtship. Your perception of men and women is woefully wrong. No one person is the same. What one man lusts for is another man's disgust." Salvarias's jaw loosened. He glanced from Wilhelm to Varila. When he spoke, his tone was lighter than it'd been in days. "Lady Varila's advances are exactly what my brother finds attractive. If she were a shy, demure woman, my brother would not find her appealing. It is her strength and worship of her own body that he is drawn to. I guarantee if she draped herself naked over a platter of roasted venison, my brother would not be able to resist her. That act would disgust you and many other men. Every person is different in what they desire."

Wilhelm chuckled. "Now that brings a wonderful image to mind. I'm rather hungry now."

Varila's eyes lit, and she grinned. "Maybe one day I'll see if your brother is right."

Wilhelm grinned crookedly. "I hope that day comes." His brow furrowed and then a rumbling, infectious laugh echoed in the cavern. He wrapped an arm around Salvarias's neck and ruffled his hair. "Tricky, Salv."

Salvarias said, "Do not be so stubborn, and I would not resort to such tactics."

Lunara watched her sister closely, hoping Salvarias's act had softened Varila's feelings. Either by stubbornness or because she didn't hear, her demeanor went on unchanged.

Turning to Neithelas, Lunara saw his head lowered and deep lines of thought carved into his olive skin. Her heart went out to him. To be so sheltered in a world of black and white, without the influence of others, and then to be thrust out into a world full of colors must be difficult.

She increased her steps until she was at his side. "I can't imagine how much you miss your home."

Neithelas nodded. "It's beautiful, peaceful, clean, and loving. I find the outside world quite different. This trip has opened my eyes to many things."

"You believe the thryn tree, I mean, what it's used for is wrong?"

Neithelas shrugged. "I'm not sure. I've seen many marriages flourish by initiating their beginning with thryn. I'm not so ready to believe."

"Time reveals much to us," Lunara said.

"Indeed, it does. This journey has reinforced many of my beliefs, but it has also shown me how empty my life is. I have no wife, no children, and no home of my own. It's time I think of such things." Neithelas gently took her wrist and held her until the companions had filed past them. "I believe it's time for you to think of such things as well."

Lunara turned to walk, but he kept a firm hold.

"Are my intentions unclear?"

"Neithelas, you're a sweet man—"

He pulled her possessively close—too close. "You presume too much!" she breathed, wrenching her arm from his grasp and stepping back.

"My lady, I believe you're my soul's mate."

Lunara gaped at him. "We've only just met. You—"

"I know my heart's desire." He fell to his knees and clasped her hand. "I implore you, expand your sight and look to one who would bathe you in love and jewels, who could offer you an entire race that would worship you!"

Lunara yanked her hand back. "I don't want jewels and I certainly do *not* want to be worshipped. I am flattered, but I'm not interested."

Before he could say another word, she whirled around and fled for the comfort of her friends. Salvarias was walking alone in the rear of the group, and she joined his side, trying to calm her breathing.

He looked up from his book. "Are you unwell, my lady?"

Lunara shook her head. "It's ... it's Neithelas."

Salvarias turned his gaze to his book. "He is fond of you."

"A feeling I don't return."

"He is a kind man, if not confused at times. Why do you not return his affections?"

She widened her eyes at him. "Is it not obvious?"

He inhaled deeply and met her gaze. "What you seek from me, I cannot give you. Neithelas can provide safety and comforts. He—"

"I don't want safety and comforts, Salvarias Laybryth," she said, begging her tears not to surface. "I want love."

Salvarias turned his gaze to his book. "That he can offer you as well."

"And if he proposed, you'd bestow your blessing upon us? Would you attend the wedding as well?"

"Yes, my lady. To both questions."

Something stabbed her heart. She bit her trembling lip and walked quickly to Varila.

Lunara didn't speak for the rest of the day, and when all was dark and quiet, and the snores from her companions started, she rolled on her side, buried her face in her blankets, and allowed her tears to flow freely.

A rustle from behind made her wipe her cheeks and snap her eyes shut. A breeze rippled by, carrying with it the light sent of lavender and the sound of whispered numbers. Once he passed, she opened her eyes and watched him sneak off to the tunnel they'd taken earlier, Adok on his heels. At the entrance, he paused and looked back. She knew he couldn't see her, but she swore he stared into her eyes. After a quick glance at the wolf, he strode down the tunnel alone. Adok whined and padded over to her, circled a few times, and plopped down against her stomach.

"He loves me, you know," she whispered to Adok, running her fingers along his soft ears. "He wouldn't have sent you if he didn't."

Adok's sad eyes sparkled, and his tongue lolled out to lick her hand. Grinning, she snuggled down with the wolf and reached out her mind to Salvarias as he began his enchantment. Once his thoughts were occupied enough and his pain started, she snuck her way in and gave him strength and support, offering what comfort she could. She doubted he sensed her, but she felt his pain reduce and his mind strengthened.

This time, she became aware of his magic as it readily accepted her gift on behalf of the mage. It imbued her with its sense of respect and appreciation. She was shocked to feel it as almost a presence, a living thing inside him. Even more startling was its level of power, how deep it was seeded in the mage, how entwined it was in his mind. She'd never felt it before. Either his magic was getting stronger, or her connection with Salvarias was solidifying despite his efforts to sever it.

It wasn't long before the hazy wave shot from the tunnel, rippling puddles and stirring up dust. It sucked back as fast it came, and when it retreated, Wilhelm stirred awake. In the faint light of the hylim she saw him shake his head and frown as he rose from bed.

Before he took one step, a pebble fell from the roof, echoing loudly in the otherwise silent cavern. Adok bolted to his feet, growling, hackles stiff. Lunara sprang up, shoving her sister awake.

Wilhelm snatched up his sword, ripped it free from its sheath, and darted toward the tunnel. Well before he reached it, a white body dropped from a stalactite to block his way. Its milky white eyes were alight with hunger, and its pointed black teeth dripped with saliva. It crouched, flexing its clawed hands as it watched Wilhelm barreling toward it.

"Hidlu?" Hunz breathed. "Impossible! These caves always be safe."

"'Always' seems to be a fond word for some people," Okulu said. "Personally, I think it's stupid." With a flick of his wrist, his dagger soared through the air and landed in the hidlu's skull, crunching through bone and spewing black blood. "Go!" Okulu barked.

Wilhelm closed the distance to the tunnel entrance, leapt over the spasming hidlu, and disappeared. Everyone else had risen and formed a circle around Lunara, thankfully blocking the flailing creature from view.

The pink glow of the hylim lit the creatures dripping from the stalactites as if they were thick honey.

"How many?" Varila asked.

"Me see eight," Durak said.

"Nine," Neithelas said, pointing to the far end of the cavern where hylim did not permeate the shadows.

"The leader." Hunz spat. "Kill him, Winsire."

Neithelas raised his bow and aimed. The arrow whistled free and disappeared into darkness. A thud was followed by a screech. Hisses and spitting calls sounded around them.

"Next brilliant idea?" Varila snapped at Hunz.

"Usually they stop if the leader's dead," Hunz retorted. "These must be hungry."

"Really? How wonderful," Okulu said, launching a dagger at the ceiling. A body plopped to the ground, taloned feet scraping, gurgling a scream. Lunara closed her eyes tightly.

"Don't they know they're outmatched?" Okulu said.

"They be starved," Durak grumbled. "They only see meat."

Neithelas released another arrow. A thud sounded in the darkness.

"Let some of 'em down," Durak growled. "Me want a fight."

"It's not my fault you chose to only wield a close-range weapon," Okulu said, launching another dagger.

A horrible screech echoed in the cavern.

Neithelas sighed. "Let us be done with this."

Arrows hissed through the air with such speed, Neithelas's arm was a blur and his bow a steady vessel of death. He dispatched the remaining five hidlu.

"You've been holding out on us," Humar said, standing straight.

"Years of practice," Neithelas said, shrugging.

Wilhelm entered, carrying Salvarias. The mage was out cold, but there wasn't as much blood on his face this time.

"It's not safe anymore," Frink said. "We walk with no sleep until we reach Catlin."

Lunara held in her groan of annoyance.

The night of walking was nothing shy of torture. Salvarias woke at some point, looking as exhausted as she felt, but walked on his own. Instead of focusing on his spell book, he took to whirling the puzzle box into odd shapes.

After a quick break for food—what she assumed to be breakfast—he joined her side as they continued their trek through the caves.

"Last night," he said, "I felt something different in your presence."

"If I focus, I can give you strength. I don't understand how I can do it, and it doesn't seem to drain my own."

"You have done it before?"

"Yes, several times, actually. And I know already you're going to ask me to stop, but I'm afraid your plea is futile." She smiled her sweetest smile. "We don't always get what we want."

Salvarias shook his head. "It is dangerous for you to try such things. We do not understand our connection. We—"

"On the contrary, I'm learning a great deal about our connection because I embrace it. I study it and try new ways of strengthening it as well as weakening it. I've learned to distance myself when you're in physical pain. It helps, though not entirely. The second time you did enchantments, I felt you slipping away. I withdrew as much as possible, but a darkness came for me as well."

Salvarias glanced at her. "Why did you not tell me?"

"What good would it have done? Once you fought your way through, I came with you. I woke tired, but nothing else."

"I am sorry, my lady."

Lunara shrugged. "Don't be. You didn't know the effects enchanting had on you."

Mithal, who'd been walking behind Salvarias, nudged him off balance. She looked over her shoulder at the horses following them. It felt odd not to lead them. She glanced at her white mare. "Does Shell like me?"

"Shell?"

"My mare."

Salvarias shook his head. "Palony is the name she prefers."

"I've called her Shell since she was a foal."

"And she has hated the name since."

"Will you tell her I'm sorry?"

"She is fond of you. There is no need for you to apologize, but she appreciates the sentiment."

Lunara smiled at her horse. "How wonderful it must be to talk to them."

"Indeed, it is."

Hours more of walking gave Lunara a nasty blister on her foot, and her leather boot finally gave way to a hole. She tried to hide her limp as best she could. She thought she was doing brilliantly until Wilhelm whisked her into his arms.

"You can't possibly carry me all the way to Catlin," she protested.

"Is that a challenge?" Wilhelm said, grinning crookedly.

Lunara settled comfortably in his arms. "I would never dream of it."

Wilhelm's rumbling chuckle echoed in the cavern.

Of course she'd been joking, but for hours Wilhelm showed no sign of tiring. When the sounds of a bustling city echoed in their tunnel, Lunara burst out laughing.

22

S alvarias did his best to conceal his robes with his cloak as they rounded a corner that dumped them at the rear city of Catlin. Disappointed was an understatement. He had seen masterfully drawn pictures and read of the glory of Cattlar, and he had assumed the Cavruls' architectural talents would have translated to all the cities. But no homes were carved in the sides of the mountain, and elaborate pulleys did not operate platforms that shot up the cavern walls to the homes of the wealthy. Instead, stone homes were erected like any other city in Dalnar. The cave mouth yawned open with no gate to bar entrance. No rivers of lava flowed nor did jewels glitter like stars on the ceiling. It was ill-conceived and mundane.

"Ye call this a city?" Durak groused. "It's not even worthy to be called a home to Cavruls!"

"We've not had time to carve the mountain to our taste," Hunz said.

"How many other cities have ye started?" Durak asked, looking around with disgust plastered over his frown wrinkles.

"Seven," Frink said.

"None of 'em be on a map," Durak said.

"Aye. We thought it wise to keep locations to ourselves for a while.

238

Catlin is just now becoming known. Mostly by Watythms," Hunz said.

"Why would Watythms venture this far inland?" Okulu asked.

"We be testing our strongest new brew on them," Frink said. "It's brandaline. The richest-looking brown mixture you've ever seen. Burns right through the throat and gullet."

Okulu grinned. "I'll have to try some of that."

Frink chuckled. "I'd like to see who can drink who under the table first. Perhaps you all would accept our offer to stay the night in our friend's home. He's got plenty of free rooms. His eleven children have up and left. It'd be our highest honor, Lord Boughlar."

Salvarias caught Humar's questioning glance and shrugged. He had yet to develop a plan or receive additional information regarding the army. As far as he could tell, time was not a factor ... yet.

"We'll stay two nights," Humar said.

"Tell me you have a bathhouse here," Varila said.

"Aye," Frink said. "Our friend has three private rooms dedicated to baths. He's as fond of them as you."

"Wonderful!" Lunara exclaimed.

"Are there stables?" Salvarias asked.

"Aye. Our friend runs them. The horses will be seen to."

Mithal nickered an approval.

Hunz and Frink's friend indeed owned a small mansion. It was the largest building in the city, constructed in what Salvarias assumed was a hasty manner based on the sloppy aligning of stones. Some windows were cracked where the settling foundation strained the glass. Durak snorted as he looked over the home.

The owner, Anard, as Frink introduced him, welcomed them graciously. When Frink mentioned Durak's name, Anard threw himself to the ground. "Lord Boughlar. Truly, it's an honor."

"Get up, ye fool!" Durak barked. "Me not a lord any longer. Address me as such again and me chop yer head clean off."

Anard scrambled to his feet and bowed. "As you command, D-Durak."

"Good," Durak grumbled. "We need baths and some strong drink."

Anard motioned to a few servants. "Show them the baths and their quarters."

They were ushered inside the home that looked as ordinary as any other. The furniture was simple, the fabrics plain, and the layout predictable.

The steaming baths were refreshing, and Salvarias and Wilhelm lingered long after the other men had left. When the water cooled, Salvarias reluctantly crawled out, dried, dressed, chanted his spell, and flicked his hand. He rubbed his smooth cheek.

Wilhelm chuckled. "Maybe you can find a spell to keep my beard short. I hate shaving."

Salvarias nodded. "I will come up with one, Brother. Have you talked to Durak?"

"He's as tight-lipped as ever. He won't even tell Humar. All I know is that Cavruls who are referred to as lord are usually head of clan."

"Indeed," Salvarias said. "Your knowledge is fact."

Wilhelm got out of the tub, dried, and dressed. "Let's meet up with everyone else. And by the way, while we're here I don't want you venturing off at night. We don't know these , and it's not safe."

"You have my word, Brother. Anard was less than surprised to see a mage, and far too accepting of me."

Wilhelm nodded. "I noticed the same."

In the courtyard of the estate, the rest of their companions were waiting along with Anard.

"It's midday," Anard said. "We'll be eating dinner an hour before sunset. My home is yours during your stay. Feel free to wander the city. Mage, the sole reason you live is because you're in Durak's company. You'll not be welcomed, but no one will kill ye while you're here."

"Thank you, Gentleman Anard," Salvarias said with a slight bow.

The rest murmured thanks, and Salvarias turned to his brother. "I would like to go for a walk outside."

Wilhelm's gaze was already fixed on the sunlight beaming through the cavern entrance. "I think that's a brilliant idea."

"May I come?" Lunara asked.

"I think we all would like some fresh air," Humar said, setting off.

Outside the cavern, Salvarias fought the urge to fling himself to the ground and kiss the fading green grasses, or to run to the nearest tree and embrace it in gratefulness for its soothing song that filled his ears. Neithelas, however, did not refrain. He rushed forward and leapt up a tree with the grace of a jaguar.

"Lady Lunara!" Neithelas called. "Join me!"

Giggling, Lunara darted to the tree and climbed, seeming to move with ease even in her peach dress that offered a lovely view of her collarbone and slender neck. She ignored Neithelas's offered hand and scaled past him.

Wilhelm wrapped an arm around Varila's shoulders and led her from the group while Durak and Humar took off on their own path.

Okulu grinned, eyes brightening to their usual grass green. He glanced around, nodded slightly to the forest, and all the weight seemed to slide off his shoulders. The smile was turned to Salvarias. "What should we do? Go woo some ladies to our beds? Get drunk off that brandaline? Braid each other's hair?"

Salvarias inhaled a deep breath. "I am far less adventurous."

"I could solve that problem. You ever been with a woman? I'm sure I can find a Watythm or two to catch your eye."

Salvarias's cheeks were hot with embarrassment. "Thank you for the offer, Okulu, but I must turn you down. Do not allow me to squelch your fun. The city of Catlin awaits your arrival with bated breath."

Okulu chuckled. "Nah, I'll visit it tonight. How about a stroll?"

Salvarias propped his aspen branch against the entrance to Catlin and limped after the merc. When the branch was nearly out of sight, Salvarias ignited his magic.

It's time to test our attempts, my wizard, his magic said. *For this, it's quite simple.*

Indeed. Salvarias closed his eyes, developed a picture of his staff in his mind, and beckoned for it. When he opened his eyes, the staff was in front of him. He caught it before it fell.

"That's new," Okulu murmured.

"It is the enchantment I am testing to prepare for the one I will cast upon your daggers."

Okulu's pearl white teeth flashed a smile. "Brilliant!"

"I am still far from perfecting it. Right now, my enchantments are linked directly to me. To make an object link to someone other than myself will be quite draining."

"No hurry," Okulu said lightly. "We'll be in each other's company for some time. You have plenty of years to figure it out."

Salvarias mused over Okulu's choice of words. Years. "Why years?"

"What?" Okulu asked.

Salvarias realized he had spoken aloud. "Nothing."

Okulu chuckled. "We're friends, Salvarias. That means we're going to know each other for a very long time."

Oddly, Salvarias could not find his voice to argue.

They eventually ended up at a stone slab that offered a bench-like seat to rest and drink in the sun. Neither spoke. Neither had to.

23

Talura tightened her robe as the spring breeze swept over the bedroom's balcony. It brought with it the filthy stink of Falar, all fish and sweat. She heard a rustle behind her and smiled when Edium's arms circled her waist. He dropped a kiss beneath her ear, recalling to her the pleasure he'd brought her last night.

"Morning," he whispered.

"Morning, love. How'd you sleep?"

A smile filled his voice as he spoke between pressing his lips against her skin. "Wonderfully. Any news from the girls?"

"Not this morning. But we just received a letter yesterday." She twisted around in his arms. The sun brightened his dark beard and hair, shimmering the flecks of emerald in his hazel eyes.

Edium sighed. "It feels like so long ago."

"How was your talk with Brenil yesterday?"

"He's a wealth of information when it comes to Wilhelm, though he never met Salvarias. I think we'll return home today. Between Idolar and Milred, I don't think there's much else to learn about the brothers. We've done what we came here to do."

Talura shook her head. "No, I want another day. There are some statements from Baker Jyfil that have sparked my curiosity." She smiled at her husband. "From what you've learned, do you approve of the brothers?"

Edium raised his gaze to look over her head at the ocean beyond. "I feel I've known Wilhelm his whole life. Any father would be honored to have him take his daughter. When the time comes, I will embrace him as my own son."

"And Salvarias?"

"I don't know him. He's as mysterious to me as the cause of thunder. If Wilhelm requested it, I would permit Salvarias in our home and would treat him with respect." He shifted his gaze to her. "You adore him."

Talura ran her nails through his short beard. "Yes, I do. I find him ... enchanting. Milred said it took her a mere month of knowing the young man to warm to him. He's serious in nature, but some of his deeds show that his heart is as vast as Wilhelm's."

Edium grunted. "I don't see it. All I see is a reserved, aloof boy. I haven't even gotten a good look at his face. It's always shadowed in that damn hood of his. He's hiding something ... I can feel it."

"There are reasons he keeps to shadows. I learned from Milred that his eyes are unique. According to her, the irises are large enough that no white can be seen. And she said they move and look more like a creature than human."

"Move?"

"Like curling smoke from a fire. She couldn't describe them any other way. She said any person seeing them felt as if they could fall into his gaze, as if he devoured all that existed within them, uncovered all their secrets."

Edium snorted. "That's ridiculous. How come you didn't mention this yesterday?"

Talura grinned. "You didn't give me a chance to talk when we returned home."

Edium's eyes glinted with familiar desire. Tilting back, she obliged him a view of her figure through her thin robe, and smiled up at him through her eyelashes. He bent and kissed her softly. The way his lips parted hers had the same effect it did when first she'd tasted him at the young age of seventeen. Her knees quivered and her stomach fluttered, sparking a heated desire between her thighs.

Lifting her in his embrace, he turned toward the bed.

"There's much we need to do today," she breathed.

Edium laid her on the bed and slid his hand under her robe. "It can wait."

A knock on the door prompted an irritated groan to rumble in his throat. "What is it?"

"A visitor, my lord," Brenil called.

Edium rose and faced away from her a moment before he flung open the door.

"Apologies," Brenil said. "He said he was looking for his nephews, the Laybryth brothers, and was told you knew where they were."

Talura hopped up from bed, snatched a dress, and darted behind her changing curtain.

"Thank you," Edium said. "We'll be down in a moment. If you would be so kind, please show him to the sitting room. Have a few guards standing by in the adjoining room. When it comes to those brothers, I'm not going to trust anyone looking for them."

Brenil nodded. "A wise decision. I'd hate to see any harm come to Wilhelm. He's a good lad."

"Thanks, Brenil. And send in my wife's attendants."

Their door closed. Her husband's worried thoughts were nearly audible.

She changed quickly and sat in front of a mirror as her attendants hurried inside. The two girls braided her hair in a matter of a few breaths and added jasmine flowers. After Talura checked herself over in mirror, she gave her thanks to the girls who left arm in arm.

Talura turned to see Edium lounging in a chair and smiling at her. "Let's go," she said, moving in front of him and holding out her hand.

Edium bent forward and lifted her foot to rest on his knee. Grinning, he picked up her dagger from the table next to him and slid his hands up her calf, past her knee, and to the center of her thigh. He fastened the weapon while trailing kisses up her leg. Once she felt it tightened, she lowered her leg and leaned over to kiss him.

"Tonight, my love," she whispered, "you may finish what you just started."

"It'd be my pleasure, my lady."

Edium rose, offered his arm, and led her downstairs. They passed through the adjoining chamber where five guards were posted. In the sitting room, a man stood in front of the window overlooking the garden. He was tall, broad-shouldered, and wore voluminous slate-blue mage robes.

"Good day," Edium said.

The man turned and smiled, extending his hand. "You must be Lord Edium Bellerum." The man's face was handsome—extremely so, painfully so.

Edium shook hands. "I am. And who might you be?"

"Mafarias. I'm Wilhelm and Salvarias's uncle."

If one did not know Edium, they wouldn't notice the tension in his shoulders, and one wouldn't hear the deadened malice in his voice when he spoke, which somehow always seemed to come across as a friendly drawl. "Ah, I've heard of you from Humar, as well as Idolar and Jyfil."

"All good, I hope," Mafarias said, grinning widely as if he were free of worry.

"On the contrary," Edium said, his smile growing.

Mafarias chuckled, though it sounded forced. "Whatever you've heard must be a misunderstanding. I was told in Serinity that you knew where my nephews were. I'm anxious to meet up with them. We were separated in—"

"I'm well aware," Edium said. "Sit, let us talk."

Mafarias's smile was quizzical, but he sank into a chair. Talura took note of his dusty clothes. He must've just arrived.

"Can I interest you in an ale or fruit?" Talura asked.

"Spirits and magic don't mix, my lady," he said. "Water and food of any kind would be most welcomed. I've not had a decent meal since I left your city."

Talura motioned to a servant standing in the doorway. He scurried off.

"So tell me how you escaped," Edium said. "From what I heard from Humar, there were near fifty soldiers on your tail."

"Slightly less," Mafarias said. "I killed a few. I barely escaped Reffil and lost them in the mountains. I knew Salvarias was headed up river so I followed it to Acklar. That's where I received Humar's message that everyone had survived the attack. I waited until his next letter, which he sent from Serinity. I heard Salvarias was the one who warned you of the blackfurs. I was happy to see your city unharmed save for a charred meadow."

"Indeed," Edium said. "Salvarias was instrumental in our victory, as was Wilhelm. I've never seen a man fight as well as he."

"He is talented."

"I'm surprised you know of his skill," Edium said coolly. "From what I've heard, you abandoned the boys. After their parents were murdered, you didn't return. Nor did you seek them when they were taken to mine in the mountains, forced into slavery for five years. Whipped, beaten, and mistreated. I must admit that I find your timing ... suspicious, and I find your care ... hollow."

Mafarias reclined in his chair and laced his fingers together. "Let's drop the pleasantries, Edium. I don't have to answer to you. You don't know me, nor do you know those boys. A man who sits in his wealth and has allowed his own daughters to roam the countryside in such perilous times will not judge me. Now, I would appreciate any information you have as to the whereabouts of my nephews."

"Go to Oblivion," Edium growled. "You don't deserve those boys and the knowledge of where they are. You've done nothing but show up in their lives when it's convenient for you."

Mafarias rose from his chair. "I can see we're not going to get anywhere. I bid you good day."

Talura rested a hand on her husband's. "Please wait, Master Mage. You must understand that we care for the boys. We spent quite a bit of time with them in Serinity, and our findings here show us that both are very special. They've earned a deep place within our hearts. We're simply concerned for their safety."

"If what you say is true, my lady, then it would behoove you to tell me where they are."

She smiled weakly. "You have a right, as their uncle, to know."

"I won't—" Edium started.

Talura held up her hand. "But I regret to inform you that we don't know their location."

Mafarias raised an eyebrow and glanced at Edium. "I don't believe you."

"I'm insulted you would think a lady of my station would lie," Talura said evenly. "I assure you, Wilhelm and his friends left without any indication as to their end destination. We've received some letters from our girls, and it appears they're heading east. That's all we know."

Mafarias rubbed his forehead and cursed under his breath. "That boy is too damn cautious."

"I assume you're referring to Salvarias?" she asked.

Mafarias nodded. "He doesn't trust many. He probably told Humar and manipulated him into silence."

Talura bit back her sharp defense of the young man. "Humar is not a man easily manipulated. Perhaps he saw value in Salvarias's need for secrecy. Regardless, I fear no one besides those in Wilhelm's company know of their location. We offer our home to you until we receive another letter from our daughters. Hopefully, it'll provide additional information."

Mafarias bowed. "You are kind, my lady. I accept your hospitality."

Edium growled.

She tugged her husband up and curtsied to Mafarias. "Please excuse us. Food will be brought in shortly."

Mafarias tilted his head and returned to a chair.

Talura led Edium from the room. Once they were out of earshot, he went into tirade about her offering their home. She listened until his anger fizzled out and his voice calmed.

"He doesn't deserve to know anything," Edium muttered. "He left those boys on their own. He's their only family, and he's done nothing for them."

"There's no point in playing games with him. We don't know where the brothers went. We don't know what it is they seek. Telling these facts to Mafarias won't do any harm. Not to mention, Humar might try to reach the mage. If he does, we could learn more. We need to build an open, sharing relationship."

Edium rubbed his cheek. "I hadn't considered that."

She smiled at him. "I noticed rational thought had left you."

Edium chuckled. "Sorry, love. I guess ..." He sighed and slouched against the wall. "I guess I grew fonder of Wilhelm than I'd thought. I don't want to see the boy hurt."

She kissed him lightly. "Your heart is the reason I married you, dear. Now, I'm going back in there and will try to smooth things over with our guest. Hopefully, I can earn his trust, and he'll share information with us."

"Just be careful. There's something about him that rubs me the wrong way."

She kissed him again before leaving for the sitting room. When she entered, she found Mafarias devouring slices of rosemary bread and yellow cheese.

"You'll have to excuse my husband," she said.

Mafarias rose from his seat and bowed. He swallowed a few times to rid his mouth of food. "Of course, my lady."

"Please sit. And call me Talura."

He returned to his chair and resumed his eating, though he did so more politely. "It seems your husband has a temper."

"He cares for the brothers."

Mafarias snorted. "Surely not Salvarias. Few warm up to the boy that quickly."

Again, Talura had to fight off her retort. "Salvarias is a unique man. He deserves no less care than Wilhelm."

Mafarias paused in his chewing, and his gaze intensified. "You're the first person to say so."

"I find that a shame. I must admit, I do tend to see people differently than most. I ... well, without sounding conceited, I have an ability to uncover certain traits in people. It's not always available to me, but when it is, I have an instant response to those I meet. Some I adore, some repulse me, and others I care neither way. The moment I laid eyes on Salvarias, I knew he was special." Talura blinked rapidly a few times, feeling her head swim for a breath. She'd never disclosed her ability to any except her husband. Smiling, she changed the subject, thankful Mafarias seemed uninterested in her statement. "Surely his mother knew what a unique child she'd birthed."

He shrugged. "He refused affection from all except Wilhelm. It's the boy's own fault. If he would open up a bit, people probably wouldn't be so intimidated by him or find him so unsettling."

"Are you saying Ashra didn't care for her son?"

Mafarias's brow crinkled, and the corners of his mouth turned down. "You may think you know Salvarias, my lady, but I assure you the boy doesn't invite affection. Matter of fact, he shies away from it. He never allowed another besides Wilhelm close to him."

"And Tobin, from what I've learned. The man raved about Salvarias to Idolar quite often. When the boy finally spoke, Idolar said Tobin came in the next morning with a ridiculous smile on his face and told any that would listen what a curious and soft-spoken boy Salvarias was. It seems the young mage became affectionate with Tobin."

"No," Mafarias said. "Talked to him, perhaps, but not affectionate. The boy doesn't permit anyone to touch him besides Wilhelm."

"Affection is not always physical contact, Mafarias."

He laughed lightly. "No, my lady. Not always."

Forcing herself to relax, she chatted with him about nothing important; weather, the price increase of beef, the shortage of barley. It must've been an hour before they fell silent. She was the one to break it. "Was Ashra your brother's daughter? Or sister's?"

"Pardon?" Mafarias asked.

"Ashra—from what I've learned—called you uncle as well. What was her relation to you?"

"Oh." Mafarias rubbed his cheek. "Sister's daughter."

"I've been told Ashra's mother is dead."

He nodded. "Taken by creatures when Ashra was seventeen, I believe. I sent her to live with Jyfil."

"Why not care for her yourself?"

"My life isn't one for a child. I wanted to give her a stable home."

"If her mother was taken, did you search for her? Are you certain she is dead?"

Mafarias nodded. "I am. No woman ever taken has escaped or been rescued. What I bestowed to Ashra was finality. We even had a funeral. It was important to me that Ashra not be left guessing. No child should endure the uncertainty that comes when one doesn't have a body to bury. She was just a girl."

"It must be hard to lose a sister."

"It is."

"And what of the brothers' grandfather, Ashra's father?"

"Oh, um." Mafarias shifted in his chair and coughed. "He died some time before my sister was taken. Tragic plowing accident."

"So they were farmers?"

"He ... didn't own one himself. He helped another farmer."

"Oh, I'll have to hunt him down."

"Tragically he died as well. No living heirs."

She arched an eyebrow. "How truly horrible."

"Times are difficult."

"Did the brothers ever meet him?"

Mafarias laughed lightly. "No. And, you'll forgive my hesitant responses. It's been some time since I spoke of it. Neither Wilhelm nor Salvarias ever asked questions about them. I think Wilhelm is too used to the unknown, seeing how his father abandoned him. He's not a curious boy."

"Based on the number of books Salvarias's reads, I think he's a very curious young man."

He shrugged. "Perhaps. But the boy never talked to me. Actually, he's only talked since his rescue from Zeeas."

"How lonely for Salvarias."

"Like I said, Salvarias's issues are created by himself."

"Are you not fond of the young man?"

Mafarias pursed his lips. "I care for him in my own way. It's hard to be close to a boy who won't allow it. Wilhelm ..." Mafarias chuckled. "Now that's a young man I adore."

Though Talura rarely used the might of her powers, she thought now was as good a time as any to break her promise of not invading another person's mind. She reached out to Mafarias, probing his heart and soul. He spoke the truth of Wilhelm. He loved him as an uncle would. However, with Salvarias, his concern wasn't out of love but ... necessity.

"Lunara has her mother's powers," Mafarias murmured.

Talura quickly withdrew. "Pardon?"

"Lady Lunara did the same when she first met me."

Talura looked away, trying to hide her shock. Lunara had never told her.

"You know enough of me to see my care is genuine," Mafarias said, leaning close to her. "If you know where the boys are, I beg you, tell me."

Talura gazed into his eyes, so beautiful, so enchanting. His voice was like the caress of a lover, and his smile immersed her mind in a fog. "Tell me," he whispered.

"I've told you," she breathed. "We don't know."

"Those boys are extremely important to me. You'll tell me if news comes?" he asked.

She nodded, unable to find her voice. His fingers caressed her cheek, and he smiled.

"Thank you, my lady. You should rest. You look peaked."

Talura nodded and rose from her chair. She moved through her estate as if submerged in a cloud. When she reached her room, she settled into bed. Sleep claimed her quickly.

She woke to Edium's worried voice and her brain thumping in her skull.

"Are you all right?" Edium asked. "You look pale."

She nodded, trying to shake the haze lingering over her vision.

"Fine, dear. I was merely tired."

"How was your conversation with Mafarias? Did you learn anything new?"

She forced herself to sit up. "Nothing. We talked of the weather." She frowned. "And ... and barley, I think." Honestly, she didn't recall much of the conversation.

"You were in there a long time to simply discuss such mundane things," Edium said, smoothing a lock of hair from her face. "I'm going to send for a healer."

Talura nodded. "Please. I have a terrible headache."

UNUPTURE STARED at the women huddled together in a cell. All wept and looked at him with fearful gazes.

Running his hands over one another, he thought of Salvarias's light voice and dark eyes. It'd been two days since Unupture had used his powers to create, and his will was failing. His power ate away at him, weakening him to the point his body shook. He swallowed, feeling as though cotton was stuffed in his mouth. He doubted Salvarias truly understood. It was like leaving a man in a desert for a week and then offering water. How could the man refuse?

Clutching the wall, he turned from the women and took a lurching step. His stomach heaved, and he leaned to the side and rid it of its contents. Once done, he ran the back of his hand over his mouth. He barely kept upright as he rounded the corner and entered another room. Caged animals squealed and growled, beat themselves against the bars of their prison. Grabbing at anything to keep upright, he went to the nearest cage and removed a trembling rat and squirrel.

"Shush," he whispered to both as he released his power, transferring the seed of the rat into the squirrel. Both wailed and twisted, contorting their bodies as Unupture's powers created new life. Breathing heavily, he slouched at the instant relief that cascaded over him. His trembling subsided, and his stomach calmed. Gently, he returned the creatures and stepped outside the room. An octril was waiting.

"God has summoned you," it said.

Unupture patted the octril's shoulder and smiled. "Thank you."

He left the dungeons and glided down the halls of the stronghold, sweating waterfalls in the warmer upper levels. He hated the swamp. How anything survived here, he didn't understand. Those things that sustained some semblance of life were of the unsavory: alligators, lizards, poisonous snakes, toads, and rats the size of house cats. Birds cawed in the stagnant air, but he'd yet to see one due to the continuous fog that clung to the ground, making visibility scarcely fifteen feet or so. No breeze ever came to rid the swamp of the stench like decayed flowers and molded mushrooms.

He envied the army stationed by the lake, the star-dotted sky they gazed at each night, at the gusty wind that cleansed the air they breathed, and of the various life that skittered across the ground and soared overhead in the open plains.

Running the sleeve of his robe across his forehead, all he could do was hope for some sort of victory. For which side, he didn't care. He just wanted it to be over.

He entered the throne room, but God was nowhere in sight. He strolled toward the dais, half lost in his thoughts. His mind wandered to Salvarias and the dreams they had shared. They were the happiest moments Unupture had ever experienced. They talked for hours, and he was beginning to believe in himself a bit more. As if he truly might have the power to deny his master.

Sounds, one moist like bare feet in mud, and the other like crunching bone stopped him. From behind a pillar, a line of blood meandered along the stones, snaking around lumps of moss and sprouts of vegetation that had pushed between stones.

Unupture turned on his heel, but before he made it a step his master spoke.

"Come, Unupture. Tell me what you've learned."

He bowed his head and turned around. "Nothing, Master. The young man continues to battle my powers. He's not yet ready."

"This is taking longer than I thought. I'm disappointed." God emerged from behind the pillar. He was free of blood save for a single drop clinging to his chin. "When will he be ready?"

"Soon, Master. Perhaps two more visits."

"Perfect timing."

Unupture cocked his head. "Pardon?"

"Sansis is on his way to claim the boy."

"He didn't mention," Unupture said, battling to keep his voice even.

"They've been trailed since Tripir and have been in the company of my servants for days. We decided to test their abilities. The brothers alone bested twenty-five of my most highly trained octrils. The battle taught us much. Tonight, thanks to the help of the barbarians, they'll be ours."

"How did you find them?"

"Some of our soldiers pieced together their little party in a tavern. The Soul tried to hide his mark, but the soldiers were not fooled."

Unupture's heart beat rapidly. "You sent Sansis?"

"Yes. Why? Are you displeased I didn't choose you?"

Unupture shook his head. "Sansis's mind is warped. He wants the mage for his own."

God arched his perfectly shaped eyebrow. "You know this for a fact?"

"Yes, Master."

"Sansis is my most trusted servant. What you accuse him of would lead to his death."

"I am aware, Master. Dethal would agree with me."

"Ah, I've sent Dethal as well. He'll ensure the boy is brought to me."

"And what of the others?"

God shrugged. "In exchange for the barbarians aid, I've promised them the boy's companions."

"A wise plan," Unupture said.

"I summoned you to tell you the Four have risen. They are conferring with one another and reacquainting themselves with Arden. Whatever they require, see to it."

"I assume Sansis hasn't found the other Guardian and Protector?"

God frowned. "No, he has not. What's worse is calling the Four has drained my powers remarkably. I must obtain the stone lest I waste away into nothingness." He waved his hand. "I must rest."

Clearing his throat, Unupture motioned hesitantly to his chin. "You have a ... a spot of ..."

God wiped the red speck from his chin. His black eyes saddened when he turned to the pool of blood on the floor. "It was not always so."

"Pardon?" Unupture said.

God sank to the first step on the dais of his throne. "I was not always this ... this creature." Unupture gaped at the tears brimming in God's eyes. "I was once carefree. I was once loved. Now look at what I've become. Look at what I must do. What I must eat to survive." God buried his face in his hands and spoke in a voice thick with sorrow. "I did it for him. I loved him. And he left me as this! A monstrosity!"

Unupture took a step forward, hand outstretched to offer comfort. Suddenly God sprang to his feet, face twisted in rage, streaked with tears, and his eyes carried so much pain that Unupture ached in sympathy.

"Leave, fool!" God belted, thrusting his arm toward the exit.

Unupture recoiled, stumbling backward, tripping over tree roots.

"Leave before I take your soul!" God yelled, marching toward Unupture.

Unupture whirled around and fled the room. He barreled through corridors, shoving aside octrils and black-armored soldiers. He bolted into his room, latched the door, and flung himself on the bed. Gripping the pendant in his hand, he slipped his consciousness free of his body.

24

Wilhelm's stomach grumbled at the long hours deprived of food as they entered Anard's home. At first, he caught a whiff of bread and onions, perhaps potatoes. He was about to groan in utter agony until the delicious gamey scent of venison and beef permeated the air. As he inhaled deeply, his stomach belted out an approval.

He swore the last few days had weakened him. How his brother survived on something as insubstantial as vegetables he'd never know. He felt Salvarias's amused gaze and winked. "Finally," he muttered. "I think I was near death."

Salvarias shook his head. "I am not hungry, Brother. I would rather rest. Feel free to eat my portion."

Wilhelm was about to argue until he caught sight of tired, dark rings framing Salvarias's eyes. "Sure, Salv." Mussing his brother's hair under his hood, Wilhelm grunted when a strong fist landed in his ribs. "Ouch!"

"Is the wolf staying in the woods?" Humar asked.

Salvarias nodded. "I will find him in the morning." He bowed to their friends and hobbled from the room.

Wilhelm trailed behind Varila, enjoying the lovely view, and entered the cozy dining hall where platters of food awaited them. He blinked aside joyful tears and chose a seat closest to the wonderful roast of mouthwatering venison. Though an impressive spread, it didn't compare to Talura's idea of dinner. He missed her meals, but what he reluctantly admitted he missed more was the sense of family he'd felt while staying at the Bellerum home. Something he'd missed after his parents' deaths.

"I think some brandaline is in order," Frink said. "Travel's been hard, and we could use a strong drink to relax our muscles."

Anard and Hunz gathered mugs and scooped a thick, dark liquid from a cask setting on a nearby table. The aroma was potent enough to burn nose hair.

After everyone had a drink in hand, Hunz raised his glass and said, "To Lord Boughlar and his friends."

All raised their glasses. Wilhelm downed his in one swallow, coughing instantly as the liquid seared his throat. His empty stomach was set aflame and sweat beaded his forehead.

Okulu laughed, clapping his knee. "Brilliant!" He shoved his flask and glass at Hunz. "Give it all a refill!"

Humar coughed while patting Durak's back to help the Cavrul breathe. Varila, who'd been smart enough to sip hers, wiped tears from her eyes. Lunara sniffed it, then set aside the cup, not even bothering to taste it. Okulu was quick to snatch it up and down it. Neithelas stoically cleared his throat ... several times.

"Potent," Humar gasped.

Frink and Hunz chuckled, taking glasses and filling them once more while everyone helped themselves to the food. With restraint, Wilhelm kept his plate to normal size.

It wasn't long before he'd chugged down four glasses of brandaline and wolfed down three portions of food. Sometime after his sixth glass, he'd cleared the table of any piles of food that had been left untouched. After his eighth glass, he found himself singing alongside his friends, something he'd never tried before, but was surprised how wonderfully he sang. Lunara must've been wincing from the volume of his baritone. He tried to sing softer.

Okulu's voice was lovely, nearly as lovely as Neithelas's. The two, arms wrapped around each other's shoulders, carried tune after tune. The three Cavruls sang enthusiastically out of key, hugging one another.

Wilhelm didn't remember what glass he'd finished when Varila moved to sit in his lap. With each new song and glass of that damn good liquor, she allowed his hand to inch farther up her smooth thigh.

He wasn't sure when it was that he noticed Neithelas had passed out, hunched over the table. Nor did he know how much more time went by before Varila sagged, limp, in his arms. Humar's head thudded on the table.

"I think we've had enough," Lunara said, tugging Wilhelm.

"She's right," Okulu said, swaying to his feet. "I hate to says it, but we probably need res'." Okulu toppled to the ground.

"Drunkard can't hold his spirits!" Durak roared. The instant he sprang to his feet, he fell headfirst to the ground, softened by a weak attempt from Hunz to keep the Cavrul upright.

Wilhelm, however, was functioning just fine. He stood and flung Varila over his shoulder. The problem was, there appeared to be three sprawled out forms of Okulu blocking his way. He gently lowered Varila to the table and assessed his situation. The three Okulus kept moving. He batted Lunara's hand away. He wasn't drunk enough that he couldn't find his way to his brother. He'd never let his mind be too muddled by spirits. One had to be alert for danger.

He took a tentative step and rested his foot on something soft that grunted. "That's not right," he muttered.

A thump and muffled scream issued behind him, and white-hot pain flared along his side. He swayed and rubbed where it hurt. It was wet. Frowning, he pulled his hand back. There was some sort of red liquid on it.

"Stab him again," someone snarled.

Another bolt of pain leached a cry from him. This one shot up his back. The room spun violently, and he almost lost his balance.

"Brother!" Salvarias called.

His brother was standing in the doorway. Wilhelm's vision blurred.

Salvarias's gaze darted around the room. His lips moved. When he raised his hand, he winced and exhaled sharply. What looked like a hazy cloud of blood puffed around Salvarias. He cried out, clinging to the doorframe. His aspen branch clattered to the ground.

Wilhelm grimaced when a jolt of pain staggered him. He suddenly felt very unstable, and his legs were nothing but limp snakes under him. He'd have passed out if fear hadn't kept him grounded.

Dark liquid matted Salvarias's robes to his side, glistening in the flickering torchlight. A trail of blood smeared down the doorframe as Salvarias slid to the floor.

Anard stepped from behind Salvarias, holding a dagger dripping blood. "A paralyzing poison," he said to Salvarias. "I've heard it burns hotter than flames."

"You son of whore," Wilhelm snarled.

A weight landed on Wilhelm's shoulders, yanking him backward, causing him to trip over chairs. Pricks of pain spread over his shoulders. Darkness pulsed in his vision.

"He's not going down!" someone yelled.

"Keep stabbing him!" Frink said. "The poison will work soon."

The room dimmed. Sweat ran down Wilhelm's face. His hearing droned in and out, revealing snippets of wet tearing that sent a new bolt of pain along his shoulders. He saw his brother's eyes brimmed with tears, chest rising in short gasps. Wilhelm's legs crumbled from beneath him.

"I'm sorry, Salv," Wilhelm mumbled.

He thudded to the floor, feeling nothing. A man robed in slate-blue stepped from the shadows. His hair was as fire-red as his beard.

"Hello, my star pupil," Dethal said.

Wilhelm's wept "no" faded into a horrible dream full of his brother's screams.

~

LUNARA STIRRED awake to a pounding head swimming in syrup. Opening her eyes, she blinked several times in an attempt to remove the fog blurring her surroundings.

She found herself in a cage with iron bars that wrapped overhead. Beneath her was a warped wood bottom. Her friends were with her, each bound to different bars, out of reach of one another unless they were to stretch a foot. The only one absent was Salvarias. None of her friends were awake and none appeared hurt except for Wilhelm. Blood trickled from wounds covering his shoulders, as if someone had used him for a pincushion. Three punctures along his side still oozed blood. He was pale, sweating, and breathing heavily.

Frowning, she twisted her wrists, wincing when metal shackles flayed her skin. Striving to fully awake, she shook her head, wrinkling her nose as the stench of wet dog assailed her. Looking over her shoulder, she noticed horse-like beasts hitched to a flat wagon bed that carried her cage. The creatures' sandy-colored, shaggy fur draped to the ground, and their heads were wide like a cow with nostrils mere slits like a snake. Fur concealed their eyes, and their hooves were flat and round. She recognized the grynfs from drawings in a book she'd read about the barbarian lands.

Straining against her shackles, she touched the welt on the side of her head. The contact sent a shot of pain into her brain and yanked her fully awake as she stifled a groan.

Another odor assailed her, an atrocious stench of piss and something else she couldn't place. Tears welled when her gaze steadied on the horror beyond her cage.

Corpses littered the streets of Catlin. Men, women, and even children had been slaughtered. It was a city of blood and broken bodies, excreted bodily fluids and groans of the still dying. Limbs with no home, entrails with no owner, and dull, horrified gazes stared at Lunara.

To the side of her cage, a small Cavrul boy wept over the gutted body of his mother, not seeming to care that her insides were soiling his shirt. A man crawled on his elbows next to a woman who was missing her head. A dog sat by a Cavrul man who'd lost his arm and lay in a pool of blood. The dog whined.

Her tears broke free.

She craned her neck to look over her shoulder. Rows of cages housed those Cavruls she assumed had surrendered. They were women and children, elderly men and boys too young to lift a weapon.

"We had an agreement, ye foul mage!" Frink roared. "You said all we had to do was deliver the boy here! We kept our end of the deal! Release us and Lord Boughlar!"

Frink was being held by what she guessed were barbarians. The savages were nearly as tall as Salvarias with a trim, muscular build. Their bodies were not left to the imagination. A strip of stained cloth covered their private area, connected to a leather belt adorned with what appeared to be bones. Their leathery-tanned skin mirrored one another, and their hair, eyes, and pigment blended into the same sandy brown. Some faces resembled the average Erthla while others were deformed: one eye socket lower than the other, lopsided ears, jutting chins too large for the jaw, or more gum than teeth. If she had to guess what a horrible disease smelled like, it'd be them. Stale, unbathed, and reeking of vomit and piss.

A savage stepped toward Frink and plunged a crude sword straight into the Cavrul's chest.

Lunara whirled her head away, and her gaze found the cage next to hers that housed Salvarias. Blood stained the wood floor, and Salvarias's wheezing breaths reached her ears. His gaze was locked on her.

"Hello, Salvarias," a voice said.

Salvarias's fear sprang up like a blow, blinding her a brief moment. Through fuzzy vision, she saw a man robed in burnt orange walking toward the cage. Translucent skin offered view of his tendons and veins, and three long white hairs clung to his balding scalp. One look into his soul showed her a mind lost to madness and sadistic pleasure. Behind him, a mage robed in slate-blue followed. The man's hair and beard were fire red. She recognized Dethal from Serinity.

"When will you trek into the caves?" the orange robed man asked Dethal when he stopped by Salvarias's cage. The man's gaze was fixed on Salvarias, as was Salvarias's on him.

Dethal shrugged. "When Wilhelm wakes, we'll see if we can learn of our mage's gift. Once we have all we can get, we'll turn Wilhelm over to the barbarians and leave with the boy."

The man nodded. "Wise. You think the boy will talk?"

"We'll soon find out," Dethal said.

As they waited for Wilhelm to wake, barbarians hauled the dead Cavruls, including Frink, into another cage, unceremoniously piling the bodies on top of each other. Those who'd clung to life were not given a choice. Barbarians ended their suffering. The dog tried to flee when a barbarian approached, but the savage loosened an arrow and the dog tumbled to the ground, its high-pitched yelp echoing in the city.

Lunara combed the bloodied streets for Adok, but the wolf was nowhere in sight. Their horses were tethered to the back of another cage.

As the barbarians continued their massacre, Lunara tried to tear her gaze from the nightmarish sight but couldn't. At one point, she'd been sick without realizing it. The stench of it brought her from her trance. Burying her face in the crook of her elbow, she wept. When the city was silent, she wept harder, feeling the loss of so much life in her very blood, the emptiness it left in the world.

It seemed an eternity passed before Wilhelm stirred awake. When he groaned, Dethal sprang upon the cage quicker than a roach to the pantry at night.

"Get him out," Dethal commanded.

The commotion of the barbarians entering the cage must have awakened Varila. Her eyes popped open, and her gaze swept over the scene. When she saw the barbarians, she quickly turned away. But it was too late.

One of the savages paused before grabbing her hair and yanking her head up. His smile chilled Lunara. "Varila Bellerum," the barbarian said. "Chesrick will be overjoyed to see you." The barbarian yelled to the men mulling about, "The woman is not to be touched. She's a gift to the king."

"Bellerum?" Dethal said. "You're the daughter of Edium?" Varila spit in Dethal's face. The mage ran a sleeve over his cheek. "It seems events are turning in our favor rapidly." He motioned to a black-armored soldier. "Send word to Lord Bellerum that his daughter was taken to the barbarian lands. Tell him she'll be handed over to King Chesrick." The soldier saluted and went out of sight. Dethal turned to Varila. "You'll be our bait."

"What do you have against my father?" Varila snarled. "He doesn't even know you."

"No, he doesn't. But we know of him. He's building an army. That displeases my master."

Varila snorted. "I think your master is a coward. Hiding in some hole, no doubt. Tell him to come out and enjoy the fun. I'd love to drive my sword through his heart."

Dethal chuckled. "Swords cannot kill him, Lady Varila. He's a god." Dethal turned to Lunara. "Ah, you must be his youngest." His eyes narrowed. "I remember you. Our mage was quite devoted to your safety at the base of Serinity."

"She's a gift to my king," the barbarian said. "To have both of Edium's daughters will please him."

"No," Dethal said. "I've already promised you the rest of them." He leveled a finger at Lunara. "She's mine."

Wilhelm was dragged out of the cage without a fight, eyes unfocused, and seemed unaware of his surroundings.

"I don't suppose you'd let me take the boy?" the man in orange asked Dethal.

Dethal's lip curled. "When did it happen, Sansis? At what point did you become so infatuated with him that you would risk the wrath of God to take him?"

Sansis shrugged. "It has been some time. It was after you used a poison on him, made him delusional. I was in his cell performing my normal dissection when he looked at me. He smiled and said: 'I love you too, Father.' Have you ever seen that boy smile? Have you ever heard him speak with affection? I've had the privilege. Ever since, I've wanted him for my own."

"Why do you trust me not to tell God what you've told me?" Dethal motioned the group of barbarians hauling Wilhelm toward a post supporting a roof overhang, and called to them, "Tie him up. Make sure he's secure."

Sansis smiled at Dethal. "Because I was the one who persuaded him to give you power. You owe me a great debt."

Dethal shook his head. "I was promised greater power than Shamir. Than Perl. Than Quinal. Yet they possess more than I."

"How do you know this?"

Dethal smirked. "Because I sensed them in the stronghold, you imbecile! How stupid do you think I am?"

"It's of no matter. God gave you all the power you could command without going insane."

Dethal jabbed a finger toward Salvarias. "How is it that he has more power than me? Even more power than the three mages?"

"I don't even have a mage's power. I can only heal. And Unupture? Even more sad. He can create, certainly. And he can penetrate the mind, uncover secrets, but he has no defense. You're the luckiest of all of us. If I were you, I'd stop complaining."

Dethal sniffed and folded his arms over his chest. "I'd like to know how you're still alive. You served Veedran. Veedran! Over a thousand years ..."

Sansis shrugged, and his gaze distanced. "Veedran granted many long lives. I am the oldest. Unupture is a mere few hundred years younger than I. Veedran was a powerful god." Sansis shook himself. "Our god is nothing compared to him."

"God is weak indeed. Yet there is something about him that tells me there is more to him than he reveals. I think he hides his power. I think he's older than you. I think he's more powerful than the boy. Tell me how he compares to Veedran."

Sansis sighed. "Veedran was a ruthless god. Full of savage power. If not for his hate, I think he would have easily defeated Zerana. He didn't have the mind for tactics, much like our master. The Four were all that kept us at war for hundreds of years."

"Did you ever meet him?"

Sansis shivered. "Once. He was nothing more than a red cloud of hate. No form to him, no compassion. Hate and a lust for blood, a hunger for souls. Raw and frightening. I pissed myself." Sansis chuckled, but it sounded haunted. "I pissed myself at the sight of my own father. But I'll tell you this. I *wanted* to be around him. I'd give anything to hear him speak my name again. To feel his touch. He ... he was a god, and any in his presence were humbled by him. Even Wilhelm here would be hard pressed to escape Veedran's allure. I once met Zerana and was equally humbled by her. Like Veedran, she had no form, just light ... beautiful, blinding light. Only the higher gods have that kind of allure, that sheer beauty that makes even the fairest maiden look like a hag. Crutar and Lakvra are nothing compared to them."

"Have you not felt that with our God?"

Sansis smiled at Dethal. "I have somewhat. His beauty, his presence. Perhaps he is a lesser god, like Crutar or Lakvra. I doubt we'll ever know."

Once the savages bound Wilhelm's arms around the post so he hugged it, they ripped off his tunic. Lunara averted her eyes at the sight of his scarred back.

Dethal turned to Salvarias. "If I were you, as soon as the poison wears off, I'd start telling us exactly what your gift is."

With a wave of Dethal's hand, a barbarian stepped forward holding a whip with sparkling metal fastened to it every few inches. Salvarias's gurgled pleas were unintelligible. The barbarian leaned back, coiling the whip behind him, and used his weight to snap it against Wilhelm's back. Bright blood dripped from the laceration.

Lunara buried her face in her arm, flinching when the whip cracked again. She counted twenty-six strikes before she heard Salvarias rasp, "Visions."

Gathering her courage, she looked up. Blood painted Wilhelm's back, staining his trews, and the sight of his meaty flesh made her gag. Tatters of skin hung off him and he sagged limp in his bindings, unconscious.

"What'd you say, boy?" Dethal said, smiling smugly at Sansis.

"Visions," Salvarias repeated, his voice stronger. "I have visions."

"Tell me all of them," Dethal ordered.

Salvarias went on to provide detailed descriptions, times and places of his visions; the one of his father dead, of Serinity in flames, the one of the men attacking the inn when she was searching for him, the warning of the hidlu in the caves, additional visions of the attack on Serinity, the revelation of blackfurs, the disclosure of the location of the orb, and finally a vision of a massive army. Dethal and Sansis listened closely, only asking a handful of questions, mainly regarding exact times. Once Salvarias finished, Dethal and Sansis shared a look that told Lunara they'd learned whatever it was they sought.

When the two men were whispering to one another, Salvarias twitched violently and, in a blink, a shard of ice soared through the air and struck Dethal in the chest. The impact catapulted him backward, leaving a trail of blood along the street

"Brandaline!" Sansis screeched. "Drug the boy!"

Sansis bolted to Dethal's side and rested a hand on his forehead. The mage thrashed wildly, screaming, clawing at Sansis's arm. The hole in Dethal's chest smoked and sizzled as the skin melted closed. Dethal's final scream contained nothing but horrible pain. Then he went slack. By his torturous cries, he might've died from whatever Sansis had done. She couldn't tell.

The small bit of magic seemed to have drained Salvarias of life, and his exhaustion rang in her own bones. Black-armored soldiers leapt into his cage and roughly grabbed hold of him. He put up no fight, his eyes unfocused, his body limp. When the commotion stopped, Salvarias was on his knees. Four soldiers held his arms, one fisted a chunk of his hair, another squeezed his mouth open, and the last dumped the contents of a wineskin down his throat.

Salvarias thrashed and retched up half the contents before another soldier clamped a hand over his mouth to make him swallow. They continued forcing him to drink, though each time, Salvarias's fight waned. By the second wineskin, he didn't struggle and merely choked it down.

Once the soldiers were done, Salvarias crumpled in a heap, groaning and gagging up amber-colored liquor.

Sansis turned to Salvarias, eyes gleaming with triumph, though over what, Lunara could not discern. "Brandaline," Sansis said, "in case you were wondering, Salvarias. Strongest spirit known. I've heard any mage attempting a spell under the effects of liquor dies. Would you like to test the theory?"

Salvarias retched again.

"I thought not," Sansis said. With a smile on his lips, he spoke to the cluster of armored soldiers. "Your men will stay behind with Dethal. He'll sleep for the night and well into tomorrow. Once he wakes, he'll provide direction. I'll follow the barbarians to Avulin with the boy."

The barbarian who appeared to be in charge shook his head. "The boy was supposed to stay with Dethal. My instructions were clear."

Sansis motioned to Lunara. "An incentive."

The barbarian grinned, a stream of drool falling between his lips. "Indeed. My king's reward will be great."

Sansis nodded. "We leave now."

Wilhelm was hauled to their cage and shackled. In no time, they lurched forward down the mountainside, leaving behind all the black-armored soldiers and Dethal.

The sight of Wilhelm's tattered body brought her a hopelessness she'd never experienced before. He was a formidable man to behold. He seemed indestructible. But now, blood flowed freely from his many wounds. His face had no color, he shivered, covered in sweat, and his usual steady breathing was labored and wheezy. He looked so incredibly vulnerable to Lunara.

Turning to Salvarias, she probed his mind, clinging to a hope that he'd be alert enough to help them. His magic was weak, fragile as a newborn, and fighting to keep connected to Salvarias. It was as if he were slowly being ripped in two. She fed the magic her strength, but instead of taking her offering, it lashed out at her, driving her back while protecting its connection with Salvarias.

The slightest surge of his magic sent a jolt of pain through him, echoed in her own bones, and he was violently ill. She withdrew from his mind as far as possible.

Throughout the day, her friends regained consciousness and cast Wilhelm worried looks, seeming to see him for the first time as a mortal man, one who bled as they. During the long hours of rocking down the mountainside, the constant strain Salvarias suffered eventually wore on her, and she had no more strength to stay awake. She merely dozed in and out of alertness.

It felt like eternity passed before the sun dipped beyond the horizon, casting the forest in deep shadows. The howl of a lone wolf chilled her while the owls' haunting question cooed all around. The forest floor was alive with snapping twigs and rustling leaves, escalating her fear with the unknown. The forest had always terrified her at night, but tonight it seemed more sinister.

The savages set up camp with quick efficiency. After the cooking fires were roaring and a huge kettle placed over the flames, several barbarians walked to the cage of dead Cavruls. Lunara stiffened in horror as they yanked a large Cavrul from the stack, stripped him naked, and used crude axes to hack the dead man apart. The savages gathered the Cavrul's members and tossed them in the kettle.

Lunara leaned her head against the bars and retched. Varila was talking to her, but she couldn't make out the words. Shock stalked the edge of her awareness, and it took all her strength not to give in to it.

As the night waned on, a fraction of the barbarians turned in for sleep while the rest patrolled camp. When the moon shone high, a shadow glided around tents and sleeping bodies. A desperate hope of rescue welled up in her. Maybe a barbarian was sympathetic to the Bellerum family. Maybe he would set them free.

Like a hurricane gust of wind, her spark of hope snuffed out when the figure stopped beside a fire, the orange flames illuminating Sansis and the hungry look in his eyes. He lit a torch and serpentined to Salvarias.

"Hello, boy," Sansis whispered as he unlocked the cage. "It has been some time since we've been together."

Salvarias scrambled backward until he was crammed in a corner. The intensity of his fear pounded her own heart as his emotion seemed infused in her blood, sending a rapid thumping in her ears to muffle sound. Pushing her mind to extremes, she withdrew from him further.

Sansis secured the torch to a holder welded to the cage and slipped inside. "I have missed you. Did you miss me?"

Salvarias shook violently. "Brother ..."

"No," Sansis said. "Scream or call for him and I'll make him pay for your mistake. Fight me and I'll do the same to him as I do to you."

The flames of the torch flickered off a blade clutched in Sansis's hand and glistened a trickle of drool falling from the corner of the man's mouth. He wrapped an arm around Salvarias's shoulders, pulling him from the corner to cradle him. With care, Sansis cut open Salvarias's robes to his waist and peeled back the fabric to display the mage's mutilated body.

Lunara desperately looked around for help, but only Varila was awake.

"We can't do anything," Varila whispered. "Don't look."

By morbid need, Lunara turned her gaze to Salvarias.

"He's yours no longer, Unupture," Sansis whispered. He grabbed a pendant hanging around Salvarias's neck and yanked it to break the tie. After stuffing it in his robes, he lifted his dagger to Salvarias's torso.

Salvarias trembled so violently he seemed locked in convulsions. "Please," he breathed.

"Shush now," Sansis said.

Lunara watched, stunned to immobility, as Sansis eased the blade into Salvarias's stomach. Dark blood trickled down Salvarias's skin, and his cry of pain was a deep exhale, fists balling Sansis's robes. As if carving a roast, Sansis sawed down Salvarias's stomach while crooning a soft lullaby she'd heard mothers sing to their babies.

Sansis set aside the dagger, licked his lips, and sunk his hand inside Salvarias. Lunara clamped a hand tight around her mouth to keep from screaming as the man withdrew some lump of red from Salvarias's stomach. Salvarias's feet scraped the wooden floor as he twitched and clawed at Sansis.

Sansis broke his lullaby to whisper, "You'll only make it worse, Son." Resting a bloody hand on Salvarias's forehead, Sansis's lips moved yet Lunara heard no words. Whatever he said caused Salvarias to flail, and his teeth clenched together to stifle his cry. He arced, causing more blood to gush out. When Sansis ceased his whisper, Salvarias went limp, and his gaze drifted to her. Sansis plunged his hand inside Salvarias again. The mage hitched and winced.

Tears raining down her face, she smiled her sweetest smile at Salvarias, conveying all the comfort she could in her eyes. He never looked away.

25

Varila stared absently at the deep lines the treading wagon left in the fine-grained sand. Dunes rose and fell like an ocean; never ending and mercilessly hot. Air was oppressively silent, baking the desert like bread in an oven. The sun had just started its nightly dance with the horizon, a bulb of orange in the dusky sky. She wasn't looking forward to night. The desert was as windy and cold at night as it was stale and burning during the day.

Her wrists were swollen in her attempts to free herself. Matter of fact, all her friends sported the same flayed skin around their shackles. Her arms ached, and it'd taken deft maneuvering to keep blood flowing up to her fingers.

She looked over at Salvarias, curled up in his cage. Blood stained the wood, and his robes were crusted with it. She couldn't get the image of his stomach closing up by some whispered command of Sansis. The skin had crawled together to form a new scar on top of the old ones. How he lived, how he didn't scream at the top of his lungs while he'd been gutted, she would never understand.

"Why aren't they listening to you?" Okulu rasped. "The mighty Bellerum family! What has your name gotten you now!"

"Shut up!" Varila said. "I told you we don't have a good reputation with these bastards!"

"Enough," Humar said. "Tell us everything you know, Varila."

"Again?" she growled. "I've already told you."

"Yes, again."

Taking a deep breath, she rushed through the story she'd told Humar twice already. "Twenty or so years ago, my father had gotten himself stranded in the desert, and the barbarians found him, took him to Avulin, and King Chesrick ordered his death by fighting in the arena. My father challenged him to a duel for his life, but the king doesn't fight. He sent in his second in command. My father beat him. That earned him the king's respect, and his life was spared. Ever since, my father has tried to start up trade with the barbarians. He thinks he can help grow them from cannibals into a prosperous, civil race. Chesrick has yet to listen. I visited once, about two years ago, and Chesrick told my father he wanted me for his queen. My father knew he couldn't openly deny Chesrick. The king would've taken me by force if he did. So my father said yes to buy us time. That night, we escaped—barely—and we've not returned since."

"Tell me about the games," Humar said.

"The fights are held in a pit that's as massive as it is inescapable. Seats circle it so the entire city can watch. Every man, woman, and child attends. The bouts are usually between wanderers who've been captured or creatures that roam the deserts. If they're ever out of combatants, they'll go to the outskirts of the desert and snag a few. Mages are very common since they find it amusing to send the bastards out there while doped up on spirits. The ale makes them go mad if they're stupid enough to use magic."

"You've heard of the treaty?" Humar said.

Varila snorted. "A treaty made over a thousand years ago by a dead goddess."

"She tried to save them."

"I don't remember the whole story," Varila said. For some reason, conversation made her feel less doomed.

Humar shifted his arms, wincing. "It was during the Long Wars.

Veedran had surrounded this area and trapped the city of Avulin, not permitting any to leave the desert. He told them Zerana had betrayed them, left them to burn alone in Avulin. Secretly, day by day, he killed crops and herds of livestock. When the people were at their lowest, he taught them cannibalism. He made women objects. Boys, warriors. The elders, meals. He was the one who developed the games, bringing captives from Zerana's army to fight in the arena he built for them—the one he made inescapable. He handed over his own creations to keep them occupied. When he gained their loyalty, he unleashed them on Zerana. She fought them and won, but they were beyond her aid. Instead of killing them, she banned them to the sands. She promised to allow them to live out their days in peace if they promised never to take sides in any war, to stay in the desert. They agreed, and for over a thousand years they've kept to the treaty."

"Me guess is a thousand years in solitude don't appeal to them anymore," Durak growled. "The goddess was stupid to make such a pact."

Varila grunted her agreement.

Once the sun dipped behind the undulating dunes, the barbarians stopped for the night. The light breeze started when the last ray of orange faded from the starry sky.

"Finally!" Okulu exclaimed. "A breeze!"

Varila didn't say anything. Soon enough he'd be cursing her for the cold night. Already she felt the fine grain sand awaken under the wind's calling, sticking to her sweating skin.

The barbarians set up a quick camp and lit cooking fires. Her stomach churned at the foul stench of their stew. They didn't offer her or her friends any, though she would've turned it down if they had. Human was something she never wanted to try.

After the savages ate, a group went to Salvarias's cage and forced another wineskin of brandaline down him. He hardly fought. Once they left, he crawled to the edge and shoved his finger down his throat until he retched. At some point, he passed out.

She tried to sleep, but found herself staring at Wilhelm's pale face, shivering body, and the blood caked around his wounds. He'd come in and out of consciousness, though never seemed of his right mind. At least the blood had stopped oozing. When not occupied with him, she gazed at her sister who looked to be in some kind of shock. Lunara rarely took her eyes from the mage nor had she spoken.

As if a crack of thunder ripped across the sky, Wilhelm jolted awake. The moonlight reflected in his dull amber eyes and danced off his enraged scowl. "Salv?" he said in a cracking voice.

"In the next cage," Humar said. "Rest. There's no chance of escape and you'll need your strength."

Wilhelm craned to look over his shoulder at his brother's cage. "How long?" he asked.

"A few days," Humar said.

Leaning his head against the bars, Wilhelm closed his eyes. He might've dozed off. She couldn't tell for sure.

And the night trickled on. The wind picked up, sending biting sand to sting her, a chill to set in her bones, and filling her mouth with grit that crunched between her teeth no matter how hard she pressed her lips together. Okulu's curses blended with the howling wind.

Once the barbarians went to sleep, the man in orange rose from his bedroll, plucked up a dagger and key, and went to Salvarias's cage.

"You bastard!" Okulu rasped. "Come over here and try that on me!"

Wilhelm opened his eyes.

"Go to sleep, boy," Humar said soothingly.

Varila fought down bile rising in her gorge when Sansis cradled Salvarias like a mother holding a terrified child. Salvarias no longer fought, he merely lay there, gazing at Lunara. Unable to watch, she turned her head when Sansis slipped the knife into Salvarias's stomach. The mage didn't scream. The only sound was his feet scraping the floor.

"No!" Wilhelm choked. Chains rattled loudly as he wrenched his arms in an attempt to break free. His struggles cracked his crusted back and fresh blood leaked from his wounds. "Leave him alone."

Sansis seemed not to hear as he studied a dripping lump of red in his hand. When he returned the organ, he rested a hand on Salvarias's forehead. The mage thrashed wildly, his screams nothing more than grunts through his clenched teeth.

Wilhelm ceased struggling and shifted until he sat sideways, able to watch without craning his neck. Resting his forehead against the bars, he said, "I'm here, Salv."

Salvarias's gaze jerked to Wilhelm. "Help ..." Blood pooled up from his lips.

"We'll get through this," Wilhelm said. "I promise. I want you to relax. Stop fighting."

Salvarias's writhing calmed, and his gaze locked onto Wilhelm.

"Good." Taking a deep, wet sounding breath, Wilhelm spoke in a tone that sounded as if they were enjoying a meal around the family table, sharing warm stories. "Remember that time in the guardhouse? The game we played? Remember how mad Tobin was when he found us: me dressed in armor, you shooting off a spell? We got into a lot of trouble." He chuckled. "I don't remember Father ever being so red."

Varila closed her eyes as Wilhelm continued the stories of times when the brothers were alone, reading together or playing a game he'd devised. It was hard to believe such a vibrant young boy was the same cold-hearted mage caged next to her. As Wilhelm's stories continued into his early teenage years, she even found herself smiling, imagining his crooked grin saving them from any punishment Tobin might've thought to carry out. It was clear their father had loved them; so opposite of the stories she'd heard about their mother. Those always revolved around Wilhelm, never both brothers. She took notice he never mentioned her in his tales this night.

Near an hour passed before Wilhelm stopped. She looked over to see Sansis leaving Salvarias's cage. The mage lay curled on the floor, gazing at Wilhelm while choking up bile and blood.

"Take a deep breath," Wilhelm said. "It'll be all right now. He's gone. You're safe."

Jerking in a small breath, Salvarias reached out his hands and moaned something that caused Wilhelm to exhale a soft sob.

"I know, Salv. I can't. I'm sorry. I want you to get some sleep."

Tears fell from Salvarias's eyes as he closed them. It didn't take long for his head to toss and soft mutters to start.

Wilhelm buried his face in the crook of his elbow, and his shoulders shook. She wasn't sure how long it was before he passed out.

26

Humar stared at the bright moonbeams glittering off the sands, seeming to reflect up into the starry sky. It would have been a beautiful sight if his heavy manacles and empty stomach hadn't reminded him that no beauty existed in his situation. The last few nights of Salvarias's disembowelments in the wretched desert had dwindled Humar's bonfire of hope to a tiny flame that barely warmed his soul.

"We'd be better off dead," Durak said softly.

Humar glanced at the others sleeping. "Perhaps. Perhaps not."

"Hope blinds you, ye thick-skulled knight."

"I'm not ready to give up," Humar said.

Durak gazed over the sands. "This not be how I imagined dyin'. I saw a great battle in me future."

"A blacksmith dying as a soldier? I didn't know you thought of such things. Or is this from your time as 'lord'?" Humar had yet to forgive Durak for keeping such a secret, or from the fact the Cavrul still refused to talk about it.

"Death is as real as me bones," Durak said. "Me not ready to face it. We be enemies of the worst kind."

Humar regarded his friend a moment, noticing a spark of fear never seen in the Cavrul's dark eyes before. "I'm not ready to die either, my friend. We just need to stay alive. We're all good with a sword. I don't think there's much we can't handle. Once Edium learns Varila was taken, he'll send his whole army to rescue us. We just need to survive."

Durak grunted. "Me be agreeing with you if Wilhelm was better."

Humar glanced over at Wilhelm's sallow complexion and ragged breathing. The boy had caught fever.

Okulu twitched violently, and his eyes popped open. He looked around before sagging against his shackles. "We're still in this forsaken desert?"

"What'd ye think?" Durak snapped. "Zerana herself would rise from the grave and whisk us off to a tavern?"

Okulu sighed. "I could really use an ale."

"It be doin' ye good to be sober," Durak said.

"Actually, it's made my temper rather nasty."

"Hush," Humar said. He nodded his head toward Sansis crossing the camp.

"Sick bastard," Okulu growled.

As Sansis passed within reach of their cage, Okulu snagged hold of the man's robes. "Why don't you try that on me and leave him alone for a night? I think you'd find I can be as entertaining."

"I don't believe so, half-breed. You're not nearly as enchanting as our friend." Sansis ran his fingers through Okulu's hair. "And I doubt your pain tolerance would match his."

Okulu yanked his head back and spat on Sansis. "Leave him alone."

"Oh, you prefer to test my theory? Is that it? Then let us do so." Sansis reached through the bars and rested a hand on Okulu's fore-head. As if his fingers possessed the strength of ten men, Sansis pulled Okulu's head to the bars and leaned down to whisper in his ear, soft enough none of the others could hear. Whatever he said caused Okulu's eyes to widened and flash with fear. Sansis straight-ened himself and said, "Now, let me heal you and purge the poison from your liver."

Okulu's screams tore from his throat while he flailed wildly under Sansis's apparently ironclad hold. Humar gagged at the foul stench coming from the bile-looking liquid dripping from Okulu's pores.

"Look at me," Sansis hissed.

Okulu's eyes were drenched with fear when he met Sansis's gaze.

"Talk to me again and I'll show you my true power."

Piss spread across Okulu's pants.

"Much better," Sansis purred. The man removed his hand and strolled over to Wilhelm.

Neithelas shifted his foot as if to offer Okulu comfort but he jerked away, curling himself up as much as his shackles would allow. He buried his face in his arm and wept as if he were a small child.

"Touch that man and I'll rip your throat out," Varila said to Sansis.

Sansis smiled faintly. "He'll die if he does not receive aid. I do so at the barbarians' behest." He slipped his hand between the bars and rested it on Wilhelm's forehead.

"No," Salvarias rasped.

Sansis frowned. "I said he'll die. He requires healing."

"No," Salvarias repeated, using the bars to pull himself to a sitting position.

"But—"

"No," Salvarias said. "Do not touch him."

Sansis arched his scraggly eyebrow. "You know what I want, boy."

Salvarias glanced at Wilhelm for a long moment before he said, "If I agree, you must give the knight my herb pouch and allow him to tend to my brother. You must never touch any of them ... ever. And you must find a way to free them."

Sansis scoffed. "I cannot free them. They were promised to the barbarians."

Salvarias shook his head. "Then I will not go with you willingly."

"And I'll heal your brother."

Salvarias's jaw clenched. His gaze switched from Sansis to Wilhelm. The defiance usually sparkling in those eerie black eyes dwindled. "So be it."

"No," Humar breathed. The boy was Humar's only hope of

finding the figure behind the darkness spreading across Arden. Salvarias was the key.

Sansis smiled. "You're a brave boy." He went to Salvarias's cage, unlocked it, and slipped inside. Kneeling in front of the mage, Sansis opened his arms. "Come to me." Salvarias's gaze flickered to Wilhelm before he shifted himself next to Sansis. The man encased Salvarias in his arms and smoothed the mage's hair. "Think of all I can do now. With no need to keep you whole, I can truly enjoy our time together." Sansis caressed Salvarias's mouth and around his eyes. "You no longer need a tongue to perform spells. And eyes ... but you have such beautiful eyes. Perhaps I'll leave those alone." Sansis's smile was filled with warmth, but, nevertheless, Humar shuddered. "We'll live a long happy life together, Son. I have one additional requirement. You must call me Father."

Salvarias looked up at Sansis with hate pouring from his eyes.

"Think of your brother," Sansis whispered. "Say what I want to hear."

Humar looked over at Wilhelm, intending to wake him so he could dissuade Salvarias from his path, but Wilhelm was already awake, his gaze focused on Salvarias, eyes glistening with tears. His lips parted as if to protest, but no words were spoken, and his expression melted into tortured helplessness.

Humar closed his eyes and awaited the one word that would decide the fate of Arden. If Salvarias went with Sansis willingly, Humar had no doubts he'd never find them. There would be no hope in tracking down whoever this "god" was before it would be too late, before cities would burn, just as the boy's visions predicted. Salvarias would hand over Arden on a silver platter to save the pain of one man. Not even death, merely to spare Wilhelm pain. The boy couldn't be so selfish. Surely, he knew he couldn't give himself to Sansis.

A whisper floated to Humar's ear, a soft word that, for the second time in his life, extinguished his flames of hope.

"Father."

LUNARA BLOCKED out Salvarias's soft moans as she smiled at him, trying to offer all her love in her gaze.

Wilhelm's anger must have boiled so deep that it'd blanketed him in silence, his stare more like a vicious animal than human while he watched Sansis explore Salvarias's insides. Neithelas talked soothingly to Okulu who still wept, trembling as if stranded in an ice storm. Bile continued to seep from him, dampening his hair and clothes while adding a stench worse than a decaying corpse.

"Someone's out there!" a savage shouted.

Sixty barbarians darted from their blankets and spread out around the camp and cages to form a circle.

"There!" another barbarian called.

Just on the outskirts of the camp, gliding through the sands as if they were a finely cared-for road, was Adok.

"Adok!" Lunara cried. With the wolf's help, they could be free. Salvarias wouldn't be victim to Sansis, wouldn't be taken from her. She simply needed to help the mage. Salvarias could save them.

Her mind awash with hope, she whirled around to Salvarias and burst into his mind. His pain nearly debilitated her, but her momentum pushed past it and she drove her strength straight to his magic.

Salvarias's scream was followed by one of her own. She felt as if some beast had sunk its claws into her body and was slowly ripping her in two.

"No! You mustn't use magic!" Sansis ordered.

Salvarias clutched his head in his hands, and a river of blood flooded from his nose. Lunara tried to wrench her mind free from his, but they were too linked, his mind fastened to hers. Another cry tore from her throat. She looked down at her body, sure to see her skin parting open and bones splintering in two.

"No, girl!" Humar ordered.

It was too late. She'd made a terrible mistake.

Sansis, eyes wild with fear, rammed his dagger in Salvarias's chest and ripped down. Blood sprayed the cage, and Salvarias convulsed violently. Sansis's cry was nothing short of sheer panic.

Hot blood spewed from Lunara's lips and spread across her stomach and chest.

"What have I done?" Sansis cried. Tossing aside the dagger, he clamped both hands over Salvarias's forehead. "Fight, boy! You must fight!"

Death was threatening to claim them both, ice cold and hungry. For the first time, Lunara felt what Sansis was doing each time he whispered to the mage, hand on his forehead. Sansis was using his powers of healing. But the power was not benevolent, and Lunara choked out a scream.

It was as if Sansis were *inside* her, groping her, touching places no one should ever touch. His powers were savage in their mending, cruel in their handling, and felt like she'd been stabbed a thousand times, tossed in a boiling pot of tar, and then sewn up with no care for her suffering. The pain covering every inch of her robbed her of vision, drowned out her own sobs and Varila's cries, and thrust her into violent convulsions.

She didn't want to experience it anymore. Death would be more welcomed. Refusing to fight, she helped Salvarias who was already reaching for the darkness.

"Fight, boy!" Sansis ordered. "I will kill your brother if you don't!"

Those words fueled a resolve in Salvarias, and he battled to live. He shoved away the clutches of death even as she clawed for its embrace. Sansis's powers were ebbing as Salvarias's body could no longer endure the mending. His heart, not yet whole, was left weak and failing. The loss of blood threatened to haul him into Oblivion. She felt it all within her body: her own heart laboring to beat, her limbs weak from blood loss.

She wept for him to let them die, pleaded in his mind, screamed at him to end it. He must've realized the depth of their connection, how far she'd dove into his mind, and the extent of her pain. One forceful shove from him freed her. The tearing of that deep connection stunned her. She sat void of emotion and physical feeling, as if floating in air where nothing could touch her. Then she plummeted toward reality. Realizing she'd merely experienced a vague understanding of Salvarias's suffering reduced her to sobs. Now, he screamed in a pain beyond her comprehension. Hating herself for leaving him alone, she tried to merge with him again to lend her strength, but he refused her.

Weakly she raised her head to see the cut on Salvarias's chest sizzle closed. She retched at the feeling of her skin melding together, the sense of her insides shifting into place, the ache in her heart from the hole that had been pierced into it.

Salvarias, cheeks streaked with tears, met her gaze. In one look, she conveyed she was fine. He, however, was not. The power to completely heal Salvarias was beyond not only Sansis's ability, but surpassed what Salvarias could endure. His body simply couldn't handle further pain, and Sansis could do no more to rectify his mistake.

Dreaded darkness came for her: the kind that brought nightmares, the kind that cut her open. Now she understood what she dreamed. It was what Salvarias dreamed. Pain. Such horrible pain.

HUMAR'S GAZE darted between Lunara and Salvarias. Both had succumbed to sleep, both were covered in blood. Varila's sobs and the barbarians' alarmed voices rose in unison, confusion making the savages halt their pursuit of the wolf and send a group to check the camp.

It took several moments for Sansis to calm the barbarians and explain the boy had tried to use magic. Once all had quieted, Sansis crawled into Salvarias's cage and covered the boy with a blanket, smoothing his hair and whispering in his ear.

Humar's disgust drove his gaze from the bloody sight to the rest of the barbarians returning from their chase. He was beyond relieved not to see a wolf dragged into camp.

Sansis tucked a blanket around Salvarias, left the cage, and locked it.

Wilhelm, voice dead of emotion, eyes as angry as a blazing fire, whispered to Sansis, "I *will* kill you."

Sansis studied Wilhelm a short moment before leaving the cages and disappearing into the dark night. He returned a short time later with the boy's herb pouch, unlocked Humar's shackles, and passed the pouch through the bars. By Sansis's haunted eyes, one could've sworn he'd lost a child of his own loins.

Sansis turned to Wilhelm. "I'm sorry. Truly. He mustn't use magic when under the influence of brandaline. I-I panicked. I can't cure his mind if he were to go mad. I had to distract his focus." Sansis looked apologetic when he said, "You must know that I love the boy. Once I get supplies from Avulin, I'll take him and leave this cursed land. I'll give him all the love I have. Those who seek him will never find him. Nor will you should you search for him. I'll give my life to keep him safe. He ... he's mine. You must see that truth. He has agreed to it."

Wilhelm's silence spoke louder than any words he could've uttered.

Sansis sighed deeply, all semblance of a weak man dropping, replaced with a glare of ugly cruelty. "So be it. You've made us enemies. I hold no ill will toward you, but I'll not look over my shoulder every step I take." He glanced at Salvarias. "The barbarians' sporting games are not easily won. I might stay in Avulin to see you meet your death. With you gone, Salvarias will have no reason to flee, no need to break our agreement."

"My brother isn't the only one who sees things," Wilhelm whispered.

Sansis's brow furrowed. "You have visions?"

Wilhelm nodded. "I'm having one right now. I see you sprawled at my feet. I see my sword dripping with your blood. Your body is sliced apart, but it's not random. No. There's a pattern. Every scar I inflicted upon you matches what you did to my brother. I'll gut your sorry ass, and there won't be anyone there to save you."

"How vivid," Sansis murmured. "I assure you, if a mere sword could kill me, I would've been dead over a thousand years ago."

Moonlight flashed on the blade of Sansis's dagger before he slid it into Wilhelm's side. The boy didn't even wince. Sansis glanced at the barbarians mulling close and shifted to block their view of the knife. "A present for you, Protector," he whispered. "A slow bleeding wound that, even if stitched, will continue to spoil your insides." Sansis leisurely withdrew the dagger, twisting it as he did. That time, Wilhelm winced. "Sleep well."

Sansis glided to his bedroll. Once he no longer looked their direction, Wilhelm exhaled sharply and slouched against his restraints.

"Check on Lunara," Varila ordered Humar.

He gently peeled back Lunara's hair and placed his hand over her mouth. Her breathing was strong, and the life beat in her neck pulsed steadily. "She's fine," he said. "Wilhelm, I—"

"Leave me alone," Wilhelm growled. He rested his head on the bars and stared at Salvarias.

Humar sank to the ground, holding herbs that would do no good.

Doomed. They were all doomed.

27

U nupture winced when God flung his hands up and shouted an ear-piercing roar of rage. Dethal kept his mild gaze locked on God, even allowing the edge of his mouth to curl in a contemptuous sneer as he knelt in front of the throne, courageously unshaken by God's spouting of every failure Dethal had ever committed.

Once God's rant reduced to a normal tone, Dethal cut in and said, "Unupture and I have told you before, Sansis has gone mad. You refused our warning. This isn't my fault. This isn't Unupture's fault. It's yours. You should've ended Sansis when he first nearly killed the boy in Zeeas."

God stopped his pacing and turned a cool stare upon Dethal. Moments passed where only the indignant croak of a frog punctured the thick air.

"You have just earned my respect," God purred. "For once, a soul willing to be honest."

Dethal laughed, but it contained no mirth. "I've been honest since Sansis first brought me to you. You've refused to listen. You only cared what that decaying monster said."

"Do not press your luck, Dethal," God said, sinking to his throne. "You've shown me disrespect. Don't take my lack of action as encouragement to continue. One more lapse and I'll feed off your soul. I'll take back what I have sacrificed to you, what gift I've bestowed upon you."

Dethal's defiant eyes flashed to submission. "Forgive me, Master."

God tilted his head. "Am I not a merciful master?"

"Yes," Dethal whispered.

"Where would Sansis take the boy?" God asked.

"I haven't a clue," Dethal said. "Perhaps he'll use his station to ensure the savages' cooperation. Once to Avulin, I suspect he'd stock up on supplies and leave Dalnar. But where ..." Dethal spread his hands.

"Do we have a portal to Avulin?" God said.

"No, Master. I used the one in the mountain to return here."

"We must send the God of Magic to rectify that situation for us."

"I will tell him," Dethal said. "I took it upon myself to send a soldier to the sands to carry word of Sansis's betrayal. He'll kill a hundred horses to beat the barbarians there. Sansis will be in for a surprise when he arrives."

"Wise," God murmured.

"There's more good news," Dethal said. "We have learned Salvarias's gift."

God's mouth gaped open, as did Unupture's.

"It was as I suspected," Dethal continued smugly. "I whipped the Protector until Salvarias confessed. I must say that this 'gift' has been nothing more than a result of his growing power. I think the boy is ... evolving."

"Tell me," God asked hungrily. "Tell me how he knows our plans."

"He has visions," Dethal said. "Some are merely paintings, if you will. Informational. Others are a play, performed out in his dreams and waking hours." Dethal listed off in detail all the visions Salvarias had confessed. "I have studied each closely, as well as the timing. I understand how he obtains them. It's you who supplies certain ones."

"Yes," came a whisper from the shadows behind God's throne. "I see your mind, mage. I see your conclusion. The blurred images are from another source, no doubt his growing power. But the ones played out before him are provided by our master, provided by the link they share. Yet how do you explain his vision of the orb? The timing of it appearing the moment he needed it?"

Dethal shrugged. "Simple. The stronger visions are when our master is focused with a clear goal. It's as if God drives the visions into our young mage's mind. The orb had eluded Salvarias because God wasn't focused on it. We didn't bother to think it might be in danger, so it was less relevant. Once Salvarias assumed he'd missed something, he subconsciously pulled from the link he shares with God. If the boy ever figures this out, he'll be truly unstoppable."

"And how do you explain the girl in his vision of Serinity?" the voice purred.

Dethal smirked. "He cares for her. No doubt the power that we've awakened supplies information he isn't even aware he seeks. He doesn't know his full capabilities. Furthermore, I don't think he can tap in to all his power. I sensed it in Zeeas. So much lies within him, but he has scarcely grazed its surface."

"You have a wise servant, Master," the voice said.

From the shadows, three of the Four stepped forward. Unupture hadn't seen them since the Long Wars, and the years had foolishly lessened his fear. But now as he stared at them, Unupture shook like a thrummed lute string, gritting his teeth to stay in control of his bladder, and forcing his lungs to breathe. All of them were in human form; legs and arms, a head and torso, but they had been forged from the bodies of Veedran's enemies, from some of the brightest of minds in Zerana's army.

Marro was nothing more than stark-white bones, writhing as if they were snakes, coiling around one another, constantly shifting and grinding together like smooth hunks of wood. The sound set Unupture's teeth on edge and raised the hairs on the base of his neck. Glowing red eyes burned from beneath its hood like smoldering coals.

Forged from the blood of enemies, Eludar was encased in skin crusted like cooled lava that wept crimson yet never soiled the creature's robes. It was inspired by the bloodleders, vile creatures in their own right. Just as they, Eludar's touch was death.

The third was Remnant, which was exactly what the name implied. Under its armor were the discarded tissue, muscle, and organs that Eludar and Marro didn't need. It was an appalling mass of gore that rose bile in Unupture's throat.

The voice from the shadows rose again, coming from a low smoldering red hue. "The Soul, the Guardian, the Keeper of Arden. You're fools to go against him. I advise you to bow to him and beg for his mercy before he unleashes his power upon us."

"No," God snarled. "I linked him to me! I made him what he is! The boy is mine! His power is mine!"

The glow stepped forward into the light. Unupture's control over his fear vanished and loosened his bladder as he stared at Devoar, the Devourer of Hope and Light, the Eater of Souls, the one rumored to have feasted on the body of Zerana. Heat simmered the air, creating a rippling aura around Devoar, reminding Unupture that melting the burning souls of Veedran's enemies had made the creature. Devoar was the ultimate strategic plotter, the most brilliant militant mind to ever exist. Armor, as much part of Devoar as the red pustule living inside that fed its existence, covered its form. The plates had the fluidity of water yet burned hot enough to melt a sword before it managed an inch inside.

Devoar's glowing lava eyes gazed out at the throne room, as if staring at an audience. "You did not make him, Master. *He* made him."

"You lie!" God snarled.

"Believe what you will," Devoar said to God. "The fact remains: The Guardian's mind isn't comparable to a human. His soul isn't weak. Your fight is near impossible."

"Near," God said. "But attainable."

Devoar tilted his head. "Yes, attainable."

In a voice heavy with uncertainty, Dethal said, "I've given another message to the savages. With us learning of his gift, there's no need

for the boy. His soul won't turn. He'll fight us till his last breath. So ..."
Dethal licked his lips. "I told the barbarians to kill him."

"What!" God roared. He marched toward Dethal, but Marro
plucked up the mage in one skeleton hand before God reached him.

"How cunning," Marro said, holding Dethal up by the arm like a
doll.

"Indeed," Devoar said. "Do not punish him, Master. His mind was
of good intention. He truly believes the Soul will never turn toward
our cause. I'm inclined to believe him. That doesn't, however, mean
the Soul is worthless. There are other ways to use him."

"Tell me," God demanded

"I can no sooner tell you than your mind will convey our plot to
our enemy. You must place your faith in me. You must let me sweep
over the lands by my own methods, which, based on your attempt, is
the wisest decision you could make. Your army could've taken over
Dalnar years ago. Your elaborate schemes within the caves have been
pointless. Serinity did not fall to you. Instead of lashing out, you
cowered like a beaten dog."

"I won't be defeated!" God roared.

"Victory comes with defeat," Devoar said offhandedly. "You
cannot achieve one without the other. Bygones. You must move past
your errors and embrace my words." Devoar turned its gaze to the
entrance of the throne room and smiled. "He is here. The Guardian."

Unupture whirled around to see a middle-aged man sauntering
in. His light brown hair glowed in the flickering torches, which lit up
his dark amber eyes. He was tall for an Erthla, covered in thick
muscle. Unupture immediately saw the resemblance to Wilhelm in
the bone structure and build. But this man wasn't the Protector,
therefore wasn't Wilhelm's father.

God bolted to his feet, his eyes wide and voice tight. "Guardian."

The man gave a flourishing bow. "The one and only."

God strode forward then snapped to a halt, gaze darting around.
"Where is your Protector?"

"He's not here ... not yet, anyway."

Unupture shrank into the shadows, using the pillars to hide his advancement on the man. The Guardian looked exhausted, dark rings around his eyes, a slump in his shoulders.

"Let's be clear up front," the Guardian said. "I don't have it on me. Kill me and you'll never know where it is."

"If you are dead, the stone will reveal itself to me," God said, though uncertainty hemmed his voice.

"No, it won't. I've got it in a nice little hiding place. You'll never find it."

God curled his upper lip. "What do you want?"

"I've seen the creatures roaming the lands. I'm no fool, and I can clearly see which side is going to win this." The Guardian's stance relaxed, and his smirk was that of a man holding the winning hand. "I also know I've never had an heir. There's no other Guardian besides me." The man tapped his crotch. "I've kept my seed free of a woman. I won't force another to endure what I've endured. My cousin wasn't so wise. But without another Guardian, I hope to free my Protector to live the last of his years with his son. Now, I've hidden the stone in a safe place. It's not even on Dalnar. So if I die, you'll never find it. Are we clear?"

God nodded.

"Wait," Devoar said. "Do not speak further."

The man looked Devoar up and down as if accessing a stock horse. "Well, aren't you an ugly one?"

Ignoring him, Devoar addressed God. "You forget. If your mind focuses too much, the Soul will gain valuable knowledge. I must speak to the Guardian alone."

God spewed what Unupture assumed were curses in languages never spoken on Arden as he stormed out of the throne room.

"How did you learn of us?" Devoar asked.

"The stone," the Guardian said. "It told me who its master was and showed me where to find him ... or it ... or whatever that thing was."

"And what is it you want in exchange for the stone?" Devoar asked.

"I want you to call off the Hunters, and I want my family safe."

The Guardian's eyes darkened. "Which, because of your little monsters scouring our land, is only my Protector and his son. But I want all our future generations protected from whatever you have in mind for Arden. I want us to be given land and peace."

"The Hunters were created but for one cause," Devoar said. "They cannot be dissuaded. They cannot be controlled."

"Deal's off," the Guardian said.

"Wait," Devoar said. The creature strolled over to the Guardian. "Tell me your name, boy."

The Guardian laughed. "I haven't been called 'boy' for years. Name is Perek."

"Come. Let us talk. Not much is known of the Guardian and Protector. With information, I believe I can help with the Hunters. As for your family's safety, I guarantee anyone of your bloodline or that of your Protector will never see harm."

Perek regarded Devoar for a moment, seeming unafraid, scrutinizing its words. Slowly, he nodded. "All right. What do you want to know?"

Devoar leaned conspiratorially in with Perek and whispered for quite a while. Try as he might, Unupture couldn't catch a single word. When Perek finally left, the other three creatures gathered around Devoar.

"What is the plan?" Marro asked.

"The Soul's doubt is as thick as his power. A trap is what we will set. We'll feed him false visions, leave a wake of death in our path, and break him down until he has lost confidence in himself. It's time for our army to march. We must send word to Vescar."

Unupture's doubts over Vescar's capabilities had vanished some time ago. The Loutsil knight was ruthless, and his mind a strategic vessel. The man's only weakness was the goddess, Lakvra. She'd seduced him to God's cause after he'd been kicked out of the Knight Council, though the task wasn't difficult. The man was all too eager to deal a wrath of vengeance upon the world he thought had forsaken him.

"Vescar will die trying to lead us to victory," Devoar said. "The man was a wise choice by God. However, God made a fatal mistake with Serinity. He should have sent Vescar, not the blackfurs."

"Edium Bellerum is the most influential force in Arden," Marro said. "God's failure could be our demise."

"Agreed. He has called us into a near unwinnable situation. I have told him to abandon Dalnar, but he has forced me to make one last attempt. If we fail, I don't want to spend time building an entirely new army."

"Divide it," Remnant said.

"A wise course."

"If we can get the Soul, why bother with a city?" Eludar said.

"There are other forces besides the Soul we must concern ourselves with. Only a fool would leave Edium Bellerum and the knight Humar alive. Lord Bellerum is a force unto himself. His care for his family drives him mercilessly to defend Arden. The knight ... he intrigues me. There is a determination to overthrow us that eats at him like acid. I think there's more to him than we know and that I can see. His emotions are hidden from me, kept close and confined."

Devoar paced, gauntlet-clad hands locked behind its back. "The Soul knows of the army, and he'll go there. No doubt, that was where he was heading. If he escapes Sansis, he'll resume his mission. When he finds our army gone, he'll follow their trail. We will leave death in our path. It's time the mind games begin. We must set traps for the Soul at every turn, we must plot assassinations for those who would oppose us, and devise new plots in anticipation of each failing. The Soul cannot foresee all and each will wear him down, chip away at his health and mind. If that's unsuccessful, we'll turn the Soul's focus from us to a new task. Of that, our friend Perek will ensure."

"Why not set a trap where the army is now?" Marro said.

"The Soul's mind will be on alert. He'll still be confident, sure of his visions, of his mission. Simple traps won't work. We must manipulate him, tear him down, make him question his every move. Make him see only failure. Then, he'll be vulnerable and willingly walk into our waiting arms."

"Sansis has broken the connection Unupture had with the Soul,"

Remnant said. "Finding the boy's fears has failed. Without that knowledge, our attempt to turn him will increase in difficulty."

"Sansis is our wolf," Devoar said. "His infatuation with the Soul has turned him mad. He'll be nipping at our heels until he finds a chance to tear us apart and take the Soul. At our first opportunity, we must kill him."

"Easier said than done," Eludar said. "Veedran made Sansis's healing capabilities ten times stronger for himself."

Marro nodded. "Indeed. He's a threat to our plans, as is the Protector."

"Ah," Devoar breathed, "the Protector, Wilhelm Laybryth the Undefeatable, as his reputation has earned him. He'll die before he lets the Soul be taken. He'll kill a thousand armies to save him. Their bond is stronger than any Guardian and Protector before them. But it's their bond that makes them careless, drives decisions that are not for the greater good of Arden. It's our blessing as much as our curse. It's time to look upon Wilhelm Laybryth as more than a mere obstacle. He's as dangerous as Sansis, Lord Bellerum, and Sir Humar. We must rattle his confidence, loosen his connection with the Soul, pry apart their devotion to one another. There are ways long forgotten by God that I must remind him of. It's time for our master to call upon his rightful claims."

"God's mind is weak, as is his powers," Marro said. "I'll lay down my life for his, but he's not the force I remember. He's vulnerable, afraid. V—"

"Hush," Devoar said. It turned toward the pillar Unupture hid behind and smiled. "We're not alone. Come from the shadows, Unupture."

Cursing himself, he stepped clear of the pillar.

"You've been a very unfaithful servant, Unupture." Devoar's eyes glowed brighter. "I see your conflict as clearly as I see the horrid goo that keeps you alive. You've stopped breeding."

"I ..." Unupture glanced between the Four, fear causing him to stammer over his words. "I ... I wanted the mage to trust me. I've been building a rapport with him. He ... It was working until Sansis interfered."

"Make no mistake, servant. I'll get our master victory. The Soul will deliver it to us, whether by his life or his willing agreement. Whatever you thought to achieve by befriending the mage isn't for the benefit of our master. Consider yourself under our scrutiny, breeder. If I were you, I'd guard my actions very closely. And I'd be very dedicated to enlarging God's army."

Devoar spun on his heel and marched to a table that had a map spread across it, the others following.

Unupture wrung his hands, hope falling to the pit of his stomach like a foul meal. He should've told Salvarias all he knew. He'd come to care for the mage. Not as a father. Not as a friend. It was something deeper. Something he'd never experienced before, neither given by him nor received from any. Love?

28

E dium stormed down the hallway of his estate in search of the mage. Ever since Mafarias had arrived, Talura had been assaulted by headaches after each visit with the man. She insisted Mafarias wasn't to blame, but Edium doubted it.

He found the man lounging on a chair in the garden. As always, Edium's anger simmered into a false friendliness. "Do tell me, Mafarias," he said, smiling broadly at the roach. "What have you done to my lovely wife?"

To Mafarias's credit, he looked genuinely surprised. "What are you talking about, Edium?"

"Don't be dull," Edium drawled. "She goes to her room with a headache after each of your visits. I find it hard to believe you two can sit and talk of the weather for hours."

"I assure you, I've not done anything to harm the lady. I would be happy to … look her over. I'm rather talented in healing."

Edium's stewing anger erupted into a raging volcano. Yanking Mafarias to his feet, Edium dealt a strong punch to the bastard's face. Mafarias reeled backward, hand clamped over his bloody nose.

"You'll never touch my wife! You stay away from her!"

"Edium!" Talura said, running up to them.

His stomach knotted at her pallid face and the dark circles under her eyes.

Mafarias waved her aside. "Your husband and I were getting better acquainted, my lady. It appears he's ... jealous of our relationship."

"That's it!" Edium yelled.

He pounced on the mage, taking them both to the ground. Edium was experienced in hand-to-hand fighting. Obviously, the mage wasn't. He didn't even try to defend himself when Edium slammed his head into the ground and then promptly beat his face.

Hands grabbed Edium and hauled him off. Mafarias rolled on to his side, gasping, and looked up with sheer hatred, a look Edium happily returned. The mage shoved himself up.

"Those boys are not your sons!" Mafarias roared, blood dripping from his split lip and pooling in his eye. "Their blood is the same as mine, not yours! Your wife is wonderful company, and I'd never harm her. She's one of those rare people who wouldn't spit on me if she saw me walking down the street."

Edium tried to yank free, but realized four men were holding his arms. "Bastard! You don't care for those boys! You left them! And my wife—"

Mafarias leaned forward and whispered in Edium's ear, "I don't like you, Lord Bellerum. I think you're a wealthy merchant who thinks he can buy whatever he wants. Those boys aren't for sale. They're my blood, not yours. I do care for them. And all your money will never buy you a different answer. If not for your wife, I'd have sent you to Oblivion. I love Wilhelm. And I guarantee I care more for Salvarias than you. So your accusations have no weight with me."

Mafarias strolled to Talura and eased her to a bench. "Your husband merely cares for you, my lady. I'll be fine."

Talura gazed at the mage with a subservient smile. Edium had never seen her submissive. With his entire being, he knew Mafarias had done something to her.

"My lord!" Brenil cried, barreling into the garden. "One of your

Cavrul merchants has just arrived. He's in bad shape and says he has urgent news about your daughters."

Edium yanked free and marched toward the exit. Mafarias was on his heels.

"You're not coming," Edium growled over his shoulder.

"On the contrary, I am. My lady?" Mafarias called, holding out his arm.

"Yes," Talura said, hiking up her dress and sprinting after them.

Edium stormed after Brenil, fury boiling his blood and causing him to step on the servant's heels.

Brenil led them through the packed streets, parting through the destitute crowd toward the front gate. Seeing the people fleeing small towns planted a seed of guilt in Edium. Without his daughters standing before him, he began doubting his choice to shut Serinity's gate to those who'd lost so much to the creatures plaguing Dalnar. But his girls' safety was all that mattered. Falar had allowed any seeking refuge inside her walls, and crime had never been higher. Shops were vandalized, merchants were run out of business, there were food shortages, and the guards were unable to obtain any semblance of order. Soon, the city would be a wasteland like Hadrium.

When they shoved their way out of the front gate, Edium saw the guard Idolar kneeling beside Rurk, Edium's newest Cavrul merchant who'd been exploring recently developed Cavrul cities. Rurk's tunic was stained with blood.

Edium sank by Rurk's side and took his hand. "Rurk, it's me, Edium."

"All he's been saying is that he must speak with you," Idolar told Edium. "I've got a healer on the way. We didn't want to move him in his condition until someone got him stable."

Rurk opened his eyes. Recognition glittered in their black depths, and he clutched Edium's hand. "They came for us. Barbarians and men in black armor. They slaughtered women and children, butchered men. I hid. Like a coward, I hid! I didn't want to die. I waited until the screaming stopped, and I snuck out of the hole I'd hidden in. Blood covered the ground, but there were no bodies. No bodies! No bonfires! No graves!"

"Easy," Edium said. "Take a breath."

Rurk shuddered in a breath and continued. "There were tracks ... like wagons leaving the city and other tracks, like men on foot heading into the caves. I-I didn't know what to do. I followed the tracks out of the city and caught up to the wagons. Inside were half the citizens of Catlin. The dead bodies had been loaded into cages and savages were ..." Rurk gagged. "Eating them. Then I saw them."

Edium's stomach twisted. "Don't tell me," he said between clenched teeth. "Not my girls."

Rurk nodded. "Prisoners. They hadn't been hurt badly, and the savages had yet to lay hands on them. I-I-I didn't know what to do. I stole the horses in the night. A wolf helped me! A wolf! It actually created a diversion, and the savage guarding the horses went to check. I-I got them free and saw the wolf watching me! It didn't attack me. It just watched me. Its eyes! It knew!"

"Easy," Edium said, squeezing Rurk's hand.

"I-I fled. I was attacked by unholy creatures and robbed by thieves. In Flitver I learned you were here. I drove a few of the horses into the ground, but I got here."

Edium raised his head to see the familiar horses of his daughters' companions, except the brown mare of Okulu and the charcoal gelding of Durak. The black stallion's flank had a good slice on it.

"How long ago?" Mafarias asked.

"Four days," Rurk said. "I'm sorry, Edium. I should've saved them. But there were over a hundred savages. I didn't know what to do." Rurk's grip tightened. "I didn't know!"

Edium squeezed Rurk's shoulder. "You did the right thing. The only thing you could."

A plump woman parted through the crowd and knelt by Rurk.

"I'll pay you anything," Edium said to Milred, his voice dull in his own ears. "Whatever you need to heal him."

"Give me room," Milred said.

"Forgive me," Rurk said, clinging tighter to Edium.

"There's nothing to forgive, friend." Edium squeezed the man's shoulder. "Rest now. I'll take care of everything."

Rurk sagged and released Edium. Milred worked to remove the man's tunic while Idolar cleared the crowd.

Inhaling a deep breath, Edium urged his anger to clear a path through his hectic thoughts. He stood and turned to his wife. Her head was held high, tears barely within her control. He pulled her into his arms. "I'll find them and bring them home."

"They'll be dead," Mafarias said. "By the time you reach the sands, they'll be dead."

Talura shuddered and buried her face in Edium's chest. He turned a cold star to Mafarias. "And what would you have us do?"

"If a fraction of those soldiers went inside the mountain, Cattlar could be in danger. You travel there. I'll go to the desert."

"No, I'm getting my daughters. I don't trust you."

"You can't make it there in time," Mafarias insisted.

"And you could?"

Mafarias stared at him a long moment. "I have a portal in the city of Xeroth. Less than two days from Avulin."

"Take me," Edium said.

"Cattlar must be warned."

"I don't care about Cattlar!" Edium roared. "I care about my girls. Take me, or so help me I'll carve out your heart and feed it to the vultures!"

Mafarias cursed and paced.

"I'm going," Talura whispered, raising her face to meet his gaze. "I'm good with a sword. I can help."

Edium would have argued, but she had as much right to go as he. And she handled a sword nearly as well as Varila. He nodded.

"Fine," Mafarias growled. "I'll take you to Xeroth and then leave for Cattlar. They'll not listen to a mage, but I've little choice since I'm dealing with a selfish idiot."

"Go to Oblivion," Edium growled.

"Will you two stop it!" Talura snapped. "We both have the same interests. We must work together!"

Edium stared off with Mafarias, unwilling to look away first.

"Your wife is correct," Mafarias said. "Let us work together to save your daughters and the only family I have left in this world."

The genuine catch in the mage's voice nearly stole Edium's resolve. But there was something about Mafarias he couldn't bring himself to trust.

29

Varila slid her forearm along her brow to rid the sweat running into her eyes. Her skin was blistered from the beating sun, her lips cracked, and the stench of unbathed, baking bodies was pungent. Surveying her friends, she hoped for some signs of improvement, but as it'd been since Sansis had nearly killed Salvarias, hope remained a stranger. Wilhelm's sallow complexion, ragged breathing, and sweat-drenched body gave clear clues that his wounds were running a healthy pace toward death. Okulu's skin still bled bile, the odor causing Varila's stomach to be in constant turmoil. He'd yet to speak, and several times during the night, she heard him weeping. Humar had sunk into a horrible depression. He reeked of hopelessness. On Durak, where blisters didn't fester, his gray skin had a rosy tinge to it. Neithelas looked like a wilted flower. Salvarias hadn't stirred once since Sansis had ripped through his chest, nor had Sansis bothered the mage again. Lunara had also remained in the clutches of sleep, her mutters and wept words nearly a reflection of Salvarias's. The ending of Sansis's disembowelments was all the good Varila could find in their predicament.

She glanced at the sun passing overhead, and then out to the sparkling sands. Above a watery mirage, a sea of square sandstone turrets climbed the faded blue sky, looming over the mirage to make it appear as if the city of Avulin had no foundation.

Their doom drew ever closer.

As the cages waded through miles of fine sand, the mirage dissipated to reveal the sprawling city of Avulin. The outskirts were nothing more than tents crammed full of people. Women walked topless with a thin strip of cloth between their legs that tied up around their hips to keep it place. Children ran through the streets with knives and crude shafted spears with a dagger at the tip. She buried her nose in her sweaty arm, preferring her own stench to that of the city.

The rickety ride reminded her that "savage" wasn't a harsh enough word to describe the barbarians. Bodies of the old, stillborn babies, and their dead mothers piled beside a vat of a greenish brown stew. Men walked with the air of a warrior, holding decrepit looking swords and axes. In the shadows of tents or right in the open, girls barely of age lay sprawled, emotionless eyes staring at the light blue skies as man and boy alike mounted them. Avulin had two purposes: fighting and breeding.

"It's so much worse," she breathed. How her father had ever thought to save such a race she couldn't begin to understand. But it was why she loved him so dearly. His grandiose ideas of a peaceful Dalnar where women were treated with respect, where mages were not persecuted, and where all lived as equals was admirable, if not foolish.

Their convoy stopped at another feeding area and the Cavruls were left behind. Only the cage carrying her and her friends, as well as Salvarias's cage, continued on. They hadn't gone far before the Cavruls started screaming.

Durak shook his head. "The fool."

The king's castle was made of sandstone blocks stacked upon one another, causing it to tower over the tents. Unlike Erthla buildings that had rounded turrets, everything the barbarians did was square with harsh angles. Attached to the side was the arena, soaring to massive heights. They were taken to a sandstone door that must have been five stories high. Upon their arrival, chains rattled and the slabs of stone ground open to reveal the arena floor, at least half mile long as it was wide.

As the cages lurched inside, she stared up with the same amazement she'd had when first she'd gazed upon it. It was a magnificent structure, no doubt built by Veedran's hand. The walls were smooth sandstone, made of what looked like one slab instead of bricks, and raised high enough that no troll or ogre would have hope of escape. Above the pit, rows upon rows of seats circled it, enough that the entire city could view the fights with space left.

When their carriage rattled to a halt, a regular-sized door opened, and a savage nearly as large as Wilhelm stepped through and strode over to them. Chesrick. A scar ran from his brow to his chin, and a crude gold crown was nestled in his tawny hair, streaked with gray that hadn't been there the last time she'd seen him.

"Ah, the mage and his companions. Welcome to Avulin! I am King Chesrick!" His gaze fell to her. A familiar sick hunger flared in his eyes. "Varila."

"King Chesrick," she said calmly. "I see you're as ugly as ever."

Chesrick grinned widely, not seeming to notice the rivulet of drool that leaked from his thin lips. "I look forward to taming that tongue of yours, whore. You'll soon be a suitable queen and gift me strong sons."

"The only gift you'll receive from me is a slit throat," Varila said.

Chesrick motioned to a few barbarians, and they opened the door to the cage. They put a collar around her neck that had a chain connected to the new shackles they put around her wrists. Using another chain attached to the choker, they hauled her from the cage and shoved her to kneel in front of Chesrick.

"Touch me and I'll rip off your cock and shove it in your mouth!" Varila snapped.

Chesrick glanced at each companion. "Tell me Varila, which one is your favorite?"

"The giant," Sansis said.

"Ah, Sansis. I didn't see you there." Chesrick motioned to a few savages at his side. "We'll start with the giant and the mage tomorrow. Brothers, from what I've been told, with an inseparable bond. Let us test if they are willing to die for each other ... and if they can."

"No," Sansis said. "The mage is mine."

Chesrick flicked his hand toward Sansis. "Throw him in the dungeons with the others."

"You forget yourself," Sansis hissed.

"It's you who has been forgotten. Our master thought you might be foolish enough to come here. When I send my report to him, no doubt he'll let me keep you for my personal amusement. Imagine it! A man who can heal himself yet has no skill with a sword. I wonder how you'll fair in the arena."

"The mage is to be handed over," Humar said, voice heavy with desperation. "Sansis's master wants him. You've been ordered. The boy can't die!"

Chesrick smiled. "Yes, yes. Indeed, he does seek the mage. But my master only cares for his body, alive or dead, it doesn't matter."

"But look at them!" Humar yelled. "Neither can stand! Neither is even awake!"

Chesrick laughed. "We have herbs that wake the mind, knight. Given one dose, both will be alert enough to fight and watch their end approach." He turned to another set of barbarians. "Throw the rest in the dungeons. Prepare the brothers. Make sure the mage gets a fresh dose of brandaline." He grabbed the chain linked to the choker on Varila and yanked her after him.

She glanced behind her to see another barbarian carrying Lunara.

"So, is that the revered Lunara?" Chesrick asked, following her gaze. "The girl no man has touched? The innocent daughter of Lord Bellerum?"

Fear pitted itself in Varila's stomach. "She's just a girl we ran into during our travels. She's sick. She needs a bed and healer."

"You know, the first time Edium came to visit me after her birth, he told me about his daughters. He was a gushing father. Rumors reach us even here, Varila. Those threatened with their lives tell far more than a gossiping merchant. I've heard of her beauty, her innocence, and of your undying devotion to her."

"What do you want, pig?" she growled.

"With you as my wife, you'll negotiate with your father. He'll have no choice but to meet my demands. Avulin will become the wealthiest city in all of Arden."

"And what do I get in return?"

"No man will lay a finger on your sister but me. Deny me, and I'll throw her into the streets."

She looked back at her sister. Blood still caked Lunara's face and crusted her dress, and no color touched her skin. Varila would do anything to spare Lunara pain, and the bastard knew it. "No one touches her, including yourself, and we have a deal."

"Don't press your luck," Chesrick snarled. "With a simple threat to you, your father would give me what I want. I'm merely offering a wedding present to show I'm a compassionate man."

Varila followed him through a door in the arena and into the maze of corridors.

"Tomorrow after the games we'll wed," he continued. "I'll send a note to your father with my demands. You'll sign it. Then your sister will be under my protection. I'll take her as a second wife."

"I want her safe tonight. She's sick and needs rest. If you leave her alone until after we're wed, you have an agreement."

Chesrick looked down at her and smiled. "Deal."

He passed through another door and entered the castle. The flowery perfume of heated oils made her dizzy. Rooms with no doors were layered in a see-through material, and rug-sized pillows offered cushions for the orgies conducted by those few who were born with no deformities, treating them like gods so as to obtain healthy babies that would be trained as warriors. Those born with defects were tossed into the streets to survive or die like the others. Avulin had sickened her since first she'd laid eyes on it, and nothing had changed. Matter of fact, it'd worsened.

Chesrick made his way down dimly lit corridors, passing rooms illuminating additional men and women slithering over each other.

At the end of a long hall, he shoved her past double doors leading to his chambers. Lunara was taken to the next room where a group of women with bathing water followed.

Chesrick's quarters would rival any ruling lord in Arden. His four-poster bed competed with the size of hers, covered in light blankets. A few beautifully crafted stone furnishings supplied a dresser, a small, two-person table, and a massive chair even Wilhelm would find roomy. On the stone table near a wall was a tray of dates and some sort of peach-colored melon. She saw opportunity in a knife resting on the tray.

"Bathe her," Chesrick ordered.

A flood of women ushered her to an adjoining room that had a steaming tub of water. She didn't fight as they unshackled her, removed her armor and undergarments, and helped her clean herself. They put her in a dress that had no point. The fabric was rough and sheer, the front cut in a deep V mirrored on the back. Once she was shackled again, the servants escorted her to Chesrick's room and bowed before leaving. The thud of the door closing sent a chill up Varila's spine.

Using her most seductive smile, she presented her wrists to Chesrick. "If I'm going to be your queen, I think the chains are unnecessary. I'm not a cannibal so I guess breads and fruits will do." She glanced around the room. "I'd like some flowers added."

Chesrick's eyes narrowed. "Why the change?"

"I want the rest of my days to be lived in peace. There's no chance of escaping without help. If I fight you, you'll hurt me. I don't want that."

Chesrick grunted and went to a table, grabbed a key, and unlocked her fetters. She motioned to the choker around her neck. He unlocked it as well and tossed it aside.

"Why don't you go lie down?" she said, moving to the fruit. "If I'm going to do this, we'll do it my way."

He untied his loincloth, revealing his manhood. That'd be the first thing she'd chop off. She grinned at him. "At least I won't be disappointed."

He grinned, allowing a stream of drool to trickle down his chin. She plucked up the platter of food, noticing his gaze fixed on the knife. She made no move for it as she followed him to the bed. He sprawled out, his gaze darting between her and the knife. The idiot didn't take it from her. No doubt he was conceited enough to think she wasn't a real threat.

She crawled on top of him and straddled him. "Date?"

He opened his mouth slightly, and she fed him one, then popped one in her mouth. The burst of sweet juice reminded her how hungry she'd been.

By the third date, his body had relaxed under her thighs. Forcing a smile, she fed him another before setting the platter aside. She draped herself over him, gliding her lips around his salty neck. His hands gripped her buttocks, fingers bruising her flesh. Sliding one hand up his chest, she moved her other lower, feeling for the tray. Her fingers touched a cold metal hilt. Soundlessly, she lifted it and gripped it tightly.

"You've wanted me for a long time," she whispered in his ear.

Chesrick grunted. His arousal made him carelessly grip her hair in his fists as his teeth nipped her neck, giving her clear access to his side, his ribs, his lungs.

"This is what happens when you get what you want," she hissed, and rammed the dagger in his side.

She yanked it free and brought it down again, but instead of stopping it, he accepted the blow and used her momentum against her, flipping her on her back, and his weight crushed her. The wound hadn't hit home. It was barely leaking blood. Cursing her stupidity, she kicked and flailed wildly, trying to throw him off balance.

He wrenched the knife from her fingers and tossed it across the room. His movement angled up, and it was all she needed to drive her knee into his groin. He howled, rolling off her, and clutched his manhood. She bolted up and ran for the knife.

His weight crashed into her again, tackling her to the floor, scrapping her skin painfully on the sandy stones. She clawed forward. Her fingertips just touched the edge of the knife's handle when he hauled her up.

He backhanded her, sending her reeling to the floor. The blow erupted a loud buzz in her ears and snatched her vision. When she shook it back, he was upon her again. His fist landed in her side and air whooshed out of her lungs.

"Wretched whore!" he roared.

He grabbed her by the hair and flung her to the bed. Gasping, she rolled off to the other side. She managed to get to her hands and knees before he was upon her again. He snagged hold of her hair and slammed her forehead into stone. Warm blood gushed to the floor and ran into her eyes. Her vision blurred and darkness flickered its invite.

He ripped aside her dress. All she felt were hands groping her everywhere she didn't want him to. She thought she was struggling—she was screaming in her mind—but he mounted her without seemingly any resistance.

She cried out when he took her. Painful tears fell down her cheeks and mixed with the blood on the floor. She heard herself sobbing, begging for her father. She was sixteen again, frightened and alone. Vulnerable and defenseless.

The mere thought and memory were enough to purge those feelings, and rage sprang her alert. She would not be a victim again.

Blinking away blood, she waited until his weight lessened on her just enough. Gritting her teeth, she bucked her head, grimly satisfied to hear the crunch of bone. His weight toppled off her. She scrambled on her hands and knees to the knife. Clutching the hilt, she whirled around to be greeted by his fist. The strike sent her sprawling, but she never let go of the weapon. She grasped it like a slave would the key to freedom.

This time, she waited for the perfect opportunity, taking his blows without fighting. Then she caught a glimpse of his manhood as he stood over her yelling. She thrust up and hot blood spilled over her hand. He howled and grabbed his groin, careening backward. Leaping on his back, she used his staggering balance to drive him to the ground, keeping a hand fisted in his hair. As he landed, she focused her strength into ramming his forehead into the sandstone.

Blood pooled under him, and his form was still. Weakly, she crawled off him, swaying at the sudden dizziness, wincing at the throbbing between her legs and the swelling of her face. Shaking a clump of his hair from her fingers, she stumbled to the shackles, snatched them up, and tripped her way to his side. Grabbing his shoulders, it took several forceful tugs to budge him. She dragged him to the bed, wrapped his arms around a post, and snapped the shackles in place.

Once he was secure, she went to the washroom and gently cleansed herself.

Tomorrow, she would sneak out during the fight and rescue Lunara and their friends. With the commotion, it'd offer their only hope for escape.

She wiped away her pathetic tears that, for some stupid reason, wouldn't stop.

It was early morning when Chesrick woke. Varila was straddling a chair she'd pulled in front of him, knife leveled at his throat.

"Scream and I kill you," she said.

He grinned. "You're a fighter. I've never seen such a powerful woman."

"It might do you good to use your women for something besides breeding."

Chesrick shrugged. "How else are we to eat unless they give us meals?"

"Try a damn crop, you ass," she growled. "How much longer till the games?"

Chesrick glanced out the window. "Any moment now."

"Does the entire city still go?"

The king nodded. "For as well fed as they were last night, there'll not be a soul on the streets."

"Are there guards?"

"If there were, they would have heard my cries and came to my rescue last night."

Varila narrowed her eyes. "What else?"

Chesrick curled his lip. "Two guards will come to get me before the games."

"Good. Now, we'll both get out of this alive if you do what I say. Got it?"

"I don't believe you."

"You don't have a choice, idiot."

A knock on the door was followed by a barbarian saying, "The games are about to begin, my king."

"Tell him you're occupied and won't be making the games. Tell him to get them started," Varila instructed.

"Start the games," Chesrick called. His gaze never ventured from hers. The bastard thought she was telling him the truth. "I'm ... busy."

Varila heard their snicker through the door.

"Tell them you don't need a guard," she said.

"Go enjoy the games yourselves. This one has been tamed," Chesrick said.

A chuckle this time. "Thank you, Majesty."

Varila waited a long moment before turning her full attention to the savage in front of her. "I want you to know that what you did will not haunt me," she whispered. "After today, I won't think of you ever again. But in Oblivion, you'll think of me for eternity."

She slit his throat, not dodging from the spray of warm blood on her face nor did she allow his gaze to leave hers. She grabbed his hair and held up his head until the last light of life faded from his brown eyes. Even then, she couldn't rip her stare away.

She wasn't sure how long she sat there. When she finally left her trance, she heard the roar of the crowd in the arena.

Rising from her chair, she went to the washroom and wiped the king's blood from her face, grimacing against her swollen eye, split lip, and welt on her forehead. Taking a deep breath, she forced her eyes to lose their haunted flicker. She dressed in her armor, feeling the security and strength it provided.

Wincing, she went to the door, forcing herself to walk normally. Anything else would give clues to Lunara, and Varila had kept her first experience at sixteen from her sister. Right or wrong, she'd fervently tried to shield Lunara from the despicable world. It was for selfish reasons. After Varila had lost her own innocence, she had fed off Lunara's naivety, vicariously living through her sister, clinging to that wide-eyed look of awe and love toward a world full of savages.

Squaring her shoulders, she eased open the door. No one guarded it. She crept to the next room, turned the key, and slipped inside. Lunara was on the bed, mumbling, eyes opening and closing, clearly not alert. She was cleaned and in a dress similar to Varila's.

Varila sat on the edge of the bed. "Lunara? Can you hear me?"

Lunara spasmed. "Salvarias ... Salvar ..." Her voice trailed off.

Varila pulled her sister to sit. Lunara wasn't limp, but she wasn't exactly stable. Tugging her to her feet, Varila wrapped a blanket around Lunara, tucking it in like a drying cloth, and wedged a shoulder under her sister's arm.

Clutching the kitchen knife, which had yet to leave her hand, she supported Lunara and left the room.

30

Wilhelm jolted awake with such violence he was on his feet stumbling backward before he even saw his surroundings. Blood pumped through him fast enough he feared his heart would give from the strain. His limbs shook dramatically, which made standing a challenge. When his back slammed into a wall, a ripple of intense pain drove him to his knees and dimmed his vision.

A roar he had thought was his pounding head was only partially so; it was a crowd. Savages jeered from seats so high up that he could barely see their outlines. The ground was hard stone, covered in a thin layer of sand. Pillars sprouted up randomly, and stacks of stones were sprinkled about, neither supporting anything. Mounted along the wall, weapons reflected sunlight streaming from overhead. A foul stench tainted the air, and he realized it came from him. Gingerly he touched the gooey holes in his side, feeling the rawness of his back and the wounds covering his shoulders. He swallowed a bitter taste lingering on his tongue.

Surveying his surroundings, his heart skipped when he saw his brother lying on the ground, robes hanging around his waist, chest caked with dried blood, the scar caused by Sansis still puffy and red.

No longer processing pain, he shoved himself to his feet and took lurching steps toward his brother.

Suddenly Salvarias inhaled sharply and scrambled to his feet, eyes wild as he stumbled back. Wilhelm sprinted to intercept him and grabbed his brother's arm.

"It's all right, Salv. I'm here," Wilhelm said, hating how weak and raspy his voice sounded.

"Help ..." Salvarias gasped.

"He's not here. Sansis isn't here."

Salvarias doubled over, and a soft cry left him as he clutched his chest, his body giving out. Only Wilhelm's hold kept him on his feet. Gasping between each word, he said, "I ... cannot ... breathe ..."

Without Salvarias's breathing concoction, the dusty surroundings would kill him as easily as whatever came into the arena.

Cursing, Wilhelm eased Salvarias to sit. "Look at me, Salv." Once his brother focused, Wilhelm took in a deep breath, biting his tongue to stop a wince when the scabs on his back cracked. "Just like me."

Salvarias sucked in a painful-sounding gasp that induced a hacking fit. Wilhelm rested a hand on his brother's back and surveyed the weapons available, quickly picking out the great sword that would be his preference. Once his brother gulped in another breath, Wilhelm refocused his attention on his own breathing, keeping it deep and steady. Though it took longer than normal, Salvarias gained minor control.

Grimacing, Salvarias rubbed his chest and looked down at the new scar. "What happened? My chest ... it hurts."

"You don't remember?"

Salvarias shook his head. "The last thing I remember, I was in a cage with Sansis. I ..." Salvarias's eyes darted back and forth. He twitched and raised his gaze to Wilhelm's, apology overflowing from his black eyes. "Brother, I am—"

"We'll talk about it later, Salv. What do you remember?"

"My magic ... I almost lost ..." Salvarias shuddered. "My magic and I were breaking apart." He winced and pressed a hand over his heart, exhaling softly. "Sansis ... he stabbed me. I nearly died."

"You've been out of it since," Wilhelm said. He tapped his brother's chin to gain his attention. "We're in the arena. We're going to have to fight." Salvarias's gaze swept over the pit, and he nodded. "Can you use magic?" Wilhelm asked.

"No, Brother. I can taste the brandaline." Salvarias spat to the side. "And something else ... vernk?" He spat again and shook his head. "They have drugged me with something."

"Bitter?" Wilhelm asked.

Salvarias nodded. "I would not trust myself to keep hold of the magic. I am sorry."

Wilhelm's stomach knotted as he rose to his feet, hauling Salvarias up with him. Trying to keep his voice light, he winked at his brother. "Good. I get to have all the fun."

Salvarias's eyes sparkled a smile as he pulled up his ripped robes to cover his scarred body. "Do not think I plan to sit this out, Brother."

Limping heavily, Salvarias hobbled over to the nearest weapons rack holding a great sword and a broadsword. He yanked both free and walked back to Wilhelm. Wilhelm went to take both, but Salvarias kept hold of the broadsword.

"You're going to fight with a sword?"

Salvarias shrugged. "What other choice do I have?"

"Stand back and let me handle it."

"If what walks out to greet us is easily defeated, I will willingly step aside, Brother. However, if necessary, I will fight."

"You've never swung a sword, Salv," Wilhelm protested. Even as he said it, he realized his brother held the sword as Humar had taught Wilhelm, his brother's stance a mirror of his own.

"I have watched you practice," Salvarias said. "I can do this."

Wilhelm saw sweat glistening on his brother's palms, and the sword tip shook ever so slightly. He ruffled Salvarias's hair. "I'm sure you can, Salv. You'll probably end up being better than me."

"Though I appreciate it, your compliments will not sway my confidence."

Wilhelm grinned. "You always see right through me." He tried to keep his frown hidden when he saw his brother wince, resting a hand over his heart, battling for a tiny gulp of air.

Beyond the towering doors opposite the brothers, a roar erupted that shook the ground and lifted up a pillowy cloud of dust. Salvarias pressed a sleeve of his robes over his nose and mouth.

"Ready, Salv?"

Salvarias adjusted his grip and nodded.

"Keep with me. Never leave my side and do what I say. Don't question me."

The tip of the sword shook steadily, and when Salvarias spoke, his voice was anything but confident. "Yes, Brother."

Wilhelm would have thought he'd relish in fighting side by side with his brother wielding a blade. Instead, it felt like a betrayal of who Salvarias was, and Wilhelm fought the urge to wrench the weapon from his brother's hands.

Inhaling a deep breath, Wilhelm faced forward, flexing his arms and legs to rid the scabs hindering his movements. Warm blood snaked down his back, and his splitting flesh felt aflame. Despite his best efforts, a groan escaped.

"Brother ..." Salvarias's voice choked off. His wide eyes were fixated on Wilhelm's back.

"I'm fine, Salv. It looks worse than it is." He tucked in his arm to keep the stab wound hidden.

"What are you not telling me?" Salvarias said, his voice trembling.

"Don't know what you're talking about."

"Brother—"

"I don't think now is the time to get into it, Salv." He pointed ahead. "You need to focus on what's going to come through those doors."

As if the world knew of the need to distract Salvarias, the doors moaned open, pulled apart by chains that rattled between the walls and left a high-pitched ringing in Wilhelm's ears. Surveying the space, he mentally marked where pillars and stacked stones could either be used for protection or an obstacle for his foe. He shuffled his feet, feeling how the sand moved underneath him. Slippery, dangerous. His brother would have a difficult time.

A bellow issued from the darkness beyond the doors and vibrated the pillars and evoked a vicious roar from the crowd. Wilhelm's mouth fell open as the beast emerged.

"Tell me that's not what I think it is," he said slowly.

Salvarias grimaced. "So it is, Brother. What worries me as well is what follows it."

Wilhelm lowered his gaze to the two minotaurs banging swords to their shields, playing to the crowd. His gaze darted up to the monster waving its arms in an attempt to stir the crowd's roar to higher volumes. Standing near sixty feet tall, the troll wielded a spiked club in its enormously large hands. Leathery, greenish-brown skin looked taut against the beast's muscular arms and legs. Its eyes were disproportionately small and slanted, whereas the mouth was overly large with spiked teeth jutting up from the lower jaw to curve over its upper lip.

"Well, luck isn't on our side," Wilhelm muttered.

A slow smile crept across Salvarias's face. "On the contrary. I see a small chance for victory."

"And that would be?"

Salvarias grinned at him. "Tigers. Two starved tigers."

Wilhelm grinned back before searching the shadows for what gave his brother hope. Then he saw them. They were chained to platforms that had risen from underground. Both were focused on Salvarias.

"They will not harm us should we go near," Salvarias said.

Wilhelm grabbed his brother's arm and sprinted for them. As he ran, he yelled, "Tell them to protect you. Just you. If I know you're safe, I can focus."

Salvarias glanced over, eyes clearly conveying his disapproval.

"Come on, Salv. You know I'll get careless if you're not safe."

Salvarias nodded.

When they met the first tiger, Wilhelm released his brother. "Work on the chain!" he ordered.

Salvarias raised the sword and brought it down against the links. Sparks flew but no damage. It wasn't rusted or ill cared for. All it would do is break the sword. Salvarias realized the same and ceased the effort.

Wilhelm inhaled a deep soothing breath and let it out slowly, relaxing his mind until nothing existed but what needed to be done. The minotaurs were taller than he, horns ill cared for, hooves dull. Metal collars were around their necks. By the scars, the beasts had fought their fair share of battles.

"This does not bode well, brother," Salvarias murmured at his side, gaze locked on the troll.

"Come on, Salv," Wilhelm said lightly, waving his sword toward the troll's legs. "I'm sure it's slow. Those legs are as thick as trees but short. And the arms are long. I'm sure it doesn't have good balance."

As if retorting his insult, the troll swung its club swiftly and showed its agility by leaping along the pit wall.

"Never mind," Wilhelm muttered.

The minotaurs sprinted forward, charging head first, barreling past the troll. A whistle and shadow were the only warnings. Wilhelm grabbed his brother and dove to the ground, narrowly missing the troll's speedy swing. By the gods, its arms were long!

Rolling to his feet, he clenched his stomach in time to accept the charging minotaur's head. The force lifted him off his feet, catapulting him backward before he slammed to the ground, sliding another few feet on his back. Gravel and rocks embedded themselves in his raw flesh, and the fine sand seemed to take off the first few layers of what skin he had left. Fighting back the darkness beckoning him, he spared a glance at his brother.

Salvarias was on one knee, sword overhead, grating against the minotaur's sword. The tiger leapt over Salvarias, tackling the creature to the ground. It ripped into the minotaur's jugular and proceeded to eat it. One down.

Salvarias limped toward Wilhelm, gaze locked on the minotaur readying for another charge. Even with the danger around them, Wilhelm grinned with pride. Though he hated seeing Salvarias with a sword, his brother held it as if it had been in his hands since birth.

A dark shadow sweeping across the ground caught Wilhelm's eye. Glancing up, he saw too late the troll's club sailing through the air.

"Salv!"

Salvarias whirled around in time to accept the club square in his abdomen. The momentum lifted him as if he were a child and launched him across the arena.

Scrambling to his feet, Wilhelm lowered his shoulder to take the charge of the minotaur. They ricocheted off each other, reeling in a complete circle. Wilhelm got his bearings first and took off at a frantic run for his brother. Fear pounded blood in his ears, drowning out the cries of delight from the barbarians, and his vision pulsed with each painful beat of his heart. His whole body felt encased in flames, and shooting pains ran all over him.

A shriek from behind sent chills up his arms. Looking over his shoulder, he saw a tiger's hindquarters gripped by the troll as it thumped the tiger on the ground. With the next smack, the cat's howl cut off, and blood rained down. The troll tossed the tiger aside and bounded toward Wilhelm.

Ahead, Salvarias was on his hands and knees, shaking his head.

"Stay down!" Wilhelm yelled.

Salvarias must not have heard. He rose to his feet, swaying as if on the deck of a ship caught in a hurricane.

The thundering ground tangled Wilhelm's feet. He nearly lost his balance. All that kept him steady was seeing Salvarias's robes matted with blood on his side. One of the spikes must have cut him.

"Stay down!" Wilhelm ordered again.

Salvarias lurched forward and picked up his sword.

The troll sprinted by Wilhelm. It closed in on Salvarias before his brother even seemed to notice the threat. It reached out a gnarled hand.

"Salv!" Wilhelm roared.

Salvarias's head snapped up, and he barely raised his sword in time to shove it into the troll's palm. The weight and momentum of the troll's reach drove Salvarias back. His bum leg gave out, and he howled in pain as he fell to his knees. His lower leg twisted in the wrong direction.

Desperation drove Wilhelm to leap on the troll's hand. He dropped his great sword and opted for the short blade of the broadsword sticking from the troll's palm. He yanked the sword free and brought it down in wild, quick stabs. The beast staggered, yelping and dancing, shaking its hand as if it burned it on a hot kettle. Wilhelm clung on for dear life, squeezing his eyes shut to keep from getting dizzy.

When finally the beast stopped, he looked down to see Salvarias crawling toward the great sword, dragging his mangled leg. From Wilhelm's vantage point, he saw the minotaur hidden behind a pillar a few feet from his brother.

"Salv! Behind you!" Wilhelm yelled.

Salvarias clutched the hilt of the sword and used the blade to help shove himself up, balancing on one leg. He hopped around, struggling to lift the sword. It was too late. The minotaur strode up to Salvarias and knocked aside his weak thrust. Latching on to Salvarias's shoulder, the beast drove its blade straight into Salvarias's stomach.

An animal-like wail leached from Wilhelm's throat. Salvarias stumbled, clutching his belly.

Wilhelm had no time to see anything else. The troll's other hand grabbed him and yanked him free of his grip. He looked up to see rotted teeth and a tongue with sores oozing pus.

"Eat him! Eat him!" The crowd chanted.

He clutched the sword in both hands and drove it straight into the troll's tongue. It shrieked and wobbled back. The hand clamped around Wilhelm loosened enough that he slid free.

He was too high, though. He fell, farther and farther, air whooshing by him, stone walls blurring into smooth, brown looking waterfalls. He landed with a thud and crack on a stack of sandstone half his size. Air left him and darkness pressed on his vision. None of his body responded to his commands to move. It felt as if his head floated detached from the rest of him. He couldn't even twitch a finger. He couldn't even *feel* his finger, his arms, legs, nothing from the neck down.

He turned his gaze to his brother lying in a heap, blood pooling beneath him. Towering over him, the minotaur held its sword overhead, readying for the final blow. Wilhelm gurgled a "no," tasting iron in his mouth.

Then time stopped. No roars from the crowd could be heard, no feet shuffling from the troll. Nothing. He looked up to see the barbarians frozen. The minotaur stood motionless, sword poised overhead. It was as if nothing existed but Wilhelm.

A shadow next to the minotaur caught his attention. It shifted in hues of gray-black, swirling like his brother's eyes. It seeped into the light, rising in waves of an inky, undulating mass. Wilhelm remembered the shadowfires, remembered their hate-filled gazes, their flaming bodies, the burning people screaming.

"No," he wept.

The form rose to a featureless body, its shadowy flame flickering like his brother's black fire. The creature screeched and another shadowfire came into Wilhelm's vision. Its deep-socketed gaze leveled on him as it walked over to him in long, jerky strides. Grabbing hold of his arm, it dragged him off the slab, through the sands, and to his brother's side. Still, he felt nothing.

The other shadowfire knelt next to Wilhelm and, in a hiss like water extinguishing flame, said, "Hear me, Protector. This boy is mine. He will do *my* bidding. Remember!"

It grabbed Wilhelm's head, and he wanted nothing more than to swat away the warm foggy feeling it left on his skin. An unbearable pressure burgeoned in his skull. Memories flooded from some dark corner of his mind. He remembered waking in the middle of the night and hearing his mother scream. He remembered the creatures standing over her. He remembered a shadowfire driving a ball of black fire into her stomach, burning her, and planting its seed. He remembered touching it and the shadowfire's words, "The boy will be mine; he will do my bidding. No longer is Arden safe." Then he remembered the day his brother was born. He remembered the man robed in blood. He remembered his uncle's words, "May the gods have mercy."

"Feel your weakness," the shadowfire hissed.

The creature shoved Wilhelm's hand to his brother's, locking their marks together. Salvarias screamed and tried to yank free, clawing at Wilhelm's arm.

"Stop!" Wilhelm roared. "You're hurting—"

His words choked off as a warming tingle flowered inside him, imbuing itself in his every muscle, in his blood, in his soul. Wounds secreted vile pus, and his broken back snapped into place. He exhaled sharply, feeling himself come alive with a power that fed him like rains fed the desert, thickening a thirst in him only the power could quench. Greedily, he absorbed it. He needed it, and with that need, he sucked more of it into him. He swore his muscles were expanding, his mind sharpening, his feet itching to experience a lightness he was sure was there.

"Stop!" the shadowfire commanded.

Wilhelm realized the power came from his brother. Blood parted Salvarias's lips, and he hitched violently. As much as Wilhelm wanted to stop, he couldn't wrench his hand free. Instead, he tightened his grip, drinking in more power, draining his brother.

"Stop!" the shadowfire screeched. It took both shadowfires to wrestle his hand from Salvarias's.

Gasping as if he'd chugged down a keg of ale, Wilhelm gaped at his healed body. There wasn't even a scar in his side where Sansis had stabbed him.

"Now you see," the shadowfire hissed. "Your strength is your worth. Your weakness is the ability to drain my son. And you will do well to remember he is *my* son. *Mine!* It is time you accept your powers from *me*, Protector!"

Wilhelm cried out as fire boiled his blood, blinding him. Blinking rapidly to gain his vision, he saw the shadowfires were draped over him, heating his skin to near unbearable. The black fire seeped into his pores, merging with his blood. He inhaled sharply when a warmth long forgotten flourished—the same warmth that entered him the day his brother was born. This power didn't come from Salvarias; it came from within Wilhelm. It was his alone.

"Look at your brother's blood," the shadowfire commanded. "Look at his pain. Look at your purpose!"

Both shadowfires plunged into his chest. Wilhelm released his pain in a roar. Fire, he was certain fire consumed him. Something slithered up his gorge, gagging him. He rolled on his side and heaved, feeling something swelling in his throat. He grabbed his neck, gasping, but nothing entered his lungs. He forced himself to cough with what precious air he had left.

He retched up what looked like two black worms along with inky liquid. The worms twitched, hissing and sputtering, smoking and sizzling, shriveling in the sunlight.

Its last words chilled Wilhelm's bones. "*I* created him. He's mine, not yours, not his."

The sands absorbed the liquid and black worms, leaving no evidence to their existence.

Gasping, Wilhelm raised his gaze to his brother. Blood trickled from Salvarias's mouth, oozed from the wound he suffered, and he looked paler than snow.

Rage—utter, inconsolable rage—surged up in Wilhelm, and his vision swirled the same hue as his brother's blood. Sounds flooded to life. The crowd jeered as if they'd seen nothing, egging the troll to finish the job.

He grabbed Salvarias's sword and thrust up just in time to stop the minotaur's downward stroke, all the while still finding strength to rise to his feet. The creature's black eyes widened. Shoving the strike aside, Wilhelm whipped his sword around and connected with the minotaur's abdomen, easily slicing halfway through. Innards spilled like a gutted cow.

After prying his sword free from the minotaur's thick spine, he glanced down at Salvarias's seemingly lifeless form and blood shining brighter than the sun. Something had to die to ease

Wilhelm's anger. He turned to the troll, to the beast that would suffer for the pain his brother endured.

Wilhelm walked toward the beast, slowly picking up speed until he was sprinting, feeling lighter than air, stronger than he'd ever thought possible. Even through his red vision, he saw everything. Every barbarians' face was clear as if they stood in front of him, he swore he could see each granule of sand, but mostly he heard his brother's shallow breathing soften with each of Wilhelm's steps. Fear would have crippled him, but purpose drove him forward.

A smile spread across Wilhelm's face, but it was nothing like his usual grin. This was the smile of death coming to claim its victim.

31

Varila rounded a corner and came face to face with a barbarian. He was more surprised than she, and his scream was cut short when her kitchen knife sank into his jugular. He flopped to the ground, gurgling.

Lunara suddenly cried out and doubled over, clutching her head, and gagged up blood. Tears rolled down her pale cheeks, and she seemed unable to breathe. Then, as if knocked unconscious, she collapsed in Varila's arms. Her sister was out cold. Cursing, Varila dragged Lunara around the corner.

Thudding footsteps alerted Varila, and she dropped her sister, whirled around, and rammed her dagger toward the flash of leathery skin she'd seen. A hand grabbed her wrist. Using her swing's momentum, she turned the savage enough to jam her knee in his groin. He howled and released her, clutching his manhood and staggering backward. She followed him, flipping the knife, and when within range, she slammed the blade into the back of the savage's neck, grimacing against the resistance of skin and muscle that parted way to her thrust.

Returning to Lunara, Varila wrestled her sister over her shoulder.

She continued through the maze of corridors until finding the one that led to the cells.

Peeking around the corner, she saw two barbarians muttering to one another as they paced. Gently, she lowered Lunara and readjusted her grip on the knife. Taking in a few deep breaths, she sprang from behind the corner and rushed the savages.

The element of surprise was definitely in her favor. The stunned barbarians stared at her with dumbfounded expressions as she charged them. Picking the first one who came from his confusion, she rammed her knife in the savage's throat. Hot blood poured over her hand, making the smooth handle slippery. Yanking it free, she whirled to the other barbarian to find him choking against the bars of a cell, an arm wrapped around his neck. She strode forward and stabbed him in the heart. The body toppled to the floor. Okulu was there, a halfhearted grin on his face, his grass-green eyes haunted, and bile still seeped from him.

She gave him a small smile. "Thanks."

He nodded and sank against the wall.

Humar's smile couldn't have been bigger. "I'd feared we'd die in this place."

"Not if I can help it," she muttered. She kicked over the dead barbarian, snatched the keys, and unlocked Humar's cell. "Where are the others?"

"The brothers are in the arena," Humar said, taking the keys from her. He went to the next cell that had Durak, Neithelas, and another Winsire that could have been Neithelas's twin and unlocked it. He opened the next cell, and a savage stepped out. Varila raised her knife and charged, shouting a warning to Humar. The knight yelled something, but she couldn't hear him over her own cry.

The savage grabbed her wrist before she could drive her weapon in his throat. Twisting her around, he bent her arm behind her back and wrapped his other around her shoulders.

"Varila!" the savage said. "It's me."

It took her a moment in her writhing to recognize the voice. Her legs gave out, but the man's grip kept her on her feet.

"By the gods, I've missed you," he whispered.

Tears brimmed when he released her. She almost didn't turn around for fear her suspicion would be false. Slowly, she looked over her shoulder. He merely wore a loincloth, and he'd caked mud in his dark hair and beard, but his bright hazel eyes glittered in the torchlight, and his smile would have shone through the darkest night.

She spun around and threw her arms around his neck, holding on too tightly, but unable to let go or find her voice.

Her father crushed her close and smoothed her hair. "We need to get the brothers. Where is your sister?"

"Around the corner," Varila said, wiping her tears before she leaned away.

Edium hooked a finger around her chin and lifted her face side to side. A familiar anger glittered in his eyes. "Who did this to you?"

"Chesrick," she said. She forced a laugh and pulled free of her father. "Trust me, he looks worse. Seems he and kitchen knives don't get along."

Edium smiled slightly. "That's my girl. You all right?"

Varila nodded. "Fine. We need to get out of here before they find him. He said the whole city will be attending this, so the streets will be clear."

Edium turned to Humar. "We'll get the brothers. Once we leave the arena, we need to get out of here before the crowd realizes what's going on. Be ready to run."

"We'll be ready," Humar said.

"Lunara can't walk," Varila said. "She passed out." Resting a hand on her father's shoulder, she said, "She looks bad, but she's fine. She's not injured, just exhausted."

Edium nodded and strode forward. Even though she'd warned him, he still gave a soft cry when he rounded the corner. He returned with Lunara cradled in his arms. "There's so much blood."

"I know, but I promise she's fine. We need to get to the arena."

"I'll take her," Neithelas said.

Varila motioned to the other Winsire. "Your brother?"

Neithelas smiled, taking Lunara from her father. "Yes. It appears he was captured."

"Let's go," Edium said, plucking up a barbarian's sword. He offered her the other one, but she shook her head, preferring to keep her kitchen knife. Furthermore, she wasn't sure she'd be able to free it from her grip.

Edium led her down a winding maze of corridors while he filled her in on his last few days. When he told her "they" had used Mafarias's portal, she interrupted him. "They? Who else is here?"

Edium winced. "Your mother."

"Have you lost your mind?" Varila snapped. "Why would you bring her to this forsaken place?"

"She refused to remain behind. Trust me, I'm not pleased by it either. She's safe in an abandoned home near here. She's with Adok and has been looking for everyone's packs and gathering grynfs. I—"

"Adok?" Varila asked. "How in Veedran's wickedness did he find you? We saw him days ago. He shouldn't have survived the heat."

"I'm not sure. I nearly killed him until your mother recognized him. Plus the fact he didn't try to eat us."

"Plus the fact he's a damn mountain wolf in the desert?" Varila said dryly.

Edium smiled over his shoulder, cheeks red. "Yes, there was that too. Anyway, we split when we got here. I was supposed to be rescuing you, but I ran into some issues. My disguise didn't work as well as I'd hoped, and I was captured yesterday. If we don't get out of here soon, your mother will come looking for me. She said she'd give me a day to get everyone out."

"Then let's hurry," she said, poking him in the back. "I can run."

He nodded and picked up his pace. She kept on his heels, the roar of the crowd giving her energy she didn't know she had left.

WILHELM VAULTED into the air and rammed both swords into the troll's left thigh. The beast reeled, howling so loud it shook through Wilhelm's bones.

Using his swords to scale the creature, he sprang from leg to leg. Avoiding the sweeping strikes of the troll, he hung precariously from his swords as he climbed farther up, slicing his way to the troll's belly.

His own roar seemed to vibrate Arden as he carved out the troll's stomach. Intestines flooded out, drenching Wilhelm in blood and bile.

The troll gurgled and shuddered as it teetered this way and that before its knees buckled and it plummeted to the ground. Wilhelm leapt aside, landing on the ground and somersaulting to safety. He sprang to his feet, both swords clutched tightly, and surveyed the arena. With no other foe in sight, he stormed toward his brother.

"Wilhelm!"

He glanced in the direction of the voice and saw Varila standing in a doorway, motioning him over. He sprinted to his brother, swooped him up, and darted through the door Varila held open.

"I need Sansis," Wilhelm said, cradling his brother close. "Take me to the holding cells."

A savage stepped into view, and Wilhelm stumbled back a step.

"It's all right," Varila said, grabbing his arm. "It's my father. No time to explain. This way." Varila entered the corridor and covered her nose when she glanced back at him. "By the gods, you reek!"

Wilhelm followed her and Edium down a maze of seemingly endless corridors. Torches sputtered dark shadows that kept Wilhelm vigilant in his watch for additional shadowfires. The creature's last words, "He is mine, not yours," played in his head and made him tighten his hold on his brother.

Prison cells lined the next torch lit corridor. His friends were free, and a fair number of dead barbarians littered the floor.

Durak limped over to them. "We were attacked." The Cavrul's side was leaking blood.

Wilhelm couldn't hear the next exchange of words. All he saw at that moment was a man in burnt orange robes standing at the bars of his cage, his sick, milky white eyes staring at Salvarias.

"Open it," Wilhelm said to Humar.

"What happened to him?" Sansis said, stepping aside so Wilhelm could enter.

"Heal him," Wilhelm ordered.

Sansis needed no prompting. He placed a hand over Salvarias's forehead. The wound closed, sizzling and smoking as skin melted together. His brother's leg cracked into place. Through it all, Salvarias never stirred.

"It's all I can do," Sansis said. "He's not well enough for me to heal him completely. You must take me with you."

Wilhelm gently lowered his brother to the floor. "So you're telling me he'll die without you?"

"Y-yes."

"Lying bastard!" Wilhelm sprang to his feet and shoved Sansis against the wall, pressing his forearm to Sansis's neck. "It was you, wasn't it? You scarred him like that in Zeeas! You're the one who cut him open! Sliced him up! Tell me!"

Sansis's eyes widened. "Your ..." He choked in a breath. "Your powers have been unleashed."

Wilhelm angled closer. "They have. And right now, I'm very angry." He rammed his sword into the man's chest until it collided with the stone wall behind him. "If you can heal yourself, do it." He yanked his sword free and watched the hole in Sansis's chest meld closed.

Leaning down, jaw tight with anger, Wilhelm whispered in Sansis ear, "I'm happy you can do that because I want you to send a message to your master. Tell him my brother is not his. He's mine. Do you hear me? Mine! Tell him to leave my brother alone. If he doesn't, no place in any world will hide him from my wrath. Tell him I'm not afraid of his shadows anymore."

Wilhelm stepped back and raked his sword up Sansis's abdomen, eviscerating him. Sansis toppled to the ground, shoving his guts into his belly. Wilhelm marched over to his brother and lifted him. "Let's go," he grumbled.

Neithelas and another man Wilhelm didn't recognize supported Okulu. The merc's hair was a bloody mat and blood dripped from a slice on his chest. Humar was favoring his left arm.

"We're in for trouble," Humar said, picking up another sword.

Wilhelm heard the angry crowd above.

"We make a run for it," Edium said, sweeping Lunara in his arms. "There are only two entrances into these tunnels from the seating above. If we're lucky, they'll trample one another before they make it to us."

Wilhelm followed Edium as he led his friends through more corridors, more shadows. He fought a rising lump of panic that Sansis hadn't lied. Taking a deep breath, he squelched the urge to rescue the sick bastard. No doubt his brother would be weak, but Sansis wouldn't risk not healing Salvarias enough to survive.

When they rounded the next hallway, the power surging within Wilhelm began to fade, shrinking to some dark place he couldn't feel. He tried to keep his mind focused on it, begged it not to leave him, not yet. Salvarias wasn't safe. Regardless, no amount of pleading or concentration could keep it lit. The red tinge that had sharpened his vision ebbed.

Shouts rang down the tunnel, and slapping footfalls sounded close. Edium cursed and sprinted ahead, the others struggling to keep up.

Edium stepped through a door and into blinding sunlight. A cluster of abandoned homes huddled in the shadow of the towering arena walls. There were several bodies sprinkled along the base of the wall's edge. They looked like they had exploded. Wilhelm was about to question what had happened when a shrill cry sounded from overhead. Just a few feet away, a man was sailing through the air, apparently knocked over the edge of the arena. He hit the ground with a horrible splat, and the back of his head burst open.

Edium whistled. Wilhelm startled when Talura and Adok emerged from a home. Talura gave them and the splattered bodies a once-over and motioned to a herd of grynfs.

"Let's go," she said tartly. "We don't stop until we're out of the sands."

Wilhelm mounted the nearest beast and clutched his brother close. He kicked the grynf's flanks and never looked back.

32

L unara clawed her way through the familiar depths of Salvarias's pain. As she surfaced from nightmares, her body felt weak, beaten, used, and defiled. And hers was merely a sense of what Salvarias endured.

A light shining through her eyelids told her somehow, miraculously, they'd survived that horrible pain. All she had to do was open her eyes and wake.

She became aware she was jostling in someone's arms. They must be on horses. She assumed she was with Neithelas. As the thought left her, she realized whoever held her had a broader chest than he. Not as large as Wilhelm, closer to Salvarias, but it wasn't him either.

Stretching her mind, she focused on everything she was feeling. Biting dirt stung her face, clinging to her sweating skin. Her arms felt pinned, tight to her sides. She was wrapped in something ... in a blanket, perhaps. Rough fabric scratched her bare breasts.

Panic sliced though the darkness and surged her mind alert. Resisting the urge to immediately fight, she cracked open an eyelid. A bare-chested savage with muddied hair held her.

Fear consumed her. Clutching tight to the blanket, she rammed her elbow in the barbarian's stomach. His grunt and gasp eased his hold enough that she shoved his arm away and flung herself off the loping creature. She somersaulted through scorching sands, crying out as she rolled, seeing vague blurs of other beasts whizzing by. Someone cursed. She gained some sense of uprightness, scrambled to her feet, and fled. She moved as if stuck in quicksand, her feet devoured with each step.

They'd catch her. The gods only knew what they'd done to her: violated her, took her innocence. Tears burned her eyes and muddied the dirt on her face. Shouts were rising from behind, barely audible through the pounding in her ears as her heart raced painfully. She was so disoriented. Sand and sky were all she saw, tipping this way and that as her vision swam with dizziness. The sands seemed to have the sole purpose of gobbling up her feet as she sank in it past her ankles.

An enormous weight landed on her and drove her to the ground. Hands were grabbing her. Screaming, she kicked wildly, throwing her arms about in blind punches.

"Lunara!" Varila's sharp voice cut through her panic.

Lunara stopped struggling to see the same savage holding her. Her sister knelt by her side.

"Help me!" Lunara cried, reaching for her sister.

"Let her go," Varila said.

The barbarian released her, and Lunara flew into Varila's arms.

"It's all right. Nothing happened," Varila said.

Lunara burst into frenzied sobs, trying to convey her nakedness beneath the blanket, screaming the words of what she'd lost to a savage. Varila held her tightly, whispering comforts Lunara couldn't hear over her own ranting.

Exhaustion and a hoarse voice finally stopped her. When she could no longer speak, she curled up and wanted nothing more than to retreat into some dark corner of her mind, one ignorant to what had happened to her.

"I want you to listen to me," Varila whispered.

Shock threatened to claim her. She didn't want to deal with any of this. She felt unclean and wanted to bathe, wash away the stench of sweat and ... and ...

"Does it hurt?" Varila asked. "Between your legs? Does it hurt?"

Lunara rocked herself, seeing nothing.

Varila cupped Lunara's face in her hands. "If you were raped, it would hurt, throbbing, sore. You need to focus, Lunara. Does it hurt?"

She gazed at her sister's calm eyes, void of anger or fear. Gulping in a few deep breaths, Lunara shook her head.

Her sister smiled. "Nothing happened to you. The barbarians put you in a different dress, that's all."

Now that Varila mentioned it, Lunara felt a rough fabric bunched up oddly against her stomach and around her legs. She nodded her understanding.

"The man you saw is Father," Varila said. "He's here. He disguised himself as a savage so he could sneak into Avulin. He rescued us. We've been on the run for an entire night and half a day."

Lunara swallowed hard and peered around her sister. Her friends were mounted on grynfs, and the barbarian knelt behind Varila. His shoulders shook with sobs and tears streaked his filthy face, but he smiled. She'd recognize that smile in the darkest caves. She bolted from her sister and flew into her father's arms.

LUNARA JERKED awake to her father's panicked voice vibrating in his chest. When she looked over his shoulder, a wall of dust greeted her. It ate up the sky, carried forward by gusty winds catapulting it toward them with the speed of an avalanche.

"Push hard!" her father yelled. "It's another half mile!"

Winds whipped her hair about and blasted stinging sands on her face. The dust-laden air made her choke in each breath and dried her mouth. The grynfs plunged onward, the tide of the storm nipping at their heels.

Her father kicked his grynf and barreled by everyone to take the lead. Squinting through the dust, she saw crumbled structures jutting up from the sands. It wouldn't even qualify as a ruined town; perhaps village if one were to stretch the definition. As they rushed past the first abandoned home, she counted ten other dwellings that had deteriorated to nothing more than a pile of broken stones. The few walls that were standing were shorter than Wilhelm.

Her father reined in his grynf behind the tallest wall. "This is the best we've got!" he shouted above the yowling wind.

Lunara accepted her father's help to dismount. Her friends would barely fit, much less be protected, and only if they huddled practically on top of each other.

"Me don't want to die in this forsaken place!" Durak snarled.

"We can't stay out here," Wilhelm yelled over the wind.

"We don't have a choice," her father said. "This wall will shield us from the wind—"

"We've got to get out of it," Humar interrupted. The knight ripped a portion of his tunic and rested it over Salvarias's face. "The boy will die!"

"I'm open to options!" her father snapped. "There's no place—"

"Hello there," a voice called.

Lunara shielded her eyes to see through the grimy air. A man in slate-blue mage robes with a flowing white beard walked toward them.

"Vuddruk?" Humar said. "What in Nevlar's damnation are you doing here?"

"You wouldn't believe me if I told you," Vuddruk said. "Come with me. There's a hidden treasure beneath these sands."

Lunara's father kept a firm hold on her with one arm and guided his grynf with his free hand. They weaved through a few piles of rubble and came to the outskirts where a waist-high wall protected a home. It'd fallen like the rest, but the pile of stones had been cleared to reveal a tunnel leading underground.

Vuddruk motioned to Humar. "It'll be a long walk. There're no options so just go straight. I'll secure the mounts here. They'll survive the storm."

"They need to be out of sight," Humar said.

"Ah, in trouble again, I see," Vuddruk said, his eyes sparking with amusement. "I think we've been in this situation before."

Humar disappeared into the tunnel, followed closely by Lunara and the rest of her friends. They didn't walk long before the light faded, casting them into utter darkness. The winds were just a far-off howl, and the air tasted sweet and clean.

"We'll wait for Vuddruk," Humar said.

"What do you know of this mage?" her father asked.

"He's helped us once before," Humar said. "I don't trust him, but we've got little choice."

A painful wheeze sounded from Salvarias.

"What's wrong with the boy?" her father said.

"Salvarias has a breathing condition," Humar said. "The sands would have killed him."

Wilhelm's voice shook when he said, "We don't have his potions, Humar. He's not getting enough air."

"I found some of your supplies," her mother said. "There were potion vials among my findings."

Wilhelm's exhale of relief echoed in the tunnel. Lunara reached out and felt the walls. It seemed to be made of smooth glass.

"Sorry," Vuddruk said from behind. "Let me get us some light. *Ecia Lumenious.*" Beside Lunara, a stallion made of pure white light appeared. "Lead the way, Sir Knight."

Lunara followed the stallion down the tunnel, which was wide enough for her to walk alongside her father, though low enough Wilhelm had to duck. Indeed, the surfaces were smooth, reflecting the light like a stained window.

"How did you know we were here?" Humar asked Vuddruk.

"The boy," Vuddruk replied. "His magic is like a beacon for mages."

"Is that how you found us outside Zeeas?" Humar said.

"In part. The boy was near death. His power was fading with his life."

"Where is 'here,' exactly?" Edium said.

Vuddruk chuckled. "You'll see. I want you to be as surprised as I was when I discovered what I'm about to show you."

"This tunnel be unnatural," Durak said.

"Indeed," Vuddruk confirmed. "I formed it with magic."

Lunara heard Durak spit.

"Fear not," Vuddruk said. "My tunnel is as sturdy as any carved by a Cavrul."

They descended until the howling winds were but a memory. A hush blanketed the group, broken occasionally by the rasping wheeze of Salvarias. Lunara looked over at Okulu still being supported by Neithelas and his brother.

"Will everyone be all right?" she asked her father, staring at the blood seeping from various wounds on Durak, Humar, and Neithelas.

He shrugged. "I'm not sure. While Varila and I were getting Wilhelm, the others were attacked. It was a rough fight from what Humar tells me."

Eternity seemed to pass before the tunnel opened to yawning darkness. Lunara shrank from the emptiness before her, feeling as though it was a silent witness to something horrible.

"No worries, child," Vuddruk said. He whispered under his breath, and torches flared out in front of them, stretching as far as she could see. Lunara gasped. Before them lay a lost city, buried in dust and decay.

"The City of Quind," Vuddruk breathed. "Long thought lost."

"How ..." Humar's voice trailed off.

"I figured a Loutsil knight would be interested," Vuddruk said to Humar. "Everyone knows the mountain that Quind perched upon slid under the sands when Nevlar struck our world. It's why the lands east of the desert have horrendous winds. It's unnatural what occurred with Quind. It changed that whole side of Dalnar, the weather and landscape alike." Vuddruk gazed over the city. "I've studied my whole life to find it. And I did."

Lunara surveyed the city she'd read about in so many stories, trying to recall the maps drawn from the memory of those who'd survived Quind's fall. Estates that had been the homes of nobles and high-ranking knights were reduced to the size of Gundar's, but each had once rivaled the king of Loutsil's marbled castle in the city of Warton. Towering above all was a structure so magnificent, so massive that Lunara could not fathom its construction. The castle had been constructed by Zerana, much like the one in Warton, and its towering heights belied engineering. Above them, the sandstone slab acting as the sky had hacked off turrets and lay waste to watchtowers. The wall circling the castle had crumbled, but even in its ruin, it was taller than any Lunara had ever seen.

"I believe the castle is what saved it," Vuddruk said. "It loomed as tall as the mountain, you know. Shot into the clouds. Once the mountain slipped under the plate of sandstone that supports the desert, the castle was knocked down, but the foundation was too sturdy to crumble. It created this cavern and preserved I'd say ... maybe a quarter of the city."

"It's beautiful," Lunara said.

"Indeed," Vuddruk said. He cleared his throat. "Let's get everyone settled and patched up."

The steep descent along crumbled rock to the street below made Lunara slip as often as her father, but he took most of her weight and the dangers. At the bottom, Adok growled at Vuddruk before trotting off into the city, not waiting for any others.

"What's with the wolf?" Humar said.

Wilhelm shrugged. "Not sure."

"Plenty of places for him to explore," Vuddruk said. He glanced at Varila and smiled. "You'll be happy to know that Lake Virknil survived. Wait till you see how water was transported from the lake to the estates' washrooms."

Lunara shared a smile with Varila.

Vuddruk escorted them down the cobblestone street, past walled estate upon walled estate. Lunara couldn't peel her gaze from the awe-inspiring intricacy of carved iron gates, nor from the meticulously chiseled statues of long-lost creatures that lined the streets and towered above her. For the first time, even Wilhelm seemed small.

The estate Vuddruk entered appeared to have survived with the least amount of damage. The upper portion had caved, leaving four stories of solid-looking stone.

"First," Vuddruk said. "I'll get the washrooms set up. There're four in total, and I can use magic to boil the water so as to speed things up. After everyone's tended to, I'll need some help retrieving your packs I left in the tunnel."

"I'll help," her father said. "I think I'm in the best condition."

Vuddruk nodded. "And Wilhelm here."

"No," Humar said. "Wilhelm needs to tend to his brother. I'll help as well."

Inside, the tapestries had decayed, and what Lunara dreamed were formerly cushy sofas and chairs had deteriorated to their frames.

Vuddruk ushered them through a series of corridors and expansive rooms, aweing her with the once-lavishness of the city.

The corridor he stopped in was lined with four doors. "These are the washrooms," Vuddruk said. "They have a wonderful system that extracts water from the lake and delivers it right to a spout above the tubs. Marvelous feat of engineering. It's one of the many things I'm studying here. Imagine being able to draw water with a pull of a lever. Brilliant!" He opened one of the doors. "This one has the most baths. Five in total. The other rooms have two each."

"The girls will have their own," Humar said. "Edium and Talura can also have a private one. The rest of us will use this one."

"Of course," Vuddruk said, casting a wide smile to Lunara. His green eyes sparkled. "You look very familiar to me, dear child. Have we met before?"

Lunara shook her head. "No, Master Mage."

"Huh." Vuddruk shrugged. "Must be my senile old mind running away from me again. Come, come, girls. I'll show you how the device works."

Her father smiled and tilted his head as a sign to follow the mage. Varila snatched Lunara's hand and led her inside the next room. Two tubs that could've accommodated three people each were positioned in the center of the room.

Vuddruk walked over to a pull dangling from the low ceiling and gave it a tug. A spout mounted to the roof sputtered, and a steady stream of water poured into the tub.

Varila yanked a handle near the other tub with the same result. She grinned. "I'll have to get one of these."

"Ha!" Vuddruk said. "Your father might be the only one besides the king of Loutsil with enough money to hire the right engineers to figure it out. All I've deduced is that it involves a large wheel holding buckets of water."

Vuddruk waited until the tubs were full and tugged the lever again to stop the water. He chanted under his breath, flicked his hand, and the water erupted to a boil.

"There," he said. "Give it a bit to cool down. Once we retrieve your packs, I'm sure someone will bring you clothes and soap. Drying cloths are in that dresser." The mage pinched Lunara's cheek and slipped from the room.

Lunara stared at her tub, unable to focus on anything else but the clear, inviting waters. Long moments passed before she broke the silence. "I don't want Father or Mother to know of my connection with Salvarias. I don't understand it, and I'm not ready to try to explain it. I'll think of something, but right now, I can't even fathom where I'd start."

"I'll take care of them."

Lunara giggled. "Have I ever told you that you're the most amazing sister?"

"Several times. And each time, I tell you I know." Varila grinned wickedly. "Sisters have to have secrets, or else they're not sisters."

"Your turn. What happened after Sansis nearly killed Salvarias? I remember nothing until waking up in Father's arms."

Varila shrugged. "Not much to tell. I killed the king, rescued you and the others. We've been on the run since."

"So nothing happened with their king? I heard them say they were taking—"

"Water's ready," Varila said, unbuckling her armor. "Let's get rid of this stink. I smell worse than an ogre."

Lunara tested the water and squealed with delight. Shedding her blanket, she gaped at the "dress" she wore. "There's no point!"

Varila laughed. "I think that *is* the point."

Lunara happily ripped it off and sank into the tub. A knock on the door stopped her sister from slipping free of her armor. She strode over to the door and cracked it open.

"I've got fresh undergarments and soap," their mother said. "I'd love to hear what you girls have been up to, but I'm afraid it'll have to wait. I reek like I spent a week without a bath." She scrunched up her face in playful smile. "Actually, I have spent a week without bathing."

Varila laughed lightly. "We'll catch up soon."

Once their mother left, Lunara leaned her head back and closed her eyes, allowing the water time to loosen the grime caked on her skin. She dozed until Varila's vigorous scrubbing woke her. Just as Lunara sat up, Varila threw the cloth across the room and hugged her knees, staring off at something that drained color from her face. Lunara was about to rise from her tub to offer comfort, but her sister suddenly reclined and closed her eyes as if nothing had happened.

Understanding stole Lunara's breath. "I'm ... sorry ... I—" Her voice choked off.

Varila studied her a long moment before speaking. "Life is not endless meadows, Lunara. You're finally seeing what it truly is: a forest full of slippery moss, frightening shadows, and starved preda-tors. But in all that dangerous terrain are flowers. When one is found, you have to make sure no predator tramples it, that moss doesn't overtake it, and that it receives the sunshine it deserves." Varila's eyes distanced, and her voice was a whisper. "I am a flower in a forest of evil. I do not bow to anything, I am not crushed by horrors inflicted upon me, and I surround myself with those who feed me the love I need."

For the first time, Lunara saw Varila as the woman she hoped to one day be: a woman who could not protect herself from the evils of the world, but one who was never defeated or ruled by them.

WILHELM LEANED in the doorway of his room, watching his brother sleep. His half-brother: half-man half-creature, created by horrors of a murderous hunger that impregnated Wilhelm's wonderful mother, his caring and loving mother.

He should hate Salvarias—hate the half-creature burning inside with the same blackfire as the shadowfires ... as his brother's *father*. Wilhelm wondered if his mother knew what'd been forced upon her or if she'd forgotten that night as he had forgotten. She was never affectionate toward Salvarias, but that was his brother's fault. Salvarias wasn't an affectionate child unless it was toward Wilhelm.

He should hate him ... it.

He should feel less connected with Salvarias. They only shared a mother. No father. They didn't even look alike. Wilhelm doubted his mother was anything but a vessel for the creature's seed, just a place to keep it warm. Wilhelm had always known ... always seen it. If Salvarias were to share his smile, women would swoon over him and wait in pairs in his bed. His brother's power was beyond anything to roam Arden. Wilhelm had sensed it when he took a portion for himself ... when he took a portion of his brother's evil. But Wilhelm didn't feel it alive inside him like Salvarias. He felt wholly healthy, abnormally healthy. Perhaps his mother was right. Perhaps Zerana's grace watched over him. But that would mean the goddess's leftover powers didn't protect his half-brother, half man, half creature ... an abomination of life. A monstrosity.

He should hate him ... it.

Yet he didn't. All that swelled in him as he watched his brother was unconditional love. It filled Wilhelm completely, consumed his heart. Evil might have created his brother, but it didn't rule him. Salvarias was strong, loving, with a heart more capable of compassion than Zerana herself. Salvarias was abomination's opposite. He was a *person* who made others look like they were the monstrosities.

"Half-brother" and "creature" would never be uttered in Wilhelm's mind again. Salvarias was his brother, wholly, and would never learn the dark truth of the shadowfires. Wilhelm would take the knowledge to his grave: both of the shadowfires' existence as well as the truth they'd fathered Salvarias. If his brother ever discovered his creator ... Wilhelm shuddered to think. Salvarias harbored an internal pain Wilhelm never understood, but he'd be damned if anything added to it. He'd spent his life shielding his brother, keeping oddities a secret, trying to guard Salvarias from harm. Though Wilhelm had failed time and time again, he could at least keep this horrific revelation secret. In this, he would spare his brother grief.

Wilhelm inhaled deeply and let it out slowly, along with all he *should* have felt. With his mind reconciled, peacefulness settled over him, as if he'd come to terms with his destiny, as if he'd correctly answered a question that had hung over him for years. He'd always known ...

Unbidden, he whispered words directed at the evil stalking his brother, "He's mine. Not yours."

"How's the boy?" Vuddruk said from behind.

Wilhelm jumped clear of his skin. He looked over his shoulder to see Vuddruk's wide grin. "I think he's fine," Wilhelm said. "I didn't see any wounds that hadn't closed."

"Want me to check him over?" Vuddruk asked.

Wilhelm didn't trust the mage and preferred Okulu. "Is the half-Winsire up yet?"

"I gave him a potion to keep him resting through the night."

With none others gifted in healing, Wilhelm nodded.

Vuddruk peeled back the blankets covering Salvarias's scarred, bruised body, and glanced over at Wilhelm. "I'm going to do a spell to help with my touch. Don't be alarmed and run me through with that sword of yours."

Wilhelm hadn't realized he was gripping the hilt of his great sword. He relaxed his hand. "How did you know?"

Vuddruk shrugged. "Magic helps us see much. I noticed it last time I helped, but the boy was too close to death for me to do any damage. He's not so far gone now."

"It won't hurt him?"

"It'll be over quickly. I wouldn't do so if it weren't necessary."

Wilhelm slowly nodded.

Vuddruk whispered words under his breath, and sea-green fog dripped from his fingertip as he pressed it to Salvarias's forehead. His brother thrashed for a mere blink before groaning deeply. "Do you know what happened to Salvarias? What caused these wounds?"

Suddenly, Vuddruk cried out and scrambled back. As it had happened with Mafarias, the fog seeped into Salvarias. His brother moaned again before he stilled.

"What happened?" Wilhelm asked.

"He stole my power." Vuddruk hauled himself up, shaking off whatever he'd suffered. "Not intentionally, mind you. His magic … it's extremely protective. It thought I was hurting him so it lashed out at me. It took whatever power I was using for itself."

"I don't think that's it," Wilhelm said. "My uncle did the same thing when my brother was born. He didn't have magic back then, not until he was six."

"I don't have another explanation, young man. The magic's link is more solid than any I've ever seen." Vuddruk shook his head. "Now tell me, what happened to put the boy in this state?"

"There was a man robed in orange who had him sliced open. He …" Wilhelm swallowed his anger and the bloody memory. "He kept my brother alive while he disemboweled him."

Vuddruk shuddered. "An old man? Looks like his skin is missing?"

Wilhelm jerked his gaze to Vuddruk. "Would you like to tell me how you know such a man?"

"Every old wizard has heard of Sansis. The man's been around since the days of Veedran. I thought I saw him years ago. I guess I did. Should've killed him."

Wilhelm grunted. "I don't think it's possible."

"Everyone and everything can die, Wilhelm. You just have to find out what kills them."

Vuddruk turned Salvarias over, examining him closely. Once done, he covered him and met Wilhelm at the door. "He'll be fine. Sansis's healing takes a toll on the body, from what I've heard. He'll be sore for days. Probably have trouble eating. The body wasn't meant to be jostled about and put back together. He must have broken something else in that bum leg. It's why it's swollen. It healed enough that he'll walk on it again, but it'll take time." Vuddruk rested a hand on Wilhelm's shoulder. "Sansis did something to the boy's heart. It's weak ... very weak. Keep that in mind on future adventures. Overexertion, too much excitement, any wound that bleeds freely, even if nonlethal, could kill him."

Wilhelm clenched his fist and nodded. "Can we give him anything?"

"I suspect he'll come up with his own remedy. Edium is going through the packs he gathered, trying to find the boy's breathing concoction. I'm sure he'll be along shortly."

"Thanks."

"Do you need any tending to?"

He shook his head.

"So be it." Vuddruk patted his shoulder before leaving the room.

Wilhelm closed the door as he mulled over Vuddruk's conversation. It was too coincidental for the mage to find them twice. Then it suddenly hit him. Vuddruk had known his name. Wilhelm went over their first meeting, trying to recall each word spoken. They'd never told Vuddruk their names. Nor had introductions been made yet. They hadn't even had time to formerly meet Neithelas's brother. Wilhelm hadn't even said hello to Talura.

A knock on the door startled him from his thoughts. Wrapping his hand around the hilt of his sword, he edged open the door and peered out.

"I found them," Edium said, presenting Wilhelm with a handful of vials. "I see you both got baths already."

Wilhelm nodded, taking the vials. "Thanks for bringing these." When Edium turned to leave, Wilhelm said, "Did you tell Vuddruk who we are? Our names, I mean."

Edium shook his head. "No. Not yet. We talked mostly about his findings in the city. He said once we were cleaned up, he'd meet us in the dining room for introductions. Why do you ask?"

"He knew my name."

"One of us probably said it," Edium said. He glanced at Wilhelm's grip on his sword. "Everything all right, boy?"

"I ..." Wilhelm slouched and shook his head. "I'm sure it's nothing. Thank you for finding these."

"Get some rest," Edium said. He smiled reassuringly before leaving the room and heading down the hall, his whistling muffled when Wilhelm latched the door closed.

A sharp gasp spun him around. Salvarias was clutching his chest, gulping for air, and his face was tinted blue. Wilhelm darted to his brother's side, propped him to sit, and uncorked the vial.

"We're safe, Salv," he said. "Drink this."

Salvarias choked down the liquid.

"Breathe just like me," Wilhelm said.

Salvarias focused on Wilhelm, tears forming, fists balling his tunic.

"You need to relax," he said. "Don't try so hard."

Salvarias's airless gasps made Wilhelm's lungs ache in sympathy, and he fought the urge to devour huge breaths. Time passed as slow as a slug. The coolness and mustiness of the room seemed amplified by his heightening tension.

"Come on, Salv," Wilhelm whispered. "For me, just one long breath."

Salvarias's feet kicked on the bed, tears finally breaking free, and then he gasped in lungsful of air.

"We're safe," Wilhelm said. "We escaped Avulin."

Once Salvarias gained control over his breathing, he sat up on his own and looked around the room. His eyes widened as he ran his hand over Wilhelm's back. "Your wounds ... How—what—"

As suspected, Salvarias had no recollection of the shadowfires, which would play into Wilhelm's plan perfectly. He had already told Humar, Durak, and Neithelas that Sansis had been forced to heal him before he'd been taken to the arena. It was a boldfaced lie, one he didn't stomach well, but one that was necessary. Edium, Talura, and Okulu would believe Humar. That left Varila, Lunara, and Salvarias. He could've fed Varila the same lie, but for some reason, he wanted to be truthful with her and trusted her to take care of Lunara. Now, he faced the one person he couldn't lie to, the one person who seemed to be able to peer inside his soul.

Smiling, he took in a deep breath. "I don't want to tell you, Salv. Something happened in the arena, something I don't understand, something I'm still digesting. I need you to trust me and not ask questions."

"Did Sansis—"

"No questions, Salv."

Salvarias's eyes narrowed. "There is something different about you."

Wilhelm shrugged off his brother's comment. "Not sure what you mean."

Salvarias swallowed hard and sagged against the wall. "You have never withheld anything from me, Brother. Not when I have asked you for the truth."

"No, I never have. I've always told you what you wanted to know. If you push me, I'll tell you everything. But I'm asking you, begging you, please don't make me. I need you to trust me on this, Salv."

Salvarias plucked up another potion vial and drank the contents. His gaze never left Wilhelm's. "If you think it best, Brother, I will not question you."

Grinning, Wilhelm ruffled his brother's hair. "Thanks. Why don't you get some sleep?"

Salvarias glanced around the room. "Is Sansis ... dead?"

Wilhelm's smile faded. For the first time, he made himself study his brother's mutilated body, forcing himself to see each wound he had turned his gaze from in the past. Now, he looked upon the full horror of what Sansis had done; at the scars stacked upon each other, the knotted burn marks, the missing pinky. Guilt fueled Wilhelm's anger and shook his voice when he said, "I know it was Sansis who cut you. I know what he did to you in Zeeas."

Seeming ashamed, as if the mutilation was Salvarias's own fault, he pulled up the blanket to cover his maimed body, eyes averted, cheeks tinted red. It cut through Wilhelm like a hot knife, reminding him of the times he'd failed to keep his brother safe when they were younger, of the bullies' beatings, the cringes, and the nightmares.

Wilhelm folded his brother close, wincing when fingers dug into his back. Jaw tight with anger, he whispered, "I swear to you, Salv, I'll kill the bastard. I'll find a way, and then I'll hunt him down. There won't be a corner dark enough for him to hide in. I swear it."

"Forgive me, Brother. I agreed to go with him ... I—"

"There's nothing to forgive. But you can never agree to go with him again. You've got to fight." He tapped his brother's chin, and Salvarias looked up at him. "I'm bound to get hurt, Salv. It'll happen, and there will be times when you can't prevent it. But I promise you I *will* survive. You can't agree to stuff to keep me from harm. You have to trust me."

"I trust you, Brother. You will never leave me."

His brother's words sounded more like a plea than a statement. "I promise I'll never leave you. If you're ever taken from me again, I'll find you. You just have to fight until I do."

A smile spread across Salvarias's face, seeming to rid a layer of cold and brighten the candlelight. Air came alive with freshness.

Wilhelm's grin grew childishly large. "Promise me you'll fight him. Promise me you'll never give in to him."

"I promise."

"Good. I want you to get some sleep. I'm going to let everyone know you're all right."

His words seemed to remind Salvarias of his exhaustion, and he sank to bed without further prompting, falling asleep before Wilhelm covered him with all the blankets in the room.

When Wilhelm opened the door, Lunara was poised for a knock, looking lovely as ever in a peach dress that gathered under her bosom, flowing freely around her frame.

"How is he?" she asked.

He stepped aside to allow her in. "Sleeping. How are you?"

"It ... it was my fault."

"What was?"

"That the man robed in orange hurt him. Our connection grants me the ability to give him strength. When I saw Adok, I thought we could escape. I shoved my strength at his magic. All ... all that came to me after I did was pain. I'm so sorry, Wilhelm."

"You didn't know what that sick man would do. You thought you were helping. It's all I could ever ask of you: to help him when he's hurt."

"Thank you." Lunara snagged hold of his tunic, pulled him down, and kissed his cheek. "You're a wonderful brother. Salvarias is lucky to have you."

He swooped her up in a hug and swung her side to side. Her soft giggle induced his grin. "I don't know if I've said it or not, but thank you for caring for him. It's nice not to be the only one."

"He deserves nothing less."

When he lowered her, he saw her gaze lingering on Salvarias. Her heart might as well have burst from her chest to announce her feelings. Salvarias, however, wasn't a man who offered affections. Not for eighteen years had his brother even looked at a woman. "You know he's not one to part with his heart," he said.

"I expect nothing from him." He was about to voice his relief when she said, "As much as I expect everything from him."

"You're like a sister to me. I don't want to see you hurt."

Lunara patted his cheek. "I know. Now go eat before your growling stomach wakes him."

She slipped by him, sat next to Salvarias, and opened a book. Almost absently, she twirled a lock of his brother's hair between her fingers. The lines of pain on Salvarias's face melted, and he inhaled a deep breath. His expression turned peaceful, and his usual tense furl loosened until he lay almost stretched out. Someday, Wilhelm would have to find the appropriate time to ask his brother the millions of questions he'd developed since Salvarias's rescue.

Casting her a wink, Wilhelm strolled from the room and closed the door behind him. He froze when he saw Varila outside her room, taking in several deep breaths, clenching her trembling hands into tight fists. When she raised her beaten face, there was a haunted flicker in her sea-blue eyes that passed quickly. She stood straight.

"Happy you're alive, you giant ogre," she said, a smile spreading. It lacked its usual mischievous flicker.

He knew. With one look he knew, and the knowledge hit him like a blow. It must have played across his face. Her eyes tightened, and her jaw clenched. She turned away from him.

Stepping in front of her to block her escape, he gently took her hands in his. She'd struggled in her bindings so long that deep scores had swollen her wrists to nearly the width of her hand. Without fully thinking, he bent down and kissed each lightly. When he met her gaze, there was a question in her eyes he knew without her voicing it. Indeed, the horrible event had changed his feelings for her. He respected the defiance in her eyes, the strength in her heart, and her fight more than ever before. And she had fought. Her blue-black eye had swollen shut, the lump on her forehead bulged the size of a pebble, and a cut on her lip had crusted over with blood. By all the gods, she was stunning. That she even thought he'd lose the care he had for her hurt.

In answer to her unspoken question, he gently kissed her forehead and lightly pressed his lips to her bruised eye.

"I killed him," she said, holding her head high, masking the pain in her eyes with fake cockiness. "I told him I wouldn't, then I slit his throat."

He hooked his finger around her chin. "Don't you dare act around me. Not me."

"You see me differently than everyone else."

"I ..." He wanted to tell her he loved her, to confess what had dwelled in his heart for some time. But he spared himself the pain. Salvarias would always come first. The woman Wilhelm would choose for a wife would have to love his brother as much as he did. That woman wasn't Varila. He lowered his head, fighting a terrible tightening of his chest.

Soft lips pressed to his. He tried to resist her, but his will failed, and he opened his mouth to her tentative pressure. She tasted like ale: sweet, fresh, cool. Her hands slid up his chest to wrap around his neck. He gathered her close, devouring her body in his arms, deepening his taste of her.

Tension drained from her stiff stance, and she melted into his embrace. Saltiness from her tears slipped between their lips and fueled his love.

"Ahem," Edium said.

Wilhelm jumped and snatched his hands back. "Sorry ... I mean ... I'm not ..." He cast Varila a pleading look.

Smiling, she waved her father away. "We'll be down in a moment."

Edium nodded. "Food will get cold. I'm sure you'll be respectful of my daughter from here on out, Wilhelm."

"I was ... I mean, of course," he stammered.

Once Edium left, Varila eyed him up and down. "Wanna tell me what happened in the arena? How in Oblivion you walked out of there looking better than when you walked in?"

"Time stopped in the arena," Wilhelm said carefully, plotting each word. "A creature helped me."

"A creature?"

"A creature I don't trust. I've met one before, and they're not nice."

Varila's brow crinkled. "Then why did it help you?"

"Because whoever is after Salv wants him alive. I was its single hope to get him out of the sands."

"What did Humar think?"

Unable to meet her gaze, he stared at their boots nearly touching toe to toe. "I lied to Humar. I told him Sansis healed me. It's what they'll believe. Except for Salv. He's not questioning me about it."

"You're not worried Humar will say something?"

"No, he promised not to bring it up."

Varila shook her head. "You and Lunara. I don't get these secrets you two keep."

"I can't let Salv find out," Wilhelm said. "There's more to it, but I swear Salv can never find out a creature helped me. He's trusting me, and I'm asking you to do the same."

Varila sighed. "You've got my word. But, one day, I hope you'll tell me with the whole truth."

"If ever there's a person I would trust in this world to share that with, it'd be you."

She grinned up at him through thick eyelashes. "Kiss me, you damn ogre."

Wilhelm obliged eagerly.

33

E dium rapped on Humar's door. "It's Edium."
"Come in," Humar called.

Edium stepped inside a room that was a replica of his: a bed void of a mattress, side tables, a sitting area, fireplace, and dresser. "I was going to see if you were ready to meet with the others."

Humar stood in front of his armor sprawled on a table. The knight's shirtless chest had a fair number of scars, surface wounds by their look—old ... very old. "Let me get dressed."

"You've seen some battles," Edium remarked.

Humar laughed lightly. "Most of these are from my days training for knighthood." He pulled on his gambeson. "Loutsil is adamant that knights begin training as soon as they show an aptitude for coordination and the strength to wield a weapon. I held my first wooden sword when I was five. By six, I held a real one." Humar began the arduous task of buckling on the shiny pieces of his armor. "Most start with wooden swords at eight. I had ... special circumstances. There was much I needed to learn, so I was awarded an early start."

Edium raised an eyebrow at the speed in which Humar assembled himself. Leg guards were done. "When did you have time to polish it?"

"We had drills in the academy," Humar said, hefting on his breastplate. "Whippings to any boy who couldn't polish it fast enough to appease the master. You learn quickly under such instruction."

"Indeed, Loutsil varies greatly from Dalnar." Edium glanced up and down the empty corridor. "Are you sure it's necessary to wear armor? Seems we're pretty safe here."

"I've worn armor since I was ten." Humar grinned. "I feel naked without it. Furthermore, it seems we often find ourselves darting off suddenly. I want to be prepared. I've not lost any piece of my armor and I don't plan to. This set I've owned since I was fifteen. Thanks to a few modifications by Durak, I've grown into it nicely."

Edium chuckled. "Good thing Talura found it. I'd hate to see your streak broken."

"I as well. I owe her."

"Where were you headed before you were captured?"

Humar paused in tightening an arm guard. "I've promised the boy I wouldn't say."

"You know I could help if you just told me what in all Oblivion is going on."

Humar shrugged his armor into place "I'm sure you could. Matter of fact, I'd love nothing more than to tell you everything I know, which would take the same amount of time as Okulu spends sipping his ale. What I will tell you is that boy is wrapped up in something very dangerous. What seeks him can only come from the depths of Oblivion."

"You're the one in charge of this group. If it's in the best interests of everyone, you should break your promise and tell me what you know."

Humar sheathed his sword and joined Edium at the door. "I'm a knight. I have oaths. I live by my word. The boy trusts me to tell people what needs to be told. Right now, I'm seeking truth to the boy's claims before I go shouting Salvarias's ... speculation across Dalnar. You're more than welcome to journey with us and see the truth for yourself. Until I deem it absolutely necessary, our end goal will remain between the brothers and myself."

"You're a fool."

Humar chuckled and clapped Edium's shoulder. "More so than you know. Come, let's meet the others."

Edium and Humar found Durak, Vuddruk, and the Winsire brothers in the dining hall. Humar strode up to one of the brothers and offered his hand. "I'm Humar."

The Winsire accepted. "Prince Arthias Frisliasi of Meitholias. My brother has told me much about you. To discover a Loutsil knight free of corruption is a rarity. You have my thanks for seeing my brother safely across Dalnar."

"The pleasure was mine," Humar said, motioning everyone to sit. The knight introduced Edium to the group before reclining in a chair. "If you're so inclined, I'd like to hear about your journey, Arthias."

"I am a prince and should be addressed as such," Arthias said coldly.

"I rarely acknowledge titles," Humar said. "They mean little to me."

"You show your heritage," Arthias sneered.

"I think grown men should act as such," Edium said, tossing a friendly smile at Arthias. "Especially when our cause is aligned. You seek to discover the identity of the darkness plaguing Dalnar, as does Humar. Throw my name in the mix as well. Men have little need for formalities when the lives of our loved ones rest with each breath we take. Dark times such as these require us to put aside our titles of empty fame."

"Lord Bellerum speaks wisely, brother," Neithelas said.

Arthias tilted his head. "As my brother wishes. My journey at the start was peaceful. I talked with many people in many cities, I listened to the trees' whispers, and I followed my own instincts. When I learned that none ventured south of the barbarian desert, I knew my destination. Keeping to the north of the sands, I headed for the coastline and the Watythm city of Xeroth. I must've skirted the desert too closely to her heart. I was captured in the night and taken to Avulin. I've lived longer than any other human combatant." Arthias tossed back his near-white blond hair, lifting his head proudly. "A bow can take down a foe before their sword can come within range to strike. I was prized and won favor with the crowd. My reward was food. I fought on because, in my heart, I knew my father wouldn't let me perish."

Humar smiled at Neithelas. "You owe your life to your brother. He left without your father's permission. He said you two were close, and he wouldn't rest until he found you."

Instead of a proud smile, Neithelas blushed and looked down at the table.

Arthias sprang from his chair. "Is what this knight says true, Neithelas?"

Neithelas rose and met Arthias's cold gaze. "Yes, Brother. I disobeyed Father."

Arthias slapped Neithelas across the cheek. "Fool! You're second heir to the throne! What would've happened if we both perished?"

"I—"

Arthias slapped Neithelas again. "Speak to me no more this day. You're a disgrace to our family."

Edium bolted up. "Your brother saved you! He—"

"Do not involve yourself in our matters!" Arthias snapped. "You don't understand our culture. You don't know of the shame my brother has brought to our family!"

"The only shame felt in this room should come from you!" Edium said. "How could you treat your brother with—"

"Please, my lord," Neithelas said. "Prince Arthias is correct. I appreciate your support, but I've disgraced my family. I must accept the consequences of my actions."

Humar rested a hand on Edium's arm and gave him a gentle tug to sit. "We'll not interfere in this matter," Humar said to Arthias. "I trust you'll take into account that without Neithelas's help, all in our party would've perished."

"And tell me why the lives of Erthlas and Cavruls should change Neithelas's punishment," Arthias said.

"There's one within our group who is hunted by the evil stalking our lands," Humar said. "A young mage who holds a high level of power. It's imperative the boy live so he can lead us to this dark force."

Arthias sank to his chair. "My brother has told me of this mage. He said the trees have sensed in Salvarias ... something unnatural."

Humar shrugged. "I wouldn't doubt it."

Edium startled at Humar's admission. "Why would you agree to such a thing?"

"We've seen things you haven't," Humar said. "Trust me when I say that Salvarias is not ordinary."

"He leads you?" Arthias asked.

Humar nodded. "He has insights none others possess. The boy will direct us to the heart of this madness."

"Insights? I can assume he is leading you to the army?" Arthias said.

Humar ran his hand through his hair. "So it's true?"

"Rumors," Arthias said. "Spoken from drunk traders who said they saw a mass of thousands yet couldn't say where nor accurately guess their numbers. Though I gave them little credit, I was going to explore the plains myself. Since the mage has led you this far, the rumors could hold more truths than lies."

"An army!" Edium's jaw dropped when he turned to Humar. "Nevlar's betrayal! You don't think it important to tell me of an army!"

"I haven't seen it for myself," Humar said. "If such a thing truly existed, I find it hard to believe none would know about it."

"Fool," Edium growled. "No one in their sane mind travels east of Treppter. By Nevlar's fury, none even travel by land to Xeroth. Those plains are unholy. Winds will tear your skin off and seasons never touch the air. It's always warm. Grasses and trees survive without rains. The rocky terrain can lame an inexperienced horse in hours. I know because I was in the army that tried to cross the plains to end Crutar's raids."

"Edium's right," Vuddruk said. "It's the perfect hiding spot for an army. We've lost too many men in that section of Dalnar. We've accepted Crutar's monthly snatching of women and girls because their loss isn't nearly what we've suffered trying to stop him."

"But the raids are increasing," Arthias said. "Hardly any women are left in small villages. Nor are there healthy men. Only the old remain."

"I don't think it's Crutar," Humar said. "One of our captors, Dethal, said 'God.' His tone was fearful. Crutar, from what I've been told by a mage friend of mine, holds little power. Dethal wouldn't be frightened of him."

"Your mage friend speaks the truth," Vuddruk said.

"What else have you learned?" Arthias asked.

"They were after Edium," Humar said, casting a wane smile. "It appears they don't like you building an army of your own. They were going to send word that Varila was turned over to Chesrick to bait you into going to the desert. You've got a target on your back, my friend. You'll need to be careful."

"What now?" Arthias said.

"I still intend to follow the boy," Humar said. "Any of you thinking of joining us should know a few things. First, I'm in charge of this group. If you come, you'll do what I say without hesitation. You'll have to trust me. Secondly, don't question the boy about his plans. Thirdly. If you value your head, you won't point out anything odd you might witness or hear from Salvarias. The boy will count nonstop, he'll fiddle with a puzzle box I find completely disquieting, he'll have nightmares where he wakes up screaming with a bloody nose, he'll wander from camp in the dead of night to perform spells, and animals are ... fond of him. Wilhelm has a short temper when it comes to his brother. Mention anything to the boy about what I've told you and Wilhelm will cut out your tongue. Any questions?"

Edium grinned. "Since you asked, what's a Loutsil knight doing so far from home?"

Humar laughed. "I thought by now you'd have figured out I'm not one to talk about myself."

Edium leaned back in his chair, studying Humar with curiosity overflowing. There was more to the knight than a keen mind, unbending emotional control, and impressive swordsmanship. Something harrowing lurked behind Humar's friendly smile.

~

SALVARIAS STIRRED AWAKE, reluctantly leaving the darkness he had roamed. It had not been frightening, nor did he feel completely alone. A presence followed him, shielding him from the usual horrors of his dreams, leaving nothing but peaceful, blessed darkness. He longed to return to its comforts, to drift in the shadow of the presence protecting him, but the realization of his lazy thoughts, the missing images of death, and the lack of whispers told him Lunara was touching him. Should he care? He was so tired. And the darkness ...

Sighing, he shifted away, feeling her fingers tug through his hair. Images raced forward of dying men, women, and children, the victims of his parents' murderer sliced across his mind and body, and screams echoed around him. His thoughts went from lazy to a whirlwind. Grimacing against the rush, he shut his eyes tightly, biting back a groan of pain.

Even with the chaos of his thoughts, he felt the hollowness of Adok and Mithal. He hoped they had escaped Catlin. Yet in all his selfishness, he desired their presence more than anything. The missing touch of Adok's mind left a hole in Salvarias's heart, an emptiness that made him afraid, alone. He would give anything to hear the wolf's rhythmic, fond tone used even when scolding and lecturing Salvarias on safety.

Once it all was within his control again, he opened his eyes, and Lunara's sweet smile greeted him. He swore he saw the sun rise in her eyes.

"Hello," she said.

Salvarias forced his body to sit, propped an elbow on his knee, and sank his head in his hand. "My lady."

"How are you feeling?"

In truth, he was miserable. His heart ached with each beat, his lungs were clogged with sand, his head thumped against his skull, and his insides felt like someone had clubbed them to death. "Fine, my lady."

"Liar," she whispered.

Soft fingertips traced down his spine, sending a pleasant shiver along his skin. As her touch glided over the numerous bumps on his back, it summoned forth the memory of the torture wall in Zeeas. Nails had reached floor to ceiling while six larger spikes jutted out from the rest to hold his weight, seeming as if they were positioned just for him. A shudder racked him as he remembered the feeling when they pierced his skin each time he had been impaled on the wall. He clearly saw Sansis's sick face as he sliced Salvarias open, felt the jab of each nail when he would twitch in pain. The memory was so vivid he found himself trembling with the cold that had plagued him from his days in the dark room.

Lunara shifted closer, sliding her fingers over each hole. Her warmth stripped away his chill, and the whiff of a spring meadow eased his mind. The tenderness of her touch banished his pain and replaced it with desire. Overcoming his selfishness, he flinched from her fingers.

You should send her away, my pet, the presence hissed.

"Are you up for a walk?" Lunara asked. "There's a lovely library here. A few books managed to survive."

He suddenly became aware he was naked and very aroused. Luckily his blanket hid his lapse in control. Squelching his weak thoughts, he shook his head. "I should see to the others."

"No need," she said, rising from the bed. "Vuddruk attended to them already. Everyone's meeting in the dining hall."

Salvarias looked around his room. "Vuddruk? Where are we?"

"Remarkably, the city of Quind." She placed a set of robes next to him. "After you've dressed, I'll tell you everything on the way to the library." Casting him another sweet smile, she left the room.

He dressed and tugged on his boots, wincing when his newly broken and newly healed leg throbbed with pain. He called forth his staff and used it to shove himself up. Grimacing against what he knew was to come, he tested a minor amount of weight on his leg. It gave immediately, and he barely kept on his feet. He mused the darkness had developed a new ploy to chip away at his body, breaking him one small portion at a time until nothing would be left.

He joined Lunara outside and followed her down a maze of corridors that tested his counting abilities as he listened to her retelling of Vuddruk's story, all the while battling his twitching free hand as it searched for the soft leather of his spell book or the sleek fur of Adok.

They stepped through a threshold to enter an outdoor courtyard with a long-dead garden. He pondered if any others would have noticed the skeleton crumpled in the dried-up pond or the wooden toy soldier clutched in the dead's hand. The alabaster statues sprinkled about—most broken and chipped—made the space feel haunted, as if their vacant eyes were watching him. The ruin of what was once surely a spectacular garden drove home a feeling of life fleeting by him, of the mortality of it all. His morbid thoughts conjured a strong sense that he would die a young man. Time was the sun burning away a precious cup of water in the middle of the desert. And he was in a race to be the first one to reach it.

They passed through another door and into a spacious, two-story room stacked floor to ceiling with books. By the looks of some, one touch would turn them to dust. A few, however, had managed to survive.

"Beautiful, isn't it?" she whispered.

Salvarias nodded. "Indeed, my lady."

As they strolled from shelf to shelf, Salvarias asked, "Tell me what happened after the caves. I remember little."

Lunara smiled up at him. "There's nothing to tell. The trip through the sands was painful for us both. I must offer my thanks yet again for saving my life. I'd given up. It was you who pulled us from Death's grip."

"I am sorry you had to experience it, my lady. I was not aware how connected we were."

"It's not your fault. Varila told me of Wilhelm's battle with the troll. He must've been brilliant."

"I do not remember my brother killing it."

"Adok—"

Salvarias looked up sharply. "Adok?"

"He's here. He—"

Salvarias ceased listening and stretched out his mind. Adok's presence burst into a rant of how Salvarias always seemed to get into trouble. He hobbled as fast his leg would allow to the door and flung it open. Adok tackled him to the ground, continuing his stern lecture and licking Salvarias's face. He threw his arms around Adok's neck and hugged him.

"I thought I would never see you again, my friend." The painful void of the wolf's presence flooded with care. "Mithal?" Salvarias asked, looking first at the wolf then Lunara.

She shook her head. "I don't know."

Adok told him someone had stolen the horses in the night. Salvarias blinked back his tears and focused on his happiness. At least one of his friends was with him.

Lunara cupped the wolf's face in her hands and kissed his muzzle. "We didn't know where you went." She turned a frown to Salvarias. "Does he mind that? The kisses, I mean."

Salvarias shook his head.

"What's he saying?" Lunara asked.

Cheeks burning, Salvarias grabbed his staff and shoved himself to his feet. He made it one step before Adok snagged his robes and growled. Keeping his gaze from Lunara, he said, "He thinks your beauty is unmatched, my lady. And ... and he would appreciate more kisses."

Lunara giggled and threw her arms around Adok, planting kisses on every inch of his face. The wolf asked Salvarias if he was jealous, and he firmly said no. He yanked his robes free and continued to study the books.

After near half an hour gathering his selections, he stared at the two tables full of his choices. Lunara joined his side and frowned. "I don't think we can take them all with us."

Salvarias sighed. "We cannot."

Giggling, Lunara examined each book, tossing some aside and keeping others. When she was done, they were down to half a table.

"Hmmm," Lunara said, gliding her fingers over the books. He shivered at the memory of her caress. "Round two," she said, grinning up at him.

This time, they discussed each book together, talking of what they had read that might compare or if they had ever heard of the book. When done, they had narrowed it down to ten.

"Perfect!" Lunara said.

"I think not, my lady. We should only take five. The weight on the packs—"

"Nonsense," Lunara said, stacking books in his arm. "My father and mother are here. They'll help carry some."

"Your parents are here? Is there anything else you are forgetting to tell me?"

Lunara shrugged, gathering up the rest of the books. "We can talk about the rest another time."

He could not believe it had taken him so long to see the deep pain in her eyes. Setting the stack of books on the table, he gently took the ones from her arms and set them aside. He angled down to try and catch her gaze. "My lady?"

She flung her arms around his neck, burying her face in his chest. Her words flooded out as she recounted the sight of the dead Cavruls in Catlin, the fear and violation she had felt when Sansis healed Salvarias, what she had thought happened to her when she woke, and the wounds she had seen on their companions. Her last word was a choking of Varila's name and held so much pain that he tightened his embrace, wishing nothing more than for his arms to take away her sorrow. She did not need to confess what happened to Varila. Her pain said it more than any words.

When Lunara finally calmed, he unfolded her from his arms, and bent to keep her gaze. "I will see to all within our company. And you do not need me to tell you of Varila's strength. I will give her a potion that will grant her a dreamless sleep and a calm mind so it is easier for her to ... come to terms with what happened."

Lunara smiled, causing tears to trickle down her cheeks. "Thank you."

Salvarias stepped back and bowed. "Shall we?"

She nodded, wiping her tears. He collected all the books he could carry and followed her from the room.

Thousands of innocent Cavruls dead, the presence said sadly. *An entire city destroyed. They would still be alive if you hadn't been in their city.*

Salvarias swallowed down the bile that rose in his throat.

I continued to be amazed that you can live with yourself.

As do I.

In his room, they deposited the books in a corner, and then Lunara led him down the hall, another set of stairs, and into a warmly lit dining hall.

Wilhelm's instant grin spread. "Hungry?"

Salvarias nodded and surveyed the room, startling when his gaze fell to an old man studying him, smoking a pipe of tobacco. The level of the wizard's skill would rival that of Mafarias. Salvarias bowed and folded his hands in the sleeve of his robes.

"Salvarias Laybryth," the old man said. "I'm Vuddruk."

Salvarias tilted his head. "My brother told me of your care outside Treppter, Master Vuddruk. Allow me to offer my thanks. Your skill is impressive."

Vuddruk shrugged. "I do what I do."

"How have you come to be our savior once again?"

"I've been down here exploring for weeks. I sensed your power. It's like a flaring torch in the darkness, boy. You should really learn to shield some of that."

Salvarias glanced at Varila. Obviously, she knew he had discovered what happened. Lunara's lowered head was a giveaway. Varila's eyes were not seeking assurances or comforts; they were challenging him to be dull-witted enough to offer pity. Her distaste of such emotion was something he easily related to. He hated those looks he received when any saw his body.

Based on the fire in her eyes, she had not caved to defeat as easily as Salvarias's mother had done. No doubt Varila fought. No doubt Varila had not permitted the man power over her. For the first time, he found a woman he respected more than his mother, a stronger woman.

Instead of looking away awkwardly, he stared right at her and tilted his head, emitting all the respect he felt for her. Her eyes softened, and she snuggled down in Wilhelm's embrace. It was the closest she had come to showing him anything less than hatred. He swallowed back the hope of one day earning her favor. Though undeserving, he desperately wanted it.

He glanced at the others and quickly concocted remedies in his mind. When he turned, Lord Bellerum was behind him offering a hand and a smile.

Salvarias bowed. "Lord Bellerum."

"Just Edium, Salvarias. You've saved my city. I don't think we're on formal terms."

Salvarias kept silent.

"Come, I have something for you." Lord Bellerum turned on his heel, not waiting for a response.

Salvarias bowed his farewell to the group and followed Lord Bellerum up the stairs, which were much more difficult to scale, and into a room similar to his.

"My wife came across your packs," Lord Bellerum said, rummaging around in a pile of supplies. "They'd burned most of your robes, but there are a few things barbarians won't touch for fear of being cursed. Mage books are one of them. Now, normally, I would leave books behind, but I don't remember you ever setting this one aside."

When Lord Bellerum rose, he presented Salvarias's spell book. He fought the urge to snatch it and hop around the room in utter joy.

He bowed as he accepted it. "You have my eternal gratitude, my lord. This book is priceless to me."

"Edium, just call me Edium."

"Good day." Salvarias walked to the door.

"One more thing, boy."

He barely turned in time to catch an object Lord Bellerum had tossed. It was Salvarias's herb pouch.

"Thought those herbs would come in handy," Lord Bellerum said. "My wife found them."

"Indeed they will, my lord—"

"Edium."

"Once again, I am in your debt. If you will excuse me, I would like to visit Okulu."

"Of course. On the right, down two doors."

Salvarias bowed and left the room. He went to Okulu's room and knocked softly.

"I'm trying to sleep!" Okulu snapped.

Salvarias grinned at Adok. "Perhaps I should come bearing gifts first."

He made his way down the treacherous stairs and found Vuddruk. "By chance do you have ale or wine?"

"Spirits and magic don't mix, boy."

"It would be for Okulu."

"Oh ... lemme see." Vuddruk rummage through a pantry and produced a bottle of wine. "It'll be potent. Been aging for a thousand years."

Salvarias bowed. "Thank you."

He hurried back up the stairs and knocked again.

"By all the gods in all the worlds! What do you want?"

Salvarias slipped into the dim room, softly illuminated by a single candle. His gut churned at the sight of Okulu seeping some yellow, foul smelling liquid. The merc's eyes were jaundiced, and his skin sallow. Blood wept down the white dressing wrapped around his head.

Salvarias lifted the bottle. "I thought you could use some comfort."

Okulu's eyes lit. "I'd kiss you if it wouldn't be weird."

Salvarias pulled a chair next to the bed, uncorked the bottle, and passed it to Okulu. "Did you self-diagnose?"

"I'll be dead in a week," Okulu said after a healthy gulp of wine.

"I've suffered some kind of head trauma. My thoughts slip from one thing to the other. Swelling of the brain, I'm sure. I have problems remembering. Had a convulsive attack a bit ago. At least now I'll die happy."

Salvarias set his pouch on the table and retrieved his mortar and smooth rock. "Would you object to living? I have a potion in mind. It has not been tested and there is a risk it might ... speed things up."

"Depends. How much more of this stuff is there?" Okulu asked, wiggling the wine bottle.

"I am sure we can uncover another bottle or two."

Okulu shrugged. "I'm game, then."

"Vuddruk told me he gave you a potion to help you sleep."

Okulu snorted. "He forgets I'm part Winsire. Not all the herbs have the same effect on me."

Salvarias nodded. "Would you like to tell me what Sansis did to you?"

Mirth drained from Okulu's eyes, turning them dark and haunted. "I've never ..." He looked away, blinking, but tears still fell. "He told me I was dying. Liver giving out from my drinking. He said he'd cure me so I'd have another thirty years to kill myself." Okulu's voice dropped to a whisper. "Not that I deserve it." He took a lengthy swig of wine.

"It would be wise to give up spirits."

Okulu sniffed, wiping his tears. "After what I felt, I think I'd rather be dead or permanently drunk so I never remember. I don't understand how you survived a year. I'd kill myself before I let that man touch me again."

Salvarias reburied the surfacing memory of battling his magic to perform the spell he had concocted to kill himself in Zeeas. Like Okulu, he had been eager to end his suffering. He poured his mixture into a mug and passed it to Okulu.

Okulu downed the potion and grinned. "You make them taste good."

Motioning to the merc's chest, Salvarias said, "Can you sit? I would like to apply a balm to the stitches."

Okulu winced and groaned as he shoved himself up, unwinding his own dressings, much to Salvarias's relief. After compiling the balm, Salvarias turned to apply it, grimacing against the pain he knew would come. Okulu snatched up the mortar and smoothed the mixture on himself. Leaning back in the chair, Salvarias arched an eyebrow.

Okulu chuckled. "Do you think you're the only one with powers of observation? I won't ask why. You don't like to be touched, nor do you like to touch others. Except that behemoth brother of yours. I'm not one to press for answers."

"Thank you," Salvarias said.

Okulu shrugged. "I'd be easier if you just tell me why."

Salvarias accepted his mortar and cleaned it. "I am sure it would." He thought of telling the merc, but his shame was too great. How would it sound? *When I touch people, I cannot breathe, and I see images I do not understand. It is because I am evil, and the innocent lash back at the monstrosity that is me.* He shook his head and packed his things. "Would you like to tell me why you do not feel you deserve a second chance?"

Okulu cast his roguish grin. "The day you start trusting me with your secrets, my friend, will be the day I tell you mine." He plopped back on the bed and closed his eyes. "Thanks ..."

Salvarias caught the bottle of wine when it slipped from Okulu's fingers, corked it, and set it on the stand. Leaving the room, he made his way to the dining hall. Neithelas and a man that could have been his twin were sitting beside Varila.

"This is Salvarias," Neithelas said. "The mage I told you about. Salvarias, this is my brother, Prince Arthias Frisliasi of Meitholias."

Salvarias bowed. "An honor, Prince."

Arthias grunted. "A mage with manners."

Salvarias quickly sat by his brother and rested a restraining hand on his arm. "I assure you, Prince, there are many mages with manners if any would choose to talk to them instead of spit on them."

Arthias snorted and turned his back to them. After forcing down a few bites of bread, Salvarias administered a potion to Durak, finding it somehow comforting that the Cavrul had not partaken in Vuddruk's offer of help and only accepted Salvarias's concoctions. Then he left in search of Humar, finding him outside the estate, watching sand sift through his fingers.

"Sir Humar," Salvarias said, bowing. "I have a balm for—"

"We need some rest. Are we in a hurry yet, or can we stay here another day?"

"I have received no further visions. I assume nothing has changed." Humar's eyes were distant, and a frown pulled down the corners of his mouth and crinkled his brow. "Sir Humar, are you—"

"It's supposed to break the curse," Humar whispered.

Salvarias gazed over the wondrous city. "Little of the Lilkous curse is documented."

Humar shrugged. "What's there to know? It's quite simple. Any child born to the Lilkous line is consumed by a maddening darkness the day of his coronation. For over a thousand years, the Lilkous line has spawned princes who turn into greedy, power hungry monsters."

"If I remember, there are three rumored cures to break the curse. Sands from the city of Quind, the claw of a griffin dipped in the blood of Zerana, or a mortal housing the power of a god."

Humar nodded. "Veedran was no fool when he set the curse upon Lilkous. All the griffins had been defeated, and Quind was under Veedran's control. No one could step foot inside the city and live."

"Indeed. Veedran was not dense."

"Agreed. I thought I might have a chance with Crutar. I assumed he was more man than god, but Mafarias corrected me. He said Crutar was a lesser god compared to Nevlar, Zerana, and Veedran, but an immortal god all the same. Mafarias told me the powers of godhood can't be contained in a mortal mind. Humans weren't meant to control it, and those who occupy human form are weakened."

Salvarias nodded. "However, in human form they can be killed. Not traditionally, but it is possible. You have not been home for some time. Perhaps Loutsil has changed. Perhaps there are those who rose up against the tyranny."

Humar tossed away the sand. "Loutsil is nothing but slavery, sexism, and racism. Women are treated like fragile glass, any lower class as slaves, and any other race as inferior. Mages rarely live to see their twentieth Birth Day. Most are found stabbed to death in alleys, or some ridiculous charge is fabricated in order to sentence them to death." Humar scooped sand into a pouch. "Loutsil kings are incapable of change, and the people are too frightened to rebel against the Lilkous line. But maybe once this is over, I can try this stuff."

Salvarias shook his head. "Those are the sands of the desert. Too fine grained to be native to Quind." He strolled ahead, studying the ground by the light of his sparrow. "Is that why you came to Dalnar? With hopes of saving your king?"

Humar chuckled. "You believe in the curse?"

"For Loutsil to live so long in darkness, can any other conclusion be drawn?"

"The citizens deny its existence. Any voicing truths to it are hanged. Nobles have much to gain from unjust rulers."

"I find it fascinating how one can close the mind to possibilities."

"Because some things are foolish to believe in. I don't know for certain that this curse is real." Humar's voice dulled. "I'm not even sure this would work if it is."

Salvarias glanced at Humar's furrowed brow. "I have never known you to be without hope." For some reason, it shook Salvarias to his core. Humar's hope was pointless, but Salvarias realized he had relied on it ever since he met the knight.

Humar inhaled a deep breath and smiled. "I do have hope. Why else would I be taking sands back to a country I promised myself I would never return to?"

Salvarias stopped at the edge of the city and pointed to a patch of large grained sand. "Then I pray to any who would listen that this remedy work."

Humar shoveled sand into the pouch. "As do I, boy. Perhaps there is a chance I can rid my land of monsters."

Salvarias gazed over the fallen city. "Only with the presence of evil can we uncover the truth of our character."

34

E dium sat in the light of a single candle, watching his daughters sleep. Whatever the mage had given Varila hauled her into deep, seemingly peaceful dreams. Lunara, the only child he'd known never to have nightmares, tossed restlessly. So much had happened to his girls over the past year he wondered if he knew them anymore.

He rose from his chair, kissed each on the forehead, and blew out the candle. On his way down the corridor, he passed the brothers' room. The door was cracked open, and he peeked inside. Both were sitting up against the wall, Wilhelm's arm draped over Salvarias's shoulders. Wilhelm's soft snore filled the room, mingled with Salvarias's fleeting mumbles. The boy's spell book had fallen from his hands. At the base of the bed, the wolf was curled up, the candlelight reflecting in its golden eyes fixed on Edium.

He was about to leave, but couldn't help notice the mage shivering. Glancing at the wolf, Edium slowly walked inside, keeping one eye on the beast. Adok watched him with a steady gaze. At the bed, he closed the boy's book, laid it on a nearby table, gathered up a blanket, and covered Salvarias.

Edium's gaze drifted to Wilhelm. He'd always wanted a son. He loved his daughters more than life, wouldn't trade them for the world, but every man wants a son. Talura, after Lunara's birth, never took with child again. His wife didn't seem to mind, and Edium's longing usually vanished when one of his girls smiled. But sleeping before him was a young man who, without hardly knowing him, had gained Edium's love and entered the sacred circle of his family. Once Varila married Wilhelm, he'd be Edium's son. His chest swelled with pride. A son.

He blew out the candle, crossed the room, ignoring the cold stare of the wolf, and slipped outside, partially closing the door behind him. When he turned, Neithelas was waiting.

"Might I have a word with you, Lord Bellerum?"

"Certainly." Edium strolled toward his room.

"I've been in the company of your daughters for several weeks. I find them both to be remarkable women."

"Thank you."

"With your permission, I would like to court Lunara. She's a woman worthy of every luxury and safety. I feel, with my position, I can offer her all that her heart desires. My hope is to show her how deep my care dwells."

"I'm not familiar with Winsires' customs of courtship."

"Nor would they be appropriate. I would suggest using Erthla customs. I can bestow gifts upon her and be in her company alone, if she so allows it. Courtship would be nothing more than an opportunity for her to learn about me in private ... respectful privacy, of course. If she so deems me worthy, I would have her hand in marriage."

Edium jumped. "Marriage? Now hold on. I don't know you enough to even think about you asking for her hand."

"You would deny her choice?"

"Well, no. I ... She ..." Edium rubbed his forehead. "If she accepted such a proposal, of course I would honor her choice. Let's just start a little slower. Give me some time to think about your request to court her. I'll answer you tomorrow."

Neithelas bowed. "Thank you, Lord Bellerum."

Edium bid the prince good evening and nearly sprinted to his room. Once inside, he closed his door and leaned against it. He wasn't sure he was ready to lose both girls at the same time.

"Edium?" Talura said sleepily.

"Here, dear." He kicked off his boots, slipped from his tunic, and crawled into bed. "How are you feeling?"

She molded her body to his, and he encased her in his arms. "Tired, but much better than I have in ages. I feel like my mind has risen from a year-long fog."

Indeed, the instant they were free of Mafarias, Talura had nearly passed out from exhaustion, but her eyes were clear of the unfocused haziness she'd been subjected to since Mafarias had arrived. Bracing for her wrath, Edium said, "I think it was Mafarias."

"Perhaps," she murmured. "You don't trust him?"

"No," he said bluntly. "I trust no man who abandons his family." Her hair filled his nostrils with the scent of jasmine.

"I'm not sure," she said. "He truly does care for Wilhelm."

"We'll talk about it later. We have bigger issues. Neithelas asked to court Lunara."

Talura sighed. "I'm not surprised. He looks at her with this heart in his eyes. I have doubts she feels the same."

"I'll ask her tomorrow. You need to rest." Even as he said it, he inched up her nightdress, trailing kisses along her slender neck.

Instead of agreeing with his words, she guided his hand under the soft fabric and moaned her approval.

35

E dium propped his legs up on the short table, leaned back in his chair, and leafed through the book Lunara had given him last night. She had hoped he'd find some meaning to it, but as he skimmed the writings, they were clearly those of a mad man.

The rise of murmurs and a deep chuckle outside his room told him the rest of the group was finally awake. He rose from his chair and opened the door.

Wilhelm was passing, holding Salvarias in a headlock while mussing his hair.

"Morning, Edium," Wilhelm greeted warmly.

"Morning." Edium held out the book to Salvarias. "I've been told you're a man of study."

Salvarias accepted the book. "I am, my lord."

"Edium. For the love of the gods, call me Edium. Lunara had glanced over it yesterday and asked that I give it a look. It appears to be the ramblings of a senile man. What are your thoughts?"

Salvarias, with the care one would use toward a newborn, opened the book and glanced at a few pages. "I would be inclined to agree with you, my lord—"

"Edium."

"However, if you are willing to part with it, I will study it in further detail when I have the time."

"Of course. I don't think you'll find anything."

"First impressions can be deceiving, my lord—"

"Edium."

Wilhelm smiled fondly at the mage. "I'll go put it in our room."

"No need, Brother. I will do it." Salvarias wiggled from Wilhelm's hold and left for his room.

Edium rested a hand on Wilhelm's arm to stop him from following and steered him inside. "I wanted to ask you about something Talura found." He retrieved a pea-sized piece of wood from his table and handed it to Wilhelm. "It was in pile of trinkets near your armor. It—"

He couldn't finish because Wilhelm's embrace crushed the air from his lungs. "Thank you, Edium! You have no idea how much this means to me."

Edium patted the boy's shoulder, gasping for air. "What is it?"

Wilhelm lowered him and held up the puzzle box Salvarias had fiddled with when in Serinity.

"Where'd you get that?" Edium asked.

Before his eyes, it shrank to the same pea-sized block Talura had found. Edium jumped back.

"It's ... it's special," Wilhelm said. "Salv has had this since we were little."

"How does it do that?"

Wilhelm shrugged and dropped it in his shirt pocket. "Not sure. And don't say anything to Salv."

"I've learned a lot about you. Your care for your brother is touching. However, I think it's ... unhealthy. We can't point out that he counts aloud; we can't tease him or touch him." Edium squeezed Wilhelm's shoulder. "You've shielded him too much. He needs to learn to deal with—"

Wilhelm shrugged from Edium's hand, and his bright eyes dulled. "Salv has learned to deal with enough. You don't know us. You don't know what we've been through. If you did, you wouldn't say such things. Salv's been counting since I can remember. I've grown used to it, and I like it. I told you he doesn't know he's doing it aloud, and he'd stop if he knew." Wilhelm's tone sharpened when he said, "And *I* don't want him to stop."

"And why doesn't he let people touch him?"

"It's none of your business," Wilhelm grumbled.

"It's not right for a young man to be so distant. Friendship and camaraderie make for strong, honorable men. You need to let others into the boy's life."

"Salv's mine," Wilhelm growled.

"Salvarias should belong to no one but himself."

Wilhelm's clenched jaw loosened, and he glanced away, cheeks tinting red. "I ... I just want him to be safe."

"Understandable." Edium smiled. "You're not a parent. You're a brother. It's natural for you to be protective of a younger sibling. I myself once had a brother, and I was the same. However, I let him have his own life, his own friends. All I'm asking is that you let Humar and me coax Salvarias out of his shell. Trust us. And Talura. She adores him."

"I trust you, and I trust Humar and Talura. That doesn't mean I'm going to allow you to make him uncomfortable or point out stuff you see that *you* think is abnormal. Salv is a very special man full of gifts. And I'll protect those gifts with my life. I appreciate your concern, but Salv is my responsibility. You'll not mention his counting, you'll not say anything about the puzzle box, and you'll never touch him."

"And if I don't agree?"

Wilhelm stood straight, towering over Edium, his eyes burning with a sudden anger. "Then I'll take Salv and we'll go our path alone."

"Your relationship is toxic."

"Maybe. Regardless, it is what it is."

Edium studied the boy for a moment before nodding. "So be it. One day, I hope you would trust me as you would trust a ... father."

Wilhelm's shoulders dropped, and he seemed to age years. "I've not met another who has cared for my brother as much as me. Even

Tobin, a man I respected above all others, couldn't stop bullies from beating up Salv when we were little. He made me leave him. He dragged me from my home." Wilhelm's voice switched from a strong rumble to a defeated confession. "Every time I left, I would come home to a brother covered in bruises, cowering in a corner, petrified of any person besides me. He wouldn't tell us who did it. He endured it all. I don't understand why he never told me. I could've stopped it."

"Surely your parents did something," Edium said. "How—"

"My brother snuck away from my mother when they would visit the market."

"That's ridiculous. She couldn't keep a better eye on the boy?"

"She was as upset as we were. Salv wouldn't listen to her." Wilhelm shrugged. "If Salv wants to go somewhere, there's no stopping him. He sneaks from camp nearly every night. Not even I can do anything." Wilhelm inhaled a deep breath. "I won't let anyone hurt him anymore. I'll do everything in my power to keep him safe, to keep him free of pain. Counting and that puzzle box help him." Wilhelm met Edium's gaze. "Maybe it's you who should trust me."

Edium regarded Wilhelm for several moments before nodding. "For now, I'll trust you. But I'll be watching Salvarias closely."

Wilhelm's sadness melted, and his eyes lit with their usual brightness. "Thanks."

Edium nodded. "You've lived a hard life, Wilhelm. You've been alone in so many ways. But not anymore. I care for you, boy. As much as you want Salvarias's happiness and safety, I want yours."

Wilhelm's cheeks tinted rosy pink. He scuffed his boot on the floor. "Let's get down to the courtyard. Humar's waiting for me."

Edium followed Wilhelm through the estate and outside into one of the many courtyards. It was nothing but hardened dirt with a few cobblestone pathways and marble planters. Humar and Durak were leaning against the wall in soft conversation. Edium's daughters and wife were sitting on the ground, heads together, giggling. He'd desperately missed the sound of their laughter. Salvarias sat apart from the group, reading his spell book and stroking Adok's ears.

"Here, Salv," Wilhelm said. He tossed something, and Salvarias caught it. In his hand, the puzzle box appeared.

Salvarias looked up and, though his face was shadowed, Edium felt a smile emanate from the boy. "Thank you, Brother."

Talura rose and kissed Edium. "I'm going inside for a bit."

When she left, he squeezed himself between his daughters, wrapped an arm around each, and kissed their foreheads. Both snuggled against him.

"We've missed you," Lunara said.

Edium rested his cheek on Varila's head. "I have been a broken man without the two of you."

He gazed in contentment at Wilhelm sparring with Humar and Durak. Not much time passed before Edium's mouth gaped open in dumbfounded amazement. The boy moved as if liquid, bending and twisting like pliable stone, more graceful than a bird of prey hunting its victim.

Flexing his fists and tensing his back, Edium thought he might give it a try. Someone had to beat the boy.

A sharp elbow to his ribs made him jump.

"Well, Father," Varila said. "Are you going to test yourself or sit here like an old man?"

"Have you sparred with him?"

Varila grinned. "Not yet. I can't have his confidence shaken when we're in dangerous situations."

After kissing each daughter's cheek, he rose and called to Wilhelm, "I think I'll give that a try."

The three men paused in the bout. Wilhelm's grin sliced across his face.

"Three against one?" Humar asked.

Wilhelm chuckled. "It would be my pleasure."

Edium glanced over at Salvarias sitting on a low wall. "Want to join us, Salvarias? You could offer some help to your brother."

"No," Wilhelm said. "He doesn't fight with swords."

Though Edium had agreed not press the boy about oddities, at least the mage could talk with others besides Wilhelm. "The boy can answer for himself. Salvarias?"

"My brother speaks the truth."

"Don't you want to learn?"

"No," Wilhelm said.

Edium looked first to Salvarias, then to Wilhelm. "Again, allow the boy to speak for himself."

"I do not wish to learn," Salvarias said.

"Why?" Edium asked. He lifted his hand to stop Wilhelm's explanation.

"I have magic."

"You could try something different."

Salvarias shrugged. "If I want something different, I merely need to come up with a new spell."

"I would've thought the arena taught you that you can't always rely on magic," Edium said.

Wilhelm stepped in Edium's line of sight, body rigid, jaw rippling. "Enough with the questions. Leave Salv alone."

"But—"

"Leave him alone," Wilhelm growled.

Salvarias appeared by Wilhelm's side, resting a hand on his brother's shoulder. "I have watched my brother spar since I was two, Lord Bellerum. I am well aware of the skill needed to wield a sword. I know the appropriate steps, blocks, lunges, and thrusts. I, however, attempted them in the arena unsuccessfully. I am sure you have noticed my limp and the fact I cannot walk without assistance. Such an injury makes swordplay impossible for me, as I learned in the arena." Salvarias glanced up at his brother and squeezed his shoulder before returning to his wall.

Edium realized the mage's staff took the place of his bum leg. "I'm sorry, boy."

Salvarias shrugged. "There is no need for apology, my lord."

"Edium. For all of Nevlar's fury, call me Edium."

Wilhelm stretched his neck side to side. In a quiet voice barely heard, he said, "Next time, stop asking questions."

Edium nodded and joined Humar's side. "Too damned protective," he muttered.

Humar smiled. "You haven't seen the half of it. He punched me once. He must respect you a great deal to keep control of his temper. Best to not ask the boy questions." Humar, apparently accustomed to these awkward moments, tapped Wilhelm's sword edge with his own. "Ready? Or do you need time to pummel something first?"

Wilhelm grinned crookedly. "Why go for something else when I have you?"

The boy lunged so quickly, Edium narrowly made it out of the way. He whirled to strike at Wilhelm's back but hesitated, thinking he might catch the boy off guard and injure him. Wilhelm's sword, however, had already moved behind to counter the obvious attack Edium should have taken. His great sword was blocking Humar and Durak's attempted swing. Even as the boy pivoted for the advantage, he winked at Edium.

"Don't be shy, Edium," Wilhelm said, dropping below a swing from Humar. "Join in anytime."

Laughing, Edium lunged into the foray.

The bout lasted longer than Edium's endurance allowed. He stopped, doubling over and gasping harsh, cold air. He was drenched in sweat. Humar called a halt, breathing heavily but far better trained than Edium.

"Let's take a rest," Humar said.

Edium nodded and plopped down on a nearby half-wall. The test wasn't completely merciful. He already felt tender bruises forming and several scores bled where he would've been fatally wounded if the boy hadn't been in practice mode. Humar and Durak were in no better shape. Wilhelm, however, had a single scratch on his arm, his breathing as regular as if he were sipping tea, and only a minor sheen of sweat shone on his brow.

"It's inhuman," Edium wheezed.

Humar chuckled. "I'd agree there. I've been training him since he was sixteen, and I've not managed once to get him out of breath."

"How do you do it, boy?" Edium asked.

"My father and I ran every morning through the entire city of

Falar. I kept it up after he died. And if we have time in the mornings, I take a run before we set out to travel."

"Endurance," Edium said, nodding in approval. "I think I'll add running to my men's training exercises."

Wilhelm grinned. "Just make sure they run in their armor. No point in practicing in light clothes if you're going to be bogged down by tons of armor."

"Good point," Edium said.

Humar clapped Edium on the shoulder. "Rested?"

"Hardly," he said. "You go ahead."

Durak nodded. "Me need a break."

Humar bowed mockingly to the Cavrul. "Age is catching up with you, my old friend."

"And that rude tongue of yours followed ye from youth, ye dull-witted bastard!"

Humar motioned to Wilhelm. "Time for special training."

The two men went to a shadowed corner of the courtyard and sat facing each other, swords lying across their laps, Humar talking softly.

With painful throbs, Edium rejoined his daughters.

"I'm disappointed," Varila said. "You're out of shape."

"You haven't been home for over a year to keep me active." Edium sank to the ground and leaned his back against the wall. "Neithelas asked permission to court you, Lunara."

His daughter's gaze lowered to her hands. "I'm flattered by his attentions, but I'm not interested."

"He's such a nice man," Varila said. "Sweet, handsome, and he dotes on you. I think you should accept. Just to get to know him better."

"I know him enough. I'm not interested."

"It's not marriage," Edium said. "All it would allow is for him to give you gifts and take walks alone."

Varila snorted. "She's a grown woman, Father. It means he can be alone with her ... anywhere. Not that he'd ever do anything disrespectful."

"Well, they don't have to be alone ... in rooms ... with beds." Edium shifted. Steering his attention from his youngest, he cast his oldest a stern stare. "And you don't have to be caught kissing in hallways. Especially when he hasn't asked permission to court you."

Varila shrugged. "His father died before he taught him proper etiquette in courting. I'm sure his mother never got around to it. He doesn't understand what he's doing is improper. And you know I don't agree with stupid rituals. I'm a grown woman, not a sixteen-year-old girl who needs monitoring. And the same with Lunara."

"Is that why you both turn the color of an over-ripened tomato every time I catch you?"

Varila chuckled. "Stop trying to change the subject." She angled forward to meet her sister's gaze. "For me, Lunara. Accept and give him a chance. If you still feel the same after a few months, I'll drop it and never mention it again."

Lunara glanced at the mage. "Is it required that I be alone with him?"

"No, you don't have to," Varila said. "But I think it'd do you some good. You've not had time away from others to really sit and talk with him."

"I swear to you, dear sister, my feelings for him won't change."

"Then there's nothing for you to worry about," Varila said. "Accept, and in three months tell me you're not interested. I'll drop it."

"It's cruel to lead him on."

Varila shrugged. "I doubt he'll stop. At least given the appropriate chance, he might accept your 'no' as final."

"I must think about it." She rose and crossed the yard to Salvarias.

"I don't like the mage," Varila said.

"I haven't decided myself," Edium said. "She seems fond of him."

"It's just infatuation. She'll get over it once she sees how nice Neithelas is."

Edium stroked his beard, watching Lunara's smiles toward Salvarias. "I'm not so sure."

~

LUNARA SETTLED beside Salvarias and peered at the pages he was so intently focused on. Odd symbols and words were written in meticulous, fluid handwriting. As she gazed at them, she swore they began to move, slithering together to create shifting patterns. The sight made her teeter, and she rested a hand on his arm.

Salvarias flinched and turned the book from her view. "You may not read this, my lady."

"What is it?" she asked.

"Spells and runes."

"I swear the words and symbols moved." She rubbed her forehead to dispel the lingering effects.

"Only mages can read them. Is there something you needed, my lady?"

"Do you take issue with my company?"

"Yes, I do."

It was going to be one of those days. Lunara looked toward Durak whittling away at a stick. "Neithelas has asked my father for permission to court me, as you suspected he would."

"You should accept his offer. Neithelas is a good man."

"How do you know I haven't already?" Lunara asked.

"Because you are here, my lady."

"It would be cruel to accept. I'm not interested in his offers of wealth and worship."

"It is the Winsire way to value such things. Do not be mistaken to think his heart holds anything less than love."

"I know what his heart holds. I've seen it for myself. That doesn't change how I feel."

Salvarias returned his gaze to his book. "Feelings are forever changing. What you think you feel today may not be what you feel tomorrow."

Lunara sighed. "Varila asked me to accept to appease her."

Salvarias shrugged. "Then you have no option. Your bond with

Varila is strong. If I have learned anything about either of you, it is that you both would do anything to make the other happy."

"The same goes for you and Wilhelm."

"Indeed, my lady."

"But Wilhelm would never ask you to do such a thing."

Salvarias closed his book and stared at his brother. "No. My brother is very careful never to force me to do anything." Salvarias's voice distanced, and she doubted he realized he spoke aloud. "The one time he did has haunted my dreams, and he has yet to release his guilt."

"What happened?" Lunara whispered.

Salvarias was still in his trancelike state. "In the slave caverns, a man sacrificed his life for mine. My brother made me leave him alone and dying in a tunnel. Alone in a place of nothing but pain. I left him."

"Summertide!" a voice roared.

Lunara jumped, and Salvarias jerked so hard his book shot up from his lap.

Vuddruk stood in the doorway. "Today is Summertide! I'd forgotten until that lovely little wife of yours reminded me, Edium. I'll prepare us a lovely feast; we'll have music, dancing, and plenty of wine!"

"Summer already," Lunara said, resting a hand over her pounding heart. "Spring went by so quickly."

"I think that's a great idea," her father said.

"Brilliant!" Vuddruk exclaimed. "You there, boy, come help me." He waved at Salvarias. "There's a few spells we can do to make the night enjoyable."

Salvarias rose from his seat, bowed to her, tilted his head to their friends in polite farewell, and left the courtyard.

Heart heavy, she strode to her father and Varila. "I will accept his courtship."

Without waiting for a reply, she bolted through the estate, up the stairs, and to the washroom. Once there, she latched the door, crumpled to the ground, and gave her tears freedom.

36

Salvarias cracked open Okulu's door and peeked inside. Candles lit the room, and Okulu was up getting dressed.

"You should be resting," Salvarias murmured.

"And you should knock." Okulu glanced over his shoulder and grinned. "But I bet you thought I would still be lying in bed, dying."

Salvarias's amazement moved him to Okulu's side. The merc's skin had returned to its olive tint, and the stench seeping from his pores had disappeared. "Truly remarkable."

Okulu chuckled and hopped into one of his boots. "I think you've got a gift with herbs. I was certain I would be dead by evening."

"How are your thoughts? Convulsions?"

"No attacks since you gave me the first dose. My thoughts are clear, and the pressure in my head is reducing."

Salvarias leafed to the back of his book, chanted his spell, and recorded the herbs he had used and their effects.

"So am I cleared to attend the party?" Okulu asked.

Salvarias ended his spell and closed the book. He studied Okulu's appearance once more and picked out the exhaustion dulling the merc's grass-green eyes, the slouch of his stance, and the occasional wince when he moved too quickly. "Though I would prefer you to rest another day or so, I cannot see any reason for you to remain in your room. I will ask that you limit your drinking to help thicken your blood. I would also ask you to celebrate with restraint."

Okulu yanked on his other boot, chuckling. "I'm sure Varila will be thrilled."

"If you ceased teasing her, you might earn her favor."

"But then I wouldn't have as much fun. It's too easy to get Lunara to blush. Varila, on the other hand, is a hardened woman."

"Indeed she is." Salvarias bowed. "Until tonight."

"There'll be dancing?" Okulu asked.

Salvarias stopped at the door and looked over his shoulder. "Yes. You should refrain from such activities."

"Shame, because if you don't ask her first, Lunara's going to be stuck with Neithelas all night."

"As she should. Neithelas is a good man. She should accept his affections." The words tasted vile.

"That's a load of ogre crap," Okulu said. "Neithelas is a smug ass. She deserves better."

"Why then do you not court her?"

Okulu burst out laughing, doubling over and clutching his stomach. Salvarias waited patiently for the merc to gain his composure.

"Lunara's like a sister to me," Okulu said. "Plus, she's far too innocent for my taste. I prefer an experienced woman, if you know what I mean."

"Unfortunately, I do," Salvarias said dryly. "You have an appetite for women that rivals my brother."

"They're pleasant company. You should try it sometime."

"I feel this conversation has deteriorated," Salvarias said. "If you will excuse me, I must help Master Vuddruk finish preparing for the festivities."

"You don't know what you're missing out on, my friend."

The memories of the dreams he had shared with Lunara surfaced. He clearly recalled the softness of her skin, the warmth of her, the supple feel of her body against his. "On the contrary," he whispered. Bowing, he left the merc and rid his mind of selfish memories.

~

LUNARA DIDN'T SPEND much time in solitude before her mother and sister burst into the room carrying fresh clothes, bathing oils, and brushes. Vuddruk heated the water for them while talking of how he'd never seen such a fine-looking group of women, which her mother took as an opportunity for polite banter that seemed to charm Vuddruk further. After the old mage left, Lunara wasted no time in climbing into the steaming waters.

Her doubt and heartache over accepting Neithelas's courtship soon faded in fond conversations shared with her mother and sister. The warm waters absorbed the weight of the past few weeks, and her sense of family encased her in a robe of love. She hadn't been this happy since she'd left her home.

As she dried, her mother held up one of Lunara's red dresses. "My goodness, dear. Your dresses have faded."

"I know," Lunara said. "Washing them in streams with harsh soaps has taken its toll on the fabric."

"Yes," her mother murmured. "I noticed Salvarias's robes were in very poor condition. The bottoms are tattered and the burgundy color looks dreadfully dull. When we return to Serenity, I'll have to fetch him some new slate robes. If he stays with us, I'd love to measure him and sew some myself—ones that actually fit him."

Lunara smiled, recalling all the times she'd sat watching her mother sew. At home, her mother was rarely without a needle and fabric resting in her lap. "I think he prefers burgundy to the slate-blue robes," Lunara said as she pulled on her dress.

"But with his coloring and hair, he'd be so handsome in blue. Don't you agree, Varila?"

Her sister snorted. "You're asking the wrong person, Mother. I don't find him the least bit attractive."

"You're not blind, girl," her mother said. "I admit, the blood caked on his face didn't add appeal, but I clearly saw beneath the layers of dirt a man who holds no equal. Haven't you noticed his bone structure? I'd give anything to have hair that shines like his. And the young man has eyelashes any woman would envy. Let's not even mention those lips of his."

"Mother!" Varila said exasperated.

Talura giggled. "I have eyes, dear, and I do notice such things."

"Well I haven't!" Varila snapped. "He's damn cold and aloof. I find those traits very *un*attractive."

"I see. Perhaps the next time he gifts us with a view of his face, you'll take notice."

Lunara realized her heart was racing as she recalled his smile when they'd exited the cart in Serenity. Without meaning to, she whispered, "You should see him smile."

Her mother laughed. "I'd pay good money to witness one."

"I'd pay to see any damn emotion," Varila growled.

"The brothers are so opposite," her mother said. "Wilhelm's emotions are quite clear at all times, don't you think, Lunara?"

She giggled. "Yes, Mother. Such a handsome man. Powerful. Gorgeous. Kind. And those eyes! I've never seen such bright amber eyes before."

"Knock it off!" Varila snapped. She picked up her armor, but their mother clucked her tongue.

"No, dear," Talura said. "I have an extra dress for you to wear."

Varila's eyes narrowed. "What are you up to?"

"Why nothing, dear. It's a party, after all. You should dress appropriately."

Lunara clamped a hand over her mouth, muffling her giggle.

"It won't fit," Varila said gruffly, though her eyes wandered to the dress her mother had brought in.

"It might be a little short, but we're both built the same," her mother said. "No arguments, dear. Put the dress on."

A smile twitched on Varila's lips when she picked up the light blue dress. Indeed, it fit her voluptuous figure nicely. The square neckline was cut too low for Lunara's tastes, but her sister was busty enough to fill it in, and her hips allowed the fabric to cascade loosely. Times such as these, Lunara envied her sister's seductive body. Next to Varila, Lunara resembled a twig.

"All ready?" Talura said.

"I think Wilhelm will enjoy this," Varila said, turning to regard her backside in the mirror. "Yes, he'll very much enjoy this."

Lunara giggled, snatched her sister's hand, and followed their mother from the room and down the stairs to the antechamber that led to the courtyard. The mages had taken great care to cover the windows that might provide a sneak peek at their work.

Upon their entry, Wilhelm shoved off from the wall, and his crooked grin spread while his gaze slid up and down Varila.

"You're beautiful," he said.

She winked. "I know."

Wilhelm had traded his armor for a white belted tunic and black trews. The light fabric rested against his chest, calling attention to his broad shoulders and exquisite physique. Making him even more attractive was the lack of conceitedness in his gaze. Lunara wondered if he even knew how handsome women found him.

"You look positively striking," Lunara said, balling his tunic in her fist and pulling him down to kiss his cheek.

"And you're lovely as ever, my raven-haired temptress," Okulu said from behind.

Lunara turned to see the merc looking as dashing as always. His eyes sparkled in the soft light, and that damn roguish grin made it impossible not to return his smile. Her embarrassment over his compliment was nothing compared to her joy at seeing his playful personality returned. She rushed into his arms. "I'm so happy you're better!"

Okulu laughed. "That mage of yours has quite the talent for healing."

"My lady," Neithelas said.

He was stunning in a green tunic that called attention to his olive skin, bringing out the violet in his eyes. His sleek hair fell effortlessly around his shoulders. Beautiful was all she could think. Arthias stood by his side, a replica of Neithelas except for his cold stare.

"Lady Lunara," Arthias said with a curt bow. "Truly my brother has not misspoken of your beauty."

She curtsied, biting her tongue to keep from smiling when Okulu rolled his eyes. "You're too kind, Prince Arthias."

Her father joined her and cast a toothy grin. "I'm famished."

"Agreed," Wilhelm said. "I think I'm going to pass out from starvation soon."

Seeming unconsciously, he pulled Varila to him so her back leaned against his chest, and he wrapped his arms around her shoulders. Rarely did Wilhelm not have someone in his arms, and she doubted he was aware of how oddly affectionate he was for a man.

"Hurry up in there!" Durak roared. "We be hungry, and it be hot in here."

"Testy Cavruls!" Vuddruk snapped from beyond the door. "These things take time. Curb your impatience."

"Damn mages," Durak pitched back. "Always trying to show off. Making things more complicated than need be."

"Cursed Cavruls with their lack of elegance and refinement," Vuddruk said.

"Wretched mages and their—" Durak started.

"I think that's enough," Humar said, a smile dancing on his lips. He still wore his full suit of armor even though they were obviously safe. She'd become accustomed to the sight, but here in a room full of men dressed casually he seemed out of place.

The doors flung open, and everyone gasped. Beyond was a scene from another place and time done in mage light. Above, conjured stars dotted the darkness of the cavern. The courtyard glowed with soaring redwood trees fashioned from white light, canopying over areas to brighten the space. Shimmering grasses with beaming flowers blanketed the ground. Within it, there were hues of pink from the hylim jars that apparently had made the journey from the dark caves to this wondrous setting. They illuminated certain draping trees, providing a place she imagined sneaking away to where kisses would not be all that was shared. Her cheeks burned at the thought. On its own, her gaze shifted to Salvarias. He strolled in the pinkish branches of one of those trees, and she was shocked to see him disappear. Indeed, they provided privacy. He reemerged on the other side, studying the tree intently. His lips moved and a branch thickened with additional leaves.

"It's wonderful," Varila breathed.

"So it is," Vuddruk said. "I think our friend has a romantic side to him."

Salvarias didn't acknowledge the comment. He continued his inspection.

"Isn't this a little ... draining, Salv?" Wilhelm asked.

"No, Brother. I am fine."

Vuddruk grunted. "The boy is gifted in the light spell. Every mage has a preferred spell. Mine is fire. Love the stuff. For some reason, that preferred spell is less straining than others. The human mind and magic are a mystery of the ages." He motioned everyone in. "Come, come."

Lunara took a tentative step forward. Unfortunately, it was clear that it was just light. She felt no cushy ground and smelled no fresh trees.

They nibbled on a variety of food Vuddruk had laid out and chatted together of nothing important. When the old mage snatched up a flute, Varila grinned.

"Who's the best dancer here?" Varila asked.

"I'm skilled," Neithelas said.

Varila grabbed his arm and headed to the center of the courtyard. "Strike it up, old man."

Vuddruk played a delightfully fast-paced tune. Indeed, Neithelas moved with the grace of the wind, easily leading Varila along and matching her pace. Her father hooked his arm with Lunara's and escorted her to the center courtyard. She wasn't nearly as skilled as Varila, but she could hold her own. In no time, she was twirling and laughing, and her father's chuckle brought wonderful memories of her childhood forward. As the songs spun from Vuddruk, she found herself passed between Humar and Okulu, occasionally Durak and Arthias, and more often Neithelas.

After several fast-paced songs, Lunara excused herself from Neithelas and made her way to the food table. Adok was patiently waiting for her, and she used her body to block anyone's view of the generous portion of salted pork she casually shoved off the edge of the table. After a rather slimy lick on Lunara's hand, Adok went to feasting.

She drank two glasses of water, dabbing sweat from her forehead, and caught sight of the brothers off to the side. Wilhelm's grin was plastered across his face as he watched Varila.

She strolled over to them. "Why don't you dance with my sister?"

Wilhelm shrugged. "Never learned how."

Grinning, she grabbed both brothers' arms and ushered them to one of those secluded places. She left Salvarias off to the side and took Wilhelm to an open area, hidden from view so as not to embarrass himself if he misstepped.

"It's quite simple," she said, positioning his arm around her waist. "All music has a rhythm." She tapped her hand on his chest in time with the current song. Quicker than she expected, he nodded. "You just step in time with the rhythm."

His first two attempts resulted in her foot throbbing, and she wasn't sure she had a big toe anymore. Because of his size, she expected him to be stiff and clumsy, but instead, he moved nearly as fluidly as Neithelas. Her lunging leaps barely kept up with him and after two songs, she felt like she'd jogged a mile.

"Good!" she praised. "You'll keep up with my sister just fine. Now go dance with her!" She shooed him away. Turning, to Salvarias, she held out her arms. "Your turn."

"Thank you, my lady, but—"

"I won't take no for an answer, Salvarias Laybryth. When those two get married there will be dancing at their wedding. As his brother, you'll be expected to partake in the festivities." She strode forward and planted his hand on her waist and shoved her hand under his, ridding his grip from his staff.

"My lady—"

"I'm not asking you to marry me, I'm asking for a dance."

"My lady," Salvarias said more firmly. "You forget. I cannot dance."

Salvarias's hand lifted, but she stopped him. "I can support you," she whispered

A new song started, a sweet melody, slow, forlorn. Taking a chance, she shifted closer, pushed down his hood, and locked her fingers together behind his neck. The white mage light brightened the churning hues of his charcoal eyes. She'd forgotten how beautiful they were, alive and seductive.

Pressing her luck, she snuck her fingers under his hair and traced a scar along the base of his neck.

His intense stare faltered. The furrow between his eyebrows relaxed. His scrunched-up shoulders dropped. The tightness of his mouth loosened. His arm around her waist tightened, closing the gap between them. His gaze drifted to her lips.

She dare not move. Her chest heaved for air, her stomach knotted with an ache she'd never experienced, her knees threatened to give out, and the entire world seemed to disappear until it was just the two of them.

Then, as it had happened in their dreams, control passed through his gaze, and he lowered his head. His hands entwined with hers and unwound her arms as he stepped back.

"I ..." He cleared his throat and looked away. "I am sure Prince Neithelas has missed your company." He dropped her hands.

She watched him grimace as he did each time he ceased touching her. She doubted it meant what she wanted it to mean. Smiling back her tears, she said, "If you ever change your mind, I'd be happy to teach you how to dance. Perhaps after your leg heals."

"Thank you, my lady."

She curtsied and left their concealment to join the festivities. She caught sight of Neithelas striding for her so she darted into Okulu's arms.

"My lovely Lunara," the merc said, lifting her in a warm hug she needed.

"I don't want to dance with Neithelas anymore," she whispered.

"The pleasure of your company is all mine," he said in her ear. "As for Salvarias, patience and perseverance, my enchanting temptress."

She looked up quickly, masking her pain with a quizzical expression.

Okulu grinned that damn devilishly handsome grin. "I think—and mind you, these are words from a drunkard—that you love our mage friend. No," he held up his hand, "I want neither an agreement nor denial. It's merely my observation." He kissed her cheek and whispered in her ear, "But, if I were to wager all the ale in the world, I'd wager it on him feeling the same."

She flung her arms around his neck and hid her face in his shoulder. His understanding and faith gifted her a brighter flame of hope.

Salvarias shook head to toe as he watched Lunara dancing with Okulu. Selfishly, he had almost kissed her; kissed a woman he cared nothing for.

You disgust me, the voice hissed.

Salvarias disgusted himself. Barely managing to get his trembling limbs to move, he kept to concealed pockets and made his way from the courtyard. He nearly fled through the estate. When he entered his room, he closed the door and leaned against it, fearing his heinous act would follow him and tempt him back to her side. Perhaps the spells were draining. Perhaps they had robbed him of a sound mind.

A knock on the door caused him to jump, and his heart squeezed painfully. Gasping, blinking aside pulsating lights of pain, he doubled over, clutching his sore chest.

"Salvarias?"

It was Talura. A mother. And he was alone. Alone and afraid.

"I"—he gasped in a huge breath—"am fine."

"Open the door."

Her tone was so authoritatively motherly that he found his hand on the handle before he realized what he had done.

"Please, my lady. I—"

"Now, Salvarias."

He ran his sleeve across his eyes and opened the door.

She looked him up and down and shook her head. "What happened? You're pale as a winter moon."

"Nothing. I—" Salvarias blinked when he saw his mother before him. It was not real. He shut his eyes tightly and begged the apparition to disappear. When he opened his eyes, Lady Talura was studying him.

"You see her, don't you?" she whispered.

Fear clamped his throat closed. How could she know? He stumbled back a step and shook his head.

A sharp edge lined her tone when she said, "Don't lie to me."

Salvarias took another step back. Was she mad? Had he done something to displease her? Her fingers pressed against a table by the entrance. There was a thick book within her reach.

He staggered backward, raising his hands in front of him. "Please, I am sorry. I am trying." Tears welled unbidden when she looked at the book. He stumbled over a chair. "I will try harder. I promise."

"Salvarias, I only—"

He heard nothing else. All he saw was his mother striding for him, book gripped in her hand. He tripped over a small table and toppled to the floor. Tears breaking free, he scrambled to the corner of the room.

"Make it leave!" his mother screamed.

"Please," Salvarias wept, curling into the corner. "I am trying."

He cried out when the book struck his legs. He curled up tighter, hiding his ribs, covering his head with his arms as she slammed the book against him.

"Salvarias!" a voice snapped.

He cowered and rocked violently, repeating his apology. The beating stopped. As he had done in his room above the baker, he dug his fingers in the mortar binding the bricks together. He wanted to escape, to fly away, to be as free as the sparrow.

"Look at me, dear," a woman said.

Salvarias shook his head and buried his face in the wall. He did not want to know what was around him. He desperately wanted his brother.

The woman began to sing. The tune was unfamiliar as well as the woman's voice, which was breathier, not as rich as his mother's.

Time passed unknown, but eventually the lovely song calmed him. When his mind surfaced from that dark place, he shut his eyes tightly to rid them of the last of his tears. He curled his fingers, wincing from the layers of skin the mortar had shed. Inhaling a deep breath, he wiped his cheeks and raised his head.

Talura sat in a chair nearby, still humming. "Hello, dear," she said in a normal tone.

Sure his cheeks were red, he tilted his head and used the wall to help him rise. "My lady. I ... I am sorry. I ..."

With a shake of her head, she retrieved his aspen branch and brought it to him. "You apologize far too much, dear. Let's get you in bed. You look positively exhausted." Humming the same tune, she pulled back the blankets, blew out the candles save one, and motioned him to bed.

He kicked off his boots, feeling his cheeks burn with more embarrassment. "There is no need to remain, my lady. I assure you, I am fine."

"Come, come," she said, waving to the bed again.

"I can put myself in bed," he said, sharper than he intended.

"Of course, dear. Now come along."

He fumbled for another way to be rid of her, but by the determination in her eyes, she had every intention of tucking him in. Feeling foolish and childish, he limped to his bed and settled in. She batted his hand away when he went to lift up the covers.

"If my mother was here," she said, "I would let her to tuck me into bed. I always slept better when she did." She raised the blanket up to his shoulders and smiled. "Good night, dear. Sleep well."

"Thank you, my lady."

Instead of leaving him to deal with his embarrassment in private, she lowered herself to a chair and began to hum again. Resigned to his foolishness, he closed his eyes. Much to his dismay, sleep came quicker than it ever had in his entire life. Soon, he was sitting in front of his parents while they spewed words of hatred and bathed him in blood and fire.

37

Varila stirred awake to a thudding headache and her own groaning voice. Her night of dancing, drinking, and stealing kisses from Wilhelm in dark corners had left her exhausted and hung over.

Lunara's giggle sounded. "You slept long. Everyone is already up."

"I drank too much," Varila moaned.

"I think you had an entire bottle yourself. How you were able to keep dancing is beyond me."

"Practice."

"I would've thought Wilhelm would share your misery, but he's as bright-eyed as ever. He drank three bottles himself."

"It'd take an entire keg to bring down that giant ogre."

"Ogre, you say? Well, I didn't know you were so fond of ogres. Your mouth was stuck to his more times than I could count."

"Knock it off," she snapped. "Wine does things to the mind." Tossing aside her blanket, she managed to sit, blinking rapidly against the candles lighting the room to the intensity of the sun. "Why so much damn light?"

"Shall we have some breakfast?" Lunara asked, holding out her hand.

Varila groaned. "I'm not sure I can eat."

"It'd do you good to get something in your stomach besides left-over spirits."

Varila accepted her sister's help and leaned on her, wishing the room would quit spinning. Lurching forward, they made their way to the dining hall. All their friends were there, moaning with heads in their hands, except Wilhelm who winked at her, and her mother who cast her motherly smile. Salvarias was absent.

Rolling her eyes at Wilhelm, Varila plopped into the nearest chair. "Damn you for letting me drink that much."

"I wasn't feeling too great this morning either, but Salv mixed up a potion. Feel as good as new."

"Get his ass down here, and tell him to make us some," she snapped.

"Shhh," her father groaned. "Not so loud."

Salvarias glided into the room and dumped some leaves in a kettle.

"Tell me that's for us," Varila said.

"Of course, my lady."

"Hurry it up," Varila said. "I think I'm dying."

"The leaves must fuse, my lady," he said, stirring the water.

Once the fragrance drifted to her, she inhaled deeply. The aroma alone eased her pounding head. A few moments later, he removed the kettle and poured everyone a glass. She downed it, coughing when the liquid scalded her throat.

"Why don't you all go pack," Humar said, dropping his forehead to the table. "We're leaving soon. Meet me in the courtyard."

"I'll get yours," Durak grumbled.

The Cavrul looked the worst of all. "How much did you drink?" Varila asked.

Wilhelm chuckled. "Two bottles. A man his size shouldn't—"

"What do ye mean, 'a man my size!'" Durak roared.

Everyone moaned.

"I'm just saying, there's less of you to fill up," Wilhelm said, his grin growing.

"Curse you to Oblivion, boy! I can handle as much as the rest of ye!" He swayed a few steps.

"Might I suggest a second cup, Durak?" Salvarias said.

"Me don't need the first one!" Durak tossed the glass across the room, splattering its contents on the marble floor, and stormed out.

"You had to say it, didn't you?" Humar muttered.

Wilhelm shrugged. "I didn't mean to insult him."

"He's a sensitive drunk," Okulu said, sprawled in his chair.

"I'm surprised you're suffering," Varila said. "You drink enough you should be immune."

Okulu shrugged. "That wine is pretty potent, lovely golden-haired warrior."

"Stop calling me that," she snarled.

"Could everyone just be quiet!" Edium groused.

"Pack," Humar said. "We need to leave."

Varila shoved herself up and followed the brothers and Lunara up the stairs. In her room, she threw her belongs into her pack. As always, Lunara folded her dresses with care while humming a melody Vuddruk had played last night. By the time Varila finished, she realized her headache had vanished.

Sitting in front of the mirror, she held up a thin strip of leather for her sister. "Braid my hair."

Lunara began the task of taming Varila's mass into a loose braid, pulling strands free to frame her face. As she stared at herself, she noticed the bruise on her temple had disappeared under the mage's soothing balms. Though her body had healed in mere days, her mind ... She recalled it so clearly. Nonetheless, she'd made a promise. Chesrick wouldn't rule her, wouldn't make her crawl into a corner like beaten dog. No, she would rise from this chair a stronger woman because of it. She'd been violated—twice—and each time she emerged with less scars. She would be damned if anyone broke her.

Smiling to herself, she inhaled a deep breath. A body was just a body. Her heart that she'd tucked behind walls of stone had been freed. Merely being near Wilhelm made her feel more powerful than the mightiest warrior. Love was a wonderful blessing.

"Ladies," Wilhelm said.

She turned to see him standing in the doorway.

"I can take your packs," he said.

"That would be very sweet of you," Lunara said.

Wilhelm snatched up both and left.

"You love him," Lunara said, tying the braid off with the leather strip.

Though it wasn't a question, Varila gathered her courage and added voice to her feelings. "I do."

"When will you tell him?"

She shrugged. "When I'm ready."

Lunara flung her arms around Varila's shoulders and grinned at their reflections. "I'm happy for you. He's the only one worthy of you in all of Arden."

Varila hugged her sister's arms. "Let's get going."

Lunara's smile faded. "I love you."

"I love you, too. Don't worry, he won't come close to replacing you."

Lunara smiled halfheartedly. "I know."

It'd be impossible for anyone not to notice her sister's uncertain voice, the slight tremble, the downcast eyes. It'd always been just them. No matter how many men Varila took to her bed, she would kick them out after she'd had her way with them and return to the room she shared with Lunara. If Varila ever married, she'd be staying with her husband. It fortified her determination to wed Lunara off to Neithelas soon.

"Come on," Varila said, rising from her chair. "Let's get down there before Humar has a fit."

Hand in hand, they left their room and joined everyone in the courtyard.

Humar was just emerging from the dining hall. "Seems our mage friend took off in the middle of the night. He left a letter wishing us luck on our journey."

Wilhelm frowned. "He said his life's work was here. Why did he leave?"

Humar shrugged. "Said he needed supplies. I assume he'll come back." He glanced around and then groaned. "Durak, where's my pack?"

The Cavrul leaned over and retched.

"I'll get it," Wilhelm said.

As he took a step, the ground vibrated.

"What was that?" Lunara asked in a small voice.

Neithelas wrapped an arm around her shoulders. "A quake?"

"Maybe it's the stubborn monster coming to claim Durak," Okulu whispered.

"Shut up, you nitwitted drunk!" Durak snapped.

"Yes, hear it?" Okulu cupped his ear. "It's calling for the Cavrul who refused to take his medicine like a good boy."

Wilhelm chuckled and took another step. The ground trembled again, followed by a far-off rumble.

Okulu frowned. "Or maybe Arden has finally succumbed to your weight."

Wilhelm took another tentative step. A tremor rippled through the ground, rising up the side of the house and freeing a cloud of dust that descended upon them. Salvarias wheezed and covered his nose with the sleeve of his robe.

Okulu withdrew a dagger, tossing it casually in his hand, but his eyes were darting around. "I have a bad feeling."

Varila withdrew her sword, as did everyone.

This time, the ground rocked without Wilhelm's step. In the distance, a clatter sounded, as if pebbles had fallen from the ceiling.

"Might I suggest we leave," Salvarias whispered.

"I need my pack," Humar said.

Varila glanced at his armor and sword. He might be missing some undergarments, but it wasn't worth risking their lives. "The mage is right."

Humar shook his head and took a step. A whistle sounded from above. Varila craned her neck to stare up into the darkness, trying to see what caused such an odd noise. It built with each quickened breath.

Suddenly Adok lunged on Humar, slamming him to the ground. The wolf grabbed the knight's wrist and bolted, dragging Humar behind him.

Okulu cursed and flung himself from where Humar had been standing. A boulder the size of a horse crashed into the ground, sending shards to pelt them. She heard her father grunt and looked up to him shaking his head. Blood speckled the ground.

"Run," Salvarias whispered.

Wilhelm responded immediately, grabbing Salvarias's arm, and dragging his limping brother forward. Okulu helped Humar up and bolted after Wilhelm while Durak grabbed Edium's arm and hurried to catch up.

Varila glared at Neithelas. "Don't you dare let anything happen to her," she said.

"Upon my life," Neithelas said. Shielding Lunara, he ran forward.

Arthias wrapped his arm around Talura's shoulders. Varila made a cursory glance at the ceiling before cursing and running after her friends.

It sounded as if a war had begun at the far side of the city. Whistles like siege-catapulted boulders hissed in competition with one another, pops of layered stone gave way under some enormous weight she couldn't begin to understand, and crashes sounded as if a troll were stuck in a kitchen.

A whistle shrieked overhead. Unable to see the pitch-black ceiling, she gauged as best she could and lunged to the left. A boulder landed within a few feet, showering her with shards of rock and a plume of dust.

"Great," she growled under her breath. "Now my hair's dirty again."

The quaking ground split cobblestones beneath her feet as she bolted ahead. A sickening, mucusy roar sounded behind her, sending chills up her neck and drying her mouth. She didn't want to look back, and Okulu's wide eyes as he craned to get a peek told her it was horrible enough.

"Run!" the merc shouted.

Salvarias's sparrow of light flittered above him and morphed into the same eagle he'd used to light Serinity. It took flight and headed behind them.

"What in Veedran's creation be that!" Durak cried.

Varila clenched her jaw and spared a glance. Off to the very rear of the city, crunching rock and homes in its massive maw, was what looked like a giant grub. Its height rivaled the tallest estate, and its length stretched past her vision. Ink-black spikes lined its glistening white body, and something bright orange dripped from its spiked teeth. It ate stone like a cow would munch on cud.

Escape was hopeless unless they could buy time to keep the collapse at the back of the city so they could make it up the tunnel and reach the sands in one piece.

Wilhelm must have concluded the same. He stumbled to a halt when they reached the tunnel and shoved his brother forward after the others who were already barreling up. "Go!" he roared.

He marched back, face set in grim determination, and withdrew his swords with that slow measured withdrawal she'd come to love. Salvarias strode after his brother.

When Wilhelm was near her, he said, "Please, take care of Salv for me."

"He's coming behind you," she said

Wilhelm's face drained of color, and he whirled around to his brother. "Get back! Go with the others."

"I am not leaving you, Brother."

Wilhelm stormed up to Salvarias, looming over him, face a thundercloud. "I said go, Salv! Now!"

"You will have to carry me out if you wish me to leave."

Wilhelm cursed and glanced behind him. Fear shone in his eyes until Salvarias's hand rested on his arm.

"As long as we are together, we can do anything," Salvarias whispered.

Wilhelm's crooked grin spread. "You'll use magic?"

Salvarias nodded.

"Good," Wilhelm said, flexing his shoulders. "I didn't like seeing you with a sword. Felt wrong." Wilhelm waved her on. "Get the others out of here."

Salvarias ran his fingers through the wolf's fur. "Keep her safe."

Adok whined and licked Salvarias's hand before loping after the others.

"I'm staying," Varila said.

Wilhelm winked at her. "I love your sense of adventure."

"You haven't seen the half of it," she said.

"Will you two please!" Okulu said, stepping from a shadow.

"We've got ourselves a little army," Wilhelm said. "The three of us will keep it busy. Salv, do what you do."

"Oh my," Okulu breathed.

Varila looked to see a pack of what she guessed were around twenty hidlu racing in front of the creature. She couldn't tell if they were fleeing or aiding it. It didn't matter anyway. She'd kill them regardless.

Wilhelm sheathed his broadsword and effortlessly held his great sword. "Change in plans. We take care of the hidlu first."

The three of them darted toward their enemy, leaving the mage alone. She pulled ahead of Okulu and Wilhelm, navigating the rock-strewn street with ease.

They'd gone no more than thirty feet before she heard a chorus of whistles and looked up to see a slew of rocks plummeting toward them. Either way she dodged, she'd die. The men didn't stand much of a chance either. Trying to find a spot she thought might be safe, she fell to her knees and curled up, covering her head, coughing in dust.

Then the air switched to a wonderful temperature and freshness drove away the musty smell. The loudening whistle stopped directly overhead. A breath passed before a dull thud shook the ground. Looking up, she saw a filmy white bubble around the three of them, and the rocks that had been bent on killing them were piled outside the shield.

Okulu's soft chuckle turned into a victory laugh as he sprang to his feet and sprinted ahead. Wilhelm's crooked grin spread when he glanced back at his brother before jogging after Okulu. The film vanished. Varila took off at a full run, keeping well ahead of the men.

Issuing her war cry, she charged into the front lines of the hidlu. Her mind numbed except for her training. Fully succumbing to instinct and drill upon drill with her father, she whipped her sword around to block an attack while rolling clear of the next. Slipping her hand in her boot, she yanked free her dagger as she rose, bringing it around in an arc to slice through the shin of a hidlu. When she rose, she saw three creatures flanking her fall to the ground, twitching and grabbing a fire shard lodged in their chests.

Blood rushed through her as she reengaged her foe, placing trust in Salvarias to aid her as he'd done for his brother. It freed her to be a destructive force of death, spinning the battle into a tale of blood that made her pant in excitement. Creature upon creature fell before her, grunting and moaning in the throes of death. It was a blur of bodies and raining black blood. Vaguely she heard another sword humming the same tune as hers. Sparing a glance, Wilhelm sliced through enemies in rhythm with her.

All too soon it was over. Only a worm roared off in the distance. Her numb mind snapped alert, and she grimaced at her blood-covered armor and was certain it was splattered in her hair. She cursed, knowing a bath was days away.

Wilhelm's swords clattered to the ground, and she looked up to see him marching toward her. A fire gleamed in his eyes that she'd never seen. It beckoned to her, primal and seductive. Then he was upon her, his arms crushing the air from her, his mouth devouring hers. Her sword and dagger slid from her hands, and she tangled her fists in his hair. A deep groan rumbled in his throat, and his fingers dug into her hips, pulling her closer.

"Will you two please!" Okulu complained.

Wilhelm's next kiss was so deep and intense that it stole the strength in her legs. Only his embrace kept her from falling to the ground. He pulled his mouth from hers and met her gaze. Fire still burned in his eyes.

"By the gods," he said in a voice heavy with desire. "You're beautiful."

She grinned. "I know."

"Worm!" Okulu snapped. "Giant worm? Anyone else see it besides me?"

Wilhelm's fire faded, and he glanced over his shoulder at the approaching creature. His crooked grin sliced across his face. "Let's go give it a welcome." He whirled around, grabbed his swords, and sprinted for the worm.

"He's got some serious issues," Okulu said.

Varila smiled. "Yes, he does."

She snatched up her own weapons and ran ahead, hearing Okulu banging behind her in his head-to-toe armor.

"Brother!" Salvarias cried.

All three stumbled to a halt, whipping their heads around to stare at Salvarias who pointed to the roof. On the smooth sandstone slab acting as a ceiling, a line snaked down its center, splintering off, creating a thick cloud of dust. Sand began to trickle through, as if a lazy waterfall. By the time it dawned on her what was happening, it became a flash flood, raining down to form a mountain no more than twenty feet ahead. And it was growing ... rapidly.

Wilhelm staggered a step. She saw his lips move, and he spun around.

"Run! It's caving!"

She glanced up to see the slab split completely in two. Both sides lurched down until they butted together, forming a V overhead with a deafening boom. She teetered backward, gaze locked above her.

The worm roared again, shaking the entire city. One slab pitched and slid free of the other, echoing a horrible crack.

"Nevlar's fury," was all she could breathe.

Whirling around, she tripped over a boulder that had fallen behind her, twisting her ankle. She cried out, scrambling up, limping forward, dragging her bum foot. Something large smacked the ground behind her, robbing her of solid ground, and spewing rocks pelted her back.

Wilhelm grabbed her arm and hauled her up, carrying her weight in his one hand as she struggled to limp forward.

A boulder plummeted to the ground in front of them. The force sent them flying backward and slammed them to the hard stone. She rolled on her side, gasping in air.

"Brother!" Salvarias's voice was filled with panic.

Wilhelm flung himself on top of her. Sand crashed down on them, dust clogged her lungs, and a whistling shadow swallowed them. More rocks cascaded around them. Wilhelm grunted. He wrapped an arm around her head. This was it. This would be her death.

"No!" Salvarias cried.

Through all the roars and cracks, the chaos of noises, Varila heard Wilhelm's whisper in her ear, "I love you."

She wasn't sure if his words were for Salvarias or her, but she desperately wished she could breathe to tell him of her love. Instead, she gripped his hand in hers.

Then it stopped. She felt the familiar soothing temperature of the mage's protection spell. The dust stilled and the thunder of the collapsing city sounded miles away. Unlike the last, this shield clung to their bodies. But that's not what she gaped at. A boulder the size of a house looked to be resting on Wilhelm's back, and high above them, a second white film covered the entire ceiling, dripping down to form a waterfall in front of the worm that clawed frantically to get through it. The slab of sandstone was no more than a few feet above the boulder floating above them.

Wilhelm lifted his head. "Salv," he breathed.

Salvarias was on his knees at the tunnel entrance, tears streaking his dirty face. "Slowly, Brother," he said, wiping his cheeks.

"We need to hurry," Wilhelm said to her. "He can't maintain these that long."

Both of them crawled on their elbows from under the boulder as fast as the shield could move with them. When free, the boulder slammed into the ground, and the film evaporated. Wilhelm helped her up and ran forward, carrying her along. He reached his brother, released her, and scooped the mage up in a hug.

Salvarias's hood fell back. His eyes were shut tightly, fresh tears trickling down his face, and his fists clutched Wilhelm's shoulders. "I thought I had lost you," Salvarias breathed.

"I'm sorry, Salv."

"We need to leave," Okulu said.

The merc wedged himself under her arm and clambered up the steep entrance to the tunnel. She looked over her shoulder at Wilhelm holding his brother's arm in his hand, leading him forward and taking weight off his leg. Behind them, the white film keeping the worm at bay and the ceiling from collapsing seemed not as vibrant as it was breaths ago.

"What's the plan?" Wilhelm asked.

"When I release the spell, the ceiling will cave," Salvarias said. "It will kill the worm. The implosion will kill us as well."

"How much longer can you hold it?"

Salvarias shrugged. "Not to the top."

Wilhelm inhaled deeply. "We need to run."

"I could not keep up. You would have to carry me, Brother. And Lady Varila cannot run on her own," Salvarias said, pointing to her swelling ankle.

"I can carry most of her weight," Okulu said. "Give her your staff. It'll help."

Salvarias passed her the staff. The mage immediately crumbled without it, but Wilhelm quickly caught him. "Go as fast as you can, Okulu," he said, wrapping Salvarias's arm around his shoulders.

Okulu sprinted forward. At first, it was awkward to keep his pace, and she stumbled every other step, cursing herself and the merc. Soon though, they found a suitable rhythm. When she guessed they were halfway up, she glanced back.

Salvarias trembled violently, his muscles under his robes tightening in spasms. Blood trickled from his ears and ran from his nose.

"End the spell," Wilhelm said. She swore it looked like Wilhelm was growing. His taut skin seemed strained to contain his bulging muscles. "It'll take a bit for the cave-in to reach us, Salv. End it!"

Sand drifted from overhead and the ground beneath her trembled. She saw a crack along the wall ahead of them, snaking up until it circled the tunnel. They passed under it as sand drizzled down.

"Faster!" Wilhelm roared. "Release it, dammit!"

She craned her neck to look over her shoulder. Salvarias's eyes had rolled in the back of his head, and blood flooded from his mouth.

Okulu cursed, and in one swift movement, she found herself flung over his shoulder. She lost her grip on the staff, and it clattered to the stone. Wilhelm cursed, sidestepped it, and scooped Salvarias up in his arms. Sweat soaked the mage's robes and beaded his face, streaking down and wetting his hair. He gagged up more blood. Her gaze locked on Wilhelm. By the gods, his skin looked ready to rip open.

Salvarias began to shake violently. He jerked, falling from quick seizures into violent trembling. She glanced ahead. There was light.

"*Rulose.*" Blood spurted from Salvarias's mouth.

"Dammit!" Wilhelm shouted.

He flung Salvarias's limp form over his shoulder, and with his free hand, grabbed Okulu's arm and bolted ahead. She swore Wilhelm ran as fast as a horse. Okulu's feet tangled, and he lost his footing. He latched hold of her before she slipped free as he hung from Wilhelm's hand like a dead rabbit.

Behind them, the roar of the cave-in was catching up. Dust and rocks pelted them. Through the haze, she caught sight of the collapse. It was close, too close for her comfort. Above all the chaos, she heard a horrible shriek, what she assumed to be the worm's dying wail.

"Faster!" she cried.

They burst into blinding daylight. Varila gaped at the pit behind them and the plum of dust infecting the sky. The sunken hole stretched farther than the city she'd seen. And the collapse still ate at their heels.

"Hurry!" Humar roared.

Okulu stopped beside a grynf and half tossed her on it. She managed to get herself upright and hissed her mount into a run behind her friends. Sparing a glance behind, she saw Wilhelm leap on a beast, hauling Salvarias with him. Her breath caught in her throat when the ground disintegrated beneath his grynf's rear feet, forcing the beast to struggle desperately with its front hooves to find solid ground. Adok was suddenly there and nipped and snarled at the grynf's heels. The beast wailed, wide-eyed, and jumped forward, finding purchase and galloping clear of the cave in.

The ground crumbled beneath Adok. The wolf slipped from sight.

Varila kept her gaze back as she plunged onward, seeing Wilhelm mouthing "come on." Then her father rode past her toward the collapse. His pack rested on his lap, and the rope used to tie it was in his hands.

"Father!" Varila cried.

Black paws appeared at edge of the dissolving sand, clawing for safety. Edium tossed the rope, reeled his mount around, and kicked its flanks. The beast took off. From the edge of the cave-in, Adok slid into view, mouth clamped on the rope. The wolf scrambled to his feet, released the rope, and loped next to Wilhelm, eyes fixed on Salvarias.

The collapse chasing them finally faded into the distance of the grynfs' long strides. Gaping at the devastation, she marveled at the size Quind had once been. Serinity was considered one of the largest cities in Dalnar, but the yawning hole was twice the size.

Once clear and safe, Humar motioned everyone to a halt.

Wilhelm had Salvarias cradled to his chest, dumping the contents of a vial down Salvarias's throat while whispering in the mage's ear. Salvarias wasn't breathing.

Fear punched Varila's lungs. Whipping around, she saw Lunara limp in Neithelas's arms. Her father and the prince were trying to wake her, their voices growing more panicked.

Lunara gasped, and with hers, so did Salvarias. He coughed up some blood and promptly went limp in Wilhelm's arms.

"Lunara!" her father cried.

"She'll be all right," Varila said, nudging her mount between her father and Neithelas's.

"Like Oblivion she will!" her father snapped.

"She's fine, Edium," Humar said. He stopped by Durak and belted his friend in the face, launching the Cavrul from his saddle. "Do me a favor," Humar said coolly. "Don't talk to me for a few days. What I had in my pack was of greater value to me than all the gold in Arden." Turning to Okulu, he tugged on his gauntlet and said, "What happened?"

"Well," Okulu said, stroking his mustache. "We had the brilliant idea of fighting the slightly large worm and was pleasantly surprised to see a pack to twenty hidlu arrive as well. Our brilliant golden-haired warrior took them down rather quickly. But during that time, the worm—only slightly larger than most, mind you—decided to make the roof cave in. Raining boulders is not a sight I'd recommend. Varila was victim to one, as you can see by her swelling ankle. In all his adoration with our lovely golden-haired warrior, our mighty Wilhelm went to her rescue, willing to sacrifice himself for her. Very honorable, but altogether stupid. There was no chance he could get her clear in time. Anyway, as I know, though some of you refuse to see, our mage friend here is strongly opposed to the thought of any of us—especially his ogre of a brother—dying. So, he cast two protection spells. One over the loving duo, then another to keep the collapse and worm at bay. From what I know of magic and based on the amount of blood I saw, he pushed himself well past his tolerance. When he wakes, he'll either have survived it, or he'll be mad."

Humar shook his head. "I'm in no mood, Okulu."

Wilhelm put his ear over Salvarias's heart. "He summed it up rather well, if you ask me. Salv's told me that pushing magic can kill a mage or make him go mad. We saw it happen in the slave caverns."

"We can't stop to give him time to rest," Humar said. "I'm sure barbarians will be here soon. That collapse sounded like a thunderstorm, and the dust alone is a beacon. It'll be a day and a half of hard riding."

Wilhelm nodded. "I'll carry Salv."

"Neithelas, keep Lunara with you." Humar glanced between the two younger siblings. "Looks like their—"

"Lunara probably just fainted," Varila said.

Humar frowned and glanced at Edium before nodding. "If you say so."

Her father's eyes narrowed. "No, she didn't faint. Try again."

Varila shrugged. "I'm sure she fainted."

"Swear it to me on her life."

Varila glared at her father. "That's not fair, Father."

"Lying to your father gives him the right to be unfair."

"Enough, dear," Talura said to Edium.

"Let's go," Humar said. "We'll discuss this later."

"Yes, we will," Edium said.

Varila had heard that tone before. Yes, they would be discussing it, and she doubted Lunara would be able to keep the secret from their parents. It was for the better. Once their father learned that Salvarias carelessly risked Lunara's life, he'd disapprove of the mage as much as Varila did. In no time, Lunara would be walking hand in hand with Neithelas, happy and safe.

38

E dium sat with Humar under a stocky tree, watching the others prepare lunch. It had taken hours of riding into the plains outside the desert before Humar called for a rest.

Lunara had finally woken. Dark rings framed her eyes and made her skin appear even paler. Salvarias had yet to wake. The long, nearly two days of flight had sobered up the Cavrul, and he had stayed his distance from Humar, often massaging his black eye. Overall, there was a heaviness to the group. Everyone looked exhausted.

"Hidlu," Edium said after a bit of silence. "Odd, wouldn't you say?"

Humar picked dry grass and crushed it between his fingers. "Extremely. Did you ever hear Wilhelm talk of his days in slavery?"

"Not directly, but he was open with Talura. She passed along his tale. Sad for such young boys to have endured so much."

Humar nodded. "That's not my point, though. Wilhelm is a gifted man. His mind ... well, it doesn't work like others. I'm teaching him a fighting technique that fewer than twenty men have mastered. His mind was made for it. His concentration, his control ... it's simply astounding. He links things, Edium. I doubt it's fully dawned on him yet since he's been so focused on Salvarias, but it will soon. He told

415

me when they were mining he felt there was a larger purpose than just metals. One day in passing, he mentioned it felt like they were tunneling *toward* something. I think whatever threatens Arden has a web that branches from Avulin through to the Cattlar Mountains. The hidlu in Quind prove my theory."

"Why would they spend time tunneling?"

"Safe passage for armies. Supply routes that can't be ambushed. The ability to cover distances undetected. Think of something more brilliant than moving right below your enemies' feet."

"You think that's how they managed the army outside Serinity without detection?"

Humar shrugged. "I think it played a role. Along with Dethal's magic, of course."

"It makes sense." Edium stared over the rolling dry hills speckled with dots of dark evergreens. "What's Salvarias got to do with this?"

Humar inhaled a deep breath. "That boy scares me more than any monster. He's not normal. Veedran's insanity only knows what this 'god' wants with him."

"You discredit what you learned from Dethal?"

"The gods residing on Arden barely qualify for the title. An old mage holds greater power than what's left here. Yet this ... thing has creatures at its disposal that Crutar and the likes could never command. It must have more power. Perhaps it's a mage."

Edium scoffed. "Surely you aren't such a fool."

"What do you think it is?"

Edium stroked his beard. "A wicked creature of Veedran's warped mind—one that has hidden in shadow. A mage couldn't command the abominations of Veedran, no matter how powerful, no matter what race. It has to be linked to the dark god."

"Interesting theory. Say it is. What's its goal? Why now?"

"Why now, I can't answer. As to its goal ..." Edium frowned. "To carry out the wishes of its master. It seeks to finish what Veedran didn't."

"A logical explanation," Humar said. "I wish we knew more. I wish I had a face. I feel like we're running blindly into a pit of snakes."

Edium clapped the knight's shoulder. "That's because we are, my friend."

Lunara strolled over and handed Humar and Edium a plate of food.

Edium grabbed her wrist. "Sit with me."

Humar tilted his head and left to join Okulu. Lunara took Humar's seat by Edium's side and snuggled under his arm. Talura sat on her other side.

"You look tired," he said, resting his plate beside him.

"I am. The last day and a half have been exhausting."

Edium picked up a chunk of bread and stared at it, hoping it could provide him the appropriate way to go about his questions. The bread didn't speak, however. "Varila said you fainted after the collapse."

"Mmm."

Edium smiled, remembering the times his youngest failed at lying or withholding the truth. "I think she was mistaken."

"I need some rest."

He tightened his arm around her shoulder, keeping her in place. "Not yet. Unless you choose to tell me the truth, we're in for a long discussion."

Lunara sagged in his arms. "I'm so tired, Father. Can't we do this another time?"

"No, no we can't."

With a heavy sigh, Lunara shifted around until she sat facing him and Talura. "So be it. There are many things that have happened since I first fled our home that I can't explain. I can simply tell you what I know."

Talura nodded. "That will do, dear."

Lunara glanced over her shoulder at the mage who was encased in Wilhelm's arms. "I have dreamt of Salvarias since I was a little girl. I'd never met him, at least, not that I remember. But every night I would walk with him through forests or gardens. We talked of books we'd read … nothing personal. The night I fled, I had a different dream. I was told that he was real and I had to help him. That's how we came to know Wilhelm. During our travels to find and rescue Salvarias, I stopped dreaming of him. Instead, he spoke in my mind. He warned me of danger and saved us." She drew her knees to her chest, rubbing her arms even though the sun baked the air. "One morning, a mere few days from rescuing him, I started bleeding. One breath I was in a chair in a tavern, sipping warm cider, and the next, I looked down to see my body covered in blood. I had cuts all over me. Everywhere. The connection I share with him goes beyond being able to communicate. We're linked mentally and physically. If he dies, I die."

Edium felt like he'd been punched. He slouched against the tree, forcing in a sharp breath.

"That's why I don't like the mage," Varila said, stepping into view. "The risks he takes are too great. She suffers because of him."

"He takes risks that will save the majority," Lunara said softly.

Varila snorted. "He could've left with you. But he had to stay. He refuses to listen to Wilhelm."

Lunara raised her teary gaze to Varila. "Would you so willingly leave me if I went to sacrifice myself to save others?"

Varila's lip curled. "Don't give me that crap, Lunara. You'd never do anything to get yourself into a situation that'd require your sacrifice or that of others."

"So it's his fault that a giant worm found us?"

"It's his fault we're on this forsaken sprint across Dalnar," Varila snapped. "With no idea what in all of Nevlar's fury we're doing."

"You're right," Lunara said. "Better he go home to Falar and ignore his purpose. Ignore the gifts he's been granted. Better to let Arden be devoured by this foul evil than risk the lives of eight to save it." Lunara bolted to her feet. "How wise you are, sister." She stormed a few steps before whirling around. "And just so you know, I asked him to stay and fight the worm. I told him to help save you and Wilhelm any way he could. No matter the cost." Lunara's tears broke free, and she marched to the edge of the camp.

Varila looked like her world had just ended. The two hadn't fought since they were little.

"She wasn't trying to hurt you," Talura said, rising. "She merely wanted you to see her point. How she feels. What she sees." She kissed Varila's forehead and joined Lunara.

Varila sank next to Edium. "What do you see, Father?"

"I see a set of companions who have grown closer than any family. They fight, bicker, and care for one another. I see two brothers who would die for each other. And I see two sisters who would do the same."

Varila nestled up against him. "Is it wrong of me to say I wouldn't cry if Salvarias died? You haven't seen what I've seen. You don't know what he's capable of."

Edium rested his cheek on top of her head. "You feel what you feel. Right or wrong. I think if you look deeper, past your anger and pain, past this odd connection to Lunara, you'd surprise yourself. I don't know the boy, but death is a harsh thing to wish upon anyone."

"There are times I feel so lost, so confused. Everything happening is outside of my control."

Edium smoothed her hair. "Life is a winding path with many intersections. Inevitably, at one point in your journey, you will veer from the main road and walk a dark path. In those times, how you handle yourself will determine who you'll be. Sometimes you can find your way back to the main road. Others, you die horribly on that dark trail. But all that matters, all you should expect from yourself, is to be courageous and never give up. It's the journey that makes us who we are, both the trails that ensnare us in darkness and those we walk in the light."

"I'm careful to never step on those dark trails. I'm not that blind. I know right from wrong."

"My dear daughter, you've walked those dark trails already. The darkness does not mean murdering people or committing heinous acts, it means being caught up in something frightening, either by your own actions or by those of others. When you were sixteen, your road was closed, and you were forced on to a dark trail. But you were brave and fought your way to the light. At one point, we all walk the roads of shadow."

"I never thought of it that way," she said softly.

"The path you are taking now will determine your character. Look at him," Edium said, motioning to Salvarias. "You walk in darkness now. Your heart is weighted, your mind muddled. The choices you make in regards to that man will forever be with you. Choose wisely. Choose objectively. Know yourself and the person you want to be. Only you can find the right trail."

Varila took a deep breath and nodded. "You're right."

Edium chuckled. "Of course."

He finished the meal with a knot in his stomach. His practices didn't align with his lecture. His family was his world, and anything that threatened them had to be eliminated. Yet because of Lunara's embracement of this connection, her approval of Salvarias's actions, he mused there was more to the story than what was seen on the surface. Perhaps he would watch the boy closely, study him, and learn for himself if the mage was a danger to his daughter.

Salvarias, for the first time since Quind, muttered under his breath. Wilhelm's eyes flew open.

"Salv," Wilhelm said, gently shaking his brother.

Salvarias head tossed back and forth, and his brow furrowed. "Help ..." He twitched and moaned, fingers knotting into tight fist.

"Wake up, Salv."

The boy curled up, hugging his stomach. Edium glanced at Lunara. She stood in the same spot, eyes distant and staring over the grasses.

Salvarias's mutters turned to short cries of pain. No one paid him much mind, and Edium assumed the boy's nightmares were the same in travel as they'd been in Serinity.

Salvarias jerked awake, gasping. He doubled over, coughing violently enough to gag. Humar was quick to offer water. The boy barely got down a few gulps before he succumbed to another coughing fit.

Edium sprang up when blood mixed with saliva fell from the mage's lips.

"We're all right, Salv," Wilhelm said, arms holding his brother's hacking body together. "You just have to breathe."

The mage fumbled in his robe pockets and retrieved a potion vial. His shaking hands dropped it. Wilhelm picked it up, uncorked it, and helped the boy drink. Enough time passed that Edium found his own chest sore with sympathy.

At long last, Salvarias gasped in huge breaths and gained control. He glanced at his brother and then around the camp. "Where are we?"

"Outside the desert," Wilhelm said, relief evident in his tone. "You've been out of it for a day and a half."

Salvarias nodded and drank more water.

"Shame," Okulu said. "I thought you might've gone mad with the amount of magic you used."

"I am sorry to disappoint you," Salvarias said dryly.

Edium's mouth dropped open at the boy's first open jest. Glancing at the other's surprised expressions, they'd never heard one either.

Salvarias rose with help from Wilhelm. "My staff?"

"I dropped it," Varila said. "It's buried in Quind."

Salvarias nodded. One breath later, it appeared at his side.

Edium jumped, sputtering out a curse before he said, "How in Oblivion did you do that?"

Salvarias retrieved a cloth from his robes and wiped his mouth. "I learned how to enchant, my lord."

"Edium. Call me Edium."

Salvarias's hooded head turned to Lunara. She smiled.

"Hungry?" Wilhelm asked.

Salvarias shook his head. "I must gather some herbs."

"I'll come," Wilhelm said.

"No need," Edium interjected. "I'll go with him."

He followed the mage from the camp and out into the rolling plains.

"There is no need for you to come, my lord—"

"Edium."

"I am sure you need rest."

He shrugged. "I'm in the mood for a stroll."

"I would prefer to be alone, my lord."

"Edium." He glanced up at the burning sun and a raven cawing in the cloudless sky. "My daughter has told me of your connection."

Salvarias's shoulders tensed. "I assure you, my lord—"

"Edium."

"I am doing everything within my power to sever it."

"Why?"

Salvarias stopped walking, and his shadowed gaze fell to Edium. "It is dangerous, my lord—"

"Edium."

"You have seen firsthand just how dangerous."

"Yet you did the spell anyway."

"With her permission," Salvarias said. "There was a chance to save her sister, my brother, and Okulu. Three lives for two."

"Ah, the majority. I think it's important you know how I feel about your majority guideline, boy. Those two girls are the center of my world. If anything happens to them, I'll have no problems hunting you down and making you pay."

Salvarias raised his head, and the glaring sun lit up his black eyes. Prepared somewhat, Edium still recoiled. No white could be seen; simply blackness so intense he was sure his soul was sucked into those dark pits, unraveled to reveal his secrets, his fears, his entire character.

"The safety of Arden is my concern, my lord. I have requested more times than I can count that your daughters remain behind. Instead of issuing your threats to me, perhaps you should shift your efforts to your own children and take them safely to Serinity. I do not wish for their company." He turned and walked away. "Or yours."

"I want Arden's safety as much as you do, boy."

Salvarias stopped and strode back up to Edium. When he spoke, his voice was tight, not lulling as usual. "Then it would behoove you to return home. What I do should be done alone. You, however, have the means to build an army and rid Arden of her shadows. Those who follow me would be an asset to you, my lord. I beg you to take them with you. Leave now and let me go my way alone."

"You listen to me, boy. I—"

"I am no boy." Salvarias's voice went flat.

"You're wet behind the ears," Edium snarled. "I'll tell you what's going to happen. We're going to see you safely to this army so I can see its size and what makes up its forces. Afterward, I'm bringing everyone home with me. *Everyone.* Together we'll fight what is plaguing Dalnar. I've seen your magic firsthand. You're the one who's the asset to my army as is your brother. You two will command it at my side."

The boy's voice switched to almost a helpless confession. "My fate does not lie here. After this, there will be something else I must do. My purpose will never see an end until I lie dead." Shaking his head, he continued in his usual soft voice. "I will not return with you. I will not rule an army at your side. That, my lord, is not my destiny."

The boy's words, his initial tone, the glint in his eyes, were filled with so much despair and defeat that it reached out to Edium's heart. In that moment, Salvarias looked so young, hopeless and helpless, frightened and confused. "What is it? What do you know? What are you hiding? How did you know about the attack on Serinity? Why do they hunt you? Trust me, son!"

Salvarias shoved back his hood, and Edium recoiled from the flare of anger in the boy's eyes. "I am not your son." He spun around but Edium grabbed his arm. Salvarias yanked free. "Do not touch me!"

Edium stared after the boy with a dagger twisting in his heart. Adok let out a low growl, snapping at Edium's legs and causing him to stumble back. After a baleful glare, eyes seeming more human than wild beast, Adok loped after Salvarias.

Edium trekked toward camp, analyzing every word the boy had spoken. Halfway, Humar joined him.

"I see you've upset the mage," Humar said.

Edium rested a hand on the knight's shoulder. "You have no children, do you?"

Humar shook his head.

"Then you haven't seen the signs. That boy has been screaming for help, Humar." He glanced over his shoulder at Salvarias huddled under a tree. "And for his entire life, no one has listened."

SALVARIAS HUGGED HIMSELF, rocking, trying to rid his mind from the memory of Tobin's betrayal. "You are no son of mine" echoed around him, ripping out chunks of his heart. He drew his knees closer to his chest and buried his face in them, begging his mind to seek another thought. It did. But what it switched to stole Salvarias's breath until he was gasping. As if he were still there, he saw the rock falling toward his brother, and the terror at almost losing Wilhelm shook Salvarias to physical tremors. He raised his gaze and picked out his brother's frame moving about the campsite, unmistakable among the others. Salvarias had barely gotten the spells out in time. If he had not, his brother would be dead.

And it would be your fault, my pet, the voice hissed.

"Leave me," Salvarias snapped.

The near-death of his brother, as horrific as it was, had forced Salvarias to push his magic to a new level, unlocking yet more power. When Salvarias's own mind threatened to abandon him in darkness, his magic had refused to allow it. It surged forward with strength and determination, saving Salvarias from the yawning emptiness of a mad mind. Its lasting impression upon him was one of mutual awe. The moment had created a stronger bond, reset their understanding of each other's limits. What they had accomplished made him ponder how much more they could do, what else they were capable of. Perhaps he did hold greater power than Dethal.

Salvarias snorted at his evaluation. Dethal could surely perform the same spells if pushed. Times such as these made him wish he could sense his own level of power, how he truly compared to those he aspired to surpass.

Lord Bellerum and Humar were not in camp but for a brief moment before Wilhelm left and headed toward Salvarias. Sighing, he shoved himself to his feet. His muscles succumbed to a fit of spasms, and his brain pounded against his skull in protest of movement. Leaning heavily on his staff, he set out to meet his brother.

White light flashed in front of him, blocking the rolling plain of dry grasses. When it dissolved, he stood in a line of stocky trees. Before him, an aqua muddied lake sparkled in the sun, and the vast field was empty. He burst from the trees and gazed at the scorched patches of earth where fires had once been and at the abandoned cages with rotting dead captives.

The sight sent him staggering back. He had failed. How simpleminded was he? Did he think the army would patiently wait for him to show and then at his request, slit their own throats?

Clenching his fist, he grated, "Do not think me weak." He would find them again. He had to. If he did not ...

You've doomed Arden, my pet, the voice hissed.

Salvarias suddenly stood in front of an unrecognizable city. Blazing buildings lit the night sky, creating a red aura around the entire city. Other than the crackling and popping of timber, the air was eerily silent as if paying homage to the ruin. Outside the city walls, children were impaled and corpses littered the fields. The stench of burning hair and flesh caused his stomach to heave.

White light flared again and streaks of azure sky, brown grasses, and stocky trees bled by him. He leaned to the side and retched.

His world tipped this way and that. Stumbling, trying to keep his balance with his staff, he lurched forward. A lump on the ground tripped him and twisted his bad leg. A howl of pain escaped as fell to the ground.

"Salv!"

Salvarias tried to rise, but his surroundings had yet to settle. The sky was above and then below. Reaching out a shaking hand, he waited a few breaths before he felt his brother's grip.

"What happened?" Wilhelm asked.

A strong arm held him upright, allowing his vision to stabilize. Shame clogged his throat. "I-I failed, Brother. The army ... it left."

Wilhelm's jaw clenched. "You failed at nothing, Salv. We've had one obstacle after another thrown at us. You've tried your best. Come on, let's tell the others."

Salvarias followed his brother to camp, fighting the waves of nausea. The fires ... children, women ... so much death.

"What is it?" Humar said. "What's happened?"

Shame prevented Salvarias from meeting the knight's gaze. "The army has left. I ... I do not know where they have gone."

Humar's disappointment, as unspoken as it was, kicked Salvarias in the chest.

"How do you know?" Lord Bellerum asked.

"I've told you," Humar muttered. "The boy has insights. He knows things."

"Well ... We'll find them," Lord Bellerum said. "We'll go to Xeroth, catch a ship, and sail up the river to the lake. That'll save us at least a day of travel. From there, we'll follow the army's trail. I can keep my men apprised of its location once we find it. I'm sure we'll catch up to it. We can warn whatever city is their target, just as you did for Serinity."

"It's too late, isn't it?" Humar asked, voice dead.

Salvarias wanted nothing more than to crawl into a hole. He felt so very small, so weak, just as when he was a child, helpless and alone. In his peripheral vision, he caught sight of blue mage robes rustling by behind Humar. Glancing up, his mother stood, arms folded over her chest, lip curled in disgust. He ducked half behind his brother, begging his mind to rid the image of her. It was not real. It was not real.

"Well?" Humar snapped.

Salvarias flinched. "A city has burned."

Ashra shook her head. "Monstrosity."

39

SUMMER 1018 A.R

S alvarias sat astride his grynf, huddled in his cloak, wiping sweat
from his brow as he had done for the last two days. He was
miserable. Though he had hidden it from Wilhelm, he had yet to
keep a full meal down—a side effect of Sansis's disembowelments—
nor had his body stopped aching from the spells he had performed
when they had fled Quind. His insides throbbed, and his sore chest
made each small breath a labor for inadequate air. After Humar had
shared Salvarias's failure with their group, the glares he had received
cocooned him in layers of depression that seemed to amplify the red
haze tainting life and prevented his body from recovering as quickly
as it should. Defeat was a bitter taste that burned his throat each time
he swallowed.

You whine like a child, the presence hissed. *It is because of you that
darkness has come to these lands. It is you who beckons for it.*

Leave me. I am in no mood for your lectures.

I am in no mood for your self-pity, but I must endure it.

Regardless of its words, the presence receded.

A sudden, near overpowering urge to turn south hit Salvarias
with the force of hurricane winds. It took every ounce of his
willpower to keep from running off. The tug turned into a physical

pull that made him sway in his saddle. His mouth dried, and his hands shook enough to loosen the reins from his grip. Taking in a soothing breath, he added the scars on his right hand to the list of things he was counting. A few heartbeats passed before he gained control over his urge. If not for the army, he would have ridden off and uncovered the mystery.

"Xeroth," Okulu announced.

Salvarias turned his attention ahead to buildings clustered on the ocean's edge, growing sparser and cruder toward the sprawling outskirts of the city, which was nothing more than randomly placed decrepit homes littered along the open plains covered in green grasses and a rainbow of flowers. Xeroth's winding streets looked as if a child had scribbled lines on parchment and the Watythms used it for city planning. Floating in the sea were ships surpassing the stunning ones Salvarias had seen in Falar. It would have been beautiful if the red haze had not infected it, making it appear as if the stones were stained with blood and the ocean soiled with it.

Okulu motioned to the scattered outskirts. "Whenever a family thinks they're going to settle down they build a home, but soon the sea calls them and they leave, abandoning what they built. That's why there's so many.

"It's an interesting race. I've heard it said that the ocean's call is so powerful, a man or woman can forget everything, including husbands or wives or children. So, the entire race looks after whoever lives in the city. Eventually, the children will start to hear the summons and leave as well, usually joining up with their birth parents. When Nevlar changed the race, he knew the oceans to be dangerous, so the urge for sailing doesn't start in a child until they're sixteen. I don't think the god thought through his plan, though. If the parent is being called to the sea, and it's too dangerous for children, then who looks after the young ones? Sad, really. It's why the race is dwindling. It's not in the nature of a Watythm to remain in one place." Okulu looked over his shoulder at Salvarias. "You'll be welcomed. Watythms worship mages."

"If that's true, why won't they sail with 'em?" Durak asked. Once again, the Cavrul had a stick and was carving it into something Salvarias assumed would be stunning. He thought it might have been a redwood, but Durak tucked it away before Salvarias could confirm.

"They think Veedran's creatures are attracted to magic," Okulu said. "Of course, it's ridiculous. There are mage Watythms, though very few. I think right now, they only have nineteen amongst their entire race."

When they reached the outskirts, the merciless sun broke free from the hazy clouds, and Salvarias pulled his hood as low as it would go. His eyes throbbed, and he felt the searing heat through his robes even as he shivered from cold. He hated summer.

"Humar and I will enter the city," Lord Bellerum said. "Watythms don't take well to strangers, but I have a nice trade business in Xeroth. The rest of you wait here while I make sure we're not all murdered."

The two men dismounted their grynfs and strolled to the inner city. The rest of the companions milled about. Salvarias dismounted and sat on a stone half-wall, burying his face in his hands.

"Are you a wizard?" a voice asked.

Salvarias looked up to see a little boy staring at him with wide eyes.

"Yes," he said.

"A wizard!" the boy shouted. "A wizard is here!"

Okulu chuckled. "Told you."

Children flooded out of homes and soon circled Salvarias. "Cast a spell!" one yelled. "Yes, set something on fire!" another one called. "No, freeze something!" one said. "I want to see something different!" another one pouted.

Salvarias whispered his light spell, and the sparrow of light fluttered around the children. They giggled with delight and chased the bird when he sent it through the fields lit pink by the fading sun. One child remained.

"I said I wanted something different," the little girl insisted, adding emphasis with a stomp of her foot, causing her simple green dress to ripple. "I've seen fire, ice, lightning, and that stupid light spell. I want to see something new!" She tucked a lock of chestnut hair behind her ear, allowing the sun to light up her startling blue eyes.

Salvarias suppressed a smile. "So be it. Permit me a moment to think." He ignited his magic.

My wizard, his magic greeted. *The child will be a witch one day. I sense it within her. Her mind is not yet ready, but the power is eager.*

Let us show her something interesting. Suggestions?

I think now might be the time to try something new, my wizard. Something truly amazing. As we have been enchanting, I've been testing the powers within you. My wizard, you can create.

Salvarias shrugged. *Of course. I create fire from nothing. I create ice. The plant spell is simple enough.*

No, my wizard. You wouldn't need the twig or seed of the plant you wish to create as you would with the plant spell. You can create life. Creatures, plants, anything that lives.

Salvarias coughed to hide his gasp. *Surely you are mad.*

Quite the contrary. However, you must control the blackfire to do so. I cannot.

I will not touch blackfire with my own mind.

Let us try the other power. It's ... lazy, content to be in the background of your thoughts. I doubt its effect will be the same. Furthermore, it seems trusting of me, almost as if it doesn't care what it's used for. I can call it forth easily and use it much more efficiently than blackfire.

I am not sure now is the time to test this.

I think it is. You'll be able to sleep all night on a ship. Please, my wizard, I'm most curious about this power and how it works. Once you use it, I can familiarize myself and gain the knowledge needed to help lessen its effect on you. Possibly, it'll prove more powerful than blackfire.

Salvarias sighed. *So be it. I am not sure I want to show her something significant that she might not be able to replicate. Allow us to create a plant. When she learns spells, she will think it was merely the plant spell. Our endeavor will be less obvious.*

Of course. To ease the strain, you need something to funnel the power to. Think of it as a component or the recipient of an enchantment. You can create without an object, but I've no doubts the strain on your mind would be tenfold. Whatever you select will hold the power and come alive with what you desire. Anything will do. A leaf, soil ... anything. Once you've selected something, form the picture in your mind. Think of smells, sounds, and characteristics. The power will do the rest ... perhaps fill in any gaps you miss.

"What is your name?" Salvarias asked the girl.

"Thia."

"Close your eyes, Thia."

She crossed her arms over her chest. "It's cheating if I can't see you do it."

"I will not perform the spell without you watching, but I need you to focus for a moment."

"Is something wrong with your face?" she asked.

"In a manner of speaking."

"Is that why you keep your hood up?"

Salvarias nodded.

"Are you disfigured? Can I see?"

Okulu chuckled. "Watythms fear nothing."

Thia snorted. "We sure don't. I've seen monsters in the oceans that'd give the bravest warriors nightmares." She reached out and ran her fingers along the side of his hood.

"I advise against it," he said.

"I'm not scared. You shouldn't be either," she said.

Salvarias closed his eyes as she pushed down his hood.

"There's nothing wrong," Thia said. "You look normal."

He heard her stomp her foot. Sighing, he opened his eyes.

"What's wrong with you? You're not deformed," Thia said.

Salvarias cocked his head, trying to determine if she was being cruel or honest. "Usually my eyes spark a level of fear in most."

"Well, there's hardly any white like mine. But that's not your fault, is it? Why would people be afraid?"

"I do not know," Salvarias said.

"I think they're pretty."

"Thank you."

The girl stuck out her bottom lip in a forced pout. "I was really hoping to see something deformed."

"You could take off your robes," Okulu said.

Salvarias cast the merc an arched eyebrow. "Thank you for the idea and insult."

Okulu winked. "How about the ear?" He looked at Thia. "He had his ear chopped off, then they burned the skin with acid."

Thia clapped her hands together. "Let me see! Let me see!"

Stifling a laugh, Salvarias lifted aside his hair.

Her smile melted into a gaping mouth. "Oh my! Who did that?"

"A very unpleasant man," Salvarias said.

"I certainly hope you're not friends with him anymore! Can I touch it?"

"If you wish."

She reached out a tentative hand and felt the bubbled skin then brushed her fingers through his hair. Images fluttered painfully: vast oceans, creatures he had only seen in picture books, lands he had yet to visit. He flinched free of her touch.

"Do you feel your ear sometimes?" she asked. "I know a man who lost his leg, and he swears he can still feel it."

"Yes, I do."

"Did the same man cut off your pinky too?"

"You are a curious child."

"How do you learn without asking questions? That's what my caretaker says."

"A wise man," Salvarias murmured. "And your parents?"

"Dead. For as long as I can remember."

"I am sorry. My parents died as well."

"Well," Thia said, standing straight. "What spell are you going to do?"

"Close your eyes."

She snapped them shut. Salvarias shifted as he realized the other companions had gathered around him.

"I want you to think of a flower," he said to Thia, blocking out

Talura hovering by. "But not simply any flower. I want you to think of a new flower. Whatever you want."

The little girl's eyebrows knitted together.

"What color are the petals?"

"Blue, like the ocean," Thia said. "There're four of them. Perfectly round and circling a yellow center. The flower is as big as my palm." She thrust out her hand to show him the size.

"And how tall?"

"As tall as I am. With leaves as soft as your hair." The little girl popped open one eye. "You have very soft hair."

"I would say thank you, but I am not sure that was a compliment," Salvarias said wryly.

Thia closed her eyes. "It wasn't an insult either. It's just something I noticed."

Wilhelm chuckled. "I kinda want to take her home. She's rather entertaining."

"Indeed," Salvarias said, closing his eyes. He started developing the picture in his mind, thinking of textures. "And the smell?"

"Like the ocean when it rains."

"Open your eyes and go sit with that man," Salvarias instructed, pointing at Wilhelm before picking up a handful dirt. *I am ready,* Salvarias told his magic.

You must be willing to receive the power. You feel me, do you not?

Salvarias had never tried this before. He had felt his magic since he could remember. It was like trying to remember when he first noticed his arms. As he focused, his mind glided over the power of his magic. It warmed him further, and he felt a click, just like what happened in Zeeas and Quind when he pushed his magic to complete spells. He had just gained another level of power, and his magic responded in a surge of delight that made him lightheaded.

I ... I never thought to strengthen our connection in such a way, the magic said in an awe-filled voice. *I feel so much more a part of you.*

Salvarias sensed it too, as if it had infused itself in his blood, in his skin.

Wonderful, his magic said. *Now, focus and find the power I am calling forth. We must both concentrate on it.*

At first, he thought it was his evil, but hidden behind that horrible presence was the other power. It indeed was strong. Even as he focused on it, he felt it lazily bubbling up inside, blooming into his awareness like a morning glory greeting the sun.

Good, his magic encouraged. *When it surfaces to the level needed, we'll know. Focus on the component and release it like you would a spell. It'll read your mind and obey your command. I think you're about to make the entire meadow a field of flowers for Thia. The power should imbue each tiny grain of soil. I'm hoping this doesn't kill you, my wizard. I didn't think of each particle.*

I could always end it. I am having doubts.

Fear not. I'll keep you safe.

Salvarias closed his mind to everything but the power and the image of the flower. Once the power had of his full concentration, it burst alive with potency stronger than what he had initially sensed, vaster than his mind could comprehend.

Then came pain so horrible it leached a howl from him. His blood and insides turned to ice, what felt like acid ate his skin, and sharp shooting pains stabbed his brain.

Fear, utter terror clamped around his throat when he sensed the power's foul anger, its loathing of beauty.

You must release it! his magic screeched.

Salvarias would rather die than let a drop of that power into the world. It gave him no choice in the matter. The power surged up, casting him aside, setting his mind aflame, and clenching his body. He heard his brother's panicked voice, but the pain had blinded sight and dulled his hearing.

His magic attempted to battle it, but clearly the power was stronger, and it attacked his connection to his magic. Lunara's strength fused with his own, and he greedily accepted it, solidifying his magic's connection and protecting it. But all he could do was keep his magic safe. Anything else was beyond him.

As if it had talons, the power clawed along his arm to the soil clutched in his hand. At the same time, it tore its way up his gorge, widening his throat. Unbidden, he rolled on his side. Salvarias clenched his jaw, screaming in his closed mouth. The power wiggled up like a barbed worm and exploded in his mouth. He had no choice but to vomit it out. A red fog poured from his lips, spilling to the ground like roiling steam. The talons along his arm pried apart his fingers. He heard himself weeping to stop, but the soil fell from his hand. The red fog liquefied, sizzling its way to the soil, leaving behind a trail of decay. Salvarias gagged up the last remnants, staring in horror at a light green sprout climbing and climbing skyward. At the top, a sea-blue flower burst into bloom.

Thia squealed with delight as hundreds of flowers sprouted. Salvarias tried to choke out a warning, but the power imploded, hauling him into a world of death. The last thing he smelled was blood mingling with the aroma of the ocean on a stormy day.

40

S alvarias jolted awake, gasping, and scrambled backward until he
felt walls on both sides.

"Salv."

Wilhelm's rumbling voice cut through Salvarias's panic and
allowed him to see his surroundings. He was in a bed. Wilhelm sat
beside him, and his companions were crowded into a small room.

"Th ..." Salvarias choked on the dryness of his throat, scratchy
like a sore throat from a cold. He downed a glass of water Talura
offered. "Thia?"

Wilhelm smiled, but it seemed haunted, halfhearted. His brother
was hiding something. "She ... was romping through a field of flowers
outside. Let's—"

"No!" Salvarias coughed, doubling over. Whatever he had created
was nothing short of evil. "You must stop her!"

"It be too late," Durak snapped. "She died! She had run far into
the field when those abominations ye created sprouted poisonous
thorns and killed her. Ye foul creature!"

"Get out," Wilhelm growled, springing from the bed. "Get out, all
of you!"

Salvarias's world went black, spiraling him to his deepest fears that were now his reality. He ignited his magic. *What have we done?*

I-I didn't know—

Never speak to me again! Salvarias shoved his magic into a dark corner of his consciousness. He turned from the scowls of his companions as they left and curled up in the corner. Outside, thunder echoed and sheets of rain thrashed the stone walls. None of it sounded above his own internal torment, his own rebuke of himself.

Ah, my poor, poor little murderer, the presence said. *What have I told you? One day you will kill. Have I not always said those words? That day has come, my little murderer.*

Salvarias grabbed his head and cried out in sheer agony. "Leave me! Leave me!" Massive arms wrapped around him, but he shoved his brother away.

"You didn't mean it, Salv. It wasn't your fault."

"Leave! I do not want you here!"

He had to flee. Flee from them all. He knocked aside Wilhelm's hands and scrambled from bed. His legs would not support him, and he toppled to the floor. A roar of thunder shook the building, creaking wood, vibrating the entire structure.

"I'm not leaving you," Wilhelm said softly.

Salvarias clawed at the wood planks, pulling himself toward the door, ignoring the splinters spearing beneath his fingernails.

So weak, my murderer. Look how pathetic you are. Look how evil you are. Killing an innocent child full of life and hope. The first and only to look upon you without fear, and you slaughtered her.

"I did not know!" He curled up, hugging himself. "I did not know!"

Pathetic! You are always so pathetic! You voiced your concerns. You knew you were wrong. You disgust me.

Salvarias had no response. He broke. He could not endure it anymore. He could not continue to hurt his brother, to kill, to spread his evil.

Familiar arms gathered him close and Wilhelm said, "I love you,

Salv. I know you better than you know yourself, and what happened wasn't your fault. I heard you say no. You were trying to stop it. Don't you remember? You were fighting it."

Salvarias latched hold of his brother, begging for some redeeming part of himself to appear.

"Listen to me very carefully, Salv. You're not evil. You didn't mean to do it. I'm so confident that I'd bet your own life on it. Do you understand me? May Oblivion rise up and take you now if I'm lying."

No dark fog snatched Salvarias from this world. He buried his face in his hands and allowed grief to ravage him into exhaustion.

WILHELM SETTLED his sleeping brother in bed, adding lavender under the pillow. Lunara sat in a chair close by, and Okulu took a spot next to the door.

"I'll get you when he wakes," she said.

Nodding, he covered his brother with extra blankets before following Okulu from the room to the main living area where his friends—or those he'd thought were his friends—waited. Their sickened gazes, except Talura, clenched his fists.

"If anybody so much as looks at him wrong," he growled, "if anyone says one cruel word to him, I'll beat their ass to Oblivion."

"What be wrong with ye?" Durak snapped. "Did ye see it, boy? Something unholy came from his mouth."

"Durak," Wilhelm warned. "I'm in no mood."

"What happened?" Edium asked.

"I don't know," Wilhelm said. "He ... It must've been some spell that went wrong."

"Went wrong?" Neithelas snorted. "He killed a little girl. When will you see the truth of what he is?"

"And what's that?" Wilhelm said, resting a hand on the hilt of his sword. "Speak carefully."

"You are blind," Arthias sneered. "You refuse to see the monster that lives within him."

"I think we need to calm down," Talura said. "Varila, take the others through town and get supplies. We could use fresh clothes as well. We'll need horses instead of grynfs."

Varila, Durak, and the Winsire brothers filed out of the room.

"Is Salvarias all right?" Talura asked.

Wilhelm sank into a chair, glaring at Humar's curled lip. "He's finally sleeping."

"I've talked with Hyde," Edium said. "He runs the city. Think of him as a ruling lord. Watythms don't go by that title, but he deserves respect when you meet him. Best of all, he's a mage. When he found out it was Salvarias who made the plant, he said magic can have a mind of its own, something about the plant spell being unstable. He doesn't blame the boy."

Wilhelm nodded. "Thanks."

"Hyde?" Okulu asked.

"Yes," Edium said. "This is his house."

Okulu groaned. "Why'd you have to pick him?"

"Is there a problem?" Edium asked.

"We'll find out soon enough," Okulu responded, stroking his goatee.

The door flung open and a Watythm entered, draped in deep burgundy robes. His pale blue skin contrasted his fire red hair, and his frame was thick and sturdy. When his sweeping gaze met Wilhelm, his mouth dropped open. He recovered and snapped it shut, furrowing his brow. He turned a steady gaze to Okulu. "Hello, Okulu. You understand my daughter would have my head should I not extract vengeance for her."

"It was a misunderstanding, Hyde," Okulu drawled, leaning against the wall. "A tragic misunderstanding. I caught her with another man. I thought our relationship was over so I sought ... comfort for my broken heart. That's when she saw me. Apparently, in her mind, our relationship wasn't over, and only she was allowed to bed another."

"You know Watythm live by their instant emotion," Hyde scolded.

"Erthlas and Winsires don't. What you did was ten times worse than what she did."

"I didn't think our fight was bad enough to cause her to go to another man. I had no idea how much I'd upset her."

"You insulted her ship," Hyde said, exasperated. "How did you think she'd take it?"

Okulu shrugged. "She was lacking in her care. I merely pointed out a rotting piece of wood."

"Then you said you'd never met a Watythm as negligent of their ship as she. What did you expect?"

"A small fight. Cessia is ... more interesting when she's angry."

"Her sister wants you dead, you know," Hyde said, a smile tugging the corners of his mouth.

Okulu's posture relaxed. "How is your youngest?"

"Feistier than her sister. Kisra's a handful of trouble."

"You'd think having an Erthla mother would have tamed her," Okulu said.

Hyde laughed. "Fressa was just as adventurous as any Watythm. Why do you think I was so attracted to her?" Hyde's smile faded, and he rubbed the back of his neck. "By the gods, I miss her. She was a great woman." Shaking himself, he grinned at Okulu. "You know Cessia's still fond of you. I think she'd marry you if you asked."

Okulu scuffed his boot on the floor and remained quiet.

Hyde turned to Wilhelm. "I look forward to meeting the wizard. Not too many out there, and that boy is talented. How long have you known him?"

"All his life. He's my little brother."

"You don't say? You two look nothing alike."

Wilhelm shrugged.

"How long has he been practicing?" Hyde asked.

"Since he was six, over twelve years."

"You realize his power is beyond measure. I'm surprised the Association permitted him to wear the robes. I would've thought they'd have killed him."

"I think they might have," Wilhelm said honestly. "But my uncle knows someone in the Association."

"Interesting." Hyde studied Wilhelm for a moment before saying, "Hold out your right hand."

Wilhelm knotted his hand into a fist.

"I see," Hyde said. "You look exactly like your father."

"How do you know Tedris?"

"I took him from Falar when he was young, about your age, over to Windlous with three other men. Took him fighting, we did. He apparently met some wench in Falar—Ashra I believe—who stole his heart after one night."

"That wench was my mother," Wilhelm growled.

"Apologies. Pleasure to meet his son." The man shook Wilhelm's hand vigorously. "Hyde's the name. This is my home, which makes it yours. Make yourself comfortable. Anything you need will be provided."

"I appreciate your hospitality. And thank you for understanding my brother's spell."

"Half, right? As far as I know, Tedris never saw Ashra again."

Wilhelm shrugged. "I'm sure you don't know all Tedris's escapades."

Hyde grunted. "He had many before your mother. None after her. He was quite taken with her. I was in Falar when his father found me and booked passage to Windlous." Hyde laughed. "The boy was popular in town with the ladies. His father even encouraged him, telling him it was important to have a son. I don't think the young man took his father seriously. Tedris enjoyed his women. I went out to a few taverns with him and discovered the boy wasn't thinking about children. He had one thought."

"Like father like son," Humar murmured, a slight smile on his face.

Wilhelm couldn't help but grin. He did like women. Soft skin. They always seemed to smell nice. But like Tedris, one woman had captured him and none other would do. Only her.

"He came across Ashra in the market the day before we were

supposed to set sail and followed her around like a lost puppy," Hyde continued. "The next morning, he showed up at the docks and told his father he'd fallen in love. He refused to leave. The choice wasn't his. His father knocked him over the head and hauled him on the boat. When he came to, he spent two days trying to dive overboard."

"You said three other men were with him?" Wilhelm asked.

"Yes. One the same age as your father. Perek was his name. His father, Brine, came along. Your grandfather's name was Rennar. Took all four to Windlous. Several months later, Rennar booked passage to Loutsil. Only he and Brine were there. I ran across your father a year after that. He was a changed man. Serious, older. Perek was worse for wear. The man looked like he'd fought a war. Took them back to Falar. They stayed on the ship, and only Tedris would leave to meet up with your friend Durak to be fitted for his armor. I caught him watching her though, following her, hidden in his cloak. When we left, I asked him why he didn't see her. He said it was for her safety and that of his son. I've seen him a few times since. Matter of fact, I just brought Perek and him over here a month ago. Dropped him off in Falar." Hyde smiled. "He was looking for you."

Wilhelm reclined in his chair. "Why?"

"Wouldn't say. He and Perek were at each other's throats though. I heard him yelling at Perek that he should have had a son by now. It's all rather confusing."

Wilhelm grunted his agreement. "Was there anything interesting about Perek?"

Hyde shrugged. "Nothing unique. Handsome man. Tedris told me they were cousins. Eyes are darker than Tedris, but you can tell they're related. Unlike you and your brother. You look nothing alike."

Wilhelm ignored it, though he caught Edium's eyes narrowing. "Any marks on them?"

Hyde smoothed his beard, smiling a knowing smile. "I saw the marks on their hands. Just as I saw it on your brother. Perek's was different than your brother's. His was a circle, nothing in its center."

Wilhelm nodded. "Thanks for telling me."

"Are you going to go to Falar and find him?"

"Why should I care about him?" Those words were bitter.

Hyde frowned. "You shouldn't disrespect your father, boy."

"I'm no boy," Wilhelm grated. "And I don't have a father. There's a man out there who was careless and got my mother pregnant. I'm the product of that." He shoved himself up and left for his brother's room.

41

S alvarias scrambled up a hill, throat tight with fear, gagging from the stench of burning bodies. At the top was the same city he had seen in his previous vision. The dusky evening was thick with black smoke roiling skyward in the stagnant air. The fires reddened the sky, illuminating bodies stacked upon one another, impaled children adorning the wall, and blood weeping down the stones.

"You did this," a small voice said.

He looked down at Thia standing by his side, skin bloated from poison and covered in thorns.

"It's your fault, you know," she said. "You killed me, and now you've killed all these people."

"Forgive me," Salvarias breathed. "Please forgive me."

"I don't think so. Maybe if you had stopped all this death. But you didn't. Instead, you took the time to make a forest of light in Quind. To dance and lounge around a city with your friends. You selfishly did enchantments that made you tired and delayed your progress. Why should I forgive you?"

Salvarias stared at the ruined city. "You should not."

"One day, I'll meet you in Oblivion. Until that day, I want you to know that I suffered horribly before I died. Just as your mother and father did."

Salvarias closed his eyes when his mother's scream pierced the darkness. By all the gods, he did not want to see her. Not tonight. Please not tonight.

When he opened his eyes, his mother's melting face greeted him. "You did this to me," she rasped. "Monstrosity! Murderer! Abomination of life! Demon Child!"

Salvarias stumbled back. "I am sorry."

"Liar! Look what they did to me!" She clawed at her face, ripping off chunks of flesh and tossing them at him. Her charred skin dripped down the front of his robes, leaving dark, wet streaks.

"Please," he begged, falling back a step. "Forgive me!"

She latched on to his arm, igniting in flames, burning him.

"Please, stop!" Salvarias wept, feeling her skin peel as he tried to shove her hand away.

"Why, son?" Tobin rasped.

Salvarias looked over to see his father, blood gushing from his slit throat, splattering Salvarias's face.

"Why did you kill me? I loved you, Son. I loved you."

Salvarias sank to his knees and shut his eyes tightly. "It is just a dream. Just a dream. Just a dream."

"Look," his mother breathed in his ear. "One for each person you've killed."

Opening his eyes, he stared down at his naked body covered in black leeches. "No!" He swatted his arms and legs. "Get them off! Get them off!"

"Salv!"

"Brother, help me!" The slick bodies burst over his skin, leaving crimson patches of trickling blood. Doubling his efforts, he raked his fingers along his arms, removing chunks of the black bodies. His fingernails cut into his skin, but he did not care. He had to get them off. They were everywhere, his legs, arms, chest ... everywhere. They were everywhere!

Something grabbed hold of his wrists, preventing him from

ridding himself of the blood-sucking creatures. He thrashed wildly, kicking and imploring whoever held him to release him.

"Salv!"

He blinked and bright amber eyes appeared. Strong hands held his wrists. He gulped desperately for air, mind awash with confusion. He had no idea where he was nor who else besides his brother was with him, nor did he want to know. It could be his mother, aflame and staring at him with shriveled eyes. Or his father, butchered and gurgling his disgust. Or Sansis ready with a knife.

Salvarias curled up, hiding in the arms that enclosed him. A chorus of whooshing air and a steady heartbeat sounded in his ear. The scent of oiled leather and sour steel drifted to him, mixed with soothing lavender.

Salvarias's magic battled to break through the wall he had erected, imbuing him with its regret and plea for forgiveness. Never. Never would he use it again. He no longer wanted it. He hated it.

The magic recoiled from his thought. It receded into such a dark corner of Salvarias's mind that he was barely aware it existed, leaving a hollow feeling in his soul, adding a horrible chill to his bones.

So utterly worthless you are, my murderer. However do you live with yourself?

Leave me!

For once, I am proud of you. You are beginning to see the burden you place on your companions. Perhaps you will be given the chance to sacrifice yourself for their benefit.

Salvarias mulled over the thought. There had to have been a purpose in his vision of the army. Perhaps it was to turn himself over to them. If they had him, maybe they would leave Arden. Maybe he was the cause of all of it.

You should drive your companions from you so when the opportunity comes for you to part ways, they don't follow you. Lessen the care some have for you. Cruelty will distance them from your evil. Cruelty will save them all. Especially her.

Another valid point.

Such a selfless thought, my murderer. So brave. When the time comes, you'll know what to do. One life to save Arden is an acceptable loss, is it not?

Salvarias inhaled a deep breath, unhinging his fingers from his brother's shoulders. *That it is.*

WILHELM PULLED his cloak closer about himself and his brother as they stepped outside Hyde's home and into the dark night. It didn't seem to help. Salvarias shivered like a rattle-tail on a desert snake.

The storm flogging Xeroth was suited for winter with its icy rains and gusty winds. The pitch-black sky told him the clouds were thick and no doubt the greenish hue of the storms caused by his little brother.

Hyde greeted them in the streets, huddled in a cloak. Salvarias folded his hands in the sleeves of his robes and bowed.

Hyde smiled broadly. "It's I who should be paying you respects, young man. Your power is amazing."

Salvarias tilted his head. "Thank you, Master Hyde."

"Don't worry about the girl, Master Salvarias," Hyde said. "Spells have a way of running away from us. I once knew a mage trying to light a campfire and ended up burning down half our wine crops. Tragic, but we didn't blame her. Magic is as wild as the sea herself."

Salvarias bowed, and his voice caught when he spoke. "You are … too kind, Master Hyde."

"Let's get you all aboard a ship and out of this rain," Hyde said.

Wilhelm lifted Salvarias in some pathetic attempt to ease his brother's burden as they followed Hyde through the zigzag streets.

"We've finally got our chance," Wilhelm said softly to his brother.

"For what?" Salvarias asked.

"Sailing. We get to go on a ship. I'm rather excited."

Salvarias's head lifted slightly. "I as well, Brother."

"Can you talk to animals in the sea?"

"Perhaps. I have not tried before."

"I don't think we'll be out far enough to see kassruls, will we?"

Salvarias shook his head. "No. Those are in deeper waters. But dolphins and seals will be abundant."

Wilhelm smiled at the lightness filtering into his brother's voice. "Whales, even?"

"I would hope," Salvarias said.

The squall abated, leaving a steady drizzle of rain. For now, it was good enough. He squeezed his brother's shoulders.

The walk through town revealed Watythms cared little for land buildings. All of them were crude in construction, and over half were so in need of repair that the roofs were caving. The only ones tended to were the taverns, which seemed to be the sole purpose of Xeroth.

Wilhelm marveled over how vastly different the Watythm culture was compared to Erthlas. For one, Salvarias was looked at with wide and welcoming eyes. Those who came in his path darted into nearby establishments, calling out that a mage was in town. Hyde, instead of receiving formal greetings and bows as Edium would receive in Serinity, was greeted by claps on the back and pints of frothing ale that made Wilhelm's mouth water. A few recognized Edium, and he was met with warm handshakes and even warmer smiles. Wilhelm preferred Watythm culture to his own. It was almost innocent, free of judgment and the fighting that seemed to rule the other races. It was as if Watythms were rather unimpressed with the stigmas and traditions other races conjured. Maybe ... just maybe he could find a way to afford a home here, a place his brother could live free of snarls and judgment.

"Mind if I ask a question?" Wilhelm said to Hyde.

"Interrogate away," Hyde said.

"Watythms seem ... unprejudiced, yet you don't let other races into your city. I'm curious why."

Hyde chuckled. "Xeroth is for us and us alone. We don't want your petty squabbles and war affecting us. We expect it when we sail from here, but this place ..." Hyde's gazed swept around him, and he smiled. "This place is our sanctuary. A place unimpeded by judgments. A place where men and women enjoy each other freely. A place where we partake in activities that other races frown upon. We do what feels good." Hyde glanced back. "What do you think about that, boy?"

"Sounds fine by me. Shame you don't accept others."

Hyde gave him a quizzical look before it switched to a broad smile. "Any friend of Edium and Okulu is a friend of mine. You're welcomed here anytime."

A flicker of hope lit inside Wilhelm. After his brother warned Dalnar of the army, Wilhelm would whisk Salvarias to Xeroth where they could live in peace and happiness. It was all he could've ever hoped for. He looked down and grinned at his brother. Salvarias's eyes sparkled, seeming to brighten at the thought of a home.

A crowd of Watythms suddenly massed around Salvarias, driving a wedge between Wilhelm and his brother. They bombarded Salvarias with questions and requests for spells. Hyde laughed, saying he was surprised it'd taken word so long to spread.

Unfortunately, the crowd's enthusiasm made them affectionate. Salvarias grimaced and dodged from those nearby who reached for him. Wilhelm would have intercepted, but he felt his brother's happiness blooming. The air crisped with freshness, the torches sputtered brighter, and life seemed to respond to his brother's joy.

Just as Wilhelm thought the storm would break, Salvarias's hood fell back and the pulse of lazy lightning was ill timed. Those close or tall enough recoiled with gasps as the flash lit up Salvarias's black eyes. Then the murmurs started as the crowd backed up. "Creature," "demon," "Veedran's creation," and other cruel words where whispered among the crowd.

Wilhelm even heard Hyde—the only other one tall enough to see —hiss, "What in Veedran's wickedness has possessed the boy?"

Alone in the center of the crowd, Salvarias lowered his head and raised his hood. His soft whisper carried to Wilhelm, holding so much pain in the one word that it tore open his heart. "Brother."

Growling in attempt to keep his fury within his control, Wilhelm shoved through the crowd, flinging people out of the way. He wrapped his arm around his brother's shoulders and glared at the crowd. "Begone," he grated. They scurried like rats. He turned to Hyde. "Get us to the ship. I've seen enough of this damn city."

Hyde nodded and swallowed hard enough that Wilhelm heard the clicking of his throat over the steady drizzle.

Wilhelm continued through the city with heavy steps as he realized that even if he found a place accepting of mages, his brother would still be unwelcomed. And he knew Salvarias had arrived at the same conclusion. His brother's pain was as tangible as a dagger twisting in Wilhelm's heart.

When they neared the docks, it was even stated more clearly that Watythms cared for their ships more than the town. Those anchored to the harbor were freshly tarred, tended to by a crew that Wilhelm mused was larger than needed. The ships were of every size and purpose imaginable. Some seemed solely made to haul goods. Those ships were home to a massive hull and an expansive, flat deck. Others were made to transport the wealthy, and the stories upon stories of cabins, ornate carvings, and girth showed that those vessels were meant for luxury. Others were as deep as they were towering, and Wilhelm thought the slightest breeze would knock them over. Some of the feats of engineering baffled him. He pondered if gods had granted the Watythms some sort of power that aided them in building such magnificent vessels.

The Watythms' source of income became apparent when he saw the ale warehouses and barrels upon barrels of wine lining the deck of cargo ships.

"Who tends to the vineyards?" Durak asked Hyde. "Me heard Watythms don't stay on land for long."

"Very true," Hyde said. "When a ship ports, those who have children too young to take to sea spend time in the vineyards. It's a rotation of sorts. No one person tends to them longer than a month."

"Where are the fields?" Neithelas asked. "I didn't see them when we came in."

"Over that rise," Hyde said, motioning to a hill that flanked the north side of the city. "Cascades down like a river. Best amount of sun there."

"Me find it odd that a race who loves the ocean would specialize in an occupation caring for land," Durak said.

Hyde laughed. "It's our love of spirits that drives us to make ale and wine. Can't live on that watered down Erthla crap. No offense."

Humar laughed. "None taken."

Hyde stopped in front of a ship smaller than the others, but no less magnificent. Its carvings were of sea creatures Wilhelm had seen in books he'd read to his brother. The mast was carved to mimic an albatross, and the sails were died a royal blue. There were a mere two stories worth of cabins.

"This'll be yours for as long as you need her," Hyde said. "She's thin enough to fit up that river and take you right to the lake. She might be slower, but this is the only captain in town that'll sail with a mage. Unfortunately, my beauty won't fit down the river or I'd take you myself."

Edium shook Hyde's hand. "I'm in your debt."

"I think I'm still in the red, my friend," Hyde said warmly. "Consider this my attempt to repay you."

"Thank you," Edium said.

After all had bid their farewells, they boarded the ship. Amid curses and kicks from the captain, sailors went to work casting off.

"You want to go below or stay up here?" Wilhelm asked his brother.

"I would like stay up, but if—"

"Up it is."

He led his brother to the bow of the ship and both leaned their backs against the railing and watched the darkness of night devour the twinkling lights of Xeroth.

Initially the rocking sensation made Wilhelm queasy, but after an hour or so, he felt right at home, breathing in the saltiness, feeling brine collect on his beard, and relishing in the speed the ship reached. The slapping of waves on the hull would have tempted him into a trance had Neithelas and Arthias not been retching over the side of the boat, holding each other upright.

"I should go below and concoct something to help them," Salvarias murmured after a rather violent upheaval from Neithelas.

Wilhelm wrapped an arm around his brother's shoulders and turned him around to face the dead of night before them. "Later. They deserve a little misery."

To Wilhelm's surprise, Salvarias didn't argue. They stayed on deck for hours, soaked and shivering, until a sight like nothing Wilhelm had ever seen blessed his eyes. Sunrise. He'd seen sunrises at the docks on his morning runs with Tobin, he'd seen them in the forests during their journey, and he'd even been privileged to see the sun peek over the undulating sands of the desert. But here, clear from anything that felt solid, he saw it glow between the never-ending ocean and the layer of clouds. A line of brightness shocked the horizon with such magnificence that he swore the gods themselves were rising. Clouds came alive with brilliant orange, and the ocean reflected it like a blazing fire.

"It is ..." Salvarias's voice choked, and a smile spread across his face. He inhaled deeply. "It is beautiful."

Wilhelm looked up at the calm gray clouds, no longer muted green, no longer sinister. He smiled. "It is, Salv."

The morning passed with Salvarias's lips moving in silent conversation as he occasionally coaxed various ocean life to the surface. Between those visits, the sound of whispered numbers loosened Wilhelm's tension, and the fluid dance of the puzzle box calmed his mind.

Midday, Wilhelm wrapped an arm round his brother's neck. "Let's get some sleep." He steered Salvarias across the deck and down into their cabin. It was smaller than he had expected, holding only two small beds, a bolted down table home to a washbasin, and a small shoddy chair. He plopped down on the bed, not even bothering to undress. His calves hung off the bottom and his shoulders spilt over into Salvarias's cot. Sighing in discomfort, he closed his eyes.

Sleep came quickly and brought dreams of dark, cold corridors where Salvarias's screams echoed, begging for help. There were so many; a maze of hallways and rooms, endlessly branching off.

Wilhelm came around a corner to find his brother curled up on the ground. The man robed in red stood over him. When the man raised his head, Wilhelm stumbled back. The man could have been Salvarias's father. Their features were identical. The single difference was the man's eyes were flat black, stagnant and malicious, void of love and care.

"He is mine!" the man hissed. "He will do my bidding!"

Wilhelm jolted awake. Salvarias stood at the washbasin shaving with Wilhelm's straight razor.

"Evening, brother," Salvarias murmured.

"Why are you shaving?" Wilhelm asked, forcing himself to sit. He shook off the remnants of the dream.

Salvarias shrugged. "I do not feel like using magic."

Those words made everything around Wilhelm stop. He no longer felt the rocking of the boat, heard the ocean pounding the hull, or smelled the brininess of the sea. Swallowing, he forced his tight throat to loosen enough to voice a question he was terrified to have answered. "Why not, Salv?"

Salvarias used a piece of cloth to wipe the blade clean and ran it down his cheek. "What did you think would happen, Brother? I killed a girl with magic. I will not put myself in the situation to do so again."

"But it wasn't your fault."

Salvarias sighed, set aside the razor, and used a cloth to wipe his face as he turned to Wilhelm. "And whose fault is it? The soil that sprouted the plants? The sun that gave them food? Or perhaps it was Thia's? She should have known better than to trust a field of flowers." Salvarias held up his hand when Wilhelm opened his mouth to object. "Your words will not convince me otherwise, Brother. I thank you for caring so much that you see no flaws in me. Truly, I do. I, however, must take responsibility for my actions. I control them; they do not control me. I chose to do the spell without fully understanding it. It was my error and a burden I must carry. Please, I beg you, do not lie to yourself any longer, and do not lie to me."

Wilhelm clenched his jaw and rose from the bed to stand in front of his brother. "You listen to me, Salv. You're special. You've gifts no other person in all of Arden has. You have no tutors, no men to tell what to do with them, no books to learn from. You're alone. Completely and utterly alone. There's not a damn person in Arden that can help you. I can't. I don't understand why you vomited red acid. I don't understand why you can erupt in black flames with no injury to yourself or the ground you walk. I don't understand why you can speak to animals. I don't understand why it hurts you to be touched by another besides me. But there is one thing I understand completely. And that's you." Wilhelm tapped his brother's chest. "I know you better than you know yourself. I'm telling you, it wasn't your fault. I know how much your magic means to you. You can't block it out."

Salvarias looked away. "I do not deserve you, Brother."

Wilhelm ruffled his brother's hair. "I say the same thing to myself every time you do something amazing."

Despite their talk, Salvarias refused to use magic.

42

S alvarias stared over the field where the army had once camped. Blistering hot wind ripped through the landscape, flapping his cloak about him, whipping his hair in his face, and threatening to uproot him. The sky was a blanket of ominous coal clouds that refused to give the land the water it urgently yearned for. Grasses were brown instead of green, and just the sight of them made Salvarias thirsty. What resembled trees were stocky, and the tops nothing but tufts of green-looking cotton. Unable to identify what was a leaf, he mused they did not qualify as trees. Neithelas and Arthias glared at them with distrust. Next to Salvarias, Wilhelm towered as tall as the trees, unwavering in the gusts, stance as solid as a mountain.

Behind them, the horses protested the winds, fighting against the sailors hauling them from the boat. Salvarias had not developed a strong enough relationship with the horses to completely calm them, nor was he in the frame of mind to do so.

Wilhelm suddenly burst out laughing. Glancing over, Salvarias saw Durak tumbling head over foot as the wind carried the willowy man off. Salvarias elbowed his brother.

Wiping tears, Wilhelm strode forward. When his brother no

longer blocked the wind, Salvarias had to lean his full weight to keep upright. Wilhelm plucked up Durak and firmly planted the Cavrul, dodging swings and laughing harder the more curses Durak spewed.

"They've marched toward Treppter," Humar yelled over the winds.

Salvarias's gut knotted. He knew what they would find when they reached the doomed city. Death, blood, and fire. It was all he had dreamt since leaving Xeroth, which was why he avoided sleep as if it were the plague. He feared the time when his mind would mercilessly haul him into the realm of nightmares. Sleep had become a foe.

"Let's mount up," Humar called.

Without asking, Wilhelm lifted Durak on to a horse. Neithelas mounted and offered his hand to Lunara. She refused, but one word from her father made her accept. Salvarias looked away.

Careful, my murderer. Do not falter in your resolve. Think of her happiness.

Salvarias inhaled a deep breath and swung himself on a light brown mare, Ness. He felt as if he were betraying Mithal, which did not help the horse's acceptance of him.

Adok growled at his side, complaining about the wind. At least the storm Salvarias had caused dissipated when they were out to sea. It would be miserable if it rained.

Gazing over the empty field, Salvarias sank further into his depression. He was a fool to think he could stop this army. One man against thousands. One man against a god.

ANOTHER DAY and a half passed before inky black smoke rose in the distance, causing Salvarias to cringe further within himself. Humar, Durak, Varila, and the Winsire brothers' cold stares and sneers added to his withdrawal. He did not want to be around anyone. He was exhausted, beaten by hopelessness and doomed by his inadequacy. Why he even bothered to continue, to urge Ness into a gallop, to cling to some hope that just one person lived, was beyond him. There was no hope. It had fled Arden.

Stars blanketed the sky when they arrived at the body-strewn fields wreathing the smoldering city of Treppter. Neithelas and Arthias escorted Lunara and Lady Talura from the scene to set up camp a few miles upwind. Though Wilhelm begged, Salvarias remained. He would look firsthand at the ruin he had caused.

Okulu, Varila, and Durak took to the fields in search of survivors among the overturned wagons and charred grasses. The crows plucking at corpses were too busy feasting to tell Salvarias all that had happened. A part of him was grateful for being ignored.

He followed his brother, Humar, and Lord Bellerum to the city gate. The walls were scorched but had not crumbled. No doubt there had been no time to fortify or even close the gate.

Lord Bellerum raised his hand to halt them. "We'll walk from here."

Salvarias looked left to right at the row of impaled children, the only objects not roasted by fires. Beneath one child, a dog was curled up around the post, lying in its master's blood. It whined when it looked up at Salvarias. Blinking aside tears, he begged the dog to accompany him, promising to keep it safe. It refused, saying it would never leave its friend's side. Adok nestled the hound's muzzle before rejoining Salvarias.

Sliding off his horse, he retrieved his staff, raised his hood as high as he could, and lowered his head. He could not meet Wilhelm's gaze nor could he bring himself to see the disappointment in Humar's eyes.

"I don't see a point," Humar muttered, patting his horse as he dropped the reins. "Everyone in there is dead."

Lord Bellerum drew his sword and waved them to follow. Climbing over the ruin of stone and wood blocking entrance to the city was difficult, but Adok helped keep Salvarias steady. Wilhelm walked a step behind, and Salvarias felt his brother's outstretched hand waiting to catch him if he fell. As comforting as it was, his shame over failing the tens of thousands living in Trepptar made him cringe from Wilhelm. Comfort was the last thing Salvarias deserved.

Once he made it over the rubble, he drew a cloth from his robes and held it over his nose and mouth to aid his breathing. It helped little.

All around were men boiled alive in armor, shriveled corpses of women, and husks of children clutched in the arms of toasted adults. Rats scurried about from corpse to corpse, nibbling through flesh. The combination of crunchy and moist bites seemed louder than a herd of horses to Salvarias, and he resisted the urge to scream to rid his ears of the noise.

His eyes found those small details he wondered if others noticed. The doll clutched in the arms of burned up little girl, the couple still clinging to each other's hands even in death, or the little boy who held a dagger that had not drank the blood it sought.

Hope fled a little further, and dread sank in a little deeper when he saw no bodies of their foes. No octrils, no soldiers in black armor, no creatures of horror. Either the army was truly undefeatable, or they had taken the time to burn their own dead.

As they drifted through the city, the scene stayed consistent: Death, blood, and fire. He walked half aware of what he saw as the other men hollered for survivors, nudging corpses that were not too badly burned. Salvarias knew better. The army would leave none alive.

Lord Bellerum spent time at one of his buildings that oversaw his trade. Salvarias vaguely heard the lord saying all his men were dead. Street by street, they made their way to the exit. Okulu, Varila, and Durak were waiting. One look and they all knew none had survived.

Salvarias rode in a listless state, heedless of his surroundings. It was dark, always so dark. He glanced at the moon covered in a thin red haze. Dark and bloody.

He had not realized they had arrived at camp until Ness stopped. He slid off, unbuckled his pack, tossed it next to his brother's, and walked from the warm fire. Wilhelm was kind enough to gift

Salvarias time alone. He was in no mood for conversation or false comforts.

He ambled through dry grasses until he no longer heard the conversations of his group or smelled the campfire. Finding a cluster of short trees, he hid himself among the stout trunks, sinking to the ground and wishing he would become one of them.

He swatted a leech he thought he saw on his arm. When he looked closer, there was nothing there. Adok leaned against him until they found their balance, using each other as a wall of sorts. Salvarias shifted to rest his face in Adok's fur. It smelled of smoke.

"Where is the light, my friend?" Salvarias whispered. "I see none. I see only blood."

Adok remained quiet.

He might have dozed lightly enough that mere vague dreams of burning cities haunted him. He glanced around, wondering what brought him from wherever his mind had strayed. It was Lunara.

"Hello," she said.

Salvarias closed his eyes, relishing in the solace her voice imbued into his heart.

Shame, my pet. She is our biggest challenge. She will always haunt you unless you drive her from you. Although you may hurt her, you will save her. If you continue your pleasant demeanor, she will continue her pursuits. Look at her.

Salvarias stood and turned to face her. The light breeze played with her hair, allowing the moonlight to catch it and change the shades, luring him into a reverie of dancing colors.

"May I join you?" she said.

Such purity. You said so yourself, my murderer. She, above all else, must remain pure. Send her away. Hurt her. Drive her from you. For once, think of someone else besides yourself.

Lunara reached out her hand, and he flinched.

"No, my lady. I prefer to be alone."

"I think you could use some company," she said. "We don't have to talk. We—"

"No," he said.

Her brow furrowed, and she reached for him again. An image fluttered in his mind of her lying on the ground, blood soaking her dress, his dagger plunged into her heart.

Drive her from you! the presence snapped.

When she reached for him again, he grabbed her wrists and yanked her close, clenching his jaw. "I do not want you or your affections. I want nothing to do with you. You are like a schoolgirl panting after a boy who does not desire her. I find it pathetic and repulsive. Now leave me." He released her and turned his back to her.

There was a moment of silence before she said, "Forgive me."

As her footsteps faded, his knees buckled, and he sank to the ground. He asked Adok to keep her company, and after a whine, the wolf trotted off.

Rain spat down from newly formed clouds and a gusty breeze picked up. Staring at the water stinging his hands, he chuckled. At least his evil storm would put out the fires. His chuckle turned to a light laugh that choked in his throat when he vomited.

43

S ix more days crawled by before Wilhelm and his friends arrived at the blazing city of Klurp. As it had been in Treppter, the bastards had impaled the children on spikes along the outer wall. As if the army meant to drive his brother further into a horrible depression, they'd piled the dead in a hill twice Wilhelm's height, blocking entrance into the city.

"Same search parties," Edium said.

Wilhelm clambered over human remains, grimacing when his hand sank through a corpse. The stench was suffocating. Once inside, he kept a hand ready to help his brother who walked listlessly behind Edium and Humar, distant gaze sweeping the streets. What Salvarias saw, Wilhelm didn't have the heart to guess. All he knew was his brother's demeanor grew more frightening daily. Salvarias rarely ate, he rode in the same numb trance as he walked now, and Wilhelm had yet to see him sleep. What had increased were Salvarias's flinches. He'd swat at something in the air or brush a part of himself, wince and clutch whatever he thought hurt him.

After a fruitless search for survivors, they found their camp. Salvarias went for a walk once he'd removed his pack from the mare, seemingly unaware he'd forgotten to unsaddle his horse. Adok padded by his side, whining and licking Salvarias's hand. His brother didn't seem to notice that either.

"We've got to get him to sleep," Talura said.

Wilhelm unbuckled his saddle, grunting his agreement but voicing the truth. "He won't."

"You need to talk to him," Edium persisted.

Wilhelm shrugged. "He wouldn't listen if I did."

"You can't let him continue like this," Edium said.

Wilhelm met the man's gaze. "I can, and I will. I know my brother. I know how—"

Salvarias suddenly hobbled into camp. He snatched up his pack and began tying it to his mount.

"What is it, boy?" Edium asked.

Salvarias jumped and looked around. His brow furrowed, and his eyes widened as if he'd just noticed he was in a room of strangers.

"Salv," Wilhelm said, putting himself in his brother's line of sight.

Salvarias looked at him and then the others. "Cattlar. The army is heading to Cattlar."

Edium nodded. "We'll push hard for the next four days."

Salvarias swung on his horse and kicked its flanks. Wilhelm retightened the saddle, mounted, and spurred his horse after his brother, leaving the others to extinguish the fire and pack up.

They rode through the night, his brother a mere speck in front of them, only seen by the light of the moon. Wilhelm urged his horse as much as he dared, ignoring the stallion's frothing mouth.

When the first rays of morning kissed the plains, Salvarias fell hard from his saddle. The horse slowed, returned to Salvarias, and waited.

Wilhelm's throat tightened as he kicked his horse into a dangerous gallop through the rocky terrain. When he reined in next to Salvarias, he saw his brother's chest rise with a slight breath. Jumping from the saddle, Wilhelm knelt by Salvarias and checked his sleeping brother for wounds. Luckily, the fall hadn't broken anything.

"We'll set up camp," Humar said, trotting up next to them.

It didn't take long to gather bedrolls and blankets. Food was less of a priority to sleep. No one bothered to hunt or remove bread from packs, much less search for firewood. Durak kindly took first watch, allowing Wilhelm to quickly succumb to exhaustion.

He jolted awake to Salvarias thrashing in his blankets, weeping for help. Shaking his brother's shoulder, it took a breath for Salvarias to snap awake. He stumbled to his feet, tripping backward, gaze frantically sweeping over the camp. One look into Salvarias's dark eyes showed his brother was half alert, half in his right mind.

"You need to rest, Salv," Wilhelm said, rising to stand next to his brother. "You're going to kill your horse."

Salvarias shook his head. "We must help Cattlar. No others can die because of me." He went toward his horse but Edium intercepted him.

"You need to sleep, boy," Edium said. "We're not going anywhere for a few hours."

"Stay here if you ..." Salvarias shook his head, staggering backward. "Get away!" he cried.

Wilhelm snatched hold of Salvarias before he could flee, grunting with each punch and kick as his brother struggled, eyes seeing something not there. It didn't last long before he passed out. Wilhelm muttered a few favorite curses as he carried his brother to a bedroll. Just as he lowered Salvarias, his brother jerked awake.

He shoved aside Wilhelm's arms and rose. "We must leave."

Not listening to any pleas, Salvarias mounted his horse and urged the beast into a gallop. Wilhelm had a fleeting thought of forcing his brother, but he quickly dismissed it. He'd promised to never do such a thing again. Salvarias was his own master.

Wilhelm turned to Humar. "How many days until Cattlar?"

"Three," Humar said grimly. "He'll kill himself or the horses before we reach it."

There was no arguing the truth.

SALVARIAS'S SORROW shoved him to his knees. Blood soaked through
his robes as it weaved its way down the sloping mountainside in
rivulets of death. Cavruls were sprawled over rocks, heaped in
grasses, speared against trees. The entrance to the city of Cattlar
yawned open and fires flickered from beyond the half-closed gate.
The Cavruls had had no warning. The army had massacred their way
inside.

A little Cavrul girl stumbled through the gate, blood soaking her
lavender dress and soot staining her cheeks. Salvarias rushed forward
and caught her in his arms as she fell.

"They're all dead," she rasped, balling his robes in her tiny fist.
"It's so cold."

"Forgive me," Salvarias wept, cradling her close. "Please, forgive
me!"

"Mother and Father burned. I heard them screaming. They
screamed so much." Her eyes distanced. "I'm so cold."

He smoothed her hair, rocking her, sobbing, begging her not to
leave him. Her hand slipped free, and her last breath sighed out of
her as her eyes dulled.

"No!" he shouted, clasping her tightly. "Forgive me!"

"Salv!"

Not another child lost to darkness. It could not happen. He—

"Salv, wake up!"

He jolted awake to a rough shake. He saw woods, thick and dry
from summer's heat. A breeze rustled through the leaves and the air
was fresh. Moonbeams shot through the trees and illuminated a
forest floor littered with pinecones.

"Where are we?" he asked.

"Less than a day's ride from Cattlar," Humar said.

Salvarias batted aside his brother's arms and darted to Ness. He
saddled the mare quickly, ignoring her pleas for rest. People were
shouting from behind, but their exact words never reached him. All
he heard was the little girl saying, "They're all dead."

He swung on the horse and kicked her flanks. Trees blurred by, the wind chilled him, and birds startled from their perches at hearing Ness thundering by.

He was too late. The city had been destroyed. The Cavruls were an extinct race now. All because of his pathetic need for sleep. Regardless of hopelessness, he dug his heels in Ness's flanks.

The darkness of night eased as the moon slid high in the sky, and next thing he knew it was dark again. The moon had crossed to the other side of the sky. He should stop. Ness was near death, and he hated himself for how much he pushed her when there was no hope. But he was driven by mad desperation. He kicked her flanks.

The sun had just peeked over the horizon when Salvarias cleared the trees to be greeted by the bustling hillside of Cattlar. Tears blurred his vision as he slid off his mare and took a few jerky steps.

Cavruls stared at him with distrusting gazes as they guided wagons into the inner city. Tents of traders not staying within the city were erected outside. There was the buzz of a waking morning, unaware of what Salvarias had seen.

Confusion broke free his tears. He had seen the city burning. They should be doomed. Why then was there no sign of the army? Why did blood not stain the mountain?

Behind him, his horse thudded to the ground. Her gasp ended, and her light presence in his mind ebbed into darkness. He looked over his shoulder to see her tongue lolled out, her eyes rolled in the back of her head, and her chest fell with her last breath.

"Salvarias?"

He wiped his tears and turned to see his uncle sprinting toward him. Behind him was Ashra, her eyes cold and dark.

"Brother," he choked, spinning around. No one was there. He was alone.

"Boy?" Mafarias said.

Salvarias looked down at his dead horse and then over his shoulder at Ashra. None of this was right. None of it was as it had been in his vision. Something had gone terribly wrong. He fell to his knees next to his mare and hugged her. "Forgive me," he sobbed.

"Salvarias," Lady Talura said. She knelt on the other side of Ness, smiling through tears.

"I-I do not understand," he wept. "I do not understand!"

"I know," she said. "We'll figure it out together."

"What are you talking about, boy?" Mafarias snapped. "What's happened to you?"

Salvarias became aware of the stink of him unwashed, his growing beard, his unkempt appearance. Gathering his knees to his chest, he rocked next to Ness, cringing from his uncle. "I want my brother."

"Where is he?" Mafarias said, his voice lashing out. "Talk to me, boy!"

Salvarias cowered and covered his head.

"I'm here," Lady Talura said. "No one's going to hurt you."

Salvarias peered at her through his arms. "They should be dead," he choked. "I-I saw the mountain covered in blood. I held the little girl."

"I know, dear. I want you to sleep," she said. Her fingers brushed through his hair. "I want you to rest now."

He cringed from her touch, wincing against the bombardment of images ... images of Lunara and Lady Varila laughing, of Lord Bellerum smiling. "I have to find the army," Salvarias said, his eyes closing on their own. Fixed firmly in front of him was the Bellerum dining hall. The family sat around a feast telling stories. It chilled him as much as it warmed him.

"Sleep," a woman whispered. "Everyone's safe."

He curled up against Ness and rested his head on her chest. "I am sorry."

A voice lifted in a soft hum, a soothing melody he had heard from somewhere before. The sharp perfume of jasmine cut into the stench of the horse and himself. Darkness wrapped around him and hauled him into a deep sleep filled with screaming women and children, burning cities, and blood. So much blood.

44

Talura wiped her tears and looked up at Mafarias. "Can you carry him to your tent?"

The mage shook his head. "I can't touch the boy. His power reacts poorly to mine. I'll hurt him. He'll hurt me."

"At least take his pack and saddle," Talura said.

She clasped Salvarias's chest in her arms and grunted and groaned until his weight shifted enough to allow her to drag him to the shade of a nearby tree and clear of the dead horse. She situated him on grasses, wishing she had a blanket to ease his trembling. A nightmare must have assailed him quickly. His head tossed side to side, and the furrow of his brow deepened.

"He's exhausted," Mafarias said, leaning over the boy. "What happened?"

"We've been traveling nonstop," Talura said. "The others are a short way behind me."

"You never sent word. I've been going mad with worry. Of course, the clan leaders refuse to meet with me. None will listen." He smiled at her. "It's good to see you again, my lady. You look well."

"My husband was right. It was you."

Mafarias winced. "It was a spell. My powers can sometimes have a mind of their own. You must understand, I knew neither you nor Edium would trust me. I had to find them."

Talura shook her head. "You invaded my mind."

"I made it weak to my suggestions. Use your powers, my lady. I did what I did for those boys."

Talura took him up on his offer. Indeed, he was not lying. Still, his actions were unforgiveable. "What you did was no different than if you had violated my body."

"My lady, I—"

Talura held up her hand. "You and I are no longer friends. I won't tell my husband. He would kill you, and your intentions were of a just cause. Nevertheless, I'll never trust you again. Find the others and bring them. There is much to discuss."

Mafarias looked truly hurt. "I'll spend the rest of my days making up for my transgression, my lady. Of that, you have my word. I never meant to hurt you."

He bolted to her horse, mounted, and hissed the mare into a run.

Leaning against the tree, she smoothed Salvarias's hair while singing Lunara's favorite lullaby, and turned her gaze to the imposing gate of Cattlar.

To say the entrance to the cave city was grand would be a drastic understatement. The doors towered high above, occupying a small section of the sheer cliff that clawed its way up to the clouds and spread as wide as three cities. The gate was taller than any in Arden and proved a god had built the city with a god's eye for engineering. Only Cavruls understood the mechanism that operated the closing and opening of the doors, explained in detail by Nevlar himself and passed down through the generations. After the attack on Serinity, her husband had been quick to commission the Cavruls to construct a stone gate for Serinity, one that would not be threatened by acid-dripping creatures alight with flames. As with all that involved her safety as well as their daughters', Edium spared no expense.

The sloping mountainside was clear of trees for a good half mile or so, allowing those not staying—or perhaps those not allowed—within the cave city a place to set up tents. The three main roads were clear of incoming traffic in the early hours of morning, making those few wagons leaving seem unusually loud as they clattered out of sight. Cattlar had always impressed her, and she found herself slouching with relief in the knowledge that they had a chance to save the enchanting city.

When her fingertips glided over something rough, she yanked back her hand. Apparently, she'd moved aside Salvarias's hair, revealing the sight of eaten skin and a missing ear. She'd never noticed it, nor had the young man mentioned it. Blinking away tears, she traced the innumerable scars on his forearm. They doubled the higher she raised the sleeve of his robes.

It wasn't long before the rest of the group burst from the tree line, save for Mafarias. Wilhelm slid off his horse and motioned her away before scooping up Salvarias. As was Wilhelm's new habit, he rested an ear over the mage's chest. Seemingly satisfied by whatever he heard, Wilhelm lowered his brother, helped her up, and joined the others.

Edium spoke to Durak. "Do you know any of the clan leaders?"

Durak shrugged. "Me not going into the city. I ... I can't."

The exhausting days of traveling had ended her husband's patience. Eyes dark, jaw tight, he said, "You can help us, can't you? You know people on the counsel."

Humar rested a hand on the Cavrul's shoulder. "My friend hasn't been home for over a hundred years. I doubt his former connections —if there were any—are still alive."

"Don't give me that horse crap," Edium spat. "Cavruls live for hundreds of years. Your race could be facing extinction, Durak. Does that mean nothing to you?"

"Not all the Cavruls live in Cattlar," Durak said. "We'll repopulate. If ye wish, I'll send 'em a note with what me've seen, though a lot of good it'd do."

Okulu laughed. "How brilliant. I can see it now. A bunch of sour-faced Cavruls open a letter that states, 'Dear Cavrul clan leaders, we think your city will be attacked by an army you've never heard of or seen. We don't know exactly where they are, but we're sure they're close. And we're pretty sure you're doomed. Love, the seven mad companions.'

"By the way, I'm not including our snooty Winsire brothers. And no offense to you, Edium and Talura, but you're both stowaways on our little adventure here."

Ignoring Okulu, Neithelas said to Durak, "Your selfishness could be the end of your people."

"Please, Durak," Lunara said. "You must help them."

"She's right," Varila said. "We don't know where that army is. Even if they're not heading here, we could use the Cavruls to help us find them and fight. You saw what they did in Klurp and Treppter. All of Dalnar is in danger."

"Cattlar must pull back to the inner city," Salvarias said. Everyone whirled around. Salvarias was shoving himself up, using his aspen branch to help steady his trembling body. Wilhelm was quick to help. "Until reinforcements arrive," Salvarias continued, "the outer gate must be closed and the tunnels to the inner city collapsed."

Durak snorted. "And why would me trust ye? We've nearly killed ourselves to get here and there's not a damn creature in sight."

Salvarias shook his head. "There is danger here. I ... I can feel it."

"Please," Lunara said.

Durak stared off at the city. "I doubt the clan council will listen to me, lass."

"But you must try," Lunara insisted.

Frown lines deepening, Durak glanced at Wilhelm. "All right. Let's go in."

Another horse trotted into view. On it was Mafarias.

"Uncle!" Wilhelm exclaimed.

"Wilhelm, my boy!" Mafarias jumped off the horse and rushed forward to accept Wilhelm's embrace. "I'm so glad to see you both well."

"Where have you been?" Wilhelm asked.

Mafarias nodded to Salvarias. "Hello, boy."

"Uncle," Salvarias said with a tilt of his head.

Mafarias warmly embraced Humar and shook Okulu and Durak's hand. "I see you've managed to keep them alive, Humar."

The knight grunted. "Our nephews have made the task challenging."

Talura frowned when Salvarias moved a step behind his brother, peering around Wilhelm to gaze at Mafarias with a frown tugging down the corners of his mouth.

"Let's get this over with," Durak growled.

"The boy and I will stay outside the city," Mafarias said. "I have a tent that'll fit both of us."

"No need," Durak said. "They'll let ye in."

Mafarias scoffed. "No mage has ever stepped foot inside the city. They'll cut us down."

"Me said, they'll let you in!" Durak grumbled.

Talura locked arms with her husband and followed the stomping Cavrul toward the gate.

Once they arrived, Durak straightened himself. "Let us in, lad," he said to the Cavrul on guard.

The young man sneered at Mafarias and Salvarias. "No mages. Ye know the rules."

An older guard stared at Durak with wide eyes. "Is that you, Boughlar?"

Durak scowled at the old man. "Of course, ye nitwit. Let us in."

The old guard fell to his knees. "Lord Boughlar! We never thought to see you again."

"Get up, ye fool!" Durak snapped. Looking around, cheeks reddened, he motioned the old man toward the gate leading to the inner city. "Escort us inside."

The old man started at the sight of Adok.

"The wolf be tamed, ye coward," Durak growled. "Now get up! Let us in!"

The old man scrambled to his feet and led Talura and her group into the outer city. Once past the gates, they paused in the main thoroughfare, giving their eyes time to adjust to the hylims' pink glow. Glancing around, she surveyed the streets upon streets of merchants and taverns set back from the grand entrance meant to humble visitors—and it adequately performed its duty. No shops or structures were near the doors, allowing one to marvel at the towering ceiling with its hylim cascading down like tendrils of falling water. Statues of Cavruls carved into the sides of the cave flanked the city, and two stood watch at the closed doors to the inner city of Cattlar—a place none others besides Cavruls had ever seen.

As they continued on, any Cavrul noticing Salvarias and Mafarias froze, and those old enough to know Durak fell to their knees as he passed. Everyone recoiled when they saw the snarling wolf.

"Lord is a title earned or inherited in the Cavrul clans," Edium said in the same light tone he used when angry. "Which was it?"

"Earned," Durak said.

"Combat?"

"Aye. The lord of my clan disgraced me mother. I challenged him to a duel and ownership of the clan. Me won."

"Impressive. So you're the fabled Lord Boughlar," Edium said with a sharp note in his voice.

"So I am," Durak growled.

"If I've read correctly, you led a war on Crutar's stronghold when you were a mere fifty years?" Edium said.

"Aye. Lost over half our men before we turned back."

"Treppter never came to your aid as they had promised," Edium said.

"Aye."

"It was said after that you refused to join any army that sought to defeat Crutar."

"What be the point?" Durak said. "We'd just be abandoned again. No more Cavruls will die for Erthlas."

"You married shortly after you returned?" Edium continued.

Durak glanced over his shoulder. "Ye obviously know me story. I'll not be baited."

"I was just curious if the rumors were true," Edium said casually.

Durak sniffed. "Aye. They be true."

Edium's upper lip curled. "How many?"

"Me lost count after a hundred."

"That's why they worship you," Edium said, disgust hanging thick on his words.

"Aye. All but one man."

By the time they reached the gate to the inner city, word had already spread before them. Twenty or so guards were all on a knee.

Talura took a moment to marvel over the statues flanking the inner gate. Reaching the towering height of the ceiling, they were meticulously etched to supposedly resemble the heroes of the Battle of the Hidlu. The two heroes were blacksmiths who'd been quick to sabotage the inner gate mechanism before a horde of hidlu had managed their way inside. The Cavruls had held the rear tunnels for a month before Zerana had arrived with an army and annihilated the hidlus.

A guard whose wrinkled face reminded Talura of tree bark said, "Lord Boughlar. Ye honor us with your presence."

"Open the inner gate," Durak ordered.

"Ye understand that mages not be permitted in our city. Ye want us to break tradition?"

"Aye, I do."

The man cast Mafarias and Salvarias a quick glance. "Might me inquire as to why these mages live while in ye presence?"

Durak growled deep in his throat. "I'll lop off your head if ye don't open that gate."

"Of course, my lord."

The inner gate lurched, grinding and squeaking, objecting loudly to movement. They waited in thick tension for what felt like hours before it parted enough to allow them to pass. Lurking beyond was even more wondrous than what they'd seen in the outer city.

A ridiculously long arched bridge connected the outer city to the inner. Flowing beneath and along the wall separating the two sections of Cattlar was liquid fire, red hot and churning with chunks of black crust. The heat was nearly suffocating, rising up in waves that shimmered the air and burst sweat on Talura's forehead, making her long for the coolness of the outer cave. As they trekked across, she stared farther along the wall where the river of lava spilled over a ledge that dropped into some chasm, which must've been carved out under the city. The sight made her leery of the stability of the ground beneath her.

Past the bridge, they continued on a path of polished road. Soon, the fire's heat faded and the unfathomably massive cavern grew cold. Flat lands now spread out, covered by different crops that grew without sunlight.

As they strode with purpose through the sunless fields, she noticed Salvarias's gaze lingering on the plants. Eventually, as if unable to contain his curiosity, the young man began to lag behind, stopping to take a quick look, caress a leaf, or bend down and sniff an odd-looking vegetable. Wilhelm would wait each time, seeming like it was a common thing to stop and study crops.

She slowed her pace, thus Edium slowed, then Humar, Okulu, and Durak, and soon they were strolling instead of walking briskly. It gave Salvarias the opportunity to examine the crops, which he seemed to gladly use. The frown lines of exhaustion that had framed his mouth, the deadened slouch of his shoulders, and the rough, lurching steps that had ailed him began to fade, and he shuffled from plant to plant with more energy than she'd seen from him in days. His soft voice carried over the group, calming her and providing almost a musical accompaniment to their stroll.

She couldn't help but smile. The young man fascinated her as much as he ripped open her heart. Obviously, he needed help, but Salvarias had spent far too much time alone, laboring on his towering walls with his own blood and sweat. His heart was so closed in that she doubted her ability to help him. She'd always thought she had a knack for it, to see the torment of others, to be able to say the words they needed to hear. But not Salvarias. He fought what he needed with fervor, as if accepting her help or care would doom him to eternal damnation.

Regardless, there was a door there. There had to be. How else could Wilhelm sneak past those impenetrable walls?

Beyond the fields, they entered another vast cavern that Durak announced as the inner city, which contained the residences of Cattlar's denizens. Along every surface of the cavern walls, houses were carved into the rock and each had a balcony that jutted out to view the city below. She couldn't count how high the homes scaled nor begin to understand the elaborate pulley mechanisms that transported what looked like giant kettles filled with Cavruls to the different levels.

The ground floor was strewn with taverns and a few specialized merchants that Durak informed them were only for Cavruls. There were no roads, just a wide-open space stretching for miles in not only width but length and height as well.

"I don't doubt the gods had a hand in the making of this great city," Neithelas said, his violet eyes wide and his mouth agape.

"Aye," Durak said, puffing up his chest. "She's a beauty to behold."

Edium, always with a mind for business, stroked his beard and said, "Ever thought of permitting outside trade in here? I think we—"

"No," Durak growled. "Ye be allowed to visit, but this is sacred ground for Cavruls. We don't need Erthlas ruinin' what we've taken such care to protect."

"Your prejudice against Erthlas runs deep," Edium said mildly.

"Me been betrayed by enough of 'em." Durak scowled at Edium. "Ye should know since you know everything else about me."

A Cavrul with a lustrous mane of slick black hair marched up to Durak and spat angry words in the Cavrul language.

Durak's normal glare softened as he responded in Erthla. "Ye know I wouldn't have if it weren't important, Muddil."

Muddil glanced at Mafarias and Salvarias. "What be the meaning of this? What of yer oath over me sister's grave?"

"Me couldn't do it anymore," Durak grumbled.

Muddil punched Durak hard enough to send him sprawling to the floor. "Couldn't do it anymore! Me sister's dead! Over a hundred years have passed since we heard from ye. Since we sang songs of praise at every rumor of a mage cut down by a Cavrul."

Talura covered her mouth as she gasped. Salvarias, who was standing near, swayed.

"Ye swore to me over her grave that ye'd kill 'em all!" Muddil said. "And now ye bring the demons into my city!" Muddil kicked Durak in the stomach.

Salvarias took a step forward, but Wilhelm held him back, eyes dark, jaw set.

"Grindia would roll over in her grave!" Muddil shouted. "Ye children would weep at the coward their father had become!" He spit on Durak.

"Stop," Salvarias said, his face twisted in sympathy. "Please, leave him."

"Shut up, boy," Durak snapped through a gasping breath. "Stay out of this!"

"Was it you?" Muddil said, glowering at Salvarias. "Were ye the one who slaughtered me sister? Who cut down me nephew and niece?"

"No," Salvarias said. "But if ever I come across the mage who committed such atrocities, be assured that he or she would not live to see another sunrise."

Muddil spat in Salvarias's face. This time, it was Salvarias that held his brother back.

"All of ye deserve to die," Muddil said. "All of you!" He scowled at Durak. "And ye best stay clear of me, Boughlar. Me in a killin' mood!"

"We need a place to stay, Muddil," Durak said, shoving himself up. "Please, for the sake of Grindia, give us yer home for a few days. Neither the boy nor his uncle will be safe in the city."

Muddil roared with laughter, though it sounded more sinister than friendly. Once he calmed himself and wiped his tears, he said, "Ye cocky son of whore! After what ye've done, you expect me hospitality?"

"We be family," Durak said softly. "Our oaths bind ye to me."

Muddil sniffed and looked Durak over. "Ye've changed." He paused a moment before nodding. "I cannot refuse family. Best sleep with one eye open. If me get drunk enough, I'll slit yer throat while ye dream."

45

S alvarias left the washroom finally cleansed of his own filth, freshly shaven, and feeling mildly alert. The spaciousness of Muddil's home continued to be a pleasant surprise. The baths accommodated him nicely, though his brother was challenged, as he was with every bath. The high ceiling granted Salvarias enough room to stand upright with only the top of his hood brushing the polished stone roof. He marveled at the craftsmanship while he walked down the corridor to the main sitting room. No surface was plain. Life-size carvings depicting each leader of Durak's clan lined the hallway. The precise, sharp corners and perfect slanting angles of the walls and ceiling were unnatural, only explained by the means in which it was created. Pausing, Salvarias rested his hand on the dark gray rock. Nevlar himself had formed this very stone. To be touching a home a god had created humbled Salvarias. For several moments, he stood in awe.

Breaking his trance, he peered around the corner. The sitting room was furnished with plush chairs upholstered in solid subdued colors, lengthy couches, stone tables, and simple woven rugs to keep the chill floor at bay. Durak was winding between the furnishings and heading for the door. Gathering his cloak about him, Salvarias waited for the Cavrul to leave before he took up pursuit.

Outside, the distant city below sounded like a bee buzzing from flower to flower. A railing on the left side of the walkway prevented one from falling to his or her death. The right side was a wall that stretched the length of two Cavrul homes. Durak had just stepped into the last door. As Salvarias passed the pulley, he took a moment to study the gears, chains, and counterweights of the device that provided such an enjoyable ride to the towering levels of the inner city. After locking the mechanism firmly in his mind to study later, he continued to the door at the end of the walkway. It was ajar. Peeking inside, he saw the home had long been abandoned. Furniture was draped in what once were cream linens but now brown from the thick layer of dust. The stone shelves were home to more spiders than old books and jars with dead plants.

Durak stood in the center of the room. Seeing tears glistening down Durak's beard, Salvarias turned to leave.

"What do ye want, boy?" Durak called.

Salvarias stepped inside. "I ... I am sorry."

Durak grunted. "For being one of them? Or for what happened to me family?"

"Both."

"Ye haven't used magic since you killed the little girl."

Salvarias nodded, unable to stop his gaze from drinking in his surroundings. Additional stone shelves sported books and jars crammed full of soil. His insatiable hunger for knowledge, for written words, made his fingers itch. He tightened his grip on his staff to keep from bolting to the shelves and snatching up all the books. "Your wife was a healer?"

"Best in Cattlar." Durak lowered his head and scuffed his boot on the floor. "Me killed a hundred and thirty-seven mages. Never did find the one who killed 'em. Me wanted to kill you. The first day ye woke after the slave caverns, me came in the dining room to find ye reading by the light of yer sparrow."

"Why did you not?" Salvarias asked.

"Yer brother. He be the sole reason you still live, boy."

Salvarias withdrew his dagger, set it on a table, and gently pushed it toward Durak. "Would another death ease your pain?"

Durak stared at the knife a long moment before he spoke. "I thought it might. Me hate ye enough to do it."

A sick hope sprang up in Salvarias, and he found himself holding his breath.

Durak shook his head. "After the last one me killed, I swore I'd not kill another unless need be."

"Why did you stop?"

"She was just a girl, young as ye be now. She was beggin' me. I ... I slit her throat. Why didn't she save herself? The others put up a valiant fight. Castin' their spells at me, cursing me to Oblivion. But not her. The lass merely pleaded."

"No doubt she was too young to know enough spells to protect herself."

"Yet ye practice as if ye be an old man."

"My relationship with my magic was ... different."

"You'll never use it again?"

Salvarias shrugged. "I hope not."

"No matter. The evil is in ye blood."

"More so than you know."

Durak glanced over his shoulder and grunted. "Ye got the look of pity in ye eyes, boy."

"I ... I understand grief."

"Ye think you do because of your parents' murder? Bah!" Durak waved his hand. "Until ye hold your little girl in your arms while she spits up blood and turns cold, ye know nothing."

"Why were they killed?"

"It was a young mage who did it. Me saw from opposite the hill. He was bad off, beaten and bleedin'. I heard him yellin' to Grindia to heal him. She refused. No Cavrul would aid a mage."

"Yet you did."

"Me told you it was for ye brother. Not you."

"Regardless of your reasons, you have my eternal gratitude. I cannot imagine how difficult it was for you to share your table with me."

Durak grunted. "No, ye can't, boy. Leave me now. Me want to be alone with me memories."

Salvarias looked longingly at the bookcase once more before taking his dagger and turning to leave. Wilhelm stood in the doorway, face twisted in anger.

"We're leaving for the clan council," Wilhelm growled.

Durak nodded. "Be along in a moment, lad. Take the pulley down."

Salvarias wrapped his arm with his brother's and steered him outside.

"Sick bastard," Wilhelm said.

"Grief can tear down the most honorable man," Salvarias said. "Do not judge him so quickly."

"It could have been you," Wilhelm said.

"But it was not."

"I don't want you alone with him again."

"Brother, he—"

"I won't hear it," Wilhelm said. "If he's somewhere by himself, I want you to leave."

"If he wanted to do so, he would have harmed me years ago. He is your friend and cared for us when he had no reason to do so, when no others did, including our own blood. We must give him our respect, Brother."

"How could you even talk to him after knowing what he did?"

"It is easy to sit in our cozy homes and point at people passing by outside while a storm is raging. We watch them battle the gale and marvel over why they did not seek shelter sooner. We call them idiots for not seeing the storm clouds. The menace in the air had spoken of rain. Only an imbecile would have missed the signs. The scent. The darkening sky. The lack of a breeze. The birds seeking the safety of trees. We laugh at them when they fall into a muddy puddle. They should have been out of the rain sooner. They should have sought shelter. It was so obvious."

"You're not making sense, Salv."

"Is what I said untrue, brother? Let us say the man who is leaning against the wind, pushing onward when a shelter is at his side, ignores it. Is that man not dense?"

"If it's right there, yes. He could get out of the rain. If he stays in it, he'll catch cold. He could die. Lightning could strike him. But I don't see how—"

"You never asked why."

"What?"

"Why did he not seek shelter?"

"You said it earlier. He's dense."

"That is what we assume. That is how we judge him. Let me ask you this: Why would *you* be out in the storm? Why would you not seek shelter?"

"The only reason would be to get you. Maybe you were …" Wilhelm's voice trailed off.

"Yes, Brother. That man might have a loved one as well. It is easy to judge what we do not understand. The same applies to Durak."

Wilhelm shook his head, but remained quiet. Salvarias was not sure why he voiced his pensive thoughts, which he usually shielded. Those gave away his pain, and he strived to keep that pain close. It was his, personal and needed in order to remind him why he stayed adrift on his little raft, floating on his lake of indifference. It must have been his exhaustion that rippled the waters, revealing—if his brother listened closely—what Salvarias so desperately wanted from others: no judgment. To be seen and not stared at. To be helped and not feared.

When they arrived at the pulley, Wilhelm ruffled Salvarias's hair. "Get some sleep."

Bowing to Lord Bellerum, Sir Humar, Prince Arthias, and Muddil, Salvarias rammed his fist into Wilhelm's ribs. "Of course, Brother."

Not intending to lie, Salvarias made his way to his room. To his dismay, Lady Talura was waiting by his door.

"How are you?" she asked.

"Fine, my lady." He opened the door and slipped inside. "I must rest."

When she reached out a hand, his mother appeared. She raised a board over her shoulder.

"Release your evil!" she screamed.

Salvarias staggered, tripping over furniture to topple to the stone floor.

Stomping after him, his mother screeched, "Release it and this will end!"

"I am trying," Salvarias said, covering his head. The board smacked his arms repeatedly before moving down to his legs as he curled up tighter to protect his ribs.

"I'm sick of you!" his mother sobbed.

"Brother, help me."

"Leave him out of this!" she roared. "You will taint him with your evil, monstrosity!"

"Please—"

"I loathe you!"

"I am sorry," Salvarias wept, wincing when his words brought the board down harder.

"Salvarias!" A woman's sharp voice cut above his mother's.

The beating stopped. Hesitantly, he looked up through his arms to see a woman with golden hair kneeling beside him and another woman with chestnut hair hovering directly behind. He glanced around the unfamiliar room, but his mother was nowhere to be seen.

The woman with chestnut hair spoke softly. "Whatever you see is not there, dear."

As his mind cleared, he remembered where he was and who was with him. His cheeks burned with embarrassment. The memory seemed so vivid, so real.

"Go to your room, Varila," Lady Talura said. "Your sister is waiting."

Salvarias trusted Varila and pleaded with his eyes for her not to leave him alone with Lady Talura. An understanding eased Varila's contemptuous gaze and softened her hard expression. She went to offer a comforting touch that he desperately wanted, but he drew back.

Her eyes flashed with her usual anger. "Let's go together, Mother."

"No, Varila. You will go to Lunara."

"But—" Varila started.

"Do as I say. Now."

Varila directed an apologetic look at Salvarias. Then she left him. Left him alone. His door clicked closed.

He was alone.

Fear edged his rational thinking. Memories of his childhood barreled at him like a flash flood, devouring clear thought. The stunning woman with rich brown hair and piercing blue eyes would hurt him.

Yes, the presence hissed. *Just like your mother. She will learn of your evil. She will cut you. She will beat you. She will do the same horrid acts your mother committed, the same ones that, even now, your mind refuses to remember. I remember though, my little murderer. Do you want me to tell you?*

Salvarias clamped his hands over his ears, thinking he could block out the voice's next words. "No-no-no."

Feel the back of your head.

Salvarias tentatively reached to find the scar hidden in his hair. Terror blazed a path through reality. He was a little boy again. Scared and alone. He scrambled to his hands and knees and fled to the corner of the room. There were soft footsteps behind him. She would hurt him. He curled up against the cold stone. Dark gray just as he remembered. Dark and cold. He made himself as small as possible, pressing his body to the rock.

She is coming, my precious murderer.

"No-no-no," Salvarias wept.

So small, so helpless, so alone. But now you have powerful magic. Kill her. Save yourself the torment. Kill the one who hurts you.

Salvarias buried his face in the corner. "No. I love her."

Weak pet, the presence barked.

Salvarias flinched, pressing his hands to his ears.

When will you save yourself? When will you free yourself from your pain? She hurt you! Kill her now!

"No!" Salvarias sobbed. "Please leave me alone. Please! I beg you!"

"Salvarias."

It was a woman's voice but not his mother's. It was soothing, filled with the gentle warmth of love. It was a lie, though. Only Wilhelm loved him. Only Wilhelm never hurt him.

"Salvarias," the woman called again.

He did not want to see who sat with him. He wanted his brother. He clung to the rock with his back to the room. A rustle issued behind him. He closed his eyes tightly, tensing his body, readying himself for the strikes of a board, or book, or perhaps the iron skillet again. He wanted something to hold him, to comfort him. He was so alone, so cold. It was so dark. Another rustle. He felt her drawing near, heard the light tap of footsteps.

"Please," he cried softly. "Please, I am trying."

A warm blanket draped over his shoulders. It smelled of jasmine. Something touched his hair, and he cringed, clawing at the rock. He wanted to flee, wanted to fly through the cracked window of his room, to be as free as the sparrow. The sparrow ...

Whatever touched him stopped. The woman's voice began to hum. It was a melody he had heard from somewhere before, a voice soft and light. The hum turned into a whispered song. He was not sure what was said, but he started rocking himself to the lovely tune. It was such a soothing rhythm of words that he relaxed. He nestled against the wall, pulling the blanket closer. The fabric was warm, as if it had been lying by a fire. He inhaled the sharp sweet smell of the little white flower. The calming words went on until he forgot someone else was in the room. All he heard was the melody, all he smelled was jasmine, all he felt was a cozy tenderness. Soon, he slipped into sleep.

SALVARIAS WOKE WITH A START. He was curled up in the corner of the room facing the wall, and Adok was nuzzling his arm. He hoped it had been a dream. He closed his eyes and battled the burning tears and lump forming in his throat. He prayed to the godless sky that when he looked up, he would be alone, that Lady Talura truly had not witnessed his reenactment of his childhood. Building his courage, Salvarias raised his head and glanced around his room. All comforting thoughts vanished when his gaze fell to Lady Talura sitting in a plush chair.

"Hello, dear," she said in her normal tone.

"My lady." Salvarias swallowed hard. His throat was dry with the lingering effects of terror.

"It's a beautiful afternoon." Lady Talura rose from her chair and glided over to the pitcher of water. "A lovely breeze has swept over the mountains. I'd love to go for a walk outside the cave. My daughters, Okulu, and Neithelas have decided to take a tour of the inner city. Your uncle has left to retrieve some items from his tent. The rest are meeting with the clan council. So, as you can see, I'm left with no company. Would you be a dear and escort me?"

His mind was too tired to find an excuse. He drank the water she offered and shoved himself up. Reluctantly, he set aside the warm blanket, snatched up his aspen branch, and followed her from his room, Adok in tow.

They rode the pulley down in silence. Once at the bottom, passing Cavruls spat at his feet, but all were kind enough not to spit directly on him. Lady Talura said nothing as they strolled by the farms and out the inner gate. The outer city was still awash with traders and laughter, blissfully oblivious to their fate.

Outside the city, she briefly spoke alone with a Cavrul before returning to Salvarias's side. She led him past tents and the outer inhabitants and into the forest. Though still not as lush as Serenity, it was the closest he had seen since leaving, and as always in the woods, a peaceful contentment eased his tense shoulders.

"I miss my home," Lady Talura said.

"The forests of Serenity and Falar are most beautiful."

"That they are." She stopped in a clearing where the sun warmed a patch of wild flowers. "Lower your hood, dear."

Her tone was so authoritatively motherly that Salvarias obeyed without the slightest hesitation.

"Raise your face and drink in the sun's warmth."

This time, Salvarias paused. He kept in shadow to avoid the cringes and gasps when any saw his demonic eyes. After Xeroth, he was not sure he had the strength to witness another cringing from him.

"Do as I say, dear."

Again, her toned demanded he obey. Bracing himself, he met her gaze.

A slow smile spread. "You have beautiful eyes."

He flinched.

She closed her eyes and raised her face skyward. "The ground is beautiful to stare at, but you must remember to drink in the light from time to time. Close your eyes and raise your face to the sun." She popped open one eye to regard him. "Do as I say."

Pulling himself from shock, he closed his eyes and looked up. Warmth blanketed over him and dulled the terrible chill he had felt since shoving his magic into its dark prison. A breeze cooled his face as the sun imbued its light into his very soul. He inhaled deeply, allowing his cares to fall from his back, the woodsy pines to drown the stench of blood that had seemed to follow him for weeks. The light blinded away his memories of burnt people, impaled children.

"You feel it?" she breathed. "Life. All around us. Inside us. Everywhere."

Salvarias nodded. "I do, my lady."

"I'd ask you to call me Talura, but from what my husband tells me, you're not one for informal titles."

"Our relationship is not informal, my lady." He felt her stare but ignored it. He was too hypnotized by his experience. Rarely did he look up, and he could not remember the last time he fully faced the sun. It renewed his hope the longer he stood there.

"From now on, when it is just the two of us, I expect you to lower your hood, dear. And you'll raise your head and view the world as others do."

Salvarias remained quiet, unsure if he would obey.

"Sit with me," Lady Talura said.

He glanced over to see her settled on a patch of grass. He sat more than an arm's length from her. When she seemed uninterested in speaking, he raised his face to the sky. Before he knew it, he was lying on his back, hands laced behind his head, mind hypnotized into blankness. Adok's heavy frame rested against his as the wolf curled up at Salvarias's side.

"Lunara told me you found the men who killed your parents," Lady Talura said.

"Yes, my lady." He was not even counting. It was the most relaxed his mind had been without touching Lunara. There was still pain, but it seemed to play in the recesses of his conscious, freeing his mind to think of nothing but the warmth seeping inside him.

"Did you know we visited Falar after you left?" she asked.

"No."

"We learned quite a bit about your brother, but very little about you."

"I knew few."

"Milred adores you. She misses you terribly."

"And I her. She was a brilliant teacher." The cool grasses seemed to reach inside his shoulders and steal his burden. He inhaled deeply, feeling the weightlessness of his body, his thoughts, the absence of fears and shame. He lived in light.

"Baker Jyfil told me what an enchanting woman your mother was and how affectionate she was … toward your brother."

A sharp pain stabbed his heart. "Indeed. She was a wonderful mother."

"Jyfil said he never saw her touch you. Nor you her."

"I am not an affectionate man." He shivered from a chill running up his spine.

"You seem very affectionate with your brother."

Salvarias shrugged. "He is different."

"Jyfil said he sometimes heard screams coming from your home. Whenever he would check, your mother said you were dreaming."

A violent tremor racked him. "I ... I have nightmares."

"You must've slept often ... most of the day and night."

Salvarias opened his eyes to regard her. Her gaze searched his face, but for what, he did not know. He sat up and looked directly at her, surprised she never batted an eye nor shied away from him. "If you have questions, please ask, my lady. But understand, I may choose not to answer them."

"I have no questions, Salvarias. What I offer is an ear to listen if you ever chose to unburden yourself from what you witnessed the day your parents were killed, or what horrors you endured while held captive in Zeeas, or the memory of your mother's abuse."

Salvarias bolted to his feet, startling Adok to his. "I must leave."

"I won't tell your brother," she said, darting in his path. "What you tell me would be shared with no one."

"You know nothing of what you speak!" Salvarias snapped, trying to move around her but she stepped in his way each time.

"I know exactly what I speak. I know you endured abuse by her hand."

"I ... You ..." Salvarias stepped back, mind reeling in a maelstrom of chaos. He had promised his mother no one would ever know. Irrational or not, he feared if anyone found out what she had done he would be separated from his brother, stolen away in the night.

"Lunara thinks you witnessed your parents' murders. She thinks that's what you dream."

"She ... I ..." Salvarias clutched his chest, battling for air.

"I saw the scars on your arms," she continued mercilessly. "I saw your missing ear."

Salvarias clamped a hand to the side of his head when he heard the knife sawing through cartilage. "I beg you ... stop." He could not breathe, and a sharp pain repeatedly stabbed his heart.

"I have watched you, Salvarias. I've watched you enough to learn of your character. I've peeked over your walls, and I've seen a wonderful young man. A man I want to know. A man I respect. A man I care for."

He gasped at the shooting pain in his heart and clutched his chest. "You do not know me."

"I know you just fine, dear. As with your brother, I've seen enough to love you as my own—"

He doubled over. "No!" he shouted, cutting off words he was in no frame of mind to hear.

"—son."

Salvarias fainted.

"Fools!" Edium boomed. His voice resounded in the circular room lined with three tiers of chairs, each occupied by a representative from a clan. He would've been in awe of the domed roof inlaid with gold and jewels had his anger not been so great. The meeting had deteriorated rapidly.

"Ye know I not be a liar!" Durak shouted. "Me saw with mine own eyes!"

Muddil snorted. "The word of a betrayer!"

"Enough!" a Cavrul snapped. "Lord Boughlar has not betrayed his race. What he swore on the graves of the dead are only for the dead's ears. You, Lord Muddil, inherited a great prize when Lord Boughlar left. Ye had his entire clan to gain by planting mad ideas in his mind."

"Don't ye dare insult my brother!" Durak unsheathed his axe.

"I'm not ye brother!" Muddil yelled, whipping out his sword. "Ye married my sister, nothing more is shared between us."

Edium motioned to Humar. The knight and Wilhelm dragged Durak cursing and kicking out of the room. Once all was quiet, Edium inhaled a deep breath. "What will you do?"

"You cannot ignore this threat to Dalnar," Arthias said.

Muddil rammed his sword in its sheath. "We'll send scouts to track this supposed army. We've got the commanders gathering half our forces to be ready if one is found. The rest of our forces will stay here to guard our city."

"Until the army's location is discovered," Edium said as calmly as his anger would allow, "please close your outer city, shut the gates, and withdraw here."

"There be four ways into the inner city of Cattlar," Muddil said. "The outer city and three tunnels in the rear of the inner city, and we've got them heavily guarded. We not fear for her safety."

Edium shook his head. "See reason! If I led an army against Cattlar, my first priority would be to divide your forces, make you fight for both the outer city and inner. You don't have enough men to defend both fronts!"

"We not be a bunch of newborns who haven't left their mother's teat!" Muddil shouted, springing to his feet. "We can defend our home without shutting off trade based on some hunch from a mage that an army is set for our doorstep. It could be headed anywhere!"

"The boy hasn't been wrong yet!" Edium pitched back.

"He has!"

Edium rolled his eyes at Durak's voice.

"What ye be sayin'?" Muddil said.

Durak glowered at Edium. "The boy thought Cattlar was already lost. We rode for four days to arrive here to help, and we find it perfectly safe."

"Are you mad?" Edium said. "You've just—"

"But I tell ye this," Durak continued. "The boy is right more often than he's wrong. I believe he believes Cattlar will be attacked. I believe it's enough of a reason to withdraw inside the city."

"Ye place the honor of your name upon it?" Muddil said, a glint of satisfaction in his eyes.

"Ye request is unreasonable," another Cavrul muttered. "It not be right to ask such a —"

"I do!" Durak snapped. "On the word of my family, me trust the boy. Cattlar will be attacked."

A hush blanketed the room. Edium held his breath as the Cavrul council shared surprised glances.

It was Muddil who spoke. "Once we hear from our scouts, we'll make our final decision."

Durak waved his hand. "Ye be fools."

Edium agreed. Disgusted, he marched out of the council chambers, Humar, Durak, Arthias, and Wilhelm on his heels. "I want a way out of here," Edium growled. "If what Salvarias thinks is true, we'll all die when the army arrives."

"I think we should leave now," Wilhelm said.

Edium grunted. "I'd love nothing more." He looked over his shoulder at Wilhelm. "You think you could convince your brother?"

Wilhelm's eyes darkened, and he shook his head.

"I didn't think so," Edium said. "Hyde sent word by sea to Serinity, but Brice is still days away. Perhaps, by some miracle, he can get my army here before we're attacked. Regardless, we'll have an escape route planned. If the boy sees the hopelessness of a fight, he might leave."

"Can we at least get Lunara and Talura out?" Wilhelm asked.

Edium laughed. "If you think your brother is stubborn, apparently you've not gotten to know my wife well enough. She'll not run from this."

"Lunara?"

Edium's laugh was renewed. "She's as stubborn as her mother. I've no doubt she'd follow the boy to the depths of Oblivion without blinking an eye." It hit him in that moment that his daughter's feelings for Salvarias went beyond friendship and deep care, beyond some mysterious connection. She loved the boy. His laughter choked off.

Salvarias stirred awake to a light hum of a now-familiar song. It comforted him and tempted him back to darkness, but he knew who sang next to him. He opened his eyes to see her sitting by his side, eyes closed, gazing up at the sun.

"Hello, dear," Lady Talura said casually. "You slept for nearly an hour. Are you ready to head back?"

Salvarias was beside himself. She acted as if she had not called out all his torment with one sentence.

She looked down at him and smiled knowingly. "I've said my peace, dear. It'll not hang in the air between us unless you allow it. When you're ready, you'll talk to me. And that day is inevitable. Until then, I'll settle for your company."

Salvarias shoved himself to sit and rubbed his burning eyes. He had no idea what to say.

A playful smile danced on her lips, and her eyes were lit with a contagious happiness. "Tell me, dear, are there any animals about?"

"I assume Lady Lunara told you," Salvarias said.

She cast a motherly smile. "She told me some. I assure you, there are many secrets she kept. Now, tell me what animals are about."

Sighing, Salvarias opened his mind to the myriad of voices around him. One slammed into him, a familiar one. Tears burned his eyes as he bolted to his feet and darted for the deep shadows of a thicket. Mithal and Lilly burst from the trees. A cry of joy left him as he flung his arms around the stallion's neck.

"My dear friend," he said. "I was so worried for you."

Mithal lowered his head over Salvarias's shoulder in an attempt to return the hug while hastily filling Salvarias in on his adventures. Grinning at Lilly's complaint that she had grown soft since she no longer carried Wilhelm, Salvarias hugged her.

He pulled away from both horses, blinked aside his tears, and turned to Lady Talura. "How is this possible? I thought they had been stolen."

"They were, but by one of my husband's traders. Your uncle brought them to Cattlar. He'd planned on meeting up with us later and thought you'd want your own horses."

Adok offered an affectionate growl at Mithal before nudging his head under Lady Talura's hand.

"He's never been affectionate with me," she said, running her fingers along Adok's ear. "But today, he stared at me for several moments then sat by my side. I think I've earned his approval."

Salvarias ignored the wolf's raving about Lady Talura being one of the most wonderful people he had met.

"He is not as vicious as he seems," Salvarias said.

Adok growled at him.

"As a matter of fact," he continued. "Few animals find him intimidating."

The wolf bared his teeth.

"I think it is because he is out of shape, disconnected with the wild," Salvarias said, picking up his aspen branch. "I am not sure he could survive without Lady Lunara passing him food under the table."

Adok snapped his teeth.

"I think you've upset him," Lady Talura said.

He glanced at the wolf. "Perhaps. Then again, I could be making a point."

The wolf ceased his recounting of Lady Talura's traits.

"Maybe one day you can introduce me to an owl," Lady Talura said, eyes distant as if she was already seeing one. "I've loved owls since I was a little girl. I used to sneak out of my room at night and climb to the rooftops so I could see them." She laughed lightly. "My father was furious each time."

"If ever given the opportunity, I will certainly do so."

She smiled at him. "Shall we return?"

"Of course, my lady."

Salvarias followed her through the forest, trying to process all that had happened to him in the span mere hours. It was no good. He had no clue as to what he felt. He was too tired to care.

"I've found out something interesting," Lady Talura said. "Apparently, you knew before I, but my daughter has an amazing gift to read people's ... souls."

Salvarias remained quiet, unsure how much Lunara had disclosed.

"I've had a little chat with her about respecting others' privacy. She said she's rarely used her gift, but she said she's in your mind constantly. She also mentioned you don't approve."

"My thoughts are my own."

"Indeed. I've told her the same, but I fear she'll not listen. She's most curious about you."

"I thank you for trying, my lady."

"As much as I agree with you, I can understand her argument. Perhaps you should explore your connection in further detail."

"As long as this connection exists, Lady Lunara is in danger. I will do everything within my power to sever our link."

Talura smiled up at him. "Fear, my dear, should not drive decisions."

"You have seen the danger she is in firsthand, my lady. Why—"

"Danger is all around. I think this connection, while it does have many downsides, is far more beneficial than detrimental. You can keep her safe, know when she's in danger, help her. If I can persuade you at all, I'd ask that you work with her to strengthen it."

"I disagree, my lady; therefore, I will continue my best efforts to distance us."

"I find that a shame, dear. But the decision is yours as much as it is hers. You understand you'll be working against each other?"

"Then so be it," Salvarias said shortly, his tone ending the conversation.

When they came to the hillside of tents, Mafarias was waiting.

"My lady," Mafarias said, bowing. "Might I steal the boy for a moment?"

She took the reins of the horses. "I'll see them to the stable."

"Thank you," Mafarias said.

Salvarias had a strong desire to run. Why, he had no idea. He never had trusted his uncle. Something about Mafarias reminded him of himself, something about his magic. Besides, when it came to Mafarias, Salvarias was certain nothing was what it seemed. The man was more mysterious than the origin of magic.

When Lady Talura was out of earshot, Mafarias said, "I see you've not had any reservations telling Humar and Edium about these visions."

"On the contrary. However, our travels have forced me to make difficult decisions."

"You trust them, but you don't trust me."

Salvarias regarded him for a moment before walking alongside him. "I do not trust you. I remember almost everything from my childhood. But you ... I do not remember you dining with us every night. I do not remember you staying in Falar for the years you say you did."

"You don't trust me because you don't remember?" Mafarias chuckled. "Don't be absurd, boy. You were too young to remember."

"As I said, I remember much. Books I read. What we ate for dinners. Tobin's stories."

"You must know that I want to help you," Mafarias said.

"Where have you been since we were separated in Reffil?"

"Fleeing. Once I got ashore, I had to run from the soldiers."

"On foot? They were on horseback."

"I purchased a horse in Reffil. Would you like me to tell you about every breath I wasn't in your company?"

"Though your words drip with sarcasm, I would love nothing more than a recount of your entire existence, *Uncle*." He allowed his own sarcasm to roll into that word.

Mafarias's eyes flared with anger, and he grabbed hold of Salvarias's arm. "We're related, boy, even if not exactly as that term means. I—"

Salvarias heard nothing else. Images bombarded his mind with the force of a battering ram. Some he recognized: Wilhelm laughing and smiling, Ashra cooking dinner, Tobin's kind face. Others were foreign. Prominent was a woman of extreme beauty, auburn hair the same as Salvarias's mother, a beaming smile, and jewel-green eyes. Then came creatures and lands he had never seen.

The images swelled in number, spiraling around him, creating a vortex of torment. His body went numb, legs crumbling beneath him, lungs laboring painfully, heart staggering to keep him alive. Nothing of the physical world existed. He was only aware of the war waging in his mind. Once again, he perched on the cliff of sanity, huddled against a vibrant tree. Instead of a ravenous red ocean, below was a chasm of knowledge, of eternity, the absence of death, the yawning hole of immortality.

Salvarias slipped. Crying out in desperation, his fingers grazed the tree root before he plummeted from the cliff of sanity.

Spells and languages he had never heard penetrated his brain, swelling his already-full mind to near-explosion, while what felt like a vice pressed against his skull. He screamed.

A power cascaded over him ... something he had felt before. The day he was born. He remembered it. It was his uncle's power erecting a shield around Salvarias's mind, trying to retrieve the knowledge that had been jammed into his brain, striving to lessen his burden.

With Salvarias's failing strength of mind, his magic surged forward on its own, angry and confused, burning his blood with long-forgotten warmth. After it realized Mafarias was the cause of Salvarias's pain, it struck his uncle. In a desperate ploy to protect Salvarias, the magic grabbed what power Mafarias was using and absorbed it, merged with it. The sensation brought forth a long-forgotten memory. In his first breaths of life, he remembered being scared and in such terrible pain, his world nothing but fear and death. He remembered a power had risen up, a familiar one—the one he used to haul souls to Oblivion. Salvarias cried out "no" when he realized the blackfire had taken Mafarias's power that day, that it was the blackfire that cursed him with magic. This time, however, it was not blackfire that lashed out at Mafarias. It was Salvarias's own magic.

We will not *die this day,* his magic commanded.

As Mafarias's power sucked into Salvarias's pores, they both groaned. The feeling was a reverse of losing hold on the energy. He felt its alien presence stabbing his skin, invading his body. His magic used the extra power to battle the maelstrom of his mind, struggling to haul him back to the edge of sanity. A surge of dizzying power strained his skin, leaching a cry from his throat.

By the gods, he just wanted it to stop.

A shrill voice pierced his ear. "Stop! You're hurting him!" It was Lady Talura.

"Leave me alone, woman!" Mafarias snapped. "Breathe, boy!"

"Brother ..." Salvarias choked on blood running down the back of his throat to sputter from his lips.

"Get away!" Talura cried.

"Come on, boy. You need to gain control."

"Salv!"

He could not tell if he screamed aloud or silently, but he begged for his brother. Then familiar arms encased him, grounding him in to the physical world and leaning him over to rid his mouth of blood.

"Breathe!" Wilhelm ordered.

Succumb to me, his magic urged. *You must let me help you. Stop fighting me!*

With safety surrounding him, Salvarias surrendered to his magic. It erupted with mind-breaking power and gathered all the information in the chasm Salvarias plummeted toward. His magic encased his fragile mind, and slowly, one word at a time, allowed the knowledge to leak into his awareness, permitting him to process it at his own pace. After what felt like hours but was surely only a few breaths, Salvarias found himself huddled against the vibrant tree, safe. He wept until dreaded darkness devoured him.

"WHAT DID YOU DO TO HIM?" Edium roared, staring at Salvarias covered in vomit and blood, lying limply in Wilhelm's arms. The last of the foggy blue light that had encompassed the boy finally settled *inside* Salvarias, which did absolutely nothing to eliminate Edium's near-panic. The boy had been clenched into a tight ball, his skin seeming to bulge against some unseen force, muscles flexing, and teeth grinding together. Now, he looked nearly dead.

"I accidentally touched him," Mafarias muttered. "I didn't mean to hurt him."

"What?" Edium snapped.

"It's nothing," Wilhelm said, wiping Salvarias's face.

Edium opened his mouth to retort, but his wife shook her head.

"Do you mind?" Mafarias said shortly, nodding to the dagger Talura held to his throat.

She lowered her weapon, hiked up her skirt, and sheathed it.

"Let's get inside," Wilhelm muttered.

Edium and his friends walked in uncomfortable silence through the outer city. Once past the inner city gate, he offered to carry Salvarias but Wilhelm refused.

The remainder of the walk was tense. Mafarias seemed truly worried about the boy, yet it did nothing to ease Edium's anger. He found his hands shaking, remembering the blood spurting from the boy's mouth. Talura appeared equally rattled. Apparently, Humar and Wilhelm were desensitized to the sight. They recovered quickly, as if it were common. Then again, Edium had witnessed enough in the short time he'd spent with the boy that he, too, should have calmed quicker. Instead, he grew more concerned each time he saw the boy in distress. Surely, whatever Salvarias was doing to himself would guarantee a short life.

Inside Muddil's home, Varila and Lunara were waiting in the sitting room. Lunara's hands were trembling.

"What can you tell us?" Edium asked her.

She shook her head. "I ... I couldn't explain even if I tried."

At the brothers' room, Edium and his family waited until Wilhelm cleaned Salvarias, changed him into a set of fresh robes, and settled him in bed under a pile of blankets. Edium ordered food from a servant and additional chairs so Talura and himself, along with their daughters, could stay with the brothers.

It wasn't long before a platter of food arrived. Wilhelm ate his fair share and finished whatever was left before moving to sit in the largest chair available. Lunara sat on Salvarias's bed with a book in her hand, the other twirling a lock of the boy's hair. Varila plopped down in Wilhelm's lap.

After everything had calmed and Wilhelm's furrowed brow showed some sign of relaxation, Edium cleared his throat and said, "Would you like to tell us what happened out there?"

"I will," Mafarias said from the entrance of the room.

Edium shifted in his chair to free his sword for easy access.

"Salvarias has a keen sense of powers," Mafarias said, gliding into the room and stopping at Salvarias's bed. "His own power exceeds any mage I've ever met, though I doubt he would believe me if I told him so."

"I thought mages could sense their own power and compare it to others," Edium said.

"Indeed, we can," Mafarias said. "I can easily compare mine to others. If Salvarias possessed such capabilities, he wouldn't doubt himself as he so ardently does. As Wilhelm would verify, the boy holds no confidence."

"It's true," Wilhelm said, leaning his head back and closing his eyes. "He never believes me when I tell him either."

Mafarias smiled at Wilhelm. There was a genuine love in his eyes that surprised Edium. "My nephew knows his brother best." Mafarias inhaled a deep breath and faced Edium. "My power is immense. It has few limits. Salvarias's power reacts poorly with mine. Touching him hurts him. What I was trying to do was help strengthen his mind. That is the light you saw. A spell to aid him."

"But Salv stole it," Wilhelm said.

"Indeed. How did you know, boy?"

"Vuddruk used the same sort of spell on Salv before he touched him. The same thing happened."

"Ah, this Vuddruk person?" Mafarias said.

"He's not to be trusted," Edium growled. "The bastard patched us up and left so the worm tunneling in Quind could have a healthy meal."

"I've told Humar that few can be trusted," Mafarias said. "We must be wary of any person or creature near the boy. Whoever seeks our young mage intends to keep him alive. What appears to be a friend could be an enemy."

"You think he's following us?" Edium asked. "To be in such convenient places raises suspicion."

Mafarias shrugged. "He did speak truth. Salvarias's magic is a beacon to other mages. It's as bright as the sun on summer day."

Mafarias turned to Wilhelm. "I have no doubt the boy will find a way to shield his power. Until he does so, you must understand that his power can be felt at a greater distance than most mages. He isn't safe until he conceals some of it."

"Can he make it disappear?" Wilhelm asked. "I mean, can he make it so other mages can't sense he's a mage?"

"Unfortunately, no," Mafarias said. "His power is too strong to do so. There will always be traces of it surrounding him. But at least he'll be able to limit the effects." Mafarias chuckled. "With how brightly he's shining now, I wouldn't be surprised if every mage across Arden knows where he is. And it's growing. Every time I meet the boy, his power is stronger."

Wilhelm's face drained of color. "If they can sense him, they'll—"

Mafarias held up a hand. "Sorry. Wrong time for an exaggeration. It's not that powerful of a beacon, but it's strong."

"Have you learned who wants him? Who this 'god' is? Why Salvarias?" Edium asked.

"Who? No. Why? I assume his power. If they or it controlled him, their forces would be unstoppable."

"So if he's on our side, then victory is certain?"

Mafarias shook his head, his voice dropping to a whisper. "His power alone isn't enough. He must choose between what resides inside him or be enslaved by it."

Edium glanced at his wife to see if she had the same confused expression as he. She did. "What do you mean, 'enslaved?'" Edium said.

"What I speak is speculation." Mafarias inhaled deeply and bowed. "I've promised to dine with Humar tonight. We've much to catch up on."

Edium glared at the mage. "You know more than what you're telling us."

Mafarias smiled. "The ramblings of an old mage who listens to too many rumors, I assure you. Why they want the boy is a mystery to me. I can simply draw conclusions based on what I know. Now, if you'll excuse me."

Edium leapt up from his chair and grabbed Mafarias's arm. "You're lying, you sack of ogre crap! Tell me how you've heard these rumors! Tell me who. For the love of all the gods, tell us! Or so help me, I'll have Muddil arrest you and shackle you in your room until you talk!"

"Uncle?" Wilhelm asked. "Do you know something? Can you help us?"

Mafarias glanced over at Wilhelm before returning his stare to Edium. "No, boy. I can't help." The mage's eyes told a different story.

"Let him go, Edium," Wilhelm said, his voice sounding exhausted.

With great reluctance and despite his screaming instincts, Edium released the mage. Mafarias smiled fondly at Wilhelm before leaving the room.

"You seriously trust him?" Edium said to Wilhelm.

Wilhelm sagged further into the chair. "My uncle has never been one to speak clearly. I have no idea what he does to survive, how he obtains money for food, where he lives, or where he travels. All I know is that he loved my mother as if she were his own daughter. He gave us magical artifacts to sell so we could afford food and clothes. He made sure the mages from the Association didn't kill my brother when they came to test him. When he's been around, he's looked after us. He's taken care of us. I can't imagine him not helping when he could."

Edium let the conversation die out and withdrew deep into his own thoughts, recalling every action the mage had made since meeting him, every word he'd spoken.

46

SUMMER 1018 A.R

Salvarias set aside the book Lord Bellerum had given him in Quind. No doubt a story lurked within what appeared to be ramblings of a senile old man. Perhaps even ancient knowledge of the old gods. Unfortunately, Salvarias was in no frame of mind to decode the book.

Glancing around his room, there was little to count. The fabrics were solid in color with no patterns, and the walls were comprised of four smooth slabs of stone pressed next to each other. Desperate to occupy some portion of his mind, he began counting the fur on Adok's head, which rested on Salvarias's propped up knees.

"It has been two days, my friend," he murmured to Adok. "Nothing. No creature, no man armored in black steel. Nothing. I am lost."

Adok's silence mirrored that of his room. It was rare over the last two days for Salvarias to have time alone. Wilhelm, Lord Bellerum, Sir Humar, Durak, and Prince Arthias met with the clan council several times a day. The extended absence of his brother had seemed to carve out an incredibly dark and painful hole inside Salvarias.

Apparently, set to fill his void, Lady Talura had taken it upon herself to occupy nearly all his time, although he would have rather spent a year in Oblivion. Being near her brought the memory of her ripping all his secrets from his grasp. Now she knew more about him than his own brother. Not only had she violated his box of hidden torment, her presence alone sent him in a spiral of delusions. Some he kept in his control, blocking his mother who strolled next to them when Lady Talura would take him on walks through the forest. However, more times than not, he was forced to relive his mother's beatings. He would wake in the corner of the room or huddled against a tree to find Lady Talura humming her sweet melody by his side. She never commented about his lapses, which he was grateful for. She seemed unbothered by his refusal to be baited into revealing further secrets from his time alone with his mother.

To add to his dismay, she apparently gained some sort of pleasure in giving him motherly orders: "finish your fruit," "lower your hood," "raise your head," "look at me when you speak." It was becoming tiresome. He had lived his entire life free from parental influence. His mother never cared what he did, and Tobin was too busy trying to win a word from him that the guard never scolded or told him to do anything. Though he had once desperately wanted the same parental love Wilhelm had been awarded, he was far too old to be receiving it at his age. Now, it just reminded him of all he had been denied in his childhood.

You're weak, my murderer. I know what is in your heart. Though you push her away, you long for her acceptance. I sense your darkest desires. As it has been the same for your entire life, you seek family. People who will accept you and your brother unconditionally. Your search is futile. No one will love you. And your brother suffers because of it.

Surely the presence was wrong. To admit what might dwell in some dark part of himself would mean to doom those he loved, if ever there were such people. If his evil did not kill them, then the fact he was a mage would put anyone he cared about in danger. He needed no one. Except Wilhelm. His brother was different: immune to Salvarias's evil and capable of besting a group of thugs bent on butchering him for being in Salvarias's presence.

Adok barged into his thoughts with questions about what had happened outside the city with Mafarias a few days ago—a moment in time Salvarias had purposely not explored. Whatever he had seen left him feeling vulnerable in a world bigger than he could conceive. He understood it as much as it was a mystery. His mind teetered on revelation. Instead of trying to discover it, he shied away from it. Whatever lurked over the precipice blocking his knowledge, he was not eager to find. Sometimes ignorance was bliss and, for the first time, his curiosity wanted nothing to do with it. He even refused the new words he had learned, new spells and magical possibilities. To focus on them, he would need to permit his magic to surface, and that was one thing he had no desire to do again ... ever. He firmly told Adok he would not relive the experience.

A flash of white light blinded him, springing alive a hope that had been dead since his last vision.

When the light faded, he found himself floating in a cavern, vast and stuffy, moldy and thick with the stench of unholy creatures. The army. Creatures hissed around an apparition of himself and parted to clear a path. He glided forward, following his own wispy form. When he reached the other end of the army, a man was waiting. His glistening black hair stuck to his black armor, and he had a smug smile.

"I knew you would come," the man said. "You're all we ever wanted. Now we can finally leave Dalnar. I am Vescar," the man continued. "You have power. My god wants it. Simple enough. You give it to him. He leaves Arden. The decision is yours to make. Are you willing to sacrifice yourself to save your home? Your brother? Or will you fight us tonight as we march upon the helpless city of Cattlar?"

Salvarias's apparition presented his wrists. He surrendered.

White light flared out the vision and streaks of gray and black raced for him. He grabbed hold of whatever was in front of him to steady himself. Luckily, he was still in bed. Sitting helped gain his senses quicker. He apologized to Adok as he unhinged his fingers from the wolf's fur.

It was a vision of sorts. He knew the location of the army within the caves. He could lead the Cavruls straight to it. He frowned. No, the

Cavruls would be massacred. Their numbers were not enough. And Lord Bellerum's army was at least a day away, and that was best case. If he had to decide tonight, reinforcements would not arrive in time to save them. Cattlar would be overtaken. This "god's" army would have the use of the caves to spread across Arden like a plague. What choice did he have but to surrender himself? Sinking his face in his hands, he thought of his brother. Wilhelm would be devastated, not to mention furious.

He will move past your death, the presence hissed. *Push him to marry Varila. Give him a reason to live. With her, he would obtain the happiness he so richly deserves, the happiness you have denied him for years.*

He will come for me.

To where? There are no clues. If there were, you wouldn't need to surrender yourself. He'll find nothing. He'll give up. He'll marry Varila. He'll be happy.

Salvarias rose from bed, grabbed his aspen branch, and left his room. He came across Muddil in the sitting room, pouring himself a mug of ale as he sat comfortably in a plush chair.

Salvarias bowed. "Excuse me, Lord Muddil. Might I ask you a question?"

Muddil glowered at him and downed an ale. "What?"

"How easy would it be to collapse tunnels farther from the city? Say a few miles north."

"Impossible," Muddil growled.

"Might I ask why?"

Muddil smoothed his beard and leaned back in his chair. "It be a web down there. Collapse one, and more will follow. What holds up the mountain are thin supports." Muddil stuck out his jaw, as if angered to admit his next words. "We tunneled too much. We weakened the foundation. Only the three tunnels that lead straight to the city are reinforced. And as me told Lord Bellerum, we've got thousands of men and women inside 'em, guarding for any threat ye dreamed up."

Salvarias bowed again when he caught sight of his brother on the balcony. "Thank you, Lord Muddil." He left and joined Wilhelm. "Brother," Salvarias greeted.

Wilhelm locked an arm around Salvarias's neck and ruffled his hair. Salvarias punched his brother's ribs before wiggling free and leaned against the balcony to face his brother. He needed to watch for lies, and Wilhelm's eyes always betrayed him.

"I approve of her," Salvarias said. "She is brilliant, strong, beautiful. She is one of the most amazing women I have ever met."

Wilhelm nodded. "I know."

"Why have you not pursued her?"

"I have ... somewhat."

"She deserves nothing shy of an honorable, kind man. She deserves you."

Wilhelm shrugged.

"No," Salvarias scolded. "We will discuss this."

"I ... I don't like the way she treats you. I always imagined whomever I married would love you as much as I do. I wouldn't be happy if we were to marry. I'd be mad at her every time she looked sideways at you."

"She cares—"

"I know all the excuses you'll make for her. I know some of my anger isn't rational. But no matter what you say, it's not going to change how I feel. Nor my decision."

Salvarias shifted to stare over the balcony. "You are most stubborn, Brother."

Wilhelm grunted, resting his arms on the railing next to Salvarias. "Runs in the family. Let's leave Cattlar, Salv. We can go to Serinity where it's safe. We've warned the Cavruls. We've given them every opportunity to prevent what's about to happen. I want us to settle down. I want us to have a little bit of peace and happiness."

Salvarias accepted the puzzle box Wilhelm offered. "Peace will be obtained for both of us, Brother. Your happiness will grant me mine." He paused his building of a bear to meet his brother's gaze. "You have cared for me past what I deserve. For eighteen years, your life has been placed on hold because of mine. I want you to marry her,

Brother. I want you to have a family. I want you to live in the Bellerum home and become a knight. Only once you have done these things will I be happy."

"What's this about, Salv?"

Salvarias rested his head on his brother's shoulder and stared at the puzzle box whirling to match the images in his mind. "I love you, Brother. More than you will ever know."

"Love you, too, Salv."

With that, his decision was made. The presence was right: alone, Wilhelm would finally have happiness. The last piece of his puzzle box clicked into place, and he held up his finished masterpiece of a bear.

"What is it?" Wilhelm asked.

"My brother."

47

The home was quiet and dark when Salvarias rose from bed. He retrieved his aspen branch and headed for the door until a tug on his robes stopped him. Steeling himself, he knelt and gave the wolf a hug.

"You must let my brother sleep. Keep Lady Lunara safe and look after my brother. You have been my dearest friend."

Rising quickly, he left his room and paused outside the door to collect himself. Fighting tears, he pushed Adok's presence from his mind, shivering instantly at the loneliness that transcended upon him. Taking a deep breath, he clung to the knowledge that his actions would bring peace to those he cared for.

Counting his steps down the dark hall, he turned after twenty-one to enter the sitting room. He continued counting toward the front door.

"Where are you going, boy?"

Salvarias whispered, "*Ecia Lumenious,*" as he turned to see Sir Humar sitting in a chair. "I have received a vision," he said.

"And what was it?" Sir Humar asked.

"I would prefer not—"

"Tell me. My patience for your secrecy is at an end."

Salvarias winced at the knight's harsh tone. At least with Salvarias's capture, Sir Humar would be free. Perhaps the knight might smile again. "It is no secret they have sought me. They have hunted me ever since I was rescued from Zeeas. The creatures do not harm me. They want me. Nothing more."

Sir Humar snorted. "You? That's it? They want a boy?"

"That is it," Salvarias confirmed. "I will hand myself over to the army this night and they will leave Arden in peace. I am the reason they attacked Serinity. Treppter. Klurp. The fault is mine. The blood of the dead is on my hands."

"And the slave mines? Taking women? What was their reason for that?"

Salvarias frowned. He had not thought of it. Shrugging, he said, "I assume because they did not have me then, either."

Humar studied him a moment. "So you're going to walk into their camp and they're going to turn around and march home? Just like that?"

"Yes. One life to save a world is a small price."

"You think they'll kill you?"

"Their god seeks my power: what I use to enchant, what I used that killed the girl in Xeroth. I assume my life will end by whatever means this god needs to claim my power for himself."

"You willingly walk to your death?"

"As I said, it is a small price to pay."

"And you're not afraid once this 'god' has your power, that he'll enslave us with it?"

"We are already well on our way to enslavement, Sir Humar. With my death, I either hope to satisfy this god or at the very least, give Lord Bellerum time to amass an army so as to be prepared for an attack."

"Wilhelm will be upset."

"My brother will eventually move past my death. He will marry Varila and live the rest of his life in peace and happiness. I could hope for nothing more."

"I could stop you. I could tell Wilhelm the instant you leave this house."

Salvarias suppressed his sardonic smile. "You welcome the opportunity to rid yourself of my company. Do not feel the need to offer false care, Sir Humar. It does not become you. You know as well as I that this is the right choice. The only one that can spare Arden."

"There was a time when I cared about you, boy. A part of you was worth something to me. I once saw great potential in you. But now ... I don't see those traits anymore."

Salvarias winced at the knife twisting in his heart. "I am a murderer. Do not feel guilt for turning your heart from me. I deserve none of your concern."

Sir Humar looked down at his hands. "Your actions are as honorable as those of a knight. It's ..." He inhaled a deep breath. "You're right. It's what I'd do. I'll pray for a painless end."

Salvarias bowed. "I wish you safety in your travels." He turned to leave and paused at the door. "You are a kind man. It has been an honor knowing you."

Salvarias ducked out of the home and closed the door. He inhaled a few deep breaths to ease the wounds Humar's words had carved into his heart. Salvarias needed no one.

The creaking pulley seemed to echo through all of Arden as it glided down the mountain. The Cavruls' leers merely fueled his need to end his misery. Life had never blessed him with complete bliss, but only granted him fleeting moments of joy with his brother: those times when they were alone, when no one judged him, when he did not judge himself, when Wilhelm's laugh would infect him, when he thought that his soul might have a chance to rid itself of evil. A foolish wish. Blind hope for the unattainable. He had been lying to himself since birth.

He sneered at his own denial. Even now, he could not admit he was lost. Even now, he clung to some speck of light within him. It was so dim though, hidden deep in his lake, concealed by the red haze of death.

Once at the bottom, he strode through the sleeping city. Few were out, and those who were seemed to change direction for an opportunity to spit on him. He made it to the rear of the city and a tunnel guarded by near a thousand men. None stopped him from leaving. "Good riddance" was murmured as many times as hissed accidents they hoped he would suffer in the caves. If he was cruel, he could merely cast a spell and collapse the tunnels. However, that would mean killing thousands of Cavruls to merely save his own life. He was unwilling to do so. Death was becoming more alluring to him.

The walk took a few hours, winding through tunnels, passing expansive caverns, fighting memories of whips and the beatings his brother had endured, gritting his teeth against the pain in his bad leg. He shivered violently, resisting the urge to ignite his magic to drive away the painful chill of its absence. His staff did little to counter the effects.

He was in a tunnel when he saw a dim light at the end. This was it. He was here. He took a moment to prepare himself. He thought he would be stronger, but the thought of dying erupted a need to live that had remained silent.

Closing his eyes, he conjured an image of his brother dressed in a fine outfit, standing by Varila in a dazzling gown. They would be married in the Bellerum gardens, no doubt. Salvarias imagined the sea, the trees, the sweet fragrance of jasmine. Standing by Varila would be Lunara. Her beaming smile would light the world. Sir Humar would laugh with Durak. Lord Bellerum and Lady Talura would shed happy tears. Okulu would pursue some wench. Perhaps Prince Neithelas would finally win Lunara's heart and give her all the happiness she deserved.

Wilhelm would be smiling. There might be residual pain in his eyes, but he would laugh. Salvarias imagined years later when his brother would hold a son. Wilhelm would be an exceptional father. With a child and wife, his brother would rarely think of him. Maybe more during spring when new life sprouting in the forest would remind Wilhelm of Salvarias's favorite time of year. Given a few years and additional children, Wilhelm would not have time to mourn the loss. He would laugh and be free.

Today, my murderer, you have earned my respect, the presence hissed.

Coming from his daydream, Salvarias ran his sleeve across his wet eyes and squared his shoulders. He strode down the tunnel to the light awaiting him.

48

Wilhelm woke with a start. The room was eerily silent, lacking the normal mutters from his brother. Groping around in the darkness, he crossed the room to Salvarias's bed. He lifted the blankets up, gently feeling for his brother. The bed was empty. Though Salvarias often snuck out, it didn't ease the burgeoning fear tightening his gut.

Then he heard it: the click of nails on the stone floor. The soft whine of Adok. Salvarias never left the wolf unless it was with Lunara.

Wilhelm darted across the pitch-black room, stubbing his toe, tripping over a table. He flung the door open and stepped into the corridor. A dim light glowed from the entrance to the sitting room. Shaking, he marched down the hall and into the room lit by a single candle. Humar sat in a chair, eyes looking as though he'd seen a ghost.

"Where is he?" Wilhelm asked.

"He had a vision," Humar said, gaze distant, his voice hoarse. "He's supposed to go to the army."

Air whooshed from Wilhelm's lungs, and his heart pumped a rush of blood that made him lightheaded. "You let him go?"

"It's the right thing to do. It's the only way to save Arden. He said his vision—"

Wilhelm grabbed the knight and yanked him up. "You let him go!" he boomed.

"I ... I ... His vision—"

Wilhelm punched him, barely using any strength, but it sent Humar reeling. "I don't give a damn about his vision! How could you let him go? How could you sit there and not tell me!"

The room filled up quickly as his friends rushed inside.

"What's happened?" Mafarias asked.

Wilhelm couldn't take his eyes from Humar. "Why can't you trust him? Why do you have to look at him with those hateful stares?"

"I've trusted the boy," Humar said, stumbling to his feet. His voice lacked the conviction of his words. "I've followed him here, listened to him. I've done what he said, what he's asked of me. Doesn't that show I trust him?"

"No! It proves you don't care about him! It proves you don't give a damn if he dies, if he's tortured. All you care about is making yourself feel good. Like you've done something to stop this evil. And what did he ever do to you? What did he ever do to any of you?" Wilhelm said, rounding on his friends. "All he's cared about is your safety, asking you to remain behind. I have to beg him every morning to let you come with us. Every day he knows something could happen to any of you. You people wanted to help us and now ..." Wilhelm's fear and anger spun his thoughts to a whirlwind when he turned to Humar. "Now you've sent him to his death, and I'll never forgive you if anything happens to him."

"That boy be evil, Wilhelm!" Durak roared. "It's time ye see it!"

"Who's the evil one?" Wilhelm growled. "How many mages did you kill? You're lucky I even allow you near him."

"Me had a reason, boy! He killed that little girl for nothing!" Durak howled.

Wilhelm gaped at the Cavrul. "Do you honestly think he meant to? Stop passing your judgment and seriously think about it. When has he ever hurt anyone? He would never do that intentionally!"

"What caused it?" Durak countered.

"I don't know, and I don't need to know! He's been tormenting himself to figure it out!"

Durak shook his head. "That boy be wrong!"

"Why? Because he doesn't laugh all the time or talk? Because he's different? Why is that such a bad thing? Why?" he demanded.

"It's not just that," Durak snapped. "His eyes scare everyone!"

"And that's his fault?" Disgusted, Wilhelm shoved the short man down. He trembled with absolute fury when he looked at the two men who'd taught him, who he'd grown up with, who'd molded him into manhood. Now, nothing but pure hatred stemmed from him when his gaze rested on Durak and Humar.

"I fear I've made a terrible mistake," Humar breathed. Tears brimmed in his eyes. "A terrible mistake. I-I'm a knight. I'm supposed to protect people ... gods help me, what have I done?"

"What do they want with him?" Edium said. "What did his vision convey?"

Humar stumbled until he collided with a wall. He sank to the ground and tears spilled over his cheeks. "His life for Arden."

Those words were a blow. The room spun. Wilhelm's legs gave out from under him, and he plopped down on the ground.

"What!" Edium yelled. "You let him walk to his death!"

"I ... I let him go," Humar said, his voice breaking to sobs. "I let him go." He looked across the room at Wilhelm. "Forgive me, boy."

Pain parted way to untamed anger. Wilhelm shoved himself up and marched to Humar. Yanking the knight to his feet, Wilhelm pounded on the man's face. Humar didn't even fight him. Anger clouded his vision, blinded him, consumed him. He hit anything stupid enough to step in front of him.

Only when he saw sea-blue eyes did he stop his next strike. His arm was coiled back, hand balled into a tight fist, Varila cringing before him. He glanced around to see all the men holding some part of their bloody faces.

"Are you done?" Varila said, arching an eyebrow.

She wasn't excused from his anger either. If it'd been her in the chair, she would've let him go too, probably even packed Salvarias a snack. "Get out of my way," he growled. He shoved her aside, snatched the candle, stormed to his room, and dressed in his armor. He knew she was in the doorway without looking.

"Humar was as right as he was wrong to let him go," she said.

"Go to Oblivion," Wilhelm muttered. He picked up his broadsword and strapped it over his back.

"Your brother doesn't talk to us. He doesn't even look at us. He keeps everything a secret. How are we supposed to feel about him?"

He wrapped the belt of his great sword around his waist and turned to face her as he tightened it. "The more you know, the more danger you're in. And why should he look at you? You recoil every time he does. Regardless of how you treat him, he cares for everyone, even you." He glanced at Adok. "Find him."

The wolf growled at Varila, making her leave the doorway. Wilhelm strode down the hall, past the sitting room filled with men groaning, still sprawled on the floor. Shame simmered when he saw his uncle passed out, blood running down the side of his face. Wilhelm didn't remember hitting Mafarias. And he doubted his uncle would have let Salvarias leave.

He paused in front of Lunara.

"He's blocked me," she said, her voice breaking. "I can't talk to him."

Wilhelm nodded and left the home. The Cavruls were at the top as always. He stepped inside the pulley after Adok and closed the door. Varila reached to open it, but Wilhelm held it shut.

"Let the men recover," she said. "We'll all go with you."

"You know what he said to me tonight? He said I should marry you. He said you were one of the most amazing women he's ever met." Wilhelm shook his head and motioned the Cavrul to pull the lever before turning to Varila. "I agree with him. You are. And I hate myself for loving you."

The pulley lurched into its hasty descent, fading her tear-streaked face from his vision.

Salvarias walked down the path the creatures had made for him. They hissed and spat, a few jeered, but he kept his eyes straight. There was a man at the end. Vescar, he was certain. Salvarias repeated that his choice was the selfless one, the right one, the one to bring peace to Arden, but with each step, Humar's words flourished a dreadful sense of wrong within him to the point he slowed his walk.

Why, if all they sought was his power, had they not taken it in Zeeas? Why, if all they wanted was him, had they sent raiding parties to take women and men while he was held captive in Zeeas? Why had they massed an army to attack Serinity when he was not even there until his vision?

His thoughts cut off sharply. It was a trick. This vision never did feel right, nor the vision of Cattlar covered in blood. Now that he thought back, the little girl seemed forced into the scene. They had discovered how he obtained his visions. They were luring him into a trap.

He nearly succumbed to insanity over his own stupidity. It was so clear. He slowed his pace further and surveyed the army. They were ready for an attack. The creatures and armored soldiers were up and equipped. Obviously, he could not defeat them all. He frowned at the thought. This was not the entire army. This was not even half of what he saw camped by the lake. His gut knotted. They had divided forces, just as Lord Bellerum had feared. They would attack the outer and inner city. Cattlar was doomed. Arden was doomed.

His sole option was to kill the commander. Maybe that would delay the attack. It was a desperate act, but it was time for desperation. He increased his pace and slid his hands in the sleeves of his robe, clutching the hilt of his dagger.

"How do you like my army?" Vescar called, spreading his arms wide.

"It is impressive," Salvarias said, stopping out of Vescar's reach.

"You're a hard one to find, boy."

"Yet here I am. Though I suppose you knew I would come."

"Ah, I was wondering why you slowed. Just hit you, huh? I guess you are as smart as they say."

Salvarias smirked. "If I was, I would not have been dull enough to fall for this ploy."

"You must admit, it was artfully played."

Salvarias tilted his head. "I admit so. How did you discover the means of my visions?"

"You told Dethal too much outside the desert. Your link—" the man looked over his shoulder into the shadows and nodded. "Never mind. I tend to ramble."

"I enjoy listening to the ramblings of my foe. Please continue."

Vescar laughed. "I think I'd rather keep my life."

"Who hides in the shadow?"

"The creature taking you to the stronghold."

"Stronghold?"

"Where God awaits—" Vescar grunted and stumbled a step.

"Show yourself," Salvarias said.

"He's shy," Vescar said.

From the depths of the shadows, a voice sounding as if two smooth hunks of wood rubbed together said, "You've realized you're doomed yet you try nothing."

Salvarias shrugged. "I have no means to save myself."

"You're planning something," the voice said. "I smell it on you."

"Come forward and see if you are correct."

A hulking cloaked figure stepped into view, as massive as Wilhelm, perhaps broader. Something slithered beneath its cloak as if alive.

"Lower your hood," Salvarias said.

"Show me your mark and lower yours," the creature countered.

Salvarias held up his left hand and pushed his hood down with his right. "Your turn." He folded his arms in his sleeves, wrapping his hand around the hilt of his dagger, readying himself.

The figure reached up and skeleton hands lowered its hood. Salvarias had seen nightmarish pictures of the Four, had read about them in books with his brother, yet staring at one now made those horrible depictions seem like a children's story.

His speck of hope, the faint dim light flickered out. "Marro."

"It is I. You see your defeat."

Salvarias had no time to understand how the Four could be resurrected. All his readings had stated they had died. Trying to push away his river of questions, he glanced at Vescar. He could kill him, but Marro could lead the army. Then again, it was Marro who would take him to God. So who would lead?

Pooling his courage, he yanked his dagger free and flicked it at Vescar. Marro was expecting him to act. The creature shoved Vescar clear, taking the dagger in the commander's place. Twisting bones devoured the blade as if it were a meal. The creature's laugh chilled Salvarias.

Desperate, Salvarias ignited his magic, stumbling back as Marro advanced. He quickly drew in the energy and raised his hand to trace the rune right as Marro wrapped its boney fingers around Salvarias's neck, constricting his breathing and lifting him off the ground until eye level. Pins stabbed his eyes. Without an outlet, his magic lost its grip on the energy. Salvarias cried out when it tore through his pores, leaving behind a puff of bloody steam lingering in the air around him.

"Is it painful, boy?" Marro whispered. "I've heard it is. Surely, a boy as intelligent as yourself knows the Four cannot be harmed by magic. Nor your pathetic enchanted weapons."

Salvarias's vision faded, his feet twitched, and his head swam with dizziness. He clawed at the bones squeezing closed his throat, gasping for air that never came.

"Don't fight it," Marro said. "Accept the darkness."

Salvarias had no choice but to obey.

49

W ilhelm hid behind a slippery stalagmite, musing that the dull pink light of the hylim seemed unusually bright as he tucked himself in as much shadow as possible. He watched the army of soldiers and creatures march past, their droning steps echoing painfully in the cavern. His brother was nowhere in their masses. The right thing to do would be to return and warn Cattlar, but he had no intention of doing so. As always, his brother's life was more important to Wilhelm than the world.

Waiting was agony. Each breath was one step farther from his brother. When the last solider finally disappeared from the cavern, Adok bolted and Wilhelm sprinted after him.

The hours of running eventually added a sharp, cold pain to each gasped breath, and his legs were wobbly with fatigue. He refused to acknowledge his suffering. He'd promised himself never to lose Salvarias again. And he never broke a promise.

At long last, Adok slowed and raised his hackles, baring his white fangs. Wilhelm inhaled a soothing breath, calmed his pounding heart, and listened. It was faint, but off in the distance he heard a clicking noise, like Adok's nails on stone. Easing into a silent jog, he took up chase.

Entering a cavern, he saw a cloaked figure larger than himself following two armored soldiers. One of the soldiers had Salvarias's limp form slung over a shoulder. His brother's hands and fingers were bound, and he was gagged.

"Give him back," Wilhelm ordered.

The figure stopped and turned. Its face was concealed in the shadows of its hood. "Ah, the Protector; the pebble in our shoe. Have you not lost hope yet, boy? Do you think you can keep the Guardian safe?"

"Guardian?"

"Now we have him, and I'll not fail my master. The Guardian is yours no longer."

Wilhelm didn't like the sound of its voice. It definitely wasn't human. The creature passed a torch to one of the armored men.

"Do you know who I am, Protector?" the creature asked.

"It doesn't matter. I'm going to kill you regardless of your name or whatever kind of creature you are." He drew his broadsword, savoring the hiss it made as it raked the leather sheath.

"I am ... Marro," it said, tossing back its hood.

Surprisingly, no fear rose at its dramatically played announcement. Instead, a grin sliced across Wilhelm's face. "The supposedly unbeatable creatures of Veedran. I'd like to test that theory myself."

A laugh sounding like bones smacking together came from the beast. "You've no fear. I can sense only your excitement. You truly think to best me with a sword? To test which one of us survives? It will be me, Protector."

"I've always been fond of a sword and a good brawl. Come on, boney," he said, waving the creature forward with his sword. "Let's see who's better."

Marro reached underneath its cloak and pulled free a curved sword with a jagged blade. "Why have your powers not ignited?" it asked. "You face doom. You face the capture of the Guardian. Yet nothing surges forth to aid you."

Wilhelm shrugged, circling with Marro, watching how the creature planted its feet, how it held its sword, where its glowing red eyes focused.

"No mortal can defeat me, boy. I suggest you find your power quickly."

"I suggest we stop the chit-chat." With that, Wilhelm darted forward. It was not a strike attempt, merely a way to learn how his opponent blocked, which foot it favored, how it flipped its sword to meet his. The creature was skilled. A fair match. Wilhelm's grin broadened. *Finally.*

Assessing his opponent with a breath of thought, he concluded he'd need both swords, even though he hadn't perfected his fighting. He yanked his great sword from his scabbard and lunged, feigning one way with his broadsword to distract Marro's eye from his great sword heading straight for the creature's side. Marro wasn't expecting it. Wilhelm's sword struck what felt like rock, sending a throbbing vibration up his arm and a dull ring to echo in the cave. Still, he managed the smallest nick on what looked like a femur.

Marro hissed and pranced back as the wounded bone slid inside the creature. Despite its mass, it moved like a cat. "Well played, Protector." A childlike skeleton finger slid between two bones acting as a mouth, as if it was already savoring victory. It was arrogant. The eagerness warned Wilhelm of the next strike. Leaning back, he ducked below Marro's whipping sword. Curving his body around, he came up with both swords, ramming them into the side of Marro. Sparks flew off bones and steel.

The creature roared, freeing pebbles from the ceiling, and deafening Wilhelm. His loss of hearing teetered him back. He flicked up his sword at the last instant to block Marro's strike.

Taking advantage of Wilhelm's disorientation, Marro jabbed its elbow in his face. Warm blood spurted from his nose and his vision blurred from tears. He stumbled, blinded by the stunning blow. Going simply off instinct, he raised his broadsword. They collided, sending a jarring pain down his left side. His vision returning, Wilhelm went on the offense, bombarding Marro with a series of movements Humar had recently taught him. It put the creature on the defense, but not for long. It picked up his pattern and countered accordingly. One parry brought them face to face, swords locked.

"I admit, I wasn't prepared," Marro said. It shoved off to put distance between them. "We've underestimated you."

Wilhelm cocked his head as if it would help him hear. "Yet your master keeps trying the same old routine." His voice sounded odd in his head, like he spoke through a pillow. "He's not learning from his mistakes. I'm not losing my brother again."

"Think about it, Protector. Your sword cannot penetrate my bones. Your strength is insufficient. This will end with your death. I give you the chance to leave now. Go and live a peaceful life."

Wilhelm spat blood from his mouth. "Only an opponent who knows he's outmatched would make such an offer." He raked his sword along Marro's, sending off a shower of sparks. "Or a coward."

With a roar, Marro lunged. The creature misread Wilhelm's parry. Instead of dodging, he angled to the side to avoid the jagged sword and drove his swords in like spears. His blades sank past bone, but not far enough before additional bones circled to protect its chest, dead center. Wilhelm knew where to strike. The problem was he lacked the strength to penetrate the layers of bones. As much as he hated admitting it, he needed the power, the one that lived somewhere deep within him, the one that had ignited and helped him kill the troll. No matter how much he begged it to surge forward, it wouldn't come.

Marro's counter-advance put Wilhelm on the defense, barely stopping lethal blows. His hearing returned to a deafening clash of steel that reverberated in the cavern. The creature had the slightest advantage of speed. Wilhelm couldn't protect himself from all the strikes in the flurry of the creature's offense. Marro's sword cleaved into Wilhelm's thigh, ripping away a chunk of flesh. He staggered back, blinking away the darkness crowding his vision. He looked down to see over a dozen scores bleeding freely, and his meaty flesh was exposed on his thigh.

Salvarias stirred, moaning and weakly struggling. Marro hissed a curse and backed a few steps from Wilhelm. "Take him to the portal!" it commanded.

Salvarias's glazed over eyes focused on Wilhelm. His brother's brow furrowed when he glanced around.

"Come on, Salv," Wilhelm breathed. "Remember."

Salvarias looked at him and then to Marro. His eyes widened and brightened with alertness. In one quick buck, he tumbled to the ground, free of his captor.

"Run!" Wilhelm roared. He charged Marro in hopes of offering a distraction. His leg nearly gave out, but he pushed through the pain.

"Your souls should he escape!" Marro shouted to the soldiers. "Get him to the damn portal at all costs!"

Adok grabbed the leg of one soldier, growling viciously as Salvarias tried to gain his footing. The soldier dealt one quick kick and the wolf yelped and skidded across the floor. He seemed stunned.

Salvarias scrambled to his feet, wrenching his hands against his binding, hobbling from the soldiers.

Wilhelm tackled Marro and pinned it just long enough to steal a glance at his brother. A black-armored soldier backhanded Salvarias, crumpling him to the ground. Before his brother even tried to rise, the soldier kicked him in the temple. Salvarias went limp. Blood trickled down his forehead.

Warmth exploded in Wilhelm, rippling a shudder down him, invigorating his mind, calling forth his anger. It wasn't the subtle build that had happened in the arena. This time, it burst alive with such intensity that a cry of pain tore from his throat. His blood boiled in his veins, his muscles bulged against his skin, and stabs of pain shot up and down his body.

"No," Marro hissed.

Wilhelm was incapacitated. He couldn't move, couldn't breathe. It gave Marro a chance to escape from Wilhelm's hold and stumble to its feet. As fast as it came, the pain vanished. Only anger was left.

A red veil cascaded down Wilhelm's vision. All fear and doubt drained from him, replaced by a desperate need to kill the creature looming in front of him, to protect his brother, to slaughter anything that threatened his treasure. A bloodthirsty grin slid in place of his normal one.

Wilhelm was on his feet before Marro's stance had stabilized. With a cry of rage, he charged, swinging both swords in a dance of alternating directions. Marro was thrown on the defense. Strike after strike, the creature's eyes widened. Spinning, Wilhelm feigned a beheading strike. When Marro ducked and sprang back, Wilhelm used the creature's own tactic against it. With the pommel of his great sword, he rammed it into Marro's eye.

The creature reeled, shrieking. Its defense faltered. Its sword lowered. Wilhelm grabbed the thickest bone around its neck and yanked it forward while at the same time he guided all his burgeoning power into his right arm. He rammed his sword straight into the center of Marro's chest. Hard bone cracked aside and gave way to a mushy center. His great sword appeared out of the creature's back.

"Now we know who's better," Wilhelm said, yanking his sword free.

Marro staggered, clutching its bones to its chest as they started falling away from its form. The stench of decay wafted from the creature, and a thick red acid oozed out of its center. The creature tossed its head back in a silent cry, and then disintegrated into a heap of lifeless, stark bones.

With the threat gone, the warming power imploded, leaving Wilhelm trembling, weak, and wincing at the slices he'd taken.

His gaze swept the cavern to find it empty. Taking a step made a wave of dizziness tip the cave. He plopped down on the ground, begging his surroundings to stabilize.

Among the bones piled next to him, the blade of his brother's dagger gleamed. Smiling, Wilhelm picked it up. "Nicely done, little brother." At least Salvarias had gone down fighting.

Adok whined urgently. Wilhelm closed his eyes and inhaled a deep breath. He brought to mind his brother's tortured body, the fear that flickered in his brother's eyes so often, and the absolute trust Salvarias placed in Wilhelm. He'd not lose his brother again.

Shoving himself to his feet, he stumbled forward, following Adok who blurred in and out.

50

E dium wiped blue-green octril blood from his eyes and squinted at the battle. They were barely holding the inner city. The fighting waged in all three tunnels, and it was merely a matter of time before the battle for both the outer and inner city was lost. They might've had a chance if the black-armored soldiers succumbed to mortal wounds. Cutting through their armor was like slicing a sweet cake, yet they fought on as if the hole gouged in their chest meant nothing. Even more disturbing, within that dark cavern of armor, Edium saw no flesh or blood. He had a sinking feeling they were not men, but some new heinous creation conjured by whoever sought to rule Arden. Humar had spread word quickly on how to kill them, but few were as precise as the knight, and getting a weapon in the tiny eye slit on their helmets was near impossible.

"It's no use!" Humar roared over the clanging of swords and screams of the dying. "We have to collapse the tunnels."

"Me brothers are in there!" Muddil shouted.

Mafarias wiped sweat from his forehead and shook his head. "Humar is right. We can't hold them off. If we collapse the tunnels, we can help close the outer gate. All we can do is wait for Edium's army."

"No!" Durak shouted. "Me not slaughter our people! If ye collapse 'em, we be trapped in here! Don't ye see? There only be one way out!"

Edium dragged Humar and Mafarias far from the foray. "How many Cavruls are in the tunnels?"

Humar yanked off his helmet and wiped sweat from his brow. "Perhaps a few thousand. The armored soldiers are slicing their way through more and more. Before long, all of Cattlar will be in there trying to hold them off."

"The creatures are not dying of mortal wounds," Edium said. "Perhaps fire?"

"I could try," Mafarias said. "But any in the path of the fire will be burned alive."

"Is there no way to cast a protection shield over the Cavruls and get them to safety?" Humar asked Mafarias.

The mage looked doubtful. "I might save a few. But I can't make a protection spell large enough and do so for all three tunnels."

"Salvarias did," Okulu said from behind. "He had one over the entire city of Quind."

Mafarias snorted. "And I've made it clear the boy is powerful. I, unlike my nephew, am unwilling to risk my sanity. I can get half out, perhaps."

"Afterward, you'll need to collapse the tunnels," Edium said. "I know Durak's worried about being trapped, but he's not thinking clearly. We can't fight two fronts."

Mafarias rubbed his smooth cheek, gazing at the fighting. "The spells will need to be extremely powerful. I can't close off the tunnels entirely, mind you. Too tall, and I don't have a Cavrul's mind for engineering. I could collapse the mountain on us. But I can make it so the army can only cross over a few at a time. We can kill them as they fall over the barricade." Mafarias shook his head. "If I do all you're asking, I'll be a heap of flesh. I'll not be able to assist anymore."

"We're used to Salvarias pushing himself," Humar said grimly. "As well as the blood. We'll prot—"

"Blood?" Mafarias asked, looking sharply at Humar. "What blood?"

"When the boy casts spells and extends himself, blood comes from his nose, ears, and mouth," Humar said. "Is that not—"

Mafarias sputtered out a few curses. "Damn him. The boy refused my instruction and now look!"

"What?" Edium asked.

"This isn't the time," Mafarias grumbled.

Edium's blood pounded in his ears. "Tell me!"

"There are long term effects," Mafarias snapped. "Pushing himself as he does might not kill him now, but it shaves years off his life and weakens his mind. He'll be a senile man before he sees his fortieth Birth Day. I never thought he'd test boundaries." Mafarias shook his head and seemed to say the next words to himself. "His mind is so fragile. Once this is over, that boy and I are having a long talk. There are rules that must be followed. Many rules."

Edium glared at Humar. "Did you know the risks?"

"Of course not," Humar said. "I wouldn't have let the boy do it if I knew."

"Oh, I forgot how important the boy's life is to you," Edium retorted sarcastically. "Sending him to his death is just your way of showing you care, isn't it?"

"Another time, friends," Okulu said. "In case you forgot, there's a war going on here."

"Get Durak," Mafarias said. "Muddil, too. Haul them forcefully if you must. Where are the Winsire brothers?"

"Up there," Edium said, pointing to a low balcony the two occupied. Arrows were released in a steady stream. The two princes would be out before they made a difference.

Mafarias nodded. "You're sure? Durak will hate you for killing so many."

Humar stared at the fighting. "It'll be a massacre if I don't. No one will survive."

Edium rested a hand on Humar's shoulder. "It's the right decision."

"Let's get this over with," Okulu said.

Edium sheathed his sword and bolted into the fighting, Humar and Okulu on his heels. Okulu easily restrained Muddil and dragged him back. Durak, however, fought like a cat trying to escape a basin of water. Axe and fists flew in a flurry of desperate attempts to block Edium's hands. Humar, braver than Edium, grabbed Durak's beard. The Cavrul howled like a crazed boar. Taking advantage of Durak's distraction, Edium knocked the Cavrul senseless and helped haul him from the fight.

Mafarias met them at the back of the battle clear of the tunnels.

The mage inhaled a deep breath and pushed up the sleeves of his robes. "A protection spell, fire, and lightning." He looked at Humar. "You'll owe me one."

Okulu laughed. "And he always collects."

Edium glanced at the innocent Cavruls. He swallowed hard and looked away when a white film rushed through the tunnel and blanketed over a chunk of the Cavruls as well as their enemies. He stared at the top of the city and found Muddil's home. His family was there along with all the children they'd rounded up before the bulk of the fighting had started. At least now, they'd be safe. Thousands to save three. It was a price he'd pay again and again. And he felt no shame in it.

SALVARIAS WRITHED IN HIS CAPTORS' grasp as they dragged him through tunnels and caverns. The soldiers moved too lightly for men in full armor, and the stench of death clung to them, an unnatural feel to their presence. As curious as he was, so was he as desperate to free himself to help his brother. The Four could not be defeated, and Salvarias would rather suffer a thousand tortures at the hands of Sansis than be absent from his brother's side to face death together.

A steady drumming of feet echoed in the cavern. Salvarias ceased his fight and craned his neck to look over his shoulder. It was impossible. He knew it, yet he distinctly heard the heavier planting of one foot.

His brother burst into the cavern, face twisted in rage, covered in blood. Salvarias heart skipped when he saw the chunk of flesh missing from Wilhelm's thigh and the sheer number of scores that bled all over. Wilhelm should have been too weak to walk.

His brother's roar of anger startled Salvarias's captors. They dropped him and wrenched their swords free in time to stop Wilhelm's charging strike. Salvarias yanked on the shackles around his wrists, straining his fingers against the thin ropes binding them. If he could just free his hands, he would be able to help his brother.

Wilhelm, after only a few parries, planted a sword in each of the soldiers' chests. Salvarias's breath caught in his throat when the soldiers advanced without seeming to notice their mortal wounds. No blood flowed from the hole.

Wilhelm cursed and stumbled back, switching to a defensive stance. "Suggestions?" he called to Salvarias.

Salvarias scrambled to the nearest stalagmite and frantically rubbed his fingers against the rough stone in an attempt to break the rope. Jagged edges shaved skin from his fingers, moistening the thread, but still it held. He glanced at his brother. Wilhelm was barely holding them off. Adok was grabbing at ankles and using his body to help keep the soldiers off balance.

Then Salvarias felt it. A power burst alive in Wilhelm. It was ... enormous, frightening. His brother gasped, staggering backward a few steps, grimacing as if someone had stuck him. It lasted a mere breath, and when whatever he endured passed, his usual innocent grin switched to be more animal-like, vicious and hungry for death. His eyes turned from open and inviting to amber coals of fury.

Wilhelm's movements blurred, his swords whirling so fast that only the torchlight glinting off steel kept them visible. The soldiers were a pincushion for Wilhelm's blades, yet they fought on.

Either out of luck or a desperate idea skillfully executed, Wilhelm's sword slid through the eye slit in one soldier's helmet. Its far-off-sounding screech chilled Salvarias's bones. The soldier spun around, clawing at its face as red acid dripped from the hole in its helmet.

Wilhelm's grin made Salvarias huddle closer to the stone.

His brother slipped his sword into the last soldier's helmet. As the creature fell, Wilhelm jabbed his blade in its chest. "Sick bastards," Wilhelm hissed. "Leave my brother alone!" He stabbed the soldier three times before he ceased his butchery. When he staggered upright, he shivered slightly, and Salvarias felt his brother's power ebb.

Wilhelm knelt beside Salvarias, patting him down for wounds. "Are you all right?" Wilhelm asked.

Salvarias swallowed hard. "What ... what happened to you?"

Wilhelm chuckled. "I'm sure I looked like some wild beast. I kind of get angry when I see you hurt." Wilhelm's smile faded. "Speaking of, what in Oblivion were you thinking?"

Still stunned from what happened to Wilhelm, Salvarias stammered out a reply. "I ... I fell into a trap. I thought I could make the army leave. Forgive me, Brother. I was foolish."

"Stop apologizing for stuff, Salv. Everyone makes mistakes." Wilhelm looked behind him at the heaps of metal. "Any ideas?"

Salvarias ignited his magic. *I sense a power within the metal.*

Please, my wizard. Can we talk?

Not now. I need to know what you sense.

Yes, my wizard. It is enchanted.

Yet no mage can enchant?

The power is very similar to me, as are all enchanted items except yours. Yours are different. But I assure you, no mage can enchant. Something else is at work here.

Salvarias shoved his magic into its dark corner. "I am unsure, Brother."

Wilhelm grunted. "Damn hard to kill." He went to work on the ropes binding Salvarias's fingers. His brother's brow furrowed in annoyance the longer he fumbled with the intricate knots. Salvarias grinned. "Knock it off, Salv. It's not my fault my fingers are stubby. You're lucky to have the dexterity you do. Wish I had it."

"My entire life I have wished for hands that were like other men."

Wilhelm snorted. "Why would you want that? Look what good it does." He uttered a few audible curses.

"Use your dagger."

Wilhelm shook his head. "The blade's too big. I could cut you."

"I am beginning to lose feeling, Brother. A small cut is much more appealing than having my fingers fall off."

"I guess you're right." Wilhelm reached into his boot and withdrew their mother's dagger. "Do you know how to get back to the city from here? I've passed through too many tunnels and caves to remember."

"No, I was not conscious after I found the army. It does not matter. Somewhere is a portal we must find and guard until Uncle arrives. I have no knowledge of them or how to collapse one, but we cannot allow any more of this 'god's' army to travel here." Salvarias turned to Adok and requested he find Mafarias. Adok licked his hand before loping off.

"The army was marching on Cattlar. I ..." Wilhelm frowned. "I'd be surprised if anyone survived."

"I felt Uncle cast several spells. I assume they collapsed the inner tunnels. If so, they could pull back and close the outer gate, or inner if the outer city has been lost. Uncle might have just saved Cattlar. Even if he has not, I have a feeling our uncle is very opposed to death. I am sure he would find a way to escape the city, and he would take the Bellerum family with him."

"Good. We'll wait here for him. Now, hold perfectly still." With achingly slow sawing, Wilhelm cut through the first rope. He grinned. "Managed not to cut you."

Salvarias chuckled. "Unfortunately, at your pace, the lands of Arden will be lost by the time you finish."

"I'm not rushing," Wilhelm said. "Those stubborn-ass Cavruls had plenty of warning. I don't care about anyone in that damn city."

Salvarias slouched against the rock and cast his brother a stern stare. "What did you do to Sir Humar? What did you say to Lady Varila, brother?"

Wilhelm shrugged. "Nothing undeserved."

"You cannot punish others for my choices."

Wilhelm remained quiet, intent on the next rope. Salvarias rested his arms on knees and sank his face between his elbows. It was obviously going to take a while. He wiggled his finger. Two down, seven to go.

He twitched when a sting sliced across his hand. He looked up to see his brother's apologetic eyes locked on him. Blood fell from Wilhelm's lips. Salvarias's gaze slid down the sword protruding from his brother's stomach. The blade yanked up, cracking through bone and tearing through flesh, spilling his brother's insides to a puddle at Salvarias's feet. Hot blood sprayed across his face.

"Mar ..." Wilhelm sputtered.

His brother toppled over. The once bright amber eyes dulled of life. Standing behind his brother's corpse were twenty black-armored soldiers.

Horrible grief robbed Salvarias of thought, sending him floating in a world of denial. His body did not acknowledge hot blood dripping down his face. His vision blocked out the dull amber eyes. His hearing refused the last exhale of breath.

No, my murderer. Awake to what you have done.

Merciless reality crashed down upon him. The agony of what he had just lost pierced through him like a thousand daggers. As his heart was about to shatter, the ugly beast of his fury burst forth. Rage seeped out of him, drenching the ground with his anger. He was blinded by it, consumed by it, aflame with it.

He wanted the army dead. Grabbing his head in his hands, he doubled over on his knees and roared out his wish.

His cry seemed to last eternity. When his hoarse voice faded, his anger ebbed with the last of it, leaving him naked in his sorrow and pain.

Slowly, he opened his eyes and looked at his brother. No smile flashed at Salvarias. No rumbling laugh echoed in the cavern. No massive hand mussed his hair. No sparkle lit the amber eyes. No arms circled him to shield him from his pain.

He had nothing.

You killed him, my precious little murderer. You killed your brother.

Salvarias's world crashed around him.

51

E dium sprinted behind Humar toward the outer city gate with what was left of the Cattlar army on his heels. For now, the inner city was within their control, allowing Edium to focus on his next goal of securing the outer city. Afterward, he would force Durak awake and, by sword point if necessary, search the caves for Edium's son.

When he barreled past the last merchant shop, his sprint slammed to a halt. The fighting had managed its way inside the city. The once grand entrance was strewn with bodies and trickles of blood ran around Edium's boots.

"No," Humar breathed.

Doomed. They were all doomed. Even with the army at Edium's back, his forces weren't enough to push the armored soldiers from the city.

"We must retreat," Arthias said.

"We can't," Muddil growled. "The inner gate be broken since the Battle of the Hidlu. She takes too long to close. We'd never get it shut before those foul creatures cut us down."

Humar snarled at the enemy. "Then we take as many as we can."

The knight surged forward, yelling a war cry that carried a tone of a man seeking retribution before his death. The Cavrul army followed, their shouts echoing in the once-glorious cavern.

Muddil held a young Cavrul back. "Send word to close the inner gate. We'll do our best to hold them here until it shuts. Warn the other clan leaders to be prepared for another attack."

"But ye be dead before it closes."

"Do as I say!"

The Cavrul bowed and ran back toward the inner city.

Okulu grinned. "I knew I'd die young, handsome, and single. I'm not sure the ladies will ever recover. Shall we?" With a wink, the merc sprinted after Humar.

Edium glanced back and sent a silent plea for forgiveness to his wife and daughters. Inhaling deeply, he ran behind Okulu.

Just as Edium reached his first opponent, the last of the Cavruls' outer army fell to the sword of a man armored in black, leaving only the inner Cavrul army alive. Between parries and dodges, Edium stole another look. Though the man wore black armor, it was clearly a human and not some cast of empty metal. His black hair was soaked in sweat, and blood covered his face. It must be the commander.

Edium kicked an octril back to give himself time to find Humar. The knight was close to the commander. "Humar!" Edium roared.

Humar slid his sword in the slit of his foe's helmet and glanced at Edium.

"There," Edium called, pointing to the commander.

Humar barked something to Okulu. The merc and Humar went into a fighting pattern that mirrored one another, slicing through soldiers, not attempting to kill but merely create a path. The sheer movements of the two men, fighting as if they were one, briefly froze Edium.

He turned his attention back to an octril who made a clumsy thrust. He knocked the creature's sword aside and arced his blade up the octril's stomach. The creature tumbled to the ground in a pile of its own innards.

Humar had broken ahead of Okulu and shouldered by the last soldier in front of the commander.

"You!" the commander roared. "You!"

Humar's grim frown switched to wide-eyed recognition then melted to a face red with rage. The two engaged each other. Humar's movements replicated those of the commander. Their lunges, thrusts, parries, and jabs were of the same training.

Edium quickly backed out of the fight, making his way behind the ranks toward Humar. "Okulu! Help him!"

Okulu spared a glance, but the merc was barely holding his own. Neithelas's arrows were all that kept Okulu alive. Edium pushed through the crowd of Cavruls.

"This fight could last for years!" the commander said. "I bested you before, I'll do it again!"

Humar snarled and narrowly made it clear of a tight jab. "You didn't finish your training, Vescar. Allow me to offer you an education."

Humar's fighting switched to a series of tight thrusts and quick jabs Edium had never seen before. The knight's sword whipped so fast, its direction was nothing but a blur. It only took two breaths before Vescar's head sailed through the air.

The fighting stopped. The army stumbled backward, their heads turning from the corpse of their commander to the army of Cavruls in front of them. Still backing up, they trampled over their own who didn't move quickly enough, and the clang of metal crashing into metal rang in the cavern. The Cavruls retreated as well, dragging the bodies of their half-alive comrades with them, and formed up new lines. A wide gap separated the two armies.

Edium's hope bloomed. Without the commander, the army seemed at a loss on how to proceed.

The enemy was at the gate when one black-armored soldier raised its sword and shouted, "Wait!" The voice sounded far away, yet all around them, echoing as if it spoke into a copper kettle.

"Leave," Humar barked, sword dripping the blood of the

commander, "and we will let you live. Retreat, and tell your master we will not be defeated!"

The soldier who had raised its sword paused and turned to the creatures behind it. "For our souls!"

The roar was deafening as well as their pounding feet as they rushed toward Humar. The knight stood tall, slowly raising his sword, feet set in their fighting stance. Edium desperately swept the cavern for some means of salvation.

"Nevlar help us!" Arthias cried, pointing beyond the army and yawning gate.

From outside the city, a tidalwave of black fire charged toward them. Cries rose from Cavruls as they spun and fled for the inner city, leaving the black-armored soldiers to their own fate.

Okulu broke out in a hearty laugh.

Humar grinned and waved his sword toward the entrance. "Behind you!" he boomed.

The soldiers whirled around. The flames reached the first creature and its scream was nothing short of horrific. It stole Edium's warmth and paralyzed him.

"It might be our death, but at least it's by Salvarias," Okulu said, standing boldly in front of the wall of fire.

Edium had no place to go. The fire's pace picked up, washing over the enemy and boiling everything in its path. From the slit in the black-armored soldiers' helmets, a red pudding-like substance exploded like a volcano.

Humar straightened himself, his face grim, but accepting. Edium closed his eyes and thought of his family burning alive, screaming in agony. He wasn't sure this was better than a death by sword.

Intense heat bathed him, scalding his lungs, singeing his hair. He gasped and braved a look. The flames licked over his skin, sizzling the hair on his arms, yet he didn't catch fire. He looked at the enemy army, now nothing more than a heap of metal and boiled lumps of octril flesh.

Okulu laughed hysterically, rubbing his arms. Humar merely stood still, trembling violently. Edium looked behind him, but the fire had not spread to the fleeing Cavrul army. No one else was aflame.

"How is this possible?" Edium breathed.

Arthias batted at the flames, stumbling backward, panic in his eyes. Neithelas grabbed his brother and held him. "It's the mage. I've seen it before," Neithelas said. "We are pure in heart. Zerana's grace protects us from that abomination of evil."

Edium glanced between the brothers and the pile of armor. He wasn't so quick to side with Neithelas. Evil didn't fight evil.

Then, as quickly as the black fire came, it sucked back from the cave, leaving billowing smoke and the stench of death and singed hair.

UNUPTURE FLED from the portal as black fire burst from it.

"Close it!" Devoar screeched.

Dethal tripped backward, muttering under his breath. Any soldier near or passing through the portal flailed about, consumed in flames, red acid spurting from their helmets.

"Faster!" Devoar belted.

The portal collapsed and the flames flickered out.

"Dammit!" God roared. "You've failed me!"

Devoar turned a dead stare to God. "I've not failed you, Master. I told you our chance for success was slim. If you quit your ranting, you'll sense a shift. The Soul is leaving the light. Arden will bathe in blood."

Unupture closed his eyes, feeling the air thicken and the freshness of life ebbing. The candleflame danced as if caught in a vicious storm. White mage light flickered out.

God cackled when the last spitting torch sighed out of existence.

"YOU PROMISED ME," Salvarias wept. "You promised." He picked up the last pile of his brother's insides and shoved them into the gaping hole in Wilhelm's chest. "You cannot leave me! You promised!" He shook his brother's shoulder. "Wake up!"

Wilhelm's head swung side to side, lifeless eyes staring at nothing.

I told you this day would come, my murderer. I said you would kill him. Look. Look at your hands. His blood is on your hands.

Salvarias raised his hands. Blood and gore dripped down his fingers, staining his robes. "No!" he cried.

You killed him. Murderer.

"Brother!" Salvarias shouted, shoving Wilhelm. "Wake up! I am scared! Please, wake up!"

There's no one left to save you. There's no one left to protect you. There's no one left who loves you. You are alone. It is time to accept what you are. It is time you faced what you've done. Tell me, my little murderer, confess to me what you've done?

Salvarias scanned the cave for help. Where was Lady Talura? Lord Bellerum? Humar? Durak? Varila or Okulu? Hugging himself, he shouted, "Lunara!"

No one came to help him. He was alone.

That is right, my murderer. You are alone.

Salvarias crumbled next to his brother. His mind began to shut down, denying what his eyes saw. Wilhelm had promised. He had promised. He would come back. Salvarias just had to wait. His brother would not leave him.

Salvarias wedged himself under Wilhelm's arm, curled up, and slipped his hand under his brother's as he had done when they were little. Wilhelm's hand did not close to engulf his, and his brother's arm did not tighten to hide Salvarias in safety. It was heavy, limp. There was no steady drum in his ear. His head did not rise and fall with Wilhelm's whooshing breaths. The familiar scent of oiled leather was tarnished by the metallic stench of blood.

Salvarias looked up at his brother's eyes, no longer bright with life and happiness. They were dull, dead, dark. Dead. His brother was dead.

Wilhelm had left him. His brother had lied.

It was your fault. You made him leave the protection of Cattlar to find you. You led him right to Marro. Tell me, my precious murderer, what have you done?

Salvarias buried his face in his brother's shoulder. *I ... I killed him.*

Say it out loud.

"I killed my brother."

Tell me what you are! the presence shouted.

This time, no doubt edged his voice, no speck of light shimmered in his soul. "I am evil."

Pain shot from him, feeling as if his insides exploded. The mountain shuddered and pebbles and dust rained down from the ceiling.

Before him once again was the cliff of sanity; below, an ocean of ravenous red fog. He looked up, but the vibrant tree was gone.

He was so terribly alone.

He slipped from the ledge and plummeted through heavy darkness toward the sea of blood.

As it had done when he witnessed his parents' murders, a strong hand reached out to him from the darkness. It was a hand that would free him from pain. A hand that would steal his mind to someplace secret, someplace unknown, even to himself. A place of nothingness, darkness.

But Salvarias had no desire for salvation. He reached down and gripped the hilt of mother's dagger. He pressed the blade over his heart.

No! You must live with what you've done! You do not deserve death!

Slowly, he drove the dagger toward his heart as he clasped his brother's hand tightly. Burning pain flared on his palm as the hand in his mind reached out and snatched hold of him.

Darkness. Utter Emptiness. Nothing.

52

SUMMER 1018 A.R

E dium clapped Humar on the shoulder, both men sharing a childishly large grin. "Salvarias you say? How is it possible for the boy to do such a thing?"

Humar's smile faded. "As Mafarias has said, Salvarias is powerful. I'll make it my life's mission to bring him to the same realization. Let's get some air."

Edium waded through the heaps of armor and dead Cavruls to the expansive sloping mountainside. It was good to breathe in the fresh scent of the forest instead of singed hair and decay. The sky had paled to the wonderful yellow of sunrise, bringing Edium a spark of peace and hope that'd left him moments before. He vaguely listened to reports pouring in that none of the enemy's army had survived. Furthermore, there were Cavruls calling for aid on the other side of the collapsed tunnels. The fire had never reached the inner city or spread past the grand entrance of the outer city.

"I assume Wilhelm found Salvarias and the boy did this?" Edium said.

Humar nodded. "We need to round up a search party. With the amount of power Salvarias used, I'm sure he'll be weak if not completely out of it."

"I'll take you to find 'em," Durak growled from behind.

Humar winced. "Durak, if there had been any other way, I would've done it."

Durak folded his arms over his chest and nodded. "Me know, ye nitwit of a knight." The deep frown lines on Durak's face softened when he looked at Humar. "Thank you. Ye saved our city." He cleared his throat, waving away whatever Humar was about to say. "So, the fire ... it was the boy?"

Humar ran a hand through his singed hair. "I've never seen Mafarias use that kind of power. I have no doubt it was Salvarias. He saved you. He saved a city that spat on him, hissed names at him, and cursed all who are like him."

Durak turned to regard the towering gate, eyes distant as he stroked his beard.

"Sounds like you've had a change of heart," Edium said, not hiding the ridicule from his voice.

"Every man has the right to see the wrong in his actions and do everything within his power to make amends for what he did," Humar said. "I was wrong. I sent the boy to his death because I don't understand him. I'll not make the same mistake. Though the boy is a mystery, the thought of anything happening to him has made me realize that I do care for him, more so than I thought. He's my nephew. He's family."

"He's not blood," Edium said.

"Nor is Wilhelm of your bloodline, but I've seen the way you look at him. You consider the boy a son. Salvarias is as much my nephew as Wilhelm, and I ... love them both." Humar shook his head. "Look what the boy did, Edium. He ... he cares for us—for this world—so much that he was willing to walk to his death. He has more honor in one of his fingers than I have in my whole body. He isn't the evil, selfish man I thought. I see it now. He hides his true self from us, though why, I don't understand. I've seen him do things—horrible things—but I'm starting to realize that some stuff is out of his control, that he hates what he did. Like what happened to the girl in Xeroth. I see now what you meant.

He's asking for help, and most of us have turned our backs to him."

Edium grinned. "You might've just earned my approval back, friend."

"With all due respect, it's not your approval nor forgiveness I seek."

"I—"

Edium couldn't finish. In the time it took to blink, rain and thunder, lighting and tremors thrashed the mountain. The tranquil morning sky morphed into a pustule of sickly green clouds, heaving with menace and intent on destruction. Lightning fingered down, striking the ground mercilessly. Dead birds plummeted from above like bolts from a ballista. The trees shriveled into husks, and the air itself seemed void of life. The forest floor became a blanket of dying insects and vermin.

"No!" Neithelas and Arthias cried, racing toward the forest.

"What—" Edium's words were cut off when a hazy wave of air cut across the landscape and crashed into him. He was catapulted backward, crying out from the stabbing sheets of rain and hail pelting him. He slammed to the ground with enough force to bruise his shoulder and knock the air from his lungs, bringing painful tears to his eyes.

Lightning lanced the mountainside, raining down chunks of rocks. Edium covered his head and curled up as stones pelted him.

"Veedran's wickedness!" Durak roared.

Edium gagged at the iron taste seeping between his lips. He glanced up to see the sky raining thick blood.

In mere breaths, it was ankle deep, a layer of dead insects floating on its surface. A dead rabbit bumped against Edium's legs, its once-white fur now matted with blood. The death of the trees had spread beyond his vision, half of them knocked over from the gale, some aflame from lightning that still lashed down from the sky as if the gods themselves were intent on destroying Arden.

A flicker of shadow caught his eye at the horse pin. It looked like it was covered in a gray fog ... or fire. Maybe it was a mere shadow. He couldn't make it out through the torrent of blood.

Then the wave receded and, with it, the clouds imploded until nothing was left but the soft yellow sky of morning. Staggering to his feet, he spat out blood, flinging it from his hands, and brushed off dead bugs from his clothes.

Arthias and Neithelas were weeping at the forest's edge as if they'd lost their family.

Humar hauled Durak to his feet, eyes wide and wild. "Get up! We have to find them!"

Durak stumbled toward the horses. "There's another entrance to the tunnels a couple miles down the mountainside. We'll try to back-track to the city and see if we can find the boys."

Edium sprinted behind Durak. When they entered the barn, Adok was waiting, swaying slightly and panting as if it'd run a mile.

Edium's gaze swept the area, but whatever had shadowed the back of the barn wasn't there anymore. As they passed stall upon stall, they were greeted by dead horses, tongues lolled out, wide-eyed, petrified expressions frozen on their faces. However, alive in the last few pins were the horses that had been in Edium's group. All were skittish and huddled practically on top of one another.

"That was new," Okulu said, striding up. He wrung blood from his hair. "Rather interesting."

"Ye fool," Durak growled. "It be the boy's evil showing its ugliness."

Okulu clucked his tongue. "I agree it was Salvarias. But I think the bigger question is what happened to him ... or Wilhelm?"

By the time they'd calmed and saddled the horses, Neithelas and Arthias had joined them. Neither spoke.

Adok took the lead, and Durak seemed content to follow the wolf. So was Edium. The beast had a special connection to the boy, and no doubt it was guiding them to the brothers.

The ride ended at a tunnel Edium didn't notice until they were on top of it. During the miles of walking through caverns and winding tunnels, dread burgeoned in Edium's gut the longer he listened to Humar's recount of all the times the storm had hit, all the times it came when the mage was in torment. Edium's morbid mind continually strayed to one heart-wrenching thought: Okulu was right. Wilhelm was dead.

He received confirmation when they entered the next cavern. Hylim lit Wilhelm lying flat on his back in pool of blood. A gruesome slice ran up his abdomen, and blood stained his torn armor. Wedged under his arm was Salvarias. Though unable to see a wound, clearly the boy had died as well. His black eyes were vacant, and his face death white.

Everyone stood in stunned silence.

Before Edium's mind succumbed to shock, grief sucked the air from his lungs and punched him in the chest. A shout of despair tore from his throat as he bolted for the brothers. His legs gave out just as he reached Wilhelm, and his weak body draped over that of the dead. Tears burst free as he clung to the son he'd never had.

Vaguely he became aware of hands grabbing him. He fought them, snarling like some animal, broken by his grief, by what had been taken from him, by what he'd never had.

As Edium was hauled to his feet, his frantic gaze turned to Salvarias. It hit him in that moment that he cared for the boy. No ... he loved him. Edium had seen what his wife had seen, even though he'd denied it. But now he felt a knife carve open his heart. His anguish erupted anew, and he fought harder to reach to the dead boy.

"He's alive!" someone yelled in Edium's ear.

It didn't sink in for several breaths. He stopped struggling and looked into the azure eyes before him.

"They're alive, Edium. Both of them."

Edium shoved away from the other men and looked intently at the boys. Wilhelm's chest rose slightly, rarely. Salvarias's eyes were void of a soul, and he looked as dead as Wilhelm, but he breathed.

"By the gods," Edium choked.

Okulu was busy fishing through a pouch tied at Salvarias's waist while Durak hastily unbuckled Wilhelm's armor. Okulu pulled out a needle and thread.

"I'll go back to Cattlar and fetch a wagon and men to help us carry Wilhelm," Arthias said.

Edium stood frozen, still trying to digest what his eyes beheld. The slice on Wilhelm should've been his death, not to mention the amount of blood he'd lost. How had the boy survived?

Edium turned his burning eyes to Salvarias as Humar gently pulled the tip of a dagger from Salvarias's chest and pried it from the boy's clenched fist. Dark blood trickled out of the wound. Humar tugged on Salvarias, and he rose to his feet, eyes lifeless, breathing rarely, blinking even less.

"What—" Edium's voice broke. He cleared his throat. "What happened to the boy?"

The boy's fingers were bloodied and his wrists burned badly. Lying on the ground was what looked like shackles, but Edium couldn't be certain. The melted metal was twisted beyond recognition. Piled in a clump of softened black armor were twenty dead soldiers, red acid oozing from the heap. How Wilhelm's sword and armor hadn't been affected, Edium couldn't guess.

Humar ripped off the edge of Salvarias's sleeve and pressed it over the boy's wound. "He was like this after his parents were murdered," he said. "It took Wilhelm a year to pull the boy from his shock."

Okulu, once done mending Wilhelm, stood and met Humar's questioning gaze. The merc's eyes were glassy with tears. "His stomach doesn't feel right. There are lumps where there shouldn't be. When we get to Cattlar, we'll have a healer check him. I've never seen anything like it, though. The wound ..." Okulu shook himself. "I think he was eviscerated."

"He'd be dead," Humar said. "His insides would be lying on the ground."

Okulu lifted Salvarias's hands, pointing at chunks of gore. "I ... I think Salvarias tried to ... put him back together. Something else must have happened. Something brought Wilhelm back from Oblivion, something healed him enough to keep him alive, but didn't finish the job. He won't live for long."

"It would be merciful to kill him," Neithelas said. "Wilhelm's suffering will be drawn out. If there's nothing a healer can do, it would be our duty."

"We'll do no such thing, you snotty bastard," Okulu growled. "Salvarias might be able to do something when he wakes."

"Okulu," Humar said. "The boy—"

"No!" Okulu snapped. "We're letting this play out."

Edium considered himself a merciful man, however, he whole-heartedly agreed with the merc. Durak nodded as well.

Humar ran his hand through his hair. "So be it."

Edium stepped in front of Salvarias and gently raised the boy's head, brushed back his blood-crusted hair, and said, "Son, can you hear me? Come on, boy. Wake up."

The swirling irises he'd seen only once were dead, motionless like an ebony lake on a summer night. Salvarias did not tremble with cold as usual, and he did not shy away from touch. He was a husk, an empty vessel.

Grief and hope brimmed fresh tears. He clutched the boy tightly and whispered, "It'll be all right, Son. I'm here, and I'll do everything in my power to bring Wilhelm back to us. Do you hear me, son? I'll fix this or die trying."

He couldn't bring himself to think anything else. The boys were too important to him, to his daughters, to his wife. Just as he convinced himself that both would survive, Wilhelm succumbed to violent seizures. It took all of them to hold him down. Edium looked away from the blood sputtering from Wilhelm's lips and seeping between his stitches.

THE RIDE UP to Muddil's home gave Edium's mind a chance to wander to his daughters. Varila would be devastated. She'd been through so much pain in her life and had finally found a man to love, one who gifted her the confidence to be who she truly was, and now that man would die. And what of Lunara? Would he return to find a shell of a daughter?

When the pulley lurched to a halt, his legs moved as if an ogre was tied to them. A part of him wanted to run away and save himself the torment of breaking the news to Varila and the agony of seeing what had become of his youngest.

Inside, the home was hushed in oppressive silence. Leaving the others to tend to the brothers, Edium trudged to the kitchen and found the latch that opened the concealed door to his family's hiding place.

A slab groaned aside, revealing the faint light of a candle and Varila standing at the entrance with her sword in hand, raised for strike. Her eyes were red and glittered with anger and grief.

"Is it true?" she asked hoarsely.

Edium glanced past her to see Lunara folded in Talura's arms. His youngest raised her head.

"Don't," Lunara whispered. "Don't you dare say it." A horrible wail choked from her, and she sprang up, storming to Edium with sorrow flooding from her voice. "I don't want to hear it! Do not say the words!"

Edium stepped by Varila's sword and pried it from his daughter's fist. "He's dying," he said softly, setting the sword aside. "It could be hours, it could be days."

Varila's chin trembled. She nodded, holding her head higher than needed. He turned to his youngest and cupped her face in his hands. "Salvarias lives. He—"

"You lie," Lunara screamed, shoving his hands away. "I'm alone! For the first time, I'm alone!"

"You're never alone. I'll always be here for you."

"Impossible," Lunara wept. "They died. He's no longer with me!"

She pushed him aside and bolted from the room. Varila followed, walking stiffly, using the wall for support. A warm hand slipped in his. He looked down at his wife's tear-streaked face. "Forgive me," he whispered.

She rose on her toes and kissed his cheek. "This wasn't your fault." She led him after their daughters.

When he entered the brothers' room, both had been situated in beds, but the blood caking them had not been cleaned. Durak was barking orders for a healer.

Lunara looked first at Wilhelm, then to Salvarias. Taking faltering steps, she wobbled to the mage. She reached out and hesitated before resting her hand over his. She wept some word Edium couldn't understand before crumpling to the floor. Talura joined her, holding her close and smoothing her hair.

Varila cast the mage a sneer before striding to Wilhelm, all the while standing tall, tears still held within her control. She sat by his side and brushed his hair from his forehead. Barely loud enough for Edium to hear, she whispered in a voice dripping with venom, "Bastard."

He wasn't sure which brother was the recipient of her comment. His answer came when she lightly pressed her lips to Wilhelm's.

53

L unara sat by her sister as Varila caressed Wilhelm's fingers. His condition had deteriorated rapidly over the last two days. The healers kept him on three herbal remedies to ease his pain. Still, his skin was yellowing and seizures wracked him several times a day. One had just passed.

"I've finally find a man I love, and he's going to die," Varila said.

They sat together for hours until Varila fell asleep. Their father and mother, always waiting, always with them, carried her from the room.

Lunara kissed Wilhelm's cheek before moving to Salvarias's bed. His soulless eyes stared at nothing. He did not shiver, did not dream, and did not sleep. He simply blinked and breathed. She ran her fingers through his hair.

"Salvarias? Can you hear me?"

It was a fruitless effort, but she tried anyway.

"Any change?" her mother asked from behind.

She shook her head.

"I'm going to get some sleep. Your father will return in a moment. Do you need anything?"

"No, thank you. I would like some time alone, though. Perhaps Father could give me a few hours?"

"Of course, dear." Her mother kissed Salvarias's forehead and left the room.

Biting her lip to keep her tears in, Lunara crawled into the bed beside him. Adok, curled up at the foot of the bed as always, whined. Resting her head on Salvarias's shoulder, she gently took his hand and ran it along her cheek, imagining what the tenderness of his caress might feel like. She didn't remember it from their dreams anymore.

Her fingers glided over a raised bump on his palm. Turning it over, she saw a black mark of a ring circling a silhouetted flame. "How have I never seen this before?" she whispered. So much of Salvarias was a mystery, and she feared it would remain so.

Adok lifted his head and stared at her with a very intent, unwolf-like gaze that flicked between Salvarias's hand and hers. Frowning, she remembered when Salvarias had traced her mark near the stream after he'd killed his parents' murderer. There'd been a memory that flitted by her; a tree and a scream.

Lightly, she ran the tip of her finger around the black circle on his palm. A pulse of blackness sucked away her surroundings, leaving her in a world of nothing but light. Something surged up within her: something warm, something loving.

The voice from her dreams echoed in her head, "We must hurry before I am too weak. Touch him and allow us to aid him."

Her heart pounded painfully.

"We do not have much time, child," the voice said. "I can help him through you. Touch his forehead as you once did."

Tentatively, she rested a finger on Salvarias's forehead. "Come from the darkness," she whispered, though the voice was not her own.

That warm feeling in her surged up stronger and locked her finger to Salvarias. As the power left her to him, it hauled her mind along with it. She left her world of light and entered a world of darkness. Initially, all she sensed was emptiness so profound she shuddered and fought the urge to scream in horror. Deeper and deeper the power fled, plunging further and further. The oppressiveness finally lifted to reveal a roiling fog of shifting hues of gray-black, tinted red. She sucked in a breath when she realized the fog was Salvarias ... his mind and soul, hidden someplace so dark and deep that she could not fathom how the voice's power had found him. When the white light encased Salvarias, his pain rippled over her own body, pulling a cry from her lips. Whatever the power used was hurting him. She doubled her efforts to wrench her hand free, but it was pointless.

Then they were rising. As they climbed toward awareness, the white light yanked her mind into that of the black fog, into Salvarias's mind. The power showed her the strain he suffered, what played before him every breath he took. Death. Blood. Fire. Screams. She wept openly. His rapid thoughts were a painful pressure on her mind, jumping from this to that, thinking so much at once ... always thinking. She leaned to the side and was sick from the chaos of it.

The power drove her deeper into the fog, passing dark holes that seeped unbearable pain. Before her, in a soft gray light, what looked like two vines materialized. One was white and glowed brilliantly. One was shadowy and black. The vines' roots were separate for a short span before they interlocked, weaving together into an intricate pattern, and as they climbed, they became more tightly entwined. It was ... beautiful and appalling. It was the product of a little girl who had wanted a friend.

She remembered the sole tree perched on the cliffside outside Serinity and the names engraved in it. She remembered Wilhelm, a young man, and Salvarias, just a boy. She remembered touching his forehead, and this same power she experienced now had left her and entered Salvarias. And Lunara had used it to force her way inside him.

The voice whispered, "Yes, it is your soul and his. When you first helped him, you stowed away with me as I entered his mind. You sensed in him a kind heart and deep pain. You wanted his friendship; you wanted to help him. Selfishly, without his permission, you

violated what another should never touch. In all your childish innocence, you enslaved his life to yours, you shackled his mind to yours,
and you imprisoned his soul with yours. He was not of his right mind
to fight your efforts. He was still lost in darkness with no inkling of
what you had done to him. I did the only thing I could to try to miti-
gate the damage you had done. I suppressed your memory of the
event, hoping you would never discover it. But his mind is unique. He
felt something different within himself, even if he did not understand. His knowledge manifested itself in a dream that called to you.
You answered, and with each dream, the connection strengthened."

"I-I didn't mean to!" Lunara wept.

The voice spoke with sympathy. "Not all is sorrow, child. I will
show you how to help him, how to use what you have done to benefit
both of you, and I will show you how you put him in terrible peril."

Memories of when she'd touched him played before her. She'd
never realized with each caress, his lines of pain had vanished; with
each touch, she'd driven away all the death, the screams, and his
chaotic thoughts. But her effect had its dangers. His mind was lazy
when with her, lacking the strength to think through challenges as
easily as he did when not touching her. He was weak to his surroundings, unaware of what threats might lurk around him. All that filled
his mind when she touched him was peace and silence. Worse than
the danger she inflicted when touching him was what happened
when she released him. All his thoughts and images battered him at
once, doubling the strain he endured until he once again controlled
them. That short moment debilitated him.

"Now you see, child."

"Fix it!" she sobbed. "Separate us! Save him from me!"

"No mortal has ever done what you have done. His mind is not
like others. Furthermore, I am not certain it would benefit either of
you. He needs you, even if he denies you. You must be patient. You
must embrace your powers and help him. There are forces that seek
his soul, child. They need him to submit to the darkness within him,
cave to their will. You must not allow it. It is up to you to find what his
soul craves; what will turn him toward the light. You *must* help him."

"I don't have any powers," Lunara said, mind tumbling toward panic. "I don't know how to help him."

"If you have no powers, then how is this happening?"

"It's you ... You ... invaded me!" Lunara yanked her hand. "You've done to me what I did to him. You are not welcome inside me. Leave me!"

"So be it, Lunara. I part with a warning and a plea. Stay close to the mage. He teeters toward a chasm of evil. He is not safe from himself. I beg of you, find me. Save me from this pit of darkness."

Blinding white light flared before her, and the room reappeared. The power fell silent and ebbed from her blood, leaving her cold and shivering, terror still pounding her life beat to dangerous speeds. She cringed from her vomit and went to rise, but snapped rigid. Salvarias's lifeless eyes were switching from pits of coal to the familiar swirling hues of gray. Staggering off the bed, she gaped in horror at old wounds that had opened up over his body, spreading blood across his robes and the sheets.

Salvarias suddenly sucked in a huge breath and sprang up. He crawled backward, falling from the bed, knocking his head against the side table. He scrambled to a corner of the room and curled up, gaze darting around wildly.

"Salvarias," Lunara said, sinking in front of him. "It's me—"

Salvarias doubled over and grabbed his head. His scream tore through the home, and his breath came in quick, sharp intakes. The door flung open and his head jerked up. He stared in absolute terror at Humar, Mafarias, Talura, and Edium.

Salvarias's face twisted in pain, and he screamed again. Lunara tried to reach out to his mind, but it was as if she were confined to a room, knowing beyond her locked door a tunnel led to him.

She waved the others back, focused on her door, waiting for her chance to help him. Suddenly it flew open. She plunged through a dark tunnel and flung open the other door, bursting inside his mind.

He cried out, looking at her with wild eyes. She sensed his memories flooding him, all his life relived, all his pain experienced again.

With his chaotic mind, each memory of his life battled his random thoughts. The spiraling feeling made her nauseous.

Reaching out a shaking hand, she forced a reassuring smile, but he recoiled from her, cringing against the wall. He had yet to recover the memory of her touch and the power it possessed.

His pain and screams continued for what felt like eternity. Tears flooded from him, and his distant gaze watched his life replay before him.

At long last, his eyes widened. "Help me," he rasped.

She grabbed hold of his hand, and he pulled her into his arms. His thoughts slowed and memories flowed like a tranquil stream. She smoothed his hair, whispering words of comfort. When his memories went to his parents' murderer's death, he broke into sobs, burying his face in her neck, crushing her to him. The torment he suffered at the hands of Sansis shook him violently, holding her so tightly she had to gasp for each breath. The little girl who had died outside Xeroth hauled him to such hopelessness she was sure it darkened the world.

Then grief. Utter, incapacitating grief. His mind spiraled to the depths of chaos. "No-no-no-no," Salvarias repeated.

"Please," Lunara wept. "He lives."

Salvarias grabbed his head, screaming out in sheer agony and doubling over. The entire city of Cattlar trembled. Cries of alarm from outside the home erupted. A fissure snaked its way up the wall.

"Salvarias," Lunara snapped.

He raised he head, eyes crazed. "He left me! He promised, and he left me!"

"No. He—"

"He left me!" Salvarias hugged himself, rocking violently. "He promised!"

Lunara grabbed his arm and gave him a firm yank. Before he could move, she clasped a chunk of his hair and jerked his head toward Wilhelm's bed. "He lives!"

Salvarias's anguished sob made her ache in sympathy. Half crawling, half running, tripping on his robes, he rushed to Wilhelm. "Get up!" Salvarias grabbed Wilhelm's arm. "You promised me!"

Salvarias slammed his fist down on Wilhelm's chest. "Get up! Get up!" He hit and shoved Wilhelm again and again before Humar pulled him back. One touch from another sent a stab of pain through her mind, causing her to lose her balance. Her father caught her before she fell. Salvarias pushed Humar away.

They stood helplessly and watched Salvarias yank on his brother, repeating Wilhelm's promise through retching sobs, ordering him to rise. No comfort could be provided.

Salvarias latched hold of Wilhelm's hand and suddenly cried out, recoiling with a gasp of pain, and clutching his head in his hands. Lunara swayed, snatching hold of her father's arm when a shooting pain lanced through her mind. Salvarias raised a confused face to his brother, looked at his own hand, and then back to Wilhelm. After a slight hesitation, Salvarias touched his mark to Wilhelm's palm.

Again, he exhaled a cry and jerked away. Again, a dagger rammed into Lunara's skull. Wilhelm groaned.

Salvarias frantically looked around and grabbed a cloth. "Help me!"

She rushed to his side.

"Tie them together," he wept. "Hurry!"

Confused but desperate, she started tying Salvarias's hand to Wilhelm's, but the instant he felt the pain of touching Wilhelm's palm, it debilitated her, and he wrenched free.

"Help me!" Salvarias sobbed, paranoia and wild hope in his voice.

Her father came to their aid. His touch combined with the pain from Wilhelm sent Salvarias swimming in torment. She withdrew her mind from his.

Mouth agape, she watched Wilhelm cough up blood, and his insides beneath the slice on his stomach undulated like an ocean in a storm.

Salvarias crumbled on the floor, clutching his head. He couldn't even cry out anymore. He shook violently, his eyes rolled back in his head, and blood parted his lips. Lunara braced herself against the post of the bed, trying to stay on her feet and overcome the pulsating darkness. She withdrew further from his mind.

"Stop!" Talura cried.

Her father ripped away the cloth binding the brothers, and Salvarias fell in a heap. Wilhelm's eyes fluttered opened.

"By Veedran's wickedness," her father breathed.

Wilhelm's brow furrowed. "What ..." He choked up blood as he shoved himself up.

"No, son," Edium said. "You need to rest."

"Get out of my way," Wilhelm growled.

Her father stepped aside. Wilhelm swung his legs over the bed and groaned. Blood spread across his dressings.

"Salv?" Wilhelm said.

Salvarias raised his head, gagging up blood. His eyes widened, and he scrambled to his feet. He looked petrified. Taking a step backward, he stared at his hand and then his brother.

"I'm sorry," Wilhelm said.

"You knew," Salvarias rasped, voice full of accusation.

Wilhelm nodded and teetered to his feet. He took a faltering step toward Salvarias, but the mage backed up.

Salvarias's eyes brimmed with tears, shock, and betrayal. Voice scarcely audible, he said, "You knew, and you did not tell me."

"I ... I didn't understand, Salv. I—"

"You left me there alone." Tears cascaded down Salvarias's face. He hugged himself, his air leaving in a rush, his distant eyes darting back and forth. His voice rose to a scream. "You left me alone!"

Wilhelm swayed. "I didn't—"

Salvarias strode up to Wilhelm and shoved him. "I had nothing!" he shouted, pushing his brother again. "You left me! You left me!"

Wilhelm took Salvarias's forceful shoves with tears trailing down his gaunt face. At long last, Salvarias's strength seemed to drain out of him. He looked up at Wilhelm, face twisted in utter anguish. "You lied to me. You left me. I ..." Salvarias hugged himself tighter. "I had nothing."

"I'm so sorry, Salv." Wilhelm went to embrace Salvarias but he shrank back. "I should have told you," Wilhelm said. "I ... I just didn't want you to worry. I wanted to protect you." Shame and sorrow drenched his voice when he wept, "Forgive me, Salv. Please—"

Salvarias flew into Wilhelm's arms, eyes shut tightly. Through a choking sob, Salvarias whispered, "My brother."

Those two words were filled with more love than Lunara's heart could bear. She turned from the brothers and planted her face in her father's chest.

WILHELM CLUNG to his brother too tightly, crushing him, trying to hold him together as sobs ravaged him. Salvarias's fingers were dug into Wilhelm's flesh, but he didn't care. Never before had he felt such self-disgust for what he'd put his brother through. He'd been so wrapped up in ensuring his brother never discovered the shadow-fires' existence that he'd ignored the power Salvarias could grant him.

When he gained control over his own tears, he raised his head to others. "We need time alone."

Edium, holding Lunara close, ushered the others from the room. Varila stood in the doorway, tears raining down her cheeks. If Salvarias wasn't still consumed by grief, Wilhelm would have marched over and kissed her with all the passion only love could bring. Instead, he smiled. She smiled back and more tears fell. Slowly, she closed the door.

Wilhelm glanced around as his hazy mind battled through the layers of pain until he recognized their room in Muddil's home. The last thing he remembered was blinding pain. By the gods, so much pain. It'd consumed him for what felt like eternity. And it still did. Nothing in his gut felt right. He was sore, and it hurt to move. Warm blood continued to spread across his chest, and he felt lightheaded enough he feared he might pass out.

Slowly, as his mind fought for clarity, he realized slick blood from Salvarias was sticking to his arms, smearing over his chest. It didn't appear life threatening, and Salvarias needed comfort, not a healer.

When Salvarias's fingers loosened, his brother pulled away, hesitantly, until they made eye contact. "How ..." Salvarias swallowed hard. "I do not understand."

Wilhelm faced a dilemma. He'd kept something he shouldn't have from his brother, though he'd done so to avoid an outright lie or trying to explain what happened while leaving the shadowfires out of his story. He was still certain the shadowfires' existence was a knowledge Salvarias should never unearth.

Unable to keep his footing, Wilhelm plopped down to sit, begging the dizziness to fade. Salvarias sat in front of him.

"I ... I don't understand it either, Salv. It happened in the arena. I was in bad shape ... really bad. I was next to you and took your hand. Our marks touched. A ... power rose up in me, fed by you. It healed me. But it nearly killed you. I think I can suck the life right out of you. I never wanted to do it again. It hurt you so badly."

Salvarias took Wilhelm's hand and studied it. "I find it odd that through our childhood, never once have we touched marks."

"I think it's because I always held your right hand, or rather, you always held my left. I think we just got in the habit, and when you found out about your magic, you wanted your left hand free." Wilhelm muttered a curse. "It would have been nice to know about this earlier—"

Wilhelm sucked in a breath when a surge of power erupted. Salvarias yanked his hand back, doubled over, gasping.

"Knock it off, Salv," Wilhelm said, closing his hand. The small contact had settled his insides, but ignited a deadly thirst. He clenched a tighter fist, fighting to keep his hand from seeking his brother's.

"Please," Salvarias whispered. He raised his gaze, fresh tears welling. "Please let me heal you."

"You've done enough. I can do the rest on my own."

"I cannot ..." Salvarias buried his face in his hands. "I cannot endure it, Brother. Please."

"I know, Salv," he whispered. "We'll be all right."

He held his brother until exhaustion finally hauled Salvarias to sleep. With effort, Wilhelm shoved himself up and carried his brother to bed. He checked Salvarias's injuries, but none required immediate help, and Wilhelm's vision was fading rapidly. After stuffing a bag of lavender under the pillow, he turned to see Varila standing in the doorway, tears dribbling down her cheeks. By the gods, she looked stunning.

"You look like crap," she said in a hoarse voice.

Wilhelm smiled slightly. He didn't have the heart to tell her he was still dying. He knew as sure as roasted venison was his favorite meal that nothing inside him was right. But he refused to use his brother's power, to drain the life from Salvarias only to save himself. He'd endure this pain a million years before he would hurt his brother again.

"What is it?" Varila asked.

He hadn't noticed she'd crossed the room. He ran his thumb over her cheek, drying her tears. "You're beautiful."

"Wilhelm!" she cried.

Warm blood flooded his mouth and darkness pounced on him.

54

SUMMER 1018 A.R

Edium sprawled out on a cushiony chair in Muddil's sitting room, staring absently at Varila who stood on the balcony, gazing over the city below. Humar sat next to him while Muddil poured four glasses of ale and a glass of wine for Arthias. Commander Brice, who'd arrived yesterday with Edium's army, was leaning against the fireplace. Edium saw so much of Unbril reflected in Brice's tactical mind. Unlike his father, Brice had not taken up Unbril's rigid, serious demeanor. The commander drained his second mug of ale and wiggled it at Muddil.

"So this army be destroyed," Muddil said, glowering at Brice as he poured another cup.

"Barely," Humar said. "Lucky for us we had a mage. Fire appears to be all that can kill them besides a swordsman with enough skill to get a blade through that slit in their helmets."

"Didn't you have a run-in with them when you rescued Salvarias?" Edium asked. "Didn't you kill any?"

"It was too chaotic to be certain," Durak said, whittling away at a stick, seeming not to care about the wood shavings forming a pile on the floor. "We wanted 'em off the boat. Nothing more. And the bunch Wilhelm fought when Salvarias was first taken were too many for the boy to defeat. He didn't try to kill them. He just wanted to get away." Durak shifted in his seat and turned to Humar. "Don't be takin' this as an insult, ye dull-witted knight, but me've been thinkin'. Ever since we first set out to find Salvarias it seems this darkness be one step in front of us. Tell me, how well do ye know Okulu?"

Humar's eyes deadened. "As well as you, my friend. Okulu has earned my trust. I've known him for years, and he's saved my life more times than I care to count. He wouldn't get himself involved in something as deplorable as this darkness."

Durak held up his hands. "I merely ask. No need to get your undergarments in a bunch. But we best figure out how they always seem to know where we were headed. We need to be wary in our travels."

Humar ran his hand through his hair. "I see your point, but I trust everyone I've confided in. This 'god' has creatures at his disposal all over Dalnar. It's just as likely they've been able to track us."

Edium cleared his throat. "Speaking of, we, unfortunately, haven't discovered who this 'god' is."

"Whoever it is might have been burned up in the fires," Humar said. "Or he could still be out there."

Edium accepted the mug from Muddil. "You don't think the person you recognized was the mind behind this?"

Humar snorted. "Vescar? He's arrogant enough to call himself a god, but he lacks the ambition to coordinate this."

"How do you know him?" Edium asked.

"He was a commander in Loutsil's army. Vicious man. Raped, pillaged, and burned. He was kicked out of the knighthood for disobeying the orders of the king. Last I'd heard he was a drunkard in Windlous. I guess that's where this 'god' found him."

"He seemed ... shall we say, surprised to see you," Edium said

Humar smiled at him. "That he did."

"So you're not going to elaborate?"

Humar chuckled. "I'm afraid not, my friend."

"Can you tell me if you trained together?" Edium continued.

"We did in our youth. I hated him from the first moment I met him. He was a boy who did what pleased him. If he wasn't skilled with a sword, I bet the Loutsil knights would have kicked him out just because he was difficult to deal with."

Commander Brice scratched his beard as he spoke. "We need to find the source of this army. Dalnar isn't safe until we do." Brice grinned toward the balcony. "Perhaps we should send Lady Varila to rid 'god' from our midst."

Varila gave a halfhearted smile over her shoulder. Wilhelm, though healed somewhat, was rarely awake, and his condition didn't seem to be heading toward the road of recovery. Whatever power Salvarias had used hadn't done enough. Of that, Edium was certain. By his daughter's haunted eyes, she'd come to the same conclusion.

Turning his attention back to the men, Edium said, "Brice is right. I think it's time to sweep through Dalnar. One side to the other. We'll kill anything that reeks of this darkness and hopefully find the mind behind it. And it's time to take care of the barbarians."

"The Winsires will aid you," Arthias said. "I thought we'd wait for this evil to pass as most evil does, but I see we must end it or else Dalnar will be lost."

Edium nodded. "An alliance would be beneficial. Winsires have developed a reputation of being an aloof race. Your aid would do much to change that."

Arthias nodded. "Yes, we have. Speaking of our reclusion, your youngest daughter's heart and beliefs fit well with my people. She would be a suitable Erthla mate for my brother. I'd hoped Neithelas would select another Winsire, but Lady Lunara's appeal is difficult to overcome. I understand his attraction, though from my observations, she doesn't seem to return my brother's affection."

Edium shrugged. "I think you observe correctly. I don't see what this has to do with your race's reputation."

Arthias sipped his wine before speaking. "Your character is well known, Lord Bellerum. You're respected among commoners, the wealthy, and the Knight Council. My brother might never be king, but his role as second heir is to solidify outside relations. I counsel you to change your daughter's mind. A marriage would not only bring our two people together, but benefit both races."

"I won't choose her husband," Edium said flatly. "She'll—"

"Within both our races, marriages are often arranged for the greater good. My brother is handsome, wealthy, respected, and adored by his people. He is a prize for any woman."

"And my daughter isn't a treaty agreement. I'll not sway her choice."

"You jeopardize our lands, Lord Bellerum. It—"

As always, his anger simmered him into a quiet, friendly calm. "Prince Arthias, you're about to insult me," he drawled. "My daughter is her own woman. I won't offer her to another man as a means to get a race to like Erthlas. I don't give a rat's ass what you think of us." He smiled. "Bring it up again and I'll rescind my offer for Neithelas's courtship and inform my daughter as to just the type of family she'd be marrying into. Make no mistake, Arthias, I'll leave Meitholias alone and unprotected. You'll have no support from my army or the Knight Council."

Arthias glared at him before his eyes widened at seeing Edium's truth. "I apologize, Lord Bellerum."

Edium sighed, knowing Talura would give him a lecture if he didn't apologize. He rose and offered his hand to Arthias. "Let us move past this. I want us united and focused on the innocent people living in Arden, not bickering over the marriage of two."

Arthias smiled faintly. "Well said."

They shook, and he returned to his seat.

Humar cleared his throat. "With no means of uncovering who this 'god' is, I fear we face a faceless foe."

A rustle from behind caught Edium's attention. Salvarias stood in the doorway to the sitting room. Edium sprang from his chair, a smile slicing his face. For the past two days, the boy had mysteriously disappeared when any went to visit Wilhelm.

"Salvarias," Edium said, striding up to the boy.

Salvarias evaded Edium's offered embrace and bowed. "Lord Bellerum."

"Call me Edium." He blinked away his hurt, but remember Talura had warned him not to push the boy for affection. Time would be Edium's ally, and parenting two daughters had instilled in him an ocean of patience. He murmured to the boy, "Join us."

Salvarias's fingers whitened as he gripped his staff and hobbled into the room, standing just behind the chair Edium had sat in. The boy took a deep breath before he said, "What we have learned is that we face someone—or something—that considers itself a god. Whatever has angered it has driven it mad. It has every intention of annihilating all within Arden. Its servants are those who followed Veedran. I—"

"Let me stop ye there, mage," Muddil said. "Veedran be over a thousand years ago. How can any survive that long?"

Salvarias shrugged. "He granted his followers extended lifespans. As for his creatures, I can merely assume the same."

Edium realized how tense the boy stood, how his knuckles were white as he clasped his walking stick, how he trembled. Lines of either pain or worry creased his mouth. The boy was barely holding himself together.

Salvarias stood for a moment in silence before continuing. "The Four have been called forth."

Gasps filled the room.

"None can defeat them," Muddil muttered. "We be doomed."

"On the contrary," Salvarias said. "My brother defeated Marro."

More gasps, and this time, Edium joined in.

"There has been a shift," Salvarias continued. "The darkness is … not as powerful here. I feel it further removed from Dalnar. I can only assume it has fled to another corner of our world."

"Do you know so because the same evil in our lands flows through your blood?" Arthias said casually.

Edium whirled around to defend the boy, but Salvarias spoke first.

"Yes."

Quiet blanked the room.

"Also, the army we fought was not all I had seen. It was half."

Salvarias waited for the grumbles to stop before continuing. "However, as I said, I do not believe it still resides in Dalnar. I advise that Lord Bellerum's plan is followed, that Dalnar is cleansed. The darkness is not done. If Dalnar is safe, when this 'god' sends his forces back, you will be better suited to address the threat."

"We'll clear the caves," Muddil said.

Arthias nodded. "We'll handle the southern portion of Dalnar, all except Crutar's stronghold. That place cannot be penetrated. Edium, you can take the northern section. I don't think we'll encounter a force large enough to defeat our armies until we enter the sands. Together, we'll take care of the barbarians."

"I agree," Salvarias said.

"Done," Edium said.

Salvarias bowed. "Thank you. If you will excuse me, I must check on my brother."

The mage walked toward the hallway and had almost crossed the threshold when Varila set her lips in a thin line and darted behind him. Grabbing his arm, she yanked him around and slapped him hard across the cheek.

"Damn you!" she snapped. "Damn you to Oblivion! Why'd you have to go? You selfish son of a whore! This is your fault! He'll die because of you!" She went to slap him again but Salvarias caught her wrist and pulled her close.

"Do you think I do not know," he grated, his usual soft voice dulled by anger. "I know what I force him to do! I do not need to be reminded every breath I take!"

He released her and stumbled back, tripping over furniture until he got his balance. Edium gathered Varila close as Humar went to the boy's side.

"He holds enough guilt," Edium whispered, leading her from the room.

His daughter's eyes were wide and stared at Salvarias until they entered the hall. Talura was waiting, arms open.

"I'll take her to our room," she said.

Edium nodded and watched the women walk down the hall.

Shaking his head, he returned to the sitting room. Humar had managed to get the boy to the balcony. As Edium walked up, Humar shot a warning look to leave, but Edium ignored it.

"Even with the army destroyed," Salvarias was saying, "the darkness will not stop. We must uncover this god's location."

"I agree. But where to begin," Humar said. "That's the true question. For now, let's focus on getting healthy, especially Wilhelm."

Salvarias nodded. "It may take some time. My potions are not working." His voice was lined with guilt.

Edium cleared his throat. "I'm sorry about Varila. I'm sure you've seen the way she looks at your brother. I've never seen her so enraptured before."

"No need to apologize, my lord—"

"Edium."

"She acted as she should. I should have known my brother would follow."

Edium ignored Humar's silent plea to leave the boy alone. "I had a brother once, younger by two years. I took him to war with me. Of course, he wanted to go; he went everywhere I went. He died on the battlefield. I was so caught up in my own fight I didn't watch for his safety. I blamed myself at first, but later realized there was no point. How would my brother feel knowing I berated myself day and night, living in misery? Guilt is a heavy burden to carry."

"With all due respect, my lord—"

"Edium."

"If you do not punish yourself, truly you betray the memory of those you have doomed. You yourself walk free of responsibility." Salvarias's voice carried an edge of warning to end the conversation.

Edium ignored it. "Forgiving oneself is not betrayal, boy."

"Forgiveness is forgetfulness and therefore betrayal."

Edium paused before he continued. "You think you guard others with this emotionless air, but it only hurts those around you."

Humar groaned.

"Do not think you know me," Salvarias said.

"I think you should go, Edium," Humar suggested.

"I don't know you," Edium continued. "But you never let a person near you but your brother."

Salvarias remained quiet.

"It's selfish not to allow others close," Edium said gently. "Friendships and love are imperative and save the soul."

"It may save one soul, but it condemns the other. It is selfish to permit a pure soul to follow one so tainted. My soul may be destined for Oblivion, but none others need follow."

Edium tried to peer into the shadows of Salvarias's hood. "You think your soul is going to Oblivion, boy?"

Salvarias's head jerked up to meet Edium's gaze, and his expression was one of confusion, as if he hadn't realized he spoke aloud.

For the second time, light fell across Salvarias's eyes. Try as he might, Edium could not squelch the shudder that racked him nor the instinctive recoil.

Salvarias's eyes brimmed with tears before he lowered his head, casting shadows across his face. "I must check on my brother." He left the balcony.

"That wasn't wise," Humar said. "He's not one to part with his feelings."

"Quite the contrary, my friend." Edium silently cursed himself for reacting to the boy's stare just as he'd hoped he wouldn't. "He parted with many insights into his mind. My wife was right."

"Bringer of death!" Neithelas hissed from the adjoining room. "I saw the forest, mage. I know what wickedness lurks within you! The trees sense it and fear you!"

"Enough!" Humar said, whirling around.

Neithelas's stood in the center of the sitting room, sword leveled at Salvarias's heart. Both Edium and Humar froze, seeing the Winsire's violet eyes glaring with anger, his blade trembling with rage.

"What are you waiting for, Neithelas?" Salvarias challenged, taking a step forward.

"Neithelas," Humar said. "There are no answers with what you're doing. You do not—"

"Stay out of this, Humar," Salvarias snapped, gaze locked on Neithelas. "Do it," he demanded to the Prince. "End it all."

Neithelas's stance faltered, and he lowered his sword.

Salvarias's fist clenched, and his word cracked out like lightning. "Coward!"

Neithelas raised his sword, new anger in his eyes. Salvarias took a step forward.

"Do it!" the mage boomed, taking another step.

Neithelas stepped back, but Salvarias took another step until the Winsire's sword pressed into his burgundy robes. Edium started inching forward.

"Kill the child of evil, Neithelas." Salvarias tossed back his hood. "Rid the world of this monstrosity! Do it!"

Neithelas visibly shuddered when he met the mage's hard gaze. Salvarias stepped forward. Edium winced at seeing the sword break through the boy's robes and the slight soil of red, but Neithelas backed up before it penetrated farther. Lunara entered into the room.

"Kill the pawn and save her," Salvarias snarled.

Neithelas's eyes set with determination. Before Edium could even move, Lunara was beside Salvarias. She rested her hand on the Winsire's sword.

"No," she whispered, lowering his weapon.

Neithelas trembled, but he didn't resist Lunara. His daughter turned to the mage, putting herself between the Winsire and Salvarias. Unspoken words passed between the two. The boy's face lost all anger and switched to a hopeless desperation. He glanced at Humar then met Edium's stare, and he swore the boy was ready to plead for something, but the mage recovered, his expression turning cold and uncaring. Salvarias bowed with silent tears pouring down his face and left the room.

Edium shook when he turned to Humar. "You must watch that boy, Humar. He needs help."

"More so than you know," a voice said from behind. Edium turned to see Mafarias gazing after Salvarias. "His soul is most fragile. There is only one capable of pulling him from the edge of destruction. And he's dying." Mafarias's voice caught with emotion. "My nephew is dying, and he's too stubborn to let the boy heal him."

～

SALVARIAS STORMED down the hall and entered his room. Wilhelm was sleeping deeply, as always—too deeply.

Such a shame your murderous soul was not killed, my pet. Here your brother lies, recovering at a rate that suggests he needs further mending, and yet you do nothing.

Salvarias leaned against the wall and sank to the floor. *I have tried. He will not let me. He insists he is improving.*

Selfish pet. Look at all you do to him. Look at the blood on your hands.

Salvarias closed his eyes and rested his head on his knees. By all the gods, he did not want to live anymore. He wanted everything to end. Losing his brother had gouged a hole in his heart. Even though Wilhelm lived, those lifeless amber eyes haunted him when awake and asleep. The red haze covering life had deepened. There was so much blood around him. So much despair.

"I cannot do this," Salvarias whispered.

Adok nuzzled his hand. Desperate for comfort, he latched hold of the wolf, burying his face in Adok's soft fur.

"I have no more strength," Salvarias said. "I cannot see him die again. I cannot bear it. Please, if there is any god of mercy listening, take me first. I beg you, save me from seeing such a sight again."

When he opened his eyes, he was huddled in the corner of his room above the baker. The silence was heavy, and his breath clouded in the frigid air. Moonbeams slicing through his window lit a roiling fog churning in hues of crimson. Wilhelm lay in the bloody haze, lifeless, eyes dull, insides bulging from the slice on his chest.

The fog snaked over Salvarias's skin, crawling, violating him, hungry. "You've killed him," it hissed. "Why fight? Just close your eyes and sleep. That is all you must do to be rid of your pain. You are tired, my pet. Sleep."

Salvarias's eyelids drooped closed.

"Yes, sleep. Succumb to me. Allow me to ease your pain."

He shuddered at the fog caressing over him like a lover. He batted at it, half conscious, half asleep.

"Come to me," it hissed, lulling his mind further into submission.

He twitched when something wet slid over his hand.

"No, my pet. Ignore it."

Salvarias sank deeper into the fog. He was so tired.

Pain shot up his arm, and he jerked awake. Adok had his jaw clamped around Salvarias's arm. The wolf let go and licked his hand. He patted Adok's head and shoved himself up. After checking on his brother, Salvarias crawled into bed.

In a blink, he stared at waves lazily rolling in from a bright blue ocean. Looking around, he found himself sitting on an endless sandy beach with wispy grasses lining it. The sun played with the horizon, reflecting its warmth in the lulling waves and sending a cool breeze to wash over him. He inhaled deeply the salty aroma. It was beautiful.

"Hello, boy."

Salvarias looked up at Tobin and smiled. "Hello, Father."

"Beautiful," Tobin said, sitting beside him.

Salvarias nodded. "Very." He inhaled again. "I love you, Father."

"I'd like to believe that, but I know differently. I saw, boy. I saw your smile. I saw your sick soul."

Salvarias's smile faded. "I did not mean it. I loved Mother. I swear, Father. I did not mean it."

"You did." Tobin's lip curled, and his voice was heavy with disgust. "You're not my son. And I don't love you."

Tobin rose, and Salvarias grabbed hold of the edge of his father's tunic, looking up and pleading, "Please do not leave me. Help me! I am so scared! I ... I do not understand."

Tobin squatted down in front of Salvarias. "I can't help you, boy. No one can. You're past saving. Don't you understand? No one, not even Wilhelm, can save your soul. Just look. Look what you did to me."

Tobin's throat slit open and blood splattered over Salvarias. He fell backward with a cry, frantically mopping the sickly warm blood from his face.

"Monstrosity," his mother whispered.

Salvarias's eyes flew open. His mother was tied to a stake, surrounded by red fog. Blood ran down her legs, and her face was bruised and broken.

"Creature of evil!" she hissed. "Son of darkness! Demon child! Abomination!"

Salvarias covered his ears, snapping his eyes closed. "Please make it stop," he whispered, rocking violently. "Please make it stop."

His mother's scream pierced his ears, his heart.

"Stop!" he cried.

She screamed again. The stench of burning flesh assailed him.

"Stop!" he pleaded.

She leaned toward him, her head skinless, hairless. "I know what you are," she whispered in his ear.

Thia appeared at her side, swollen from poison, foam on her lips, covered in thorns. "He's evil," she said in a small voice. "He killed me."

"No," Salvarias wept. "I did not mean to! I swear I did not mean it!"

"Die," his mother hissed. "Why won't you just die?"

"Brother! Help me!"

"Die!" she screeched.

Salvarias's hand held a dagger.

"If you die, you'll save me," Thia said. "Just die. End it."

Wilhelm rose up in the distance, gutted. "Why'd you kill me, Salv? I took care of you. I protected you. I loved you when no one else did. Yet look what you did." Wilhelm pulled out organs and chunks of intestines and presented them to Salvarias. "Just look what you did to me."

Salvarias rammed the dagger for his chest. Some invisible force stopped him. "Please," he begged.

Then everything disappeared. No one was around him. Nothing but darkness. He held his dagger, the tip resting against his chest. He tried to drive it in again but suddenly a spring meadow appeared. It was serene, pure, littered with bright flowers, wreathed by towering pines. He inhaled deeply, smelling crisp air and sweet flowers. Puffy white clouds floated by, shading him while the veiled sun provided warmth that reached his soul. He dropped the dagger and looked around.

Lunara stood by his side, smiling.

"What is this?" Salvarias whispered.

"A dream, nothing more," she said.

"You are with me," Salvarias said in understanding.

She smiled sweetly. "I am."

Salvarias sank to the grasses and stared at the brilliantly blue sky sneaking peeks between the moseying clouds. He should force himself awake. She was touching him, tainting herself with his evil. Soft fingers ran through his hair, her nails gliding over his scalp, sending a relaxing shudder down his spine.

"I've learned what my touch does," Lunara said softly. "I do not ask for your affections, I do not expect anything from your heart. All I ask is that you sleep. You've nothing to fear in this dream."

"Please, I beg of you, convince my brother. I cannot bear to see him so weak. I think he is dying. He must let me help. He—"

"Shhh," she whispered, and gently pushed him to lay back. He gazed up at her eyes, so alive, so caring. Soft fingers brushed aside his hair, and her whisper was carried on a breeze that lifted him free of all his worry. "I swear on your life that I will persuade him. Now sleep."

Salvarias closed his eyes and slept on a bed of grasses with no blood, no roaming dead, and nothing came to hurt him.

55

V arila peered inside the brothers' room to see both sleeping. Lunara was there, sitting beside Salvarias, caressing his face, tears brimming in her eyes. Varila clenched her jaw to fight the bitter remarks that flooded to her lips. She stepped inside, closed the door, and went to her sister.

"What happened?" Varila asked.

Lunara smiled, blinked a few times, and shook her head. "It's nothing."

Grunting at the lie, Varila made her way to the center of the room and plopped down in the chair her father frequented. In deep reverie, she absently watched her sister eventually succumb to sleep, her hand never leaving the mage's arm.

Curling her lip in disgust, she turned her attention to Wilhelm. He was standing, swaying at the edge of his bed, wincing when he took a step.

"You should sleep," Varila said in a sharper tone than she intended.

"I'm tired of sleeping," Wilhelm mumbled. Using the backs of chairs, he made his way to her. Seeing him so weak threatened to form another lump in her throat. She was as tired of crying as he was of sleeping.

She stood in front of him and forced a smile. "You're never going to get better if—"

"I love you," he whispered. "On Salvarias's life, I would've never loved another woman besides you. I haven't told you because he'll always come first. Always. And I knew you'd never accept him." He ran his fingers down her cheek and looked as if he would say more, but shook his head instead.

Varila glanced over her shoulder. Could she ever look past what Salvarias had done? When she turned to Wilhelm, deep pain passed through his eyes. He was serious. He'd never be with her. He'd give up the love they shared for the mage.

He swayed again, face paling another shade. Turning from her, he staggered toward his bed.

Her love for him surged up with such strength, she stood in front of him before she realized she'd moved. "I love you, too. With all my heart. And like you, Lunara comes first. How many times has he nearly died, taking her with him? You have to see this from my perspective. Imagine if the roles were reversed."

Wilhelm looked at the ceiling, his brow furrowed. "Everyone looks to him to stop what's happening to Arden. Humar, Durak, you, Lunara, even your father. Do you know how many times I've heard Humar say it? He was even willing to sacrifice Salv. He sent him to his death. No, I don't think I need to see it from your perspective or anyone else's. Even Lunara puts pressure on him. Just in a different way. If you want to hate someone, hate me, because I'm the one telling him to let you all come along. Think of the times she's nearly died. It's because Salv had to save us. Maybe he was right. Maybe we should've gone our way alone."

Varila's gaze steadied on Salvarias sleeping peacefully for the first time since she'd met him. "No." She inhaled a deep breath. "No, you wouldn't survive without us. We've all made mistakes on this little journey of ours, but we've helped each other through them. He needs us as much as you."

"I just want him to have a normal life." His voice was heavy with an exhaustion that went deeper than his wounds. "I want him to have stability, an actual home he's safe in." He ran a hand over his face, muffling his voice. "Who's going to protect him?"

"I don't understand," she said. "He had a home for half his life. It's not like—"

He shook his head. "Not Salv. He's never had a single place he could call home that was safe. In our own home, he was riddled with sicknesses from the beatings he took from bullies, he was petrified of others, and he cowered in a corner. After our parents were murdered, we lived on the streets for a year before we were taken to the slave mines. After we escaped, we stayed in Durak's storeroom for two seasons before he was kidnapped. Even then, he suffered abuse at the hands of Dethal. Don't you see? He never had a *home*. A warm, safe place filled with love and people who would die protecting him. I had it. I was never scared all through my first sixteen years. I had everything I could have wanted. But Salv never has."

She felt a pang of pity for the mage, remembering his words in the caves. She understood, more so than Wilhelm, that Salvarias's home above the baker had been a house of horrors.

Varila ran her hand down Wilhelm's cheek, feeling his whiskers tickle her palm. "My father has taken you and your brother into our family. He loves both of you as his own sons. My father will give you and Salvarias a home. Our home. You'll be welcomed there. He'll see to Salvarias's safety. Every guard in Serinity will look after him. No one will spit on him, no one will hurt him."

"And how will you treat him?" Wilhelm asked. His eyes grew serious, tinted by some unvoiced desperation. "Will you take care of him like you do Lunara? Will you protect him?"

"Give me time. I can't change overnight, but I swear I'll look at your brother without prejudices. If he is the man you think he is, I'll see it for myself. And then, yes, I would protect him like I do Lunara."

Varila's life beat increased when his scratchy finger hooked around her chin, raising her gaze to lock with his as he bent down.

When their lips were almost upon one another, he whispered, "I love you."

She melted to him, closing her eyes and submitting to his soft kiss. His raspy breathing made her pull away, and she helped him to bed, covering him in blankets to help his shivering.

"You should let Salvarias heal you," she said, brushing his hair from his face.

"I'd rather die." Wilhelm winced and closed his eyes. "I won't hurt him ... again ..."

She leaned down and whispered in his ear, "You're hurting him now, you stubborn ass."

He'd already fallen asleep. She kissed his cheek and gazed at his handsome features as she mulled over what she'd just been stupid enough to agree to. She doubted she possessed the ability to con herself into seeing in Salvarias whatever Wilhelm thought he saw. The mage was cold and aloof, carrying himself as if he were too good for the rest of the world, always serious with demon eyes that made her shiver merely from the memory of them. He'd killed in brutal ways and laughed about it, he'd created things as if straight from the mind of Veedran, and he'd nearly killed her sister more times than she cared to count. How could someone capable of such things possess admirable qualities? And what in all Oblivion did her sister see in the mage?

She meandered around the room, rummaging through her feelings. Eventually, without meaning to, she stood by Salvarias's bed. With his frown gone, his face relaxed and peaceful, demon eyes closed from view, she grudgingly admitted her mother had been right. He was somewhat handsome. His ink-black hair reflected the dim light in the room, framing his perfect features ... too perfect. Unable to resist, she ran her fingers through his wavy hair. It was silk, just like Lunara's. Unfurled and stretched out, his robes rested against his body, sinking into each indent to reveal a muscular man, not scrawny as she had thought. She glanced at Lunara sleeping by his side. Their children would be breathtakingly beautiful.

Turning to Salvarias, she studied him again. "Somewhat handsome" no longer fit. He was probably the most gorgeous man she'd ever laid eyes on. The longer she gazed at him, the more painfully handsome he became, so much so that she had to look away. Now, she understood her sister's physical attraction. But anything else was beyond her understanding.

Their children? Where had that thought come from? Annoyed and cursing herself, she returned to her chair, plopped down, and caved to a light doze.

When she woke, Wilhelm was walking around the room, leaning heavily on furniture, wincing, grunting, and sweating like he'd been working the forge nonstop for an entire week. Lunara was also up, twirling a lock of Salvarias's hair in her fingers.

Wilhelm winked at Varila. "About time you woke up."

"We need to talk, Wilhelm," Lunara said. "I'm sure, on this subject, Varila will agree with me."

Wilhelm shook his head. "I'm not touching our marks again. You saw what happened, Lunara. You know better than anyone else, I'll kill him."

Out of the corner of her eye, Varila saw Lunara's pleading expression. Indeed, Varila wholeheartedly agreed with her sister on this subject. Setting her jaw with determination, she rose from her chair and stood in front of him, hands on her hips. All the nice pleas had failed to persuade him, now it was time to see if flat-out cruelty would work. "You're a fool. He's miserable. I don't know him like you do, but even I can see the amount of pain he's in every time he looks at you. Surely you're not blind to it."

"You don't understand. I'll kill him."

"He's dying already," Varila said sharply. She'd seen a truth none others had witnessed. She'd seen it in Salvarias's eyes after she'd slapped him. The mage was giving up, hopeless and guilt-ridden. She'd heard him weeping behind closed doors, heard him retching through sobs. "All he holds is guilt, and each time he sees you struggle to get out of bed, cough up blood, or too weak to eat, he dies a little more. You're killing him. You. No one else. You."

Wilhelm flinched. He glanced at Lunara who nodded, eyes brimming with sympathy.

"She's right," Lunara said. "He's sinking into a depression that I doubt he can recover from. You must allow him to heal you."

"I can't stop," Wilhelm said flatly. "Once I feel the power, I can't stop taking it from him. I'll drain the life right out of him. I'll kill him just to save myself. That means you'll die too. No, I'm not touching our marks."

It hit Varila like a battering ram. He'd spoken in past tense earlier, and his request to protect Salvarias was clearer than water. He knew he was dying, and he was willingly letting it happen.

Varila slapped him. She was furious at him for giving up, for ignoring all the help that surrounded him. Both brothers were locked away in their own world, not permitting help, too proud to ask for it, too close to allow another within their circle. "You bastard!"

Wilhelm must have been too stunned to speak. He just stood there with big eyes.

"When will you get it through that thick skull of yours that the two of you are no longer alone? When will you end this seclusion you've trapped yourself in? Dammit!" She clenched her fists, trying to calm her tone. "You. Are. Not. Alone. We're here. We can help you. Once we think you've healed enough, we'll pull you free. We'll *make* you stop." She took a step closer, rose on her toes, stared directly into his eyes, and whispered, "One of you must let someone inside. Let it be me. Trust me. Please."

Wilhelm gazed at his brother for several moments before turning to Varila. His eyes and tone were dead serious. "If anything happens to him, I'll never forgive you. If I live and he dies, I swear I'll ... I'll trust you, Varila. Gods be damned, I'm trusting you with his life."

She knew exactly what his unvoiced threat would be if she let Salvarias die. "I know," she said. "And he won't. We'll make sure of it. If need be, we'll even divide it up into two sessions. Remember, I want him to live ... for Lunara's sake."

Wilhelm hobbled over to Salvarias's bed and sat at the end next to Adok. "When he wakes, we'll do it."

They talked of nothing important as time crawled by. Wilhelm's fidgeting seemed to increase with each passing breath, and she feared he'd change his mind if the mage slept much longer.

At long last, Salvarias stirred awake. He looked around with a furrowed brow. "What has happened?" he asked, sitting up in bed.

"He's agreed," Lunara said.

Salvarias's eyes lit when he looked at Wilhelm. "Truly?"

Wilhelm nodded. "Though I don't think it's a good idea."

Lunara rose from the bed, and Salvarias's handsome face grimaced, and his usual frown painted over his relaxed features. Still, she couldn't find fault in his appearance. She glanced at Wilhelm, noticing for a second time that the two looked nothing alike.

Salvarias sat forward and offered his hand. At Wilhelm's hesitation, Salvarias scooted closer and extended his hand farther. "Thank you, brother," he whispered.

Wilhelm grunted. He unraveled the dressings so Varila and Lunara could see his wound. After a pause and deep breath, he grabbed Salvarias's hand. The mage gasped, doubled over, and yanked his arm to free himself, but Wilhelm's grip was stronger.

Varila sat mesmerized. Within a breath, Salvarias balled into a writhing heap of a man. Wilhelm's insides and muscles heaved against his skin as if alive. He exhaled deeply and began hacking up chunks of bloody mucus. Lunara was quick with a bowl.

Salvarias ceased squirming. He lay still, staring at the ceiling. The parted skin on Wilhelm's chest crawled toward one another, mending together like melting wax to erase any signs of his wound, or even a scar. He groaned, his breathing deepening into a strong whoosh of air.

"Let go," Lunara whispered.

He exhaled sharply, readjusting a tighter grip on his brother. A pool of blood parted Salvarias's lips.

"Wilhelm," Varila said, shaking his arm.

Lunara sank to her knees, face death-white. "Varila, stop him."

"Wilhelm," Varila snapped, yanking on him.

He didn't budge, didn't open his eyes. She swore he was growing, expanding. She screamed for help, her gaze darting from Lunara's paling face to Wilhelm's expanding body to Salvarias convulsing and choking on blood.

Suddenly her father and Humar were there. Between the three of them, they ripped Wilhelm's grip free. He gasped, stumbling to his feet. Salvarias shuddered and closed his eyes.

"What in Nevlar's fury are you four doing?" Edium roared. He turned Salvarias on his side. More blood spilled out.

Wilhelm's eyes widened. "Salv!" He shoved Edium aside and scooped up his brother, resting an ear over Salvarias's heart.

"He's sleeping," Lunara said, using the bed to pull herself up. "He'll be fine, Wilhelm. He just needs rest."

Edium glared between the three of them. "Explain."

"Salvarias wouldn't take no for an answer," Lunara said. "He *needed* this, Father. Wilhelm and Varila did nothing wrong."

"Like Oblivion they didn't," Edium growled. "You wanted a pony when you were three. I didn't give you one because you wouldn't know how to take care of it. Just because you want something doesn't mean you get it."

"I didn't say want," Lunara said softly. "I said need."

Edium looked between Varila and Lunara before his clenched jaw relaxed. "Next time, come get me. I'll help. Why don't you girls go eat?"

Varila was about to object when her father shot her a look she knew all too well. She took her sister's hand and left.

HUMAR NODDED to Edium as a sign now was as good as time as any for Humar to grovel for Wilhelm's forgiveness.

Edium squeezed Wilhelm's shoulder. "It's good to see you healthy."

Wilhelm grunted, finally loosening his hold on Salvarias though his gaze never left the boy.

Humar smiled at the "good luck" face Edium cast his direction before the Lord made his way from the room. Humar waited until the door closed, and then turned to Wilhelm.

"What do you want?" Wilhelm growled.

"I was hoping to talk to you," Humar said.

"I have nothing to say to you," Wilhelm said. Grabbing a cloth from the stand next to the bed, he cleaned blood from Salvarias's face and settled the boy under a mound of blankets. "Leave, Humar."

"We're going to talk first."

Wilhelm rose, fists clenched, eyes a storm. "Get out. I've nothing to say to you. And I'm in no mood to listen to your crap excuses."

"I offer none," Humar said. "I only offer apology."

"Go to Oblivion."

Humar ran his hand through his hair. He wasn't sure what he'd been expecting, but he had thought Wilhelm would be quick to accept an apology. "I was wrong to allow him to leave."

"Damn you to Oblivion."

"I'm serious, Wilhelm. I—"

"And I'm serious, too. I don't want your help anymore. I don't want you anywhere near my brother. You let him go." Wilhelm's jaw clenched. "You let him. You handed him over without a second thought."

"I was wrong. I don't know how to make you understand." Humar glanced at Salvarias, head tossing, words muttered. "Your brother is going to stop this evil. I have no doubt. I did before, but I don't now. It's not just him, though. It's you, too. Both of you are the key. These powers you have … this link you two share is meant for something important." Humar knelt in front of Wilhelm, bowed his head, drew his sword, and laid it the boy's feet. "I swear on all my oaths as knight, on my own soul, that I will lay down my life to protect you both."

A long moment passed before Wilhelm answered in a dead voice. "He'll forgive you. All you'll have to do is say sorry, and he'll forgive you quicker than a Watythm can drink a glass of ale. He'll offer up his trust in one breath. Because once Salv trusts someone, they could stab him in a dark alley and he'll still follow them."

Those words tore a hole in Humar, exposing his shame.

"And he'll spend his energy getting me to accept your apology," Wilhelm continued. "He'll tell me how irrational I'm being, that he was the one who pressured you to let him go, that it was his fault. He'll tell me to be more understanding, that he's given you no reason to trust him. He'll remind me of all the help you've given us. So, for his sake, I'll go along smiling at you, joking, sparring, as if nothing happened. I'll save him the trouble of persuading me to accept your apology. But you ... you'll live knowing that when I smile, I'm spitting in your face. When I spar, I won't stop my blows. You'll know I don't trust you. And you'll know that I've shoved your apology back up your ass. Stay here and grovel to my brother, because he's the only one with compassion enough to forgive you for what you've done." Wilhelm smirked. "If I know Salv, he'll be the one who'll end up apologizing to your worthless ass."

Wilhelm strode by him. Humar knelt frozen in place as he listened to the door click closed. He sat until his legs were numb and his heart had been chewed raw by his own chastisement before he heard Salvarias's weary voice.

"Sir Humar?"

"I shouldn't have let you go," Humar said hoarsely.

He heard a quick rustle, and the boy knelt in front of him. "It was my fault, Sir Humar. I manipulated you into allowing me to leave. Please forgive me for forcing you to endure this."

Tears battled free. Humar wept as he hadn't wept since he'd killed his father. He released his pain in loud sobs, knowing that Salvarias never left his side, that the boy sat there with compassion reaching out to him. It only wracked him with shame.

When he quieted, he raised his gaze. "I've betrayed your friendship. When put to the test, I abandoned you. I don't deserve your forgiveness. All I ask is that you trust me. All I ask is that you let me help you. I beg you to believe me when I say I'll lay down my life for yours."

Salvarias's intense black eyes burrowed into Humar's soul, and he opened himself to the boy, permitting Salvarias to see whatever it was he searched for. The probing stare robbed Humar of breath, hauling him into the swirling black fog of Salvarias's eyes, spiraling him down further, breaking him until he saw the rawness of his own soul. His dark past, his pain. But then he saw his hope, his care for others, his want for a better future for Arden.

Salvarias broke the stare, and Humar gasped and shuddered back the violating feeling.

"You are a man worthy of whatever you desire, Humar. But your soul must not hold guilt for what happened."

Humar gazed at the boy, feeling as though he truly saw Salvarias for the first time. "Forgive me."

Salvarias studied him a moment before he whispered, "Always, my dear friend."

56

SUMMER 1018 A.R

Humar watched the city of Cattlar bustling below. From his perch on the balcony, the Cavruls reminded him of how an ant hill looked: dots moving around with seemingly little purpose. A hive of bodies with agendas he wasn't privy to understand.

"Have you given any thought to what we talked about last night?" Edium asked.

Humar regarded the man for a moment, trying to decide his best course ... and that of Salvarias. He doubted the boy would be returning to Serinity and was certain Salvarias would not want to join Lord Bellerum's army. "I have, and I must disagree. Salvarias can't be tied down to an army, traveling from one side of Dalnar to the other. We need to be free of obligations. We need flexibility. Furthermore, I don't like the idea of the boy chasing the creatures that have hunted him. It's like handing him over."

"I have a sizable army, Humar," Edium said, voice tight. "I can protect the boy better than you can."

"You could if he let you. But we both know he won't."

Edium winced and looked back over the city. "I don't want him out of my sight. Him or Wilhelm. Let's not even get me started on my daughters. Varila and Lunara will undoubtedly follow the brothers."

"Yes," Humar confirmed. "But I've kept everyone safe. At least, as well as I could in our situations."

Edium shook his head. "You misunderstand. I know you'll take care of them. You're an honorable man and you've sworn your life to those boys. But ..." He ran his hands over his face, sighing heavily. "I just want to be with them."

"Times are difficult. We can't always have what we want. It's best for Salvarias. Deep inside, you know I speak the truth."

"I could hand over my army to Brice and journey with you instead."

Humar's mouth dropped open. "You can't rest the fate of Dalnar in the hands of a young man who hasn't seen his twenty-sixth year. He has no tactical knowledge, and he's not seen war. You'll send your entire army to their deaths. No." Humar shook his head and looked back over the city. "You're needed here, my friend. As Salvarias said, Dalnar must be rid of her shadows. This evil will return, and we have to be prepared." Humar glanced over his shoulder and saw Salvarias approaching from the living room. "Morning, Salvarias."

The young mage bowed. "Pleasant morning, Lord Bellerum, Humar."

"You look better," Edium said.

Salvarias tilted his head. "Thank you, Lord Bellerum—"

"Just Edium, Salvarias."

Salvarias ignored Edium and addressed Humar. "When you have a moment, I would like a word with you."

"I have one now," Humar said, clapping Edium on the shoulder. "I'll find you after Salvarias and I chat."

Edium opened his mouth as if to object, but snapped it shut and curtly nodded before striding from the balcony.

"You've upset him," Humar murmured when Salvarias joined his side.

"It was not my intent."

"He's a sensitive man. He thinks he's earned your trust."

"Lord Bellerum's path does not align with mine."

"I assume you've not had any visions."

"I have not, and I doubt I will receive more. They will not be foolish enough to repeat their ploy. Even if they do attempt such stupidity, I will not be duped again."

"I've been thinking, how is it they knew of Tobin's death? Of the exact moment the men entered Lunara's room in Sundil? And then there's the hidlu attack in the caves."

Salvarias nodded. "I too have been consumed with solving that puzzle. I have a theory, nothing more."

"Let's hear it."

"There are two types of visions I receive. One is an image, a painting almost, hazy in its exact meaning. The other is as if bards conducted a performance. It plays out before me. It is the second type that is linked to this 'god.' The first is merely a ... feeling, a warning. It is blurry, unclear. When I first saw Tobin's body, I did not recognize him. Only after we were attacked did I connect them. The men ambushing you in Sundil were the same. I saw a group of men on a set of stairs. It was more a feeling of danger than the actual situation. The same with the hidlu. I did not know the visions were so accurate in their timing."

"Where do you think they come from? Your magic?"

Salvarias shook his head. "I do not believe so. I have not ... discussed the possibility with it, though."

Humar startled. "You talk to your magic?"

"I am a firm believer that magic is not natural to us. The difficulties we face with it prove my point. My magic and I developed a very strong relationship in Zeeas, and it strengthened with time. We are as separate as two souls, yet it is as if we live in the same room, hear each other's thoughts, sense each other's emotions."

"How interesting. I've never talked to Mafarias about it."

"Magic is different for each mage. What I feel, my uncle might not."

"So this blackfire ... what is that?"

Salvarias paled, and his voice trembled when he spoke. "A power that I fear more than anything."

"But it killed them. It's—"

Salvarias's eyebrows stitched together. "Killed who? I have only taken one man's life with it. I will not do so again."

Humar searched Salvarias's face for some sign of withholding information. The boy didn't have a clue. "Salvarias, you used black-fire when your brother died. It swept through the tunnels and the outer city. It killed everyone."

"It was not me. I ... I was too distraught ... I could not have ..." The boy shook his head vehemently. "I ... cannot ... It was not me. Perhaps there is another who holds the same power. It was not me. There are effects of using that power, and I did not, nor do I, feel any of them."

Humar smiled, nodding. "It's all right, Salvarias. If you say so." Perhaps once the boy fully recovered, his mind would be open to listening to the truth. Or perhaps Humar was wrong. Maybe it wasn't Salvarias. But who, then? Mafarias had been supposedly passed out. "So what now? With no visions ..." He left the thought hanging.

Salvarias seemed to fold inward. "I am at a loss, my friend. There is something I am meant to do. I have said it to my brother before, though he does not believe me." His fists clenched and his jaw tightened. "I *feel* it: a tug on my mind, a whisper in my ear. No matter how hard I focus, I cannot discern its meaning. These visions, none of them have been my destiny." Salvarias shrugged as if the gesture would rid his feeling. "I have no idea what to do next. With no visions that I can trust, I am clueless as to my purpose. I am left with one option."

When he didn't speak, Humar said, "Which is?"

"To travel to the swamps and find Crutar's fortress. I can only assume that is where this 'god' operated from. No other place in Dalnar is as isolated."

"No one who has ever ventured there has returned to live past a week."

"Which is why I feel this trip should be made alone." Salvarias glanced over, a wry smile on his lips. "I, however, expect I am in for a long argument."

"I'm flat-out saying no. I'll take you there. There's no way in Oblivion you're traveling alone."

Salvarias inhaled a deep breath, and his head shifted to look below. "I know my brother will follow as well. I can accept his accompaniment, but the others must remain behind. Lady Lunara will not remain unless all others do. She must not come."

Humar chuckled. "She's as stubborn as you. I doubt I can convince her. When do you want to leave?"

"A few days at most, if possible."

Humar frowned. "You need time to recover."

"Time is not our ally, my friend. We must be swift."

Humar couldn't help his smile whenever Salvarias spoke the word "friend." It was lined with a care few were privileged to receive. He wondered if Tobin had been gifted hearing the word "father" from the boy's lips. "I'll do what I can. Okulu will help me plot our travels."

The boy shifted his stance. "You understand, the visions before Cattlar told me of our destination. I knew what awaited us. I knew what to expect. Now ..." His voice trailed off, and he shook his head. "The way is dark, and I am fumbling through a wilderness that is foreign to me. The dangers are tenfold."

"They have as much right to fight as you. They want a chance to save those they care about. They know the best way to do so is to aid you."

"Fools, the lot of them."

"Heroes, all of us."

Salvarias raised his gaze and light fell across his black eyes. Humar found the courage not to cringe. Though he had dredged up his hidden care for his nephew, nothing could soften the demonic quality of the boy's eyes.

"I am no hero, my friend."

"You are, boy. In the end, it'll be you who saves us."

"You know nothing of what you speak. You do not know what lurks within my soul."

Humar smiled. "I think it's the other way around. I'll tell them of the dangers, but the decision will be theirs."

Salvarias shook his head. "Death stalks us, my friend. You *must* see it."

"Death hunts everyone. Times such as these are welcomed."

"Welcomed?" Salvarias said, a hint of exasperation in his voice.

"Rarely are we able to show our courage, and too often we forget what life is worth. Difficult times remind us of how precious each breath is, and rediscovering that reverence of life will bleed into future generations. Too long has Arden roamed in complacency. It is time to awaken and rebirth ourselves into a better world. Times such as these give us the push we need."

"But at what price?"

"The more incredible the change, the higher the price." Humar smiled. "I know you don't carry any hope, but rest assured, I carry enough for the both of us. We will win this. And Arden will be reborn into the light."

"With all my heart, I hope you are right, my friend. Yet ..." Salvarias sank his head in his hands. "All I see is death, blood, and fire. Hope has been sliced open, burned, and murdered."

"One day you'll see your worth and the light that guides you."

57

SUMMER 1018 A.R

Salvarias rose early in the morning, hours before Wilhelm would wake. Snatching up his aspen branch, he counted his way to the door. A faint orange glow coming from the sitting room lit the hallway, not granting him the stealthy exit he had hoped to achieve. With Adok nipping playfully at his heels, he left his room and peered inside the sitting room. Varila was curled up in a chair, staring at the steady flame of a candle. He doubted she would put up an argument, and there was still a chance he could sneak out. Her back was to him, and she faced away from the door.

Gliding from the hall, he made it halfway before she spoke.

"Where in Nevlar's betrayal do you think you're going at this hour?"

Salvarias slouched in defeat. Still unable to meet her gaze after he had unjustly taken his anger out on her when she had slapped him, he kept his head lowered as he turned to her. "It is early, my lady. Are you not well?"

"Don't change the damn subject."

"I am going to the lava streams. I want to examine the armor our enemies wore."

Varila shoved herself up. "I'll go with you."

"I prefer to go alone, my lady."

"And I prefer you stay in your room so your brother's heart doesn't stop when he wakes, but we don't always get what we want."

"No, my lady, we do not." He scolded himself for not controlling the hint of annoyance in his voice. Clearing his throat, he bowed. "Forgive me. I meant—"

"Don't apologize," she said. "It's nice to see an emotion from you." She snatched up her sword and strode to the door as she buckled it on. "Coming?"

Adok snarled at her as she passed. Salvarias almost laughed aloud when she growled back.

At the bottom, they left the pulley and began the long walk toward the city gate. He added the globs of spit lining his path to the list of things he was counting.

The early morning carried the somber silence of a city ravaged by horrible bloodshed. Those who were out plodded along with slumped shoulders, and their gaze fostered a haunted flicker, as if they were expecting another army to burst from the stone itself. He had learned over five thousand men and women lost their lives in the battle.

More bodies to add to your growing number of victims, my little murderer, the presence said.

At the gate, he found the heaps of black armor. Red acid had eaten through the metal, twisting the helmets into ghastly shapes. At the suggestion of Salvarias and Mafarias, a group of Cavruls had been assigned the task of melting down the metal in hopes to rid it of its power.

Salvarias stopped beside the lava stream being used, and with no other option to help him answer his flood of questions, ignited his magic.

Yes, my wizard, his magic greeted in the same moping tone it had used since they had killed the little girl. Even with its dejected demeanor, its warmth flowed through Salvarias's blood, reminding him of the terrible absence of his magic's presence.

Let me be frank. I despise you. However, there are answers I must obtain. That will be our relationship. I will use you as I see fit. Do you understand?

I will serve you however you wish, Master.

Salvarias swallowed the bile that rose in his throat. Hearing the word "master" from his magic churned his stomach. *I sense no magic in the lava. What do you sense?* Salvarias asked.

Indeed, the fires have purged the enchantment. The magic is broken, useless.

He picked up an arm guard and turned it over in his hand, breathing a sigh of relief that his theory had proved correct. *The enchantment ... it feels like a prison. A trap.*

Agreed. Its captive is what made the armor function. It was linked to the red pustule inside each of them.

Captive ... I wonder, with the gods gone, who ushers souls to the planes of death?

A curious question. Why do you ask? his magic said.

Merely a desperate grasp for explanation. I have no further need of you. Be gone.

Salvarias shoved his magic into the dark corner of his mind, shivering instantly.

"I hate you," Varila said softly.

Salvarias grimaced against the knife twisting in his chest. He tossed the arm guard in the lava and rose to face her. "I gathered as much, my lady. Let us forgo false pretenses and speak plainly. I find you a suitable wife for my brother, and I will do everything within my power to secure your union. I assume he has requested something of you?"

"He said he wouldn't marry me if you and I don't get along, if I don't learn to love you as much as he does."

"A truly unreasonable demand," Salvarias said. "He loves you because of your strong opinions. To ask you to go against who you are is unfair, though I doubt he understands the ramification of his ultimatum. I hope by now you have learned enough of me to know my brother's happiness is all I desire. You will give him that happiness."

"Not unless you and I can get along."

Salvarias studied her a moment before carefully placing a proposal of his own. "A truce. I will tell him we talked this day and worked through our differences. If you merely refrain from commenting on my actions in front of him, we may feign some semblance of getting along."

"You want to lie?"

"I will not lie to him. We have talked and have worked through our differences. I have accepted our relationship as have you. We have 'worked through it.' As for your comments, you may express them when we are alone. In order to obtain his happiness, I do not think I ask too much of you."

Varila gazed into the lava river for several moments before she nodded. "We can agree. Do you think Wilhelm will buy it?"

"I will ensure he does. His marriage to you is what I desire, and he will see the truth in that statement."

Varila raised her head and regarded him with an expression he could not quite guess. "Thanks," she said.

Ah, it was gratitude—an expression he had yet to see from her. He bowed. "It is my pleasure, my lady. Shall we return?"

The walk toward Muddil's home was quiet. The farms were blanketed in a deep hush that made the thud of Salvarias's staff seem too loud. He tried to avoid staring at the dried and withered vegetation, knowing full well that when his brother had died, he had probably killed every living animal and plant within Cattlar. How only his horses and Adok survived was a question he strived to answer. Like before, he became dreadfully bored of uncovering the truth, and his mind wandered to other musings.

It was because of the silence and his pensive thoughts that he noticed the slight prickle along the base of his neck, the sense that something was amiss. Just as he posed the question to Adok, the wolf hunched and snarled at both the left and right fields while quickly conveying that a group of Cavruls lurked in clusters of tall, dead crops.

"What is it?" Varila asked.

"Adok is edgy," he said in his normal tone. He leaned her direction and whispered, "We are surrounded by a group of Cavruls. I do not know their intentions."

"Great," Varila muttered. "Is there ever a time danger doesn't follow you?"

Salvarias thought back on his life. "No, my lady."

"NOW!" a voice roared.

A band of eleven Cavruls sprang from the crops, axes and swords drawn, barking commands in Cavrul. Once again, Salvarias had been underestimated. He had learned the Cavrul language during his study with Dethal and listening to Durak mutter under his breath all things he hated about Salvarias.

Quickly identifying the leader, Salvarias sent an ice shard straight for the man's chest. It struck home with a sickening thump. Varila charged two Cavruls, cutting them down with one fluid strike.

Salvarias chanted as he drew in a sizable chunk of energy. He traced his rune and was pleasantly surprised to see six shards. He sent them to the group charging Varila.

"We need her alive!" a Cavrul growled. "And don't harm the mage!"

"Bastard!" Varila yelled, chopping off the Cavrul's head.

A terrible thud was followed by Varila's howl of pain. An arrow protruded from her shoulder. She doubled over, clutching her wound, and staggered backward.

Fury dimmed Salvarias's vision. He strode toward the Cavrul. The arrow loosened toward him, whizzing through the air. He muttered the spell under his breath and flicked it aside with a wave of his hand and a gust of wind

The Cavrul's eyes widened, and he dropped his weapon. "Don't kill me!"

Salvarias latched on to the Cavrul's throat and lifted him eye level. Jaw tight with anger, he hissed, "Why her?"

"B-b-bait for you and your brother," the Cavrul stammered. "The entire Bellerum family and the knight. I swear, we weren't going to kill anyone!"

"Who sent you?" Salvarias demanded.

"I-I don't know! He was cloaked. The meeting was arranged outside the city by one of the black-armored soldiers. I swear we were told to avoid you and your brother, but we had to obtain the family. They said to do it only if the attack on the city failed. I swear that's all I know!"

"And in exchange?"

"The safety of our families!"

"You knew about the attack and you did nothing?" Salvarias's voice cracked from how loud he shouted.

"W-we were doomed! The council wouldn't believe you, and I knew how large the army was. We should've never won. If not for the fire, we'd all be dead! I was told this was only a precaution in case something failed, a contingency plan! I never thought I'd have to carry it through. I swear, that's all I know! By the gods' mercy, please don't kill me!"

"You are a traitor to your people!"

Rage exploded from beneath Salvarias's placid lake. Black flames erupted over him, licking his skin with a hungry yearning for blood. Images of death and murder flooded him.

From dark shadows, he leapt on to a passing trade wagon and rammed his dagger in the driver's stomach. With no regard for the man's life, he tossed the body from the seat and took off with the goods.

He fell hard to the ground, crying out as the wagon wheel rolled over his legs. Alone, crippled, bleeding, and in blinding pain, he wasted away for the entire night before death claimed him.

Murder after murder Salvarias reenacted as the killer and relived as the victim. Wound after wound slashed across his body, burning painful tears in his eyes. Once his power had pulled every horrible deed from the Cavrul, Salvarias trembled with anger and pain. Twenty-three people had suffered horrible deaths at the hands of the Cavrul suspended in his grip. He leaned forward and whispered in the Cavrul's ear, "Oblivion awaits you."

"No!" the man screeched.

As he had done before, he poured the pain of the Cavrul's victims into the man, driving each physical and mental wound into the

Cavrul's body and mind. The man's scream tore through the fields, echoing in all its tragic understanding. The sound spread a smile across Salvarias's face and fed his blackfire to engulf the Cavrul. He watched in blissful content as the man's bulging eyes dulled of life.

He blinked, and the black doors of Oblivion rose up before him. The gray fog surrounded him in warmth, driving away the chill of death. His smile widened when he saw the ghastly displayed faces, and he chuckled when his gaze found the scarred man, still screaming in horror.

"His sentence is yours to assign," the fog whispered.

Salvarias touched the door, and it swung open in eagerness. He looked down at the man kneeling at his side. "Know the pain my brother would have endured should her life have been taken. Know my fury should any member of the Bellerum family had come to harm." He grabbed the Cavrul and shoved him through the door. The gate thudded closed, and the man's racking sobs split Salvarias's smile into a toothy grin.

The fog brushed over him in approval, tasting sweet, feeling warm against his skin, and imbuing him with sensational power. He breathed it in, allowing it to consume him.

"You have done well," the fog said. "Son of Shadow and Fire, Spawn of Anger and Retribution." The fog wrapped around him in an embrace that filled Salvarias with comfort. "My cup is brimming with pride."

In a blink, he stood on the road cutting through the field of crops. Supported in his hand was a charred corpse. He dropped it and stumbled back as the murderer's crimes assailed him all at once. His body ached from each wound he suffered, and his cruel mind restrained him to a world of torment. Raising his trembling hands, he saw blood spilling over his fingers, trickling down his arms. His stomach heaved as he leaned over and retched. So much death. So much blood. He needed to flee. He had to run from the abomination that was himself.

"Salvarias," Varila snapped.

He tried to focus on her, tried to push aside the images of death flashing before him. It was no use. They bombarded him mercilessly.

He staggered backward, unable to tear his gaze from the blood dripping from his fingertips.

Salvarias, Lunara called in his thoughts. *Help us!*

Her voice and fears hauled him from the cusp of insanity, yanking him painfully to reality. Her terror threatened to infuse itself in him, and he blocked her overbearing emotions. Shaking violently as he gained a tiny level of control, he set off for the home as fast as his leg would allow, focusing his thoughts on suppressing his pain to deal with later.

At some point, his mind cleared enough for him to remember what had sparked his anger. He looked over at Varila's pale and sweating face. She had broken the shaft of the arrow and had a hand pressed to the wound. It was not mortal, and he slouched with relief. His brother would have been devastated if anything happened to her.

Taking a risk, he reached out his thoughts to Lunara. *How many?*

Her fear sprang up, nearly causing him to lose the small amount of rational thought he had solidified. *I-I don't know,* she wept. *Mother took me to the hidden room in Muddil's kitchen. I can't hear the fighting anymore.*

Grinding his teeth in expectation, he pushed the pains in his leg aside and increased his pace to a jog. Each jarring step flashed spots in his vision. When they emerged into the inner city, there was no sign anything was amiss.

"They must have ambushed them in the home," Varila said. "No one was able to call for help."

Lunara's grief slammed into him with such force it halted him and drove the air from his lungs. *What happened?*

Father! Durak! They're hurt badly! All the attackers are dead, but ... Father!

She succumbed to her emotions, and he flung up a wall before he was overpowered by her fears. He jogged forward, gasping for each painful breath. The pulley in the distance seemed to move farther away, making him pay for each dear step with near-unbearable pain. When finally he entered it, he was only half aware he did so.

The heavy winds of their ascent dried the sweat that had trickled down his face and cooled the heat of his pain. He gained his breath and stood a little straighter. Varila was watching him.

"The fight has ended," Salvarias said. "But your father and Durak were wounded."

Varila nodded but said nothing.

At the top, both rushed from the pulley and burst into the home. There must have been near twenty bodies littering the floor. Blood splattered the walls, dotted along furniture, and pooled under bodies.

"Salv!" Wilhelm exclaimed.

He found himself scooped up by his brother. "Lord Bellerum? Durak?"

"This way," Wilhelm said.

Salvarias first went to Lord Bellerum's room. Lunara and Lady Talura were on either side of the lord's bed, tears raining from their eyes and ashen-faced. One look at the man and Salvarias knew death was in the room. A slice up Edium's abdomen had nearly been deep enough to empty him. He had lost too much blood.

"Take me to Durak," Salvarias said.

Wilhelm headed down two doors to a room at the end of the hall. Durak was on a bed, cursing Humar, who held him down. A dagger stuck up from Durak's shoulder, far enough from anything vital.

Salvarias darted to Lord Bellerum's room, shed his cloak, and rolled up his sleeves. "I need my herb pouch." Brice, a man Salvarias had met once, paced the room. "Commander Brice, please take Lady Talura." Salvarias nodded to Neithelas who folded Lunara close and pulled her from her father.

You have to save him, she begged in his mind. *Promise me! Promise me you won't let him die!*

He glanced up at her supported by Neithelas, her eyes filled with dread. The mere thought of having her experience loss, to have her father wrenched from her grasp far too early in her life was unacceptable. "He will live." It was a foolish promise. He knew it the instant the words left his mouth. But a part of him could not endure losing Lord Bellerum. The promise was for his own sanity as much as hers.

Why, was a mystery. He did not need the man. He did not need anybody.

"Here," Okulu said, thrusting Salvarias's herb pouch at him.

Accepting it, Salvarias fought to toss away the deaths his blackfire forced him to relive. Even as he opened his pouch, he twitched each time a knife pierced his skin. As he laid out what herbs he had available, his bloodied hands shook so bad that he dropped some and accidentally crushed a leaf.

"It's all right," Talura said. He looked up to see her at his side, hands and dressed stained with her husband's blood. "Take a deep breath."

Salvarias forced in a long breath and let it out slowly.

She smiled. "Do what you can, Son." He saw clearly in her eyes she suspected her husband's death. Even so, she did not beg Salvarias to help. She merely smiled through her tears and whispered, "Regardless of what happens, I will always care for you."

For the first time in his life, he found a person who expected nothing from him. And if he failed, he truly believed she would still care for him. Her acceptance fueled his determination. He turned from her and went to work on saving a man who had more to live for than Salvarias ever thought a person could be blessed with.

VARILA GAZED at Salvarias's graceful fingers as he handled the delicate herbs as one might a newly hatched butterfly. She was vaguely aware of Wilhelm's arms around her waist, holding her up when her legs no longer supported her. Her sister had calmed completely, looking as though their father had already made a full recovery.

Time blurred by. The scene faded in and out. People floated by, conveying words of comfort she chose not hear. She vaguely heard Salvarias order no one to help her. He sent away healers and, at one point, was in front of her, looking at her shoulder. Next thing she knew, she was lying on a bed with a blanket modestly covering her naked body.

Salvarias peered over her, saying words that droned together. Wilhelm was there, pinning her arms to her side. Pain flared along her shoulder, shooting up her neck and down her leg, fading her surroundings to a white haze. She screamed, but whether in her mind or aloud she didn't know. When she came to, she was propped up against Wilhelm's chest.

Salvarias passed a cup of some liquid to Wilhelm who helped her drink it. It was pleasantly sweet, and she caught a whiff of honey. "You must sleep, my lady," Salvarias said.

She realized she'd been battling the urge to succumb to darkness. "My ... father," she said.

"Rest," Salvarias whispered. His voice was a breeze that kissed her mind, lulling her into submission.

When next she woke, her grogginess had vanished, leaving her vision bright and her mind alert. Wilhelm sat in chair close to her bed, and his crooked smile spread.

"Good to see you up," he rumbled. "How do you feel?"

"Fine. That brother of yours has a knack for healing." She didn't want to know, but the question came out before she could stop herself. "My father?"

Wilhelm's smile faded. "No change."

She sat up, forgetting she was naked, and the blanket slid to her waist. Wilhelm was none too quick to turn away. If she hadn't been ridden with worry, she would've allowed him a longer view. She rose from bed and fetched her armor. It'd been cleaned of blood but the hole would need repair. Durak could mend—

Her thought cut off sharply, and she jerked her gaze to Wilhelm. "Durak?"

"Recovering well. I've learned a few new curses from him."

"I assume your brother took care of him as well?"

Wilhelm chuckled. "Wouldn't let another soul near him."

She dressed in fresh undergarments and buckled on her armor, wincing at the soreness of her shoulder and the shooting pains that occasionally snaked down her spine. Once done, she followed

Wilhelm to her parents' room. Upon entering, she was greeted with warm smiles and a rush of people.

Her mother sat in chair beside Salvarias, both looking equally disheveled. The white flowers she stuck in her hair each morning had wilted, and strands of hair had strayed from her braid. She'd changed dresses, but looked as though that was as long as she'd allowed herself to be absent from Edium.

Salvarias had obviously not bathed or changed since their encounter with the attackers. Blood still stained his clothes, and his face was shadowed with new stubble. Lunara was the only one who seemed unbothered by their father's death-white face and sunken eyes. She was smiling broadly.

"How long has it been?" Varila asked.

"A day," Lunara said. "Here, sit." She moved a chair next to their mother.

Salvarias rose from his chair and knelt in front of her. He reached for her, stopped, and curled his fingers back. "Would you please move aside your armor, my lady, so I can see the wound?"

With a fair amount of difficulty shifting the leather, she did as he asked. He studied it for a moment before nodding. "It is healing well. You will have full use of your arm."

She nodded, not able to form words as the light caught his eyes. They were haunted, terribly haunted.

He checked on Edium before announcing he would return after seeing to Durak. Once he left, she turned to Wilhelm. "He needs sleep."

"He's refusing," Talura said. "I've tried to tell him the same. We all have."

"You need some too," Varila said.

Her mother smiled and reached out for her hand. "I've dozed a little. I'm fine."

Her tight hold told Varila otherwise.

Lunara, beaming that pure smile, said, "Salvarias said he'll live. That means by his will alone, Father will survive."

There was so much confidence in her voice that Varila almost believed the mage could perform such an act.

The day passed with no change in their father. He lay motionless, his color switching from blue to ash to sallow. With each color change, Salvarias mixed a different potion.

Varila's own need for sleep pounced on her early in the evening. As if reading her mind, Wilhelm lifted her from her chair and carried her to her room. He settled her into bed, and before he turned, she grabbed his hand.

"I don't want to be alone," she said.

He kicked off his boots, crawled into the bed beside her, and enclosed her in his arms. He kissed her cheek and whispered in her ear, "You'll never be alone."

With that, she drifted to a deep sleep.

The next day followed the same routine. Her mother looked better. Salvarias looked worse. His hands trembled violently, and he barely ate. Durak was up and about, despite Salvarias's protests.

That night, Wilhelm slept with her again, though she'd told him to stay with Salvarias. She marveled over how Wilhelm could leave his brother's side when Salvarias appeared so ill. She wouldn't have been able to sleep if Lunara were in the same condition. Then again, Salvarias had been wrought by sickness so often that, sadly, she'd become desensitized to it.

In the early hours of morning, she left her room with Wilhelm at her side to find Salvarias waiting in the hall. He looked like a walking corpse and trembled like a leaf in a wind storm.

"There is no change," he said. "I fear I am at a loss. I have tried every remedy I know, my lady."

Varila refused the tears threatening to emerge. "Have you told my mother? Lunara?"

"Regretfully, their condition is worse than yours. Lady Talura is not sleeping. She is exhausted and in no state to receive such news. Your sister ... I told her ..." He looked down at his feet. "I told her he would live. She was foolish enough to believe me."

Varila bit back her snide comment. "How long does he have?"

"Hours," Salvarias whispered.

The words pressed her back against Wilhelm's chest. A strong hand rested on her shoulder, seeming to give her strength to stand straight. Her father would not want her mother or Lunara to witness his death: to see that spark of life fade from his eyes, to feel his skin turn to ice.

Inhaling a deep breath to steady her voice, she said, "Send them away. Tell them you need room to work and it's too crowded. Tell them I'm helping you. Everyone else needs to go."

"I am sorry, my lady."

Varila nodded and strode into her father's room. Salvarias repeated what she had said and, in no time, they were alone. She sat in the same chair she'd occupied each day and stared at her father, fighting her tears the entire time. She could see him slipping away right before her eyes.

Selfish bastard ... Abandoning his family ... Dying before meeting his first grandchild. Shoving herself up, she went to his side. "Listen here, old man," she said. "I have no intention of losing my father yet. I want you to be there when I get married. I want you to meet my first child. So wake up, you bastard! Your damn family needs you!"

She stormed from the room. She couldn't look at him anymore. She was furious at him, and though her feelings were absurd, she was in no mood to be rational.

AFTER VARILA LEFT, Salvarias sank beside the bed of Lord Bellerum. Failure, bitter and all too familiar, tainted his mouth, burned his lungs with each pathetic breath. He was useless. Completely and utterly useless.

It is because of you he has died, my murderer, the presence hissed. *Do you think they would have targeted such a man if he was not acquainted with you? His death is your fault. His blood is on your hands.*

Lord Bellerum's breathing softened, slowing to the end of his life.

Any moment now and he would fade from this world. Another good soul taken while the parasites of humanity lived.

Salvarias shut his eyes tightly and wadded the sheets in his fist.

Lunara would have her father ripped from her at such a young age. She had been foolish enough to believe in something as pathetic as Salvarias, and now she would look at him differently. She would see him as all others did.

As anger built, his lake rippled.

Another person would leave him. Lord Bellerum would desert him just as Tobin had done. Just as Wilhelm had done.

Salvarias raised his gaze to the man who had looked at him with care and compassion brimming in his eyes. The man who had called him son. The man who would now abandon him to deal with his evil alone. The man Salvarias wanted as a father.

The foul beast dwelling in the darkest place of Salvarias's soul burst to life.

A deep voice echoed in the room. "Do this freely and only once as it is *my* soul that shall pay the price for his life. The power is yours to command. Submit to your desires. Bring back that which was taken from you. Demand it, son of Fire and Shadow. Demand it!"

Closing his eyes, he succumbed to his raw rage and fueled it with a cry of grief.

58

V arila was halfway to her room when her fury wavered, staggering her, making her cling to the wall for support. Her father would die alone.

She bolted down the hall to his room and flung open the door, expecting the worst. What she saw was harrowing.

Salvarias was knelt beside her father's bed, body covered in black fire, lightning flickering within it. His animal-like howl carried so much anguish she was sure it would cause the walls to weep.

"Live!" Salvarias screamed.

A horrible pain burrowed into Varila's heart, twisting and hollowing out a hole, leaching heat from her. She heard herself repeating the word "no" and felt her head shaking in denial.

"I demand it!" Salvarias roared, and within his voice was a power that made her cringe. "You will live!"

The black fire burst forth to fill the entire room.

"No!" Mafarias called from behind. "You can't, boy!"

The intense heat of Salvarias's power forced her to turn away. Mafarias grabbed her and whirled around. A familiar calmness draped over her and the white film blurred her surroundings. Even with the protection shield, Mafarias cried out, driving both to their knees. She faintly heard him whisper, "By our fate, help your son."

A deafening boom came from the room, throwing her and Mafarias across the hall. Then it all stopped.

Mafarias unrolled her from his arms. She scrambled to her feet and rushed inside her father's room. Dust hazed the air, seemingly suspended in time. Except for the bed, every piece of wood furniture had disintegrated into a heap of splinters, and the stone pieces had been reduced to a pile of gravel. The air was dry and hot, and the stone walls, floor, and ceiling were cracked and still vibrated. Crumbled in a corner was Salvarias, locked in convulsions, blood spurting from his mouth with each choking breath.

Her father suddenly gasped and sat bolt upright.

"What has he done?" Mafarias breathed.

Varila didn't care. Her father was alive. She leapt over piles of splinters and dissolved stone, and flew into his arms.

"Where am I?" Edium gasped. "What happened? Where's your mother? The men ..."

She gaped at his smooth chest, free of the gash that had nearly gutted him.

"Boy!" Her father leapt from the bed and darted for Salvarias.

"Stay back!" Mafarias shouted, blocking Edium's way. Mafarias thrusted a cloth at Wilhelm, who'd just barged into the room. "Help your brother."

Wilhelm snatched it and shoved it in Salvarias's mouth to stop him from biting his tongue.

"He can't do this," Mafarias breathed, repeating the words under his breath as he paced a section of the room.

"What in Oblivion is going on?" Edium demanded.

Lunara pushed everyone aside, including Wilhelm. She cradled Salvarias's head to her chest and whispered inaudible words in his ear.

"What happened, Uncle?" Wilhelm snapped.

Salvarias's convulsions eased, and Lunara pulled the cloth from his mouth, all the while still talking to him. Blood poured out of his mouth and stained the front of Lunara's dress. By her pallid complexion and shaking body, she endured pain as well.

"Your brother has done something terrible," Mafarias said. "He's used his power in a way that it should never be used. He's upset Balance."

"Balance?" Edium said. "What are you talking about?"

Mafarias cleared his throat and yanked his robes straight. His back was smoking and the slate-blue fabric was singed. "The world is held in balance at all times. What should happen happens. You were to die, Edium. Salvarias pulled from Balance. He restored you against the Laws of Power."

Her father staggered, groping at his chest, his face lighting with memory. "How could he do such a thing? He's just a boy."

"A boy with remarkable power," Mafarias said. "If I'd ever known he possessed the ability, I would've educated him. Now, Balance must be restored."

"Restored?" Edium asked.

"It will choose how and when, but it will equal itself."

"It was my fault," Lunara said. Salvarias was slack in her arms.

"No, it wasn't," Varila scolded. "I heard him say it without you ..." Her voice trailed as she sucked in an understanding breath.

Lunara's tears spilled over her cheeks, and she cradled Salvarias's head to her breast. "I made him promise me. I made him!"

Varila, for the first time, felt a tinge of care toward the man who'd saved her father.

Salvarias jolted awake from horrid nightmares of death. A single candle illuminated an unoccupied room with two beds. Stomach churning from the horror flashing before him, he scrambled from bed and tripped his way out the door. He lurched to the next door and flung it open. Another bedroom. The next door was the same. The third, and none too soon, offered a washroom. Chanting his light spell, he barely found the washbasin before becoming ill.

His hands left glistening red prints on the stone table as the blood of all those he had killed dripped down his arms, staining his hands with death. He stripped from his clothes and crawled into the bathtub's freezing waters. Shaking violently, he scrubbed himself vigorously to no avail. Bile threatened to rise again as he frantically clawed at his skin. He had to get the blood off. He had to. It was oozing into his soul, tainting that precious part belonging solely to him.

Glancing around, he saw a straight blade for shaving. He clambered from the tub and retrieved the knife. He slid it down his forearm. More blood. Sobbing, he fell to his knees and sank the blade underneath his skin, desperate to rid himself of his flesh before the evil seeped into his soul.

"Salvarias."

He looked up to see Lunara knelt in front of him. "Help me," he sobbed. "I cannot get it off! I cannot!"

She took the blade from his hands, dunked a cloth into the water, and wiped it over his arm. He cried with relief when the blood disappeared. Shaking and weeping, he allowed her to clean it from him until he saw no more.

"You're safe," Lunara said, setting aside the cloth. "You saved my father. He lives."

He recalled the lord's life fading, and then something had happened. The voice behind the stable hand of his mind—the one that had saved him after his parents' murder and his brother's brief death—had spoken, urging him to use blackfire. Frantically trying to recover memories, he searched for new victims but found none other than those of the Cavrul and scarred man. Only the faint feeling of sorrow was left by whoever owned the hand that had saved him. Yet another presence living within him. Who was Salvarias in all that occupied him? Which voice was his amid the many echoing through his mind?

Grabbing his head, he doubled over on his knees and wept, "Leave! All of you! Be gone from me!"

"Look at me," Lunara whispered.

He raised his head and met her calm gaze.

She smiled and brushed aside his hair. "You need to let me help you."

He had been so terrified that he had erected a wall, completely blocking her from his mind. How he achieved such a feat, he did not know, but now that he realized it, his wall dissolved at her request, even without his command. Her strength surged up in him, calming his mind, subduing the death until nothing flashed before him.

With his mind controlled, he used her touch to file away the victims of the Cavrul with those of the scarred man. They were there, but processed and tucked into the background of his thoughts. The bludgeoning, stabbing pain reduced to bearable.

"Forgive me," she whispered. "What I asked of you was unfair."

Tears trickled down her cheeks. The sight made him ache. He never wanted her to experience pain. He never wanted sorrow to touch her. "My lady, you—" His voice caught when her fingers brushed through his hair. "You did nothing wrong."

She smiled, causing more tears to break free. "You forgive too easily. What I demanded of you was horribly selfish. I never meant to hurt you. Never ..." Her voice trailed off in a soft sob.

"Whether you ask it of me or not, my lady, I will spare you from pain if it is within my ability. I swear, you did nothing wrong."

She flung her arms around his neck, her body shaking with silent sobs. Gathering her close, he buried his face in her hair. He was not sure how long they sat in each other's arms, both crying softly in their own torment. Eventually her shaking stopped and she breathed easily, but he was reluctant to let her go.

At long last, he unraveled her arms and sat back on his heels. The absence of her touch rushed forward his frantic mind, and he grimaced against the onslaught.

"Dress and meet me outside," Lunara said.

His cheeks burned when he realized he was naked. She rose and left the scent of a spring meadow in her wake.

He took a moment to wrap the cut on his arm before he pulled on his robes. Needing further time to collect himself, he picked up the straight razor and found the mirror. He hated shaving this way. It made him look at himself, and he had avoided mirrors since first his mother had forced him to see who he truly was: a monstrosity with demon eyes.

He cut himself a few times, but he was eager to end the experience. Once done, he inhaled several breaths, called his staff to him, and tucked his hurt beneath the surface of his lake to deal with later. His shaking reduced, and he left the washroom.

Lunara was leaning against the wall waiting for him, Adok by her side. "You look much better," she said.

"Thank you." Adok nuzzled his hand.

"As I said, my father lives. I don't know what you did, but thank you."

"I am not sure it was me, my lady." He glanced up and down the quiet hall. "Where is everyone?"

"They've gone to Durak's old home. The city is conducting a Cavrul ritual to honor their dead. Muddil and Durak wanted to go, but because of the attack against my family, Ilumar suggested they hold their own private ceremony in Durak's home. They'll be gone for the entire night. The ritual is sundown to sunup."

"And why did you not attend?"

She smiled and held out her hand. "Come. It's time for me to collect on one of our wagers. I feel like reading, and I don't want to be alone."

"I am tired, my lady. I—"

"You won't hold your end of the bargain? I did beat you. Palony made it to the ledge before Mithal."

Salvarias's exhaustion robbed him of excuses. He nodded, though he did not take her hand. Smiling, she led him to the sitting room where a warm fire crackled.

She studied the bookshelves, selected a volume of Cavrul tales, and then settled into a small couch. She patted the seat next to her. He propped his staff against the back of the couch, called for its light, and sat beside Lunara. She did not accept the distance he had chosen. She handed him the book and drew his arm around her shoulders. He inhaled deeply the smell of her hair and savored the relaxation of his mind before opening the book.

Because he had read since he was six months old, he had mastered absorbing the words ridiculously fast. Once he finished the page, he waited for Lunara. After a moment, her hands fidgeted together.

"Have you finished?" Salvarias asked.

She looked up and giggled. "A little bit ago. I tend to read fast."

Salvarias turned the page. He read both then studied her until she raised her head and smiled sheepishly. "I guess I'm not as fast as you."

"I had scarcely finished, my lady. We read at nearly the same speed."

"How wonderful," she said, eyes alive with warmth and joy. "I guess that means we can read books together so we don't have to wait until the other finishes before we can talk about them."

A smile snuck out at the thought, and he said, "I would love nothing more."

She giggled and snuggled closer. "Splendid."

Halfway through the book, he realized she was sleeping. Reading no longer interested him. Her features captivated his attention: the fullness of her lips, her thick eyelashes, the smoothness of her skin, her arched eyebrows calling focus to her large eyes. Her breasts rose and fell with each deep breath, and her collarbone beckoned him to trace it. His hand twitched to touch her cheek and run through her hair.

In need to rid himself of temptation, he untangled her from his arms and gently lowered her to the couch. After covering her with a blanket, he went to the balcony and watched the mourning city. An echo of forlorn singing barely reached the balcony, and far below the people holding lit candles seemed so few for a city the size of Cattlar. Of course, many had died because of him. Their numbers would have been greater if he had not been such a fool.

It was not long before he sensed her. Without needing to look, he knew she stood behind him.

"May I join you?" she asked.

"Of course," he said, motioning beside him.

As usual, she did not take his hint. She squeezed between him and the railing, and her gaze locked him in place as if he were shackled there. She pushed his hood down, and he reveled in her direct stare, in the fact she never shied from his demon eyes. Her hands slid up his chest, gliding over his shoulders and sneaking under his hair until gentle fingertips touched his neck. Softly she asked, "What is our relationship, Salvarias?"

Memories surfaced of the times she had helped him, stood by his side, defended and supported him. Try as he might to stop, he recalled each moment of their dreams: her intelligence, her strength, her vulnerability.

Somehow, this beautiful, pure woman had found a way aboard his raft set adrift on his lake of indifference. Her fingers glided along its pristine surface, sending ripples he was ashamed to see. Ripples he had longed for his entire life.

His hand shook violently when he raised it, allowing it to hover above her hair. His chest tightened at the mere prospect of reliving a moment from their dreams. That moment when he had felt each silky strand fall between his fingers, that moment when he had touched her. Breathing became difficult the longer he stood paralyzed, fighting temptation and need.

"Salvarias ..." she breathed.

Selfishly, he tainted her.

Sleek strands caressed his hand, and he closed his eyes, delighting in the feel of it. Peace calmed his shaking and lifted the weight from his shoulders and chest. He breathed deeply, slowly gliding his hand down her hair, weaving his fingers amid its mass, relishing in the wave of tranquility cascading over him. Nothing existed around him; no sounds, no death, no voices, no worry over his destiny, no curious questions. Nothing but her.

Even as he bathed in peace, he knew he could not love her. Nor could he continue to lie to himself about their relationship. They had grown up together, shared stories, romped through a field of dead.

Never could he accept her love or offer his. Yet he could no longer ignore the friendship that had evolved so effortlessly in their dreams. He was tired of lying to himself, of denying himself her company and conversations, of cruelly pushing her away when it went against every fiber of his being. He did not want to be that man anymore.

"Tell me," she said. "What am I to you?"

Slowly, reluctantly, he opened his eyes and met her gaze. "My dearest and oldest friend, my lady. A friend whom I will do anything for, a friend I will cherish until the last of my days. But never—*never* — can we be more."

He bowed and left the balcony. He hoped she understood. He hoped the tears he knew were pouring down her cheeks were tears of acceptance. He hoped the ache in his heart would lessen with each step, but it did not.

59

SUMMER 1018 A.R

Salvarias twitched awake to a shadowed room absent of his
brother's rumbling snore. The flickering flame of a single candle
caressed the hard lines of the room and bore a tunnel through blackness to illuminate slate-blue robes pooling on the floor around a
chair.

Adrenaline surged through Salvarias. He kicked at the blankets,
unraveling himself from the pile. Scrambling backward, he pressed
himself into the corner of the room where his bed rested, forcing his
strained mind to remember a spell. A familiar voice spoke.

"It's just me, Salvarias."

A breath passed before Salvarias's panic receded enough for him
to realize it was his uncle who spoke.

"You all right?" Mafarias asked.

Salvarias's fears dried out his mouth. He did not want to be alone
with Mafarias. He wanted his brother. Adok jumped on the bed,
baring teeth at Mafarias.

Salvarias's fears ebbed enough for him to form words. "I am fine,
Uncle."

"I wish you would trust me, boy. I truly care for you. You must
know this."

Salvarias remained quiet. He was listening more to Adok's offer to rip out Mafarias's jugular. Reaching out, he petted the wolf's ears.

Mafarias sighed audibly. "We need to talk about what you did to Edium. There are rules that must be followed. Your power must be kept on a leash. You cannot bring souls back from death."

"He had not died yet."

Mafarias's brow furrowed. "You healed him?"

"I ... I am not sure what happened."

"I've also learned of your antics with your magic. You can't push yourself. You'll lose your mind before you see your fortieth Birth Day."

"I am aware of my limitations, *Uncle*. I do not need your help or guidance."

Mafarias's eyes narrowed. "Why do you say uncle with such sarcasm?"

"Why have you lied to us? Why did you lie to our mother?"

Mafarias shifted in his chair. "I don't know what you're talking about."

"Do not think me a fool, Mafarias. I would rather you refuse me the truth than for you to continue this charade. I heard what you said when you touched me."

"Finc. You want the truth? I'm not your uncle, but I am related to you, boy." Mafarias chuckled. "I keep calling you and Wilhelm 'boys' but your brother is a grown man now. And you're into your first year of that label."

"You knew us as boys. You have not known us as men."

There was a long pause before Mafarias spoke again. "You were never a boy, were you?"

Salvarias remained quiet. Indeed, he had never known childhood innocence. Horror was what Salvarias had seen since first his brother's amber eyes disappeared into a red haze of terror. Within his few breaths of life, Salvarias understood the human condition. He saw the capabilities people possessed: the forest of bad and the splinter of good.

"No," Mafarias whispered. "You were an old man with your first breath."

"What is it you need, Mafarias?"

"I wanted to give you a little gift ... something I found in my travels."

Mafarias rose and his shadowed frame stopped at Salvarias's bed.

"*Ecia Lumenious*," Mafarias whispered. A crystal the mage carried glowed with a soft white light. A book was offered.

Salvarias accepted it. "Thank you."

"I'll let you get some more sleep. I assume you won't tell your brother about me?"

"Until I know the full truth, I will not burden him. He cares deeply for you, and your deceit will hurt him."

Mafarias winced. "You're a harsh man, Salvarias."

"Only when I am being lied to by the last *blood* relative I have. And only when my brother is in danger because of those lies. If there is nothing else?" Salvarias motioned toward the door.

Mafarias sighed. "You really should trust people. I want to help you." He walked to the door, opened it, and paused. "What did you see when I touched you?"

Salvarias shuddered at the memory. "Eternity."

Mafarias gave a slight nod. "Interesting. I'll be gone by morning. I was hoping you would be receptive to my attempts to educate you in regards to your magic, but I can see that isn't a possibility. You need to study, boy. You don't know the harm you put yourself in. You don't understand that there are powers out there—forces that rule the worlds, the gods themselves. Balance is a cruel mistress, and she must be kept or else the consequences can be terrifying. Sometimes we must live with what happens. Edium should've died. You know it, and I know it. Now, you'll be forced to pay for what you did. If ever you want me to explain it further, I would be happy to. Until then, you need to be careful."

"I appreciate the warning. Where will you go?"

"My business is my own. It's not safe if I'm with you. It's best you travel alone. Humar knows how to reach me. If you need me, all you have to do is ask, and I'll be there."

"You could help us, Mafarias. I know you could."

Mafarias shrugged. "Perhaps, but there are dangerous games afoot. I'm helping in my own way. Now, if you'll excuse me."

"My brother will be upset if you leave without passing along your farewells. As I said, he is fond of you."

"I'll say my goodbyes tonight." Mafarias doused his light. "Don't leave your brother's side, Salvarias. You're in danger. You need his protection."

When the door clicked closed, Salvarias's held breath exploded out. He rested his head on the wolf's shoulder. "Thank you, my friend."

Adok growled, upset Salvarias had not allowed him to bite Mafarias.

"*Ecia Lumenious.*" Salvarias's staff propped against the side of the bed lit.

Adok huffed and circled the same spot several times before nestling in the blankets. Salvarias ran his hand over the faded brown leather of the book. It had seen better days. It was such a shame for literature to be neglected. He opened the inside cover and paused when he saw a dried-up bloody fingerprint next to an inscription.

> *To my son, Salvarias.*
> *May you forever remain curious and never change*
> *your pure heart.*
> *I will love you always.*
> *Tobin*

His TEARS WERE INSTANT. Tobin's words, "You are no son of mine," echoed in the room. His father's blood trickled down the walls, and the man's hazel eyes brimming with horror and disgust flashed before Salvarias. Remembering the pain of rejection almost broke him. He could not endure it again. Never could he see love withdrawn. Never could he afford another the opportunity to inflict such deep sorrow on him again.

Curling up in his bed, Salvarias hugged the book and whispered, "I need no one."

He half believed himself.

AUTHOR NOTE

Thank you for taking time to read my story. I hope you found it enjoyable. If you have questions, comments, or would just like to talk, you can reach me through my website (booksbylkevans.com) or send me an email at booksbylkevans@gmail.com.

www.ingramcontent.com/pod-product-compliance
Lightning Source LLC
Chambersburg PA
CBHW022232020726
47496CB00004B/859